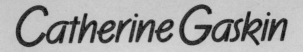

Catherine Gaskin

THE CHARMED CIRCLE

AVON BOOKS ◆ NEW YORK

AVON BOOKS
A division of
The Hearst Corporation
105 Madison Avenue
New York, New York 10016

Copyright © 1988 by Catherine Gaskin Cornberg
Front cover printing by Charles Geer
Published by arrangement with Charles Scribner's Sons/Macmillan Publishing Company
Library of Congress Catalog Card Number: 88-26401
ISBN: 0-380-70778-0

First Avon Books Printing: April 1990

AVON TRADEMARK REG. U.S. PAT. OFF. AND IN OTHER COUNTRIES, MARCA REGISTRADA, HECHO EN U.S.A.

Printed in the U.S.A.

RA 10 9 8 7 6 5 4 3 2 1

FOR SOL
yesterday, today, tomorrow
with love

1

August 1940

Chapter One

I

IT WAS A BALMY, sunny afternoon over the southeastern corner of England. Julia tried to learn her lines, with one ear cocked to the long oasthouse where her mother practiced—over and over again one small phrase from the Mozart sonata—was it K. 331? Julia could never remember the Köchel listings. She sighed as she listened. It was difficult enough to live up to a father who was a famous actor, twice as difficult to have a mother who was regarded by many as among the finest pianists of her time. Her mother was leaving on tour soon, not just a tour of the provinces, but of the United States, a tour arranged by the Ministry of Information. Officially it was to raise funds for refugees— Which refugees? Julia had asked, since the world seemed to her full of them. Unofficially it was to bring Britain and its need to the notice of every American newspaper, every magazine, every radio station that could be persuaded to photograph or interview Ginette Maslova. It should not be a difficult task, as the memory of Ginette Maslova's famous father, the Russian conductor who had scaled the heights of the American musical scene, was still fresh. Her mother was to play in benefit concerts, and she was a very persuasive woman. She might be regarded as a great pianist; she was also, even in her forties, a very beautiful woman. Her marvelously slender, tall figure, clad in one of the shimmering concert gowns that Julia thought of as miracles of color and brilliance, her little speech at the end of the concert, slightly accented by her native French, appealing for help for refugees, would be, in fact, one of the best propaganda machines Britain

3

could send to the U.S.A., whose help was needed so desperately.

The "Phony War" had ended at last. The declaration of war last September had sent children, and many of their mothers, fleeing from the cities. Those who could manage it had gone overseas. They had left the cities, and nothing had happened, no air raids, no bombing. Many had returned, bored by "the country," which they didn't understand or like or feel comfortable in. But now Dunkirk was over and done with, the British Expeditionary Force had returned, almost intact, but without arms or the means of defending their country, much less waging war. And Goering had at last decided to send his Luftwaffe to bring Britain to surrender, as France had surrendered. The Battle of Britain was now raging in the skies over southeastern England. The people were leaving the cities again, fearful. And Julia's mother worried over the polishing of one tiny phrase of Mozart.

Julia went back to the lines she was trying to memorize. Cordelia was an impossible role—far better to have been Regan or Goneril. But Cordelia had been assigned to her, so she must play it for her teachers at the Royal Academy of Dramatic Art, well aware that she would be judged more harshly because her father was who he was.

Her mother, perhaps in frustration because she could not achieve the perfection she desired, had abandoned the Mozart sonata. That would be for cities in the U.S.A. not large enough to have symphony orchestras, in which she would give recitals. She now launched into the first, slowly building chords of the Rachmaninov Second Concerto, a work that always brought audiences to their feet, the irresistible concerto, the big tearjerker. That she would play, along with the Tchaikovsky First, the two Brahms, the Beethoven Fourth, wherever a symphony orchestra existed. She would endure battered, ill-tuned pianos, inadequate orchestras, mediocre conductors to raise money and sympathy. She would also play with the greatest, and be worthy of them. Her mother, that seemingly delicate figure, was renowned for playing the huge works usually requiring the strength of a man. Julia tried to pull her attention back to what she was memorizing: ". . . *in the most terrible and nimble stroke* . . ." She stopped.

The noises overhead forced themselves upon her. They were

at it again. The Germans had come over to bomb the airfields in this corner of England to dust, the fighters had come to escort them, and to destroy the terrier-dog defiance of the Spitfires and Hurricanes of the No. 11 Group of the Royal Air Force Fighter Command, who fought with manic determination to defend their fields. On everyone's mind was the knowledge that with Fighter Command defeated, the cities would lie open to the bombers. So the squadrons scrambled to their planes, on a telephone order, many times a day, fought day after day. The pilots were more valuable than the planes, which, with difficulty, could be replaced. The trained men could not. Only last week a fighter pilot had come down in Anscombe Wood, there, darkly gathered at the ridge of the low hill within Julia's gaze. Watching the parachute and the man descend, farmers had gathered with shotguns, and where they didn't have shotguns, with pitchforks. They had waited for the enemy and had found a British pilot. He was unhurt, except for his pride. He had lost his plane, but he had seen his opponent in the aerial battle turn into a deep spiral, trailing smoke and flames. The farmers had given him food and beer and driven him back to his airfield. He had thanked them and said he would be flying again tomorrow. They never even asked his name, just what soccer team he supported. He had replied, with a distinct Welsh accent, that he played rugger. That was the acid test to distinguish friend from foe, who might be landing in an RAF uniform.

Julia heard the *crump crump* sounds of bombs landing behind Anscombe Wood. The Germans must have been trying for Biggan Hill again, and now, on their return run to France, were letting their bombs fall at random. Nearer there were the shriek and whine of fighter planes engaged in deadly combat. She never thought of going to the Anderson shelter constructed in the vegetable garden. No one ever used it. But the sound, the noise, made the study of her lines impossible.

She went to the long French windows cut into the fabric of the fourteenth-century manor house, and her eyes searched the skies above. She could see nothing. She opened one of the doors, its glass crisscrossed with strips of paper, and stepped out onto the lawn. Across a neat green stretch, in the oasthouse, which had been converted long ago, when her mother had first come to England, into a music room and a library, her mother's playing had not paused. They were all so used to it now. She had reached the big crashing chords at the end of the third movement; Julia doubted that when her mother played she heard anything else at all. Then, as she listened to both sounds, the first, tightening premonition reached her, the first clutch of fear. Something still out of sight, but close by, was happening. The whine of an engine became shriller, like the death cry of an animal. It came hurtling into sight at last, a flame-engulfed machine, spinning, weaving, wildly out of control. The noise now was thunderous, blocking out whatever her mother played—if she played at all. Even she must have stopped. There was an actual sensation of heat as the fireball descended. Involuntarily, Julia stepped backward. But the glass doors offered no shelter or protection, any more than the ancient wood-and-wattle building did. The aircraft skimmed the trees of the orchard, coming from the direction of Anscombe Wood. It seemed to bounce off the trees once, and lift, and then it plowed on. She saw it hit the oasthouse. The world was all flame and heat, and the smell of instantly burning old dry wood—heat and dust. The shock from the impact threw her backward. She hit her head on the edge of a footstool.

When she raised herself again the oasthouse was engulfed in flame, like some gigantic pyre. It was barely possible to distinguish even the shape of the aircraft in the twisting, burning wreck. The building and the plane were melded into one. The engine of the plane, living a demonic life of its own, plowed through the end of the oasthouse and into the tall beech hedge. Julia started to run, but the heat and the shock waves pushed her back. She tried to cover her face but could not. For an instant she thought she saw a figure writhe within the inferno. But it was only for a second or two. She stood there and saw her mother, the piano, the books, the long beams, everything, consumed. In the last moment she was aware of consciousness, she saw, as some kind of cruel fantasy, that the fuselage of the plane, which had endured for some minutes, bore the well-known three rings of the Royal Air Force.

It had been one of their own that had killed her mother.

Her father, Sir Michael Seymour, reached Anscombe only hours after Julia telephoned the theater. He was in rehearsal for *The School for Scandal*. He had stood with Julia as firemen combed the wreckage, at times laying his bare hands on the still-smoldering beams as the search for his wife's body continued. When he saw that pitiful thing they finally brought out, he was forced to turn away, staggering, clasping a hand over his face. His arm went about Julia's shoulders blindly, seeking her support. "Oh, my God! . . . my darling . . . my beloved . . ." What was laid on a stretcher was light and of no substance, covered quickly with a blanket. They found no other body there. The French doors to the drawing room still stood open, their glass smashed despite the tape, the frames hanging askew. The furniture and carpet were soaked with the water the firemen had poured on the small manor house of Anscombe, a jewel set in the sweet beauty of the Kentish countryside, when its wooden shake roof had been threatened by sparks from the inferno of the oasthouse. Overhead the German bombers from France, with their fighter escort, had begun another run toward the airfields of England.

She took her father into the dining room, away from the sight of the oasthouse. Stella, who had passed from the role of nanny to the family, to housekeeper and general dogsbody, brought sandwiches and tea. Apart from Cook, she was the only domestic staff they had left. Stella sniffed, her eyes puffy from weeping. "Eat!" she commanded Sir Michael. He didn't seem to hear her. Julia went and brought a bottle of brandy. The bottle rattled against the glass as he poured, and then drank the draft in one swallow, and poured again. He sat and consumed the next more slowly, staring unseeingly at the uprooted rose garden, which had been sown with vegetables.

"It's been on the six o'clock news," Stella announced. "As if she was—like the Queen or something. . . ."

"She was!" Michael shouted. "But she was like nobody else!" He drained the glass. The telephone rang.

"It's started," Stella said. "Shall I answer . . . ?" She looked at Julia.

"No—I will."

The calls kept coming all evening. Julia was aware that an extra operator had volunteered at the little local exchange to help handle the many calls. "I'm so sorry, Miss Seymour," the two operators each had said. One added, "Such a lovely lady. We'll do our best, but there are so many calls. . . ." And amid the logjam, Julia was aware that there would be the despairing calls from her two sisters.

Just after eleven o'clock, an official RAF car arrived. No less a figure than a Wing Commander alighted. He was led by Stella to the dining room. As Michael Seymour rose to greet the officer, he staggered. He had refused all food that evening, but had sat stolidly drinking.

"I had to come, Sir Michael. Simon's the name. I'm stationed at Hawkinge." Hawkinge was one of the bases on the very front line of the battle, one from which the airmen had to scramble many times a day to try to intercept the German fighters and bombers as they crossed the perilously short strip of the English Channel. He remained standing, even though Michael had waved him to a chair.

"It was one of our chaps whose plane hit here. I'm his CO. He's one of our very best. Won a DFC when his squadron was in France. Great pilot. Bit of an ace, really. He's brought down a lot of German planes. He was badly shot up today, but he managed to bail out. Got smashed up as he landed, too. Hands badly burned. They've patched him up after a fashion. The latest report was that they think he'll live—but he's got a lot more to go through before he flies—if ever he flies—again."

Michael shook his head. "Look—very decent of you to come. I appreciate your effort—the time. With all that's going on. But I really don't want to know. I wish him the very best of luck, but I don't want to know anything about him. All I know is that those boys are fighting—and dying—every day. Had one of them come down just over the hill the other day. They're all brave young men—and if we survive, we'll probably owe it to them. They're fighting a front-line battle in the air, and we happen to be underneath. Not his fault. The fortunes of war . . ."

In a gingerly fashion the Wing Commander had responded to Michael's increasingly impatient gestures for him to be seated. "I thought, Sir Michael, that was what you might think. I really didn't want to intrude. But when this chap came out of the anesthetic, some idiot let it drop that it was all on the wireless—about your wife—about Lady Seymour—er, Madame Maslova. He made one of the nurses swear that she'd ring Hawkinge. Someone, he insisted, was to come to see you to say . . . well, what can one say? How can he possibly say he's sorry? I have come to represent him. We all regret civilian casualties, but to have killed *her* . . ."

"Might have felt worse if his plane had plowed into Canterbury Cathedral. My wife was mortal—as we all are. None of us is a monument. She can't have felt anything for more than a few seconds. She was at the piano. She would probably have described it as the perfect way for a musician to go. Ah, but—or, for God's sake, man, have a brandy. Simpson, is it? Have a good stiff one. It helps. . . ." Julia realized her father was terribly drunk.

"Not a monument, no . . . wouldn't have wanted to be. A real woman. The young man, whoever he is, shouldn't feel that it was an uncommon death. Tell him that. A plane dropping on the cathedral would have been a loss of our heritage. Diving into a row of houses could have killed a dozen women . . . a score of women. . . ." The marvelously controlled voice, controlled even in grief and drunkenness, went on. The Wing Commander moved uneasily on the edge of his chair, taking swift sips of the brandy Julia had poured, listening, as people had always listened, to her father. The famous, handsome face, lean, dark-eyed, the chiseled chinline bowed toward the glass, had already taken on deep lines Julia had never seen before, as if a knife had carved them downward. Lines she had been rehearsing that afternoon came back: ". . . *in the most terrible and nimble stroke . . .*"

He spoke of her mother with love, and that was the truth. It seemed unimportant now that he had had several affairs with other women. In time, as had her mother, as had her sisters, Julia had come to see that the affairs were just that—affairs. Her father loved women. He admired and desired them. The long periods when he, or Ginette, had been on tour and he was alone had been the reason for those affairs. Other women were the objects of desire or admiration. His wife was both of these, and much more; the woman he truly loved. All of that was in his voice now—self-reproach, anger, near-despair. "I loved her, you see," he repeated to the Wing Commander. The blackout curtains were drawn, and the room lighted by a single lamp. Michael Seymour's expression was utter desolation. Now his eyes, as well as his voice, wept.

In the hall, the telephone rang yet again. Julia went to answer it, and the Wing Commander took the opportunity to leave. He shook Michael's hand. "I'll tell our young man. . . ."

"Yes, tell him. Say . . . say 'a necessary loss.' We all make sacrifices. Must do . . . thanks for coming. . . ."

It was, finally, Alex on the phone. "It's taken hours to get through." Julia's eldest sister's voice was firm, unwavering. "They said at the theater that Father had left long ago. They've been very decent here—laid on a car for me. I'll be there before morning." That would be a car from *The Record*, the newspaper for which her sister worked. "How is Father taking it? Yes . . . as I imagined." Alex's tone dropped to a low pitch. "Did you . . . did you see it happen, Julia? God!—like that! You could have gone, too! I had to wait here until we'd gone to press. I haven't an idea where Greg is, but I expect he'll turn up. I never know what he's covering. We're getting reports of a lot of enemy action. It's front-page news, you know. About Mother. I saw our story for the morning edition. It didn't seem real. There's a picture of her. I had to accept it when I saw that. My favorite picture of her. I wish they hadn't used it. She didn't seem to belong so much to me as to everyone else."

"She did belong to everyone," Julia said softly. She guessed from the silence that tears had started for Alex, tears postponed and swallowed back all evening while she finished whatever she had been working on for the paper. It was typical that she would have seen the paper go to press before accepting the gesture of the press baron, Lord Wolverton, who owned *The Record*, of the offer of a car to take her home.

Other women would have broken down and wept, would have left their desks. Not Alex. It was these qualities in her, rather than her striking good looks, which resembled their father's, that had captivated the man, Greg Mathieson, who was one of the Wolverton syndicate's best-known and -respected correspondents. He was divorced, with one child, and fourteen years her senior. Like most journalists, he seemed perpetually broke. It did not seem the sort of marriage someone like Alex Seymour might have been expected to make. Her parents had counseled waiting, offering neither approval nor disapproval. Alex had waited a year, and then, when Greg Mathieson had finally returned from his assignment with the British troops in France, where he had waited with them on the beaches of Dunkirk until almost the last moment, sending dispatches when he could, enduring the strafing and the exposed position, wading into the sea to climb aboard almost the last of the armada of little ships that had come to take them home, Alex had waited no longer. She had married him in June, with no word to her parents, and two friends from *The Record* as witnesses. Michael and Ginette had made the best of it. Alex was twenty-six and had waited long enough. The Seymour flat in London was too small for the occasion, so Michael had hired the River Room at the Savoy and invited all their friends to celebrate—all their friends and, it seemed to Julia, half the staff of *The Record*, as well as Lord Wolverton, who was a longtime friend. The worlds of theater and music and journalism had gathered, and Michael and Ginette had smiled, as if the marriage had been their idea all along. "It can't last," Julia had heard someone say as she sipped black-market champagne among the throng. "A bloody waste of a girl like that . . ."

Julia did not agree. She liked Greg Mathieson. She liked him even better as she began to read his pieces. He was the rare combination of a man who could analyze the battle action he observed, whether it was the German sweep into Belgium, the Dunkirk evacuation, or the simple, small triumphs and tragedies of war. This morning his report in *The Record* came from an undisclosed airfield somewhere on the southeastern coast. Daily he watched the scramble to the hastily refueled aircraft, waited for the often depleted squadrons to return. Today, instead of commenting on the count of numbers of British and German aircraft shot down, he had chosen to write a story about the nonreturn of a pilot whose dog had waited in vain, had refused to eat or rest, had howled, and greeted the landing of each aircraft with hope, and then had slunk off in growing despair. The dog's name was Tuff. On the third day the Squadron Leader, newly promoted because of the death of a friend, could stand the howling no more. He had risked an hour off duty and taken the terrier to a small cottage some miles from the airfield, near the village pub where the squadron all went when there was time. The cottage housed eight children, six belonging to the family, and two evacuees. He had hoped for distraction for the dog. Greg had gone with him. On its front page *The Record* had carried a picture of Tuff, perched on a rocking chair, surrounded by eight adoring faces, being fed a biscuit. It was on such things that the country's spirit, at this moment, also fed, and Greg Mathieson knew it. And it was in such a way that they would report the death of Ginette Maslova, depicted as a heroine, and the grimmer details would be omitted.

Later, when Julia felt she could not possibly take any more

phone calls, when her father had fallen into a drunken but not peaceful sleep in the big bedroom he had shared with Ginette, clutching the worn gray rabbit that had been his wife's good-luck mascot and that had accompanied her to every concert, waiting in the dressing room—later, when even Stella had gone to bed, the phone rang again. From the kitchen Julia had gone to answer it. She was in her dressing gown, waiting for Alex, waiting to warm the milk and stir in the cocoa. She knew that this time the call would be from Constance—Connie. The familiar, loved voice was strained but in control. She was at Bently Priory, Stanmore, the headquarters of Dowding's Fighter Command. She worked there as a plotter in the Operations Room. "I've just come off duty. It was pretty fierce. They didn't tell me until then. They've got a car going to Hawkinge, and they'll drop me off at Anscombe. I have seventy-two hours' compassionate leave. I'll be with you soon."

Connie—she would bring warmth and order to everything; her calm presence might even help make some sense of the carnage, soothe the futile anger Julia felt at the taking of a precious life, might even drive away, for a time, the stench of charred old wood. She was midway in age between Alex and Julia; she had always seemed the fulcrum on which the other two had teeter-tottered in their relationship, sturdy, immovable. In the dazzling array of talent and temperament in which she had grown up, Connie had seemed like a fixed lodestar—while aspiring to no stardom. Constance. How well she had been named, Julia thought, and it was not for the first time. How she ached for Connie's presence when she knew it would be all right to give way, to let the tears flow. Their father would pass into her care. The affairs of the house would flow through her hands. They would lean on her, as unconsciously they had been doing ever since she had emerged from childhood into sturdy adolescence.

Julia heard the sound of wheels on the gravel. Alex would have directed the driver past the front door and around to the back of the house The painted-out headlamps, which gave only slits of light, would have shown little of the wreckage of the oasthouse. But it was a night of a bomber's moon. All night the skies above had been heavy with the sound of their motors, the drone of the bombers, the sharper whine of the fighters. The moon would have shown too clearly, hurtfully, the twisted mass of the beams of the oasthouse that had fallen in upon themselves, fallen on their mother. Julia switched off the kitchen light before pulling back the blackout curtain from the door. In silence the two sisters put their arms around each other. It seemed for minutes that they stayed that way. No tears came, but Julia sensed the heartbeat that was as swift as her own, the choked words that would not immediately come.

Julia remembered the other presence. "Would . . . would your driver like something? There's cocoa . . . perhaps a whiskey?"

"Thank you, but I'd better be on my way." He wouldn't want to intrude, Julia thought. He might be hungry, or longing for a drink, but he would have seen the outline of the oasthouse as plainly as Alex had. No more than the Wing Commander would he want to stay.

They sat for a long time close together at the corner of the big kitchen table, almost huddling as if trying to gather comfort and stength from each other. In fragments Julia told the story in the random words she could find. The sound of the bombers and the fighters began to taper off. A bird had started to utter its first cry of the day in the beech hedge where the engine of the plane had come to rest. Perhaps it had lost fledglings in the fire. Perhaps it merely called to its mate.

"She was practicing," Julia said. "She kept playing one little phrase of Mozart over and over—you know how she was. Then she seemed to get angry with it. She played the Rachmaninov—straight through—not stopping to go back on anything. The sounds of the planes almost seemed like an orchestra—accompanying her. Perhaps she felt that way, too. I don't think she ever stopped playing until the plane hit. I couldn't hear. It was too close."

Alex's hand went tentatively to Julia's face. She traced the line of both eyebrows. "You were pretty close to the fire. Did you know your eyebrows are singed? And your hands . . ." In a most uncharacteristic gesture, she raised Julia's hands to the light and close to her own lips. She touched the bandages Stella had wrapped about both palms. "Does it hurt, love?"

Julia shook her head. She had hardly noticed this small pain beside the greater one. "The doctor came. He gave me something for the pain. And he gave Father something, too—it's sort of knocked him out. That, and more than half a bottle of brandy. It really hasn't begun to hurt—not yet. I keep thinking of her—"

"Don't!" Alex said curtly. "It can't have been more than a few seconds." She went back to what Julia had told her their father had said about it not being as bad as Canterbury Cathedral taking a direct hit. "He can't have meant it."

"He would have. A histrionic gesture, I suppose—but he can't help being what he is. You must tell Greg that. It might be her finest memorial. He *did* love her so. He's like a child now, clutching her rabbit. . . ."

The early dawn had come. Above them the skies were silent, radiant. It seemed that the weary warriors who battled for supremacy in that sky had, for a time, withdrawn—but only to regroup again. Except for the birds, now in full chorus, the world seemed hushed. A sweet, soft English morning, in the waning of an English summer. It should have smelled of roses and dew. But the smell of ancient charred wood hung over it, and the achingly cold touch of death.

The sound came at last, momentarily stilling the birds' calls. The gravel spluttered against the old walls of the house as the car roared up. There was no hushed reverence in the sound. It was immediate and urgent.

Connie stepped out of the passenger seat of a rather beaten-up military car. She paused to say something to the occupant of the backseat—perhaps offering hospitality, as Alex had. Then her hand went up in a trim salute. The backseat passenger would be an officer on the way to Hawkinge. They had had, from Bentley Priory, to cross London in the blackout and make their way to Kent. They had managed it in remarkably quick time.

The light from the kitchen streamed out, the blackout no longer needed. The Seymour sisters were known in the worlds of the press and the theater for their good looks. From their parents they had inherited fine bones, long necks, and jawlines that could never photograph badly. They all moved with a kind of liquid, lightning grace that was their mother's gift at the keyboard, their father's gloriously smooth presence on the stage. "The sensational Seymours" they had been called, even young Julia, who had barely passed out of adolescence. Only Connie did not seem to be aware of how she struck others, unaware of her own beauty. But she had inherited the best of both her mother and her father. She was the middle child, and the best of all the family had.

She pushed her cap back off her unpowdered face, her blue

uniform baggy and wrinkled after the long night on duty, the long ride. One thick, unflattering stocking had begun to slip over the sensible military shoes. Her weary, anguished face was still as beautiful as the English morning.

She held out her arms to them, and they came running. "Darlings . . ." Worldly-wise, Fleet Street—hardened Alex, and young Julia, still groping for her way in the world, came running. Connie's arms encompassed them both. Their heads bowed together, and at last they wept.

Above, as the light grew, the first RAF scramble of the day went up, to repel the invaders. The brief peace of the morning was gone.

II

Two DAYS LATER, Ginette Maslova was buried in the churchyard of the square-towered church of Anscombe, which dated from Norman times, and was recorded in the Doomsday Book. Greg Mathieson had joined his wife and her family. It was he who was mainly responsible for getting what remained of the oasthouse demolished. At first Michael had objected: "It should be her memorial. . . ." But his farm manager, Harry Whitehand, had interjected with the sureness of someone who knew Michael as a friend. "Don't be a fool, man! It's a danger to anyone who goes near it. You want some kids to get killed when that last wall comes crashing down? Look—we'll do something. Later. Plant if up with something pretty. When there's time . . ."

Michael had given in and retreated once again to the dining room and the ever-present bottle of brandy. Harry Whitehand had brought two farmhands and a tractor. Greg Mathieson had helped rig the ropes, and the whole household had flinched as they heard the crash of the falling rubble, and the dust had once again clouded the air and choked them. The windows of the drawing room were boarded up until they could find a glazier and glass to fix them. And overhead the battle still had raged.

When it was time to bury Ginette Maslova, they had all walked the mile along the dusty country lane to the church where her coffin lay. The gasoline for cars could not be spared. It was as beautiful a day as the one on which she had died. Michael, holding Connie's hand, walking with Julia at his side, Alex and

Greg, Stella, Cook, Harry Whitehand, and all the farm workers
and their wives following had audibly gasped as they had approached the village green, the cricket pitch, the church shaded
by its oaks. All around the green, horse-drawn vehicles, tractors,
and whatever other form of transportation people had been able
to manage, were gathered. A quiet crowd of villagers and what
were still thought of as "the gentry" of the neighboring estates
stood waiting. Flowers, gathered from cottage gardens and the
few picking borders not already plowed under for vegetables,
lay piled against the coffin.

"Who would have imagined . . ." Michael murmured. "I
thought they hardly knew her."

"They knew her," Alex whispered, almost fiercely. "They
knew her since the last war. They loved her because Grandfather
did. And then they loved her for herself. We were all born here.
They don't forget that."

People had come from London, either by car, using precious
gasoline, or by the unreliable train service, which must have
taken many hours. Some great names of the world of music
stood there, the world of the theater, from Fleet Street, humbly
silent as the family passed among them. Hands were outstretched in sympathy, the rough hands of farm workers, the
smooth hands of those who earned their living in softer, but not
easier, ways. Julia saw several large, important-looking cars
parked about the green. She looked around for the face of D.D.—
David Davidoff—the producer, impresario, probably the family's
closest friend, who had been part of all their lives. He stood
with tears pouring down his jowly mid-European features, just
inside the lych-gate. With him stood Lord Wolverton, Alex's
boss—"Old Wolfie," as they had called him from childhood.
His English reserve would not permit him the luxury of tears,
but his features were hauntingly sad.

The story of Ginette Maslova must have been in the minds of
many as the service was conducted, as they had sung the old,
familiar, comforting hymns. The organist of St. Paul's, Christopher Lloyd, had managed to make his way down from London, and he struggled valiantly with the old, gasping organ.
They sang hymns that bound them together in this moment of
their country's greatest peril, and another wave of German
bombers with their fighter escort crossed the English coastline.

As they moved out of the church, Christopher Lloyd played "My Country, Thee I Vow."

Many of the congregation, Julia realized, could remember when Ginette Maslova had come to Anscombe at the beginning of the First World War, the bride of young Michael Seymour, whom she had met, and married, some said in such reckless haste, in France, lingered with him for a brief honeymoon, and then, in the fact of the German advance and at Michael's order, had departed with her parents for England and to Anscombe. She was already pregnant with their first child. They had all been received with gracious bewilderment by Michael's father, Guy Seymour, whose family had farmed Anscombe's nearly eight hundred acres for so many generations that they had almost lost count.

It had been disappointing and painful for Guy Seymour to realize that his only child, Michael, would not follow him into running the farm, but had, while at Oxford, chosen, instead, to become an actor. There was no history of such a thing in the family. But his son was already beginning to make a small name for himself on the London stage and in the provinces when the war had broken out. Michael had at once joined the Army and gone to France. No one quite knew how he had had the time or the opportunity to woo and win his young bride. That the marriage had not had her father's approval was evident. Igor Maslov's name was beginning to be known well beyond the Continent—a controversial but increasingly popular conductor. He had left Russia with his wife, Svetlana, and their ten-year-old daughter after the 1905 Revolution because he had fallen out of favor with the Imperial Court and beause he considered the Czarist rule too repressive. In France they began to call their daughter Ginette.

He had been encouraged by his friend Diaghilev and often conducted the unfamiliar scores of the Ballets Russes—scores by Stravinsky, Ravel, de Falla. To make a living he had conducted what audiences had expected to hear, though the Germans thought their native composers, Brahms, Beethoven, Schubert, came out sounding too much like Tchaikovsky. He had been on the podium when his daughter, Ginette, had made her debut at age twelve, in the Mozart Twenty-first Piano Concerto. He and his daughter had been invited to America, and had had notable triumphs, though Maslov dismissed the American audiences as "provincial," and was too well aware that the appeal of his beautiful child had outweighed his own.

Then he had sternly returned her to her teachers at the Paris Conservatoire, telling her she still played like a child and must now grow up in music. By seventeen she was again playing for audiences, assured, authoritative beyond her years. Maslov had been jealous when one Paris critic had written: . . . *a rare talent that can only flower to greater beauty.* He had been furious when she had secretly married this unknown and virtually penniless young British officer who aspired to be an actor. He had declared that Ginette was still a child at heart and did not know that heart. But as the German armies had swept toward Paris he had heeded the pleading of his son-in-law and crossed the Channel to England. He and his wife had spent an uneasy two weeks at Anscombe, taking for granted the ready hospitality that Ginette's new father-in-law, a widower, had offered. They could stay as long as they liked, he said. As long as it took to win the war and free the country to which they wanted to return. No one any longer talked of its being over soon.

But the Maslovs had no taste for the country. It was a place to visit, not to live. They longed for their musical and literary friends. Igor was offered a guest conductorship in London, and they had gone eagerly. There was talk of another American tour. They kissed their daughter a fond farewell, and they talked of being there when the baby was born.

That left a quiet, homesick, almost inarticulate Ginette alone with her father-in-law. Where she had expected him to be stiff and correctly English, she found him gentle and concerned for her, in a way he never made too obvious. If he was disappointed in the profession his son had chosen, or the wife he had chosen, if he grieved that there was not a younger son to carry on at the manor of Anscombe, he never said so. With the growing knowledge of the slaughter in Flanders, there was serious doubt that his only child would survive at all. He did not hope for the miracle that Michael would suddenly turn to farming, to caring for the small, beautiful estate; he just prayed that he would return alive. He did not even express the hope that the child Ginette carried would be a son.

In those months of waiting for the baby's birth, Ginette's father gave concerts in London. He and Svetlana paid another visit to Anscombe and tearfully told Ginette that he must take up the offer of an American tour before the baby was born. It was, after all, necessary to earn one's living. With typical Russian impulsiveness Igor had given Ginette all the money they had managed to save from his London fees, saying she must not be a burden on this too-kind Guy Seymour, whom he privately thought stultifyingly dull. He had bade her take great care of their grandchild, to practice her music, and to sing to her child so it would be born with music in its soul. He was tactful enough not to mention that there was no piano at Anscombe. Ginette had never felt more alone in her life as she saw them off at the station, they obviously relieved that a duty was done and that only music lay ahead of them in America. They were facing a perilous and uncomfortable journey across the Atlantic and seemed quite lighthearted about it. "Are all Russians so . . . so careless of danger?" Guy had asked Ginette.

"Fatalistic—and melancholy. So they laugh and get drunk to shut it all out," she replied.

Guy Seymour realized her aloneness, her solitude. Unknowledgeable in music himself, he had realized that she starved for it. When her parents had gone, he had apologized. "My dear, how could I have been so blind? Of course you need music. I will see what I can do. . . ."

Even in those days of the 1914—18 wartime scarcity he had found the materials and somehow found the men to put into repair the oasthouse, where the hops had once been dried. It had been used as a playroom by Guy and his brother and had been let go back to spiders and dust when they had grown up. He refurbished it as best he could and begged the loan from a friend of a baby grand piano. He had the chimney swept, and he lighted a fire there every morning to dry the place out. He had spent three days in London in the unaccustomed pursuit, for him, of music manuscripts. He was amazed at the stacks of music Ginette required. "After the baby," she said, "a teacher . . ."

"But surely . . . well, I thought you already *knew* all this music stuff."

"I am only beginning," she said. She was touched and warmed by his kindness, by his concern for her. She began to hope her child would be a son, who would not turn out to be an actor or a musician but would farm the fields of Anscombe as the Seymours had done for so many hundreds of years.

While her body grew rounded and bigger with her child, she

had gone back to the scales and arpeggios; shyly Guy asked her why she didn't play any *music*—music as he understood it. "I have been away from it for a long time. I am afraid of the way I would sound. Warming up, first, Father." That he understood.

"Is it terrible for you—all this music?" Ginette asked. "You would rather something you used to dance to . . ."

"Not at all," he said, and meant it. "I'm learning there's far more than that."

On a day close to the birth, he had brought her a glass of sherry in the oasthouse before lunch. He had carefully watched her diet, as he did her health. She had raised her glass to him. "Now, a little Mozart, I think. If you can forgive the fumbling, the wrong notes. I hope the baby does not hear too well." She had played a Mozart sonata for him, a seemingly simple thing, which he guessed was not simple at all. She had been amazed to see tears in his eyes. "I have disturbed you?"

"No—you have made me very happy." This beautiful girl, born in Russia, as foreign a being as he could have imagined, was suddenly the daughter he had never had, the sister he had never seen, the mother he had loved, the wife who had died too young, after she had given him only one child.

She gazed at him across the piano. "You have given me so much. Such calm here. Peace in which to let my child grow. He will be a very strong child. He will grow up here and be the one you wanted Michael to be. He will be here when he is grown up—when his foolish parents have gone on making music and play-acting, and he will farm Anscombe as you have, and walk the fields. He will be Russian in his love of the land, and he will be English in the way he cares for it. He will be christened in the church of Anscombe, and he will be called Guy Michael . . . and tucked at the end, so his other grandfather will not be hurt, we will put Igor. But he will be English. . . ."

But the telegram that went to Michael in France read: *A beautiful daughter, Alexandra, has been born. Ginette and baby well. Love, Father.*

"I'm sorry, Father. Next time a boy. As soon as Michael comes home, we will make another baby. And it will be a boy. For you."

"It couldn't matter less," he had replied, looking adoringly at his granddaughter. He had stayed near Ginette during her labor, and had been terrified that she might die, as so many of his family had. "Get strong, and play your music to your baby. We will want you both well when Michael comes home."

An ancient wooden cradle had been placed near the fire in the oasthouse. For two years Ginette had played her scales, had played Bach and Beethoven and Mozart, and had watched her daughter begin to crawl and then to walk. Once a week she had gone to London for a piano lesson, feeling guilty because she did no useful work. "Your time will come," Guy had said. "It is your duty to preserve your talent—even to preserve your hands. The world has as much need of your kind of woman as those good souls who hoe their vegetable patches and roll bandages."

Anscombe was too small, too medieval in its layout to be requisitioned as a convalescent hospital, so Ginette finally prevailed on Guy to let her offer voluntary help at the home of one of his neighbors whose house was being used as a hospital. She began humbly, washing dishes and scrubbing floors. Guy fussed over her hands and somehow found lanolin, which he himself, without the slightest self-consciousness, rubbed into them. Gradually, as news of Igor Maslov's success in the United States began to cross the Atlantic, the hospital authorities pressed Ginette into service to do a little Sunday afternoon entertainment for those they nursed.

At first she had simply played at a badly tuned piano in the hall of the mansion, the popular songs they requested—"Keep the Home Fires Burning"; "Tipperary"; "Rose of No-Man's-Land." She had sung the lines, and the French-accented voice had enchanted them. Then someone had realized that she was a musician in her own right, and more as a compliment to her than to please the men, had suggested she play something of her own choosing. So she played, at times, a little Mozart, Chopin, Schubert. One day, when there had been no one available at Anscombe to take care of her child, she had brought Alex, as she was called, with her to the hospital. At the end of a long day of being cared for, and spoiled, by the kitchen staff, the tired child had slumped on the floor against the piano, sucking her thumb. Then Ginette had sung, in Russian, a lullaby. There was no applause at the end—the child had fallen asleep—but tears welled in the eyes of the men. The golden-haired mother had picked up her very dark-haired child and bowed her good-bye. Hands had reached out to touch her as she passed. "Looked like a painted picture, she did, with the kid an' all," one of the

men had said. "A madonna," the Medical Commandant, who
had been passing and stopped a moment to listen, had commented. Some of the women, who had also served at that hospital, had carried that memory to Ginette Maslova's funeral
during the Second World War. Country people have long memories.

They had had a telegram from a hospital in Reading, England,
that Michael had been sent there after being wounded in France.
Guy had held Ginette's hand in the train as they had journeyed
to see him. "It can't be so bad," he said, to comfort her. "The
bad cases die in France." He didn't mention that the bad cases
who survived got sent home to England.

It was a shrapnel wound to his leg. They had waited through
anxious days because the doctors feared gangrene would develop
and the leg would have to be removed. Michael joked feebly
through the pain. "Well, at least it wasn't my face. I would have
spent the rest of my life playing Richard the Third." After long
weeks, with the danger past, he had been sent to the hospital
close to Anscombe, where Ginette worked, and had seen his
daughter for the first time. He had sat with the other men and
officers for the little Sunday afternoon teatime concert Ginette
gave, holding his daughter like a precious charge and gazing
with adoration at his wife. Then he had been allowed back to
Anscombe to convalesce. He had sat each day on the lawn, or
inside the oasthouse, and listened to his wife practice, walking
at times to keep his leg exercised and to keep Alex from disturbing her mother.

"My darling—I don't know how I had the temerity to marry
you. You belong on a world stage, like your father, not a housewife buried in the country."

She had shrugged. "All in good time, Michael. In good time.
I am young. An artist needs to grow. I grow here in this peace,
the beautiful place your father gives to me. I grow with Alex. I
am not a bad mother, am I, Michael? Not a bad wife to you?"

Their lovemaking was both tender and passionate, and they
were both more mature than the lovers who had come together
so briefly in France. But when the convalescence was over and
Michael was ordered back to France, Ginette had wept for more
than his going. "I am not with child," she had said, sobbing,
to Guy. By now she felt that her most intimate thoughts could
be shared with him. "I had so hoped . . . I am afraid, Father.

He goes back again . . . so few return." She had increased her work at the hospital, now being trusted with more than menial chores. She resumed her once-a-week piano lessons with her London teacher, who had scolded her for some rustiness in the playing but complimented her on the changes in her approach to it. "At last you play like a woman, not like a precocious child," he had said. "I begin to think you will match what your father predicted for you."

Alex was growing, and learning to ride a very old pony at Anscombe. Her grandfather taught her, and she wept stormy tears when she was not allowed to accompany him on his tour of the estate. "Later, my pet, when you are older. And poor old Pony is too tired to carry you all the way. . . ."

The war ended, not in a blaze of glory and victory, but in a terrible exhaustion of great armies that had fought each other to a standstill. Michael returned with the rank of major and a DSO. He also joined the ranks of those looking for work as an actor—no longer so young, but with his good looks refined and rendered like steel. "We have all been case-hardened," he said. "I don't think now I could ever play Romeo." But he played numerous minor Shakespearean roles and won some individual praise for them. He did his stint in playing in repertory companies through the provinces, enduring the discomforts, the separation from his family with good humor. Ginette prepared for her first London recital and told him she was going to have a child. Unlike Michael's modest successes, her recital was a triumph, and critics and impresarios realized that Igor Maslov's daughter had not burned out as a prodigy and must now be regarded as a serious talent.

Constance was born at the end of 1919. Her grandfather Maslov had returned, with Svetlana, for a series of concerts in England. He listened with grave composure while Ginette played. "You have become better than I would have hoped." He shrugged and held his palms upward. "Though how you have managed to do it in that bourgeois backwater I will never know. Though I do admit Peter Danilovitch is not an unworthy teacher." Peter Danilovitch had been known as the St. Petersburg Conservatoire's best piano teacher. He had moved on to Paris two years before Maslov himself and then had established himself in London. Ginette had instinctively sought him out as her teacher.

"But now you need others—other influences," her father continued.

"I have a child—and a young baby. There is a limit. . . ."

He shrugged. "So? Women are always having babies. Did that stop Clara Schumann? She had eight and was the greatest pianist of her time after Liszt. As soon as the baby is old enough to travel and I have finished this tour, you will come to us in New York. I will select your teachers—"

"I have a husband, Father."

He shrugged again. "So? Let him find a job in New York for a year. Let him stay at home and take care of the babies. Who cares? This marriage was a mistake from the beginning. Though the old man"—he referred to Guy Seymour, who was the same age as he—"has not done badly by you."

"He has been the world to me."

"So you no longer love your own father . . ."

The tug-of-war started and did not end. Ginette appeared at Queen's Hall as soloist in the Beethoven Fifth Piano Concerto, with her father conducting. It was a charity concert for war veterans. She was immediately offered a contract by HMV to do the full Beethoven cycle with her father. But the recording would have to be in New York. "Not yet!" her father decreed. "She needs more training. When my daughter records, it will be the best. She must come to New York to study for a year. For two years." Igor Maslov was very dissatisfied with the current recording techniques and did not wish to commit Ginette or himself.

Michael packed her off on a ship with her parents and the two children and a young nanny, Stella, whom Guy Seymour paid for. "I'll be with you soon," Michael promised her. He had a tentative promise of a part on Broadway.

It was nearly six months before he came. He was the alternate lead in a group that would perform Shakespeare on Broadway and then go on tour throughout the States. He stayed at Ginette's parents' large apartment on Central Park West, in a strange, Gothic-like building called the Dakota, and silently witnessed the world of music flow in and out. Only a few of his own group were admitted. "They don't understand actors," he said simply to Ginette. And it was true. He suffered the silent disapproval of his father-in-law for the months he was in New York and nearly choked on his hospitality.

"Keep your money, my boy," Maslov had said grandly. "Actors always need money. And I can easily take care of expenses here."

"I heard Mozart died a pauper. And I can take care of my own children." It was true that Maslov was enjoying great success as a conductor. He traveled regularly to Boston and Philadelphia and Chicago. What irked him was that he had not been offered the permanent conductorship of any orchestra. Reluctantly he recorded the cycle of Beethoven symphonies, still not happy with the sound he heard—but they brought money and added to his audience.

Michael chafed under Maslov's patronage and was glad to set off on tour. He hardly knew his own children, and they didn't understand his role as father. Ginette worked ceaselessly for her coming Carnegie Hall debut. Alex constantly cried for Anscombe and "Grandfather." They all knew she meant Guy, and that did not please Maslov. On Michael's opening night in Chicago as Hamlet—the first time he had ventured on the role—Ginette telephoned to wish him luck and to shout down the crackling line that she was pregnant. "Soon, my darling—soon. I will make this debut here. I will do the concerts with him in Boston and Philadelphia. And then, when your tour is finished, we will go home. Our baby will be born at home with Father."

"Home?" he echoed with some bitterness. "Where is home?—and who is Father?"

"Home is Anscombe. Father is Guy. And you are the father of our son. This time it will be a boy."

The schedule was completed as she predicted. Michael had scored something of a triumph during his tour, and he had been able to hone his parts without being under the eagle eyes of the English critics. He radiated a new confidence, and a presence on the stage that made him outstanding. He had even dared to make himself into Caesar in *Caesar and Cleopatra* in a special, short run arranged in New York, and he had brought it off. It was the first time he had played Shaw, and the reviews were excellent. Ginette was heavily pregnant when they arrived in Southampton. She fell into Guy Seymour's arms. "Home again, Father." Maslov, still angry at her departure, had gone to San Francisco to conduct the newly opened Opera, and then he journeyed to Los Angeles to the novelty of conducting at the Hollywood Bowl. He was becoming a conductor known to the masses, and that made him suspect in musical circles.

Ginette's child, born at Anscombe in 1921, was a girl. They named her Julia Svetlana, after Guy Seymour's mother and Ginette's mother. Ginette gave concerts in London and Manchester three months after Julia's birth. Her father came over to conduct her in the five Beethoven concertos at a series of concerts at the Royal Albert Hall. Michael had an unprecedented four-month run in *Hamlet,* and the critics, some grudgingly, were beginning to write of him as being, perhaps, in the long tradition of the great Shakespearean actors. Ginette added the two Brahms concertos to her repertoire and broke away from her father's yoke to play them as she wanted to, under other conductors. She toured France and Scandinavia, having added Grieg and Liszt and Rachmaninov to what some people were beginning to call a "flashy" repertoire. But in Paris she had given a recital of Ravel only, and the critics had claimed her as one of their own, recalling her debut, at twelve, in that city.

She had come back, exhausted, thankful, happy, to Anscombe, to find that Michael had contracted to open on Broadway in *Outward Bound.* It was a run-of-the-play contract and so would be of indefinite length. Ginette rested and then went to Berlin, much against the wishes of Michael, who still had mixed feelings about all Germans, to play in two concerts with Furtwängler. That engagement finished, she followed Michael to New York, and this time they had their own apartment. Stella was still with them, and Alex had been left at home with "Grandfather." She was eight years old and had a governess. She had been adamant that she did not want to go to New York: "I like it here better. . . ."

Maslov had been furious at the independence of his daughter and son-in-law, declaring the Dakota apartment had plenty of room for them all, including the babies. But he could not keep himself away from his granddaughters, and he showered them with gifts they did not comprehend. He was plainly jealous of Michael. They were barely civil to each other. Ginette had been engaged to do a series of concertos with her father as conductor, and a new sense of struggle began to be heard when they performed together, Ginette imposing some of her own interpretations and tempos on her father. They collaborated in one of the first radio transmissions of a symphony concert; the public had grown fascinated by the tales of the clashes of temperament between father and daughter. "It's that Furtwängler!" Maslov roared. "He has ruined her!"

Michael had heard himself say, "I think he's made her."

"And what would you—an Englishman—know about music?" Maslov had found his niche with the public, but he remained faithful to his Russian heritage and to his friends, trying, whenever managers would permit it, to slip the music of Stravinsky into his programs, to play the music of the Diaghilev-inspired ballets *Firebird, Petrushka,* even the outrageous *Rite of Spring.* He conducted Ravel's *Daphnis and Chloë,* de Falla's *Three-Cornered Hat.* He remained, as most Russians did, eternally homesick for his native land. He played Russian music in a way no other conductor seemed able to match, and in the Tchaikovsky piano concertos he and his daughter were a perfect match of soul and fire.

Away from Maslov, Ginette and Michael enjoyed New York as only those who had tasted its success could. Michael hired a white Rolls-Royce to drive Ginette about the city; he bought jewelry he could not afford for her—trusting that the money would show up somehow. He demanded that each new concert gown should be a masterpiece. "You want the dress to be more than the music?" Maslov had stormed. Between them, Ginette and Michael spent every penny they earned. They partied and dined and danced, after the theater, in the spirit that only the new Jazz Age would know, but were wise enough and professional enough never to let such energetic romps sap their strength for their tasks.

"You bring serious music into disrepute" was Maslov's verdict on his daughter's behavior. He disapproved of the late suppers at Sardi's, where Michael always had a prominent table. He disapproved of most of the American attitudes Ginette adopted, and Ginette shrugged off his disapproval. Ginette and Michael quarreled and loved, and lived life with the full enjoyment of the young who know they were both exceptional people. After two concerts in San Francisco at which her father did not conduct, Ginette came back to New York and Alex's grubby, ill-spelled note: *Grandfather is sik.* Ginette canceled several concert engagements and booked herself and the children on the first available ship after receiving an evasive reply to the cable she sent to Guy Seymour. Michael could not leave the play, and he tended to be dismissive of the idea of his father's being seriously ill. "You can't go on the notion of a child, Ginette. She could have meant he had had a cold."

But she did go, and was rapturously welcomed at Southampton by Guy and Alex. "My dear, but it's nothing," he had protested. "Perhaps I've been overdoing it a bit. That farm . . . always something to be done, and precious little money to do it with. Doctors don't know what they're talking about half the time. A few little chest pains. Everyone my age has them." But she thought he looked strained, and he seemed to breathe heavily after any small exertion. "You shouldn't have canceled those concerts. You shouldn't have left Michael."

"I *should* have left my father," she retorted. "We were on the verge of coming to blows. Perhaps I shouldn't have left Michael. But we were living too much . . . what is it? . . . the good life. Drinking, staying up late . . . bad for both of us. I don't think he'll stop because I am not there. But as for me, I have used you as an excuse to come home. I need rest and quiet."

She returned to Peter Danilovitch for some lessons, some consultations about her deepening ideas on interpretation. She practiced daily for long hours in the oasthouse, which was beginning to be transformed into a room of rare beauty. Books lined one whole long wall, French windows gave more light, there were two pale silken Persian rugs on a newly laid parquet floor. One concert in San Francisco had bought her a Bösendorfer piano. She had set aside enough money from hers and Michael's spending sprees to install central heating in the manor house, and she extended it to the oasthouse. She played with her children and watched them grow. She got to know Alex again. She was happy, but impatient for Michael's return. The run of *Outward Bound* had been extended. *I miss you terribly,* he wrote. *I'm being good, but life's boring without you—Sardi's after the theater, and then early to bed.* That couldn't be earlier than 2:00 A.M., Ginette knew. *I want to get back to you, my love, and my babies. Kiss them for me. I long to be in your arms again.*

Guy Seymour appeared well enough to Ginette. His vigor seemed restored. He was cheerful, and clearly delighted to have her and the children at Anscombe with him. The governess was an extravagance, Ginette thought, but without her they would have had to think about a boarding school for Alex, and that Ginette could not bear. Between the governess and Stella, all

the children's physical needs were taken care of; she and Guy
supplied an overabundance of love. She decided to accept an
offer to appear in two concerts with Sir Henry Wood during the
Promenade season, to play the two Brahms piano concertos. Guy
Seymour proudly escorted her to both and sat in the dressing
room, clutching the worn gray rabbit she had carried with her
since her first appearance onstage with her father in Paris. Michael sent extravagent baskets of flowers on each night. *Home
soon*, he cabled. *Handing over my part to someone else.*

But he did not come soon enough. He was in the last week
of his appearance in *Outward Bound* when Guy, dining quietly
with Ginette after the children were in bed, suddenly slumped
forward at the table, sending china and silver clattering to the
floor. He slid from his chair and lay among the pieces. They
made him as comfortable as they could, with a blanket over him
and a pillow under his head. Ginette forbade the brandy that the
cook thought was the remedy he needed. The doctor arrived half
an hour later, but by that time Guy no longer responded to Ginette's urgent voice. "I'm sorry, Mrs. Seymour. He's gone. I'm
so glad you were here with him. He was very fond of you, you
know. And he wouldn't let me tell you how serious I considered
his condition to be. Just said: 'I refuse to be an old nuisance.' "

By the time Michael reached Anscombe his father was buried
and Ginette was bereft. He comforted her as best he could and
cursed himself for delaying so long. "I was never much of a son
to him. Never did any of the things that might have made his
life happier or easier . . . except marry you."

"Hush," she replied. "You did what you had to do. No one
can make a farmer out of a man who wants to act, or the other
way around. *I* cannot be the daughter my father would like me
to be. He would like me unmarried, without husband or children. With only him in my life. He wants me as his puppet doll,
playing just how and what he directs. *Your* father gave me a
home, love, and the freedom to be and do what I wanted. It is
a debt I can never repay."

Michael stayed with her quietly at Anscombe for a few weeks.
Then she saw his restlessness begin to emerge. "I have to earn
a living for us, darling. Can't live off you. Perhaps we should
sell Anscombe—have a big house in London for all of us."

"You cannot sell Anscombe! I would never permit it. I promised your father one day there would be a son. . . ."

He had looked at her incredulously. "You can't seriously think we must hang on to Anscombe just for that! There may never be a son. And I can't farm the place and work in the theater as well. We'd have to employ a steward . . . we'd have to—this place *eats* money. My father spent his whole life trying to repair the neglect and mistakes *his* father made. To pay off his debts. We're barely breaking even now. We could sell it, and live so comfortably—" He stopped as he saw her obdurate expression. "Well . . . at least let's have a flat in London. Staying in digs and hotels isn't right. A place for the children . . ." His features softened and he bent and kissed her. "For a son, if he comes . . ."

There had been no son, or any other child, much to Ginette's disappointment. They had lived the peripatetic lives of an actor and a working musician, Ginette more often touring than Michael, as he had settled into longer runs on the London stage, often declining Broadway because it meant being away from home too long. The London flat was convenient, but Anscombe was, for Ginette at least, home and refreshment. Her fame grew, as Michael's did. She played a few times a year with her father, their differences never entirely resolved. But a wary respect had grown between them. They made their peace, and her marriage to Michael, now that he was successful, received Maslov's reluctant blessing. The debts on Anscombe were finally cleared, and improvements were made. Ginette gratefully walked the fields with Harry Whitehand, the steward. "There must be a lot of peasant in me," she once said to him. "I have a feeling for the land. . . ."

In the mid-twenties had come what sounded to Maslov's ears as the miracle of electric recording. He enthusiastically engaged Ginette to make the Beethoven piano concerto cycle with him. It was an enormous success with the public, which before this had lain beyond their reach. He was furious when she then accepted Toscanini's invitation to do the two Brahms concertos. Toscanini then recorded the Rachmaninov and Tchaikovsky concertos with her. The dislike and jealousy Maslov displayed toward Toscanini were well known. Toscanini, aware of the near-idolatry in which he was held in the United States, behaved as if Maslov did not exist. But he had lavish praise for Ginette Maslova, and they made other recordings together, while Maslov fumed. She then angered both men by making recordings with

Furtwängler, Toscanini's great rival. The fury and the storm delighted Ginette and amused Michael. "Few people would dare be so independent," he said. "You've offended three great conductors. . . ."

She shrugged. "If I'm any good, they will want me again."

The frenetic twenties passed into the far more somber thirties. The children grew, and mostly they remained one another's friends. Ginette saw to it that they were separated as little as possible, especially when she was away on tour. They all eventually attended the same school. Ginette kept on Stella, who could take care of the small crises that arose when Ginette had to be away from them. All their vacations were spent at Anscombe. They grew used to their father being only a Sunday visitor there. They grew used to the sophisticated, bohemian world their parents inhabited. They hardly realized it was an unusual childhood.

They all went to see their father act—he was at his best in Shakespeare but could turn a nice show of comedy and satire in George Bernard Shaw. The playwright himself came several times to Anscombe. They attended their mother's London concerts. They were permitted to be present at some of the parties their parents gave, in which the worlds of music and theater mixed. They became used to the famous and the fashionable. Alex finished school and went to Girton College, Cambridge. Ginette sighed. "She is almost a woman. . . ." Ginette was happy with her life, overlooking Michael's occasional flirtations with other women. For her there had ever been only one man. She intended to keep him.

Her father came regularly to conduct in London, and always when he did, Ginette would appear in concerts with him. She gave an annual concert tour in the States. The battle of temperaments went on between her and Maslov, more muted now. He still bitterly resented his daughter's seeming disloyalty in accepting engagements to play with Toscanini. He never attended any concert at which she did so.

Ginette was grateful for the rock of security she and Michael had built in their marriage when the cable came that Igor Maslov had been killed and Svetlana severely injured in a train crash on their way from New York to Chicago. She and Michael and Alex were on the first ship leaving Southampton. Ginette received the news of her mother's death during the Atlantic crossing. The double funeral in New York was an event that the whole music world turned out for, and because of Michael, the theater world also paid its respects. Toscanini appeared, and no one could guess from his demeanor that any question of a rivalry between him and Maslov had ever existed.

"Maslov was a great show-biz man," Alex heard as she trailed and somehow lost sight of her parents in their procession up the aisle of the church. "He could play an audience like a violin."

Sadly, Ginette closed her parents' New York apartment, sending most of their treasures, the signed portraits of the famous, the collection of her father's recordings, the beautiful antique pieces her mother had indulged in as her husband's success grew, the jeweled Russian icons, the three Fabergé pieces, to Anscombe. Michael and Alex had had to return almost at once. Ginette could linger a little, supervising the packing, gazing from the windows of the half-stripped apartment as the dusk fell over Central Park. Had she ever told her father she loved him? That their quarrels had been the difference of temperament, not dislike? Had he been aware of the joys and jealousies of her marriage to Michael, the shared love of their children? If he hadn't known, it was now too late. She wrote loving letters to Michael and each of the three girls. They, if no one else, must know how much she loved them.

Michael was seduced into going to Hollywood, mostly by the money offered but also the thought of gaining a much wider audience, to make two films. He had come rushing back to Ginette when the news of his affair with a costar had become the source of too much gossip. This time he really feared that even Ginette's fierce loyalty would not stand the strain. "My darling . . . forgive me. I don't believe that until I thought I might lose you, I ever realized how much I love you. You are my soul. . . . Without you I don't believe I would—could—exist."

That next year he had played his first Lear. Ginette had watched him prepare for this supreme test and recognized a new maturity in him, as if his world had truly been shaken and he had been afraid. He was an enormous success. The critics spoke of "A new Seymour—one whose depth we have not seen before!" In the New Year Honours List he received his knighthood. Ginette was both Madame Maslova and Lady Seymour. She and Alex accompanied him to Buckingham Palace, where he knelt before the King and was dubbed by the sword on both shoulders. He was considered young to have been so recognized in the theatrical world, but there appeared to be few commentators who begrudged him his honor. The party they gave on the evening of his investiture was enthusiastically attended, and Ginette believed that most of the congratulations were genuine. There were laughter and champagne and toasts to Michael.

But in the background, in the corners where people stood and talked seriously, there was the *frisson* that lay over that whole year of 1939. Most of them feared war. They all hoped it would not come.

It had come in September, but it was nearly a year later that the line of battle was drawn in the skies over the Southeast of England. Two weeks after Ginette Maslova was killed, Goering turned his bombers aside from the airfields and directed them against London and other big cities. Afterward the historians would say that the Battle of Britain was then won, but the Blitz had just begun. This no one knew on the day that Michael and his daughters, his son-in-law, with all the attending farm families, had walked from Anscombe to the church and had seen the green ringed with vehicles. Then they still anticipated invasion. The famous there mixed with the unknown and the humble in that sea of faces. Michael moved through them in a daze, shaking hands, unable to speak a word, his great, beautiful voice stilled.

It seemed to Julia that a horde of people followed them on the walk back to the house—those who had come from London, friends from around Anscombe. A tea was waiting for them at the house, preparations Michael had not been consulted about. He had thought only of Ginette in those days since her death; that others besides himself and his family would want to stand by her grave, would take enormous trouble to do so, had not occurred to him. His own grief was enough, he had implied. She must know, that fragile bundle of bones, that only he in the world loved her with such passion, such reverence. Even her daughters, his beautiful children, had loved her in a different way. He didn't need the rest of the world to be there with them. He was silently resentful of their presence, knowing it to be kindly meant but unwanted.

At the house he went at once to bring up bottles of whiskey from the cellar, poured drinks lavishly, downing his own first one in a gulp, and quickly pouring a second. It was the only

way he knew that the pain of the presence of others, while he
wanted to be alone with Ginette, could be endured.

"There must be a memorial service in London," D.D. said.
"This is just a handful of the people who would have liked to
be here. She was a wonderful woman, Michael," he had protested as he saw the head shake of refusal. "You owe her this.
Owe it to your friends. Look, let me take care of things . . . I'll
start the arrangements going."

"I don't want—"

"Life goes on, Michael, and mourning one's friends is part
of it . . . life *will* go on. . . ."

Six weeks later, with London suffering the nightly hammering
of the Blitz, St. Margaret's Westminster was packed with those
who had come to listen to words spoken about Ginette and Michael, their talents, their laughter, their marriage, their love. It
was impossible to speak of one without the other. The music
was sumptuous; D.D. had had no difficulty in bringing together
a sizable orchestra, because almost every musician in London
had wanted to be part of the service to honor Ginette Maslova.
A famous contralto sang:

*When I am laid in earth . . . remember me!, but, ah, forget
my fate.*

At the conclusion of the service Michael had walked with an
expression of stone down the aisle, Alex beside him, Connie
and Julia following. He did not wait to shake the hands of any
who had gathered; it was evident he only wanted to be away
from the throng.

D.D. had provided his Rolls and enough gasoline to bring
them to the service and return them to Anscombe. The last words
of D.D. as he had stood beside the car had been: "As soon as
you're ready, dear friend, I will fix up a little something for you
in London. Cannot have you off the stage for too long. . . ."
Nothing was said about *The School for Scandal,* which Michael
had been rehearsing and had abandoned. Michael did not reply.

Connie had been given two days' leave, and Alex was returning to Anscombe with them. Michael sat in the passenger seat
beside D.D.'s driver, who was too old for the forces but did his
stint as a fire watcher. When at last they cleared the suburbs of
London, leaving behind the devastation of the bombing, the gaping holes where buildings had stood, the cratered roads blocked

off, Michael had turned piteously to the three women seated in the back.

"What will I do now? What in God's name will I do now?"

Alex spoke, bluntly, her words as swift and sure as the knife of a surgeon who must cut away a diseased part. "You will do what you have always done. You will go onstage and play your part. It is your duty, Father. It is the only thing left to do."

Chapter Two

MICHAEL DID NOT return to the stage, as Alex had urged. He returned to nothing but an indulgence of his grief. The London Blitz had virtually closed the theaters. At first they had been closed by government order, then reopened by public demand. But the night-after-night hammering that London took did not encourage audiences to attend, and when they did, they were mostly servicemen on leave, and others looking for a good time. Comedies and music hall were what they demanded. "I won't be missed," Michael had said.

"You're simply using it as an excuse," Alex had said. "There must be something you could do."

But he had fallen into a lethargy from which none of them could rouse him. Alex was living with Greg Mathieson in their London flat. They seldom bothered to go to air-raid shelters, preferring to take their chances. Greg was often gone for days at a time, on assignments to various parts of the country. Occasional pieces by Alex now carried her byline. She was encouraged by Lord Wolverton to write the kind of upbeat pieces that would raise morale, stories of courage and heroism, stories of simple acts of endurance.

"It's all the 'Britain can take it' stuff," she had once said with some bitterness to Julia. "I could almost be writing the scripts for *Movietone News*—all for export to America. What I don't write is that people are often cowardly and dead scared. They fight each other like dogs in the shelters for the better places. They don't share their food or their pillows. Sometimes they're downright cruel. I've even seen people looting the bombed-out buildings—if there's anything left worth taking. Of course, there *are* heroes—plenty of them. The firemen, the ambulance men and women, those incredibly wonderful women who just rush out and keep them supplied with tea and sandwiches. The air-raid wardens. The other night I saw—well, I saw a fireman just sort of swept into a kind of firestorm. Buildings on both sides of the street burning like mad, and the suction just—just, well, swept him in.''

''And what were you doing so close to it that you saw this?'' her father had demanded. ''You take stupid risks, Alex. There's enough to write about without going into the battle itself.''

''How can I know the battle if I don't see it?''

Michael had turned back to his whiskey and did not reply. The days had shortened into winter, and he sat by the fire in the dining room—the one room (apart from the kitchen, where the Aga stove was kept going) that they kept heated. He sat there, on his lap an open book that he rarely attempted to read, a glass of whiskey by his hand. Julia began to wish that the cellar had not been so well stocked before the war. She and Stella and Cook ran the house; Julia did not return to the Royal Academy. She sensed it would be a near-fatal act to leave her father alone in these months. Instead she worked every hour of daylight around the farm, mucked out the stables that housed the farm horses they had been obliged to return to for pulling the plow and the farm carts, boiled up the swill and cared for the pigs, fed the poultry, and reared rabbits that she could not bear to see slaughtered. She began to learn to drive a tractor—they had only two. She made friends with two Land Army girls who had arrived and who lived with the wife and children of their former gardener, who had joined up. But her true job, she knew, was to keep her father alive through these first terrible months when his will to live had seemed to desert him.

Christmas provoked no feeling of festivity. Julia's twentieth birthday in early 1941 passed almost unnoticed. She sat with her father and Stella at night and tried to make conversation, but there was little to talk about except the bombing of their cities and the shipping losses in the Atlantic, which were only briefly mentioned in the papers, so the morale of the civilian population would not be further undermined. Much, though, was made of the British offensive in the Middle East and the taking of Tobruk; then they began to hear about a German field marshal named Rommel. Back in September, when their heads had been sunk in grief, Germany, Italy, and Japan had signed their Tripartite

Pact. The omens for the future they only grasped at the times when Greg visited, and talked of the reality of what might happen.

In this winter of darkness, Michael went back to reading Ibsen, Strindberg, and Chekhov, relearning the parts, and he asked Julia to cue him on his lines. She listened and discovered again why her father was held to be a great actor; sometimes she would learn a part to play opposite him, however inadequately. "Someday, Pet, when you're older, you could make a great Hedda Gabler. And Nora in *A Doll's House*."

But Stella, who sat and listened, would shiver and remain silent. "It's all so depressing," she once complained to Julia. And more often than before, she retreated to the kitchen to listen to the popular radio programs with Cook.

Julia tried to get as many of Michael's friends as possible from the theater to come to Anscombe. Their company brightened him. D.D. came whenever he could, and Lord and Lady Wolverton. Julia helped Cook and Stella to try to turn the simple meals they served into something festive, always knowing that what they did was propped up by the excellence of the wines the cellar afforded. There were brief resurgences of spirit in Michael during these times. Occasionally someone could make him laugh. But no one could seriously urge him to return to the theater when there was scarcely a theater to return to. The Ministry of Information was becoming interested in the thoughts of producers who wanted to make what were virtually propaganda films, but there had been no victories for the British to boast about and therefore no likely subjects. Someone had suggested historical subjects, which would remind people of the victories of the past. Scripts based on Wellington and Nelson and Drake lay around the house, unread by Michael.

Only one thing seemed to interest him during those months. Piece by piece, using a horse and cart and sometimes just a wheelbarrow, he had cleared the debris of the oasthouse. The bricks that had not crumbled were neatly stacked in one of the barns; a few of the beams not completely consumed by the fire lay beside them. No one asked him what he intended to do with them. When the ground was completely clear, he requested a hand rotary cultivator from Harry Whitehand, and he hauled hundreds of barrowfuls of well-rotted manure from the piles around the cow barns. When the earth where Ginette Maslova had died was completely prepared, he began to make the rounds of his neighbors to beg cuttings from their roses, even uprooting whole rosebushes where they still remained. Most rose gardens, like the one at Anscombe, had been dug up and replanted as vegetable gardens.

Michael brought out the old charred beams and with Harry Whitehand's help had built a trellis for the climbing roses. "Later—after the war—we'll use the old bricks to put a wall behind it, for shelter." Some people thought it morbid. Alex had urged him to reseed the plot with grass.

"Oh, do leave him be," Connie had said. "It's what he *wants*. A grave in the churchyard doesn't mean anything to him." He read everything he could about roses, a subject that had never interested him before. He asked for advice. In February he saw the first tender buds begin to swell, delighted with those bushes that gave life, mourning over those that had failed to survive the transplanting.

"I can't believe Father is reduced to this," Alex said. "Tending a rose garden and fondling a whiskey bottle."

"Time," Connie counseled. "For God's sake, Alex, give him time. We all grieve in our own ways. He must be allowed to grieve."

"Perhaps you're right," Alex replied rather grudgingly. "But I'd like to see him out there doing something for living people, not burying himself with the dead. And *you*. Julia—when are you going to shake yourself out of this? When are you going to *do* something?"

Julia looked down at her broken nails, her callused hands. "I don't feel exactly unoccupied."

Greg Mathieson's even tones broke in. It was one of the few times that they were all together at Anscombe, one of the times when Connie was able to get leave to coincide with a visit from Alex and Greg. "Listen—all of you! Don't *you* start quarreling. That's the last thing your father needs. Connie's right." He looked directly at his sister-in-law. "I suppose I should add, 'as usual.' But that isn't the way I mean it. There is a time for grieving, and everyone does it in their own time, and in their own way." He turned to his wife. "If I got killed—"

"You'd better not get killed," she retorted sharply, "or I'll murder you. If you got killed, I'd probably work myself to death to try to forget it. So that'd be two of us."

How fiercely beautiful she looked, Julia thought, as her face
had colored with emotion at the very possibility of her husband's
death. She was so dark, like their father, with his eyes and brows
and hair. Connie, seated beside her, looked tired after coming
off a straight month's night duty at Bentley Priory. She was wearing an old sweater and corduroys, but in her their mother's classic beauty was undimmed. She had been the only one to inherit
her blue eyes, she had the exact shade of her corn-colored hair,
that sweep of long neck and jaw. Everyone regarded her as the
best-looking of the three sisters, and she seemed unaware of it.
Julia didn't know what to think of her own looks. She felt that
her features were still unformed—mixed up. She had her father's
dark eyes and a darker blond hair than Connie's, straight dark
brows in an oval face. They weren't the sort of looks that would
readily get her ingenue parts in the theater. Perhaps, she thought,
she'd be one of those actresses who played bit parts until they
were old enough to play character parts, whose careers amounted
to nothing much. She reflected on the nightly pounding of the
cities by the Luftwaffe and even dared to let the treacherous
thought creep in that there might not, after all, be any career.
Perhaps this truly was the end for Britain.

The wind gusted and howled around the house. Would this
be the winter of their defeat? It was heresy even to think of such
a thing, but she guessed that many secretly thought it.

She began to collect the cocoa mugs from the kitchen table
and take them to the sink. Their father had gone upstairs an hour
ago, nursing a glass and a bottle. She knew he craved sleep and
got little of it. Many nights she had heard him moving through
the house, making his way by the light of a flashlight that shone
through the gap between the bedroom door and the old, sloping
floor. It was as if he sought her mother, and yet knew the search
was useless. Sometimes she got up and brought him to the
kitchen, to sit before the Aga while she made cocoa, thankful
that, because they lived on a farm, they were never short of milk.
Sometimes he sat in silence, sometimes he talked of the early
days of his marriage, the times when Alex had been the only
child and he mired in the trenches of Flanders. Sometimes he
talked of the years when she and Connie had been born. He
talked of her grandfather, Maslov, and was able to laugh at the
battles they had fought for possession of Ginette.

"What a stupendous old tyrant he was!" he had said in unwilling admiration. "I never knew if he was really as good a conductor as he and some his hangers-on made out. He had a good press—and quite a few critics. But he was flamboyant enough to stay on center stage. His music was like that. He certainly knew how to conduct a row, and I mostly came off the worse . . . whenever I've had a row scene on the stage, I've modeled myself on Maslov. Ah, those were the days, Julia. Your mother and I—loving and quarreling. But we knew the quarreling wasn't important. The love was. . . . I hope you have a love like that someday, Pet. Something that sweeps you off your feet and you can't say no to. I hope it isn't disastrous. I hope it's something great and glorious. I wish you what I had."

He would stare at her. "I see so much of her in you. An expression . . . the way you move. More than the others." His face often looked haggard under the rumpled, dark hair. He wore a baggy old dressing gown, sometimes over a sweater, added for warmth. There was little of the famous actor about him at those times. He looked like a careworn man, older than his almost fifty years, who thought his life had ended in the holocaust that had consumed his wife.

Now Julia looked at her two sisters, but particularly at Greg, the only man among them. He, too, wore old, comfortable clothes, and she thought she saw lines and some gray hairs that had not been there when he and Alex had married. Smartened up, in his war correspondent's uniform, he looked younger, nearer to Alex's age. He rarely talked about the assignments he was sent on. What he wrote appeared in the newspapers—as much as the censors would allow. Some things he wrote were for overseas consumption—mainly aimed at the United States. She guessed that he was briefed on more secret things, things that the Ministry of Defense deliberately revealed to a chosen few in the hope that knowledge, not ignorance, would ensure that they did not pry any further, ask no more questions. He had been with General Wavell, and then, more importantly, with his field commander, General O'Connor, in North Africa as they had defeated the Italian forces, and had been at Bedafomm when the Italian Army had surrendered. The road to Tripoli was open, but the Allied troops were held back. Perhaps Greg knew why, but his dispatches did not hint at his knowledge. The British were then engaged only in the air and at sea. Greg had been recalled to London by Wolverton. There must be some other place for him to go. There, inevitably, would be other partings for him and Alex. Julia thought she saw the knowledge of it sometimes in the small, quick, intense looks that passed between them.

The next afternoon, a Sunday, as they had sat in the unexpectedly warm March sunshine and had tea on the lawn while Michael had wandered away to look again at the swelling buds on the roses, Greg had told them that he would be making a journey to Washington. "This Lend-Lease Bill the Senate has just passed is vitally important to us. Wolverton wants some interviews with those senators who backed it most strongly—the reasons why. If I'm lucky, there just might be an interview with Roosevelt. Wolverton is quite a chum of Elliot Forster. His papers have given Roosevelt his biggest backing—and God knows how many hundreds of them he owns, as well as his string of radio stations, not to mention *Insight*. He's not a 'hands off' proprietor—his editors think as he does, or they go. Through him we might just swing that interview. . . ."

His thoughts were far away, on the possibilities of such a meeting, and Julia didn't doubt that he had already begun framing his questions. He didn't say how he would get to Washington—the long, uncomfortable journey by military aircraft, or the slower, infinitely more perilous journey by ship, zigzagging in convoy, all portholes blacked out, constantly wearing a life jacket, and with the ever-present sense that any second could bring the swift wake through the water that meant the passage of a torpedo. Alex's face assumed a look of blankness, as if she feared to envisage that journey. She certainly would not speak of its dangers. She would not betray now, or ever, any sign of the fear that might clutch at her heart.

A chill little wind blew over the garden, reminding them that it was still March. Alex shivered and got to her feet, extending her hand to Greg to pull him up. "Too cold out here." Michael came toward them, finishing his inspection of the rose garden; his walk was shambling. From that distance he seemed almost an old man. Connie started to put the tea things together on the tray. "But it will soon be spring," she said. "How long will you be in Washington, Greg? Long enough to see the cherry blossoms?" She rose, holding the tray. "I'm sorry. I ought to know better than to ask questions like that."

He grinned at her. "You're darned right. I'll be there as long as it's fruitful for me and the powers-that-be to keep me there. No dates in this business, Connie. No promises, either. If I do a good enough job . . . well, who knows how these things go?'' He put his arm around his wife's shoulders, and as they walked across the lawn he bent and kissed her cheek; it was almost a gesture of comfort.

''He's trying to prepare her for the fact that he could stay a long time,'' Connie murmured to Julia.

''She already knows,'' Julia answered quickly.

Behind them Michael said, ''Someone told me soapy water was good for roses. Keeps off the green fly. You'll save the soapy water, won't you, Julia.''

''Yes, Father. Of course.'' Connie had an instant's vision of Julia hauling the sparse bathwater down to the rose garden, along with all her other chores. She and Alex, with their specified jobs, didn't, she thought, have much idea of what Julia actually did at Anscombe; she suspected that it was much more than she was given credit for. Julia had once, vaguely, hinted at joining one of the forces, but it had been no more than a hint. They all knew that she would stay at Anscombe until their father broke out of the web of grief that bound and made him almost helpless.

He was, Connie thought, a rather indulged man. She thought of the thousands who had suffered a similar loss, or worse. Some had returned to find not only their houses but also whole families gone. She thought of the gray-faced men and women she saw on the train on her infrequent journeys to Anscombe, her few trips to central London, people who walked through the rubble of the bombed buildings to their offices, weary from a night without sleep, but expected to go on with their jobs, some of whom would arrive to find their offices bombed or blasted, and they would begin the process of relocating in cramped and some-times almost intolerable conditions. Some started again from nothing, and were expected to do so. Her father and his rose garden seemed a million miles removed from the grim endur-ance of the populations of the big cities.

In a bleak mood she followed the others into the house. Early tomorrow morning she would return to Bentley Priory and the job of tracking the remorseless waves of bombers that came nightly from France. Would her father ever stir from that deep pit of gloom in which he seemed to wallow? If and when he did, it would be because Julia had stayed with him. She felt angry with both her father and Alex—her father because he seemed unaware of his selfishness, Alex because she did not recognize the job that Julia did for them all. When the spring came—finally the spring—would it be any different?

The spring did come. The days grew longer. The fields all around Anscombe were dotted white with the new lambs. The hedgerows began to leaf and blossom. Michael watched his roses anxiously and still refused ever to accompany Julia on her shopping trips to the nearby towns. There was little to buy, and each trip made her more aware of the damage suffered by the coastal towns, battered and with their beaches ringed with barbed wire. They were a microcosm of what she imagined London must be like. Neither she nor Michael had been in London since her mother's memorial service in October. It began to seem as if she would never be free of her father or Anscombe again.

Catching sight of herself in a mirror in a clothing shop in Tunbridge Wells, she stiffened with a sense of shock. Was this she?—Julia?—this too-thin girl with her hair dragged back for convenience and tied with a piece of tired ribbon, she with gaunt hollows in her cheeks and an ungirlish look of weariness about her? At Anscombe there never was time to look in mirrors. But what did it matter? Everyone around her was tired and strained. She completed the purchase of a sweater for her father, counting out the precious ration coupons, and made her way back to wait for the bus.

The April afternoon had grown warmer as she walked the mile from the village green where the bus set her down. Anscombe Manor looked peaceful as she topped the rise from the wood and looked down on it. The countryside around was pockmarked with the damage of the aircraft that had come down as the fighter had descended on Anscombe itself. But the metal heaps of the craft, enemy bombers and fighters, and their own craft were always cleared away—useful for something, if only for scrap metal. The swelling green of spring covered the ugly gashes where they had fallen. She began to see some sense in her father's labor to remove the ruin of the oasthouse, the struggle to make some little thing of beauty where ugliness and death had reigned. She even paused for a few moments by the rose garden to admire the rapid growth of the bushes, to recognize the promise they held for a June flowering. Then she went on to the kitchen to unpack her meager bits of shopping.

Cook and Stella were in the kitchen, and so was a young man in an RAF uniform, wearing the stripes of a Flight Lieutenant. He sat with a mug of tea and a slice of bread and butter in front of him. As Julia entered, Cook thrust a jam pot close to him, but he either didn't want it, or was reluctant to accept one of wartime's luxuries. He rose awkwardly when he saw Julia.

"Well, here you are, Miss Julia," Cook said. "You look as if you could do with a cuppa—"

Stella said, "This is Flight Lieutenant James Sinclair, Julia. I found him hanging over the gate, looking at the house. I could see he hadn't known the road ended here. . . . He'd got a bus over from Sparrow's Green—just wandering. He's in a convalescent hospital there. I thought the least we could do was offer him a cup of tea."

"Yes . . . yes, of course." It was tradition to offer servicemen whatever hospitality could be afforded—especially those who wore the RAF uniform in this part of the countryside, which had been so savagely fought over. But never before could she remember a serviceman wandering down what was really a private lane from Anscombe. There was nothing in Anscombe except the church, and a pub, which didn't open until five. He probably didn't even know that there was no bus back to Sparrow's Green that afternoon. He looked not only lost but also very uncertain.

"Had any luck with the shopping, Miss Julia? Your father will be glad to see you back. He heard some flak over the coast, and of course he's always expecting another." Cook turned away and got the kettle off the Aga, making a fresh pot of tea. "Well, Sir Michael's out with Harry Whitehand, looking over the lambs, I dare say. Don't know if he really sees them, but at least it gets him out of the house, and away from that bloody . . ." She caught herself. "Away from brooding over the roses."

Julia noticed that Stella was swiftly laying a tray, even laying a tray cloth, a nicety they hadn't bothered with for a long time. Delicate cups and saucers replaced the mugs. The plate of bread and butter, the jam pot, and the addition of some raisin scones were placed on the tray. "Julia," Stella said with the ease of one who had been giving her orders as long as she could remember, "why don't you and the Flight Lieutenant have tea in the drawing room? I opened up the windows, since the afternoon was so warm. It's pleasanter there. And you can let Cook get on with supper. . . .''

What is Stella trying to do? Julia wondered. It was one thing to ask a stranger in for a cup of tea, another to begin entertaining him as if he were a friend, or would become one. Julia dropped her packages on her chair. "Oh . . . all right," she said, and realized that her tone sounded ungracious. She was remembering the glimpse she had caught of herself in the mirror of the clothing shop. How long had it been since she had cared what a man's gaze on her could mean? How long since she had been aware that her hair was lank and stringy, her face without a trace of makeup, her nails broken and chipped, her body too thin underneath the good wool skirt and sweater that were relics from that time when it had been possible to buy such garments? She felt some color come to her face and was furious that she could not control it. She tried to avoid all airmen these days. They might have flown over and defended their house and land a hundred times—a thousand times—since the battles began last year, but she wasn't yet prepared for the sight of any one of them in the kitchen of Anscombe. Then she looked at him fully, and some instinct told her that this was no ordinary young man who had just strayed down their lane. There was something in those clear blue eyes that was not quite so innocent, nor so young, as his age might be. He had straightened himself to his full height— she thought he was about six feet—as if he were bracing himself. As she let her eyes stay on his face she saw the scar down his left cheekbone, saw where the line of his blond hair grew in a ragged way, as if a bullet had clipped it. She felt some shame at her churlishness.

Stella carried the tray to the drawing room. The French doors, which had had only half their glass restored, the rest boarded up, stood open to the lawn and the rose garden. The sun revealed the dust on the old, once-polished boards but brought out the silken sheen of the rugs. Stella laid the tray on a low table. "There, Julia—relax for a while. I expect your father will be back shortly. I've set a cup for him."

The young airman had followed slowly, as if he, too, were reluctant to make this move. Julia noticed now that he carried a cane but did not use it; he had a barely perceptible limp.

"Please sit down." He lowered himself onto the edge of a sofa. He was facing the open French doors, and sunlight fell on his face. Julia began to realize one of the other things that had flustered and bothered her. He was astonishingly handsome, with classic features that not even the scar on his cheek, on which she could now see the fading marks of the sutures, or the ragged crease at his hairline could mar. It was the sort of face, photographed in profile, that managers like to place on the billboards outside their theaters.

"Will you have more tea?"

"No, thank you. Have some yourself. You look—"

She gulped at the tea. "Yes, I know how I look. As if I've been dragged through a hedge backward. One forgets so easily . . . how things were. The way one used to look and the things one did to look that way."

"You look beautiful to me," he said, simply. "I don't find it easy to flatter people, Miss Seymour. Perhaps that's the Scot in me. I didn't come here to flatter anyone. I'd rather not be here. I didn't walk down that lane by accident. Walking that mile from the village was about the hardest mile I've ever traveled in my life. It's the extra mile no one wants to travel."

She put down her cup. "What on earth are you talking about?"

He gestured with his hand toward the rose garden through the French windows. "I heard about it. I heard someone talking about it in the hospital. About your father making a rose garden. Things that people as famous as your father—and your mother—do, get talked about. One can't help hearing things. Even my mother wrote from Scotland. A small item about the rose garden in a newspaper, she said."

"Yes—I suppose it would find its way into newspapers," Julia answered, her tone stiffened with hurt. "They think he's mad, of course. They think he's become a crazy old man, trying to bury his wife."

"Not crazy," he objected. "Loving. Grieving. Trying to do something to replace death with life."

"And what's all this to you? Why is it so special? Plenty of people are grieving these days."

"I have my own particular grief. Shame, if you want to call it that. I killed your mother, Miss Seymour."

Her hand flew to her mouth, trying to stop a cry of pain, of disbelief. "You—"

"Yes. My plane. The one I bailed out of. I thought I was

clear of all the towns around. Just open countryside. Chances of falling on a building are pretty remote. If anything, the wood up there''—he jerked his head sideways—''it should have stopped it. I had plenty of time to survey the land as I walked down the lane. But when I bailed out at that height, I really didn't have much idea what would stop it. I couldn't see very well. . . .'' The faintest gesture, which he immediately checked, indicated the furrow above his left eyebrow. ''We all hope, with a bit of luck, that the craft will carry on out to sea and hurt nothing and no one. I had no such luck that day. Survived, that's all. But I brought death to one of England's greatest families. I tried a dozen times to write to your father. But I couldn't. It's impossible to write to say you're sorry you killed someone. That you've killed a great talent as well as a lovely lady. That you've brought grief, not just to a family, but to the thousands she didn't even know but who loved her. I couldn't write it. I had to come.''

''You *didn't* have to come.'' Julia rose abruptly from her chair and went to the security of the open window, where she could keep her back to him. ''We didn't know your name. Didn't want to. Your CO came over, as you'd asked, but he never said your name. We never inquired if you'd survived—the operations. I suppose we didn't care. You needn't have come. You *shouldn't* have come. It would have been better if you hadn't. . . . I don't think any of us thought about the man involved. But I can remember . . . yes, I do remember my father saying to your CO that it was better than the plane dropping onto Canterbury Cathedral—or a whole row of houses where it might have killed a dozen women and children. Canterbury—yes, that would have been worse for the nation. But we lost *her.* I wish my father hadn't said that. People say these things when they are in shock. Naturally, he said something rather theatrical. But if it gives you comfort, then believe it. He did say it. But still . . . you shouldn't have come.''

Behind her, she sensed that he had gotten rather clumsily to his feet. ''For my own sake, I had to. Since I couldn't find the words to put on paper, I had to travel the extra mile.''

She rounded on him. ''Is it because it was Ginette Maslova? Because it was Michael Seymour's wife? Would you have gone to a demolished row of houses and gotten down on your knees? Would you have made a pilgrimage to Canterbury? No! You wouldn't! That plane would never have made it to the sea, and you know it. If you had stayed with it, trying to guide it away from everything, you would have been burned alive. It was your *duty* to bail out. We all know that. We need pilots more than we need civilians. You couldn't have controlled that plane. I *saw it*. I saw it from this window. The propeller had been shot away. The tail-plane section was half gone. The engine ended up plowing into that beech hedge—shot to pieces. We knew that. We saw it taken away. You survived to fight another day, Flight Lieutenant. You owe no one any apologies. You don't have to share our grief. In fact.''—she lowered her voice—''we don't want you to share our grief. I wish you'd go away.''

He picked up his cap from the arm of the chair and reached for his cane. ''You may be right. But I shared a lot of your grief, and my own guilt as well. Because I knew Ginette Maslova in other ways.''

''What do you mean—you knew her?''

''Please don't make the mistake of thinking that because I'm wearing a uniform I don't have any thoughts except flying. We become anonymous in this uniform. What if I told you that my mother took me twice, when we were in Edinburgh, to hear her play? That we have some of her recordings at home? A couple of my chums from Scotland who were with me at Oxford joined the RAF Volunteer Reserve the same time as I did—we were learning to become fliers before war was declared. I never believed in the Munich Pact, so I got ready. Well, that last summer before the war I dragged these two up to London to hear your mother play at the Proms. Yes—they liked her—the whole occasion, but they couldn't understand why I wanted to hear a particular pianist. I couldn't understand my own fascination with her, either. I don't know a damn thing about music.''

''It isn't necessary to *know*—it's what you hear, and feel. . . .''

He responded to the softening in her attitude. ''I only saw your father once—in *Hamlet*. I suppose he was great. All the critics said so. I just know I preferred listening to your mother play. You come of a very extraordinary family, Miss Seymour.''

She was looking at him very closely now, as he stood in the sunlight. He couldn't have been more than in his early twenties, but he was a veteran; the scars of battle showed on his body and in his mind, in the twisted sense of duty that had brought him here this afternoon. Her first estimate had misjudged him; his features were far stronger than those belonging to young men whose picture is posted outside a theater. The gash cut into his scalp was much deeper than she had first noticed. If he had been hit a little farther down, his brains would have splattered the plane. For the first time, to her shame, she saw that the skin of his hands was mottled, with strips of fire-red where skin must have been grafted. The skin still looked raw.

"Sit down," she said, her words coming in a burst. "For God's sake, sit down. Here . . ." She was pouring tea into a second cup. "Drink it if it kills you. I suppose I need to talk some more. . . ." With immense relief she saw him sit down on the sofa; cap and cane went on the floor. She heard the cup rattle in the saucer as she handed him the tea. "Of course it's taken courage to come here. It wasn't necessary, and—"

"And it wasn't wanted," he interjected. "Perhaps I did it for myself—as a sort of act of penance. As if I ever could be absolved."

"It's not for us to grant absolution. I see you're wearing quite a row of ribbons. Your CO said you were one of the best."

"Just a serving member of the RAF, Miss Seymour. We're all the same whether we get medals or not. I believe, and so do all my chums, that some of the best of us go down, and get damn all in the way of recognition. Medals don't matter when you're up there. They guarantee nothing. You trust your squadron to protect you, and you do what you can to protect them. We didn't think about medals in the days when they were trying to take out the airfields last year—Goering's big gamble. It was our job to shoot them out of the sky before they shot us. We didn't think much about the people below, either. Couldn't. You went up there to bring down German planes. Up and down again. Refuel. Wait for the next lot. Until one was numb. Killing on reflex action. But when I heard about Ginette Maslova I felt I'd killed too often."

"Please—don't! We live with it. My father called it a necessary sacrifice."

"But how I wish it hadn't been I who did it." He paused. "I expect in about three weeks they'll pass me fit for duty again. So I felt I must come before that. . . ."

She felt herself shiver. The afternoon was not, after all, so warm. "You think you might be killed, so you came here while you still could. You didn't have to go through this awful business. *We* would never have known. Shame on us that you had to make this journey. We should have made inquiries. One of us should have gone to see you in the hospital. I think war makes us selfish and hard. My sister Alex says so. She writes about it. So does her husband, Greg Mathieson. Heroes and cowards—they're all mixed up. I think we've been cowardly in not asking about you. It was something my mother would never have forgotten or overlooked. Why didn't we ask about you?—she would be ashamed of us. . . .''

"Never," he said. "Not *that* lady. I only heard her play. Saw her on a concert platform a few times. I don't think she'd be ashamed of anything any of you did. She was too warm and human a person for that—at least that's how she came over to me. It was my choice to come. None of you said a word of blame or accusation. Your father, even in those first dreadful hours, was forgiving. Understanding. I'll go back to duty feeling a little better. I've at least talked to you. I've seen the rose garden. I think it was my mother writing about the rose garden that forced me to come. She is not a sentimental woman—far from it. She didn't actually *say* I should come. But now she will know I've done—''

"What she thought was your duty?"

"No. For her it would be a very personal decision. All she will know is that I have traveled the extra mile."

"So she knows—about Mother? You were able to tell her?"

"When I found I just *couldn't* write to Sir Michael, I wrote to her about it instead. It helped a bit. Then she sent me the little cutting about the rose garden."

"The rose garden has probably been his salvation. It's the only thing he's done since—since she died. That, and drink. He looks on it, of course, as a memorial to her. It means far more than whatever words we'll finally put on a stone in the churchyard."

She saw the pain in his expression. She got up and went to sit on the sofa beside him. "I'm sorry. We all share it. She would have seen her death as no more and no less than any other woman's. She was very much aware that great talent is something that is visited upon one. In most cases it is the most terrible burden—something that has to be constantly lived up to." She felt herself, almost without volition, extend her hand to him. "We accept her death. Won't you?"

He took her hand as if it were something precious she offered. His hand in hers had the feel of something mangled, both rough and smooth. She felt the stretched tightness of the skin between thumb and forefinger. *"Will* you be able to fly again?''

"They say so. In ordinary circumstances they probably wouldn't put a crock like me back into a plane. But so many of the experienced pilots are gone. Because I was in the Volunteer Reserve I was ready when we were sent to France—got experience there until we got thrown out. Not all my chums were so lucky—even if they were damn good fliers. Now they're sending up raw kids who've just finished a very quick training course. They go pretty quickly, poor devils. Some didn't, at the worst time, clock up more than a few hours' combat. They hadn't learned the tricks of how to dodge death.''

She looked down and realized she still held his hand. "I'm glad you did—so very glad. . . .'' She felt the color mount in her face. She busied herself with the tea things. "Look, do try the blackberry jam. I picked them last September. The lane is always loaded with them!'' Without his consent she covered a piece of bread with the jam. The blackberries had been picked when she herself had been seeking any sort of distraction she could after her mother's death, as her father had begun to toil at the rose garden.

"We're lucky,'' she went on, trying to cover his silence. "On a farm, one can always cheat a little. Butter and jam. Sometimes we feel ashamed—and sometimes we just don't care. I hate to admit it's cheating, but that's what it is. I suppose we've cheated in quite a few ways. My father served in the First World War, and he hasn't forgotten how things were. They say actors are not practical people—but he certainly could see this war coming a long way off. He was convinced it would come. I can remember him giving us loads of money—more than he could afford, I suppose—and telling us to stock up on warm clothes. He stocked the cellars until they wouldn't hold another bottle. Hoarding. That's unpatriotic—now. But not then, before war was declared. He couldn't bear the thought that any of us would go without— not if he could provide. It was especially important to him that my mother would have everything he could possibly provide for her.''

She saw with satisfaction that he actually bit into the bread and jam. She found herself smiling at him, something that would have seemed impossible just short minutes ago. "You see, he suffered from father-in-law trouble. He resented the fact that, in the early years of their marriage, my grandfather Maslov was so much more successful than he was. My grandfather, being Russian, enjoyed throwing money around. He seemed to have especially enjoyed, my mother told me, being able to shower his daughter with things her husband couldn't give her. So as soon as my father *could* afford it—whether he went into debt or not—he just lavished things on her. On us girls as well. Nothing was too much. To this day, I still don't dare ask him about the overdraft."

He put the plate aside and leaned toward her. "You're very kind to me—Miss Julia. You're as kind and forgiving as he was—in what must have been his worst hours."

"I think there's little or no sense of hatred—or malice—in my father. He's a very human human being, full of faults. Rash, impetuous, given to fits of temper that blow over. But hatred or meanness isn't in him. In neither of my parents. They were, I suppose naturally, quite a bit more temperamental than most people. Rows were everyday things. Blowups! But that was all they were. They loved each other deeply. Forgiveness was a part of both their natures. They would think poorly of me if I didn't feel the same way."

"Thank you. I cherish those words."

"Then please eat up my jam." She had to do something to cover the emotion they both felt. In talking of her parents, in talking of forgiveness, she felt she had made a long stride in that direction herself. A sense of calm fell on her; she had taken a giant step in the direction in which their lives had pointed. She could face whatever came in the future with a touch of their maturity.

"I remember," she said, and her voice amazed her with the dreamlike quality of recalling, "I was trying to learn Cordelia at the time I picked the berries, and getting the lines all mixed up, and wishing there was someone to cue me. I was thinking of trying to be an actress then. That's sort of slipped away—over the winter. It seems pretty frivolous now. I think I'll join up as soon as—when Father's ready to go back to work. It isn't frivolous for him to act. He's needed. I'm not. My middle sister, Connie, is in the WAAF. She's stationed at Bentley Priory—in the Operations Room," she added with pride.

"Operations Room!—Those girls do one hell of a job there. We owe them a lot. Those and the ones who are fluent in German and man the radar stations along the coast and listen to the Germans talking on their intercom. That meant that at the worst time, we were warned in advance, and were up in the air, waiting, instead of being sitting ducks on the ground when they came over. But then we owe it to the girls in all sorts of ways. They kept the tea coming, and the bacon and eggs. Women have nursed and babied me all these past months. I love women," he said, simply. "They're the greatest."

"Some of them are. We all think Connie is. She never talks about what she does. It's almost saintlike the way she keeps her mouth shut about the bigwigs who come to visit. No one would ever know from Connie that Dowding was in charge. She makes me feel more than a little ashamed at times. And Alex—she's been in the thick of the Blitz. You might have noticed her byline sometimes in *The Record*. She got her job there because Lord Wolverton—we call him Old Wolfie—is a good friend. She started as a glorified tea girl, and then they began to send her out to report society functions and things like that. But when the men began to join up, the women were given more important jobs. You probably know her husband's name—Greg Mathieson?"

"Most people do. I've read his pieces and listened to him on the radio . . . oh, since Dunkirk, I suppose. Quite a hero, I think—although he doesn't blow his own horn. I even caught that broadcast he gave from Washington after he'd interviewed Roosevelt. I've tried to catch him whenever he's been on the radio. I've listened a lot to the radio these past months—there hasn't been much else to do."

"There isn't much else to do here at night, either. Just read—and listen to the wireless. Father put the wireless in the dining room, so he could listen to *his* sort of thing. Cook has always had her own set in the kitchen. She listens to all the entertainment shows. Stella decides where she wants to be. She used to be our nanny, and then she began to be a sort of dresser to our mother—and as you've probably noticed, she still bosses us all around. We can only keep the Aga in the kitchen going, and one fire in the dining room. It's hard to remember how warm and cozy this house used to be. My parents always had their comforts, whether they could afford them or not. My mother needed to be warm to practice. My father doesn't mind who knows that it was her money that paid for the central heating to go in. He's always called it the Brahms central heating. My grandfather Guy inherited a load of debts from *his* father, and the farm needed so much spending on it, there wasn't really much left over for luxuries. But I do remember fires in all the bedrooms when I was small—I suppose because we had so many of the farm workers' wives who were glad of jobs here at the house . . . oh, I'm running on. Life's changed for all of us, hasn't it? Do you think it will ever go back to being what it was?'' Her tone was faintly wistful.

He shook his head. "I don't expect it will. God, I can hardly believe how young and raw I was when I joined the Volunteer Reserve. Flying was a piece of cake. Even out in France. Good fun. Then when we got back here, and we knew we were fighting for our lives—well, it wasn't fun anymore, and I'm beginning to wonder if there'll ever be times I'd think of as 'fun' again. No . . . I don't think things will go back to what they were . . . no more than they did after the last war. Even the rich began to notice then that not nearly so many young women were willing to go into service for almost no wages. And not many young men were content to work for a landowner without the hope of ever working for themselves. My parents found that out. My father had had to let out most of the land to tenants—he farmed as much as he could himself, but it was never easy. . . .''

Almost automatically he handed over his cup to have it refilled, a gesture of trust and intimacy that warmed her. "We had fires, too, I remember—and someone to tend them, but not nearly as many as we needed. Now—like you, my mother heats just two rooms. The kitchen, of course, and what, in grander days, used to be the housekeeper's room. She lives between those two rooms—she and the dogs and cats, and in the scullery she puts the odd lamb or two when the ewes won't take them. She's got one 'treasure'—as we used to call them: Janet. She almost grew up at the castle. She's a marvelous cook—and will turn her hand to almost anything. Occasionally they get a bit of help with cleaning, but precious little. And that's all she has to take care of a bloody great pile that variously dates between the thirteenth and seventeenth centuries—a Scottish castle, towers and all. She goes to bed up in one of the towers with three hot-water bottles, and three dogs who sleep on the bed for warmth.''

"A . . . a castle? With towers?"

"A castle. Not a pleasant, warm, charming manor house like this. My father might just as well have been Thane of Cawdor. That's what the place reminds me of. Tall and big and cold, with dungeons, not cellars, and a guardroom with an earth floor, and a portcullis that's rusted into place. It's on a small island a wee bit out into a loch. There's a sort of causeway, and then three spans of a bridge, and a drawbridge that's half rotten. My mother's farming a couple of thousand acres, but a lot of it is hill farming—land that will carry only sheep. She's as tough as they come, and she looks too old for her age and too tired to care."

"Where in Scotland?"

"Inverness is our town—city, if you like. Capital of the Highlands. She's the daughter of an earl, and she married a minor chieftain of our clan. Obviously for love, because it certainly wasn't for money."

"You don't talk about your father."

"I hardly remember him. He killed himself in a hunting accident when I was about four. He was out looking for deer—for us to eat, not for the pleasure of the hunt. Nobody could understand how he'd been so careless. He'd been used to guns all his life. Must have slipped or something. They found his body in the bottom of a sort of ravine in the forest."

She began to understand his courage in coming here. "I'm sorry. You have brothers—sisters?"

"No, worse luck. I had a brother. He was killed when he was young. If there'd been someone besides me, my mother would have had more to spread herself on. But I was the only one—the one who had to take my father's place. I had to inherit. I think she once had the chance to marry again—to marry well. She was—still is, I suppose—a very handsome woman. But that would have meant leaving Sinclair. She would have had to turn over the management of it to someone else, and I wouldn't have grown up there. I was meant to grow up there and eventually take my father's place. There's a very strong streak of Scottish feudalism in her. Very clannish. She nearly lost the whole bet the day my plane came down."

Julia shifted her cup uneasily. He was very blunt, this young man. He laid no aura of romance over a turreted castle and an aging woman who kept guard over her son's inheritance. "She must be thankful you're alive."

"Thankful is hardly the word. She *expects* me to stay alive. I have to come home to my inheritance. I have to take over from her. She wants me married, and with children. She's even got the girl picked out for me. She was angry with me when I went into the RAF before I married her. She was angry with me for not going home to the Highlands as soon as they said I was convalescent. It would have been an excellent time to begin to court Kirsty."

"Why didn't you?"

"I suppose I wasn't sure that was what I wanted. I wasn't sure Kirsty would want *me*. Something of a crock. And I was having thoughts, too, about whether it was fair to marry a girl, and perhaps leave her with a child, when I knew that my life in the air was worth . . . I think I'll wait until after the war before I chance making any woman a widow."

"And this Kirsty—will she wait?"

He shrugged. "Who knows? She's a great girl, full of spirit. Intelligent. She grew up in the country and knows a lot about farming, which is why Mother wants her. And she has money. That would be useful. In Mother's view."

"And yours?"

He looked at her directly, and his mouth twisted in a rather bleak smile. "Perhaps that's what I couldn't quite take. She was *too* right. I think I could have had her for the asking, so there must have been something that wasn't right for *me*. We were good friends. Nothing more. I thought there should be more than that. So that's why I didn't go back to Scotland when they said I could go to a convalescent hospital. I stayed at the hospital at Sparrow's Green listening to the planes going overhead every night. I would rather have gone to Sinclair. In my own way I'm as wild about it as Mother is. I love that crazy old ruin. I love the country. Perhaps I was keeping away from Kirsty—or perhaps I was just being practical and remembering that I'd get this leg in working order sooner if I stayed where the weather would let me get some walking every day. The snow's pretty deep around Sinclair. It would have meant sharing the kitchen fire with the dogs. Not what the medics were advising."

So the winter of their grieving, Julia thought, had been the winter of his struggle back to life, with the thought that at the end of it would be a return to his squadron, and perhaps only a few more hours of life in the air left to him.

"So you decided you'd come here. In case there wasn't an-other chance."

"That's about it. I didn't know whether it was the right thing to do. I just did it." Once again he reached down for his cap and cane. "But I'm glad I came." He pulled himself up off the sofa and held out his hand. "I think I'd better be shoving off. Taken enough of your time. If you feel like telling your father—"

"I don't think I will. Perhaps he thinks you're dead. He's never mentioned the pilot. . . ." It was impossible now for her to associate him with that flaming missile that had come down and obliterated the oasthouse and wiped out her mother's life. He had a life of his own. A name. A personality. A background. "Just those few things he said when your CO came. Perhaps—much later . . ."

The warmth of the April afternoon had left them. The late sun now lay slantingly on the floor. She went over to close the French windows, wishing, for no reason she could name, that she could invent a reason for him to stay a little longer. At the window, she stiffened. "O God—here he comes." She turned back to James Sinclair. "Don't say anything—not about her. *Please* don't!" She raised her voice. "Father—you're late for tea. Shall I get some fresh?"

"I'd love it, darling. I'm parched." He was walking toward them from the direction of the rose garden.

"Father, this is Flight Lieutenant James Sinclair. Stella found him in the lane—rather lost. So she brought him in."

A broad smile lighted her father's face. "So Stella picked him up, did she? Brazen hussy . . ." He held out his hand. "How do you do, sir? I see why Stella picked you up. Gave you some tea, did they? Good. Well, you can stay and have another cup with me. Do go off and make it, Julia, dear. I'll just take the Flight Lieutenant to see the rose garden."

"Well, really, sir, I think I should be shoving off. If I miss that bus from the village back to Tunbridge Wells—and the con-nection on to Sparrow's Green—I don't think I'll make it back tonight."

"What—have they got you locked up somewhere? Hospital?"

"A convalescent hospital. They're pretty free and easy, though. They encourage one to get out, when it's possible. They just don't want us lost or straying."

"Well, as a matter of fact, I don't think there's another bus back to Tunbridge Wells this evening. . . ." Julia knew that her father would be the last person in the world to keep bus time-tables in his head. "But our steward, Harry Whitehand, has to go into Tunbridge this evening—some frightfully important farmers' meeting—more food for the nation. I think some big-wig from Whitehall is coming down to tell them what's expected of them. So using the petrol's all right. Harry can easily make a detour to Sparrow's Green. So you can stay and have some tea with me. And Julia, bring in a couple of glasses and some Scotch, will you? We'll take it into the dining room. Start the fire. But first I'll take the Flight Lieutenant and show him the rose garden."

Her father turned away, and for a moment James Sinclair looked back at Julia with an expression of near-desperation. But she simply nodded, and indicated that he should follow her father. He had come to face this, and now he must face it. Her father's voice drifted back. "It's quite new. I just began planting it this . . . well, last autumn. Everything else's been turned into vegetable plots. This is . . . this is rather special."

He stayed, having tea again with her father before the newly lighted dining room fire, tea that her father hastened through so he could produce the whiskey bottle and pour generous measures for them both. Julia had murmured something about going out to help Cook and Stella. "Nonsense, my dear. I've just inquired about dinner—supper, I suppose we have to call it. Cook's got steak and kidney pie all made up—rather less steak and kidney than we'd like but rather better than they're getting in the towns. And apple tart. She's sitting here with her feet up, knitting. I told her to put it forward a bit so Jamie here"—he had already dropped the Flight Lieutenant title—"can stay and have a bite with us. I've telephoned Harry Whitehand, and I had Jamie phone his convalescent place. They know he's all right and will be delivered back to the door. So you can just join us for a drink."

Unhappily, she poured herself a weak gin. There was now no way to warn her father, to tell him whom they harbored in their midst, whom he willingly and cheerfully invited to stay and eat with them. There was no way James Sinclair could escape the hospitality heaped on him. It was the convention of the times—

all servicemen were welcomed and offered hospitality. James
Sinclair belonged to that very special group that Winston Churchill had forever labeled ''the few'' who had saved Britain in its
most desperate hour. Her father had been able to read some of
the colored stripes on his uniform. One of them proclaimed that
he had won the Distinguished Flying Cross. Michael regarded it
as an honor to give the best the house could offer to an authentic
hero. She noticed that her father did not mention his own medal
from the war that now seemed so far away.

She went upstairs to wash, and to change her clothes, something she scarcely ever bothered to do now before dinner. Generally she was just too glad to slump in front of the fire, wiggling
her tired feet, at last freed of their boots, in the thick socks that
Stella had knitted. But now, after she had washed, she powdered
her face, put on a little lipstick, and brushed out her hair, which
surprised her by springing back to some life. She even used a
precious drop of the perfume she still possessed. Her mother's
dressing table held at least a dozen crystal bottles of different
perfumes, but no one would have dared to touch them, or suggest they be used before they evaporated. Ginette's clothes still
hung neatly in their closet. Her concert wardrobe, swathed in
muslin, had always occupied a small room of its own. It hung
there, untouched. No one would have dreamed of suggesting to
Michael Seymour, even in this time of rationing, that anything
should be given away. Ginette Maslova's possessions, like the
rose garden, were something he must be allowed.

She slipped back into the dining room, and her father rose to
pour her a stiff Scotch. He glanced at her in appreciation. She
wore a scarlet wool dress she had not put on for almost a year;
she had found it surprisingly loose at the waist. ''Very nice,
dear. Have I seen that dress before?''

''Probably dozens of times, Father. You don't think I bought
it in Tunbridge Wells, do you? Nor can you imagine how many
coupons I'd have to give up for it. By the way—I bought you a
sweater. That one's seen better days. . . .'' She didn't mention
that his chest of drawers was crammed with cardigans and sweaters, all of them cashmere, and not for digging the rose garden
in.

He looked down at the edge of one sleeve, which had ragged
threads hanging from it. ''Seen better days . . . I suppose it
has.'' His features contracted, as if in a momentary spasm of

pain. It occurred to Julia that this was probably the first time for many years that anyone but her mother had bought clothes for him. "Thoughtful of you, my dear. I'm sure you should be using the coupons for something pretty for yourself. . . ."

"You did all that before the war, Father. What do you expect me to buy—two pairs of large navy-blue knickers with strong elastic top and bottom, which is all that's on offer now?"

The spell of his self-absorption was broken. "No, Julia. Not that. I would hope not that!" He was busy filling up the glasses again. While she had been upstairs he had gone to the cellar and brought up a bottle of claret, which was open on the sideboard. She recognized it as one of his better wines. Obviously James Sinclair had earned some appreciation from him. Julia and the airman exchanged a long glance while Michael was busy with the glasses. Silently he shook his head, indicating that he had said nothing about his involvement in her mother's death. The small but vital lie they had contracted to act out was now a pact between them. When Michael said, "Well . . . cheers . . ." they looked at each other, then quickly away, as if the moment were too intimate and fragile to hold against the reality of what they had done.

Stella brought in the steak and kidney pie and the apple tart together and laid them on the sideboard. There was whipped cream and a generous slab of cheddar cheese. His face alight with anticipation, Michael poured the wine while Julia handed out portions of the pie. "How nice to have an unexpected guest," he said, raising his glass to James Sinclair. "Come back again, young man, before they put you up in one of those infernal flying machines. We'll look forward to it. . . ."

Too soon for Julia they heard the soft honk of Harry White-hand's car outside. They switched off the lights in the passage and saw James Sinclair to the door by the light of a flashlight. They ducked around the blackout curtain. The night was still and the sky clear. Suddenly, over in the direction of Dover and then all along the coast, they saw the searchlights of the antiair-craft batteries pierce the darkness and the too-familiar drone of the aircraft heading toward London. The guns had started their pounding, trying to pick the elusive specks from the sky. Then, closer to them, they saw the dim glow that told them incendiary bombs were dropping when planes had been stricken and had not the fuel to make their target, which was London, and were turning again to try to make their haven in France. "Doubt there'll be much of a meeting in Tunbridge tonight," Harry said.

Michael grasped James Sinclair's arm. "You'll have to stay, old boy. Nothing else for it. Plenty of room . . ."

Despairingly, Julia felt herself dragged farther into the vortex of their lie as Michael went back and happily settled himself before the fire, after producing a bottle of brandy. He had reached the point where he had begun to tell one of his myriad stories of the theater, always somewhat embroidered, sometimes out of context but always delivered with the wit of an unsurpassed raconteur, and in the voice and tone that had made him famous. He continued while Julia and Stella went to make up a bed. "Nice for your father to have company," Stella said. "It's too lonely for him down here. He misses company—it makes missing your mother that much worse. He should shake out of it and do something. . . . Well, I mustn't pass judgment. We all have our ways. That's a nice young man. I wonder why he wandered down here? Young servicemen usually stick to the towns when they're allowed out."

"He said he wanted to get out into the country. He comes from a country place. Scotland, of course—the Highlands."

Stella was silent for a moment as she tucked the pillow into its linen case, her gray hair falling in soft wisps from the severe bun she wore. She had a once-pretty face, gently worn with time. "Well, we all have our reasons, don't we? I would say he's had a hard time, that young man. I don't know how bad the leg was, but that scalp wound came near to putting an end to him. No hair will ever grow there again. And his poor hands. Nearly burned to a cinder, they must have been. Of course, Cook dotes on him already. I remember he just stood there in the kitchen door, after I'd invited him in, as if he weren't certain he should come in. She took one look at him and put the kettle on the stove. And I'm sure she was glad she had the pie all ready. Plenty to go around. Sensed your father would want him to stay." She was laying out fresh towels and a pair of her father's pajamas; she had brought out a new toothbrush. "We'll sterilize it after he's gone. Can't waste it. Now you run on down and keep them company." She placed fresh soap on the edge of the washbasin. As Julia opened the door, Stella threw a few words over her shoulder. "You look pretty tonight, dear. Got a little color in your face for a change."

At eleven-thirty Julia went quietly upstairs, having contributed nothing to the conversation between the two men—hardly a conversation at all, but just an audience, which her father craved. The level in the brandy bottle steadily diminished. The bombers and their fighter escort seemed to have finished their runs over London and had headed back out over the Channel. With the light out, Julia drew aside the curtain in her room, smelling the sweet, sharp chill of the April night. In a far pasture there was the bleat of a restless lamb. She could see the fires of Hastings and the glow of the sky over Dover. Would they never stop coming? Would there never be an end to this nightmare? Would James Sinclair live only a few hours, or a few minutes when next he flew up to intercept them?

It was very early the next morning when she came down to the kitchen, dressed in her corduroy pants and thick socks, ready to put on her boots and go down to help round up the cows for milking. Cook, as usual, was ahead of her. "He's gone, dearie. He found out what time the early bus left from Anscombe and said he didn't want to trouble us anymore. Pity—he could have stayed here just as well as that dreary convalescent home. He said to thank you—and Sir Michael, of course. Your father was sound asleep when I took him his early-morning cuppa. Looks as if he needs to sleep off last night."

Julia nodded, swallowed her tea, and chewed quickly on a piece of bread, unable to say anything. What had she hoped for—a cheery breakfast with James Sinclair when the milking was done, watching him devour a plate of fresh eggs and their own home-cured bacon while they talked? Had she no imagination not to realize what misery last night must have been for him, trapped with her and her father, acting out the lie she had fabricated? Acting out the silence because he had not dared to break the interdiction she had laid against him saying to Michael Seymour the words he had come to say? She had denied him the absolution he had sought. He would have been glad to have the words said, even if they had evoked a cold dismissal by her father. Instead he had received warmth and hospitality, and she had made his weight of guilt all the greater. He had walked the extra mile, and her own naïve good intentions had rendered the journey and the resolve useless.

She walked the half mile to where the cows were pastured, calling to them, and watching them come at a deliberate pace,

glad to hear her voice, needing to be milked. She thought that
she would never be able to work the sheep this way—she had no
command of a dog, and sheep were reckoned to be obstinate, if
not stupid animals. She patted the leader of the herd as she came
through the gate. "Hello, Primmie." She thought the cow turned
her head at Julia's doleful tone. "Well, Primmie—I think I blew
it. I'll probably never see James Sinclair again."

But they heard from him—a thank-you note from the convalescent hospital, a little stilted in tone. What else could it be? Julia
wondered. Only two more weeks before he went back on duty,
she thought, if he passed the medical exam, and, given the need
of pilots, that seemed more than likely.

Then something else arrived. It was a weekend when Connie
had leave. She had brought a young man down to Anscombe
with her, Flight Lieutenant Kenneth Warren. Although he wore
the uniform of the RAF, he peered at them myopically through
thick spectacles. "He's an aide to Air Vice Marshal Dowding,"
Connie had explained in her telephone call alerting them of her
arrival. "Intelligence—that sort of thing." He was a tall,
stooped, dark-haired young man with a forgettable face, his features straight and undistinguished, as if they had been arranged
for a dummy in a shop window. Michael had waited expectantly
for their arrival at Anscombe Station. He drove a pony and trap
with some style but little expertise, and his face wore a bemused
look when they all arrived at Anscombe in time for tea. It was
the first time Connie had brought someone home on her brief
leaves. "Can't make it out," Michael almost whispered to Julia
when Connie and Kenneth Warren were unpacking in their separate rooms upstairs. "He hasn't a word to throw to a goose.
Looks like a bit of a goose himself to me. But we'll see. . . .
Perhaps Connie's sorry for him. Can't be all empty up top, if
he's an aide to Dowding. But Connie . . . a gorgeous girl like
her . . . I thought when she finally did break down and bring
someone home, he'd be a real killer, like Jamie Sinclair."

Julia winced at the word "killer" and then smiled. "He's got
hidden qualities, Father. And he's probably terrified of you. You
haven't forgotten that you're famous, have you?"

He returned her smile a little ruefully. "Does it matter, Pet?
Well, we'll do our best by Connie. Make this a nice weekend

for her chum Kenneth. I don't even like his name. I wonder if he'd mind if we called him Ken?"

The conversation through tea and supper was wooden. Michael got little help with lowering the level of the whiskey bottle, and no comment at all on the fine burgundy he opened. Brandy later was declined. Ken, as he allowed himself to be called, was tight-lipped about his work and refused utterly to speak his boss's name. He did, however, offer a precise and good analysis of the aims and mistakes of the Allied forces thus far in the war—as good though not as colorful as Greg Mathieson would have done. He also had some predictions for the future, especially the desert war that the British were now fighting in the Middle East. "But we are doomed in the Far East," he concluded dryly.

"What do you mean—doomed?" Michael demanded, almost angrily. "Why, we haven't even got a war going there. No one can take Singapore from the sea. The Germans can't spread their navy that far. They're too busy blowing up our shipping in the Atlantic."

"When the Japanese come in—as they're certain to do—they will take the whole of the Malay Peninsula. They will *walk* down through it. They will enter Singapore by the back door."

"Look here—better not let anyone hear you say that," Michael objected, alarmed. "It's a preposterous idea. And you're not supposed to spread gloom and despondency."

"I only say things like that when I think the company can be trusted not to repeat them," Ken Warren answered. "You did ask my opinion."

"Yes—I see. Well, an interesting idea," Michael said, groping for words. "I hope for all our sakes you're wrong."

Ken Warren didn't reply, not did he appear apologetic. They had learned that he was the son of an accountant, had degrees from Cambridge and the London School of Economics. He had joined the RAF a year before the war broke out, having correctly predicted that that was what would happen and sure that by joining up early he would find his right niche. He had always known that his eyesight would bar him from active service, but they began to understand that in his quiet way, he could well have been an invaluable and also an almost invisible aide to whatever chief he served. He had known that he was destined to use his mind, not his body, in the service of his country, and his masters, swiftly realizing this, had placed him where he could do exactly that. Connie had told them that his only brother had been killed at Dunkirk. His parents had been bombed out of their house in Hampstead and now lived in cramped conditions with his aunt in a semidetached house in Putney. "He seems such an incredibly ordinary chap," Michael had commented to Julia when they carried the last tray of glasses to the kitchen and rinsed them. "What on earth does Connie see in him?"

"Perhaps having grown up in *this* family, she finds someone like him a nice, undemanding change," Julia offered. "And anyone with half an eye can see that he worships her."

Her father grinned at her and shrugged his shoulders. "You mean someone nice and 'unstagy'—no big temperament, no big scenes. Peace and quiet. Can't say I blame her, really. But next time it'll be someone different. Beautiful girl like Connie can just lift her finger and they'll come running."

"She hasn't shown much sign of lifting her finger in the past."

"There'll be others," her father predicted confidently. "You just see."

The mail came the next morning when they were all assembled in the kitchen at the sort of breakfast Julia had hoped for with James Sinclair—eggs, bacon, toast with generous mounds of butter, three different kinds of preserves from the pantry where Cook stored them from previous years, cream with the coffee. Ken Warren helped himself in a way that earned beams of approval from Cook. His thin, stooped frame looked half famished, Julia thought. She found herself urging more toast and butter on him and won a warm look of gratitude from Connie. It was then that Stella brought in the mail. A few letters, bills, and two packages.

"What's all this?" Michael said. Both packages were addressed to him. He opened the first, rather clumsily wrapped and tied. From it he produced a thick, navy-blue hand-knitted sweater and a note from James Sinclair. *Dear Sir Michael, My mother is an indefatigable knitter and seems to think I get through sweaters at the rate I grew out of my pants when I was a kid. I have three of these already. With your permission, sir, I'd like to offer this for work in the rose garden. Please do accept. It comes with my renewed thanks for your most generous hospitality. James Sinclair.*

"Well, this is a great present," Michael said, fingering the thick, evenly knitted ribbed garment. "I wonder how many coupons the dear lady spent on the wool. I really don't need it, but it would seem churlish to refuse it.''

Connie reached over eagerly and took the sweater from him. ''Well, *if* you don't need it, I know Ken does. He lost all his civilian clothing when his parents' house was bombed. I don't think I actually insult her if I say that Ken's mother isn't much of a knitter. He could use it. . . .''

Ken Warren turned scarlet as they all looked at the sleeveless pullover he wore. Inexpertly and loosely knitted, it seemed to hang on his bony body in thin folds. Connie held up the new sweater, measuring it against his shoulders. ''Yes, that would do very well. Winter may be over, but next winter is on the way. I'm sure it would fit under his uniform. Who did it come from?''

Between them Julia and Michael told the story of the night James Sinclair had spent with them. ''Well,'' Connie said, ''that's pretty good work on your part, Stella. Sweaters like this don't come with every lonely airman lost in the lane.''

''Nor this, Sir Michael,'' Stella said. She had been carefully unwrapping a very expertly wrapped and tied package—several layers of brown paper, hard to come by now, and beneath that, many layers of newspapers, which grew progressively damper as she went to the heart of the bundle. The very first shoots of a fully rooted rosebush had not even withered in the days it had taken for the package to travel. *Dear Sir Michael, My son has written of your most generous hospitality to him. In return I offer this from my very northerly garden. If it can flourish here, as it does, it surely will blossom for you in that much kinder climate of Kent. It is, by the way, a deep crimson in color, somewhat like the velvet gown your wife wore in one concert she gave in Edinburgh that James and I attended. I realize it's now a little late for planting where you are, but I have left a good ball of earth and trust it will take well in its new home. Sincerely, Jean Sinclair.* On the outside of the packing the return address read: Lady Jean Sinclair, Sinclair Castle, via Newton, Invernesshire.

Tears stood out in Michael's eyes. ''How incredibly kind of her. Jamie must have told her about the rose garden.'' Gently he touched the severely pruned bush, felt the dampness of the heavy ball of earth around its roots. ''She didn't say what its name is. Looks as if it's a reasonably young plant, from the pruning cuts. Could have a lot of years left in it.'' He put butter on the last of his toast hurriedly. ''Well, I'll get at it at once.

Can't let it dry out when she's gone to all this trouble." His eyes screwed up in concentration. "Deep crimson. I think I know just the spot for it—among a couple of pale ones where it'll show well. Deep crimson velvet . . . you know, I do believe I remember that dress. She used to keep it for places where she thought the concert hall would be cold. It'll be out of date now, of course. But it's probably still hanging up there in her wardrobe room. She could never bear to part with concert gowns. Some were for Tchaikovsky, she used to say, and some for Beethoven. I can remember a lilac chiffon one . . . she looked like a lovely iris in it. I think that was for Mozart. . . ."

Connie said briskly, "Kenneth and I will give you a hand, Father. We could go and bring a barrow of manure from the barnyard."

Michael blinked, as if he doubted Kenneth Warren had ever seen manure. "Yes—and I'll make a start on the hole. Make sure you get right into the heart of the pile, where it's well rotted. And bring some straw for mulch around it." His face had brightened, anticipating this addition to his beloved garden. "Maybe we'll call it the Lady Jean."

They had their morning coffee at the group of teak pieces of garden furniture that Michael had placed at one end of the rose garden. They had once faced the old rose garden, and so had escaped the fire. He eyed his new prize, standing nicely erect, the soil firm about it and swathed in damp straw mulch, to which the manure clung. He raised his cup to it. "I think she'll do nicely, even if it is a bit late in the season. I'll see that she's kept well watered to get her through the first spell. . . ." Julia had the feeling that Lady Jean Sinclair had somehow taken over a corner of a garden in Kent. "We should telephone that young man and ask him over. It must be terribly boring in that convalescent place."

Ken Warren's lips curved in his first relaxed smile Julia had yet seen, and his face was totally transformed; it spoke of a quiet, almost hidden humor, a pleasure in unexpected things. She felt herself warm to him. "Not before I escape with this sweater, I hope, Sir Michael." He fingered the good, thick wool with a gesture of possessiveness with one hand as he raised the other to put in his mouth the last of the three scones he had eaten. "I've grown very attached to it in these few hours. I hope the chaps in the mess don't mind the smell of manure. I shall tell them I've been digging for victory.''

Michael returned his smile, and his expression seemed to indicate that he also just might find the saving grace of humor in this rather unlikely young man Connie had brought home. "I'd bet James Sinclair wouldn't notice. And if he did, I'm sure he wouldn't begrudge it.''

Connie leaned over and placed another scone in Ken's hand, which he acknowledged with a nod before starting to eat it at once. "It isn't,'' he said, "that my mother *wouldn't* knit something like this for me—but she's . . . well, she's not very gifted along those lines. She's a very sweet lady, and I love her, but she isn't particularly good at—well—doing things. She's never learned to cook. Before the war, it wasn't necessary. My father took pride in the fact that he could afford help in the house for her. She's always been rather delicate, you see. My father . . . well, he comes from a rather humble background. He is old-fashioned enough to think he married above himself. He wouldn't marry until he could afford a house—a good house—for her. He worked like a dog to get himself ahead and even launched his own firm. Starting out on . . . well, sort of a wing and a prayer. Then my mother's father died and left her *his* house. It was a big Victorian pile. Quite an undertaking for my father, but he thought of it as something she had been born to, so we all moved there. I think it broke his heart to give up that rather sweet little place we had in Henley—on the river. The house in Hampstead had a big garden—that meant employing a gardener, as well as two maids and a cook. They went as soon as the war broke out, and of course they couldn't keep on Cook when they were bombed out. I think my father's deeply ashamed that my mother's living with his sister and her family in a pokey little semi in Putney. But it's handy to his office in the City. He wanted to send her to a guesthouse they used to go to in Cornwall, away from the bombing, but she's refused to go. My brother's death hit her badly. She clings to everything that's left.''

"So do most of us, old chap. Your father sounds like a splendid fellow. Not afraid to take risks. I sympathize with him. An actor's life is not noted for security. It's one long search for a new role, and not even bread and butter if one doesn't come along. When I remember the early days . . . and the days after the war when I was trying for better parts . . . if it hadn't been for my father and Anscombe, my wife and children wouldn't have had a roof over their heads. Her parents were dead against the marriage. I think she must have loved me, or she wouldn't have chosen a penniless actor. Strange what marriages turn out in the end to have make good sense—almost against reason.''

''Well . . .'' Connie's tone was almost muffled. ''I promised Julia we'd have a good turnout of the linen cupboard.'' The dishes clattered noisily together. ''Of course, we're not *throwing* anything out. But you did tell Mother to stock up before the war, Father. There are some sheets that are starting to get thin, and Mrs. Whitehand would be glad to turn the sides to the middle . . . with three kids she's—'' She paused, listening. ''I do believe our sister Alex has arrived.'' She dumped the tray back on the table. ''It is! It's Alex and Greg! I telephoned her before we left with just the faint hope that she might get here. And Greg with her.''

They all rose expectantly. ''I didn't even know Greg was back in the country,'' Michael said.

''He wasn't—until yesterday. Flew back in one of those Lend-Lease bombers Roosevelt is sending us. No doubt it'll be a great story. I wondered if he'd have thawed out by now—or have the energy to come down here.''

Alex was driving, and she brought the car to the kitchen door. She and Greg started across the lawn to them. After kissing and embracing her father and sisters, Alex was introduced to Ken Warren. Briefly, the same look of puzzlement that had greeted him last night crossed her face, to be swiftly erased. ''So glad to meet you. Connie asked especially for us to hurry to get here. Greg just had time to file his story. We borrowed the car from *The Record*. Greg's dying for some sleep, but we have three days, and he'll sleep better here than in London.'' Stella was already bringing a fresh pot of coffee and scones to the group at the table. ''We didn't have any breakfast . . . came straight from Fleet Street.''

It seemed to Julia that Greg, in his rumpled war correspondent's uniform, his eyes puffy from lack of sleep, looked infinitely older than when she had last seen him. She made allowances for the journey by plane across the Atlantic, the stop in the Azores, the cold of the aircraft, the fatigue, the necessity to file the story about what it was like to fly in one of the stream of bombers and fighters that had started after the Lend-Lease

Act had been passed by the American Congress. But he had aged beyond that. He gulped the coffee eagerly, and even more than Ken Warren, he grabbed at the scones. "Great . . ." he said. "Food and fresh air. God, I'm going to sleep like a log." He stretched out in the chair, turning his face up to the springtime sun, reaching for another scone, eating it at a more leisurely pace. "Great to be back. Great to know something like this still exists. . . ." He looked around at the three women, and a slow smile spread on his face. "Lord, Sir Michael, you have raised a bevy of beauties here. I brought a few little bits and pieces from Washington. Strictly forbidden. You've heard of nylon stockings, I suppose? Well, now you're going to be the proud owners of three pairs each."

Connie looked down at her thick lisle stockings. "I wouldn't dare bring them back to the barracks. They'd be pinched. . . . But still, they *would* be nice for the odd evening out." She glanced quickly at Ken Warren. His expression registered blankness, as if he tried to suppress near-panic. "Well, I'll *make* you take me out dancing one night. We'll go into the West End. . . ."

"You know what a rotten dancer I am."

Connie sighed. "Well, a girl can dream, can't she? I'd like the Savoy, and a chance to wear nylon stockings for my birthday." She looked across at Greg. "Any more goodies?"

"Greedy, aren't you? There are a few more things. Lipsticks. A fancy sweater each, nice-smelling soap, bath salts. I ran out of ideas then."

Alex put her hand across his. "Forgive me if I look like the cat who got the cream. He brought me the most gorgeous underwear I've ever seen—except for Mother's. My belated honeymoon present, he said."

Ken Warren was blushing violently, biting his lips. "Well—Constance, if you'd really like a night out . . ."

"I just said I did, didn't I? I'll take a pretty dress back to the station and hide the nylons." She ran her hands through her hair, which, now released from her service cap and the tight roll that the services demanded, shone like gold in the sun. "Oh, Lord, sometimes I get so tired of being patriotic . . . I long to kick up my heels. Have a party—"

"Then why don't we?" Michael said. "With you all here—I met Archy Alderson at the station yesterday. Billy and Ted are

home for a few days. I'll fix it with Cook and Stella—all the
best things we've been hoarding. A welcome back to Greg. A
toast to my lovely darlings who've kept me alive since . . . since
August.'' His voice nearly broke, but he hurried on. ''Greg,
you'll help me pick the wine. The best the cellar has. Alex,
where did you put those jazz records . . . ? I haven't been able
to find them.'' They understood that that night there would
be none of Ginette Maslova's records played. But there would be
music in the house for the first time since that fiery day in August. ''We'll roll up the carpets in the drawing room. Light a
fire there. I'll go and telephone the Aldersons right away.'' He
hurried away from them to the house.

Alex gazed after him. ''Poor darling—is he really any better,
Julia? Or is he just putting on a show for us?''

''He's better—in spots. He brightens up when there are people
around. And then there are days when he's in such a black mood
I'm afraid to speak to him.''

''If only he had something to do. If only someone would *push*
him back into the theater. Surely there will be something for
him soon. The raids are starting to taper off. People are coming
back to the West End. I'll telephone D.D. See what's happening
. . . what's around. D.D. hasn't been down recently, has he?—
well, petrol's getting a bit scarce even for *him*. Old Wolfie asked
me the other day when Father was going to come back. I said
'soon.' That's all I could say.''

''The trouble is,'' Connie said, ''that being Michael Seymour
he can't just take any old thing. It has to be a lead in a *good*
play. Rack your brain, Alex. He *needs* it.''

Later that afternoon Michael tapped at Julia's door. ''Darling,
everything in the kitchen and dining room looks very festive.
I'm so glad you got out the best china . . . Cook and Stella are
thrilled. Billy and Ted Alderson are dying to see you again—a
bit of luck they're both on leave. And old Archy and Milly are
delighted to come. I've been a selfish old brute, keeping you
buried away here, with no company—no boyfriends. What happened to all the young men you used to go out with at RADA?''

''Well—they're in the services, naturally. Some of them write
to me. At any rate, none of them was special. Just boys . . .''
The days at the Royal Academy of Dramatic Art seemed a lifetime ago.

"I'll try to make it up to you, Pet," he said. And for a moment his hand rested lightly on her cheek. Then he held out a muslin-draped garment he had carried over his arm. "Here . . . just as a favor for me. Wear it, if it fits. You're just her height, you know. Connie looks more like her—but you have her expressions, her movements. . . ." Slowly Julia uncovered the gown of deep crimson velvet.

"Oh, I couldn't! Not one of her concert gowns! No one should ever wear any of them!"

"*You* should. Her daughter. Her beloved youngest—the baby of the family. Do it for me, darling. Tonight. It won't be an unhappy memory for me, I assure you. I'd love to see you in it."

Julia looked doubtful. "If it fits . . ."

"That's my darling. Tonight we'll be a family again."

Being a concert gown, it had been made on classic lines by Molyneux. The armholes had been deeply cut, with many folds, and the sleeves tapered to slimness at the wrists. All her mother's gowns had had to have deep armholes to allow her easy movement at the piano. Julia peered at herself uncertainly in the mirror. Had she grown an inch in the past year?—her father was right. The length was perfect. It was slightly large at the waist, but a long tie sash pulled it in. She had washed her hair that afternoon, and she let it hang loosely on her shoulders. The lipstick from Greg was a good match. She smudged a little dark powder on her eyelids, as they had taught her at RADA. It wasn't quite Ginette Maslova who stared back at her, but it certainly was her daughter. She experienced a faint *frisson* of apprehension. Whatever her father said, she was playing a role. Tonight she was supposed to bring Ginette Maslova to life again. Some part of her rebelled against it; she couldn't—wouldn't—do it. Not even for her father.

But earlier than she had expected, she heard the sound of car wheels on the gravel drive. Now it was too late to change, to say the dress didn't fit. She was made up for her role; she would have to go through with it.

She ran downstairs, knowing that she was the official hostess of the evening, expected to be there to greet their guests. Her father waited in the hall, looking almost as he had before last August. He was freshly shaved and bathed, his dark hair gleamed, he wore a black tie with his dark green velvet smoking jacket. His face wore an expression of expectancy and pleasure, which heightened as he saw her.

"My darling—you are *beautiful!* Almost the image of her. I really didn't expect . . . Oh, Pet, what a joy for this old man." He caught her in a quick embrace. "She would be so proud."

The knocker sounded against the ancient oak door. But Julia heard no sound of mingled voices, as there would have been if the four Aldersons had arrived—instead, just the sound of a car being driven away. "What . . . ?"

Carefully Michael turned off the lights and drew back the blackout curtain. "Come in, dear boy. Come in!"

A tall shape moved around the curtain, and the door was closed; her father put the lights back on. "Very good of you to have me, sir. Good of you to send the car . . . it's a great treat. I was going to Scotland early tomorrow, but my mother won't mind an extra day's wait. Not when I tell her . . ."

Michael was moving ahead of them into the drawing room, bright and scented with the sprays of hawthorn Julia had taken from the hedgerow, warmed with the fire. "Come along, dear boy. What will you have to drink? Other friends are coming— two of their boys on leave. And my family around me . . . just like old times . . ."

James Sinclair, walking now without his cane, managed to halt Julia before they entered the drawing room. His face was anguished. "I almost said no. Almost said I was leaving for Scotland tonight. But I came—because I had to see you."

Michael was waiting for them by the drinks tray. "What shall I pour you? Nice we have these few minutes together before the others come down. Harry Whitehand was delighted to go and fetch you. We've seen enough of the war around her to know that we owe you a lot. A little petrol won't be missed in a good cause. Now tell me—what do you think of my Julia? Doesn't she look marvelous? You must tell your mother that we brought out the crimson velvet gown to honor the rose she sent, and her memory of my wife."

"Beautiful, sir. Beautiful. Very much like your wife. I've never forgotten *her.*"

Michael turned his back, as if he needed a second's grace to control his feelings. "Will it be Scotch?" he said. "You're right. No one could forget her. . . ."

The evening progressed as Michael had wanted it. Everyone exclaimed over Julia's appearance and made her realize that before this, she had seemed hardly more than a child. They examined her with new eyes. She sat at the opposite end of the table from her father. The pâté, made from scraps in the larder, was marvelously successful; there was leg of lamb, accompanied by Nuits St. Georges; the *pot au chocolat* was rich with cream and real chocolate. The Alderson twins, Billy and Ted, were both lieutenants in the Army, and on embarkation leave. "Can't be anywhere else than the Middle East," they said cheerfully. "Could stand a bit of real sun. . . ." They threw themselves into the spirit of the world they had hardly glimpsed before leaving school and that they didn't understand would never return again.

James Sinclair danced with Julia, his foot movements slightly awkward but his arms and hands expressively warm and close. "You smell like a rose," he said, his face brushing her hair. And then: "I thought I could never come to this house again. I thought I could never face him. I'm deeper into this lie. But I couldn't help it. I had to see you. I made my mother send that rosebush. God knows what she really thinks about it all. . . ."

"We've got to forget that we ever knew," Julia said. "It was an unknown plane that came down, and the pilot was saved. That's all we know. That's all we remember . . . from now on, that's all we'll remember."

Michael had had Stella secretly prepare a room for James, and he stayed the night. He left the next morning to catch a train from Anscombe Station to London, to change there for a train to Edinburgh and on to Inverness. Stella urged a large breakfast on him, and Cook had prepared sandwiches, fruit, and a wedge of cake. "No knowing how long train journeys take these days—what a long way home, young man. Stella showed me on the map." They, all of them, including Stella and Cook, gathered at the door when Harry Whitehand drove the car around. There were handshakes and good wishes. James Sinclair looked as if he wanted to bend and kiss Julia, but he had never kissed her, and he would not do it for the first time before an audience.

"You'll be posted back to Hawkinge, I suppose," Michael said. "It's only around the corner, more or less. Let's not lose sight of you. Julia and I will be here. . . ."

They waved him off. Julia had thought of going to the station with him, but that would have proclaimed a feeling of which she was not yet certain. But she felt a wrench of loneliness, of depression, tug at her as they returned to the breakfast table. She helped Stella fill the cups with another round of coffee and urged more toast on Ken Warren, which he eagerly accepted. Cigarettes came out. Michael did not smoke, because he was afraid it might affect his voice, and Julia followed his example. Ginette had not smoked; she had so disliked the nicotine stains on her father's fingers, and she thought cigarette holders affected. Julia had once or twice seen Connie puff awkwardly on a cigarette, as if she regarded it as something that made her seem older, but Julia noticed that now she did not, and she guessed it was because Ken Warren did not smoke. Greg and Alex very nearly chain-smoked, in the fashion of most journalists. Chairs were pushed back. The warmth of a sunny May day drew them to the garden. As Julia and Connie helped Stella with the dishes, short stabs of conversation drifted through the open window. "Those Alderson boys . . ." Greg's voice. "Going off to war as if it were going to be some lark . . . it's no joy out in the Western Desert."

"No sense of history," Michael said. "Haven't they read anything about the First World War? That's the way we went then."

"They haven't been blooded," Ken Warren said. "If they'd ever been in France . . . but, then, who am I to talk? I'll probably never be near the front lines, no matter where they send me. I'll always be at my boss's side, getting on with the paperwork—"

"Someone has to," Greg interjected. "And don't think that behind the lines is always safe. You've been in as much danger at Bentley Priory as anyone who's seen out the London Blitz. . . ." The talk drifted to possible theaters of war. Ken stuck to his argument that Singapore was a target and that the Japanese would eventually come through what were believed to be the impenetrable jungles of Malaya. Greg gave him some sharp arguments—the need for the battleships to remain in the Atlantic and not being needed for the defense of the Far East. "But I give you that there's lots of talk in Washington that the Japanese will give it a go, despite all their reassurances to the contrary. But to go through Malaya . . . well, that's a bit far-fetched. They'd have to have huge land forces and fight off the

American Navy. . . . If they try . . . well, the only good thing would be that it would bring America firmly into the war. . . ."

Julia and Connie went upstairs to make beds and tidy rooms. It never occurred to either of them that Alex might come and help. She was no longer totally part of a woman's world; she had moved beyond it. It was her right to sit outside with the men and argue the possible ebb and flow of war. "I've never even heard her mention a ration book," Connie said. "She's always so well dressed . . . or she can make herself *seem* to be. She and Greg are well matched, aren't they? I sort of feel she could go anywhere with him. Almost do his job . . . Alex has toughened up, and she's growing away from us. . . ." They heard again the voices on the lawn as they moved into the room Alex and Greg shared. "Oh, God," Connie burst out, "I do wish they'd stop talking about the war. I'm sick and tired of it. Last night was such fun, wasn't it? Almost as if the war had never been. Except Mother wasn't there. But you looked marvelous, Julia. For a second . . . when I saw you, I almost believed she had come back. What a strange but rather beautiful idea of Father's. . . . He likes James Sinclair, doesn't he?" She said the words with no particular emphasis, though she might have asked it directly of Julia.

"It seems so. But then, he likes anyone who turns up and gives him a few hours of conversation and takes his mind off—"

"Did Stella really pluck him out of the lane?" Connie asked. She was holding up against herself the silk crepe de chine nightgown Alex had tossed on the bed. "I suppose this is one of the spoils of Greg's trip. . . . Very sexy, isn't it?"

"Yes, of course she found him there, and brought him in. It was a lovely afternoon, and he was just riding buses around the country. He just happened to get off at Anscombe and he wandered down the lane." She was further into the lie.

"He's terribly handsome," Connie said. "And a hero. Poor Ken. I think he feels quite swamped by all these glamorous people around him. I had the hardest time persuading him to come. I think if he'd dreamed that Greg and Alex would show up, he'd have backed out."

"He seems to be holding his own pretty well," Julia observed, laying the precious nylon stockings Alex had dropped on the floor across the arm of a chair, giving the last pull to straighten the bedspread.

"Oh, he's not a dummy. It's just that . . . well, he doesn't seem to know how nice he is . . . once you get past the thick glasses and the scholarly stoop. I thought it was so touching what he said about his father and mother. He'd be just the same with any woman he married. Always looking after her—wanting to give her the best."

Julia looked at her sharply. "Is that what you want, Connie? Do you want to marry him? Does he want to marry you?"

"Good God! He'd never dream of mentioning marriage. Certainly not yet . . . not before we'd known each other much longer. And I don't think he'd ever marry as long as the war goes on. He wouldn't want to think that he could turn a wife into a widow—or, God forbid, there would be an orphaned child."

"You love him?"

Connie avoided her gaze. "I don't know. I think if he asked—"

"Oh, Connie, you're the best of us three. You're beautiful and kind and sweet. There have to be other men you'd look at. Someone—someone a little more exciting."

Connie turned from the dressing table, where she had been wiping up some of Alex's spilled face powder. "Exciting!" Her face was flushed, her expression almost angry. "Don't you think we've had enough excitement in this family? Our grandfather Seymour was the only sane man I ever knew when I was growing up. Everything else was chaos. Quarrels and rows and makeups. Lavish presents, and always the bills that couldn't quite be met. Grandfather Maslov behaving like every stage Russian even Father could think of. The ups and downs—the swings and roundabouts. I've seen it all, Julia, and so have you. Alex is starting down just the same road. I hope I don't. . . ."

"What about me? What do you think will happen to me?"

Connie shook her head. "I have no idea. Father is dragging you behind him, and *he* doesn't know where he's going. You'll have to break loose, Julia. Somehow. He won't come out of his dream reverie about Mother until someone shakes him out of it. Julia, you have to watch out—think of yourself a little. Perhaps it was a mistake to wear that dress last night."

"It was a mistake. I *know* it. Perhaps I'll join one of the services. But it seems so cruel to do it abruptly. And if I discuss it with him, he'll try to talk me out of it—"

"Hey!—you up there! You two chambermaids!" Alex's voice reached them from the garden below. "When can you drag yourselves away from your gossip? Drinks are served!" She stood on the lawn with a tray of bottles and glasses. From the kitchen drifted the smell of rabbit pie. It could have been any peaceful Sunday in the country.

After lunch they went their own ways—Alex and Greg to their room—"Got to catch up on some sleep," Greg said. But before they slept they would make love, Julia knew. Connie and Ken Warren set off to walk the country lanes, fragrant with Maytime blossom. Michael dozed over a book in the drawing room, the French windows open to the view of his rose garden. Julia experienced a terrible sense of aloneness. She pictured James Sinclair on his long train journey north, a journey to see his mother and his home before he went back into active service again. She went to her room and lay on the bed—like an old woman, she thought, having her afternoon nap. From Alex's and Greg's room she heard the stifled sounds of laughter—the laughter of loving friends. Hard not to feel envy—even jealousy. She buried her face in the pillow, thinking of James Sinclair. Time soon to go down and help Stella make tea. Cook had the afternoon and evening off. Cold lamb and baked potatoes for supper. After tea she would go and bring the cows in and help Harry Whitehand with the milking. There was always the milking . . . and the dozens of other chores that made up her day. And when they were all gone, there would be her father alone again, retreating to his silence and his drink. Her hands clenched in futile revolt. How much longer could she stay here like this? James Sinclair could be killed, and she might never see him again. Did he think of her as he journeyed northward? How infinitely remote and far away that Scottish castle seemed to be. He would be lost to her behind that portcullis rusted into place; he would cross a rotting drawbridge to a world where she could not follow. Uncharacteristic tears slid silently down her cheeks.

She did not see the Rolls because she crossed to the kitchen door from the milking parlor, but there was a bustle within the kitchen from Connie and Stella that alerted her that something

had happened. And down the passage from the drawing room
the sound of the voices reached her. Not the somnolent early-
evening voices, when drinks were just being poured, but animated voices.

Connie jerked her head in the direction of the drawing room.
"He's come."

"Who's come?"

"D.D. Don't you recognize the voice?" Julia saw for the first
time that D.D.'s driver sat at the big table; he was drinking tea
and munching scones contentedly. He grinned at Julia and half
rose to his feet. "Miss Julia," he said politely.

"Go in," Connie said. "He's been asking for you. Stella and
I are getting together some supper—and a few extra touches.
There's plenty of pâté left over." D.D. was a noted gourmet.
Her father's stock of precious wines would be raided fur-
ther, Julia thought as she hurried along the passage in her thick-
stockinged feet, having shed her boots on the kitchen porch.

"D.D.!"

He got heavily to his feet. "My child! So good to see you!"
He embraced her and kissed her on both cheeks. His Hungarian
accent was still strong. Julia privately thought that he cultivated
it as part of his flamboyant style. "And what part are you playing now, darling? Is it Rebecca of Sunnybrook Farm? Or Heidi?
No, too old for that. Is she one of those Russian servants from
Chekhov? What do you say, Michael? Are there, or are there
not, hayseeds in her hair?"

"Don't tease, D.D. Julia's been doing her share around the
farm—like everyone except me. All I've done is make a rose
garden."

"Then shame on you, Michael, for letting this rose grow wild!
Have you never heard of cultivation, my friend?" The bulky
figure in his expensive suit stood back from Julia a little, but he
kept one hand on her shoulder. "Unpruned, untended, she will
straggle into thin shoots running off in all directions, with hardly
a bloom to be seen. For heaven's sake, she could even go off
and marry some farmer, and then the theater will have lost
something precious."

Julia felt a flush invade her face and a sense of anger rising.
"For heaven's sake, D.D. I haven't even finished at RADA yet.
The theater's lost nothing but another clumsy ingenue. If the

theater still exists . . ." She went and gratefully took the glass of Scotch that Greg had poured for her.

D.D. shrugged and resumed his seat. "The theater will always exist, child. We old hands know that. And it must have its fresh blood. For the actors, the producers, the directors—always the lure of just one more curtain rise, one more production that might mean fame and fortune. Like the children we are—I acknowledge. Always playing our games. But what a splendid game it has always been. Such risks—such chances—and such rewards!" He raised his glass to her solemnly. "But you are both blooming and running wild at the same time. Don't wait too long, Julia. You should have been on the stage long before this. You've not been blooded by even a one-line walk-on."

"Not my fault," she muttered into her glass, wishing someone else in the room would help her. "With what's happened in our lives . . . the theaters closed, and half the West End in ruins, or so they tell me. Where would I get a one-line walk-on, to start with? I haven't been wasting my time," she added defensively.

"Nor has she," her father said, at last trying to come to her rescue. "The times are hardly normal, D.D."

"Nothing is normal, and it never has been. There will never be the perfectly right time to do anything. We have traditions and a culture that must be kept alive, no matter what. That is what our Prime Minister believes. We will carry on—no matter what happens. Already, since the bombing is less, the people are coming back to the West End, hungry for what the theater can offer them. Escape from the grimness of their lives. They want—no, *need*—the play to go on. What a propaganda coup for our enemies if the theaters should be permanently dark for the duration. It would be conceding a defeat where they have no victory."

Julia sipped her drink. "You're right. Of course you're right about that. I just don't see what it's got to do with me."

The big man's shoulders went up in another exaggerated shrug. "If you and Michael choose not to hear me, darling—"

"Well, you haven't *said* anything yet, except that I'm going to seed." She looked around at the others assembled in the room, Alex rigidly controlling her expression so that her handsome face was unnaturally cool and uninvolved, Greg smoking and watching as if some new, amusing game was being played out for him to watch, Ken Warren determinedly staring at the carpet, his shoulders hunched over the glass held with both hands. She suspected he wished he were anywhere but here.

"Well, darling, I have this little idea . . . no, I have this *big* idea. I want Michael back with me. He owes me a production, since he walked out on the last." He raised a hand to stifle any protest that might come. "All right. The circumstances were understandable. What is not understandable is that he should betray such a wonderful wife by letting his talent, like yours, Julia, go to seed. I propose to him something. He turns it down. He turns it down, not only for himself, but for you. I find such selfishness hard to forgive. Almost cowardice—"

Greg cut in. "That's a bit strong, Mr. Davidoff."

The big, fleshy face turned to him. "And what do *you* know about it, Mr. Smart Guy? Go and interview your presidents and prime ministers and leave those who know *this* end of the business to run it. If I say 'selfish'—if I even say 'a coward'—that is what I mean."

"*What* do you mean?" Julia demanded. "What do all of you here know that I don't?"

"Only, darling, a lovely idea I have, and that Michael rejects out of hand. Not just for himself, but for you. I come here to him to say we are reopening the St. James Theatre. A bit bomb-shaken, a bit dusty—but usable—perfectly usable. I propose to him that he make his return to the stage in one of his greatest roles and that you should play with him."

A coldness engulfed Julia. She gulped at her drink and started to choke. Tears streamed from her eyes.

"Need I say that I propose to open with *Lear,* with Sir Michael Seymour starring?"

"And me?" Julia managed to gasp out between her choking breaths.

"You? Why, my dear, you'll play Cordelia, of course. Who else?"

Julia put her drink on the low oak stool beside her. "You're mad, D.D.! I've never set foot on the stage professionally, and you expect me to play Cordelia! I'd be laughed off it. I'd disgrace Father. What a field day the critics would have. You said it yourself. I haven't even had a one-line walk-on yet."

"And what will you do instead? Spend your life here? You and Michael together. Marry your farmer. Or grasp your chance—which I think is your destiny. What actress in history has ever played Cordelia to her own father? I tell you, it will be a sensation! What a return for Michael. What a chance for you!''

"A chance I can't take. A chance to be laughed off the stage." She swung to face her father. "You were right to say no for me. But not for yourself. Someday you must go back. If D.D. thinks *Lear* will be wanted at this time, then you must do it. You must do *something*. But you don't have to carry me on your coattails. In time I might be able to do something on the stage. I've always dreamed of it and meant to work hard to get it. But *this* is preposterous! Fail or succeed, I'll have to do it on my own." She turned to look at each of them. "Can you imagine Father's return to the West End ruined by the amateurish performance of his daughter? I would be glad to take the humblest role at the Old Vic if they'd have me, but I won't let my father be made a laughingstock—they will call him a fond and foolish old man for staking so much on an untried actress. Even worse that it's his daughter.''

"Understudies have stepped into roles and became famous overnight." D.D. neglected to name one.

"Understudies have the indulgence of the audience. I would meet only the critics with their knives out. You'd be throwing me to the lions.''

With an air of great sadness, D.D. took up his drink. "I thought you had more in you, Julia. You refuse this challenge—this *great* chance—because you lack courage. You have been a good and dutiful daughter, helping her father through his most tragic hour. Now I see that that is *all* you have been. It is easier to stay here, going to seed with him, than return to the world. Yes, my dear, the world is hard and cold. It is tough. Who ever said different? It will be tough no matter what you do. Who needs the easy path? Go—join the Old Vic, if they'll have you. Do your walk-on parts and know what a coward's heart you have. Or stay and live with your father in his retreat, which is a shameful waste. But you will not venture out for him . . . oh, come, I am ashamed of you. You—like daughter to me. My very own idea of what Cordelia should be. But I have been proved wrong. You have not Cordelia's love, nor her courage. I am mistaken, after all. You are a pale image of Cordelia. Not her stuff at all. Tell me, my dear, why did you bother to go to RADA at all if you don't know what chances you must take? I am willing to employ you, at a beginner's salary. I will be merciless on you. There will be no charges of nepotism, even if I do regard you like a daughter. Can you imagine someone like Julian Tredwell agreeing to direct this production if he thinks a rank amateur is going to ruin it for him? Your own father will train you—you will be, *are,* Cordelia. You have shared his pain and his sorrow and exile and become a woman because of it. Go out and show the world that it is so. Prove you are no coward. If Ginette Maslova sat here she would urge you to take this chance. I knew Ginette. I knew her heart and soul. A child who first faced an audience at twelve years of age under the baton of that old tyrant, her father. Are you her daughter? Are you Michael's daughter? Or are you some changeling left on their doorstep? If so—well, then you'd better wait until someone is ready to do *A Midsummer Night's Dream.* But don't expect to play Titania. You might be offered the role of a fairy in her entourage. You disappoint me, Julia. I thought you made of different stuff. You are letting down both your father *and* your mother.''

Julia looked around at all the faces again; only Ken Warren avoided her gaze. She now read Alex's expression more truly. Did it say "I dare you?—I dare you to go out into the world as I did—to grow up.'' And Greg Mathieson, man of a thousand encounters, worldly-wise, a shrewd judge of character and of a situation. Was he sitting there, as he had sat at the ringside of so many spectacular events, waiting to see if this little, quite unimportant domestic tangle would sort itself out? Had she really grown into a woman, as Alex and Connie had? Last of all, her father. Here she expected support for her arguments. He knew the theater through and through. He knew what misery could lie in wait for her, the beguiling trap she might let herself walk into. Surely he could see for himself how D.D. was playing this? Even if he was throwing her to the lions of the critics, he must surely know that D.D. would reap a tremendous publicity coup. Success or failure, she would be written up in every newspaper and magazine. Success might please their friends; her failure would give satisfaction to so many of those who envied Michael his success. It was unfair to be compared to both father and mother at the one time. Not even Alex had had to experience that. Connie had shown her courage in her own way.

But what she saw in her father's face was not the determination she had expected. D.D. had said Michael had already declined, but she suspected it had only been a faint protest. He wanted her to do this thing that could destroy her. He *needed* it. He needed a reason for going back to what he had been born to but since last August he had lacked the will to face. She saw it now. She would be there, with him, as she had been with him all these months at Anscombe. She would be both his Julia and his Cordelia. Ah, but D.D. was clever—and cunning. When it came to the storm scene, she would truly be Cordelia. Her father needed her to help him back. He would lean on her and rant against the storm and the unkindness of fate and ungrateful children. It didn't much matter what she did, *he* would triumph. He would grope his way back to his old world, and he would lean on her all the way. And she would support him.

"Father? What do you think?"

Carefully he rose and went to the tray to refill his glass, so that he did not have to face her. "It's up to you, Pet. I don't want you to do something you don't feel you're ready for. But I can't stand in the way of a brilliant chance. . . ."

There, that was it. If she didn't go with him, he would stay behind with her. He would go only if she did. It was he who was throwing her to the lions, the lions now being her conscience.

"Well, if you think it can be done . . . if you really want to take this chance with me . . ."

The tension visibly relaxed, as if a collective sigh had escaped them all. Greg lifted his glass to her and came out with a phrase he must have picked up somewhere in the world: "Good onya, mate."

She gulped the rest of her drink and mutely held out her glass for more.

Chapter Three

I

THE WEEKS THAT FOLLOWED—the nightmare weeks, Julia forever labeled them in her mind—went by in a blur of work, tears, and the all-pervasive smell of dust. Sometimes she woke from a few hours of sleep, sleep disturbed by nightmares of apprehension—to find the dust choking her, and she was back again in the hours and days that followed her mother's death. It was a different sort of dust—dust mingled with the ancient soot of a city, as if someone constantly stirred the embers beneath a devil's brew pot. After seventy-six consecutive nights of bombing, the last major raid on London had come on May 20, 1941. After that the raids were spasmodic. The Germans had failed in their attempt to break the spirit and morale of the people but harassed them intermittently so that an air of uncertainty hung over the tired population. Exhausted people went about their work with gray faces and half-alive expressions, living in makeshift accommodations, still taking to the shelters at night, not believing that the raid they had come to think of as inevitable would not come. In June the Germans had broken their pact with Russia and turned their forces eastward, so the pressure on Britain was eased; most people would not believe they were now allies of the Russians. They only knew that they went about their jobs and their work. They produced more and more aircraft. They listened to news of their armies in the Western Desert, listened to news of the shipping sunk in the Atlantic while trying to reach a nation that could not feed itself. They counted those numbers against the numbers of German submarines reported sunk, and the figures did not make sense. They shook themselves slowly from the apathy and shock that were the aftermath of the Blitz and did not know whether to trust what their leaders told them—that they would, in the end, prevail and would not go under to tyranny— or whether their exhaustion was just the dying gasp of their whole endeavor.

Julia began, privately, to think that the whole exercise D.D. had dreamed up was totally mad. She saw the devastated city and wondered who on earth had the will or the wish to fill its theaters. Whether she did well or badly in D.D.'s scheme seemed hardly to matter now. Who would be there to see it? And yet she put to rights their flat, miraculously untouched except for some shattered windows; learned which shops she must register at for food rations; and went through the motions of an opening of *King Lear* planned for July. She went before her former teachers at RADA—those who were too old for call-up, or were female—and read, rather than played her part. She still didn't know it perfectly. They passed her out "with merit." Did they have much choice? she wondered. A student with a ready job guaranteed, the daughter of Sir Michael Seymour, protégée of David Davidoff, she would not have been failed unless her work was atrocious. With them, also, there burned the need, as D.D. had said, to keep the theater alive. It was their own life's work, their own effort. They did it along with all the other duties that life entailed—the alternate nights as air-raid wardens, their work with the St. John's Ambulance, the Red Cross, the sheer drudgery of their day-to-day living, the necessity to keep going. As Julia did her half-playing, half-reading before them, prompted by her father, she wondered if some of them were not asleep there in the darkness beyond the stage.

With Michael she attended a number of plays, amazed at the audiences they attracted. Tired people in their office clothes mingled with the no less tired who had dressed for the occasion. She had dinner at the Savoy with Alex and Greg and realized that half of the dining room had been partitioned for diners who could not get home that night and would sleep there. The cellars of the hotel were available as air-raid shelters. All around her she saw the law of the austerity meal that must cost no more than five shillings being flouted—the extra was simply added to the wine bill. At the Savoy they had their dinner with Greg and Alex, Connie and Ken Warren, which Julia sensed was their leave-taking. Greg said nothing, but Alex's air of apprehension and heightened gaiety betrayed that another parting was imminent. "Do you remember our wedding reception here?" Alex said. "Father and Mother thinking I had made a dreadful mistake, but putting a good face on it." She smiled across the table at Michael. "You were wrong, of course, and I'm still thankful you made a jolly occasion of it. It's something I'll always remember." Around them other diners became aware that the table was occupied by the Seymour family. It was the first time since the memorial service that Michael Seymour had been seen in public. Julia saw how the occasion revived him—the very fact of being back in the city that had given him the motivation for his work, given him fame, had at last touched in him the taproot from which he drew his strength to live and to go on. Julia began to understand even more deeply that whether she did well or badly as Cordelia, her consent to play with him, to continue her support, would be his salvation. The fact that she had brought her father back to the stage, that she was there if he should stumble or falter, was of prime importance. D.D. had had a stroke of genius in casting her in the role of Cordelia. She was that in real life.

In the midst of the dust and rubble she began to long for the peace of Anscombe—especially now, since the bombers and the fighters no longer went over with numbing regularity. She longed for the sweet, warm smell of the dairy; she wanted to rest her head against Primmie's broad side as she squeezed gently at the teats that gave so willingly, so plentifully of their milk. She longed for the scents and sounds of the country. She, the daughter of two parents who had made their lives and fortunes from cities, from crowds who came to see and hear them, began to feel that she was lost. Ambition, which had once propelled her to the Royal Academy of Dramatic Art, was gone. She was here to serve her father. Sometimes she telephoned Anscombe to ask Stella and Cook how things were. She denied to herself that she also telephoned with the need to know if James Sinclair had ever again shown up at the kitchen door. He had not. There had been no letter from him, apart from a note from Scotland to thank Michael again for his hospitality. Sometimes there was enough gasoline to allow them a visit back to Anscombe. Nothing waited for her—no letter, no word. She ate the good food—the eggs, the butter, the rabbit stew. Her father enthusiastically tended the rose garden, although Stella had taken it on as yet another task.

For her, there was nothing. James Sinclair might be at Hawk-inge, or anywhere else in the country they might have stationed him. But he sent no word. He was gone, in the classic pattern of men in wartime.

II

JULIA BELIEVED that her father worked himself back into the theater through her; she had much need to be coached, re-hearsed, given behind-the-scenes direction that did not come from Julian Tredwell. Her father spared nothing of himself or his knowledge. He taught her every trick in the book that would serve this role. He even taught her how to upstage himself. "Pet, try to forget it's your own dear old Dad. Go for stealing the scene whenever you can—and good luck to you. If you can steal it from me, you're no amateur, because I certainly won't play down to you. This is a highly professional business, Pet. And a greedy one. We all snatch for the limelight. Don't you miss a moment's opportunity for that. It comes your way rarely. But it's sweet, Julia. It's sweet. Wait until you hear the applause. . . . We will work together, you and I, Julia. But I won't carry you. With whatever is left of integrity in me, I have promised myself that—and you. In the end, you will do it on your own, or not at all."

With her stomach twisted in a tight knot of nerves, Julia faced opening night with her father. At the last moment he gave her a glass of champagne. "You're going to be great. Think of your-self first, but don't forget to react to the others. They'll be watch-ing *your* face as you listen to the others. And your old Dad's here with you. . . ."

It was an interminable night. To Julia's amazement, the the-ater was packed. Yes, it was a fine night in July. The raids now were intermittent. People badly needed entertainment in any form, and Sir Michael Seymour's name was enough to draw them. In her need to perform well, she lost her feeling of being thrown to the lions. She was one of this company, and together they had to make a success of this production. Whether she sank or swam hardly mattered. She was one of many. During the intermissions her father refrained from saying anything of sig-nificance to her, except a murmured, "You're doing just beautifully, Pet." Her greatest encouragement came from a stagehand she knew only as Bert. "You just go on giving it to 'em, Miss Julia. They're with you. I seen too many in my time not to know. Big and small. I can smell an audience. You got 'em!"

The applause afterward was mostly for her father, but as always he gestured the other members of the cast on to share the bows and curtain calls with him. Cook and Stella were in the stalls, along with Alex and Connie. Lord Wolverton had brought his wife and a party of friends. There were many friendly faces out there to welcome back Sir Michael Seymour, to watch with no small interest the debut of his daughter. But it was from none of these known, friendly groups that the first insistent cry went up: "Julia . . . *Julia!*" Somewhere far back in the house a familiar voice called her name. Gradually it was taken up by many in the audience. Finally, in response to the insistent demands, her father beckoned her to come and take her bow alone with him. Tears were in her eyes and nearly broke through her makeup. The first crimson rose landed at her feet. She picked it up, kissed it, and handed it to her father. The house erupted with roars of approval. At last she knew what it meant. Single red roses continued to land at her feet. She tried to gather them all up. Then the flowers in sprays and baskets were brought on. Her father summoned back the whole cast to take another full curtain call. The whole house seemed to be in an uproar. Desperately she searched beyond the footlights, trying to find the face of the man who had first called her name.

They all came backstage. More than her father's dressing room could accommodate, and many more than the humble one Julia shared with two other members of the cast. The party, and champagne, spilled out into the corridors. Her father embraced and thanked each member of the cast. There was a glass of champagne for each of them. Julia went and found Bert, who was on the stage with the rest of the stage crew, cleaning up. She toasted him and offered him his own glass. "I'll never be able to thank you. . . ."

He grinned at her. "Nuffing, Miss Julia. At my age if you can't smell 'em, you ain't been in the theater. You got the stuff of the old man in you. An' you look like your mother. Don't get many combinations like that. . . . But don't you forget there's tomorrer night, an' the night after . . . an' the night after that.

It's learning to go on, no matter 'ow you feels, that sorts out the men from the boys . . . in a manner of speaking, like.''

It was there, on the almost empty stage with Bert, that James Sinclair found her. '' 'Ello, 'ello,'' Bert said. "If it ain't bloody Romeo come to fetch you, dearie. Enjoy your night. It ain't always like this. Bloody hard work, and sometimes little thanks for it. . . .''

Jamie's arms were around her, and he was kissing her, the thorns of the huge sheaf of red roses in his arms piercing her shoulders. '' 'Ere, mate! Watch it! Crack Miss Julia's ribs and she won't be able to take a deep breath tomorrer night. There's more than one night in the theater, y'know.''

Jamie behaved as if Bert didn't exist. "God, I love you," he said. "I cried like a baby for you. I didn't know if I dared to come backstage, or if they'd let me. But in the end no one could stop me.''

"I think I died a little when I heard your voice. You started it, didn't you? You came up the aisle and threw the roses, didn't' you? Jamie, how I've missed you! Why didn't you write? Why didn't you telephone?''

"Not fair," he answered. "I had to leave you alone. When I read you were going to play in *Lear* with your father, I kept out of the way. You were going beyond my world, Julia. You were following your parents. Into places I don't belong.''

She caught his hand firmly. "You belong. Come and join the party." But before she left the stage she bent and kissed the wizened cheek of the stumpy little stagehand. "I know you brought me luck, Bert." She did not add that, carefully wrapped in a silk scarf, in a drawer in her dressing room was the worn gray rabbit her mother had carried with her to each concert.

He winked. "I'll be seeing you, dearie, in a lot more parts, and you won't have your Dad to help you through them. But you done him proud. You'll sign a photo for me, won't you? The missus—she hates all the photos of the beauties I bring home, but I says to 'er, I says, 'Look 'ere, me girl, that there's a star. An' don't you forget it.' An' tonight I'll go home and tell 'er a star brought me bleedin' champagne and kissed me. A few others 'ave done it, mind you. But only a few . . . I'll remember it forever, dearie. Now you get on with your Romeo. . . . One day I'll see this little lady play Juliet—only her Romeo ain't going t'be 'alf as 'andsome as you. Flier boy, ain't you? And lots o' medals to prove it. Good luck to y' both.'' The experienced old eyes had taken in Jamie's scarred hands, the cleft in his skull that had nearly ended his life. ''Guess yer must be one o' them 'eroes Mr. Churchill talked about. Well, why wasn't y'there when they bombed me little house in the Whitechapel Road? Been living with me bloody sister ever since then, and it's bloody 'ell. But get on with it, Flier-boy—Sir!'' He gave a tiny, almost mock salute, then strolled over to his mate, where a piece of scenery needed moving.

At the party D.D. gave at the Ritz, which included Lord Wolverton's group, Julia unashamedly reveled in the role of a woman in love. It was something she was incapable of hiding now. She insisted that Jamie be seated at her side during supper. D.D. was on her other side. He often interrupted their conversation, as if somewhat jealous of the attention she gave to the young man. ''It's all very well to be in love, darling. I've been in love hundreds of times myself. Such a nice feeling. But you mustn't let it stand in your way. Marriage and babies . . . the babies come whether one has thought about them or not. Hardly the life for a young woman who has only just started to make her mark. I have plans for you. . . . This *Lear* has been a great success, but no Shakespeare runs forever. We must find something a little lighter for you next time. And then I read an interesting film script the other day. Not a great thing . . . but properly produced and played, it just might make it. A young girl—like you—in love, with war all around. It would be inexpensive to produce. . . . There's a growing market now in the States for those kinds of films. Heroes . . . unsung heroines . . .''

She hardly heard him, but she smiled. ''Yes, D.D. But who said anything about marriage? Jamie and I hardly know each other.''

''Darling heart, that is not how it appears to me. Any man who can cause the sensation in the audience he did tonight . . . You are both madly in love with each other. Do be careful. . . .''

She heard her own laughter. ''Careful! What's there to be careful about? In a world like this? A bomb could fall on us right at this moment—just like the Café de Paris. This could be my last night, as well as my first night.'' She piled what was probably illegal caviar onto toast and gulped it greedily. ''I'll take life just as it comes—like this!'' Then she turned back to Jamie and raised her glass. "Here's to us. Don't stay away again. Not ever!''

In the flush of refinding Jamie, in the remembered glow of the applause, she was hardly conscious that the early editions of the newspapers were due, and the reviews. All hailed the return of Sir Michael Seymour; all seemed to intimate that the personal tragedy he had suffered since his last appearance onstage had heightened his powers, gave more weight to the giant role he had played. For his daughter, the reviews were mixed. Some welcomed "a bright new talent." Some seemed to withhold judgment: *One would wish to see her again in a role where she did not play so personally to her father's image. In some aspects she is the perfect, unforgettable Cordelia. It remains to be seen if she can play any other role.*

"You will play a hundred roles—and more, darling," D.D. assured her. "You have got away with it, you know. I feared so much they might just take out their wicked little knives and carve you up just because you *are* his daughter. It was a risk I had calculated. We won, darling. We won."

She turned her head and looked at Jamie. "Yes—we won!''

In the ladies' room, where the sisters went to get their coats, their party being the last to leave the hotel that night, Alex touched her cheek lightly. "I'm so proud of you, my love. I wish Greg had been here to see you. He was more than a bit skeptical that you could carry it off." Greg had been sent to Egypt and was working closely with General Alexander's staff. Dispatches from him, written from a forward position in the desert, were regularly appearing in *The Record*. Alex carried on with her own work, her byline appearing more and more as she reported the home front—"except for what the censors won't let me write," she had once said with some bitterness. And now: "This James Sinclair—it's serious, isn't it?''

"Serious? It's serious with me.''

Alex laughed. "Well, I can't see a Scot going off his head and scattering roses at your feet unless it's serious with him, too. But don't pin too much on it. It's war. He's flying again, isn't he? I rather think fliers have a somewhat shorter life expectancy than war correspondents—though, God knows, Greg's just as likely to be blown up as the soldier beside him.''

"Oh, don't!'' Connie almost wailed. "Why do you make it

seem so inevitable? Plenty of men survive war. Why, even Father . . . imagine surviving four years of that horror in the First World War.''

"And Ken Warren?'' Alex asked. "Do you love him, Connie? He doesn't seem half good enough for you, but is it serious?''

Connie's face tightened. "I don't see that that's any of your business. He may not be glamorous, or even good-looking. He doesn't do a glamorous job. But it's just as essential as any other. Why do you keep running him down, Alex? What's it got to do with you? You married the man you wanted. Why can't you leave other people's lives alone?''

Alex snapped the lid of her powder compact closed. "Sorry, Connie. I should keep my big mouth shut. But I can't help thinking . . . well, even in that dreadful uniform, you're by far the best-looking of us all. And the nicest. You'd have made a great Cordelia to our poor father, half-crazed with grief, if Julia hadn't been there to do it for us all. But I can't help seeing how men look at you. I hope before you make up your mind about marrying Ken Warren, you'll come and have a good talk with me. I'm the old married sister, remember? Wickedly wise in the ways of the world.''

"Kenneth and I aren't even thinking of getting married. He's far too responsible to marry in wartime, when one or the other of us could get killed. . . .'' A faint blush spread on her delicate skin. "Neither of you understands him—or me, I think. And what's more, I don't care.''

"Easy . . . easy,'' Alex said gently. "It *is* none of my business, except that I care about you. Sorry, Connie.'' She slipped on her coat. "I wonder why the most extraordinary things get said in the powder room.'' As the other women of D.D. and Lord Wolverton's party entered the room, she closed ranks with her sisters. "It's been a most marvelous night, hasn't it? Seeing Father back up there on the stage, and our wonderful little Julia with him.''

"There you go, again,'' Connie muttered. "There's nothing little about Julia. Or me. Don't be so damn patronizing. . . .'' She tugged her cap farther down on her head and marched out of the room. Alex stared after her, her expression startled. "Well, she's certainly grown up while my back's been turned. Never thought I'd hear Connie use a word that was even mildly blasphemous.''

''When one thinks of what she must hear used all around her every day, I'd hardly wonder . . .''

''And you, too, little one—oh, sorry, I musn't use that word again. Difficult to get used to the fact that the baby of the family is also grown up.'' Then she turned her full attention to Lady Wolverton. ''Yes, I hear from Greg as regularly as the mails allow—and as much as the censors will let him say. Actually, I learn rather more of what he's up to from the dispatches to the paper. I haven't the faintest idea when he'll be home . . . if he'll be there for the length of this campaign. I suppose events—and Lord Wolverton—will decide that.''

Lady Wolverton turned to Julia. ''You must be so pleased with this evening. But it's just the beginning, my dear. And what a handsome young hero to come and throw roses at your feet. I remember once meeting his mother on a visit we made to Scotland. Years ago. Our hosts took us over to tea at the castle. He was a little boy then . . . and what a handsome women she was. Still is, I suppose. With a family history that takes in the whole of Scottish history. How lucky he was to get out of that crash with his life. One can see from that head wound it must have been a pretty near thing. I don't know how these men do it. I mean . . . climb back into those planes and go up again . . .''

Her words caused Julia to shiver slightly. Lady Wolverton touched her hand. ''You're tired, dear. No wonder, after such a night. Your father's waiting outside.'' She kissed Julia's cheek affectionately. ''How you've brought him back to life, my dear. A double triumph for you. We're all so pleased. . . .''

Lear ran for three months, which was considered a great success for a play of that nature in the middle of war, when audiences were mostly looking for something to laugh at, or with. The tightened knot of stomach muscles became a familiar thing for Julia before she went on each night. ''Not to worry, Pet,'' her father counseled her. ''It happens to almost everyone. The good ones, that is. Once you begin to feel it's easy, then you're going to slip. Every performance counts. Some nights you don't feel like it . . . it's the last thing in the world you want. Those are the nights when you must give it all you've got.''

She and her father continued to share the flat, and their lives continued in the routine dictated by the theater. "I wish you could have a place of your own, Pet. You're old enough, and you should be breaking loose from the Old Man. But with the city bombed half to bits, it would be hard to be as comfortable as you are here. Especially with Agnes to look after us." Agnes was a middle-aged cook and cleaning woman who had worked for a family not only dispersed by war but whose London house had been bombed. "She's the most delicious snob, isn't she?" Michael had remarked after the first interview. "She was so busily weighing up whether working for us who are just mildly famous equaled working for a baronet's family who are filthy rich."

But Agnes did keep them clean, and as well fed as the rations and supplements from Anscombe would allow. Julia and Michael stayed out of each other's way as much as possible, knowing that they must come together each night, and for the Wednesday and Saturday matinees. They were scrupulous in trying to avoid any questions about whatever private life the other might have. Julia began to understand what Michael had meant when he'd said she should have a place of her own. Before, there had only been Anscombe, this flat, and her mother and father. She had wanted nothing else. But before there hadn't been James Sinclair.

He came to London whenever he had sufficient hours off duty. He would telephone her, and she would leave a ticket for him at the box office. Afterward there were always roses. She chided him for his extravagance. He laughed at her. "What else do I have to offer you?" They found a few small restaurants where they could eat quietly, and most people did not recognize her. "That's good, Pet," Michael would remark when she said she was going out to supper after the show. "Enjoy what you can."

Slowly he was easing back into life with his friends in London. Julia knew she no longer had to sit with him, and the whiskey bottle was no longer his constant companion. She sensed that with the prospect of the play, he had gone back into training, like an athlete. Her time as companion-nurse was over. She blessed D.D. and, once or twice, when he insisted that she join him with other friends for dinner, she told him so. "Darling child, think nothing of it. Selfish of me, really. I wanted Michael back at work. He's made a lot of money for me, you know— now, and in the past."

"And you've produced one or two flops with him in the lead that have cost you money, D.D. We all know about them."

He waved the thought aside. "It comes out about even. One doesn't count in friendship. I just happened to have the right idea about you two at the right time. But, of course, you must now begin to do things by yourself. We cannot have too much of this father-daughter act. Not good for either of you. What do you say to playing in *The Importance of Being Earnest?* As Gwendoline, of course. You're not up to Lady Bracknell yet. I think it's just right for the West End now. Lots of laughs and style. We'll dress it as lavishly as we can. . . ."

She drew her breath in. This time it would be alone, unaided by her father's presence, his strength on the stage, his ability to get her through a scene when she might falter. "When?"

"In time to catch the Christmas trade. When people come up to town again for shopping. When they're feeling in the mood for a good time."

"I've never played anything but this role. Do you think . . . ?"

"Yes, I think. Otherwise I wouldn't be suggesting it. It isn't a *big* role, Julia—but I think you will do it very nicely. A touch of class and wit. I want you back onstage as soon as possible. Before people have had time to forget there's a Julia Seymour as well as a Michael. We would go into rehearsal in late October— early November."

"That means—if I took the play—I'd have a few weeks off."

"Of course you'll take the play. What else is on offer? Or is there something you're not telling your old D.D.? Don't ever keep me in the dark, Julia. I'm willing to act as your unpaid agent, as well as your producer, but you must always tell me what offers come your way. If your career is properly guided, you could really make something of yourself—in your own right. And yes, of course there would be a few weeks' break. Any special plans?"

"No, nothing. Perhaps just a quiet time at Anscombe—learning the part. I'm still not used to the raids starting up at any old time, just when Goering thinks he'll give us a night's shaking up. The Luftwaffe don't bother with Kent much now. And surely—surely lightning can't strike in the same place. We've *had* our bombing."

"Well, Anscombe's very convenient to Hawkinge, isn't it?

That's where James Sinclair is stationed, I think? Dear heart, I hope you're not really serious about this young man. Oh, yes, it's a wonderful thing to be in love. I expect you'll be in love many times. Part of growing up. But what can he give you? A moldy old castle in the depths of the Highlands! How could you manage that, and a life on the London stage?''

"Perhaps he can give me love.''

"Ah, yes . . . love. How long does it last when the children come, and the boredom sets in, and the lights of the London stage are very far off? Don't rush into anything, Julia. Talk to your old D.D. first.''

"I won't forget,'' she said curtly, feeling as Connie must have when her relationship with Kenneth Warren was questioned.

But when she told Jamie of D.D.'s plans for her when the run of *Lear* was finished, he was quiet and thoughtful. "I'll be at Anscombe, Jamie. We can see a lot of each other. . . .''

"Yes, we'll do that. You need a rest, Julia.''

"I'll get it at Anscombe. Stella and Cook will put me properly back in my place. There's no 'star' treatment at Anscombe. I'll be out gathering up the cows early in the morning, cursing them when they're slow to milk, mucking out after them. I suppose I'll just do whatever Harry Whitehand tells me to do. And *he* does what he's told, too. The Ministry of Agriculture just comes around these days and tells you what you've got to plant, and what animals you can keep. And lets you buy ammunition to keep down the rabbits. Do you know how many acres of food a good-size warren of rabbits can consume if you just let them breed? And to think I've been raising rabbits for food . . .''

He smiled. "Yes, Julia. I know. I'm supposed to be a farmer. Or I will be if I get through this war.''

"You'll get through it,'' she said fiercely. "You will! You've had your one big chance to get killed, and you didn't take it. It's a special sign. You're going to come through everything now. You're going to go on right to the end.''

"If you say so . . .''

"I do say so. You just listen to me.''

But when *Lear* closed she spent only a few days at Anscombe, and then was on her way north to Inverness with Jamie. He had managed ten days' leave. "I know rather too well where you live, and how. It's time you came to see where *I* live.''

She was almost reluctant. "Must I? Couldn't we just stay here at Anscombe?"

"Why? Why don't you want to come to Scotland?"

"I'm afraid," she said, frankly. "I'm afraid to meet your mother. I'm afraid of how she'll compare me with that girl, Kirsty, she wants you to marry. Just afraid, that's all. I've never been to Scotland . . . I don't know how things are done there."

"Well, we're past the stage of being savages," he said, his tone almost rough. "We don't eat strangers. We're nearly civilized, I think you could say."

"I'm sorry," she said. "I know what you have in Scotland and that it's produced some of the greatest scholars and scientists. It's just . . . well, I wish we could have this time at Anscombe."

He signaled for the check from the waiter at the small Italian restaurant at which they had eaten dinner. "You don't want this to go any further, do you? You want to keep your girlish, uncommitted love. You want the romance but not the reality. You want to stay safely with Father at Anscombe, in a world where you're known and secure. Well, my dear, that's what you shall do. But not with me. I have my leave, and I'm going north. I'm going to *my* home."

So she sat with him through the long, weary hours of the train journey that took them overnight to Edinburgh. It was a slow journey, with many unscheduled halts on the way. They missed the morning train to Inverness. As they had crossed the River Tweed and were in the Border country, she couldn't repress a shiver, which Jamie instantly noticed. "Yes, Julia, we are a different race. You lot—especially you lot down around London—are Anglo-Saxons. We're Celts. Up in the Highlands we're Gaels."

"And I'm half Russian," she retorted. "My grandfather was a revolutionary—or almost."

"Well, then, we'll make a great pair, won't we?"

"Who said anything about making a pair, great or otherwise? I've accepted your mother's kind invitation, which you extracted from her, I'm sure, to take a little break in the Highlands. Such a polite invitation, and warm as a cold hot-water bottle. How can she thank us for such generosity as we have given you, etc. . . . Of course she doesn't want me with you. She doesn't want me at all. She wants you alone, or with the Kirsty girl."

"I may love and admire my mother, but I'm *not* tied to her apron strings. I don't intend to live my life to please her. And whom I love, I love."

She remembered the words, holding them to her like a shield as the train was finally drawing into Inverness station two hours late. But the woman who stood waiting for them on the platform mentioned neither the wait nor the raw cold of the October day. She gladly accepted her son's embrace and then turned to hold her hand out to Julia. "Welcome to Scotland. I understand it's your first visit. I do hope you'll enjoy your little time with us."

She had very fair skin, the delicate kind of skin that wrinkled early if not indulged and protected. Hers had not been. But her jawline was firm and the bone structure of her face very beautiful, Julia thought. She had clear, blue-gray eyes to which the smile on her lips did not quite carry. She had a slight and delightful Scottish accent, which made her voice seem warmer than she may have intended.

She was very restrained. It was only the second time she had seen her son since her one visit south when his life still hung in the balance after his crash. But she did not exclaim over how he looked, nor note the improvement in his movements since that brief trip back to Scotland when he had been passed fit for active service. She led them from the station to a dilapidated station wagon that stood outside. The real welcome came from the three dogs—two Border collies and a golden Labrador, who flung themselves out when the door was opened and leaped over Jamie in an ecstasy of delighted barking. He half-squatted to let all three put their paws on his shoulders, to lick his face, to nuzzle the breast of his uniform coat.

"Well, they certainly haven't forgotten you," Lady Jean said. "Of course, I told them you were coming, but one is never sure of what an animal remembers." Was this, then, her subtle reproach for the long months of his convalescence when he had stayed away from Scotland?

"These old devils would never forget. I sneaked too many goodies to them when they were puppies. Julia, these are the hounds who will bother you all through your stay. The collies are Angus and Duuf, and I don't expect you to tell them apart. The Labrador is Rory. And you lot be careful with this young lady. She's a great star of the London stage and not used to rough and tumble."

"What do you mean?" Julia demanded. "Wasn't I up every morning with Harry Whitehead milking the cows, and mucking out, and doing all the odd jobs? . . . Not quite up to repairing the tractor, but near enough."

"Well, my son didn't tell me you were so multitalented, Miss Seymour," Lady Jean said as she supervised the loading of the baggage. She directed how they would be seated in the car. "You'd better sit beside me, Miss Seymour. We'll put Jamie in the back with the dogs, because they'll give him no peace if they're not with him."

The old car rattled into shuddering life. Slowly they drove through the city, with its Victorian castle on the hill, a mixture of medieval streets and lanes, old houses and new ones. "We've had such a lot of battles through the centuries that not much of the old survives," Lady Jean said to Julia. "But you must come in with Jamie one day and see the worthwhile things." They were heading out of the city, meeting much horse-drawn traffic. "Though I hope you've no ambition to keep Jamie standing out in the hope of seeing the Loch Ness monster. But then, old Nessie's been a great attraction for tourists to Inverness—that is, in the days when we had tourists. Even then, not many ventured this far north. Except for those who came to shoot or fish, we're a mite chilly for your average tripper. And a mite strange, too. They don't feel quite comfortable here, those from south of the border."

And that told her, Julia thought, exactly where she belonged and should stay—south of the border.

Forever Julia would remember her first sight of Sinclair Castle. They had gone south of Inverness, and then turned off the main road that continued on to Elgin and Fraserburgh, driving through a forest of mixed conifers and broad-leafed trees, with outcroppings of rock, and a narrow stone bridge that spanned a white rushing stream. It was near to sunset when they emerged into the relatively flat land that lay around a small and now tranquil loch. The road had twisted through the forest so they approached from the east, and the castle was silhouetted against the last of the pale, low sun. It was approached along a narrow causeway that jutted into the loch, and this in turn gave way to another narrow, three-arched bridge. Part of one of its towers, almost a ruin, stood gauntly against the sky; the rest, a huddled, tall, dark mass of stone, showed only one light to the approaching travelers. All around the loch the flat land gave, in some places gradually, in others sharply to the lower slopes of hills, with a range of mountains standing far behind them. Across the still waters of the loch Julia could discern two lights in locations that seemed to be miles apart. It was a scene of breathtaking beauty and of extreme desolation and loneliness. Instinctively Julia reached up and drew her scarf closer about her neck.

The dogs, who had been dozing in a pile over Jamie's legs and lap, suddenly came to life as they scented home, knew by ear the sound the wheels made as they crossed onto the bridge. They sounded a deafening homecoming cry.

"You're home again, Jamie," his mother said. "We know one day it will be for good. You'll come back to us forever."

"Well—of course," he said dismissively. "I never think otherwise. It's where I belong."

His mother said nothing, but in the growing darkness, as they rattled over a wooden drawbridge that led from the last of the stone arches, Julia could almost sense her smile, an inward smile, the smile of possession. They passed under the portcullis Jamie had once mentioned. Julia had thought it figurative, but it actually existed, and undoubtedly, as he had said, was rusted into place. Lady Jean gingerly eased the station wagon between walls that could, Julia thought, have been eight feet thick. They were in a small inner courtyard, and a light over one door was the one they had seen when they had emerged from the forest.

Jamie had the far door open, and the dogs tumbled out. He opened the door on his mother's side and then ran around to Julia. "Don't be afraid. In the morning it's bright and beautiful, and all the ghosts have gone to their rest."

"How many ghosts?" Julia asked.

"It depends," Lady Jean said. "It depends on how sensitive one is to these things. We've had one or two guests here who were reputed to have 'the sight'—they reported not only ghosts we knew about, but a few extra as well. Those we put in the doubtful category."

One half of the double entrance door, which had a weathered coat of arms engraved in the stone above, was opened, and light spilled out. Julia realized that here, in the isolation of this situation, they had little care for the blackout. What bomber would be headed for a target so far north, a lonely prick of light at the edge of a loch in the wilderness? Above her, reaching high into the swiftly darkening sky, three high towers rose. A light touch of wind blew from the loch and sang against the castle walls, like an ancient sigh. "Welcome back, Master Jamie," a woman's voice called. "Aye, 'tis grand to have you home again."

Jamie's arms enfolded a woman Julia judged to be in her forties. "Glad to be back, Janet. Julia, this is Janet—Miss Julia Seymour."

Julia found her hand grasped by a strong, rough one, and she was half-led, half-pulled toward the light of the open door. "He said you were a bonny one. I never knew him to lie."

Jamie carried the bags, the dogs preceded them, and they went first into a smallish stone hall, which in turn opened into a very large room, with a carved wooden staircase leading to a gallery that ran around three of its stone walls. The ceiling of this room was lost in the darkness above. A few sconces on the walls were lighted, and a small fire burned in a huge fireplace.

"Extravagance, Janet," Lady Jean said.

"Well, it's only a wee bit of a welcome. It isn't every day we get Master Jamie back home." Despite the fire, the great stone hall struck chill into Julia's bones—or was it her spirit? "You'll be wanting a wash, I'm thinking. And I've set the whiskey by the fire. There're jugs of hot water in the rooms, all ready."

Jamie carried the bags up the stairs and led the way along the gallery. "The Red Tower Room," his mother directed.

He looked back in disbelief. "Oh, Mother, not that! Julia will be lost in there."

"It is our principal guest bedroom," Lady Jean replied. "I wouldn't offer her less."

Shrugging, he led the way along a short passage and then up a few winding stone steps. His mother moved before him to lift the heavy iron latch on an oak door. It swung open to reveal a room that commanded the whole space of one of the towers that Julia had seen from the courtyard. Three large windows were clothed in red silk that was faded and beginning to shred. The four-poster bed was hung in a similar fabric; the bedcover was red velvet and stiff with ancient embroideries. The bedhead was carved with the same coat of arms as in the courtyard, and this was repeated in a shield carved in the stone above the fireplace, where the fire that burned did almost nothing to cut the chill. There were chests and stiff dark chairs of the Jacobean era, and one massive wardrobe, a concession from Victorian times, Julia guessed. On the washstand a flowered china bowl and jug stood, with a pile of towels, and a cake of soap in a cherry-red patterned dish.

"The bathroom, Miss Seymour, is a rather long hike. Back down this little passage, and it's the second door on the right—or you can go through the dressing room and on into the bathroom, which connects with it. But the dressing room is very dusty—we have very little help. Everyone's gone into factories or the forces. Janet has only one young girl, Morag, to help. I'm afraid Scottish castles are a proper muddle. The few bathrooms we have are the last word in Victorian modernity. Sometimes the hot water gets here, sometimes it doesn't. The Sinclairs stopped putting in bathrooms about the turn of the century, when the money started running out. At least, before that happened, they had the good sense to put in a bathroom downstairs, where some of the servants slept—so that's where *I* have my baths. To have a few water closets back in those times was a great thing, considering the difficulty of getting the plumbing into a place like this. Mostly the family took their baths in front of the fire—but then there were legions of servants to bring the hot water. Jamie wrote me that your house is very old—like this. But then you never had quite the need to fortify yourselves in the way the Scots did. All these towers—very good for repelling the enemy but rather awkward to live with now. Both the weather and the peace you enjoyed down there have made life easier for you since your Elizabeth's time."

"Ours is a quite unimportant small manor house," Julia said, thinking of it longingly, for all its narrow, twisting corridors, with bathrooms and closets squeezed in wherever space existed, with the central heating that the Brahms concertos had paid for. "No one would have thought of fighting for it. It was never a fortified house." She resented the allusion to "your Elizabeth." Until Queen Elizabeth had died and James VI of Scotland, Queen Mary's son, had become her heir, there had never been a joint ruler of England and Scotland. Would her whole stay here be one barrage of small barbs about the differences of their cultures?

Jamie laid her suitcase on top of one of the oak chests. He cast a last, dispirited look around the room. "Not the coziest place on earth, Julia. But don't worry—they're all rather friendly ghosts.''

"I rather suspect," Julia replied, "that it depends on which side of the border you come from.''

He tried to smile at her and failed. "Well, when you're ready, we'll be waiting downstairs in the hall. If you need anything, give a shout. And you're not quite alone up here. My mother sleeps in a room almost as big as this in one of the towers opening off the gallery, and I'm on the floor above her.'' The thought gave her little comfort.

They left her, and she raced to the fire, holding her chilled hands to it, daring to add some extra coal from the scuttle. Ancient cast-iron radiators stood beneath the windows, but they were stone cold. She hung up the clothes she had brought— good, sensible, warm clothes, as Alex had advised, and the long velvet crimson gown of her mother's, in case Lady Jean had planned some dinner party. Now that she had met her, she rather doubted that would happen. She went cautiously along the narrow stone corridor and found the second door on the right. She opened the mahogany door to a bathroom of sumptuous Victorian size and fittings, and icy cold. There was an empty fireplace, and what was meant to be a hot-towel rack, which was cold. For a few moments of bewilderment she couldn't find either bath or toilet in the midst of the mahogany paneling. Then it occurred to her that the magnificently worked window seat was, in fact, the lid of the toilet. Above it hung a chain with a ceramic pull, decorated with a blue *fleur-de-lis* pattern; the cistern, too, was encased in mahogany. The pan of the lavatory was also decorated with the *fleur-de-lis*. After she'd used it and pulled the chain, the noise of water seemed to gurgle and plunge through an unimaginable labyrinth of pipes, eventually, she supposed, to arrive in the loch below. Only a large mahogany-framed mirror above what looked like a chest of drawers directed her to the washbasin. The lid she raised was also mirrored underneath, and the same beautiful blue-and-white pattern greeted her. The water that ran reluctantly from the tap at the washbasin was cold. But the soap was fresh and sweetly scented, as if left over from the days before the war. A blue and white handle on what looked like a very large wardrobe allowed her to slide back a mahogany panel that revealed a huge bathtub, again in the magnificent *fleur-de-lis* pattern. It occurred to her that whichever laird of Sinclair had installed the bathrooms, and the attempt at central heating, still had had strong Jacobite leanings, favoring the ancient French cause of Mary, Queen of Scots, and Bonnie Prince Charlie.

She went back to the Red Tower Room, keeping her hand on the stone wall and treading carefully, because the way was so poorly lighted, and the stones beneath her feet worn. The room looked no cozier than before, but on one of the chests she saw a small, prettily arranged bowl of asters—she supposed the last of the autumn yield in this far northern place. She washed in water from the jug that was now lukewarm, and changed her skirt and sweater—defiantly wearing a red that almost matched the color of the room. She added a paisley-patterned cashmere shawl, something else from her mother's wardrobe that her father had insisted she take. He had been very concerned about this visit to Scotland, anxious that she enjoy herself and yet worried that she would not be warmly welcomed.

"I have a feeling about Lady Jean," he had said when she had offered the letter of invitation to him. "Despite the rosebush and this invitation I have a feeling that she would rather that Jamie did not bring an English girl back to his home. But, Pet— it can't hurt." Then he shook his head. "Or perhaps it will. I think I see what Jamie is doing. He's showing you what it's like up there—even if it is a castle. He's madly in love with you, but he wants you to know what his life after the war will be. He'll never desert Scotland. You do know that, Julia? And you are set on an acting career. You can't manage that from Inverness."

"You talk as if we were married. We haven't even talked about it ourselves."

"But you're both in love," he said with great gentleness. "In war one makes hasty decisions—because you don't really believe there will be a future afterward."

"*You* married Mother in wartime."

"That's exactly what I'm talking about. We married and we both knew I had only a slim chance of not getting killed. But at least I was sending her and her parents to safety. And close to a city where they both could pursue their careers, whether I was there or not." He shrugged. "I presume too much. James is a gentleman in that he's showing you what *his* home is like. When he asks you to marry him, there will be no surprises."

"You do presume rather a lot."

"I do, Pet. I do. Forgive your interfering old father. Your trip should be a very . . . a very enlightening experience."

These words were in her memory as she came down the great oak staircase to the dim hall, the light of the fire the one bright spot. But then Jamie came forward and took her hands, and the atmosphere seemed to alter, or her courage was renewed. The dogs, too, added their welcome with whipping tails, which threatened to upset the glasses on the low oak stools about the fire.

Lady Jean had changed into a severe green gown with a high neck, which suited her magnificently. "Do come closer to the fire, my dear. Have a dram, or would you . . ." She looked doubtful, as if just remembering where her visitor was from. "I'm sure we could produce a gin and tonic if you'd prefer it."

"Whiskey, please," Julia murmured. She wrapped her shawl closer around her and leaned toward the fire.

"Are you frozen?" Jamie said as he poured the whiskey. "Water?" She nodded; she noticed he drank his neat.

"It's a pity about the heating," Lady Jean said. "We used to be reasonably comfortable when we were allowed enough coal—and when we had help to stoke the boilers. Now, of course, there's not enough of either. But it's nothing to the misery some people suffer, so we just try not to notice it. And say less about it. Here, do try some of these—we call them Scots Toasts. Janet has made them especially for you. We don't get them every day. I haven't decided if it's Jamie's homecoming or the daughter of a famous actor and a musician that has inspired this activity, but enjoy it while you can. Of course—I should have added a famous actress. Janet saw a write-up of your father's return to the stage in *King Lear*, and the . . . the glowing reviews about you. Of course it was she who helped me dig up the rosebush. . . . Janet will do anything for something or someone who interests her."

The Scots Toasts turned out to be small pieces of fried bread spread with a mash of finnan haddie, kippered herring, or flaked salmon, all done in thick cream. Julia murmured her appreciation. "Janet will be pleased" was all Lady Jean said. Jamie filled her glass again.

Dinner was in the long, formal dining hall, again hung with the ancient regimental banners, smoke-dimmed portraits of stiff-faced ancestors, the antlered heads of stags, an array of swords and shields that decorated the Great Hall. The dogs went obediently to cushion-lined baskets before the fire. Cock-a-leekie soup was served by a young girl Jamie introduced as Morag, then fried venison collops, tastes that were totally unfamiliar to Julia—not at all like the dishes that went under these names for her before. When she commented on this, Lady Jean replied. ''Ah, well—Janet is an excellent cook, and she uses the traditional Scottish recipes and ingredients. Fortunately we can still get most of them. The Scots have never been big meat eaters— except for venison and game. We sell our beef to the English, and live off what the rivers and the sea give us, as well as the forest and the moors. Scotland was, and still is in many ways, a poor country.''

Perhaps she discerned Julia's glance at the silver candelabra, the silver flatware engraved with the Sinclair crest, the faded splendor of the paneled room about her. ''There were times when the Sinclairs had much more land. Some of it went to pay debts. Some of it just fell into neglect. We could have much more fine acreage for cattle if we could find the money to drain the land. It's gone so boggy in places, and the cattle won't stand that. We have some hill farming in sheep, and Jamie's father did plant out a great deal of acreage to forestry—the land was too poor for anything else. But that's a cash crop that takes many years to grow. We must wait for our reward on that.''

Jamie shifted in his seat uncomfortably. ''Mother, you paint the worst picture. We're not quite on the point of being sold up, and after the war, when I get going on the place . . . well, it will be different then.''

''Yes, Jamie—I think of the time and wait for it. Wait for your energy and youth to come and do what I cannot. In the meantime, Miss Seymour, we are short of everything as well as money. Don't imagine we dine in this state every night. There's a housekeeper's room next to the kitchen that is our living and dining room—at least that and the kitchen we can keep warm. For the farm, we are left with middle-aged and old men, and a very meager ration of petrol to run the farm machinery. But then you probably know all this, since you live on a farm yourself. We've dust-sheeted and closed off a number of rooms—those we don't have to walk through, such as here and the Hall. There's a drawing room, but it's too damp for use, and a fine library. The whole of the North Tower has been closed off . . . but then, it should be closed off. It's in a rather dangerous state of decay. We have to be as self-sufficient as possible here. The snow-drifts in winter can keep the road through the forest closed for weeks. . . .''

Jamie had cleared the plates, and Lady Jean went to serve the pudding. ''This is called Holyrood pudding, and Janet must have been highly excited at the thought of Jamie's homecoming to make it. Milk and semolina, butter, egg whites—all the rationed things, of which we have plenty. Janet never hesitates to raid the food we send to market. And it's covered with her almond sauce, which is sheer luxury. I dread the Ministry of Agriculture turn-ing up one day to ask why we aren't producing more, or—God forbid—taking a poke around the pantry.''

They had shared a bottle of good red burgundy with the meal. ''There's little enough of it left, though,'' Lady Jean said. ''We're not short of whiskey—one has one's contacts and one's friends. The Highlands, of course, are dotted with distilleries, and it's not an industry that needs much labor. Old men serve it per-fectly well. But it's getting the barley that's the trouble. We're supposed to export the whiskey, though, to pay for the guns as well as butter. But one cannot expect the Highlanders to go without their dram. It's been both the blessing and the curse of this country. Children and wives go hungry because men must have their whiskey. . . .''

''If you're finished, Mother . . .'' Jamie scraped his chair roughly back on the wooden floor. ''I must say I'm damn sick of hearing the long dirge about how meanly we live here. It's a good life, when there isn't a war on. We have enough of every-thing we really want or need.'' He looked almost pleadingly at Julia. ''You're giving Julia such a bad impression. All depriva-tion and poverty. It's damn good inheritance, and when I come back I'm going to borrow money to put it to rights. I'll clear land and drain it. I'll double the cattle herd. There are new strains of hill sheep I want to experiment with. There's still enough land if one has the will to work it. It's just that you've been without Father so long . . . it's a tough job for a woman. . . .''

Lady Jean rang the silver bell to indicate to Janet that she and Morag could clear the table. Jamie pulled back her chair for her. ''Yes, Jamie, I'm sure you could do all those things—given the money. It *does* need a young man's freshness and enthusiasm, so be sure to come back.''

The dogs rose as they left the table. They returned to the fire in the Great Hall. Julia watched as Lady Jean seemed to bite back words of reproof as Jamie added more logs. It was quite deliberate, of course, this tale of poverty. It was probably true, in many respects, but the point was being made that if she and Jamie married, she would not bring with her the money that this place so desperately needed. Julia was filled with a sense of desolation. She dropped into the seat before the fire she had had before and pulled the cashmere shawl closer about her. The suddenly leaping flames lighted the Sinclair crest on the backplate, and on the firedogs. Jamie was filling small glasses from a decanter. ''Here—try the aristocrat of whiskies—this one's The Glenlivet. You'll surely sleep soundly after that.'' Julia sipped, and tasted her first malt whiskey. It was very strong, but a drink of incredible smoothness and subtlety. ''You mustn't take all that Mother says too seriously. She was brought up in a far less comfortable house than this—although the history of her family embraces about every famous event you can name. But somehow they always seemed to back the wrong horses—and not much money or land stuck to their fingers.''

''Poverty is no shame, James,'' his mother said tartly.

''No—just lack of money. I can remember the wind whistling through broken panes in your father's castle. I'll bet it's in an even sorrier state now.''

His mother's stern expression softened to something near sadness. ''Your uncle doesn't care for the place—he's more comfortable at the farm in Ayrshire. With no money spent on the castle, it's falling down. It breaks my heart to think of it. Only a couple of old women and a caretaker there now, and they're threatening to move to the mainland when the war's over. The place will be abandoned then. We gave plenty of men to our Scottish causes, but we seem to have been unlucky in the women they married. Hardly an heiress among them. Married for love . . .'' She turned to Julia. ''I'm one of the Macdonalds of Clanranald, and the castle is in the Western Isles. At one time we held sway along most of that coast. But it's all gone. Ruins against the sky . . . very picturesque . . . for the tourists—''

''Oh, for God's sake, Mother! Those days are gone . . . finished. A hundred or more years ago.''

''One's pride is not.''

''And one can't eat history or pride. After the war I have to get on with the job here. It's not impossible. I'm reading everything I can lay my hands on about agriculture. We've come out of the age of crofting, you know. . . . It was a mistake for me to go to Oxford, to read history like a gentleman. I should have learned something about agriculture instead.''

"An education never hurt. I was determined you should have those three years of your youth to enjoy. Mentally, you would have been better prepared for the task you faced here. But . . . yes . . . I mustn't keep returning to the past. It's a vexing habit. Of course you will do all you say. I have no doubt. It is hard to wait until this war is over. But it seems we have hardly begun the battle yet. What does your brother-in-law, Mr. Mathieson, say, Miss Seymour? How does the tide of battle really go?''

"He isn't allowed to write that, Lady Jean, even if he knew. Alex hasn't had a letter for some time. She thinks he is on the move somewhere, but not even her boss, Wolfie—I'm sorry, Lord Wolverton—will tell her where. We just hope it isn't Russia. . . .'' They all now lived with the dread of what a German victory in Russia could mean. The Germans were pressing on relentlessly; Leningrad was cut off, and some reports said the Germans were almost at the edge of Moscow.

"We will hope he is safe, my dear. And not in Russia.'' Her tone was kinder than Julia had yet heard. "Of course, we must wait for the Americans to come in . . . surely it cannot be too much longer.''

"It will take something to *force* them in,'' Jamie said. "There's so much isolationism in Congress, Roosevelt can't stir a further inch without seeming to be pushed.''

"Then we will hope for a good hard push,'' Lady Jean said, with more spirit in her tone. "I *cannot*—I refuse to believe we will go under, and yet if we don't get America as an ally soon . . . Ah, well, what's the use of talking about it? We must all do our various jobs and get on with it.'' Julia had the distinct impression that for Lady Jean, acting on the stage in time of war was no real job at all.

Janet entered with coffee. Jamie poured more of The Glenlivet. When Julia demurred, he simply handed her the glass.''Drink it. We had a miserable journey here. I want you to sleep like a log tonight, and wake up ready to see this small bit of heaven that I think this place is.''

"I'm thinking, Master Jamie,'' Janet said with the confidence of a longtime friend as well as servant, ''that maybe it's no wee bit of paradise to others who are used to maybe a wee bit more excitement. But still and all . . . a fair enough place it is. Not that I've been much farther than Edinburgh, Miss Seymour, but what I do see at the cinema . . . ah, well, now, that's another world.''

When she had gone, Jamie laughed softly. ''Is she still as mad as ever about it, Mother? The cinema and the film magazines, and all that?''

''Absolutely. Every Wednesday, without fail, unless the snow-drifts are too high, she walks to the main road and picks up the bus into Inverness. And next morning I can't get a cup of tea until I've heard the whole plot of whatever picture she's seen— and if it isn't that, it's the latest on the private lives of the newest stars, or her favorite stars, or those she's betting will become stars.'' She looked at Julia. ''Don't be surprised, my dear. Under that plain exterior lurks the heart of a true romantic. All that Janet never had in her life, and all that she will never be, is up there for her on the screen. Truly, I think she lives a fantasy life in the darkness of the one-and-thrupenny seats. The Wednesday matinee and the end of the war are all she lives for. *You,* through your father, are the closest she has come to such glamour. She knows your father's films by heart. He didn't make many, did he? I'm not too well up on these things. But whatever he has made, you can be sure she's seen them all—probably three times, as they come around again.''

Jamie rose and snapped his fingers. All three dogs got up eagerly, tails wagging. ''I'll take them out, Mother. Bed, Julia. You look all in.'' But instead of leaving her at the bottom of the stairs, after she had said good-night to Lady Jean, he climbed the stairs to the gallery with her, which, lit by only one light, was nearly in darkness. There, where his mother's gaze could not reach them, he bent and kissed her lips tenderly. ''Don't think for a moment that I feel as restrained as that seemed. If I had my way, I'd carry you to bed. But I've been patient this long, and I intend to go on until you're sure. Julia, do you think you could stand this place?—I mean, if I were here with you all the time . . . ? Unfair question. But think about it? Sleep on it. It's nothing to what you could have if you went on in London. You know . . . something like Janet's dream of a star. I wonder why I ever brought you. I should have lied like a trooper and tried to marry you to some romantic image of the life of a Scottish lady of the manor—or the castle. Well, now you know the castle, and you can pretty well guess what life is like here. Yes, I was a fool. I should never have brought you—''

"If I've fallen for a fool, then you're an honest fool. Kiss me again, dear fool. I think I shall love you forever."

This time his hands pressed her shoulders against the stone wall, and his lips searched hers with growing passion; one hand slipped down to her breast. "Dear God, Julia, I'm dying for you. . . . Go and dream uneasy dreams. But you needn't lock your door. When it is time I will love you with all my heart and my body. Will you ever be mine as I want you, Julia? What can I offer except this run-down place and a life of hard work?''

"Yourself," she whispered.

From far below his mother's voice drifted up. "Jamie, the dogs are impatient. And I'm longing for you to come back here to the fire so we can have a good, long talk.''

A talk, Julia realized, from which she would be forever excluded, the intimacies of mother and son. She groped her way up the twisting steps in the half dark, tears and a despairing, almost last hope in her heart. Hope about what? She would be a disastrous wife for Jamie, and they both knew it. The one who knew it best was Lady Jean Sinclair.

She finally went to sleep with tears still wet on her mother's gray rabbit, which she had brought as her good-luck mascot.

But she woke in the morning from a deep sleep that had contained no hint of presences strange to her; no violent dreams had disturbed her, no ghostly visions had penetrated it. She woke to Janet's cheerful presence, a tray with tea and a thin slice of buttered bread on the table beside her, and the sound of the curtains being pulled back on huge wooden rings that rattled together with an almost musical sound. Swiftly she thrust the rabbit under the pillow.

"Ah, there, isn't it a very fair day you've brought with you?" Janet made it sound as if the weather were within Julia's gift. Ignoring the tea, Julia sprang from bed, without bothering with her robe, and ran to the windows. Bright sunlight poured in. The loch and all the land around glistened with colors that made it seem a new creation, born in that very hour. The water was still, and as fresh as a mirror into which no one had ever before looked. The pasturelands about it were the gentle grazing ground of cattle, rising to the hills where the white dots of sheep could be faintly discerned. And behind the hills were the mountains she had barely been able to see last evening—the peaks of some of them dusted with early snow, the sight of which brought no foreboding to her. It was part of the enchantment of this scene, a new, fresh world laid out before her. No wonder it so tied and chained Jamie's heart.

They ate breakfast in the more cozy atmosphere of the house-keeper's room. It was a large room—perhaps several rooms thrown together when there had been money to do it. It contained a dining table and chairs, and drawn near the fire two long sofas and several upholstered chairs. In a passage opposite the housekeeper's room were a number of small rooms—the estate office, rooms for Janet and Morag, the unbelievable luxury of the bathroom for the servants that Lady Jean had mentioned—the whim of whichever laird had put in bathrooms in the towers and attempted central heating. Lady Jean's greeting to Julia was civil but lacking in warmth. Perhaps the good, long talk with her son last night had not been much to her liking. The morning newspapers had not yet arrived, but the radio brought the news. The fighting in the desert war, the siege of Leningrad, the nearness of the German troops to Moscow, the dread possibility that it might fall, were all there. Openly Jamie kissed her when she knocked and entered the door Janet had directed her to; then he turned off the radio. "The news will come when it does," he said to his mother. "We'll have our days together, won't we, Julia?"

He said it with the defiance, with the lack of care they had all adopted. Life had to be lived now—that was the creed for them all; she saw it everywhere about her, the frantic embraces of lovers, of greetings and partings. She looked at Jamie with love, and the happiness spilled out about her. The dogs rose to greet her.

"Do you take porridge?" Lady Jean asked.

"No—I hate it," Julia answered. Why should she pretend, and choke down something she had loathed from babyhood?

"A pity," Lady Jean said dryly. "Scotland lives and grows on oatmeal. But then—there's always toast. . . ."

Happily Julia piled her toast with butter, which seemed to be there in abundance, and Janet's marmalade. But there were also bacon and eggs. Whatever Janet stole from what was designated for the Ministry of Agriculture, she made sure that they themselves did not go short.

Jamie had planned a picnic for them both, but before they left the castle, Julia demanded a tour. "Oh, damn—must we?" he answered. "It's such a great day—not raining, for once." Reluctantly he had shown her some of the principal bedrooms—one called the Blue State Room. "Far too grand a title . . ." It had once been the State Room. The curtains and embroidered bedcover told that, but it was otherwise bare and spartan. He took her on to what was called the Culloden Room, and the Prince Charles Suite—both grand in size and style, with intricately paneled walls laid over the old stone that was their foundation. The Prince Charles Suite had an anteroom, with a beautiful stretcher table and upright wooden chairs, of the Jacobean period. Everywhere the furniture was shrouded in sheets, and dust was thick on the handpegged wooden floors. But all had magnificent views across the loch, or into the road through the forest. "There's a tradition—unconfirmed—that Bonnie Prince Charlie spent a few days here before he moved on to Culloden House—which is only a few miles away—to meet with his generals to plan that battle. And pretty badly planned it was. I'm sure you know most of it—the slaughter of the clans—the end of the Stuart cause. Well, whether he did stay here or not, of course my family was involved in the cause. And when the battle was over, we were as heavily penalized by the English as any family. We lost the incumbent laird—he died in the battle. His younger brother was only nine. The best land we had was forfeited. The object was to reduce those who had supported the Stuart cause to poverty, to break up the clan system as fully as they could. We were forbidden to wear the tartan. Oh, it's all the sort of thing my mother dwells on too much. Look—do you really want to see the other rooms? These are the so-called grand ones." He showed her some of the rooms that were reached by steeply pitched stone stairs in the upper parts of the towers. One of them was his, strewn carelessly with his possessions, the bed unmade, the view over the loch of stunning impact. "Yes—I know," he said. "From here it makes one feel as if one owned the world. All very well. But think of what it means to bring wood and coal up here for the fire. My brother's room is in this tower—my mother keeps it locked. There's an ancient bathroom—but these days I have to go down to Janet's bathroom beside the kitchen to get any hot water. Whichever laird put in all these modern conveniences depended heavily on a ready supply of coal and a hefty man to stoke the boiler. I hardly need say the boiler is on its last legs. There isn't any hefty man, and there's precious little coal. Above your room—the Red Tower Room—there're a couple of rooms like this, but they've been abandoned to the dust and the spiders.'' Lastly, after knocking, he put his head into the room his mother occupied. ''I don't think she'd mind. She's never here this time of day. . . . It's called the Rose Room. A pretty faded rose, as you can see.''

Like the other rooms, it had its four-poster bed, but the furniture and curtains were covered in chintz—just discernible as having a rose pattern. An ancient rose-patterned carpet lay on the floor. The room was tidy in the most extreme fashion; almost the only indication that it was occupied was the array of silver-framed photographs on the chintz-skirted dressing table—photographs of Jamie's father, in uniform; his brother, Callum, dark-haired and handsome; a photograph of Jamie as a baby, held by his mother, with Callum, wearing the kilt, beside her. She had been a very beautiful young woman, Julia thought. There was a photograph of Jamie when he had been at Oxford, seated with a cricket team. ''My friends—the Hendersons,'' he pointed out. And then a single photo of him in his RAF uniform, a young and tender, untried Jamie, not marked with the scars of combat or the death of friends.

''She comes up here as soon as the snows have melted, and only retreats down to a little room near Janet's when the winter cold drives her out. As you can see . . . the view . . . faces west. As far north as this, she is often in bed before the sun sets—she gets the last of the sun.''

They retreated, Julia feeling that she had indeed intruded on someone's very private sanctum. Hastily Jamie showed her the drawing room. It was a long, narrow room—squeezed along the side of the Great Hall, and with only the aspect of the front courtyard. Then they went to the library, reached by another stone passageway off the Great Hall. Julia expected nothing better than the drawing room, but she gasped when she saw it. It was a full two stories high, and at one end might have connected two of the towers, but the end was closed off. A narrow gallery ran along the upper level, and the whole room, except where the

three great mullioned windows gave an unexpected view of the
loch, was lined with books. "Well, the laird who completed this
must have had a bit of spare cash and a yen for books. Some of
them are pretty good." Julia gazed at the thousands of leather-
bound volumes, many of them showing signs of mold. There
were two great fireplaces in the room, but it was evident that
neither had held a fire for a long time. The chill of the room
was deep and intense, but it was possessed of a lonely kind of
grandeur, a thing of beauty at the end of a narrow, dark passage.
"I've never had time to go through all the books," he said. "I
suspect there are some that might bring quite a penny or two at
auction—but of course Mother would never hear of selling anything. Like selling the family silver. What I see in some of them
is a couple of new tractors. Had enough? Let's get going. This
is all the past. It will be the future when I have enough money
to do something with it. For the moment, we just leave it to its
dust sheets and the spiders. . . ." He pulled at her arm hastily
and slammed the door behind them. Something about that beautiful room upset him. Whether it was that its neglected splendor
troubled him, she could only guess.

Jamie had arranged to borrow the station wagon, and it was
filled with gasoline he had taken from what was meant to be
reserved for farm use. "Oh, what the hell! I've earned this one
little fling!" It had been packed with a picnic basket and with
two rugs woven in the Sinclair tartan. The dogs waited expectantly. "This is going to be *our* day—just us! Before we have to
go visiting the neighbors, or they come to us." Unspoken between them was the thought that he might be returning to an
overseas assignment. They had shared the good fortune that since
his return to active duty he had not been assigned to the fighting
in the desert. Perhaps his slight disabilities had not allowed that;
perhaps he was still being assessed for his fitness. But his squadron, made up now mostly of newcomers, was still based at
Hawkinge. So few of the original members were left. Fighter
Command perhaps rightly thought of it as a novice squadron,
no matter its brilliant and blazing record of enemy kills. Only a
few—a very slim few of Churchill's famous "few"—were left.
The squadron was kept in place because the raids on London
and other great cities continued erratically, the Luftwaffe dispatched by Goering to keep Fighter Command off balance, although they knew that most of the German thrust had been turned

east in an attempt to crush the Russians before the winter froze machines and men into inaction, if not death. As the autumn days had grown shorter, Julia knew that something of great import must soon happen in their lives, dictated by the Russian winter. But now she deliberately cast it from her mind—whatever it might be—finding her delight and comfort in Jamie's company, in the beauty of the world he opened up for her.

The island in the loch on which the castle stood was bigger than she had realized last night. There were two more inner courtyards overlooked by the three towers; there was extensive stabling for horses, though it was now tenanted by two oxen and two donkeys. "Horses are a prewar luxury," Jamie said. "When the tractor breaks down, we use the oxen. The donkeys are just for odd jobs—bringing in firewood, carting things from here to there." But there was one horse left. "Catriona," Jamie called her, stroking the dappled gray head, opening up the stable door to run his hands over the smooth, shining gray flanks. "How are you, old girl? Looking pretty good to me. She was the one thing we could not part with," he said softly as he fed the mare an apple. "Actually, she does do her bit—we almost always use her in a trap, but she doesn't consider it beneath her dignity to pull a cart, though she's not, and never will be, a cart horse. There's a bit of Thoroughbred in her, and she enjoys a jump—more than a bit mixed up, I'd say. My mother used to ride her—and she was my great joy before I went to Oxford. William Kerr's kids—he's the steward—keep her exercised if there's no work for her to do. She's as gentle as a lamb, and the kids adore her. And they take good care of her." Julia had already noted how beautifully she was groomed, the fresh hay and water in the stall, the fresh straw on the ground. "My mother likes to think she has some Arabian blood in her—that's because her grandsire was a stallion Mother brought with her from the West when she married, who was almost pure white. Mother dreams of Andalusian horses—the Lippizaners of Vienna—she likes to think there's some of that strain in Cat. The countryside around here is littered with a lovely mix of off-color horses that the stallion sired. My father never charged stud fees. He liked the fact that the commonest old mare could be mated with a blood sire. He was a great believer in raising the level of everything—and everyone. At least that's what I'm told." He gave Catriona one last pat, blew gently against her nostrils, and closed the half

door of the stable. "So old Balthazar used to have marvelous
summers out in the meadows with as many mares as he cared
to cover. They seemed to like it. Catriona is probably his granddaughter. We didn't keep records. I have just the vaguest memory of being taken out to see him—at work, let's say. Oh, look,
here's William Kerr, come to bid you welcome."

A smallish, wizened-faced, middle-aged man approached
them from a neat white dwelling that formed part of the stable
complex. Julia had already noted that the parts of the castle that
were not in ruins were well kept, a policy of money wisely
spent, she thought.

The two men shook hands. The welcomes said, Jamie introduced Kerr to Julia. "Ah, hasn't Janet already flown over to tell
us that the loveliest creature she's ever seen outside of the cinema
had come to grace the castle."

"Well spoken, Mr. Kerr," Jamie said. "I've been struggling
for months to find words like that." They were taken to William
Kerr's house to meet his wife, a stern-faced woman who civilly
offered them a cup of tea. "We've just finished breakfast, Mrs.
Kerr." Julia felt herself being scrutinized with care but reserve.
"It's well you're back, Master James. The last visit was far too
short. . . ." The reproof was clear. Jamie chose to take no notice of it. Julia realized that she was being blamed by more than
one for keeping Jamie at her side. Jamie inquired politely about
the children. "Rachel and Colin are, naturally, at school now."
He gestured with a slight show of affection and pride at the little
boy who peered shyly around from the back of a chair. "Dugald, here, our latecomer, has a few years yet before he joins
them." When Jamie commented on how well Catriona looked,
William Kerr replied, "But she's their great love. On weekends
we have to say, 'No one rides Cat until the homework is
done. . . .' " They exchanged some talk about the farm. "I'll
come and have a real talk with you later, Mr. Kerr," Jamie said,
with a hint of impatience. It was clear that he did not want to
waste this radiant morning in domestic discussion when the world
he wanted to show Julia still waited.

They drove over the bridge and the causeway and into the
forest. About halfway along what Julia later judged was about a
two-mile stretch, near a little bridge which spanned the stream,
she noticed a small cottage half-hidden in a clearing that was
being encroached upon relentlessly by young saplings. It had the

deserted air of a place that is never used. No smoke came from its chimney; no family washing hung on an outside line.

"It's been empty for years," Jamie replied to her question about it. "We couldn't keep all the workers we would have liked—someone who might have lived in that cottage. It's just used now as a sort of shelter when we're out gathering windfalls from the forest. Although I get angry every time Mother brings it up, it is true, of course, that the whole estate needs a lot of money spent on it. But I'm damned if I'll spoil this leave by worrying over what I can't do anything about until the war's over. . . ."

"Everything will happen when the war's over, is that it?"

He shrugged, as if disturbed by her comment. "Don't see how it can be otherwise. I *have* to come back here and work the place myself. Mother has done her best all these years. But she's tired—you can see that. She's been alone too long. It's not that she isn't very capable. But somehow the whole thing seemed to wait for me to grow up. And the war has further postponed all that. So the waiting goes on. I have to survive, Julia. You can see that. But that wasn't why I bailed out of the plane that day . . . if I could have hung on, I would have. . . ."

She placed her fingers lightly on one of the scarred hands on the wheel. "We agreed not to talk about it, Jamie. Do you imagine it would have made any one of us feel better if another life had gone with my mother's? Everything from that plane was shot away. Leave it alone. It's done. It's our secret—shared with your mother. And I don't think she'll ever want to talk about it."

They drove on in silence until they emerged from the forest and onto the main road. Jamie nodded toward the fields of stubble on one side of the road. "Those are ours. Some of the best land we have." They passed a cottage where a woman rushed to the door to wave. Jamie returned her wave. "One of the tenant farmers. I'll have to stop and have a word with her on the way back. I'm afraid they'll all expect to be visited, and they'll be frankly curious about you. . . ." He nodded again to the land on each side of the road. "Here's where we grow barley and wheat. When my father was young we used to own all the way to those far hills. I suppose we were prosperous then."

"What happened?"

He sighed, and the old engine almost covered the sound. "The usual. No, not gambling, for once. Not the usual sort of gambling. My grandfather was certain he was a financial wizard. He put his money into flybrained schemes. He had a ready ear for every crackpot who swore he could turn dross into gold. He wasn't content to be just prosperous. Oh, no—he meant to be the richest man in Scotland. I don't say that everyone he trusted with money was a rogue, but there must have been a fair few in their number. He didn't like being a minor little local laird. He wanted to be a really important man—not just a gentleman farmer. A vain little poppycock, I suppose is how I'd characterize him, although I never really knew him. I remember an old man. A bit touched, was what they kindly said about him. Quite mad, I would have said. Still poring over schemes to get rich while he continued to sell the land that would have kept us at least comfortable. In the end my father had to act to take power of attorney from him, before we were absolutely ruined. He didn't live long after that, and of course people blamed my father. I don't, myself, thinking about it, see what else my father could have done. . . .''

They drove a number of miles along the road, mostly passing small cottages. Sometimes there were large stone pillars and wrought-iron gates that marked the entry to some grander property. "We won't go calling on neighbors today, Julia. Today is just for us."

Then he turned off the main road onto a rough track, which Julia thought was certain to bog the old vehicle down. But Jamie drove skillfully, slewing the car from side to side, avoiding the places where pools of water had settled into the ruts. Here the land was open and uncultivated; heather, now past its August glory of purple, was brown. "Good shooting—or it used to be when we had game-keepers. My mother used to make a little money by letting out the shooting before the war. If people were willing to pay, she would even put them up at the castle, and she played the lady of the manor very well—at the same time helping make up the rooms in the morning and giving a hand in the kitchen." They were climbing quite steeply and finally reached the place he sought. They were on high ground, a steep bluff that overlooked the loch. They went to the edge, which gave a view of the castle on its island.

"We're actually on Sinclair land here, but you can't reach the castle except by a long hike along the shore. . . ." Julia saw from a different aspect the scene that had so enchanted her that morning. There were patches of cultivation, and pastures for the cattle, the same white dots of sheep stretching up into the hill-sides. The sun glowed warmly at its noon zenith. There was a mirror vision of part of the castle reflected in the stillness of the loch.

"Jamie—it's so beautiful."

He took her hand. "I almost wish it weren't. If it were pouring with rain and shrouded in mist you'd get a truer picture of what it's usually like. But there it is—my whole world, Julia. All I have, and all I ever want. Apart from the money to make it a bit better. But I'll earn it. I know I will. After the war things will be different. My father pulled it free of debt, but I'd gladly mortgage the whole thing again to give it new life." He sighed. "Well, that's what I say. That's what I dream. One can always dream, I suppose."

"Only very dull people don't have dreams," she said softly.

He went back to the car and started carrying the picnic basket and rugs to the place where they had stood. The dogs ran around sniffing in the heather for rabbits and hares, their waving tails sometimes the only mark of their presence. "Aren't you afraid they'll get lost—wander off?"

"Not them," Jamie said as he spread the rugs. "They'll always have an ear cocked—perhaps looking for a handout from the basket because you're a stranger, and they've already reckoned that you're softhearted. But at the first sound of the engine starting up, they'll be jumping into the back, no matter what. They know where they live, and who feeds them. Country dogs don't often get lost. If they decided to make their way back along the shore, they'd be waiting for us with tongues hanging out when we got back."

They ate the ham and cheese sandwiches Janet had packed, the chicken legs, the Dundee cake. They washed it down with small tots of whiskey poured from a silver flask and drunk from small silver cups. Jamie produced these from a leather container made especially for them, a relic, Julia thought, from more lavish times.

When they had finished and after Julia had shared some of the sandwiches with the dogs, who had come back to claim space on the rugs, Jamie lay back, put his hands behind his head, and stared at the sky. What appeared to be a hawk of some kind circled above. "We have a pair of golden eagles nesting here," he said. "Our own special treasure." He fixed his eyes on the bird. "Now that I've told you all my poor dreams, Julia, what do *you* dream of? Tell me. Do you dream of seeing your name in lights above the title—when the lights go back on again? Do you dream of being up there on the screen, which Janet thinks must be very heaven?"

She shrugged and looked down at him. "I wish you hadn't asked. Or I wish you'd asked some night when we were having dinner in London, and the answer would have seemed obvious. I spent years studying at RADA with just that thought—but because of Father, I wanted it to be the stage rather than the screen. He didn't . . . well, he didn't enjoy Hollywood, or filming very much. But it paid well. I thought I would follow him, and I would fight like a tiger to get parts I wanted. Well—you know what happened. I got a plum part, and I'm lined up for another, and I'm not at all sure that's what I really want. I prepared all my life to be my father's daughter, but when it came to playing that on the stage, that's all it felt like—a stage, and I was only there to support him. He doesn't need me now, and I wonder if I need the stage, or the name in lights. I'm not a great natural, as he is. He strides the stage, and he dominates it, as he does the audience. His is the face and the figure everyone watches. Even in the few films he made, it was the same. A natural photogenic quality. A gift of presence. I don't believe I've got it, and I don't think it can be learned. And somehow, now, I don't care very much. I've enjoyed the applause—and the red roses. Oh, I loved the red roses from Jamie Sinclair. But I don't think I *care enough*. I hate the thought of a lifetime of discipline—of keeping up ballet classes, and voice classes, if it isn't going to get me right to the top. The top is a long way off, Jamie, and I may never make it. I'd mind that—just being mediocre. I'd hate people—worse, I'd hate critics saying, 'What a pity, with a mother and father like that.' Sometimes I envy Connie. It isn't that she isn't ambitious. But she's ambitious for much simpler things. I think she would like a steady husband and a family. A modest measure of happiness. *That* isn't easy to achieve, either."

He was silent for some time, absentmindedly playing with Rory's soft ear. Then he sat up and stared down at the castle on its island in the loch below. "And I am bound here. I can't live anywhere else, or for any other reason. I was born to this, and

I can't shake it.'' He paused; then he said, ''It would have been different if Callum had lived.''

''Callum?''

''I told you I had an older brother. Years older than I. We weren't companions. Too big an age difference. But everyone adored him. He would go shooting and fishing with my father. *They* were companions, more like brothers than father and son. It was really for his sake that my grandfather realized that he would have to hand over affairs to my father, or there would be nothing for Callum to inherit. My mother thought the sun rose out of him. I was an unexpected afterthought. I think they were quite pleased when I was born, but in their hearts they already had the perfect heir.''

''What happened?''

''We're not sure. Just the empty, capsized boat in the loch. He often went fishing alone and was perfectly capable. But storms here get up very suddenly. The wind sweeps down from the mountains, and there are waves enough to swamp any small boat. They never forbade him to do anything, you see. He was so capable—so damn good at everything. Even if there'd been someone else with him, it could have happened just the same way. It nearly killed them—my parents. Even as young as I was I can remember that they were seized with a kind of rigor. Hardly able to think, or give directions. It was the steward we had at the time who organized the search of the shores of the loch— every man and woman on the estate joined in, and every neighbor sent their help and came themselves. It took about three days to find him. Washed ashore on the other side of the loch. His hands were tangled in fishing lines. My father could not understand how Callum got himself into that situation. For months after that Father hardly spoke. He didn't want to talk to the children of the estate workers. He didn't want even to *see* me. I wasn't very old, but I knew what it felt like to feel guilty. I was alive, and Callum was dead. I think I realized later that if I lived three lifetimes I couldn't make up for what they had lost. My father drank quite a lot, I remember—something he hadn't done before. My grandfather died—some say of that shock. And then my father went off and did the same thing that had killed Callum. He went shooting alone in the forest—it was deer-hunting season, and he was used to stocking up the larder. But this time he didn't ask his friends—it had always been a sort of social occasion before. And he didn't take a gillie with him. To go shooting alone is against the rules. Just as it's against the rules not to break your gun when you're walking through the woods. He hadn't broken his gun—or perhaps he was stalking a deer and was into the kill. We don't know about that, either. We think he slipped from a craggy place in the forest. They found him at the bottom of a sort of ravine with half his head blown away. Of course, there was talk. Some people said he was a crazed man. Others just said he was a damn fool. But whatever—it left my mother alone, with just me. A poor enough legacy.''

Julia felt anger. "Jamie, I won't listen! You're worth more than that. You're her life. She hangs on every word you speak.''

''More's the pity. She should have something more to anchor her life to. The war might have been bad for me, but if I go—then I go! Death doesn't bother me. It's what I leave behind for her to carry on. I sometimes wonder if I didn't let the Spitfire go that day just a fraction too soon, thinking that somehow I had to survive . . . for her.''

Julia began quickly to pack their plates and the remainder of the food back into the basket. "We agreed we wouldn't talk about that. You're morbid, Jamie. It's nonsense to think you have to get yourself through the war just to come back here to have care of an inheritance. You have to live for yourself! Not for a castle, or a sacred trust. Not for your mother.'' She got to her knees, but he pulled her back down beside him. This time his kiss was more urgent, more demanding than last night's.

''Damn!—I want you,'' he said. "I ache for you. But it can't be yet. Not until I'm sure that that's what *you* want. Not just a quick roll in the hay, but forever. So, if you don't mind, I'll try to live for you, if for no other reason.''

She disengaged his hands from her shoulders. "Jamie, we'll take it one step at a time. Being as sure and careful as two people who are in love can ever be. People in love aren't careful. Love makes you reckless, not sure and careful. One day at a time . . . Come on. Let's go. I'm tired,'' she added, striving to keep the tension out of her tone. Perhaps her mood was overlaid with disappointment. She wanted him, and he would make no move to take her. "Honorable Jamie. Not taking advantage . . . Perhaps you expect *me* to wait forever. I'm not Connie. I really don't know how to be sure and careful. I'll grab at just a little

time—if that's all we've got. But now—now I'd like to go back.
I can still feel the aches from the train. It's getting cold. . . .''

Her mood had changed from peace and equanimity to doubt
and mistrust. Michael had been right. Jamie had brought her
here to show her what he was committed to, what he would
return to if he came through the war. There was no woman
stronger than this legacy of sadness and dwindling hope. He
lived only to struggle upward from the depth where the deaths
of his father and brother had left him. She began to wish he had
never come to Anscombe that day in spring. She wished she had
never seen his face, wished she had never laid her eyes on his
hands. Just then a chill wind whipped up from the loch. Looking
around for the last time, she saw that mist had come in to ob-
scure those far, snow-touched peaks of the mountain range. Jamie whistled the dogs into the back of the station wagon. They
drove away in silence. When they passed through the forest, it
seemed darker than before. She knew now that somewhere near
to here his father had died. She had a further, quick glimpse of
the forlorn little cottage that the forest had almost overtaken. It
had become a place of sadness. Then the vision of the loch and
the castle came to them. Here his brother had died. Physically
she tried to shake off the thought and memory of death. Then,
as if he had known the wild mixture of her emotions all along,
his hand reached out to take hers briefly as they rattled over the
drawbridge. "I'm sorry, my love. All these wild outpourings.
Just put it down to my coming back here. Coming back—well,
I wish sometimes I need never come back. They all expect too
much. I know it. They expect too much of any woman who's
fool enough to marry me. And yet I'm stuck with this. There's
no need for you to be buried here, Julia. The world holds better
things for you. Don't let all this trap you, as it's trapped me.''

That night dinner was in the housekeeper's room, as breakfast
had been. Lady Jean had not changed, so neither did Julia. She
drank her whiskey with her legs stretched to the fire, where all
three dogs lay. The talk was mostly between Jamie and his
mother—talk of friends and neighbors, or cousins and more distant kin. Inevitably there was bad news of deaths and injuries,
things his mother had not told in letters. There had been some
deaths and injuries among those who fought, and among those
too old or too young to fight. The Glasgow docks had taken a

fearful hammering from the German bombers, and a young cousin had died as his ship berthed at Strathclyde, having survived yet another perilous Atlantic crossing. Another cousin, a girl of twenty, had died from shrapnel wounds she received as she helped man an antiaircraft gun post. And there had been births. More young kin scattered all over Scotland. Photographs to show. All the things of a family life Julia could not share.

Dinner was soup and fish and beef, pudding with heavy cream. "Janet really does not take much notice of the austerity measures—and most certainly not when Jamie is home. She cannot see that the little she keeps back will make any difference."

"She isn't far wrong," Julia said. "In London, if you know the right places, there's always enough—and not as well cooked."

"Don't tell her." Lady Jean managed a smile. "It will only encourage her. Dear knows, she eats little enough herself. But at times like this her pride is involved. You both must eat the best she can provide, and she's ingenious about where she gets it—and rather unscrupulous. Barter is the great thing. Fish for eggs. Ham for game. That way, you see, no ration coupons are involved. She thinks she's inside the regulations."

This evening, as they sat around that simple table, without the silver candelabra and dishes, the mood was more relaxed. Often Julia found Lady Jean's eyes on her, but she asked no questions about their day, except where they had picnicked. "Good for Jamie to have a day off. But we must try to visit a little—and invite some people here. His last visit was so short, there wasn't time for any of that. But people will expect to see him this leave." She seemed to be indicating that Jamie did not belong to Julia alone.

The whiskey and wine seemed more potent than the night before. Julia said, "If you don't mind—perhaps I'll go to bed. The journey up here—or perhaps just the bracing air today . . ."

Jamie was on his feet immediately. "You won't take a walk by the loch first? Clears the head. You'll sleep marvelously."

"I think I'll sleep marvelously, in any case."

Lady Jean nodded in approval. She couldn't keep them apart, but she welcomed every sign that perhaps they were not as close as he feared. "I know Janet has already put hot-water bottles in your bed. Put more coal on the fire," she added expansively.

"Would you like a brandy to take upstairs?" The solicitous hostess, eager to be rid of her.

Jamie saw her, as he had last night, to the top of the stairs. Without last night's blazing fire, the Great Hall seemed vast and cavernous, devoid of life, yet haunted by too many centuries of history. He kissed her gently, almost absently, as if he knew the doubts that swirled within her, and would do nothing to assuage them. "Sleep well." She might have been one of those numerous cousins and lesser kin they had talked of. In the silence of the Red Tower Room she pulled back the curtain a little. Utter blackness greeted her. No sign of stars, no sheen of water. As she stood there, the first spatter of rain hit the glass. Soon it lashed more strongly. By the time she was ready for bed, the handmade lead gutters and downspouts, stamped here and there with the Sinclair crest, as she had observed in the courtyards that morning, were already running with water. She slipped into the huge bed and gratefully felt the touch of the hot-water bottles against her feet.

Her sleep that night was troubled and fitful. There was a dream of hands lifted desperately from the water of the loch, hands entangled with fishing lines. She woke shivering from that dream and sensed that she was not alone in the room. The fire had died, but its red embers remained. Was there some vague image there by the great carved mantel?—something in a flowing robe, man or woman she couldn't tell? But the gentle sigh she heard that seemed to be the end of a sob was that of a woman. Or was it nothing at all? The wind also sighed about the castle and moaned in the chimney. She half sat up, and the image was gone. Then she lay down and pulled the blankets about her ears, willing to hear no more of what this place might reveal to her.

But she was still awake in the morning when Janet brought her tea. The curtain rings rattled back as before, and the cheerful voice was telling her there was a wee bit of rain but that it would clear by evening. She didn't need to look from the windows to know. The mist and rain pressed against them, and the ashes were dead and gray in the hearth.

"Janet, was there . . . was there ever someone in this room who was very unhappy? Someone who wept?"

"Ah, if you go back over the centuries there might have been scores, Miss Seymour. But the one they see most—those who do see or hear her—why, that could be the Lady Ellen. Very

young, she was. No more than fourteen. The laird of the time
abducted her—ah, it was always happening in those days. Hundreds of years ago. They plundered and murdered and abducted—all for the money, or because they thought *they'd* be
murdered. Terrible harsh times they were, and these old walls
have seen the lot.''

''What happened to—to Lady Ellen?''

''She was fatherless, poor child. Her lands went to the laird.
She died in childbirth. But her son lived. Myself, I've never seen
nor heard her. But some say they do.'' She peered more closely
at Julia. ''Master Jamie didn't tell you, did he?''

''No, nothing—he said nothing.''

Janet poured tea into a dainty china cup. ''Then it's best you
say nothing. It will not please them to know that you have been
disturbed. Or perhaps that you even know anything about Lady
Ellen. I'll get a tongue-lashing from Lady Jean. Ah, but Mistress''—she had slipped back into the old Scottish form of address—''it would be a strange house that has stood as long as
this one without its tragedies.'' Her face brightened as her ha-
bitual cheerfulness came back. ''But then we've had our times
of joy and happiness as well. Like every other family. . . . Well,
Mistress, Morag will be up in a few minutes with the hot water.
And a good, hearty breakfast will take away any wee stirrings
in the night.''

III

THE DAYS OF JAMIE'S LEAVE sped by, and they seemed hardly
ever to be alone together. If someone did not come to lunch,
then they were bidden to lunch at some of the adjoining estates.
Dinner parties were given for Jamie. There seemed an anxious
wish on the part of those who entertained them that Jamie should
have the best sort of welcome. It was evident that the Sinclairs
were a popular family. Many of the people to whose houses they
were bidden were of Lady Jean's generation. To welcome back
a young man was part of the yearning, sternly suppressed, to
see their own sons and daughters back among them. In Jamie's
case there seemed a special warmth, Julia thought. He was one
of the famous ''few'' of the Battle of Britain. He had been decorated for gallantry and service. He was an air ace who had

barely missed death—Lady Jean must not have told her neighbors and friends the full extent of his injuries, but they could be clearly seen in the first minutes with him.

The welcome for Julia was somewhat more reserved. Firstly, she was a stranger. They were polite enough to welcome her because Jamie had brought her. But their good manners were overlaid with just the faintest hint of mistrust. She was not one of them; she came from that far-off world of the stage, and her mother, though famous in her own right, was, after all, a Russian, and therefore totally strange. Her father might be a knight but was one of those ''stage fellows''—a breed they scarcely met and who were generally thought of as being of the unstable kind. But she evoked an amount of curiosity also. The story of her Cordelia to her father's Lear, his disappearance from the stage after his wife's death, and his return with his own daughter as his support had penetrated even the Scottish papers and magazines. Julia wondered what the reaction would have been if these Scottish gentry, these welcoming neighbors and friends had known the full truth of the complex relationship between herself and Jamie, the secret she had said must not ever be talked about, even though she knew Jamie was tortured by it. Even the story of the rose garden in place of the oasthouse was known— though Lady Jean was hardly likely to have talked of the rose-bush she had contributed. But somehow the news had gotten out. One day of glorious autumn weather, as Julia strolled in the rose garden that graced a fine Georgian house built when the need to fortify great houses had gone, the owner, a courteous, handsome man with vivid blue eyes and in his mid-fifties, she judged, talked to her of it. ''A lovely idea of Sir Michael's—to make a memorial rose garden. I keep this one up myself. Can't spare a gardener for purely ornamental things like this—but we've put as much ground into vegetables as we can manage. This was my wife's great passion. I keep it up for her. The only thing that comforts me about her death was that she didn't live to know about our sons' deaths.'' He paused for a moment. ''I'd be extremely honored if Sir Michael would accept a bush from here. Now might be a good time to lift it, as everything's pretty well gone dormant for the winter. You might take it back with you, perhaps. . . .''

It was the first time she had felt genuine warmth and sympathy among those who had been her hosts. Tears were close to her eyes. "That's extremely kind of you, Sir Niall. At first we—the family—thought his obsession with the rose garden was somewhat morbid. My sister Alex was really firm that the area should just be seeded into lawn. But now we see the point. Perhaps it kept him sane through those first months after her death. Certainly the labor of clearing the site—preserving whatever materials were left after the fire—for when he can build walls for the rose garden was the best thing he could have done. Otherwise, I'm afraid, in the hours when he wasn't working, the whiskey bottle was his companion. That's passed now. . . ."

A kindly hand, obviously worn from his work in the garden, touched hers. "I understand perfectly, my dear. We all seek escape from tragedy in our various ways. It is good to know Sir Michael is working again—trying to put it behind him. Here in Scotland, although we don't get much chance to see these things, he's regarded as having played the best Macbeth of modern times. We're not quite out of the world, you see."

As they walked quietly among the now pruned and leafless bushes, he spoke again: "Does Jamie ever mention my boys . . . the Hendersons?"

She whirled to look him fully in the face. "The Hendersons! Of course! Oh, how stupid of me! But I've met so many people in these few days . . . his best friends . . . not just chums. Friends. They were in his squadron. . . ."

"They'd been friends all their lives. Jamie and my younger son, Ian, were the same age. The elder one, Gordon, was only a year older than those two. They grew up together. Gordon went to Oxford a year before the other two followed. But they all joined the RAF Volunteer Reserve. My sons"—his voice wavered a little, and he looked firmly at the well-tended earth about the rosebushes—"Gordon was killed first. And then Ian—just a few days later. It was the day after Ian was shot down that Jamie came to grief. I often wonder if his concentration wasn't disturbed by his feelings about losing his friends. They were going so quickly then . . . during the Battle of Britain. It must have been a desperate situation. Watching your squadron shot to pieces . . . and losing your two best friends in such a short time. Jamie has some hard memories. . . . You can hardly imagine what it was like for Lady Jean and me in those days. Just to know he survived, never mind how badly he was shot up. We had to have something left to live for. I'm afraid I stake a large claim on

Jamie's affections, because he's just about all I've got left. I pray
he survives this wretched war.'' He lifted his head to look directly at Julia. ''Do you care for him?''

''I love him.''

He nodded. ''That's all the answer I need.''

For Julia the most difficult day was when they were invited to
Darnaway for lunch. Since the day was fair and no rain threatened, they hitched Catriona up to the trap. ''She must be seen
to earn her oats sometimes,'' Lady Jean said, but it was said
lightheartedly. Julia suspected that she was looking forward more
to this luncheon than to any of the others. Darnaway was the
home of Kirsty Macpherson, the girl Jamie had told her his
mother preferred for his wife to all others. The girl with beauty
and money.

The family had gathered in the hall of a splendid eighteenth-
century Robert Adam house to greet them. Behind the house
was the remainder of an ancient keep that had once sheltered
members of the family, their servants, their cattle, and any who
swore allegiance to the chieftain in times of trouble, just as at
Sinclair. But here they had been able to abandon the discomfort
and inconveniences of the ancient building, demolish the out-
houses, and leave it, restored but not inhabited, to represent
their former fighting history. They had been fortunate in the
lands that surrounded the castle, good arable and pasture. There
was no hill farming at Darnaway. They had been fortunate in
members of the family who had sought their fortunes abroad—
investing in sugar plantations in the West Indies, Lady Jean said.
That also would have meant enjoying the profits from slavery,
Julia thought. They had made wise investments in the Scottish
shipbuilding industry, unlike Jamie's grandfather, who had gam-
bled everything on new inventions that had failed. The family
owned two whiskey distilleries. ''Best of all, I suppose,'' Lady
Jean said, when she had come to the end of the recital of good
fortune that had made and kept the Macphersons rich, ''was that
at crucial moments in their history they made good marriages.
Some families have a genius for it.''

Embraces were exchanged as the two families met. Julia was
introduced to Sir Allan and Lady Macpherson, then to Kirsty.
Kirsty's welcome to Jamie had been cordial but not excessive.
Julia found marvelous green eyes turned upon her. ''We're so

happy you could make this long journey up here. Jamie's letters
have been full of how kind your family has been to him." She
really was beautiful, Julia thought. The pale, perfect oval of her
face was framed by shining auburn hair. She was slim and of
more than middle height, with a long neck and a jawline that
was accentuated by the crewnecked cashmere sweater she wore
above a pleated skirt—the Macpherson tartan, Julia didn't doubt.
She wore no jewelry except a silver brooch, which probably
represented the clan badge and motto.

"We didn't ask anyone else," Lady Macpherson said. "I'm
afraid, selfishly, we wanted Jamie to ourselves for these few
hours. We haven't seen him for such a long time." Julia had
already been told they had a son, Harry, serving in the Navy.
"We suspect—though, of course, he can't tell us—that his ship
is heading for the Far East." She gave a little sigh as her husband poured the drinks. "And now that I'm over my little illness"—Julia had been told on the way there that it had been a
major operation from which she had taken a long time to recover—"I think Kirsty will be joining the WAAF. That leaves
only our little Una, still at school. But if this wretched war goes
on much longer, even *she* will be old enough to join up." She
beamed a false smile at Julia. "But you, dear, don't have to
think about such things. You will be in demand on the stage,
and even if you did join up, they'd just send you around entertaining the troops. Quite necessary, no doubt. . . . How very
dull life has become here in the Highlands since the war. No
one visits anymore—never farther than a few miles. Most of the
servants have gone; the help on the farm—or at least the sons—
have gone, leaving us only the middle-aged men. You haven't
noticed problems like that, I suppose, Miss Seymour. Such a
glamorous world you live in—"

"Julia lives on a farm that was right under the action in the
Battle of Britain," Jamie cut in. "And she works in London.
There's precious little glamour in it, Lady Macpherson."

"Oh, dear." The lady looked flustered. "I've put my foot in
it again. Allan, dear, fill Miss Seymour's glass. Can't you see
it's empty? Kirsty, pass those little things, whatever Cook's
dreamed up. All the servants, Jamie, have asked me to tell you
how glad they are you've been able to manage a visit. And that
you're well again. Won't it be wonderful when it's all over and
life's back to normal."

"I wonder if it can ever be," Kirsty said. "Any rate, I don't intend to be left out any longer. I want to be able to look anyone in the eye when it *is* all over and say I did my humble bit."

"I keep telling her there's absolutely no need to join up. It's not yet compulsory. She's doing so much work here with the Red Cross and the—"

They still managed to retain an elderly butler. "Luncheon is served, m'lady."

As they drove back to Sinclair the weather turned, and rain poured down. Julia could only think miserably that Kirsty Macpherson was indeed beautiful and graceful and fully at home among her people in the Highlands. And she was rich. Because of the dark sky, the castle loomed over them suddenly. Julia felt her shoulders, already shrugged deeply into her raincoat, hunch even further. Water was trickling down the back of her neck. She thought she hated Sinclair and all it stood for, a world in which she would never belong. She would be glad when the visit ended, which would be the day after tomorrow. She would go, gladly. She would never come back. They drove around to the stable yard so that Jamie could dry and feed Catriona. The kitchen door opened to admit them. "Ah, it's drowned you must be," said Janet. "Shall I pour a wee dram, Lady Jean, to drive out the cold?"

Julia unwillingly shared a glass with Lady Jean in the house-keeper's room. There was a spurious friendliness between them. "Such a lovely house, isn't it—Darnaway? And don't you think Kirsty is beautiful? Augustus John painted her portrait. It wasn't commissioned. He saw her once in London—her coming-out year just before war broke out. He asked to do it. Such a pity there wasn't time to see all their paintings. And they have such a wonderful ceramics collection. Oh, I've been to such grand balls in that house. You didn't even see the ballroom, did you? There are portraits of Victoria and Albert presented to the family after they had stayed at Darnaway. . . ."

At last Jamie joined them. "Cat's beginning to show her years, I think," he said. "More than happy to see the stable."

"We all are, my dear," his mother said. "I so much want tomorrow night to go off well, but it's been a big burden on Janet and Mrs. Kerr and Morag—"

"What the devil are you talking about?"

"No need to be so affronted. I just planned a little dinner

party. I would have done it last time, but you couldn't spare more than two nights here. It's your last night here, Jamie—for heaven knows how long. I just asked to dinner the people who have been kind enough to entertain us.'' Her tone dropped to a reproachful note. ''Your last night, Jamie . . .''

He tossed back his whiskey and went to pour another, silently taking Julia's glass from her and refilling it also.

''You'll wear the kilt, of course, Jamie,'' his mother said.

''Damn and blast . . .'' was all he answered her.

The kitchen was in a flurry of activity all the next day. Jamie grabbed Julia's hand after they had eaten a cold lunch of ham and Scotch eggs. ''Come on—get your coat. If I see or hear any more of this I might just decide not to turn up tonight.''

He was silent as they made their way through the old walled garden, which presented a picture of neglect, weed-choked and faintly melancholy, and into the vegetable garden, which the Kerrs kept up and divided the produce with Janet. ''Something else to do after the war,'' Jamie said dismissively. They made their way around to the drawbridge and the causeway. The dogs had followed automatically. ''She must *know* I didn't want any of this nonsense. I said I wanted a quiet leave, and it's been nothing but tea parties.''

''Your friends haven't seen you for so long.'' Julia felt she had to say it, though the words came unwillingly.

''I've haven't enjoyed being peered at quite so closely,'' he answered. ''They've all been gauging how close a call it was for me. One of the reasons I stayed away so long—I didn't want them to see me shuffling along with the cane. But I'm back on active duty. That tells them I'm well. One of the things I most balked at, though, was that Sir Niall had to see me alive and well—when he had lost both Gordon and Ian. They were great chaps. I was lucky to grow up with them. The whole place feels so odd without them around. . . .'' He turned off at the end of the causeway. ''You haven't walked along the loch yet—well, I grant you, there's not been much time between lunches and tea parties and so on. . . .'' He gestured to the three dogs. ''Come on, you lazy brutes. What a dog's life you have. No one now to keep you from getting fat and lazy.'' Then his mood of complaint seemed to break. He bent and fondled the Labrador's head, and as the two collies pressed around him, he stroked them all.

"Oh, you're not such a bad lot. Can't be helped that there's nothing doing here these days. Look, Julia, look at Rory. What a wonderfully soft mouth he has—a great retriever. Well, my pets, it's a long and boring war for you, too. But we'll get through it. I'll work your tails off when I get back. . . ."

There was a touch of winter in the wind that blew off the loch; a dark, lowering sky hung about them. Jamie pulled Julia to him as they walked. "Too cold for you out here? The first snows will be on us soon. It's lonely up here in winter, Julia. I suppose you've imagined that. Perhaps that's why we make such a song and dance about being together when we can . . . it was churlish of me to begrudge Mother her little party. She has long months alone."

His train of thought seemed to flow on naturally. "I suppose this damn castle adds to it—being stuck out here on the loch. Now, if we'd been placed like Darnaway, or Finavon, Sir Niall's place, all this might have been fertile, arable land. As it is, we have to go miles just to herd the cattle. Lambing time is very rough. I suppose the Sinclairs thought they'd gotten themselves a nice, secure spot when they built where they did, but it's damned awkward now. Even the drawbridge is breaking up. I suppose you've noticed that the arches of the bridge from the causeway are starting to crumble. These old places . . . a real pain in the neck."

"Oh, shut up, Jamie. You do love to grumble. You wouldn't have it any different, even if you could."

He laughed, then bent and kissed her. "Well, a *bit* different." Then he whistled to the dogs. "Let's climb up into the forest. Now that most of the leaves have fallen, it's rather a beautiful place."

They scrambled through the rocks of the shoreline and into the steep side of the forest. Conifers mingled with oaks and beeches, and underfoot was a carpet of damp leaves. The dogs ran joyously ahead. "If we're lucky we might spot a buck or a doe—that is, if those rascals don't frighten everything within earshot. They've really gotten very undisciplined. No one to keep them in check."

The magic of the forest closed about them, and they walked in silence, Jamie giving her his hand over the steep and difficult places. There were great outcroppings of rock to which trees precariously clung. "Needs a bit of clearing out," Jamie observed. "Not very good wood management, but then we don't have the men for it. One clean sweep of the deadfalls here would give us wood for a couple of years for the fires."

"I didn't realize what a nagger you are," Julia said. "You've hardly stopped complaining about things since we arrived. Can't you just accept what is, and know nothing can be done about it until . . . until later?"

He caught her and swung her around until she faced him. "I just need *you* to know that. Nothing can be changed until later. But that doesn't mean I don't see what needs changing. Can you bear it here? Can you be patient through all the years while I try to change it?"

"Are you asking me to be here then? Are you really asking me?"

"I keep putting it in roundabout ways. I'm afraid to ask, because I'm afraid of the answer. Just take it as said. You'll answer in your own good time."

He walked on, and she had to hurry to catch up. "If that's a proposal of marriage, it's the funniest I've ever heard."

"Had many proposals of marriage, Julia? I suppose you have. Some must have been hilarious. Some must have been quite tempting. Those years at RADA—you must have met some interesting men."

"Boys," she said. "Not very interesting. Boys hoping to be men, hoping to be actors. And most of them terrified of coming near me because of who my father is." She shrugged and added laconically, "No, Jamie, I can't say I've had a proposal of marriage that was quite meant to be that. So we'll count yours the first." She tugged at his coat sleeve. "Want to say it again, just so I'll be sure?"

As they kissed, the first drops of rain fell through the remaining leaves. "Oh, damn! You'll get soaked again. Look, we'll have to make a dash for it down to the road. It's pretty steep here. Think you can manage it?"

"Yes . . ." but she sensed his reluctance. He whistled to the dogs and then turned quickly through the trees until they came to the edge of the steepest part of the forest they had yet traveled. He half-lifted her through the worst places, leading the way in others, showing her where to hold the limbs of trees, where to place her feet. The rain grew steadily heavier, but his features expressed a feeling that had nothing to do with discomfort. His look told her this was a place of special significance, somewhere he did not want to be. "Was it here, Jamie? Was it here your father . . . fell?"

"Yes," he said tersely. "A place I never meant you to be." They had reached the bottom, where a narrow stream ran, and began the ascent of the other slope. "Not so far now," he said, "not such rough going." His mood seemed to brighten as they reached the top. "You know—you're in very good shape. You look so ethereal. . . ."

"Oh, for heaven's sake, what do you think we train for? Titania's fairies? How much energy do you think it needs for my father to put on one of his fight scenes? Hamlet isn't always languishing around, you know."

"From the feel of you, I think you could probably manage an Army assault course. Good, we're getting there. Do you see the road? It's easy now. . . ."

"There's the little house," she said. "Can't we stop there? It's a good mile back to the castle. Perhaps the rain will ease off."

He looked at her wet hair sticking to her cheeks. "Well—perhaps we'd better. Not that I can guarantee it's much drier than out here." He touched the door of the cottage, and it gave under his hand. He looked dubiously at the roof. "Well, it's still almost in one piece." She was surprised to find a slate floor beneath her feet. "I don't know why I imagined it would be an earth floor."

"No, not this place. It was the usual old Scottish ben-and-butt—just two rooms, and one tacked on the back later. There's the remains of an old wooden bed in the other room. The man, McBain, who had it was a gamekeeper for my father. He added the other room as the kids came along, and dug a well. I suppose he did the floor as well."

"What happened to him?—if he put in all this work he must have expected to stay."

Jamie shrugged. "I don't know. All I know is that he went off to Canada rather suddenly, with his family. It was sometime close to when my father died. I wasn't paying much attention to anything else then—ah, look, there's dry wood still. Before the war I used to come with the men when we did a few days' timber cutting in the forest. We always used to come here to eat our lunch if it was close enough. It was generally chilly enough for a fire—nearly always is in Scotland by the time the leaves have fallen. We'd make a fire and eat our lunch, and I don't think food ever tasted so good to me. I remember the flasks used to come out. Come to think of it, this was probably the place where I first got just a little bit drunk. I seem to remember they wouldn't let me handle an ax or a saw that afternoon. Self-preservation.'' While he talked he was breaking off little twigs from the slim, dry branches, and he put a match to them. ''Hope the chimney still draws, or we'll be smoked out.'' But the thin smoke spiraled upward, and he laid on bigger sticks. ''In a minute I'll chance something heavier, and we'll have a decent fire and a wee dram.''

''You haven't got a flask with you!''

''Hardly ever without it up here. *Uisge-beatha.* Water of life, we call it. Ah, there . . .'' The fire was gaining on the dry wood. ''We always made it a rule that whatever we burned, we put back the same amount, cut and ready for the next time. But the forest's grown too damn close now. This used to be a nice, open space. I can remember that man's kids playing in the sun.'' He looked more closely at the roof. ''I'll have a word with Kerr and see if he can't spare a couple of men and a few hours to see to the slates. Pity to let it all go. Though God knows, there are enough of these old places dotted over the estate—empty, just falling apart. But this is close enough to the castle to perhaps be of some use in the future. When the war's over—oh, damn the phrase, but there's no other way to say it—when the war's over, I think there'll be men and families looking for jobs and some-place to live—almost anyplace.'' He looked around more closely, though the curtain of rain cut off almost any sight of the road or the forest; the glass of the small windows was filmed with the dust of years. ''I had some pretty good times here, Julia—with the men. I wasn't the young laird when I worked with them and shared their smoked sausage and their dram. They talked to me as if I were a man and said things to me my mother would never have said. These were the people I wanted you to meet, Julia. Some of them are dead now. But enough are still around— probably their kids are in the forces, too. Yes, it would have been better if we'd gone through the whole estate, drinking tea and eating scones, and drinking whiskey and listening to what they had to say to me. Far better than these bloody tea parties. Well, next time . . .'' He added a stouter log to the fire, then filled the cap of his flask and gave it to her. ''Just toss it back—

don't sip. It'll get right down into your bones.'' He eased the
raincoat off her shoulders. ''God, you're soaked.'' He took off
the woolen cap she wore and fluffed up her hair. ''Lean into the
fire, you silly fool.'' He took off his scarf and tried to dry her
hair. ''Can't have you going back with pneumonia.''

She dropped her coat on the ground, careless of the dust of
the years, the mud trailed in. She sat there before the fire and
reached out a hand to give back the cap. ''Fill it up for yourself
and come and sit by me and keep me warm, Jamie.''

He spread his own waterproof on the ground beside hers. He
refilled the little silver cap and eased himself down beside her,
the movement to his injured leg still not quite easy. He tossed
back the drink. ''Want another? And then perhaps we'd better
go, rain or no rain. Because if we stay . . .''

''Yes, Jamie. If we stay we'll finally make love to each other.
What do you think, Jamie? I think we'll stay . . . it could be
that we'll stay together forever?''

''You'd stay here—with me—forever?''

''Forever. I have no home except with you. You're in my
heart, Jamie, however inconvenient it may be. However difficult, and perhaps not very sensible. Even foolhardy. But I love
you, and I can't help it. I can't bear the thought that you'll go
away, and maybe you'll be killed, and I'll live forever with the
thought that you never had me as your own—and that I didn't
have the courage to give myself to you. I want you, Jamie, just
the way you want me. There's a war, and maybe our time is
very short. I want to remember—''

He stifled her words with his mouth. ''You can't know how
much I want you,'' he said, his lips moving against hers.
''Fiercely, terribly. But loving you with it . . . always loving
you, I'll love you until I die, Julia.''

She lay back on her coat. ''But you won't die, Jamie. You'll
live because I need you so much. You are my future—and my
past. We'll love together all our lives. And we'll begin right
now.''

''You'll freeze . . .'' he said as he began to undress her.

''Not with you, I won't. You'll be gentle, Jamie? I know you
will. For me, it's the first time.''

''The first time . . . in a humble, rather dirty little hut in the
middle of a wood. I had planned much better than this.''

''A palace could be no better. . . .''

"Ah . . . oh, so beautiful," as he stroked her breasts, as he bent to kiss them. "Look how beautiful the fire is. How the rain sounds on the roof . . . ah . . ."

He was slow and gentle the first time, and then later, after they had lain wrapped in each other's arms, heads pressed into each other's shoulders, the second time was more tumultuous, as if they were aware not just of the day passing but of time itself, the very era in which they lived. They had to use time as it hurried away—a phantom leaving them as the woods grew darker. Each second together seemed to be marked off on a finite clock. Neither could say how much time was left to them. They used what they had. The witnesses to the passion of their coupling were the dogs, who pressed their wet coats against the naked, entwined bodies.

They got back to the castle when it was fully dark. "We took shelter in the old McBain cottage," Jamie said carelessly, without apology. "But we got wet, in any case."

"I was beginning to worry . . ." Lady Jean said.

He shook off Julia's wet outer clothes in the little porch of the kitchen door. "Ah, don't you remember I know every inch of this place like my own hand? I took Julia in out of the rain and built a fire. Must ask Kerr to try to get some more dry wood put there. . . . It was like the old days, but much better with Julia." He loooked his mother straight in the eyes. "Oh, yes—better in every way."

"I see. . . . Well, you'd better go up and get changed. You just have time. We've fired up the boiler, so there should be plenty of hot water."

"Time! Oh, yes, we have plenty of time. All the time in the world, don't we, Julia?" They had come in through the kitchen, and Janet had offered them a cup of tea in passing. Surveying the flurry of the dinner preparations, Jamie declined. "Maybe we'll take a drink up to our rooms."

"The fires are lighted. Your hair, Miss Seymour . . ."

"Her name is Julia, Mother. Surely you know that now. And I'm sure she can dry her own hair. . . ."

He paused in the great Hall, where a huge fire burned, to fill two glasses. "I'll be drunk before the evening even begins," Julia said, and then giggled. "Do you think she knows?"

"Who cares? She'll know soon enough."

"Dear heaven," Janet called out to them as she came sweeping across the hall with another tray full of glasses. "And haven't you let the dogs bring all their mud onto the floor Morag spent half a day cleaning!"

Boisterously Jamie put his arm around her shoulders and kissed her cheek with a loud smack. "Now you can't be angry with me, Janet . . . my last night. Is this the way to send a warrior back to battle?"

"Oh, shush now, Master Jamie, getting around me with your tongue. Aren't I a stern enough body when I have the mind to be?" She slapped the tray down and turned back to look at them both. "Well, you make a bonny couple, you do, at that. Miss Julia looks as if she's been dragged through a hedge backward, but a bonny sight, for all that. You really should be in the moving pictures, Miss Julia, where *everyone* could see you, instead of those poor few who pack into the theater. But you will . . . mark my words. I'll look for the day."

Calling to the dogs, she scurried briskly away, and Jamie gently took Julia's arm and led her upstairs. "Are you all right, my love? Did I hurt you? I would never hurt you, if I could help it, Julia."

"The divine hurt of a woman's life—if it's the right man. I've been pawed and grabbed at, and I've landed a good right hand from time to time. Today I invited you, Jamie. You came home to me, and it was the most wonderful feeling in the world. The McBain cottage will be the palace of my life."

There were actually a few inches of hot water to run into the huge bathtub. Julia bathed quickly, and rinsed out her blood-stained pants in cold water, not caring what anyone thought. Let them think what they liked. Soon she would marry Jamie. Nothing mattered beside that—no one's good opinion, no one's disappointment. She could fight them all now. She dried her hair and sang, experiencing a lightheartedness she had not known since she had entered this castle. On top of her head, she swept up her long hair and thrust a few pins in it, letting little tendrils trail on her cheeks and neck. Did they think that merely getting wet hair would stop an actress from looking good? Very discreetly she applied makeup, using the techniques of the theater, so that her eyelids were faintly shadowed and her mouth appeared to have no lipstick on it, although it was very defined.

Then she took out her mother's crimson velvet gown—the rose gown, she now called it. Janet's cooking had added the few pounds she lacked, and she filled it nicely. Her breasts swelled warmly at the neckline. Just before she turned away from her mirror she paused and touched those breasts. Jamie had kissed them. Forever they would be different.

And far below, in the Great Hall, she heard the first, rather unearthly sound as a lone piper warmed up, a sound both plaintive and melancholy, and in this ambience, heart-touching.

For several minutes she remained in the darkness of the high gallery, taking in the scene below. About eight of the guests had already arrived. They had expected, in the depth of wartime, a festive evening in their own tradition and had dressed for it. Every man wore a kilt and a velvet jacket, with buttons of silver. They wore sporrans of soft fur and silver-buckled shoes. The women wore either a tartan-pleated silk skirt with a white blouse and a sash of silk tartan pinned to the left shoulder and tied at the waist on the right, or a dress of plain color, again with the sash. The clan brooches were of silver, and some, by the flashes of light from the fire, had their heraldic symbols discreetly outlined by tiny jewels. Lady Jean stood in their midst, wearing a severe black dress, the bright Sinclair tartan slashing it with color. The piper had moved up to the other side of the gallery from where Julia stood. He strode back and forth, the tune brighter now. Julia realized that her hand shook just a little on the banister as she descended into the light. Jamie looked up, saw her, and at once came forward. He wore the kilt, as his mother had asked, his velvet jacket was black, his frilled and ruffled shirt had obviously been freshly laundered and made ready for this occasion. "This is too much, Jamie," Julia whispered to him. "It looks like something from a stage set—or more, the cinema. Even the piper . . ."

"Sometimes I'd like to curse my mother. But you have to understand that it's no great thing here for them to dress like this. They do it naturally. The man up there with the bagpipes is one of the farm workers who happens to have a talent with the instrument. If we seem to be in fancy dress, I assure you we aren't. But Mother does carry her little schemes a bit far. I had hoped for a quiet last evening. . . ." He dropped her hand as more guests arrived. "You'll have already met them all. It's Mother's thank-you for their hospitality. Her one chance for a

little festivity. She won't be going out all through the winter,
and there'll be precious little chance for any of these other families to have something to celebrate. So be tolerant with
her. . . .''

The last arrivals were the Macphersons. Lady Macpherson
wore a little tartan vest above her pleated skirt—perhaps for
warmth, Julia thought. Her clan badge holding the silk sash in
place was set entirely in diamonds; diamonds were on her delicate hands. She greeted Julia. ''What an English rose you are
among all us thistles, my dear. Allan, doesn't she look divine?
Such a gown . . .''

''It was my mother's . . . used for concerts. My clothing coupons would never stretch to it.''

''And you don't have a tartan, do you?'' Kirsty said. She wore
long diamond earrings that blazed against her auburn hair and
long white neck. She wore a white crepe gown that showed no
sign of having been inherited from anyone, with the clan sash
tied about it. The badge that held it in place, like her mother's,
was jeweled, but the figure of the cat with upheld paw at its
center was picked out in tiny emeralds and rubies. ''The tartan
takes us poor Scots through so many occasions. All you really
need is a skirt and a blouse and the sash, and you're perfectly
dressed.''

Julia bit back the tart response that rose to her lips. Instead
she said, smiling, ''No, we don't have nearly such a neat and
decorative way of getting through every social occasion. May I
ask what your clan badge stands for? It looks remarkably fierce.''

''Most clan badges and mottoes are fierce'' came the reply.
''We're a fighting nation. The motto of the Macphersons is
'Touch not the cat bot a glove'—which really means 'without a
glove.' ''

''Remarkably apt,'' Julia answered. ''I can see one should
take care in dealing with the Macpherson—''

She was interrupted by Sir Niall Henderson. ''I brought it,
my dear. The rosebush. For you to take with you tomorrow. All
wrapped up in wet sacking. I say, you do look splendid. You
must forgive us old fools for dressing up this way. We don't have
many legitimate excuses these days.'' He glanced around the
Great Hall, the shining floors, the bowls of early winter jasmine
that brightened the corners, the pieces of shining family silver
that Lady Jean had brought out and polished. He cocked his

head to the skirl of the pipes above them. "Oh, it does my heart
good . . . pray God we'll see the old times back again, whatever
the sacrifices we must make. Jean, my dear, did anyone tell you
that the young Robertson boy was reported missing in action in
the desert the other day? We can just hope he was taken prisoner.
Those Italians are worthless, but I fear what the Germans may
do."

"I'll write to Margaret," Lady Jean said. "Her most loved
child, I think. He came so late to her. . . . How sad . . ."

"Now, I shouldn't have told you. Don't want to spoil your
evening. . . ."

Julia was served whiskey from a tray carried by a man wearing a kilt whom she belatedly recognized as William Kerr. Jamie
was back at her side. "Well, Mr. Kerr, I didn't expect to see
you here—doing this. A little beneath you, isn't it?"

"Not if it's for Lady Jean, Master Jamie. I would pitch in and
do anything to give her the evening she's been hoping for since
the news came that you were shot down. I think that day she
never expected to see you alive again. This is the evening she's
dreamed of. Why should I not help out? Mrs. Kerr's going to
be waiting on table to help Morag."

Jamie stayed at Julia's side all through the drinks period, but
they were separated when William Kerr finally, with a faint show
of embarrassment, announced dinner. Lady Jean was seated at
one end of the long table, Jamie at the other. Lady Macpherson
was on his right, Mrs. Gilcrest on his left. Kirsty was placed
almost opposite Julia. Julia found to her relief that Sir Niall was
next to her. She thanked him again for the rosebush. "Father
will be thrilled. I know he'll rush down to Anscombe to get it
planted. . . ." He asked her carefully, courteously, about the
intensity of the Battle of Britain as it had raged in the skies above
Anscombe, being careful to avoid any direct mention of her
mother's death but avid for details of the last days of both his
sons. "It must have been terrible—living right under it all. I
understand the bombers and Messerschmitts had only the fuel
capacity to stay a short time on the raids, so they must have been
coming and going endlessly. . . ."

"I can remember," Julia said, as she described what it had
been like, "one of the farm workers saying to me, 'Looks like
we had a real fine harvest of Messerschmitts this year.' We didn't

really admit that so many of them were Spitfires and Hurricanes.''

''Well, thank God Jamie survived his episode.'' He was silent for a while, perhaps thinking of his sons, who had not. Then he turned his attention to the soup as they were finishing it. ''Now this, to you, my dear, may seem like any ordinary beef soup, if a bit hearty, since it's nearly a stew. But the old Scots name for it is 'skink.' Tell them that when you go back across the border.'' They were being served now by Morag and Mrs. Kerr with smoked salmon. ''Don't look so surprised, my dear. This may not be the Savoy, but these are salmon from our own rivers, and we all have our own smokehouses. We turn a blind eye to a bit of poaching, as long as some is left as a wee gift at the house. Ah—look at Lady Jean! How radiant her face is . . . for this one evening, at least, she's a happy woman. . . . Now, what's this? . . . ah, well, she's done us proud. Her Janet must have worked like a dog. . . .'' When the salmon plates were removed, the piper had descended the stairs and placed himself by the doors to the kitchen passage. Morag and Mrs. Kerr held them open as Janet, in a severe black dress and starched apron, marched out to his tune, carrying a great silver dish that contained something Julia had never seen in her life. ''Haggis!'' Sir Niall exclaimed. ''Well, that's a treat. Can't seem to get anyone to make it these days. Now, don't be frightened of what you think is in it. Just enjoy the taste.''

''Sheep's stomach, isn't it?'' Julia said dubiously.

''Sheep's stomach is only the skin that holds it. It's a sort of sausage. The *haute cuisine* of all sausages.'' After it was served, he tasted it anxiously. ''Haggis Royal, I'd say, from all the different things in it.'' They had been drinking good wine, and their glasses were never empty, but they were now served small glasses of whiskey. ''Pour it over the mix, my dear,'' he advised her. ''Ah, yes—this lovely nutty-flavored brown oatmeal, mutton, anchovies, cayenne—Janet's got it all.'' He raised his glass to Lady Jean. ''Marvelous, my dear. A real treat.''

Julia took the first forkful, aware of Kirsty's eyes on her. Even if it was hateful, she would eat it. To her surprise, it tasted very good and had a marvelous texture. It was accompanied by mashed potatoes and rutabagas. ''That's traditional,'' Sir Niall assured her. ''Trust Janet to get it just right.''

Julia felt she was being challenged when the haggis was withdrawn and the dessert served. It looked something like trifle but tasted richer, and she wondered if her stomach could stand it. " 'Tipsy Laird,' it's called," Kirsty said from across the table. "A mix of sherry and brandy."

"Potent," Julia said with a gasp. "And terribly filling . . ."

"I suppose an actress has to watch her figure very carefully," Kirsty remarked.

"What's wrong with her figure?" Sir Niall barked. "Looks perfect to me. And I'm no mean judge, Kirsty."

Julia smiled her gratitude. There began a little round of toasts and short speeches—mostly to wish Jamie well. Other names were recalled. "Jean, just for one magic night, has brought back the good old days. May they and peace soon return to us all. May our sons and daughters—the sons and daughters of Scotland—return in health to us. May this war, finally, forever, end wars."

Julia never knew how anyone summoned the energy for it, but after dinner the piper played reels, and that little company formed up to dance. Julia hung back, refusing even Jamie's request to partner her. "I haven't an idea of how it's done. I'd only make a fool of myself."

"Oh, come on! Everyone is half drunk. No one will notice." But she still refused and saw him take Kirsty as his first partner. They all performed what seemed to Julia some intricate patterns, and she was more than ever glad she had refused even to try them. But she was aware of Jamie's disapproval, as if somehow she had let him down. She kept her seat by the fire, and Sir Niall gratefully retired to sit beside her. "Old leg injury plays up when I start this sort of caper. Getting a bit long in the tooth for this sort of thing, but it does make a grand sight, doesn't it? In the right setting, among friends. The only better sight would be if all our young men were out there with Jamie. How we miss them—especially the ones we'll never have back."

William Kerr continued to circulate with his tray of drinks. The cries of the dancers grew wilder and louder, but somehow no one ever went beyond the bounds of correctness. There was no careless swinging of partners, no one raised their arms above a certain level. It was revelry but not carousal. Janet and Morag and Mrs. Kerr had lined up at the end of the Hall to watch the dancing, glasses served to them also, as if it were an understood thing that they all belonged to this one festive evening in the darkness of war.

It took Julia a long time to fall asleep that night. She knew she had eaten and drunk too much, but it was the glow of her happiness in the memory of having become, finally, Jamie's lover that lighted a spark in her much more potent than the spirits she had drunk, something that the heaviness of the food would not blot out in sleep. "I love him . . ." she murmured in the stillness of the Red Tower Room. "I'll love him forever . . . forever. Come hell or high water . . . or the bloody Highlands, for that matter. They won't take him from me."

She slept at last, but when she woke it was not yet dawn. Once again she thought she heard the sobbing that trailed away to a deep sigh. She raised her head from the pillow, and once again a vague shape seemed to stand by the mantel, discernible only by the last red glow of the embers of the fire. Her head spun from the effects of the wine and the whiskey. Did the shape move, almost turn in her direction, an imploring hand outstretched? "Ellen . . . ?" she whispered. "Lady Ellen . . . ?" She felt no fear, only compassion. Did the figure turn away— shrink back on itself? No, it was not there at all. She told herself she had heard nothing, seen nothing. But she did not sleep again.

Chapter Four

I

THE WORLD JULIA RETURNED TO made her feel that she had forever suffered a sea change. The rites of passage had been made. For ten days she had lived in a world of supposed peace, the landscape untouched and beautiful and yet full of tension. She had known hope, despair, and love. She came back to the present tension of a world very much at war, the streets only partly cleared of rubble, the barrage balloons, the ever-flying dust, air-raid shelters, lines for food and for every other necessity. It was a world in which war and the talk of war were ever-present. A world in which death was beside one on the street as well as in the Western Desert and in the Atlantic. She realized she was returning to the world of theater, where competition was as keen-edged as the war itself; pride, envy, generosity, and greed were its hallmarks. She had begun to question the concept of what a hero was in her father's world.

Since it was Friday, she continued her journey on to Anscombe, saying good-bye to Jamie at the platform of the station where the line split, he to report back to his squadron at Hawkinge. She kissed him, and knew that she had grown older by as many years as she had already lived. She hadn't telephoned ahead to Anscombe, so there was no one to meet her. She walked the two miles from the station in pitch dark, carrying her suitcase and the rosebush. Stella opened the kitchen door to her, the blackout curtain carefully drawn. She had returned to a world that was no longer carefree or careless.

She was drawn into the warmth and welcome of the kitchen. Stella and Cook exclaimed over how well she looked, even after the long journey. But even as Cook examined her face and asked questions, she was frying an egg and bacon, scraping butter on bread. "You've gained a little weight," Stella said. "Which you needed. I thought, myself, at the end of *Lear,* if that child doesn't get some rest, she's going to collapse. You've borne your father's burden for too long. It looks as if you've put it off now."

Cook turned from the sputtering frying pan. "Not a child anymore, if you please, Stella. She's a grown woman. Proved her worth. She isn't in your nursery anymore."

"Yes," Stella said with surprising humility. "I keep thinking back to the days when you all needed me in one way or another. Even your mother. I remember when I once went with her on one of her tours when her secretary was ill. . . . Well, you'd better eat that, Julia, while it's hot. I'll go and telephone the London flat. I can't imagine why you didn't stop there to see your father."

"I wanted to come home . . ." Julia replied, and cut into the egg, dipping bread into the running yolk. She ate, and tried to answer Cook's questions about the food she'd had in Scotland and how the kitchen at Castle Sinclair had been appointed. Stella returned. "Your father was home, for once. Had a couple of friends with him, of course. One was Mr. Davidoff. You're expected for rehearsal on Monday afternoon. He hopes you've learned your lines. Just as well I phoned, because Sir Michael will be here tomorrow. He'd forgotten to let us know. I told him about the rosebush. . . . He's bringing Mr. Davidoff with him, and possibly someone else. . . . He said not to meet him at the station. He'll come by car. . . ."

"Isn't it amazing how some folks always manage to get things other folks can't . . . such as petrol," Cook remarked dryly. "We'll have to hustle in the morning, Stella, to get rooms ready. I just wish we had some nice soap to put out . . . like it was in the old days. Now, let me think . . . I'd better make some pâté from the scraps. . . ."

She made it sound as if the old days of careless plenty were a hundred years ago and would never return.

But it was not D.D.'s Rolls-Royce that turned into the driveway at Anscombe the next morning. It was a stately Daimler, with an old man in a chauffeur's uniform at the wheel. There was D.D.'s voice as he emerged. "Dear child . . ." Her father's arms were about her. "How wonderful you look, Pet. It's done you a world of good. . . . Ah, and this . . . Luisa, may I present my youngest daughter, Julia. Julia, Mrs. Henry Radcliffe."

An immaculately gloved hand was extended to her; the face, clothes, and figure seemed to have sprung instantly from a fashion magazine. How could any woman in England at this moment be so well turned out? Her shining dark hair, under a neat, veiled hat, seemed to have come directly from the hairdresser. Her makeup was subtly applied. There was the warm scent of good perfume.

"My dear, I am so happy to meet you. I admired your performance as Cordelia. I was asked by D.D. to the first night, but unfortunately my job—it's the Red Cross, and it does often keep us up late at nights—prevented me from being there that evening. But I made a point of seeing *Lear* later. What a wonderful beginning to what I'm sure will be a great career. Following your father—"

"Luisa, please . . ." Her father's tone begged jokingly. "No more of that. Welcome to Anscombe." The chauffeur was bringing suitcases, and the food hampers that D.D. always seemed able to procure, from the trunk of the Daimler. Julia still stood speechless, hardly able to take in this vision of perfection. It was another shock of returning to a world where it was still possible for a woman to look as Mrs. Henry Radcliffe did. A jerk on her arm from her father focused her thoughts on the moment. "Oh, yes . . . welcome to Anscombe. . . . Please do come in." She was acutely conscious of her worn and dirty corduroys. That morning, in the cold darkness, she had presented herself at Harry Whitehead's cottage and then helped him bring in the herd. "Old Primmie's hanging on," he had said by way of greeting, "and damn me if she's not in calf again. I thought she was past it now. Well, now that you've finally come down from the footlights, I'd be grateful for a little help. We're training another Land Army girl, but she's a bit thick. Or perhaps I should have said citified. . . . You look well, Julia. Had a good time up there in those Highlands? You'll have to tell me about how they manage their farms. . . ."

A million miles or years away. Julia was now conscious that probably she still smelled of the barnyard. Stella and Cook had come to the door, both, by virtue of long standing, being introduced to Mrs. Radcliffe. D.D.'s hand restrained Julia as the others moved inside. He whispered to her, "Darling, be nice to her. She is rich. *Rich!* She has a lot of interest in the theater, but I have succeeded in interesting her in this little film I plan for you. I've been gathering up-front money, and the most comes from her. Now I shall go to work on the Ministry. Mostly a propaganda film, of course, and it may do very good business in the States, where, of course, we need box-office money. Dollars. Your role isn't very large, but it's one of only two female roles. Very important. The world will see your face, instead of a few thousand on the London stage. Darling—do you have to look so *dirty* as this?" Then he flicked his hand impatiently. "No—I'm wrong. You look almost exactly as you should look for *Return at Dawn,* or whatever we shall call this film. All you have to do is see off your hero, and gaze at the planes as they return, counting them. I'm not sure whether your hero survives or not. We haven't gotten that far with the script. But we will photograph you very nicely, and I wouldn't doubt that offers of other films will come pouring in."

"Who is she? . . . Mrs. Radcliffe?"

"She comes of a very grand Spanish family. She married a Frenchman—the Comte de . . . oh, something. One of the wine families. Wine was a sideline with him, but it gave them a nice château for entertaining. He was primarily a banker, considerably older than Luisa, and he wisely transferred as much money as possible to New York. He became very ill just before it became evident that France would fall. He sent her, and loads of jewelry—and probably money—to England for safety, and died in his bed in Paris just a little after the Germans arrived. She married Henry Radcliffe—surely even *you* must know his name? Another banker—they tend to move in the same circles. Widowed. He got himself killed in the Blitz, being a hero. No children of either of Luisa's marriages, and no stepchildren. Quite—or almost quite—alone in the world. Sad, a woman so beautiful . . ."

"With all that money—sad," Julia said sharply. "Most men would be afraid to marry her now, in case they just happened to die. Or does she only marry rich men?"

"The rich of good families marry the rich of other good families, you know that, darling. After all, they seldom meet anyone else."

"Then what is she doing in *your* world—in Father's world?"

"She's a woman of great culture. Brought up to the theater and music—finishing schools. You know how *grand* grand Spanish families are—"

"No, I don't really. Never met any."

He tapped her chin. "Naughty girl! You must be nice to her. She could be a great help to your career."

"And Father's career."

"Now, that is quite uncalled-for! Your father's career needs no help. He is just coming back into his world. The companionship of a woman like Luisa Radcliffe is good for him. Don't be jealous, Julia. It's not like you. Now, please organize some coffee, and go upstairs and change those disgusting garments."

"Can't—I'll have to be out in the rose garden helping Father in half an hour. Cook will already have coffee on the way."

"Well—I can see your little stay in Scotland has put more than roses in your cheeks." Then he smiled at her fondly. "Well, darling, you were bound to grow up someday. I hope you haven't thoroughly neglected to learn your lines. You're supposed to be a professional now. . . ."

A short while later they were all in the rose garden, watching Michael planting his new rosebush. "I wonder what it's called? Very nice of that man—what's his name?—to send it. Nice ball of earth on it. Did he say what color it is? No? I suppose you forgot to ask. Well, we'll just have to put it in this spot and hope it won't clash. . . ."

"What a charming idea, Michael," Luisa Radcliffe said. "This garden in memory of your adored wife. I do predict that in the future you will become a great rose-grower. . . ." She gestured expansively. "I think after the war, when they let one do these things, you should take in part of that next field. One garden opening into another—a touch of mystery." She glanced back from where the oasthouse had been to the manor house. "What a charming place this is. So sweet . . . so English . . ." Except for her very dark hair and her faint, attractive accent, she looked, Julia thought, exactly as the lady of the manor might have done before the war—though perhaps just too expensively dressed. She had changed into a skirt and sweater of fine cashmere, shoes not too high-heeled, a subtle gold chain around her neck, plain gold earrings. All the understatement that money and good taste could buy. She had even pulled on pigskin gloves to hold the bush steady while Michael shoveled earth around the roots and tamped it firmly into place. D.D. surveyed all this from a bench. He still wore his gray flannel Savile Row suit. Gardens, for him, were things to be looked at, and strolled in if the grass was not wet.

Julia washed and changed for lunch, recklessly dabbing on a little perfume to restore her confidence. Luisa Radcliffe puzzled her. Her charm and overt good manners were undoubted. She was handsome rather than beautiful, but she carried herself as an undoubted aristocrat. No doubt her Spanish pedigree was as long as her beautifully coiled black hair. Would she be near to forty years old? Julia wondered. If so, then a forty with the agile, exercised body of a girl half her age. She had seen such faces in books of paintings from the Prado. Haughty, confident, long pale hands emerging from lace and limply holding a fan. A Velázquez face. Nothing resembling the rather daubish faces of the Seymour ancestors that hung at Anscombe. It proclaimed them English country squires and nothing more. Luisa Radcliffe could move in any wealthy circle in the world she chose, and would, probably, make another wealthy marriage. What was she doing amid the rough-and-tumble of the theater world? Of course, it amused the rich to dabble, but Luisa Radcliffe did not look the kind to waste her time merely dabbling in anything. Then, as Julia went downstairs, it occurred to her that her father was not only a great and famous actor, he was also an extremely handsome man. Sometimes women like Luisa Radcliffe fell in love. Having all the money she needed, perhaps she now sought something that had eluded her.

A fire had been lighted in the drawing room. Dark November clouds scurried across the sky. D.D. poured champagne for her. "Enjoy it, darling—hard to come by now. Next time we drink it, I hope it will be to toast you on the first night of *Earnest*."

"Supposing . . . supposing there's nothing to toast. Supposing I don't live up to it."

Luisa Radcliffe's voice was calm and even, but it almost carried a threat. "The daughter of such a man as Michael does not even entertain such thoughts."

Julia wanted to retort that she was her mother's daughter also, but in the presence of this woman, her mother's spirit seemed to have been banished from the house.

At one o'clock they listened to news from the BBC that was

both bad and good. The Germans were attacking Moscow, but the Eighth Army seemed to be regrouping for a fresh campaign in the desert. More shipping losses in the Atlantic. "Has Alex heard from Greg?" Julia asked her father as they went in to lunch.

"Not recently. There haven't been any dispatches recently in *The Record*. She says she suspects he's on the move to Singapore. Not even Wolverton will tell her."

Lunch went on until it was almost dark; they lingered over the wine Michael had brought up from the cellar, and then port. Julia took little part in the conversation, trying to stifle her yawns. It had taken a whole twenty-four hours to travel down from Inverness. She slipped away to check that all was well in Mrs. Radcliffe's room—the principal guest room. The room was fragrant with potpourri, and she had clipped some amaryllis and arranged it with the last two blooms on the climbing rose that draped the kitchen door. They had long since used up their prewar supply of scented soap, but she had raided Stella's special storeroom for some bath salts. The sheets were linen, the towels still thick and plentiful in the adjoining bathroom. She hoped the hot-water supply would hold out. They had dared to turn on the central heating—for which extravagance they might be cold later in the winter. But she felt her father expected this from her.

Then she changed back into her corduroys to help Harry Whitehand with the milking. He had the cows already herded into the barn and was washing them off. "Bit late, Julia," he said. "But you've got fancy guests this weekend." Mrs. Radcliffe's chauffeur was lodged over the garage, and Mrs. Whitehand had had to scurry to get the apartment ready. He would eat his meals in the kitchen with Stella and Cook. It was evident that Mrs. Whitehand already had learned some of Mrs. Radcliffe's history.

Julia leaned against Primmie's side and pulled rhythmically at the teats. Her thoughts were on Jamie, and the fierce ache of missing him. All day she had heard no planes overhead. Was he thinking of her now? Did he feel this strange emptiness? "Julia—Primmie's been dry for the past five minutes. You're no more help than that ruddy Land Army girl." Harry Whitehand's voice came from close behind her. She sprang up from the stool and knocked over the pail of milk. "Oh, damn!" Then she burst into tears.

Instantly Harry's arm was about her. "Here, there's no need to get so upset. There's more where that came from. But it's not the milk, is it? Look, don't worry about the rest. Go back to the house and have a bath—if they've got the water. You looked great this morning, and now you look all done in." She was grateful for his kindness and didn't attempt to explain her tears. But she paused for some minutes outside the kitchen door in the windy November darkness, making sure there would be no sign of tears for Stella's discerning eyes to see. She was greeted by Cook when she entered. "You missed a telephone call from Squadron Leader Sinclair. . . ." Squadron Leader. He had been promoted. He would lead his squadron until the war was ended or until he was shot down. No matter where they sent him now, he would be out in front, expected to lead, no matter if it was to death.

Next morning Alex caught one of the few Sunday trains from London and arrived in time for lunch. It was raining, and she was wet and looked cross when she reached the house, having walked from the station. "I don't know why I bothered. I should have stayed in bed. But I rang the flat, and Agnes told me you were all here. I suppose I just got a yen to be here with you. I haven't seen Father for weeks. . . ." Julia followed her upstairs to her room when she went to wash. She carried a glass of sherry for her.

"Here, this will warm you up a little. It's wonderful to see you, Alex."

Surprisingly, her sister leaned over and kissed her on the cheek. "You look good, Julia. A bit changed. I suppose you're still hopelessly in love with that Scot? Was his mother the gorgon I've been imagining? The Scots can be so . . ." She shrugged. "None of my business." She sipped the sherry appreciatively and then started to comb her hair and apply powder and lipstick. "I suppose I'd better go down and make the acquaintance of the particular gorgon we've got downstairs."

Julia gasped. "How can you say that? You haven't even met her."

"I hardly need to. She's in the newspaper columns every other day. Doing her bit for the war effort, of course. In a very well-tailored Red Cross uniform. Neat as a pin. But always, it seems, in some very glamorous company. Mostly taking care of the needs of generals—that is, when she isn't at a nightclub. She's been seen quite often with Father. I suppose that's what got me down here today . . . curiosity. I suppose she plays the country lady just as smoothly as everything else. . . .''

"She can't be *that* bad. She's very elegantly turned out, I'll give you that—''

"And she's a self-centered bitch," Alex snapped back. "Did D.D. give you some story about her being sent away from France by her loving husband to England and safety? The way I hear it is that she left behind a very sick man who hardly knew what was happening to him. She's happily drawing on all the dollars he left her piled up in New York, and wearing as much of the jewelry as is appropriate to wear in wartime. I expect most of *it's* in New York, where the bombs can't get at it. What I can't understand is why she isn't there herself, having a nice, comfortable war. Oh, well, she did happen to meet Henry Radcliffe when he was just poking his head up into the world after his wife's death. He stayed on in banking, since he was too old for active service, but one heard bits about him being one of Churchill's unofficial cabinet. He was a *very* clever man—as well as being a nice man. I met him once. He had to go and make a hero of himself in the Blitz, when he should have been minding his own business instead of dashing into some building and rescuing some family who were too dazed to move. Went back for the bloody dog, and the whole place toppled in on him. *She's* come through it smiling, though—or so it seems from the newspapers. And a whole lot richer. As if she needed to be. Is she angling for Father?''

"I don't know. I'm not as quick at spotting these things as you are. Any rate, if she's like that, would he want her?''

"You can never tell. You have to realize, Julia, he's not going to stay married to our mother's memory forever. He's still, in the eyes of many people—well, a relatively young man. And handsome as the devil. Famous. Distinguished. He may be Father to us, but he cuts a figure in the world. He's going to find a woman eventually. I just wish she would be a gentle little nobody.''

"You don't like competition, Alex.''

"I don't think I'm going to like Mrs. Henry Bloody Radcliffe.'' Then she shrugged, and drained the last of the sherry. "Well, nothing I can do about it, if that's the way the land lies.''

"You may not have to do anything about it. Father has taste. And don't forget whom he was married to."

"Father is a man—like all men."

At the head of the stairs, Julia stopped her. "Alex, I've never known you quite like this. What is it? Not Mrs. Radcliffe . . ."

Alex shook her head and quickly passed her hand across her eyes. "Of course it isn't Mrs. Radcliffe. Father will do as he likes, when he likes. I just wanted to see you both today. I get so lonely. I haven't heard from Greg for weeks. It seems months. I don't know where in the world he is, and I don't think Wolfie really knows, either. Last dispatch was from Hong Kong, but that was weeks ago. He seems to have vanished. Or forgotten about me. Oh, God, Julia, I do miss him. I've discovered that there's something terribly sensual about me that Greg completely satisfied. Without him, I'm hungry all the time. I would snatch at any man—except that it can't be just any man. Not after Greg. I just wait—and hope he's alive. You know, of the three of us, Connie's the smart one. It would only be by accident that Ken Warren got killed. He'll always be in some relatively safe place." She started down the stairs, then looked back. "Well, Julia, that's you and me. The risk-takers. What would anyone expect? Look who our parents are."

Before they entered the drawing room, from where the deeply accented voice of D.D. held forth, Julia stopped her again. "You know who you looked like just then—all fierce and angry and tense? You looked for all the world like Grandfather Maslov."

Alex's face broke into a grin. "I hope not mustache and all!" She was laughing as she entered the room.

They returned to London late that afternoon, Michael, D.D., and Luisa Radcliffe. Alex went with them, grateful not to have to endure the cold, slow journey by train. Julia declined the offer of the ride. "But darling, you are to be at rehearsal tomorrow afternoon," D.D. protested.

"I'll be there," Julia said. "And I'll know my lines. I feel I owe Harry Whitehand a little help. It's Sunday. The Land Army girls don't work . . . ."

"What nonsense," Michael said sharply. "Harry is getting on perfectly well without you. You'll have to get up at the crack of dawn tomorrow to—"

"Leave it, Father," Alex said crisply. "When did Julia not

do what she said she'd do?'' He shrugged and accepted what he could not alter. He must have sensed Alex's attitude toward Luisa Radcliffe, although she had been restrained and civil to their guest. Julia had been more guarded. She had seen them off, already wearing her clothes for the milking parlor. All she wanted was to put some distance between herself and this new situation that had developed. She needed a few more hours alone, conscious that she would have had to return to her father's flat. Tomorrow she would return to the theater and to work, but that was tomorrow. She opted for one more night of independence. She worked solidly with Harry Whitehand for the hours needed to bring the herd in, wash and milk them, feed and water them. He thanked her for her help and offered her some lanolin for her hands.

She ate in the kitchen with Stella and Cook, mostly leftovers from D.D.'s hampers. They were companionably silent; or was it, Julia wondered, that neither of the other women wanted to comment on this new guest at Anscombe—perhaps hoping that there would not be another visit? Why should there not be? Julia wondered. Alex was right. Why should anyone expect their father to remain in perpetual mourning for Ginette Maslova? Nothing stood still. . . . In the hall, the telephone rang. Julia ran to it. "Julia?" Jamie's voice.

She knew why she had waited here.

"I wonder how soon we can get married," he said. "Have you thought about it?"

She felt dizzy with joy and hungry with wanting—the sort of hunger Alex had spoken of, a hunger and an emptiness she had never experienced before.

"Soon, Jamie . . . please. Soon."

Three weeks of adjusting to the disciplines of the theater again, the direction of a man to whom she was a well-known stranger, finding her way with the new cast, all without her father's comforting, protective presence. At first she groped her way through her part, in awe of the great lady of the stage who was playing Lady Bracknell. In the beginning she played a humble and fluttering Gwendoline and knew she was doing it wrongly. All the experience of *Lear* seemed useless; she was a raw amateur fumbling her way into a new character. She was miserable and confused. At last she begged her father to come to a rehearsal. He

waited until it was over and then took her for a drink at the Ritz.
"Not at all bad, Pet. A little bit stiff in places. No use telling
you to relax. One owes it to the audience to give a performance—even if it's only a couple of lines. But you'll have to
leave Julia behind and step into the skin of the character you're
playing. You'll have to *be* Gwendoline. Seemingly demure, en-
gagingly pert, determined to have her own way, even with Mama.
Remember how I taught you not to miss any chance of upstaging
anyone? Even if this is Dame Lillian Kenton. It's just possible
to steal a bit of her thunder here and there. You can't let yourself
be afraid of her. Respectful of her formidable talent, yes. But
afraid—no. It isn't easy. It never will be. Not even your old
father does it without some anguish and a lot of mental preparation. We'll have an evening alone, tomorrow night, you and
I. Run through it. I can't tell you exactly how to play your character, but there are a few tricks this old dog knows that may
help you. . . . I have to run now, Pet." He rose and signaled to
the waiter. "You stay and have another. Less lonely here than
at the flat. Agnes isn't the best company. Where's that Sinclair
fellow these days?"

"On duty. He's around, but I don't see him. He telephones
me. We're going to get married soon."

He sank back into his seat and asked the waiter for a second
drink for himself. "I thought it might be that. Want to tell me
about it?"

"What's to tell? We're in love. He's asked me to marry him.
I want to. I want to very much."

"I never really asked you about the time in Scotland. You've
looked alternately radiant and sad ever since."

"Isn't that what being in love is like? I thought it was supposed to be a grand passion. I remember once that you wished
me the sort of feelings you and Mother had for each other."

"At your age, it has to be a grand passion, or it doesn't exist.
When I married your mother—well, we seemed to be the oddest
pair in the world. But we were perfectly in tune with each other.
It didn't matter a damn what anyone else thought. If it's not that
way between you and this Sinclair chap, then don't do it. Be his
lover, if you must be, but don't marry him unless you believe
you can't live without him. Saves a lot of heartache in the end.
I wonder if he's considered what it's like to be married to an
actress. You're not going to be the little wife at home all the

time, Julia. You're going to be a woman who works. After the war, when he goes back to his Highland castle—''

"We'll come to that when it really is 'after the war.' All that matters is *now*."

"If you hadn't said that, I'd have said 'Forget it.' " Then a smile broke across his face. "What can I say, Pet? Good luck!" He raised his glass to her. "In my mind it's less than ideal, but it's you who'll live your life. And to Jamie Sinclair: Happy landings. He doesn't know what he's taking on. But then, none of us do. Want to come to dinner with me and Luisa tonight? Just to celebrate . . . there'll be a few other people. . . .''

"No, Father, thank you. I'll celebrate when Jamie can be with us."

He swallowed the rest of his drink. "It's a hell of a risk. A hell of an adventure." He leaned over and kissed her cheek. "Well, Pet, to live is to take chances. Somehow I think I fancy him more than that fellow Connie is determined to wait for. Too safe and solid. Perhaps that's what she needs, poor sweet. None of you ever did have a safe and solid childhood. You're more like Alex than I thought. She's going through hell over Greg. *That* wasn't a suitable marriage, either. It just might work—after the war."

"Does everything have to wait until after the war?"

"More or less. We're all on hold now. Not our emotions— our loves. But we can hardly say we can shape our own destinies. That's being done out there, somewhere—by forces and events we can hardly imagine. Take what you can while you can, Julia. Sort it out afterward. When there's time. Time is compressed now. Don't be like Connie. Grab at life. Take the risk. Now, that's the worst advice a loving father could give. But I'm damned if I know how to say anything else and not sound like a pompous and hypocritical ass." He kissed her again and left.

In a mood of defiance, she ordered another drink. It would be cold in the bus line. Next week she would open onstage with one of the greatest actresses of their time, without the help of her father. Her slender talent would be shown up for the insubstantial thing it was, or she just might pull it off. But there was one certainty: She would marry Jamie and love him forever.

II

JULIA WENT DOWN TO ANSCOMBE on the Sunday before the play opened. She went because she needed one last day of peace, and because Jamie had a twenty-four-hour pass and they would have that time alone together. She had begun to feel the need to escape the confines of the London flat, fearing that she impinged on her father's privacy, although he was seldom there. He did not speak much of Luisa Radcliffe, but she suspected that he spent most of his free time with her. Mrs. Radcliffe lived in a large, elegant house in Wilton Crescent off Belgrave Square, and she still retained those members of her husband's staff too old to be called up, such as her elderly chauffeur, who gladly acted as substitute handyman, and when pressed to, as a sort of butler. He also gave his two nights a week as an Air Raid Precaution Warden. Everyone seemed to have a second, voluntary job, except the people who formed Julia's world—the people of the theater. Many of the men had joined up. Productions still continue all over the country, but young male actors were hard to find. The one who played opposite her in *The Importance of Being Earnest* was there only because he had what he called "a dicky heart."

"My career will do just fine out of this war, ducky," he had once said to her, "if I don't keel over on the stage one night." He was on call every Sunday as an ambulance driver.

Jamie arrived at Anscombe before lunch, and they ate with Stella and Cook in the kitchen. But Stella brought them tea in the dining room where a fire burned and left them to themselves. Julia carried a tray of cold supper to the dining room. They talked. How many hours did they talk—and of what? Hands and arms entwined. The talk of lovers, which could have sounded trite and banal to anyone who listened. But the words, and more particularly the silences, had a meaning that only lovers would have recognized.

Jamie went out to say good-bye to Stella and Cook just as the BBC nine o'clock news came on. The announcer's voice carried confirmation of the surprise Japanese air strike on Pearl Harbor. Casualties and losses were not known, but they were thought to be extensive; there were unconfirmed reports that capital ships, moored at their berths, had been lost. The loss of their crews was not calculated. Jamie, who had been waiting with his coat and cap on, suddenly swept Julia into his arms and kissed her. "God help the poor bastards, but they're in now. The Americans are in the war, hook, line, and sinker. Sorry if that's in poor taste." In turn he hugged Stella and Cook. "You understand what it means? No more Lend-Lease. We're in it together. We've got an ally. We're not alone anymore. God, how did the Japs manage it? Was everyone asleep because it was Sunday morning?"

When he was gone, the three women sat together drinking cocoa, speculating what it was like out there in the now-important Hawaiian Islands. They hadn't even thought of the American Pacific Fleet having its base there. For them, the war at sea was the Atlantic. Julia got an atlas. "Well, they can't invade America! That's preposterous!" Her finger traced along the islands of the Pacific, the Philippines, the long trail of land that led from India through Burma, through Siam and Malaya down to Singapore, island group by island group even down to New Guinea and Australia. Before this, they had only been names in the geography lessons to her—lessons that Stella had started her on. Alex would have seen this long ago, and her anguish over Greg came sharply into focus. Stella's lips twisted sternly. "If they've already inflicted so much damage, it will be a longer war than anyone ever thought of."

But outside, in the cold darkness when Jamie had kissed her good-bye, she remembered his words: "It is the beginning, but only the very beginning, of the end. We *will* come through it, Julia, you and I and all the rest."

She wanted to believe that very much.

The play opened the following Thursday night with a greater success for Julia than she had dared hope. The whole production was warmly praised, and she had a few lines in the notices to herself. *Julia Seymour shows an unexpectedly nice flair for the comic.* Another paper said: *It is good to see that Julia Seymour can hold her own on the stage without also holding on to her father's coattails.* Naturally, the bulk of the praise went to the great actress whose name headed the cast; the bouquets were hers, as Julia knew must happen. She had warned Jamie well in advance that there must be no repetition of the red roses being thrown, no calling of her name. He had obeyed, but applauded with wild enthusiasm from the stalls, where he sat with her father and Luisa Radcliffe, D.D., Alex, and Connie. But Julia's tiny dressing room, which she shared, was filled with so many red roses it was difficult to move.

They had gathered for supper afterward, waiting for the first editions of the newspapers, at Mrs. Radcliffe's house. But they had already sensed triumph from the reaction of the audience, and it was a relaxed group who drank champagne and ate food from the cold buffet, which contained many delicacies not now usually seen in the shops. Ken Warren had managed to get to the theater for the second act. "Last-minute holdup," he apologized to Connie. But her expression was made radiant just by his presence. His long, rather lugubrious face melted into a shy smile as he congratulated Julia. "You seem well on your way now. I hear there's a film coming up." Behind his thick glasses, his eyes seemed both kind and concerned, as if he wondered what possible attraction the uneven, uncertain future of an actress could hold. Then he engaged in an animated conversation with Alex about the results of the Japanese entry into the war. By now they knew more of the extent of the devastation at Pearl Harbor, the massive losses the U.S. Navy had suffered. "Of course, now the factories will start pouring out matériel," he said, "but I wonder how far the Japs can get before there can be a turning point. I think it would be a terrible mistake to underestimate them. . . ."

Alex's face seemed pinched with anxiety. "I agree. No one I talk to is very optimistic about any quick victories. Greg's managed to get to Singapore. *The Record* got a dispatch from him this afternoon. It will be in the morning editions."

Everyone was trying to forget what the week had actually been like, for these few hours to forget the stunning disasters that had followed Pearl Harbor. The day following the Pearl Harbor attack, Japanese bombers had destroyed British air power in Hong Kong, and this morning's news had been of the British battleships *Prince of Wales* and *Repulse,* steaming from Singapore to cut off Japanese communications, being sunk. It was a disaster none of them had quite absorbed yet. Julia wondered if some of the laughter in the theater tonight had not been to gain release from the tension and dread the week had brought.

Julia had whispered something to Jamie, and he had nodded

eagerly and put his arm around her shoulders. Julia asked her father to make the announcement that she and Jamie were engaged and would marry "soon." The champagne glasses were raised and toasts and congratulations offered; but Julia sensed that some of the good wishes heaped on them seemed hollow. "Darling," D.D. said, "you haven't forgotten that you have a run-of-the-play contract? And after that there is the film. You know I count on you for that. After tonight no one doubts you are an actress."

"Most actresses get married sometime."

"For you—better later than sooner. Give yourself a chance to get really established. Waiting a little can't matter."

"I don't *want* to wait. Jamie and I have waited long enough."

D.D. shrugged his heavy shoulders. "Well, darling—just remember not to get pregnant. It does seem to cramp an actress's style." He turned away, his face registering disapproval.

Alex put her arm around Julia. "Well, my love, you've done it. And who's to blame you? Your flier boy is handsome enough to take any girl's breath away. And don't listen to D.D. Now that Greg's so far away, I wish I'd had the courage to go ahead and have his baby. It would give me something to hold on to—some part of him. But, of course, I thought there was plenty of time for babies. But not everything can be postponed. Especially in war." She gulped at the whiskey she had exchanged for champagne. "God knows when I'll ever see him—now that all this has happened. But he's safe in Singapore, at least. He'll wangle transport out of there, somehow. But knowing Greg, he'll just want to get closer to the war, not farther away."

Luisa Radcliffe came to offer her congratulations. She exclaimed prettily over the modest ring Jamie had given Julia. For some reason she looked more pleased over the announcement than anyone else in the gathering. "Well, don't you see," Jamie said quietly to her when their hostess had left them, "you'll soon be out of her way. Alex is married, and Connie is blindly committed and firmly in the WAAF. There was only you between your father and her. She'll be glad to see you safely removed."

"I've never stood between my father and Mrs. Radcliffe . . . or anyone else."

"Yes you have. You symbolize the mayhem of that day. You were the closest thing on earth he had after your mother was killed. No—after I killed your mother." He stopped her protest.

"He's felt he had to look after you the way you looked after him in those months when he was like a helpless child. Now *she* will take over."

"You really think she wants him? It's not just a little flirtatious distraction for her?"

He smiled at her and smoothed a wisp of hair back from her forehead. "You're still an innocent, aren't you? Maybe that's one of the reasons I love you so much. Of course she wants him. She's got everything else. She is bored with the world of safe, dull marriages in the banking world. Now she'd like to move on to something more glamorous. She'd like a bit of glitter in her world. She's a young woman, Julia—comparatively. Though at your age you don't think so. She likes first nights. She would like Broadway and Hollywood. She's got enough presence and enough money to outshine any actress she's likely to come up against. She's not afraid of competition. To notch up two marriages before you're forty—without a divorce—that's quite an accomplishment. She doesn't need money from your father. She wants status and recognition. She doesn't just think she's a worthy successor to Ginette Maslova. She's going to singlemindedly promote and help your father's career far more than any woman who had a career of her own ever could find time to do. Why do you think she's investing in this film of yours? She might want you out of the way, but she'd like you famous, too."

"Jamie!—I didn't think you could be so cynical. You sound like Greg—or Alex."

"I'm not stupid, Julia. But she might not be the worst person in the world to entrust his interests to. She'll take very good care of him and his career. I don't doubt that for a second."

III

THEY WERE MARRIED three days after Christmas. Julia wondered if Jamie even noticed the ceremony. In his mind, he was already married to her. It was held in St. Paul's, Covent Garden, a church much loved by the acting community. It was the first occasion on which Jamie had been able to arrange a three-day leave. Her father had offered her her mother's wedding dress, but Julia knew how this could affect Jamie, so she borrowed the simple white silk suit Alex had worn for her own wedding in a registry office.

As many of Jamie's friends in the squadron as could get leave attended, but they were few. "Can't leave the place denuded," he had said. Other Army and Navy friends stationed in the South turned up, some his distant cousins. There seemed a solid phalanx of uniformed men on the groom's side of the church, all of them invited by telephone, hurriedly. Lady Jean came down from Scotland and occupied the front pew on that side, accompanied only by Sir Niall Henderson.

That there was a wedding in a church at all seemed unreal. They were among the darkest days of the war; the desert war seemed a stalemate, with the British retaking a place called Benghazi but with every possibility that it would be taken back from them by the Germans. On Christmas Day Hong Kong had fallen to the Japanese, and they had invaded Burma. In an atmosphere of tight-lipped tension, which might have disguised near-panic in those who could read the maps and had some idea of the paltry numbers of British aircraft guarding the Malay Peninsula, Julia was married in a ceremony arranged and made beautiful, she recognized, mostly by Luisa Radcliffe. The right things had been done: There were flowers, there was organ music, enough guests were assembled to make the occasion seem festive and important. She had even reminded Jamie of something he had forgotten: a wedding ring. Afterward the reception was at the Ritz. Julia felt guilty about what this must have cost her father—there were all the little extras that only Mrs. Radcliffe could have thought of. It was as unlike a wartime wedding as any could be, with flowers and a three-tiered cake and an official photographer. They would eventually have their scrapbook, like any other married couple. But after the kisses and congratulations, the speeches, the toasts, as Julia moved among the crowd, there was the ever-present talk of the war. The Japanese were hitting all along the Malay Peninsula, and there was some talk, among those who might know, that the airfields there had been practically denuded of planes in order to serve the battle in the Western Desert. With Jamie beside her, Julia realized she was being kissed by the Wing Commander who had come that terrible day to try to convey the sorrow and anguish of a young pilot whose plane had taken Ginette Maslova's life. He held her shoulders for an unexpectedly long time and looked her fully in the face. His words were low and intended for her and Jamie only. "A most happy and unexpected outcome of a tragic day, my dear.

I'm sure your mother would have blessed this marriage. And never worry—I'll never speak of it to a soul.'' But a little coldness went through Julia as she realized there were many others who must have known—the person who had told Jamie in the beginning, stretching on through how many others who had nursed him, men in the squadron, not all of them dead. But she looked across to her father's face, bright and animated, laughing, remembering other weddings, accepting good wishes for her and Jamie. He was a long way removed from the man who was stupefied and drunk on whiskey after the shocking news of his wife's death on that terrible day. If he ever were to learn of Jamie's involvement he would now see it for what it was— entirely accidental. But she still hoped he would never learn. Surely no one could be so cruel as to tell him?

Lady Jean and Sir Niall seemed an island to themselves. They sat together at a small table on little gilt chairs, forking the food, drinking the champagne sparingly. Lady Jean's face wore a mechanical smile; behind the smile was a sort of mask of desperate resignation. What she had thought could not happen had happened. This stranger to their country and to their whole way of life had become the wife of her only son. All her hopes, plans about Kirsty Macpherson were gone. She looked at the world of show business about her, of cheery young men in uniform laughing at jokes she could not understand, of malicious little bits of gossip on which the theater thrived, and Julia knew that to her it was a world totally without substance. From it Lady Jean Sinclair could expect nothing. And what would she expect of the children of this young woman her son inexplicably had chosen to marry? The doubt, the dislike, even the fear were plainly there behind the smile.

Alex kissed Julia and left early. Julia knew that she would go straight back to the office, where the wire service tapes might tell her something more about Greg. Connie was there, and in the absence of Ken Warren, who hadn't been able to get leave, she was, with some bewilderment, trying to cope with the numbers of young men who pressed her with champagne and more wedding cake and tried to get a telephone number where she could be reached.

Then D.D. was at Julia's side. "Almost time to say good-bye to your guests, darling. Two hours to curtain time. No doubt there'll still be a few left even after the show's over—but I don't suppose you'll be interested in coming back here. . . ." He lingered for a moment. "By the way, did your father tell you? I've managed to persuade him to take on the Professor Higgins role in *Pygmalion*. I've got the theater and the director. He'll go into rehearsal next month. Now . . . don't look like that! He's had long enough being idle since *Lear* closed. And *no,* I should not have waited for you to be available to play Eliza. That would have been too much of a good thing, right after Cordelia. The critics would have nailed you. They'd be saying forever that you couldn't do a thing without him. Far better where you are, darling—and the script for the film is coming along nicely. You'll have plenty to occupy your time."

"Somehow," Jamie said as they quietly left the reception. "I never imagined my wife would have to work on our wedding day."

Julia chose not to take the remark seriously. "That's the world you married into, love. Do you think I'd let the understudy take over? . . . She just might be better than me."

He sat through the performance. He had invited his mother and Sir Niall to attend, but Lady Jean pleaded fatigue from the long journey the day before. She would leave again early the next morning, while Sir Niall stayed on at his club for a few extra days. He had been delighted when Julia said she would send a ticket for the show. "I'll turn up with flowers, just like those stage-door Johnnies, even though you are an old married woman now." She went through her performance with more verve than she had thought was left in her. It had been the greatest day of her life, and the glow remained with her. They returned to the Ritz and were amazed to find that the tag end of the reception guests were still there. Had she really been away at the theater, taken on another skin, played a part, and still the old life continued, as if she had never been absent? They had a late supper with her father and Mrs. Radcliffe; D.D., who had been at the theater to monitor her performance; and Sir Niall. They were in the suite booked for them for three nights, the bills paid by her father. "You'll want your time to yourselves," he said, smiling on her benignly.

"Except for the evenings and the Saturday matinee," D.D. added.

"Jamie will be gone by Saturday," Julia reminded him. "This

is a wartime wedding, D.D. We're lucky to have even this time. . . ."

Her father gracefully dropped his own key to the London flat into the middle of the table. "Well, my darling Julia, I think you're entitled to more than that—as long as you can have it. Your old Dad won't be coming back to the flat for a while. Mrs. Radcliffe is kindly putting me up. So whenever Jamie has leave, he knows where to head, and you have the place to yourself. Except for the dragon lady, Agnes."

Her marriage had signaled his complete return to a life of his own. Ginette Maslova would not be forgotten, but she had taken a step backward into the shadows of his life. The past was the past, treasured memories, but like old photographs, in still life. Luisa Radcliffe, handsome, smiling, supremely assured, was the present, moving, living. Feeling her own happiness with Jamie, their future together, how could she begrudge her father his own future, no matter with whom it lay? She remembered Jamie's words. "She'll take very good care of him and his career." She put the key into Jamie's hand and smiled at Luisa Radcliffe. "That's very kind . . . yes, very kind. My father is lost without someone to take care of him."

Better to make peace now. Better to let her mother slip into the shadows. Her father was a man who needed a woman, as she needed Jamie. They would keep of the past what they most cherished, his memories of an extraordinary wife, she of a mother who had been like no other of her knowledge. On this, her wedding night, she was vividly reminded of her time with Jamie in the cottage in the forest of Sinclair. Back to her memory also came that vague shape by the mantel in the Red Tower Room—the shape that had no substance, the sob that might have been a sigh or merely the wind in the chimney. She leaned over and kissed her husband. "Never leave me, Jamie," she whispered.

"I never will. Never on earth—or in heaven. I will never leave you. . . . We promised forever—and that doesn't mean only 'til death do us part.' "

Death was the reverse side of his life. Death had brought them together. Her father and Luisa Radcliffe seemed to fade out of the room as they looked only at each other. Their coming together in bed had the feverish longing of two young people in love, conscious of time and war inevitably ticking away their deadly seconds. To Julia it was different, it was still miraculous, and they made love many times that night, sleeping briefly and coming together again. But the first time had been unique. She remembered the cold flagstones, the brief pain, the smell of the woodsmoke, the bodies of the dogs pressed against theirs. The first, greatest, unforgettable love lay back there.

Through January and February Julia played every night, and every night prayed Jamie would get leave. There was little of it, and Sundays, without the theater and without Jamie, were hard to bear. Jamie had told her there was talk of the squadron's being moved to Lincolnshire. "Just guesses," he said. "The Russians are screaming for us to open a Second Front, as you know. That would mean fighter escort for bombers. Of course, we can't open a Second Front at this time; it would be suicide. In theory, we're still guarding the narrowest strip of the Channel, but the Germans have sent just about everything they've got to the Russian Front—and are locked in there. And what's not there has gone to North Africa. But we still have to maintain a defense force here. Goering just might take it into his head to send over a thousand bombers one night, and there has to be someone minding the shop."

"Do I detect a trace of boredom?" Julia asked lightly. "You want more action? Haven't you had enough? You want more medals? More campaign ribbons?"

"I want you. . . ." Their time together was short and precious. Agnes served their food silently, and with more graciousness than Julia had thought her capable of. At the wedding she had spoken briefly with Lady Jean. While she mistrusted actors and their world, she knew quality when she saw it, she had once remarked to Julia. "Your husband doesn't have a title, does he? He's not a baronet . . ." The last words were spoken with snobbish hope.

"No, Agnes. His mother is the daughter of an earl, but he's just the local laird."

"But after the war—when he's home, you will be mistress of Castle Sinclair, won't you." That seemed to satisfy her needs.

After the war. It seemed an almost unimaginable future for Julia.

* * *

The unimaginable future seemed to grow to an unimaginable nightmare. They had welcomed their American ally, but the thought of defeat was still there. The German advance had bogged down on the Russian Front, but they were not defeated; in the Western Desert they continued to fight over, lose, and retake outposts in an eternal attrition. But the Japanese advance in the Pacific was frighteningly swift. It became a possibility that the American Pacific forces would be broken before their aid in Europe and Africa could contribute much of substance. Horrified, Julia traced the swiftness of the Japanese rush down the Malay Peninsula. She returned from the theater one night in the middle of February, smiling to herself as she saw the light in the sitting room still on. Jamie had had unexpected leave. But it was Alex who sat there, smoking, the remains of a glass of whiskey on the table at her side.

She didn't rise, just looked with a kind of despairing numbness at Julia. "Singapore's fallen," she said. "It's come over the wires. General Percival has been forced to surrender. There's no news of Greg. He filed his last story from there only half a day ago. It's possible . . . it's possible he didn't get away. Bloody fool! He could have gotten out. War correspondents aren't combatants. They don't have to stay to surrender."

Silently Julia took Alex's glass and refilled it. She poured a small drink for herself. "How can you say that until you know? There were plenty of ships leaving in these last days. He could—"

"A cable from him to *The Record* would have priority. He wouldn't need to send a message to me. I would know he was alive."

"He *is* alive—until you know differently. He could have gotten out on anything. A plane to one of the nearby islands. A small boat without radio." She spoke brightly, and yet she felt fear. A smell of fear and defeat seemed to hang about Alex like the cigarette smoke. She went to the kitchen, where Agnes always left a plate of sandwiches prepared for her return, and brought them back to the sitting room. "Here—have some. I'll bet you haven't had a bite. . . ."

Alex shook her head and lighted another cigarette from the butt of the last. She held out her glass silently, and Julia went to refill it. "He didn't have to bloody well *stay!*" she said vehemently. "Some pigheaded idea of being a hero, filing dispatches while the ship goes down. That would be so like him. . . .''

She talked—it sounded more like raving to Julia—until her words became slurred and almost meaningless. All the resentment of her long separation from Greg came to the surface. ''The most I know about him comes from what he writes for the paper. His letters are little scraps—a few lines. He loves me. He's very busy—very rushed. There's lots of action. He isn't allowed to say any more. *'Keep your chin up, lovely. I'm counting on you.'* They're the last words he wrote to me.''

''Oh, Alex, come off it!'' Julia cried. ''Those aren't the last words. You talk as if he's dead. He isn't dead. He's just in some place where he can't get through to you—or the paper. Have you looked at the maps? There's the whole of Sumatra and Borneo—all the Dutch East Indies. Thousands of little islands—''

''And they'll be the next places the Japs take.'' Alex spilled ash over her dress and the carpet when she waved her hand dismissively. ''His only chance was a ship to Australia. And the last of them would have gone days ago. Oh, damn him—*damn* him! How I hate heroes. . . .''

Eventually Julia got her into Michael's bed, wearing a pair of pajamas her father had left behind. She took the last cigarette from her fingers and put it out firmly. ''Sleep. There'll be news in the morning.''

In the morning there was no news of Greg, only fuller details of the appalling surrender of the ninety-thousand-man garrison of British, Australians, and Indians at Singapore, in what had been thought of as the impregnable fortress. Its useless guns faced out to sea, and the enemy had come overland. Alex stayed at the office for long hours each day, refusing to return to the flat she had shared with Greg. Each night Julia found her waiting when she returned from the theater. She ate almost nothing, smoked and drank too much. Her face grew gaunt, and if she had not known differently Julia would have thought the lines on her face had been put there with greasepaint. ''Old Wolfie walked through the newsroom this evening and saw me. He practically fired me. Said the copy I'd been turning in was lousy—they haven't used any of it, that's for sure. He told me to go home and straighten myself out. But before he did that he took me up to his office and someone produced smoked salmon sandwiches—how *do* these people keep getting such things? We had

a couple of stiff drinks. He talked about what he thought I should
do in the future. Something about America. Washington. We
have a bureau office there, and staff, but no women. He'd like a
regular column on the war seen from Washington—by a woman.
Human-interest stuff, I suppose. Not too important. But, you
know, he's the patriot *extraordinaire*. He wants a woman journalist to interpret events in Europe and Russia and North Africa
as *she* sees them. Stories about women in the armed forces,
women in factories—and ordinary mums coping with rationing
and bombs, and bomb-blasted houses. I'm to be ready to go on
the radio, or on lecture tours at the drop of a hat. Anything to
spread the word that there's the European side of the battle to
be won. Not to let them forget. Not to let them think that it's all
out there in the Pacific.''

"But that's great. You'll do it perfectly. . . .'' Julia's voice
trailed off as she saw the tears begin to run down those haggard
cheeks of Alex.

"Don't you see? Don't you understand? He thinks Greg is
dead, or captured. He doesn't think we'll be seeing Greg very
soon—perhaps not ever. Not a word since Singapore. Java's surrendered. We lost the Battle of the Java Sea. We're losing and
giving way everywhere. If the Japs get to Australia, it'll be a
goner. If Greg were free, he'd have found some way to get in
touch by now. He isn't free, I know. And he's probably dead. I
told Old Wolfie I knew he'd been trying to find out something
through the Red Cross. But it's all chaos, and no one knows
anything. I said I'd think about Washington. And he sent me
home in a staff car. Or rather, I said I'd come here. I can't stand
the flat anymore—with Greg's things around—and silence. Julia,
how would you feel if Jamie were killed? If he were dead?''

No comforting words came. Only the truth. "I think I'd feel
dead myself.''

IV

IN MARCH D.D. replaced Julia in the play; he had decided that
the script for the film was now ready, and they would begin
filming at Pinewood before the end of the month. "You need a
little rest, darling. Looking a bit peaked. Go down to Anscombe, where you can be near that flier husband of yours. We'll

be arranging a few visits to Bomber Command stations—just so you'll get the background feeling. He'll explain anything you need to know. Might as well make use of a hero while we've got him. . . . Now, don't look like that! I didn't imply he's going to die. He just may be transferred abroad . . . though where there's left to send him, God knows.'' His gloom reflected the continued advance of the Japanese in the Pacific, apparently unstoppable, a sort of weary stalemate in North Africa, and the sense that the Germans were only waiting for the spring thaw to begin swallowing up further huge territories in Russia. ''But the film will be good. The Ministry is very anxious for it to make . . . good propaganda.''

''The trouble is that I don't believe in the script,'' Julia said dispiritedly. ''I just can't see us making any raids into Europe at all, never mind one of that size.''

''We will, my dear,'' D.D. said through a haze of smoke. ''Only a foreigner knows the British as well as I do. They are quite mad.''

Before filming started on *Return at Dawn*, as the script was called, Michael Seymour married Luisa Radcliffe. It was a surprise to no one. It had simply been a matter of time. ''It can't go on like this, Pet,'' her father had said quietly to Julia. ''I know this war has turned convention on its head, but I can't go on living with Luisa without marrying her. Don't mistake me . . . she's made no demands, set no deadlines. We're just two lonely, rootless people who have come together and are trying for our own little bit of personal happiness in a very doubtful time—like you and Jamie. We're keeping it very quiet. A registry office, and just our friends at Luisa's house. Luisa doesn't want a big fuss—Ginette's and her husband's deaths are too close. But I'll want my three girls around me. Try to bless this marriage, Julia. Somehow I care more about what you think than about Alex and Connie. Perhaps because you were Ginette's favorite. Connie would be loyal, no matter what I did. Alex will never be reconciled to it, because she doesn't like Luisa—oh, don't think I don't know that. I thought life ended for me that day Ginette was killed. A large part of it did. But somehow my body didn't die. I need a woman, a marriage, a home. I suppose I'm hopelessly old-fashioned. . . .''

Very gently she reassured him. ''That's what I want with Jamie. Connie wants it with Ken Warren. Alex is hurting because she doesn't have it with Greg anymore. You're entitled to your piece of happiness, Father. Grab it. Don't let it go.''

"Bless you, Pet.''

The ceremony and reception were low-key affairs by the standards of the wedding Luisa had arranged for Julia. But the press got wind of it and jostled each other and the three sisters on the steps of the registry office. But Michael and Luisa smilingly posed for photographs, both there and at the entrance of Luisa's house. The ghost of Ginette Maslova took one further step back into the shadows.

"Well, she got him,'' Alex said with some bitterness to Julia at the reception. Alex looked worn and tired and had taken little trouble with her clothes, but still she retained the indefinable air of chic and assurance that had always been hers despite the general air of shabbiness and "making do'' that marked most people's clothes these days. She had lost pounds in weight as the weeks had gone by, and there had been no news of Greg. Lord Wolverton was urging her to take up the post in Washington and was growing impatient with her refusal to make up her mind. Julia had a sense that Alex believed that if she waited here in London news would come sooner of Greg, as if leaving here were a betrayal. But Alex did not speak very much of Greg anymore, though she continued to use her father's bedroom at the flat.

"I don't think it was a matter of 'getting' him,'' Julia answered. "It is something he wanted. He's entitled—''

"Of course she got him. She always meant to. It was a matter of waiting, of making herself indispensable to him, of always being there, the way Mother never could be. That—and pots of money. Just as well Father's talent is incorruptible, or she'd begin to manipulate his career. Rather the way she's doing with yours.''

"*Mine!* What the hell do you mean?''

"Well, it's mostly her money in this film, isn't it? She'd like a nice success for you. It would look good for Father. An acting-dynasty sort of thing.''

"Rubbish!—it's D.D.'s film.''

"And D.D. takes the money wherever he can find it.''

"And why not? That's always been how the theater keeps going. You're jealous, Alex, and more than a bit stupid. It isn't like you. Don't begrudge him whatever happiness he can manage to grab. You're too old to be resentful of a stepmother, for heaven's sake. Did you expect Father to live like a monk for the rest of his life? And if she has money to make his life easier, then all the better. He's always been short of money—you know that. Most actors are. They don't handle it very well. And any rate, he spent an awful lot on us. Fancy schools and university don't come cheap.''

Suddenly Alex gave a wry little laugh. "You know, you've touched a sore spot. I *am* jealous—just a bit. When I don't have Greg, I want to keep Father for myself. I expected him to hold my hand. But he's holding Mrs. Radcliffe's instead.''

"Lady Seymour's hand," Julia corrected. "Better accept it.''

"Yes—Lady Seymour. That used to be our mother's name—'' She broke off. "Oh, damn, I can see Old Wolfie bearing down on us—beaming. It makes me sick. Everyone's so damned pleased. He'll say the usual things about how good it will be for Father to be settled—and then he'll start up again about Washington. I really don't want the job. It sounds a bit too much like cutting and running. I'm not even sure of what I'm supposed to do. . . .''

"You'll make it your own, as you've done with everything. It would be a great experience. You'd be mad not to take it.''

"What you're saying is that Greg won't be coming back, and there's no point in my hanging around here.''

"I'm not saying anything of the sort. You're turning sour inside, Alex. If you can't have Greg back for a while, then accept the challenge of this job—even if it's only as a distraction. *Grab it!* How many women get offered anything like that? Greg would despise you for being unprofessional.''

"Unprofessional! No one ever called me that!''

"Ours is a professional family. We've always been. You know what Greg would expect of you. Go and do it.''

Alex deposited her empty glass on a waiter's tray and requested whiskey. "I need fortification," she said. "Not only is Old Wolfie pushing his way steadily here, but also here's Connie with her long drink of water in tow. I can't, for the life of me, think what she sees in Ken Warren. I hear that after Dowding left Fighter Command, Ken was transferred into some hush-hush job in the Ministry of Defense—a Whitehall job. Intelligence, no doubt. That should keep him nice and safe for the duration.''

"You really are turning into a witch, Alex. Can he help it that he'd never be allowed on active service with those eyes? In his quiet way, he's probably quite brilliant, and someone has to do the deskwork. Only he never talks about it.''

"Oh, I don't doubt it. He'll follow in the shadow of the mighty and take care to make himself indispensable. He'll be one of those faceless, anonymous people who suddenly end up getting knighted for no good reason that anyone can see except the Prime Minister. At the end of the war he'll slide into the Civil Service and end up as someone's Permanent Under Secretary—''

"And what's wrong with that?" Jamie was beside them. "Not my style, but old Ken has a lot going for him behind those glasses. Don't underestimate him, Alex.''

"Not you, too, James Sinclair. I really can't take any more flak.''

"Then stop making yourself a target for it. Try smiling, just for a minute. You used to be a good sort, Alex.'' He kissed her briefly on the cheek to take the sting out of his words. "Now *smile!* It's your father's wedding day. Smile for him, if for no one else.''

She did manage a smile as Connie and Ken Warren pushed their way to them through the crush. "Here's Ken," Connie said breathlessly, as if they hadn't noticed him. "He managed to get away after all. Doesn't Mrs. Radcliffe . . . I mean . . . well, what are we to call her now?''

"Try Luisa," Jamie said. "Asking her gracious permission, of course. Somehow I don't think she'd object.''

"Yes, I'll do that," Connie answered. "I do think she looks lovely. Don't you? And I think she'll make Father happy. It must have been such a lonely time. Now he has a home—a base— someone to look after him.''

Julia looked at the smiling Luisa across the room and knew that what Connie said was right. But something in her still longed for her own beloved, temperamental mother, the one of brilliance, near-genius. The one whose house or life was never quite as orderly as it might have been but who had been capable of flashes of such warmth and love that no one had ever taken seriously her erratic flaws. Her encompassing talent had reached out to hundreds of thousands of people. Her laughter had been rich and true, her tears had been from the heart. She had had all the tempestuous passion of her Russian ancestry. She might have retreated farther into the shadows on this day, but Julia could still hear her voice, hear her softly sing the almost forgotten lullabies of her own childhood, feel herself held close to that warm, scented breast, know her kisses, feel the ache of her frequent departures and the fervent joy of her returns. She had neither Alex's jealousy nor Connie's calm acceptance of this marriage. For Julia, no other woman would touch the memory of Ginette Maslova.

She reached for Jamie's hand and held it tightly. "You must go and congratulate Father. And wish the bride happiness. She did her best to give us a lovely wedding—"

"She did her best to shove you out of the nest," Alex said. She turned and faced her employer, who had at last made the passage to her side. "We were just discussing what we should call our stepmother. . . ."

Michael and Luisa left for three days in a house in Somerset that a friend had loaned to Luisa. Jamie and Julia were packing for the journey to Anscombe, where they would spend the rest of Jamie's three days of leave. Agnes hovered around them with the coffee pot. "It doesn't taste like much, I'm afraid. But the best we can get these days. Wasn't the reception beautiful? Isn't Lady Seymour's house beautiful? Exquisite taste—anyone can see that, although they told me so much had been put safely away until the war's over. . . ." She was once again enjoying the association with wealth, but still a little anxious about her own position. "You'll still be keeping on this flat, Miss Julia? I mean . . . you're sure to be back on the stage again once the film's over."

Julia wished she had not mentioned it. She guessed that Jamie was still of two minds whenever he was reminded that his wife had a job—a career, almost, even if a fledgling one. The time beyond the war was not settled in their own minds. The question of how one carried on a career from a remote Scottish castle still was not resolved. She guessed he welcomed the film because if she continued in that direction, there could be long gaps between films, and therefore she would be at home with him. But it all belonged in a realm almost beyond their imagination— the end of the war.

Alex quietly entered the flat just as they were about to go to the station. Something utterly desolate in her expression made Julia rush to her side.

Alex spoke one word: "Changi."

"What?"

Alex allowed herself to be guided to a chair. Agnes poured coffee, but Jamie went to the liquor cabinet and brought her a brandy.

"I—we—the paper's just had word through the Red Cross. Greg was captured with all the others when Singapore fell. It doesn't matter that he's a noncombatant. No one gets out. He's in a prison called Changi. That's all we know."

"He's alive . . ." Julia said tentatively.

"Alive," Alex repeated. "Yes, alive. I'm grateful. But when will I ever see him?" She quickly swallowed the brandy and turned to Jamie. "When will the end of the war be? Your guess is as good as mine." She continued to ramble on in that vein for a few moments, asking unanswerable questions. Then Jamie touched her shoulder. "Come on. It's time to go, or we'll miss the train. Julia, can you throw a few things into a bag for Alex? A toothbrush—whatever else she'll need."

"To Anscombe?" Alex protested. "I can't leave London. There might be more news. Wolfie sent me home—but I don't know what I'm supposed to do. I suppose he didn't want me weeping all over the office. Bad for morale. I'm supposed to be such a sympathetic but tough reporter of other people's misfortunes. I suppose he thought it would be better to have me out of the way."

"He sent you to your family, Alex," Jamie said. "You're with us. To swear or weep or curse the gods. No matter what. Any news they get will come to Anscombe. You're coming with us."

"I don't . . ." She stopped. "Well, you *are* family, Jamie, and you bear the scars of war. Until this minute I didn't think of you and Julia as quite real. I mean . . . a real marriage. Just something that came because of the war. But it's more than I thought." She reached for the brandy again and then fumbled for a cigarette, which Jamie supplied. "All right . . ." It was said a little grudgingly. "I'll come. Better there than back at Greg's flat . . . alone. I suppose I've got to get used to the feeling that 'alone' could be a long time."

"Yes," Jamie said. "That's what you've got to get used to, Alex. Like a lot of other women."

"I've never been like other women."

"You are now."

* * *

Alex stayed at Anscombe through Jamie's remaining two days of leave. Julia wondered what was wrong with her own feelings that she had a sense of resentment that Alex took all their time and attention, a time she had wanted so badly with Jamie. But she was there—telephoning either the office or the Red Cross, or going on long walks with them unwillingly. "I never was a country person. You know that, Julia. I hate walking. . . ." They avoided the village of Anscombe, where she would encounter too many people who knew her and would ask about her husband. When questions were asked, Julia or Jamie answered them and let Alex walk on. Once Alex did pick a few daffodils that were still tightly in bud, and she asked that they go to their mother's grave. She laid them there. "I'm a simpleton," she said. "I haven't got any time or place for grief. I didn't know how to handle it when Mother died. I still don't. I think of Greg as dead—and yet he isn't—not yet. One hears the Japs aren't too kind to their captives. Too many mouths to feed. And we haven't got any Jap captives to strike some quid pro quo. Sort of 'You be nice to ours, and we'll be nice to yours.' Well, belatedly, I've laid flowers on my mother's grave. I wish, instead, I could send a few cans of corned beef to Greg. Let's go home before I get more maudlin. Let's raid Father's cellar tonight. A couple of bottles of his best. I don't suppose it will matter. From now on Mrs. Radcliffe will replenish his cellar. I'm beginning to see how her money might be useful—but I hope to God he didn't marry her for that reason—"

Remembering her talk with her father before he had married, Julia cut her off sharply. "No more of that, Alex! They are two lonely people who found each other—who needed each other. They have as much chance of happiness—as much right to it—as anyone else. Father has never done anything purely for money in his life. No one goes into the theater for money. No one marries a young musician for money. He needs money, but he's always scraped it up from somewhere. But he would never marry for it."

"Well . . . well! I stand rebuked." Alex put her arm through Julia's and began to lead them all from the churchyard. "My little sister's grown up since she married, Jamie."

"And you'll realize it even more when you stop calling her your little sister."

She smiled at him, the first attempt at a genuine smile they had seen since before Michael's wedding. "You know, Jamie, I don't think I ever can. I don't mean it patronizingly. In many ways Julia's much wiser than I. But she was such a sweet and pretty little thing—with her golden hair that I so much envied. I once thought I was jealous of her because she was the youngest, and my parents adored her. But I really wasn't. I always knew that if something big came along that threatened her, I'd be there to protect her. She doesn't remember the times when both Mother and Father were away, when I really was the big sister. Connie was never any trouble. She was always so supremely sure that everything would be all right. But Julia used to fret—she doesn't remember that, but she did. And I tried to make her understand that they would always come back." She gave a last glance to her mother's grave, with the unopened daffodils. "Of course, it doesn't always work that way. . . ."

That night, as they drank two bottles of white burgundy with jugged hare and apple pie, Alex grew pensive, less frenetic than she had been. "Well, I suppose I have to make plans—if anyone can make plans. Greg is in a Japanese concentration camp. I can sit and mope here, where everything and everyone in the office remind me of him. I can push myself on you two and move into the flat, play on your good nature and sympathy. Or I can do as Julia said Greg would want me to do. I can take the Washington job and make what I can of it. I have no specific brief from Wolfie. Just do what I can to make the Americans remember that we have a need over here—and that we, too, have lost thousands of serving men in the Pacific. I can write things for *The Record* so that people here will understand our new ally better. The fact that I have a husband in a prison camp could gain me a little extra entrée. I could use his name with all his old buddies in the press corps. I can use Father's name. God help me, I'll even use Mrs. Radcliffe's—no, Luisa's—name if it will get me anywhere. Those banking circles are as tightly knit as our little worlds." She raised her glass to them. "I'll choke off this self-pity that I so much despise in another woman. I'll make you—I'll make Greg proud of me."

"I'll drink to that," Jamie said. "And I'll hold you to it."

Jamie went early the next morning to catch the first bus from Anscombe. "How quiet it seems without him," Alex remarked when she came down to breakfast in the kitchen. "I think I'll miss him, though he isn't exactly the rowdy type. I like your man, Julia."

"Thanks," Julia said and scraped butter sparingly on her toast. She looked down again at the newspaper, and then back at her sister. Alex's appearance was better than Julia remembered it since the news of the fall of Singapore and Greg's dropping from sight. She looked, for once, as if she had slept. The end of doubt had seemed to bring its own relief. Perhaps her half-decided plans of the night before had cracked the hard shell of her pain, had given her a kind of future, however tenuous. "I think I'll telephone Wolfie today and tell him I'm taking a little break here—telephone Father with the news about Greg." She had refused to allow anyone to telephone the house in Somerset where her father and Luisa were staying. "It isn't fair to break in on them. After all, there's nothing they can do. They should be back by this evening. Father's only four days away from the play—and D.D. was stretching it to do that. I suppose he thinks the publicity made up for it. Have you noticed how the public loves a wedding in wartime? If it's something notable, it always makes the front pages. I suppose they think it's a sort of guarantee that other people—important people—are expecting this mess to turn out all right in the end. . . ."

"Stop talking, Miss Alex, and eat," Stella said, thrusting a plate with a fried egg and one slice of bacon at her. "Of course it's going to be all right in the end. Whoever thought otherwise?"

To Julia's surprise, Alex began to eat the food in front of her and didn't start to argue.

Alex stayed all through the remainder of the two weeks Julia had before starting on the film. She telephoned her father daily and even asked, occasionally, to speak with Luisa. She had a long conversation with Lord Wolverton and accepted the job offered in Washington. "I think they're all very relieved," she said. "Old Wolfie really has been very patient with me . . . humoring me. Perhaps because he liked and respected Greg so much . . . now I'll have to do the best I can for him." She labored over the very short letter she was permitted to send through the Red Cross to Greg. "God knows when he'll get it." She made inquiries about sending food parcels, but the Red Cross was uncertain of deliveries. "No one seems to know how to handle the Japs just yet. It's all too new to them—to us. I can't remember when we've had an Asian enemy before."

"Half of Russia is in Asia," Julia remarked. "They weren't declared enemies, but they weren't friends until Hitler broke the pact."

"Sometimes you surprise me," Alex said. "Those are the sort of things *I'm* supposed to remember. I've grown up thinking everyone in the theater lived inside their plays and weren't really aware of half of what was going on around them. That's a notion I'll have to drop. Though with Father—"

"Father is different. He's very special. He is a very special actor. Don't expect him to be ordinary."

"Perhaps it's just as well he has Mrs.—Luisa. She seems an extremely practical type. Have you noticed . . . I mean how careful she's been not to come charging down here, full of solicitude, and beginning to take over? Do you realize it, Julia? This is probably the last time we'll ever be alone here together. After this it will be Luisa's home as well as Father's. I think she'll tread carefully, but I think we can expect changes—in time. Of course, there are some things she'll never change." She gestured through the window at the rose garden. "Perhaps she'll even be clever enough to enhance them. Well, Father made something of beauty where other men might have left a fireweed ruin. You realize, don't you, Julia, that with all her money she's never going to shift him out of this place? Even when the war's over, there's never going to be a grand country house somewhere. Father will never let go of what the Seymours have held for all these years. At one time he would have done it—but not now. Heritage and history have overtaken him. She'll have the ghosts of the Seymours as well as Ginette Maslova to fight."

"She's clever enough not to try to fight either. But you're right, Alex. We'll be guests at Anscombe from now on."

Alex shrugged. "Tough luck. We were born and mostly grew up here. Not a bad beginning. She can't take that away from us." The clock struck six, and instead of going to turn on the news on the radio, Alex rose, went to the liquor cabinet, and poured two whiskeys. "We'll let it go until the nine o'clock news, shall we? I've thought war all day, trying to write that pitiful little letter to Greg. What is there to say to someone who probably feels as if he's there for eternity?" She handed Julia her drink and indicated the film script Julia had been studying. "What's it about?"

"Why don't you read it?"

Alex shook her head. "I tried a couple of Father's scripts a couple of times. They didn't make much sense to me—so disjointed, with all those film and stage directions. Not my sort of thing. I'm strictly nonfiction, as a matter of taste and training."

"Well . . ." Julia began slowly, groping for words. "Well, you have to understand it's a low-budget picture. Big on emotion, short on props. Made strictly with the cooperation of the Ministry of Defense. In fact, we've all been told to keep pretty quiet about the subject, but of course it will get out. D.D.'s got permission to do some shooting inside Bomber Command bases—so you can guess the theme. It's set in a little village somewhere on the East Coast—Norfolk—Lincolnshire. The script doesn't say. The village had been virtually cut off by the expansion of the base. Only people who live there—people who have passes—can get in or out. It throws them together, whether they want it or not. No petrol to get out—no cars. Just bicycles. And a delivery van twice a week." She sighed. "I really don't know how to make something so slight seem like a film—even if it is a low-budget one. D.D. keeps insisting that it's the quality that matters."

"And who do you play—the village horse?"

Julia smiled. "Maybe the village idiot is what I'll turn out looking like. No—I'm from outside. Only allowed to rent a little tumble-down cottage because I'm married to a pilot. Oh, yes—D.D. cast me well, though there's a very big difference between fighter and bomber pilots. Well, I'm just there—pregnant, and trying to get used to that cut-off village. Waiting every night with the hope that my husband will be allowed home for a few hours. My neighbor is the local aristocrat, whose house has been taken over as officer quarters. She hates the whole situation but takes it in a sense of *noblesse oblige*. She doesn't like me, and she doesn't like the young Canadian navigator from the base who turns up and insists that he's related in some very distant way. He also insists on coming and helping her with her vegetable garden, and bits and pieces around the place. It isn't patriotic to send him away, and anyway, she needs the help. She isn't used to doing for herself—"

"Sounds like this lady has got the whole film for herself."

"When I tell you that Dame Audrey Fellowes is playing the role, then you *know* she's got the film."

Alex gave a low whistle. "How did D.D. land her? She's a big fish."

"The way he lands everyone. An appeal to their sense of patriotism—or whatever ruse he used before the war. Believe me, when he finds the right film for Father, he'll have his services for nothing. Luisa will see to that."

"So—go on—you're pregnant and waiting for your man, and the old aristocrat is trying to fight off the kindness of the young Canadian, who, I'll bet, is as lonely as hell and would rather be working in *your* garden, but he can't because your husband's a buddy."

"Why don't you write the rest of the script?"

Alex held up her hand. "I'll stop interrupting."

"The old lady has cancer—is beginning to be aware of it. The audience knows, but no one around her knows. The bombers are training over the North Sea almost every day. Sometimes there's a fighter escort. Neither I nor the old lady ever knows if it's training, or maybe, one day, the real thing."

"No one has made a bombing raid on the Germans since we gave up in France."

"Didn't I tell you it was a propaganda film? D.D. will be using plenty of free clips of training missions from the MOD. Well, one night they take off, much later than usual. Both the girl and the old woman are aware of it. And more bombers than the base carries join up with them. Fighter escort goes up—stays as long as their range will allow. But the bombers are away much longer—hours and hours. Just before dawn the fighter escort goes up to meet them, to beat off any fighters going up from the German side. We—the old lady and I—know it's been the real thing. They've been on a real bombing mission pretty deep into the enemy territory. We both stand at the wire fence of the base. We'd counted them out, and now we try to count them in. They come in ones and twos. But we see from the way they're landing that they've been shot up. There's no formation. Some land there that don't belong to the base. We lose count. It gets lighter. We see the ambulances. Then all the sound is gone. No more planes approaching. Mechanics already starting to work on the planes they've got on the ground. It's full daylight. The planes are a long way off. Some of them askew on the runways. Some right off them. We can't read numbers. So we go back into my cottage and make tea. It grows into a really beautiful morning. We leave the door open . . . waiting. I see someone cycling up the lane. It's the Canadian. They've been on a *huge* bombing raid deep into Germany—just to show the Germans we can do it. He tries not to tell me, but he can't get out of it. It's been reported by other bomber teams. My husband's plane had been seen going down in flames. No one reported anyone bailing out from it. So he's reported missing. No one says 'presumed dead,' but I know it. I put my hand on my belly because the baby had just given its first kicks. The Canadian takes the old lady back to her cottage. I wait through the day. One of my husband's pals comes to tell me—more or less officially. And I just sit there in the long twilight watching the Canadian working on the old lady's vegetables. She's going to die, but she's still got him.''

Alex seemed to take a long time before she spoke. She refilled both glasses. ''It sounds like the sort of film where you're going to have to do a lot of looking at the sky, and the old lady's vegetable garden, and down the lane.''

''That's about it.''

''You'll do it beautifully. Just keep thinking of how Connie would have stuck it out, and you'll do it beautifully.'' Was Alex's voice husky? In the growing dimness of the room Julia thought she saw an unusual brightness in Alex's eyes, as if there were tears to be shed—tears she had denied herself during all these weeks of waiting for news of Greg.

They went into shooting, and Julia had to be coached in every scene by the director. She found herself confused and depressed. The closeness of the cameras distracted her, as well as the sense of many people clustered just beyond them, people who were all professionals in their particular work, not a theater audience. She only had a few lines to say at a time, but they were done over and over as the director called for another take. She felt as if the camera were boring down into her very nerve ends, and sometimes the director was only feet away from her. Dame Audrey was friendly but slightly distant; she passed out no tips on acting before the cameras, but she evidenced no displeasure at having to work with a novice. Between takes she sat and knitted socks—navy and khaki socks. ''Used to do it when I was a young girl. Soldiers always need socks.'' In the end the director had her knitting socks as she observed the young Canadian toiling in her vegetable garden, unwanted, unbidden. She and Julia were filmed frequently at the wire fence and the painted backdrops of the bomber base. The scene came when they stood there, each trying to identify the planes as they came in, but saying nothing. When the director called, "Cut! Print it!" Dame Audrey nodded to Julia and smiled. "Well done, child. The hardest thing of all in acting is saying nothing."

Two days after the filming was finished and ready for the cutting room came the news of the first one-thousand-bomber attack by the RAF on Cologne. D.D. was exultant. "We're dead on time! And on target!" There had been minor, less heralded sorties by Bomber Command, but never anything of this strength, and never had they penetrated so deeply into enemy territory. For Julia the news only brought a sense of horror and of nightmare-ridden sleep. She saw herself clinging to the wire, counting.

For the first time since filming had begun, she went back to Anscombe. She could be near Jamie, and they might have time together. But she remembered her talk with Alex. Never again would Anscombe belong entirely to them. Luisa was there, mistress in her mother's place, her father's wife. Julia approached warily.

She found only small changes. Some furniture had been rearranged, some strange pieces had appeared, probably from Luisa's Belgravia house. There were some small luxuries—good soap, more abundant hot water—though she didn't see how Luisa had managed extra coal supplies. Food packages came regularly from America. "I am so fortunate," Luisa said. "So many good friends are so kind." There were canned foie gras and caviar and large cans of good crackers. Cook looked at them rather askance, but since she lacked the ingredients to make them, she was forced to accept and serve them. She became clever at disguising the taste of canned stew. Anscombe had always had a small herb garden, now tended by Stella, which was made full use of. It seemed Luisa was no stranger to cooking, and she was tactful in making suggestions to Cook. "They sent me to a school to learn how to cook so that if I married a poor man I'd always know how to make a dinner from almost nothing." she explained to Julia. There had been little chance, Julia thought, that she would have married a poor man—until she had the money to afford to marry Michael.

Her father had now finished the run of *Pygmalion* and was enjoying his time of quiet at Anscombe. The relationship between him and Luisa seemed calm and almost uneventful, as if they had been married a long time. He spent many hours with Harry Whitehand, talking over farm matters, proud that they were making their production quotas, and even, in some things, surpassing them. In the early summer mornings and the evenings Julia went back to her task of herding and milking, helping the Land Army girls get through their tasks more quickly, and earning them more time off. Jamie came over and spent three nights. She felt her marriage renewed, and the nightmares began to ease.

Daily her father tended the rose garden, and often Julia saw Luisa, gloved and with pruning shears, helping him. But whatever she did, pricking out seedlings from the greenhouse, putting a hoe skillfully around the potatoes, gathering and hanging herbs to dry, making a last-minute sauce with smoothness and flavor that even Cook had to admire, she was always the immaculate figure who had first appeared at Anscombe. The black hair, caught into its classic chignon, never had stray tendrils, her hands were soft, her skin nourished by good cosmetics she freely acknowledged came from America. "I'm at a sensitive age, my dear," she once acknowledged to Julia. "Every woman approaching forty with a husband like Michael is." She laughed lightly. "I'm still afraid of every beautiful and brilliant young actress who crosses his path." But she did not mean that, Julia knew. She was still the utterly self-assured creature they had first known. She feared no one, so she could afford to be generous. But Julia noticed that there were few times when she could be alone with her father. There was no talk that did not include Luisa. Luisa actively encouraged Jamie's visits, however short they had to be. Julia must be occupied, and Michael must not be left alone. Luisa had a way of managing Stella and Cook, lavish in praise but equally firm in dictating how *she* liked things to be done. The days of Ginette Maslova were over, though her memory would be honored. The reign of Luisa Seymour was not only begun but also well established.

A precious letter had finally reached them from Alex while Julia had been filming. Alex had made the journey to Washington through neutral Portugal and taken the risk of the Atlantic crossing, with life jacket always at the ready. She had almost the status of an accredited war correspondent because of the mission Lord Wolverton had entrusted to her. He had written letters to his friends and business acquaintances and to his military contacts, asking that Alex be granted any courtesy within their power, that she was not to be regarded just as ''a woman's writer'' but a worthy successor to her distinguished husband. He wrote to the President's press secretary, reminding him of the interview the President had granted to Greg Mathieson and suggesting that at some time Alex Seymour might be given the same privilege. *It will not be time wasted for the President. All our newspapers will carry it front page. Anything to cement the alliance.*

And, fatefully, he had written privately to his friend Elliot Forster, the proprietor of a large empire of newspapers and radio stations. *Look out for her, please. She's had a bad knock, but she's as tough as they come, and she's a good journalist. Open doors where you can.*

Chapter Five

I

WITH THE FILMING DONE, Julia was in time to witness the late-summer blooming of Ginette Maslova's rose garden. Luisa had already made sketches of how it would be extended. "We shall use the bricks from the oasthouse for a wall, and there will be gates—very beautiful wrought-iron gates with a long walk stretching back, and more high walls so it will trap all the warmth and keep out the winds. This"—she nodded to the long strip of garden—"is just the prelude."

Michael smiled at her in gratitude. "What a lovely idea, darling. I shall look forward to working on it with you."

Julia then knew that Luisa had already divined the truth about Michael Seymour. He knew little about the land and could never have endured the life of a gentleman farmer, but he could not now be parted from the Seymour lands. Luisa would add and build on, and do what she wanted, when it was possible, but it would be at Anscombe and nowhere else. Sensibly, if she wished to keep her husband, she would accept that; she appeared to have done so. By now Julia had seen pictures of the *castillo* in the hills near Granada where Luisa had been born; she had seen the château amid its vineyards that Luisa had inherited from her first husband. She knew there was a Georgian house, now a convalescent hospital, within its seven hundred acres in Gloucestershire that had belonged to Henry Radcliffe and that was now Luisa's. Whatever she chose to do with the château and the stately Georgian pile, she seemed to understand that this far more modest house would be her country house as long as she remained married to Michael Seymour.

With the summer had also come the sickening news of German successes in Russia—the siege of Sebastopol began, and in North Africa the Eighth Army once again retreated before Rommel. But at Midway in the Pacific the U.S. Navy had sunk four Japanese heavy carriers. *There is the faintest feeling here*, Alex wrote from Washington, *that in the Pacific now we just about have parity with the Japanese, but, dear God, there's such a hell of a long way to fight back—all that territory to be retaken.* The Battle of the Coral Sea in May, in which the Japanese had been defeated, seemed to have marked the limit of their advance, and Australia had been saved. *By a whisker* was Alex's comment. She seemed to have thrown herself into her new life in Washington with vigor; when the almost unknown General Eisenhower was appointed Commander in Chief, Europe, she had a piece about him ready, and it was meant for popular consumption in the British press. She had well researched his background, his family, and skirted over his lack of combat experience. He became for the British the boy of a simple background from a place called Abilene in Kansas, who had won out over all the more famous names to take the supreme job of the reconquest of Europe. *Elliot Forster arranged for me to interview Mamie Eisenhower. She doesn't seem to have the faintest idea what her husband's heading into. A nice enough, but rather unsophisticated woman.* Julia noted how often Elliot Forster's name cropped up in Alex's letters, but then, she wondered, why shouldn't it? As the owner of several hundred newspapers in the States, of radio stations, and the influential magazine *Insight*, and therefore a power in Washington, he had seemed to have taken his friend's, Lord Wolverton's, request to "open doors where you can" seriously. Greg's name was seldom in Alex's letters, because there was little or nothing to write about him. *We hear now about what hells the Japanese prison camps are. All I can hope for is his survival until they finally give in, and I know that's years away. I've had only two letters from him. I've written dozens myself. They don't seem to get through. I can't tell him how the war's going, to raise his hopes, because those letters would certainly be stopped. And what can he tell me about life in Changi that isn't perfectly awful? And they certainly wouldn't let that through. I feel so powerless to help him. I just work as hard on my stuff as I can and hope he'd approve. I keep clippings of everything I write. I tell myself one day he'll read them.* She described her small Washington apartment in a house in Georgetown. *It's near enough to the center of things, and I'm very lucky to have it. Washington's crowded to the skies, as you can well imagine, and housing's difficult. I wouldn't have got it if Elliot Forster hadn't put in a word with the woman who owns it, and who's decided to rent the top floor while her husband's serving in the Navy. Elliot took me to the Washington Press Club, where he addressed a luncheon yesterday. I was thrilled to be his guest—even though, naturally, with all the bigwigs there, I wasn't at the top table. There's so much going on here—I really feel as if I'm part of things. I was one of a dozen reporters allowed into one of Roosevelt's "off the record" press conferences in the Oval Office the other day. We can only report "unofficial sources," but everyone knows what that means. I love being here, living in a city that hasn't been bombed to pieces. But I do feel terribly guilty when I think of how comfortably I'm living, and Greg's probably half-starved.* And then her old anger broke through again. *But why the hell didn't he get out while he still could? He knew what his job was. It was to report the war, not molder in a prison camp. And I always thought he was such a clever man. Always more than one step ahead of the others in knowing which way the wind would blow. He was always such a restless soul. I can't bear to think of him caged up. . . .*

Michael read the letter with some sadness. "She's trying too damned hard. I'm glad she's not in London. Being in Washington she's not encountering memories of him around every corner and pub in Fleet Street." Before she had gone, Alex had given up the tenancy of the London flat and stored Greg's belongings. "It would have been requisitioned for someone else," she said. "You can't leave empty flats in London." Julia remembered the book-lined warren of rooms in an old house near Covent Garden and knew that its absence would be something else of a changed world Greg Mathieson would have to adapt to when he eventually returned. They also learned from Lord Wolverton that Alex had instructed that Greg's salary, which *The Record* still paid, be turned over to support his child by his first marriage. It was so easy to forget that Greg Mathieson had ever been married to anyone else but Alex.

Michael was preparing for a film—"another propaganda venture by D.D." was how he described it. "He's so certain yours is going to be a big hit, Julia, he's gotten much more ambitious

. . . it's the Navy this time. I'm supposed to be descended from a line of old sea dogs—the skipper of a destroyer escorting convoys across the Atlantic, doing the whole dramatic, heroic thing. I hope no one finds out I get slightly sick in a rowboat on a millpond on a still day. Most of it will be faked, of course, but there'll surely be times when I'll have to get out on the water. The Navy likes the idea, so we're getting full cooperation. I shall feel such a fraud. They'll have to make me look a bit younger. . . ."

There was, however, nothing for Julia at that time. Nothing in the West End was offered to her—there was no play suitable. And there were no film scripts with a part for her. "One of those empty periods," she said to Jamie. "I suppose if I were truly patriotic I would join a touring company. Get out into the provinces. It would be very useful experience. The sort of experience I've never had. But that would take me away from you. I'm a bit of a help here on the farm, and as I'm married, they can't conscript me. I can't sing or dance, so I'm useless to the ENSA concert parties. Can you imagine me standing up and reciting *The quality of mercy* . . . , etc., to a hallful of soldiers dying for a good laugh, or the sight of a shapely leg?"

"They'd whistle the roof off for your legs, my darling," Jamie said. "But I rather doubt *The quality of mercy* . . ."

"I could formally join the Land Army instead of just giving Harry Whitehand a help when it's convenient."

"And bureaucracy being what it is, you'd probably be sent to deepest Wales instead of being left right here, where you belong. But, of course, the money would make us rich. What do they pay Land Army girls, anyway?"

"One pound, eight shillings a week," Julia said promptly. "I ought to know. I hear enough about it."

Harry Whitehand now loved his Land Army girls. He had shaken his head over them at first. "What will these townies know?" Later he said to Jamie, "They're wonderful with stock— just the way Miss Julia is. I've taught some of them to drive a tractor in a day. All the jobs we thought women couldn't do. They've worked alongside me ditch-digging, and hedge-laying, up to the top of their rubber boots in water. I never thought I could work with women on a farm. Now I'm shouting to the Ministry for every one they can send."

Jamie was still leading his "circus" squadron. He didn't like the lightness the name implied, but he well understood the importance of keeping the enemy engaged and whole squadrons pinned down in France to counter the bombing raids. "We're strategically useful, and we do shoot down our share. But still, it doesn't seem like real fighting. Not like the old days . . ."

"You want to leave me, then?" Julia teased him. "Go where the big action is. You'll be here, Jamie, when it's time to invade France again. You'll get your own back for the time they pushed all of you out of France."

"I hope so," he said fervently. "There's a lot I want to get my own back for."

Michael was on location in Northern Ireland, filming the necessary background shots for *Atlantic Approaches*. Luisa had not asked to accompany him. "I wouldn't dare. Think of what they'd say about a useless wife cluttering up the scene when she should be at home doing her job." For all the fact that she seemed always present when Michael wanted her, she did manage to keep up with the Red Cross committee in London, and when at Anscombe she attended the village hall to help with the Women's Volunteer Service. "They don't mind what you do there, or who you are, as long as you do something useful." She was often at the convalescent home where Jamie had spent so many months, helping in the kitchen, writing letters for those whose injuries would not permit it, supporting those still unsteady on their feet to walk in the grounds.

"She isn't what I first thought her," Julia admitted to Jamie. "She's so much tougher, and ready to work. I thought those marvelous hands would never go into dishwater, but they do more than that."

But it was a different Luisa she discovered one morning as she started down to the kitchen for early breakfast before going out for the milking. She heard strange sounds coming from Luisa's bedroom. She hesitated a long minute before tapping on the door. There was no reply, but the choking, guttural sounds went on. So she opened the door gently and looked in. The great double bed that Luisa and Michael shared was empty, the sheets thrown back in disarray. The sounds came from the connecting bathroom. Very quietly, ready to retreat, she tiptoed forward. What she saw at the bathroom door stopped her. Luisa, in an exquisite satin and lace nightgown, was on her knees before the toilet bowl, retching almost convulsively, but her stomach now

only yielding a little bile and water. As she watched, Luisa's
hand went up to flush the bowl once more.

"Luisa . . ." Julia's voice was very hesitant. Perhaps it would
have been better if she had not come in. Whatever was wrong,
perhaps Luisa would prefer it to remain private.

The dark head turned; for once her hair was not restrained,
and fell about her shoulders and body with luxurious warmth.
But there were stray tendrils that Julia thought could not exist, and they clung to her face, wet with sweat. She collapsed
into a sitting position on the floor, one hand still holding the
bowl for support; with the other hand she weakly gestured Julia
to come to her. Julia knelt beside her.

"What is it, Luisa? Can I help?"

Julia lifted the light, slender body easily under the armpits
and supported her back to the bed, straightening the sheets and
blanket, plumping up the pillow. "Are you feeling terrible,
Luisa? Forgive me, but I couldn't help hearing—I was just going
past the door . . ." Without thinking, she put her hand to Luisa's
head, brushing back the sweat-soaked hair. "Just a minute . . ."
She went to the bathroom, wrung out a facecloth in cold water,
and grabbed a crystal jar of such size she guessed it must have
contained cologne. Very gently she bathed Luisa's face and hairline, her neck and shoulders. Then she lavished cologne on the
cloth and wiped her again.

"Ah—how kind," Luisa breathed. "How much better that
feels. I think it's over. For this morning, at any rate." Her large
brown eyes, slightly hollow and dark-ringed looked directly at
Julia. "I think . . . I hope . . . I believe I am with child."

That curiously old-fashioned expression struck Julia to the
heart. "Oh, Luisa . . ."

One of the long, pale olive hands sought hers. "For me, it is
the most wonderful thing. All my life I have wanted a baby—a
child. I hope Michael will be happy. With my first husband . . ."
she shook her head. "Then with Henry . . . for about two weeks
I thought it was possible I was pregnant. But I hadn't consulted
a doctor. And then he was killed. If I had been carrying a child,
it left me then. I was never sure . . ."

"Shall I send for the doctor . . . ?"

A weak smile lightened Luisa's face. "What? For a little
morning sickness? He has many more demands on his time. I
saw a doctor just when Michael left for filming in Northern Ire-

land. He was almost positive, but we are having tests done. From what I now know, we really don't need them.''

Julia was almost without words. ''It means a great deal to you?''

''You cannot imagine. I love your father. I know Alex finds that difficult to accept, but it is the truth. I have longed for a child—but most particularly by Michael. But, you see, I am very old to be having a first child. It will be difficult to carry this child. I realize I must be a—a sort of invalid for the whole time it takes.'' She gave a wan smile. ''I so hope it will please Michael, when he returns, to know that he will be a father again. I hope for a strong and healthy child, so I shall be very selfish and rest as much as possible, as the London doctor told me I must, if I am to carry it to full term.''

She touched Julia's arm. ''I see that the idea does not dismay you.''

''Why should it? It's the most natural thing in the world. A happy thing. Of course Father will be delighted. Why shouldn't he?''

''One never knows, my dear. At his age—at my age. Perhaps he just hoped for years of contentment, with nothing to bother him. But I so much wanted . . . but . . . ah, Julia . . .'' She relaxed back into the pillows. ''I am of a Spanish family. They regard women without children with scorn. My sisters married Spaniards, and between them they have many children. They pity me. At last . . . at last, with Michael's child . . . There is nothing more on earth I could wish for.''

Julia sat back on her heels. ''Let me help you. Let us all help you.'' How could they have ever doubted this woman—she and Alex. She absolved Connie from that judgment. This was a woman who loved her husband and longed for a child. Everything in Julia cried out in sympathy for this last hope of the exhausted woman lying on the bed.

''We shall all help. I promise you. You will have your baby—a healthy, happy baby. And my father will be so delighted. I hope it will be a boy. It would make a nice change for us all.''

The thin hand gripped Julia's again. ''You are very generous—kind . . .''

''I'll bring you up some tea. Some toast—without butter. Perhaps you'll be able to keep that down. At other times . . . well, that old saying 'You'll have to eat for two.' ''

She went downstairs, faintly bemused, wondering, as she prepared tea, what sort of difference this would make to her father's life—to all their lives. But fervently, with all the death she had witnessed, had read about, and had heard spoken of around her, she uttered little prayers for this child's life.

After a month her father returned from Northern Ireland. He took the news of the baby with, at first, silent wonderment, and then with boyish enthusiasm. "Good God!—at my age! What an old goat people will call me. It's the most marvelous thing." He said later to Julia, "Dear Luisa . . . I had no idea she wanted a baby so badly." He touched his daughter's cheek. "She tells me you have been very good to her. I would have known it, Pet, even if she had not told me."

He was working for the next two months at Ealing, finishing the film. Then her own film, *Return at Dawn*, was released. It had instant praise from the critics, and there was almost as much praise for Julia as for Audrey Fellowes. Luisa came up to London for what was called a "premiere" but was really just a first showing. Afterward, at a quiet supper—Michael insisted that everything now be quiet—at her Wilton Crescent house, with only D.D. present—Luisa observed, "I didn't realize what a good actress you are. Forgive me. Perhaps it's that I don't understand the language as well as you think I do. But in the theater I get so distracted by the people around me. I can't get lost in the play—and the intervals are a complete distraction. But there in the dark at the cinema I felt you very much. You have so little to speak—and yet so much to say. Being pregnant—the growing love for the old woman who would soon die, for the young Canadian. And that country lane, with only one figure cycling down it. The expression on your face. You photograph very beautifully, Julia. Some women who are beautiful do not photograph that way."

D.D. was exuberant. "Didn't I say it all along? Once I saw the screen tests and the first rushes, I knew we had it made. I just feel in my . . . my guts that it will be a hit in the States. And when Michael's film follows that . . ." He beamed on them all.

When Jamie came to Anscombe two weeks later, he was smiling and shaking his head. "Well, of course, it's all over the base. What did the Old Man do to deserve a film star as a wife? Really,

Julia, you're impossible to live up to now. Being a stage actress is one thing—a lot of the chaps never went to a theater in their lives. They've vaguely heard of your father, and that's about it. But the cinema—that's something different. They've all taken their girls to the one-and-sixpennies on a Saturday night. That's the big time. And your pictures in the papers and magazines. I swear that if my squadron didn't think I might spot it, some of them would have you as a pinup.''

"I'm not Betty Grable yet—nor likely to be.''

"I'd swear on oath that your legs are as good. And *she* can't act her way out of a paper bag. I wonder when I can get to see it. It wasn't very nice of you not to invite me to the first night.''

"There wasn't a 'first night.' No glamour. Did you tell them at the base that I get just as dirty every day as any other farm worker?''

"No. Why spoil the image of the beautiful Julia Seymour?''

"My name is Julia Sinclair, remember?''

A shy little note came from Castle Sinclair, from Janet. *Oh, I thought you were lovely, Mrs. Sinclair. I've been twice into Inverness now to see it. I cried my eyes out—such a sentimental body I am. Lady Jean said she would go to see it when she collected enough petrol coupons. Then Sir Niall swept up and took her off one afternoon. She didn't say very much, except that she thought it was all very good. And that you were very talented. From Lady Jean that's praise indeed. I don't think she ever expected to have so many famous people in the family— remembering your mother. Quality was what she wanted—she doesn't know what to do with fame as well.*

Jamie got a week's leave in the late days of September and demanded that they travel down to a hotel in the depths of Cornwall. "We've never been really alone, Julia. The flat in London is fine, but it still belongs to your family. And the same at Anscombe. We never had a real honeymoon. I refuse to go to Sinclair. I won't have you deferring to my mother again—though Scotland is beautiful at this time of year. But we must have a time to ourselves. . . .''

They had a week of almost perfect weather; from their small hotel they walked the lonely beaches and coves, or the clifftops where the barbed wire kept them off the beaches. They were drenched when they took a picnic lunch on Dartmoor; they lay among the heather and made love, careless of the wet and the sudden chill. They came back to dry off before the fire that the hotelkeeper had decided to light in their bedroom. He had recognized Julia from pictures in the newspapers and magazines; he respected the ribbons Jamie's uniform bore. He even sent up a complimentary bottle of champagne. "You'd think we were young lovers instead of an old married couple," Julia said.

"We *are* young lovers. Always will be."

She smiled. "Remember how it was the first time? The little cottage . . . the fire you made? How you taught me to make love?"

"Remember it, dearest. Every precious moment of it. Remember it when I'm away from you."

"You're going away?" Her voice was suddenly sharp with anxiety.

"I think so. I didn't mean to tell you. I think this is sort of embarkation leave. Only they don't tell you. You just notice a few signs of preparations for us to move out."

"Where?"

"I don't know. And if I did, I couldn't tell you. It can really only be to North Africa. There's nowhere else to send us. The Americans are running the show in the Pacific. I sort of sense they're getting ready for a big push against Rommel in the desert. But I've been at Hawkinge so long, I expected to be there when it was our turn to invade Europe. I wanted that, Julia. I wanted finally to be back on French soil again."

"North Africa! Oh, God, I won't ever see you. It's so dangerous."

"Not more dangerous than what we do almost every day here. Tempting the Luftwaffe up to meet us. I know that blasted coast so well, sometimes I almost wished I were in Bomber Command and had the chance, someday, to smash the hell out of it. The range of the fighters is so short. . . ."

But they tried to speak of war as little as possible. Rommel's destruction of Tobruk with thirty thousand men in June had been felt as a national disaster second only to the fall of Singapore. The Germans had advanced all summer along various fronts in Russia, thrusting toward Stalingrad and Rostov. But the first major victory had been won in the Pacific when the airfield the Japanese had built at Guadalcanal in the Solomons was taken. To Julia, studying the maps, it was a deadly seesaw, with Jamie's life in the balance.

"When . . ." But she let the questions about the future die on her lips and gave herself up to the joy of solitude with her husband, of loving him, of learning as much of his mind and body as she could. She sensed what she was doing—trying to store up all she could of him against a time of parting, of absence. She had begun to hate any mention of the film *Return at Dawn*. In that film her love, her husband, had not returned.

It came two weeks later, a telephone call early in the morning when Julia had just come in from milking and was hungrily eating breakfast. "Julia!" In the background there were sounds as if Jamie were making the call from the mess. "This is it, my darling. What we talked about. Can't talk about it now. I'll see you soon—sooner or later."

"I'll be waiting." There were no other words she could find to say. "I'll be waiting—for no matter how long."

II

WITH JAMIE'S GOING, a strange lassitude fell on Julia. She went about her tasks on the farm routinely, finding little now to talk to the Land Army girls about. She did the milking, drove a tractor, and mucked out and spread manure on the fields, with her mind a strange blank. She discovered after two weeks that that vital element was missing—she had nothing to look forward to. If Jamie had been sent to North Africa, then there could be no forty-eight-hour leaves, not even a few hours when they could meet in a Folkestone tearoom. It might be an endless time before his first letter came. She was hardly interested that *Return at Dawn* had opened in New York to extremely good notices. D.D. was ecstatic, telephoning her that the film had been booked into one of the major circuits. "There'll be some journalists coming down to Anscombe to interview you, darling. Don't dress up for them. Just wear those awful Land Army girl things. I want these pictures and interviews to show you as close to the girl in the film as possible. No glamour."

She went through the interviews as routinely as she did her everyday job, sometimes wondering if she wasn't playing the part of the hayseed rather too heavily. There were questions about Jamie, his DFC won in France, the bar added to it during the

Battle of Britain, questions about her relationship with her father as an actor, about her future role when she went to live at Castle Sinclair. Ginette Maslova was mentioned. Sometimes she was obliged to take some particularly well-prepared journalists on a tour of the rose garden, which was becoming famous. But the hayseed atmosphere vanished when Luisa entered, quietly announcing lunch or tea, immaculately groomed, radiating her air of distinction and sophistication. A few times her father was at home, and every interviewer craved a little time with him, wanting his opinion of *Return at Dawn,* delighting in the added spice his presence gave to the interview.

Alex wrote from Washington: *You were wonderful. I've seen it three times, and even the great Elliot Forster came once and pronounced that you were pretty good—especially playing beside someone as formidable as Audrey Fellowes. He didn't tell me, but I know from "other sources" that he's given the word that all papers and magazines are to feature articles on you. And I don't believe he's doing it because of his friendship with me. He's got too much integrity as a journalist himself for that. It would be rather the other way around. He'd almost bend over backward not to do that if he didn't believe you've got great talent. I'm proud of you—and you're still my little sister, no matter what anyone says.* Her letter did not mention Greg.

The first letter came at last from Jamie. *You can guess where we are because of the sand in the paper. Not the most comfortable bivouac, but then we got rather spoiled at home. Rather different kind of flying, too—new tricks to learn.* Then some sentences heavily inked out by the censor. Jamie had not yet learned the restraint that writing to her imposed; there had been very few letters during their marriage—mostly hurried notes or telephone calls arranging meetings. She now followed the North African campaign with special care, learning what she could from the censored dispatches of the war correspondents, learning to interpret some of what they could only hint at but not say. It was mainly tank warfare, and it was evident that the British had been heavily supplied with American vehicles. They heard a great deal about a place called El Alamein and, finally, a great victory there. Then came the great operation that they would learn was code-named Torch, the invasion of northwestern Africa in a joint exercise by British and American troops under Eisenhower. Julia wondered where Jamie was in all of this great operation. She had only one message to send him: *We are going to have a baby.*

The news was received with hoots of laughter by her father. "My dear, how absolutely wonderful! But it's the damnedest thing—both my wife and my daughter pregnant at the same time." But he was delighted and solicitous at the same time. "Pet, you must stop all this farm work at once. It's too heavy. I won't permit it, and when I told Harry Whitehand, he was absolutely in agreement. If one of his Land Army girls got pregnant, he'd send her straight back home. Can't have you dropping the baby in the field like a calf. Take up knitting, like Luisa— that will have to be your war effort until the baby's born. And put away those scripts D.D. keeps sending you. Filming's tough work. There'll be plenty of that after the baby's born. Think of it—my first grandchild!"

Luisa heard the news with a gratified smile and the hint of tears in her eyes. "Ah, my dear—so wonderful, Jamie will be so pleased." Luisa was having a difficult time as her pregnancy advanced and had given up going to London altogether, and even to her WVS work at the Anscombe village hall. On the orders of her Harley Street doctor, she rested most of the day. "He told me," Luisa confessed to Julia, "that that was not what he told most of his 'mothers.' A healthy amount of exercise was desirable, even helpful. But I am an 'elderly'—oh, I can't remember what word he used, but it means that I'm very old to be having a first child. And there's been that little bit of 'spotting'—which is a bad sign. Michael is for putting me to bed altogether until the baby's born, but I have insisted that a gentle walk in the garden every day is necessary, and I shall not die of it. So I walk around the rose garden several times, and wherever else I am permitted that's within sight of the house. And I always know Stella is watching me from one of the windows. You must follow my diet—it seems to work." Luisa ate a number of small meals a day, as much fruit and vegetables as could be managed. "Never let yourself be hungry, my dear. It only brings back the sickness. . . ."

However cheerful her talk, Luisa did not now look well. Her faintly olive skin had grown sallow, her eyes more deeply recessed, with dark smudges under them. She kept saying that she felt well, and she ate her small meals regularly, without protest. Her slight body seemed overburdened with the weight of the child. She found it difficult to sleep, appeared always weary. But the first weeks of 1943 were brightened with the news of Allied victories in North Africa and Russia, the collapse of Japanese resistance in Burma. Michael had refused any further stage or film work so he could be with Luisa.

Two letters came from Jamie on the same delivery, one written weeks before the other. *We're pretty busy, as you probably know, but unless I'm in the thick of it, I hardly think of anything else but you and the baby. Do take good care of yourself, my darling love. I wish more than ever I hadn't been sent abroad. I find myself imagining all kinds of things—teaching him to ride and fish, walking in the forest with him. Almost for the first time in my life I'm glad of Castle Sinclair. It begins to mean something other than a burden that my mother has carried for me. Now I'll work it cheerfully, because it will be for our son.*

Supposing it isn't a son? Julia wrote.

His next letter, which didn't reach her until almost the end of January, replied, *Don't worry. There'll be others. One of them's bound to be a boy.* She worried about this deeply clannish streak in him, hitherto unrevealed. He did care far more about his inheritance than she had suspected. It would figure very prominently in the way their child was brought up. This had been no light, wartime marriage, made in haste, with the future still to be discovered. The future lay there ahead of them both, in Scotland, at Sinclair.

Letters came from Alex full of her doings in Washington. They often read her pieces in Wolverton's papers at home; she sent the clippings of the pieces she wrote that appeared in American newspapers. She had sent clippings of the articles published about Julia and *Return at Dawn*. The letters were bright, growing more hopeful as she studied the turn of events in the Pacific, North Africa, and Russia. *Someday,* she wrote, *someday we'll wake up and find the tide really has turned. I hear so little from Greg. I suppose it's as much as he's allowed to write. But one hears such horror stories of the Japanese prison camps. . . .*

In a letter to Julia, she added a page marked *For you only.* It was a cry of pain and guilt. *Don't tell Father or Connie. But I can't keep it to myself another moment. Elliot Forster separated from his wife two months ago. They have agreed on a divorce. I really don't think she cares very much, just so long as she gets enough money. He wants to marry me as soon as the divorce is final. And I want to marry him. I'm so ashamed and sickened by my betrayal of Greg. I thought it could never happen. Wasn't my love strong enough to bear this time of separation? I thought it would last forever. I am miserable, and yet everything about Elliot compels and commands me. He's so dynamic, and I suppose just sheer sexual hunger, the sense of aloneness, was too much for me. I don't feel proud to be writing this. I find myself praying about it, trying to rationalize it—square it—with God. And yet all I hear is the cry from the Garden of Gethsemane "Could you not wait and watch one hour with me?" I have loved two men, but Elliot is here, alive, in the flesh, my lover. Greg has become a shadow. I look at his photo every day and know that that man no longer exists. Whatever emerges from that terrible place, Changi, will be a different person, someone I no longer know. He cannot have come through that experience unchanged, and I also have changed. But one thing I have promised myself, and told Elliot. I will not, until Greg is released, write this to him, nor will I divorce, and marry Elliot—not if it takes years for Greg to be free. Not even if I lose Elliot over it. I just cannot write that sort of letter to a man in a prison camp. But it is becoming harder and harder to write to him at all, knowing that I am lying by not telling him. So I will have to go on lying. But most of the time I despise myself—except for the times when I'm with Elliot. Then Greg slips even farther into the background. But I am a woman in love, and I don't know how to deny it.*

Julia found tears both of anger and pity in her eyes. How their destinies were all shaped by the men they loved; such different futures stretched before her and her sisters. Perhaps Connie would be the only one to experience an untroubled love, an unquestioning faith, the only one not to see any life apart from her husband's stretching before her. If they both survived the war, she and Ken Warren would marry, and thereafter Connie would happily submerge her identity in his. Julia found herself almost envying the thought of such an uncomplicated future. For Connie there would be no storm of torn loyalties, or conflict of ambitions or interests. If Ken Warren were lucky enough to keep her, he would have the perfect wife.

Although Luisa's baby was not due until February, in January Michael moved her back to the Wilton Crescent house so that she could be near her doctor. There was an unspoken anxiety in

Michael and Julia about her; she looked so frail and thin, despite the mound of her belly. Her cheeks had long, hollow lines drawn down them. "She looks as if she's starving," Stella once whispered to Julia. "And yet I know she chokes down every mouthful she can. I've never known a woman to want a child so much. And I think she's really a little older than she says. . . ."

At the end, Luisa asked Julia to come to London with them. "I've grown to depend on your company. I know I am such poor company for Michael—but at least in London he will be able to see his friends. I am selfish—yes? I want to take you away from the good country air, and back to London. But it's only for a few weeks. I would be forever grateful. . . ."

But it was not for weeks. They had been installed in the Belgravia house, with Stella and the old butler-chauffeur, along with Agnes, who had been taken on by Luisa when Michael had given up his flat, for only a few days when Luisa went into labor, which was four weeks premature. Michael rushed her to the Harley Street Clinic. She labored there almost a day and a half, with Julia and Michael taking turns to sit with her, bathing her face and shoulders, trying to comfort her, she panting and sometimes crying out in pain. In Michael's presence she tried valiantly to stifle the cries, because his sense of guilt and fear was very plain. "I should never . . ."

Luisa smiled weakly. "I shall soon have my heart's desire. I shall have our child."

Finally the doctor said he could no longer postpone a cesarean section. "She just doesn't have the strength to endure any more of this. The baby seems well—alive, kicking, struggling to be born. In the right position. I don't like a forceps delivery. Might damage the child—and your wife's not up to it. Just one swift cut and it will be all over."

Luisa had been afraid of an anesthetic harming the baby, but Michael made the decision for her. The baby, a boy, was born well and healthy, though weighing just less than five pounds. Luisa woke from the anesthetic, and tears came when she learned she could not hold her baby or nurse him. A day later she viewed him in the incubator and held out her arms imploringly toward him. "Not yet, my darling," Michael said. "He must be a little stronger—and you must, also."

There was more anxiety about Luisa than the baby. "Has she ever had rheumatic fever?" the doctor asked. "If so, she never told me. Her heart always sounded healthy enough. But she's been seriously weakened by this struggle—just the struggle to hold on to the baby all these months. Of course, she must never try to have another."

But two weeks passed; the baby gained weight, and Luisa came back from the pale and shadowy world she had seemed to inhabit. Remembering the quick recovery of Ginette after the births of their three children, Michael was puzzled and upset. Luisa became strong enough to laugh at his anxieties. "Oh, don't worry, my darling. I come of a strong line. It's just that I am so old. Older than I believe I told you. Old enough to make it a kind of madness to have a first child. But perhaps age and longing have made me . . ." She laughed, for the first time with the sound of real laughter. "Perhaps I am a little mad. But now . . . now I shall have the joy of you and the baby as well."

"If a baby was all you wanted, you should have picked a younger man," Michael said, his tone gruff with emotion.

"I wanted you first," she said. "The baby is an added blessing." Neither of them seemed to care that Julia was present as they spoke.

They stayed two more weeks in London so that Luisa and the baby could be seen by her doctor. Then he ordered her back to Anscombe. "And if you know what's good for you and the baby you won't come back here until things are very changed. Stay where the air is clean, where you have plenty to eat, and there's no chance of air raids." Occasionally the Luftwaffe did return to the major cities, to shake and send the population back to the hated shelters. But over the southeastern coast the fighting had virtually stopped, except when the fighter squadrons went up to intercept the enemy. They still heard the planes overhead, but they were no longer troubled by the rain of falling planes in the fields around them. Tentatively, Michael had suggested to Luisa that they take up the small part of the Gloucestershire mansion not occupied as a convalescent hospital. She firmly refused. "You would never be happy there, and we would probably be very uncomfortable. It is large"—she shrugged—"difficult. Anscombe is small and warm, and we have all the things there that our child will grow to love. It is *your* home. It will be his greatest, best inheritance. . . ."

She could have said, Julia thought, nothing to please Michael more. The affection he had had for Luisa now turned to a kind of adoration that included the child so unexpectedly brought into his life. "A son . . ." he mused to Julia. "I had always thought it would be a girl. An addition to my family of girls. I hardly see myself as the father of a baby son. What shall I do with him . . . ? By the time he's twenty I'll . . . I'll be an old man."

"He will keep you young. You will never be an old man."

And once he knew that Luisa and the child were well, he went vigorously back to the stage. He went into a new comedy by an author who was well tried and popular. "Just for a change . . ." He played the part of a man many years younger than he, and he played it convincingly. Julia marveled at his youthfulness, his lighthearted attitude onstage and off. "You have renewed him," she said to Luisa, "you and the baby." Michael could now come to Anscombe on Sundays only. In London he went to a gym every day, reshaping himself for the role D. D. had persuaded him it was time he played once more, Hamlet. "You now truly understand what madness and death are, my friend. You can make yourself look like the young Hamlet. But you will play him as the veteran actor of—dare I say it, or will you demand twice the money?—an actor who approaches genius."

"You Hungarian liar" was Michael's comment. "You are a flatterer of genius."

With patience and serenity, Julia waited out the days and months until the birth of the baby early in July. She liked to be with Luisa and her baby, who had been named John Carlos. "There cannot be two Michael Seymours," Luisa said. "John is a good English name, and my father will be very pleased to be so remembered." Julia eagerly watched the development of the baby and helped to care for him, glad of the chance to learn how to care for her own.

She hardly seemed to notice when it was announced with some excitement in the press that she had been nominated for a Hollywood Oscar for best supporting actress. It also came as some surprise to her when fairly sizable sums of money began to come to her through D.D.'s office. At the time she had been making the film she had been paid the nominal scale and had expected nothing more. It had been part of learning her trade, and she had been grateful for the experience. She had barely noticed the clause in her contract that gave her a tiny share of the gross once the initial investment had been earned back. The unexpected success of the film in the States had made the vital difference. *I'm glad to hear you're earning some money while you're sitting still waiting for the baby,* Alex wrote. *But don't forget that Luisa is earning far more, since she put up about half the backing for it.* Julia privately thought Luisa was entitled to every penny of it for backing such a dark horse. She put the money into the bank, thinking of what things it would buy for her child. Luisa scolded her for being so simple. "Let me introduce you to some of my friends who understand money. They will increase it for you, I guarantee. It is only a small amount, but they will do it as a favor for me."

Julia agreed, but would part with only half the money in each check. She realized she was naïve about money, but the local bank seemed so safe; she hated to see so much of it disappear into others' hands, to be invested in ways she did not understand. Both her father and mother had always spent whatever money they earned; she vaguely remembered that her grandfather Guy had by long years of thrift and modest living finally paid off the debts his father had accumulated. Perhaps her mother had inherited something on the deaths of her parents, but as they also had been prodigal spenders, she doubted if it could have been much. Now, for the first time, she realized she was close to someone to whom money meant large amounts, amounts to be worked and manipulated, amounts that turned into ever larger amounts. It awed her slightly and made her take the advice Luisa proffered. But she said nothing about money in her letters to Jamie. She knew instinctively that it would upset him; he wanted to be the provider for his wife and child. He accepted the fact that she lived at her father's home, and he knew the allowance from his salary as squadron leader would provide anything extra she needed. That part seemed normal to him, just as if she had been at Castle Sinclair. He was, in that respect, she thought, just as old-fashioned as Ken Warren.

March, while it brought encouraging news from all the theaters of war, was also the worst month recorded for sinking of Allied shipping in the Atlantic. So much of naval support had been diverted to the North African campaign, trying to protect the vital supply lines, that the Atlantic convoys were more and more at the mercy of the vastly increased German U-boat packs. Julia knew that Jamie must be somewhere involved in the Allied thrust to take Tunisia, but he never wrote from which point.

Roosevelt's declaration at the Casablanca Conference with Churchill that only "unconditional surrender" would be accepted had served to strengthen the German resolve—both in fighting and enduring the increasing bombing of their homeland. This time, unlike the First World War, there would be no armistice.

But March also brought to Julia the nearly unbelievable news that she had won an Academy Award for best supporting actress. The news came on the first bulletin they listened to while they ate breakfast in the kitchen. Julia's mouth dropped open with a look of such complete surprise that Stella began to laugh. "Didn't you ever think what's bred in the bone won't come out? It's early days yet for you to be winning awards, but remember your father and mother were winning them all their lives. Remember it, my girl. You have a lot to do yet in life to come up to your parents. But still . . ." She rose from her seat and came around the table to plant one of the rare kisses Julia could remember from her on her cheek. "But perhaps I didn't remember to tell you that *I* thought you were very good, too. Of course, my opinion counts far more than any of those people out in Hollywood. Who do they think they are, anyway? Just a lot of film people. You are an actress—"

The door burst open and Luisa, who was still ordered by her doctor to rest in bed each day until at least ten o'clock, was there, hair flowing, her dressing gown open, the baby, Johnny, a yelling bundle in her arms.

"It is marvelous—*marvelous!*" She flung an arm around Julia and nearly dropped the baby. Julia rose and pushed Luisa down into a chair. "You mustn't excite yourself, Luisa."

"Why not to excite myself?" she demanded, momentarily losing her almost total command of English. "It is a moment of great excitement! Stella, perhaps some champagne? With orange juice, of course." The canned orange juice, as carefully guarded as the champagne in the cellar, came from the States. "Oh, I am so delighted. Michael will be overjoyed. You—his favorite child."

Julia laid her hand on the yelling baby in Luisa's lap. "Not any longer. And I don't mind giving way to this one."

D.D. telephoned almost at once. "I realize, darling, that you didn't seem to think a thing of it when you were nominated. But that you *won*—it will be a big help at the box office."

Dame Audrey Fellowes telephoned. "You thoroughly deserved it, child.'' Calls came from other actors, and even some she barely remembered from RADA. After the six o'clock news, Connie phoned. "I've known about it all day, but I've been on duty, but bursting to talk to you. Ken has just telephoned. He sends his congratulations. I think he was too shy to call you directly. He says he's beginning to get rather frightened of our family.''

"Frightened?''

"Too much talent—and money—around. In a way I'm glad I have him to myself because I feel he doesn't mind that I'm not like the rest of you.''

"Oh, Connie! You're the best of us! The brightest, the nicest—the most beautiful.''

"Oh, I don't hold a candle to any of you—but I'm so happy this has happened. So proud. I'm so happy Father has Luisa and the baby. There's so much unhappiness in the world, I'm so grateful for the precious bits of happiness we have. If only Alex had Greg back . . . Do you think Jamie knows about it yet? They must listen to news broadcasts wherever he is. It's been on every news broadcast today. Something to cheer people up. 'Britain can make it as well as take it' sort of thing. Must go, darling. There's a line waiting for the phone, and I've run out of change. . . . I'll be down to see you all as soon as possible.''

Did Jamie know? Julia wondered. He must, in some way. She knew he would be pleased, and yet a little troubled, as this must seem inevitably to draw her a little more into the world of theater and films and farther from the world they intended to inhabit together. But he would put his doubts aside, as she would. In time everything would be worked out.

The surprise call of the day came from Lady Jean. "I am told by Janet that she will immediately hand in her notice if I do not congratulate you at once. Truth to tell, Julia, we *have* been trying at various times during the day and were never able to get through. The news is all over the estate. It's been on the local Inverness news. Now, that is real fame up here, Julia. Believe me. I never thought I'd care a hoot about who won what in Hollywood, but so close to home, it's different. Sir Niall also sends his congratulations. He's been trying to get through to you, also. As excited about it as a schoolboy. You have won a true friend there, Julia. I hope you will remember that in the future—if you should happen to need him.''

"I'll remember it," Julia said, a mood of somberness suddenly falling on her with the realization that in some way she had managed to touch the imagination and pride of a people so far away whom she had barely met, but people who would be a great part of her life in the future. It seemed as if she had been partially forgiven for not being Scottish. She went to bed but was unable to sleep. Someone unknown to her, one of D.D.'s Hollywood friends, had been present to accept the award in the unlikely event that it came to her. D.D. had believed in and hoped for what she had barely thought about. What had it been like? she wondered. A glittering occasion? Or quiet, because it was wartime? But a humble little film, made on a shoestring, was, momentarily, famous. She was momentarily famous. It was almost dawn before she slipped into sleep, exhausted by excitement and emotion. In one sense she felt fraudulent; the director, whom she had resented because he had demanded so much, should have had the award, not she.

The renewal of life came, as always, with the spring. Daffodils, planted many years ago and multiplying into thousands, bloomed beneath the swelling buds of the orchard trees; the lambs born in January and February, and now independent of their mothers, gamboled across the spring-green meadows. Julia listened to her mother's recordings and hoped the baby within her would bear some imprint of Ginette Maslova. Luisa's baby thrived, and so did Luisa. The gauntness of her pregnancy had left her; the bloom that should have been hers then, now came to her. She was kind to Julia, heaping the best of the things that came in the packages sent from America by her friends, and by Alex, upon her. She herself washed Julia's long hair in luxurious shampoo. One of her friends, whose children had outgrown their nanny, sent that lady, Brenda Turnbull, to help with the care of Johnny and the baby who soon would be born. Stella was indignant. "Doesn't she think I'm capable of taking care of children? I've done it all my life—from the day Miss Alex was born, and before." Remembering how many years ago that was, Julia was, for the first time, struck with the fact that Stella herself had aged. Why did one not notice this in the people one was always with? For a few days there was a constraint and a sense of resentment around the kitchen table. But gradually Stella relinquished what had been her first job at Anscombe, since Luisa now always referred to her as "our housekeeper." Brenda Turnbull was wise enough to bide her time until Stella's hostility had dampened. With skill and ease she looked after Johnny and talked eagerly of the time when Julia's baby would be born. "My father was Scottish," she said. "How Lady Jean must be looking forward to having a grandchild." She appeared to know the history of that branch of the Sinclair clan well. Again Julia marveled at how the rich could still find servants such as Brenda Turnbull at a time when more and more women were directed into factories, if not drafted into the forces. Stella and Cook were beyond being drafted into anything, and their tasks in helping run a farm were "reserved." Somehow Luisa must have gotten Brenda Turnbull into this favored position. Michael didn't ask questions about this; he just rejoiced that Luisa could enjoy her hours with their son without being overtired and that there would be someone to help with Julia's baby when it arrived and who would be there if Julia should, when she was ready, take another stage role or another film. They had a smooth time, Julia thought, for people in the midst of war, and felt some guilt over it. Agnes and the aged chauffeur-butler kept the Belgravia house running for whenever it was needed. It was a little world of privilege that Julia slightly mistrusted, feeling it could not last.

April came—Julia wondered again why T. S. Eliot had called it "the cruelest month." Everything about her bloomed and flowered, and her spirit felt at ease. Calmly she awaited the coming of the baby, reading and rereading Jamie's letters. The first that related to the Academy Award reached her.

I don't know quite what to make of it. Marriage to a film star was something I hardly bargained for. Will you ever be content with the humble life, which is all I can offer you? Was I ever the callow youth who rushed up the aisle and threw roses to you at Lear? Now I would lay them at your feet, if I could find them in this roseless, war-blasted land. But the rose of our love grows within you, my darling. Then he quoted from memory from Yeats, something that surprised her. *Had I the heavens' embroidered cloths . . .* And on to the end. *Tread softly because you tread on my dreams.* She saw from the first word that the censor's hand had hovered over the whole poem, perhaps wondering if it was some kind of code. But he had relented. She savored it. How much she didn't know yet about Jamie. She remembered how he had talked of his dreams as they picnicked on the bluff overlooking the loch and Castle Sinclair. The pros-

pect of the years of discovery before her seemed only the sweeter.
She didn't care if she never stood on a stage again, never made
another film. She had a husband, a child, and an abundant future.

How could anything so cruel come out of the perfect peace
of a warm April afternoon when she and Luisa, with Johnny at
their feet in the antique cradle in which all three sisters had been
rocked, sat having afternoon tea on the bench by the budding
rose garden? They didn't see whoever it was who brought the
telegram. All they knew was Stella's hesitant walk across the
grass toward them; she held the envelope behind her back until
the last moment. Silently she handed it to Julia.

*The Ministry of Defense deeply regrets to inform you that
Squadron Leader James Sinclair has been killed in action. . . .*

His death had occurred on the fiercely fought Mareth Line
only weeks before all vestiges of Axis resistance in Africa ended.
Later, Julia found it impossible to forgive time for what she
considered a monumental blunder.

When Julia became aware of external things besides her dry
grief, April had handed to them its own fickle punishment. Rain-
storms swept across the green meadows. Ewes and lambs huddled against the hedgerows for shelter. But the air was sweet and
clean, rain-washed, as if no ugliness such as death could be-
smirch its purity. She lay on her bed, her hands placed against
the child in her belly, guarding it as if death could strike here
also. She hoped Jamie's death had come in one rapid burst of
fire. She hoped he had not lived to ride with his stricken craft
down to the inevitable end in the barren soil of such a foreign
place. He had been a man of mountains and of a green but harsh
land, a man who had known the loch in its calm and its savage
moods. But his death had come in the desert. The same kind of
arid hardness grew in her as the tears of grief refused to come.
She had to endure for the child's sake, because that was all of
James Sinclair that survived. She had to endure so that one day
the child might know the land of its father.

They were very quiet in the house at Anscombe. After the
first few hours they did not attempt words of sympathy, because
the words seemed to fall on stony ground. Gestures were made
toward her—an extra effort to tempt her with little luxuries at

meals. The very best wine was brought from the cellar. She ate and drank because she knew she must. Her father took two nights off from *Hamlet,* in which he had just scored a triumph—two nights he could not afford, since his understudy was not what the audience had paid to see. What it all lacked, Julia thought, was the ceremony that usually accompanied a death. There was no body to be laid in earth. That, if there had indeed been a body left in the wreck of the plane, had been done hastily and with scant ceremony, which the war raging about them and the heat of that alien place demanded. At last Julia consented to a memorial service in the church in Anscombe, but a service of her own devising. The vicar, with some puzzlement, agreed. It had enough of the traditional things to rank as a religious service. They sang the Twenty-third Psalm, Julia choking on the words. The lesson was read—she asked Harry Whitehand to do this, and his broad Kentish accent seemed to bring them close to the land she loved and for which Jamie had, ultimately, died. Then her father went to the pulpit and read the last words Jamie had written to her:

> Had I the heavens' embroidered cloths,
> Enwrought with golden and silver light,
> The blue and the dim and the dark cloths
> Of night and light and the half-light,
> I would spread the cloths under your feet:
> But I, being poor, have only my dreams;
> I have spread my dreams under your feet;
> Tread softly because you tread on my dreams.

After that, on a portable gramophone at the back of the church, was played Ginette Maslova's piano recording of Chopin's Second Sonata. When it was ended, Julia rose, walking between her father and Luisa. The village congregation was puzzled and disappointed. Where had been the words to commemorate one of the heroes of the Battle of Britain, James Sinclair, DFC and bar? Where had been the rousing, stirring music, the music that made everyone feel that the sacrifice had been worthwhile? This eccentric ending to the service upset some and convinced others that Julia had hardly cared about her young husband. It was said she had not yet shed a tear over him. She had been the waxen image of beauty as she had walked from the church. The late

April sun, returning as if to grace this strange event, bathed her face and dark-golden hair with warmth. Her swollen body and palely etched features gave her a Madonna-like look. She carried last Easter lilies in her hands and wore no hat but some dark, veillike thing of lace that did not cover her face. They were not to know it had been borrowed from Luisa and was a symbol of Spain. She laid the flowers on her mother's grave and set off to walk the mile back to Anscombe.

At Anscombe they served tea and sandwiches and discreet whiskey to those who had come a long way, from London and farther. A number of the press had followed the walking procession to the house, and some of them had managed to pass themselves off as Alex's or Greg's friends. They wanted to know the reason for and the origin of the poem Sir Michael had read. Some of them had managed to take it down in shorthand; it would appear in some of the papers the next day. Julia sat on a sofa flanked by her father and Luisa and would talk to no one.

D.D. and Lord Wolverton were there, Connie had a forty-eight-hour pass, and Ken Warren had managed to get away from London to be present. He gravely took Julia's hand and said nothing, which she thought displayed exquisite taste. Slowly the people left. The late April evening light flooded through the windows where Julia had stood when Jamie's plane had plowed into the oasthouse.

When they were all gone, and only her father, Luisa, and Connie were left, Julia said, "Now that that is done, I will go to Scotland. Our baby will be born where Jamie was born."

Nothing they said could dissuade her—arguments that the journey was impossible for a woman in her stage of pregnancy in the wartime-crowded trains, that she would be better to rest at Anscombe surrounded by the people who loved her, who had cared for her since childhood. Her baby would be delivered at the cottage hospital when the time came, or, if she preferred, at the Harley Street Clinic where Luisa had been so skillfully delivered, they argued. She just shook her head. "It is what Jamie would have liked, though he never did ask it. It is what I want. When our child grows up, I want it to know where it belongs."

"Surely any child of yours belongs as much here as up there." Her father's jerk of his head indicated what he considered a barbaric land beyond reaching or understanding.

"None of you understand. I have to go to where the child's home will always be. Jamie's only child. If it is a girl, that branch of the clan will have died with him. If it is a boy, that is where he should grow up. It's better that he comes into the world knowing that."

Her father said, "Then there's nothing I can do but take you up there myself. . . ."

"I'll manage. You can't be away from the play that long. I wouldn't permit that."

"Then why, for pity's sake, are you doing it at all? Driving me out of my mind with worry?"

"Brenda would be glad to go with Julia," Luisa said, "if that's what she's determined upon. Though I wish . . . Ah, the two babies could grow up here together, like brothers. Why take him away from all this, Julia?"

"Because he belongs up there. He has to know his inheritance."

The matter was solved when she telephoned Lady Jean to tell her of her decision. "You and your child would be welcome here, of course." Nothing in her tone to indicate pleasure, nothing to tell Julia that she was not making a mistake. With Jamie's death, perhaps Lady Jean had thought his life completely finished. She did not speak of the child's inheritance, or the continuation of a name. Her last words were, "I will see what arrangements can be made."

An hour later, Sir Niall telephoned. "I will be privileged," he said in his old-fashioned manner, "to come to London to escort you to Sinclair. These wartime trains are no place for a pregnant woman without a man to fight for a seat for her." Then he added, "Lady Jean is almost beside herself. She thought all that was Jamie was gone from her forever. Never for a moment did she consider that you would actually wish the child to be born at Sinclair, in Jamie's home, in his country. She made the mistake of thinking of you as a foreigner. If she sounded strange to you, my dear, think no more about it. She is dumbfounded. She had no words to say to you. I know her so well. . . . I will telephone when I know my final arrangements. But it will be within days. We cannot have you delivering the future laird of Sinclair in a Durham waiting room."

Sir Niall came and spent one night in Luisa's Belgravia house. Luisa came up to London for the occasion and was with Michael

when they went to the train together very early the next morning.
They hoped, with luck, that they might reach Inverness the same
day, though Sir Niall was definite in his promise that if they
were held up by heavy military traffic on the lines, or even a
bombing raid, he would take Julia off the train and find hotel
accommodations somewhere. He was wearing an immaculately
cut suit of ancient vintage, in tough Harris tweed, and he carried
the cane he usually used when he walked the hills and moors.
"You see," he said jokingly, "I am ready to defend her, and
her seat, from all comers." He looked askance at all the luggage
that came with her.

"I couldn't help it. Those are mostly things for the baby.
Luisa's got so much from American friends—good warm things.
Shawls, diapers, blankets. And people have given up coupons
to knit things. I couldn't leave them behind. . . ." He nodded,
and he and Michael pushed their way into a first-class coach
with the bags, which took up a whole luggage rack. Other people
scrambled on after them. But Sir Niall had triumphantly secured
a window seat for Julia. She kissed her father and Luisa good-
bye and asked them not to wait. Trains were so often late in
leaving.

Julia saw her father's eyes bright with threatened tears. "It's
not too late. You don't have to go. . . ."

"I have to go."

It was a long day on the train, with people crowding the corridors and waiting in line for the rest rooms. Very occasionally
it was possible to buy food at the stations, but Luisa had packed
a bag with food that would have lasted them for two days. She
had provided several thermoses of tea, which Sir Niall tried to
get refilled at every station, and four half bottles of wine. Sir
Niall offered sandwiches and crackers around the compartment,
but most people, seeing the obviously pregnant woman who
might have needed them, refused. Some were offended by the
sight of so much food and disdained to touch any of it. Sir Niall
had no difficulty disposing of it to the rows of servicemen, with
their duffel bags, who stood in the corridors. Then someone
recognized Julia, linked her with the face in the papers. Many
did not know her husband had been killed, and pieces of paper
were passing for autographs. Sir Niall wanted to protest, to ask
for her to be left in peace, but she refused that. "It's part of the
whole thing," she said. "They stand out there, hour after hour,

probably hungry and thirsty, and look in at us eating and drinking. A lot of them have seen *Return at Dawn*. All they ask for is a signature on a scrap of paper. Jamie would be ashamed of me if I didn't give at least that."

He nodded but then added, "I hope, my dear, that you won't live your whole life by some idealized pattern of what you think Jamie might have wanted. He was a remarkably brave and likable young man, but in most respects quite ordinary. You're not going to put him on a pedestal, are you?"

She had no answer.

They changed trains at Edinburgh. The last train to Inverness was getting up steam as they hurried toward it, Sir Niall having commandeered the only, elderly porter in sight by the sheer act of bribery—of holding out a pound note. When the guard, in the dimness of the platform, perceived that it was a pregnant woman trying to keep up with the porter, he held his flag and his whistle until he was sure she was safely on board and seated. They had no difficulty over seats. Few people were traveling at that hour of the night from Edinburgh into the heart of the Highlands.

It was after one o'clock when they reached Inverness. Sir Niall's hands helped Julia from the train, but soon, in that darkness, she felt Lady Jean's hand under her elbow. With surprise she felt her cheek brushed with the swiftest of kisses.

"Welcome home."

She passed the next two months in an almost dazed state. Her body grew almost unbelievably heavy and clumsy; her ankles were swollen. She went to a specialist in Inverness and made arrangements for the baby to be born in a hospital there. He had refused her urgent request that the baby be born at home. "This is wartime," he said brusquely, as if Julia hadn't known it. "We are very short-staffed. I could not make that journey myself, and we cannot spare a midwife to wait around. . . ." It was the local general practitioner, Dr. MacGregor, from Langwell, who saw her regularly. "You're good and strong—well nourished—a young woman. The right time to be having a baby." Julia spent almost all her time in the housekeeper's room, where they both sat and ate their meals. Janet kept a fire going there, whether it seemed necessary or not. Each day Julia set off on a walk across the drawbridge, and the arched bridge that led to the land, along the road though the forest to the little cottage where she and

Jamie had sealed their love. She would have preferred to be alone, but Lady Jean insisted on accompanying her. "Exercise is all very well—and beneficial. But this is such a potholed excuse for a road. If you fell—or—or something else happened, there's only the faintest chance of any casual traffic—only the farm machinery, or Mr. Kerr in the car. I should only be waiting for you, in any case. You have not come this far to miscarry. I cannot have your family say that you have been neglected. Not .cared for . . ."

That was about as far as Lady Jean could let herself go in expressing her feelings. She never mentioned Jamie's name, but Julia thought that it was from stoicism, an indulgence she would not permit herself. Julia shared with her the letter she received from Jamie's Commanding Officer, giving a brief description of the action in which he had lost his life. *He took protective action to shield a brother officer whose plane was already under attack from two enemy fighters, at very great risk to himself. He paid for that act of gallantry with his life. His brother officer, although badly wounded, managed to bring his plane down safely and has survived. To mark this action of extreme bravery, witnessed by several other men engaged in the battle, I intend to recommend that he be decorated posthumously. Since he had already been decorated with the DFC and bar, I think the Distinguished Service Order might be considered. May I add, along with my deep sympathy, the certainty that he was not only respected and admired by the whole squadron he led so outstandingly, but also was held in true affection by most of them. He is missed, as the brave and the true always are. Had he survived this campaign, I am certain he would have received promotion to Wing Commander.*

Julia saw Lady Jean's lips twist, as if she struggled to control their trembling. Silently she laid the letter on the table and left the room.

Almost all of the last month Julia spent sitting with her legs, which were becoming alarmingly swollen, propped up on one of the sofas in the housekeeper's room. Janet came frequently from the kitchen to inquire if she would like a cup of tea or "a wee bite to eat?" Packages arrived almost daily from Luisa and Alex—more baby clothes, cans of jam, and crackers. "Do they not understand that we are a farm here, and not short of a thing or two?" But Janet did exclaim over the soap and shampoo and talcum powder and some of the exquisitely lace-trimmed baby garments. *All my sisters are knitting ferociously for this first grandchild of my husband,* Luisa wrote. Julia wondered how these women found the energy or inclination to do so for an unknown woman when they had all just come through their own tragic, bitter civil war in Spain. Letters as well as packages came from Alex. *I am very busy, and just as well, because I don't have much time to think of anything but the job. If I think about Greg, I grow frightened and guilty and depressed. I've not heard from him for over five months. Does he sense my letters are mostly fakes? He's quite clever enough to be able to divine that, however I labor to make them seem normal. But can I pretend I live here like a nun, when he must guess I don't? It's difficult not to bring Elliot's name into every other sentence, and yet never to mention him would look wrong, too. I'm so in love, Julia—I really believe that. And yet so unsure. Elliot keeps pressing me to tell Greg. A divorce would be swift if I wanted to make it so. But it also could kill Greg. I just hope one of his Fleet Street pals, over here on assignment, doesn't take it into his head to write about the gossip that's all over Washington about me and Elliot. Surely no one could be so cruel. I think of you often, my dear little sister, bearing your child and your sorrow, and wish I could help. Part of me thinks you mad for rushing off to your Highland wilderness, and yet I do believe I understand the reasons why you have done it. It is just the romantic, foolish, wonderful gesture you would make. If, someday, I have Elliot's children, I hope I will love them to that degree.*

After the first night, Julia, at her own request, slept in the Red Tower Room.

Lady Jean asked, "Would you not be more comfortable in a room—well, at least a *smaller* room? Even one of these down here, near the kitchen, and Janet, even though they're really only servants' rooms—"

"Ah," Janet interrupted, "let her have her way. Pregnant women do have strange fancies. I always knew Mrs. Sinclair had strong feelings for the Red Tower Room, as if she had known it for a long time. But I'll just be taking up residence for a while in the wee room beyond—and the bathroom's only a step beyond that. I'll leave a wee bell so you can ring if you want me during the night."

"Well," Lady Jean said, "as it's summer, I can see your preference for a light, airy room, with the sight of the sky and the loch. And with Janet near you . . ."

It had been Janet who had told her about Lady Ellen, without knowing, with certainty, that Julia had heard or seen anything in that room. The details had been told reluctantly, as if Janet did not wish to believe the story of a haunting spirit. She had not mentioned it again, perhaps afraid that it was no fit subject to discuss with a pregnant woman—the story of a woman abducted for her money and her lands, married against her will, dead in childbirth. Night after night, as the fire died to embers, Julia tossed, trying to find some comfortable position for her grossly uncomfortable body. Once, waking when the song of the birds about the loch told her it was dawn, she thought she glimpsed that vague shape against the great chimneypiece carved with the Sinclair arms. This time there was no sobbing to remember, just that faint, almost unheard sigh. Did it forebode well or ill for her and Jamie's child? She had chosen to come to this room where another woman had suffered so that her silent, nearly dry weeping would have companionship. Had she deliberately opened herself to another tragedy? Would this truly be the end of his branch of the Sinclair line?

But it was not so. A week before she was due to go into the Inverness hospital, she woke to the feeling of wetness. The waters had broken, and she already, too soon, felt the first contraction. She reached and rang the bell. Janet came. "What is it, Mrs. Sinclair? Are you not well?"

"It's come, Janet. The waters have broken. I'd better dress, and you'd better tell Lady Jean we'll need to go now." She indicated the bag, packed and ready. "I've a feeling it won't be long. . . ." She had been sitting on the edge of the bed and then suddenly fell back as another savage pain gripped her. It was the sort of pain she had never experienced before, as if her very insides were straining and tearing and wanted to come apart. "Oh, God—I didn't think it would be as bad as this."

Janet had drawn back the curtain to let in the growing light of dawn. She came back and peered closely at Julia. "How long since the first pain?"

"Just a few minutes. It came before I rang the bell."

Janet swung Julia's legs back onto the bed and covered her with the blankets. "I've not much experience in these things, never having had a child myself. But I saw all my brothers and sisters born. It seems to me a wee bit soon for the pains to be coming so fast. I'll go and tell Lady Jean. I'll not be more than a minute," she said reassuringly. "You'll not be alone. . . ."

Lady Jean came, wrapped in a shabby gown, her hair in a long, thick plait falling across her shoulder. "Janet tells me the pains have started." She took Julia's hand and stroked the damp hair back from her forehead. Just then another contraction seized Julia. She managed to hold her mouth shut against the cry that wanted to come. Lady Jean looked at the watch on her wrist. "How long between the contractions, would you say?"

Julia shook her head. It seemed that she had barely time to recover from each searing pain, a chance to draw breath, before the next came. In silence Lady Jean waited, her eyes on her watch. The pain came soon again. Julia turned her head away, clamping her lips on the sound that wanted to tear itself from her. "I must phone Dr. MacGregor. I cannot think this is a false labor, even though it's a first child. And it may be safer to keep you here. I'll have a word with him. Janet, you know what to do with the bedclothes. Please make her as comfortable as possible. I'll call Mrs. Kerr. Perhaps she can help. . . ." She left quickly, and Julia, through a haze of pain, felt there was a slight sense of panic. Lady Jean had had only two children, and both of them would have been born here in Castle Sinclair. But she was not more experienced than Janet. Dimly Julia tried to remember what she had read to expect at this time. She sensed it was all happening more swiftly than anyone had expected, especially for a first child. She felt she wanted to go to the bathroom, but Janet forbade her to move. She brought a bedpan, and with swift, neat movements managed to move Julia to the other side of the bed while she rolled back the sheet and the underblanket, and inserted fresh ones, moving Julia once again to do it on the other side. She inspected the contents of the bedpan. "There—that will make you feel better." She was moving with great efficiency. "Oh, didn't we all do first-aid classes when war was threatened. And they included childbirth when and where it wasn't expected. I prepared myself for this—if it happened." She rushed to the bathroom and came back with a jugful of water. "Ah, we must have it hotter. But I'll just wash my hands and then give you a thorough wash—all over, Mrs. Sinclair. A blanket bath, it's called. That will see you easier before I go and ask Mr. Kerr to start stoking the boiler—but I'm sure Mrs. Kerr has already thought of that.'' She paused as Lady Jean reentered the room.

''Dr. MacGregor said to stay where you are until he gets here. It may be false labor, in which case, when the pains ease, we can call the ambulance. But it's a risk now to try to get you to the hospital in a car. Not even he fancies a delivery in those circumstances, though I'm sure he's known worse. . . . How are you feeling?''

''Like hell,'' Julia answered truthfully. ''When the pain comes, it's like hell. And when it's over, I think I'm in heaven.''

''Yes, my dear. The most wonderful—and terrible—experience of a woman's life. I was sure I was going to die myself. Do not be ashamed. It is better, I think, to scream than to bottle it in. There's no one but ourselves to hear. This old place has heard the cries of many a woman in childbirth—and cries of torture, I'm sure, if the whole truth were known.'' She checked that the sheets and underblanket were dry. ''Janet is so good—clever and quick. As soon as she's back, I'll run and throw on some clothes. And I must wash up, thoroughly. Oh, dear God, why don't we have running water in all the rooms? I would never forgive myself if there was an infection.''

''My fault.'' Julia smiled at her feebly. ''I did insist on having this room. I felt—feel—at home here.''

''Not your fault, my dear. We'd have had to lodge you permanently in the housekeeper's room to have you near running water. Sometimes I curse this old place—as much as I treasure it.''

Julia could hardly believe what she had heard. Janet entered the room with another jugful of hot water and a basin. ''Mrs. Kerr is in the kitchen, opening up the dampers on the Aga, and Mr. Kerr is at the boiler.''

''Stay with her a moment while I get dressed,'' Lady Jean said. ''And I'd better get the car out . . . Dr. MacGregor told me not to telephone ahead to the hospital yet. But surely a first baby cannot be coming as quickly as this. She's not built for it. Those narrow hips . . . Ah, well, we'll see. . . .''

She was gone, and Julia felt the pain rip through her and gave her first cry. ''There,'' Janet said, '' 'tis better to let it out. But, oh, my dear lady . . . if only men knew . . .''

''If men knew, there'd still be babies,'' Julia whispered.

"You are right."

Lady Jean was back, and Janet went to the room next door and dressed swiftly. Then she stripped off Julia's nightgown and washed her thoroughly; Julia could smell the disinfectant in the water. Then a clean nightgown. Mrs. Kerr knocked and put her head in the door, wishing Julia a brief "Good morning" and then pausing to look at her. "Good luck, Mrs. Sinclair." She had brought yet another jug and basin. "We'll have the water good and hot in no time." Then, surprisingly, she added, "You have a fair morning for a birth." She indicated the radiance at the windows, the reflection of the light that came off the loch with the rising sun.

Julia heard the heavy, deliberate tread on the stairs. This was no hurrying woman. Dr. MacGregor paused in the doorway. "Ah, well, I suppose film stars always do things differently. But in the end, Nature is all the same, isn't it, lass?" His tone was gentle, very calm. He removed his jacket and rolled up his sleeves, going to the basin of clean water and scrubbing his hands. "Aye, it's a bonny morning you've chosen for it. How many times have I tried to get through snowdrifts to a woman? Poor wee things; 'tis not their fault, nor choosing. Now just let me have a look at you, lass, and see how things are going. . . ." He felt her pulse, placed a thermometer between her lips, and then firmly but with practiced hands felt her bulging belly and placed a stethoscope to listen to the baby's heart. "Spread for me a little, my dear. Ah, yes . . ." Another contraction, more powerful than any of the previous ones, racked her. When it was over he put the bedclothes back in position. "I think we'll just hold on here, Mrs. Sinclair. Everything seems normal to me, except the speed with which your young one is coming. I expect he'll be in a hurry all his life. The uterus is beginning to dilate. A journey to Inverness might not be good for you now."

"Then it's a boy?"

He smiled. "Bless you, my dear. It will be some time yet before doctors have that kind of knowledge—if ever. But whoever it is, is in the right position and should not cause too much trouble. Except that no man ought to say that to a woman in labor. It is a particular pain we men will never experience."

"How long?"

He shook his head. "I cannot say. An hour or two . . . a bit longer. You're in the first stage. I take it you've been having wee preparatory contractions for the past few days?''

"Yes—but it wasn't due for a week, so I didn't want to bother anyone, or go to a hospital before I had to. But this . . ."

"Well, we'll not fuss you. There's some time to go. When we reach the second stage, you'll have to do some work for yourself."

"Well, then, Doctor, I think you could maybe do with a wee bite of breakfast, if there's time," Janet said.

"There's time. But someone must stay with Mrs. Sinclair."

"I will stay," Lady Jean said. "Of course."

In the time that followed, the time that was timeless to Julia, Lady Jean sat in a chair by the bed, reaching to take Julia's hand when there was a contraction. Many times she bathed her face and neck and arms, replaced a pillow that had become drenched with sweat. She administered a few measured sips of water. Dr. MacGregor came back, a large cup of tea in his hand. He finished it, mostly staring out at the loch. Then he scrubbed again and examined her. "Not quite there yet . . ."

For the first time Julia felt frightened. Why had she spurned the idea of a hospital? She could have gone two days ago. "They probably would have sent you back home again," the doctor answered calmly. "And you would have had a bone-wrenching journey for nothing."

The second stage of labor was even swifter than he had anticipated. She pushed and relaxed at his command, wanting to push until she had freed herself of a burden that had become almost unbearable to her. Several times she heard her own cries, but it was all mixed in a terrible confusion of fear and pain; did she see the light from the loch reach its noon zenith, or was that all part of the alternating light and dark through which she seemed to pass? Steady now . . . the head is well through, and I must position the shoulders. Well, then, relax, my dear. No more pushing. Coming nicely . . . coming . . . coming . . . ah, there now. You have a fine young son, Mrs. Sinclair. And here he is, ready to bawl his lungs out." Swiftly he cleansed the mouth and face of the baby. "Listen to him! His first breath, Mrs. Sinclair. He no longer needs you for oxygen. Well, I'll just attend to the cord there . . . so." Once again he wiped the baby's face, head, and mouth. Then a quick wipe over the baby's body with a warm cloth. Janet had a blanket, newly warmed before the fire, ready.

The baby was wrapped in it, but Dr. MacGregor moved it down from his head. "Place his ear close to your heart, my dear. He will be missing the warm, dark, comfortable place he's been growing in all these months. Let him hear his mother's heartbeat again so he'll know he's in the right place—that the new world isn't all cold and frightening."

Softly she kissed the soft, fair fuzz of his small skull, striving to make some sense of the tiny, wizened features. She felt Dr. MacGregor's hand pushing upward on her abdomen while he pulled to release the rest of the cord, helping to remove the placenta.

"There—as clean and neat as I've ever seen. No tearing!"

"Oh, he's beautiful. Oh, Jamie . . . Jamie . . . You will never see him." She had cried out, screamed, even sworn, she remembered, while the terrible pain had gripped her. Now in the peace that followed, she felt the tears begin to slide helplessly down her cheeks.

"You have your son, my dear. So far as I can see, a very healthy son. And you are a healthy, strong young woman. You will go on from here and make his life as well as your own."

Afterward, after she had been washed and had fresh sheets and a nightgown, after she had fed her child for the first time and he lay sleeping in her arms, when drowsiness was beginning to overcome her, Lady Jean brought roses to the room. "Just to help get over the smell of the disinfectant." She bent to look at the baby. Her lips twisted in a smile that was half pleasure, half anguish. "Do you know, I just cannot think whom he reminds me of. Must be someone I knew rather well . . ." The sadness left her eyes. "Of course he's the image of Jamie."

Julia wondered how they imagined they could see in those crumpled features a resemblance to anyone who ever lived. But they both saw with the eyes of longing. All that was left of Jamie lived in the child. That was what they saw.

Julia opened her eyes wide. The light was still bright at the windows. "What time is it?"

"A little after two o'clock. Janet has just given the doctor a good lunch."

"So early still? It seemed a long time."

"Dr. MacGregor said it was remarkably quick for a first child."

Reluctantly Julia relinquished the baby into Lady Jean's arms, to see him laid in the old-fashioned rocking cradle that had been used by Jamie and, before him, his brother, Callum.

She felt herself sliding toward sleep, the memory of pain already being erased. "You do know, don't you? I was—no, I think he was—determined that he would be born at Sinclair."

Chapter Six

I

A FEW DAYS AFTER the child was born—he was already being called Alasdair, after Lady Jean's father: Julia was determined there would only be one Jamie in her life, and Lady Jean was equally determined that he would not be called Callum—she walked down to the housekeeper's room. Janet held the baby, and Julia held tightly on to the banister of the suddenly frighteningly steep and long flight of steps. Only Dr. MacGregor encouraged her in this. Lady Jean and Janet would have kept her in the confines of the Red Tower Room, and the longest journey would have been to the awkward bathroom. "Ah, nonsense—all for the better, so long as she doesn't overdo it."

So she sat and nursed Alasdair on the sofa and complained to Janet that the fire was too hot. "It's almost July. We don't need a fire in here in the middle of the day."

"Ah, well, just to be safe." Julia read over the messages that had come from the family. Lady Jean had telephoned and cabled the news of the baby's birth. On the first Sunday she was downstairs, Julia talked to her father and Luisa on the telephone. She reread Connie's excited letter and Alex's cable. *Delighted you and the baby are both well.* She reread Jamie's letters. She carried the baby out onto the old seat in the overgrown walled garden. Beyond the high hedge was the vegetable garden, which the Kerrs tended. There was not enough help available to have the old flower and rose garden plowed under for vegetables. The Kerrs were barely able to keep the vegetable garden itself in good condition. So Julia sat among the ruin of the formal garden, saw sadly how the weeds and briars had taken over in many places and how even the rose garden, which Lady Jean desperately attempted to keep in order, was drifting into decay. It had been October 1941 when she and Jamie had strolled through here, and it was now July 1943. In the months since Jamie's death she had taken little notice of what was happening to the world outside her own grief. Her only experience was grief and the determination to carry the baby to full term. May, when she had been careless of anything but those two facts, had seen the surrender of the Germans and Italians in Tunisia. The desert war in which Jamie had died was over.

Sir Niall came to her there in the old garden, on his first visit since the baby had been born. "Well," he said gruffly, "I suppose all babies look alike, except to their mothers. He seems a bonny little lad to me." The baby waved his tiny fists. "Going to be a fighter, are you?" He turned fully to Julia and asked, "Do you regret coming up here? It would probably have been a lot more comfortable to have stayed where you were. What do you think you'll do now?"

"Draw breath, for one thing," she almost snapped at him. "Why? Has Lady Jean sent you to tell me I must vacate the place as soon as we can travel?"

"What utter rubbish! She wants no such thing. Now she has her only grandchild, she wants him under her eye. I was thinking about you, my dear. What sort of future do you have—*here?* This is a lonely, rather desolate place—particularly in winter, and most particularly in wartime. We have so few young people left here now. I'm sure they told you Lady Macpherson has died. Kirsty joined the WAAF more than a year ago. She's somewhere in Lincolnshire, I believe. Did they tell you her brother, Harry, went down when the *Prince of Wales* was sunk?—before Singapore fell? I have as much as I can do to keep my farm running. I'm desperate for help. The Land Army girls come and go. I'm damned grateful for them, but sometimes they're here just for a harvest, and then the Ministry moves them on. It's the same all over the region. I suppose it's the same in Kent, but you have better weather there—and a longer growing season, so the Ministry sets higher quotas for you. Your father seems very busy. I read he's got another film coming up. Something very patriotic, I don't doubt, and meant to send us out of the cinemas singing 'There'll Always Be an England.' Well, someone has to do it. Everyone does what they do best. That's why I asked you what you're going to do now. You've had your baby. You've quietened some of the grief in Jean's heart—perhaps a little in your own. It was a mad, quixotic, romantic gesture to come here at all. But I don't see your life here. You belong to a different world. I think you'll miss it very much.''

"Alasdair's life is here. That makes a difference.''

"You can't give your whole life to a child.''

"Many women do.''

Janet was coming toward them down the weed-choked path, carrying a tray. "I thought a nice cup of tea wouldn't go amiss.'' The three dogs—Rory, Angus, and Duuf—were at her heels. They thrust their noses toward Alasdair, already, in these few days, having realized that something pink and warm and smelling of talcum powder was living beneath the shawl and cap. He put out his fist toward them, not yet aware that they were something different from those other beings that peopled his new world. Janet set down the tray on the seat between Julia and Sir Niall.

"No doubt when he's aware that there are animals in the world, he'll be just like his father with them. Jamie always had a wonderful hand with animals.'' Sir Niall took up one of the hot buttered scones and divided it among the dogs. They ate eagerly and looked for more.

"Sir Niall! Do you think I do my baking for dogs? I brought these out for you and Mrs. Sinclair. And it's almost time, Mrs. Sinclair, that you came in. It's growing a mite chilly out here, even with the sun. I'll leave the tray for you to bring in, Sir Niall.'' The dogs stayed, hoping for more, and got it.

"Well, Julia? What is it going to be? Do you think you'll stay here?''

"When Alasdair is weaned, I'll think about what I'll do.''

"By then it will be winter. If you can survive a winter in the Highlands, I suppose you can do anything. But don't waste yourself in the mistaken belief that you must do everything for your child now that you have him.''

"I'll just wait a while and see what happens.''

The high walls began to cut off the sun. Sir Niall gathered up the tea things, and they walked slowly back to the castle, going, as usual, to the kitchen door. Hens and roosters scattered before them. Lady Jean had just finished putting out their feed.

"Come in, Niall—come in.'' She relieved him of the tea tray

and put it down on the kitchen table, where Janet was peeling potatoes. "Sit down with me for a few minutes." She went before them into the housekeeper's room. "There was a news bulletin about ten minutes ago. An Allied invasion of Sicily has begun. No details yet. So I suppose we're going to Europe by the back door."

She was pouring small glasses of malt whiskey for them all. "Yes, you, too, Julia. A little can't hurt. I feel it's something we must toast. Perhaps a real turning point." She shook her head rapidly, as if to blink away tears. "Jamie would have been there. . . . Ah, what's the use? He went when he had to."

Julia found herself echoing Alex's words—"How I hate heroes!"—and was aware of the look of unutterable shock on the face of Lady Jean. It would be a long time before she would be forgiven those words. In her arms, Alasdair began to whimper. "He's hungry."

Sir Niall tossed back his drink and left them. Julia fed Alasdair before the fire, aware of the stare of outrage and hostility on Lady Jean's face. While she had been carrying Jamie's child, much, if not everything, had been forgiven her. If she stayed until winter, if she stayed through the winter, it would be a time of unease. Weariness overcame her. She had lived for Jamie, and afterward, for his child. Suddenly she had no more strength. She was only twenty-two. How would she fill the future when she could barely contemplate getting through the next hour?

But the days and weeks seemed to fill themselves. Alasdair took a great deal of her time; the rest she filled by helping Janet in the kitchen. Her strength came back rapidly. Her body began to resume the shape it had once had. "You must do all the exercises the doctor told you about, Mrs. Sinclair," Janet urged her, while at the same time admonishing her to "take things easy, now." They had a crib that was rolled between the housekeeper's room and the kitchen, so the baby was always with them. It was too much trouble to carry him all the way back to the Red Tower Room, and once there, he could not be left alone. So he learned to sleep passively amid the noise of the pans being washed, the fire being stoked. The dogs, particularly Rory, became his companions and guardians. He regarded them as part of his world. At least twice a day, when the weather permitted it, Julia carried him around the kitchen yard and to the stable yard. He was a regular visitor to Mrs. Kerr's kitchen. Julia held him upright so he could try to focus on Catriona's head as it emerged from the stable door, looking for a carrot or an apple, or the lumps of sugar that Julia, without guilt, stole from the supply that came from Alex and Luisa. On the calm days she carried him across the bridge to the beginning of the long road that ran through the forest. Lady Jean had produced the ancient, high-wheeled baby carriage that had served Callum and Jamie, but Julia preferred still to carry Alasdair. "That thing gets caught in all the ruts, and anyway, all Alasdair sees is the sky. I want him to see *things*." She answered Janet's question lightly, "In fact, I *do* do the exercises—faithfully. But why does it matter to you so much?"

Janet looked at her with mild astonishment. "Why, surely you'll be making another picture soon? You can't just . . ." She looked around the big old kitchen, flagstoned, with its ancient oak dresser holding dishes, the Aga stove that had seen better days and needed repair. "You can't just *stay* here. You're a film star, Mrs. Sinclair. They'll be asking you to make more pictures. A waste if you stayed here . . . although it's home to me, how can it be for one such as you?"

Even Janet's evident friendliness did not mask the fact that she was a stranger in their midst. They didn't expect her to stay, no matter what she said about Alasdair growing up there. "Well, in summer," Janet once said, "we'd hope to see you. Wee Alasdair has to know where he belongs. But you, Mrs. Sinclair, are different." She didn't mean it unkindly. It was simply a fact they all recognized.

In late September Connie had a week's leave and came to Sinclair. Julia realized the degree of sacrifice in this; Connie could have been available to see Ken Warren each evening but instead had chosen the long, uncomfortable journey north. "I felt I had to come," Connie said as Julia drove her from Inverness to Sinclair. "None of us has seen him. Father's only grandchild—a nephew for Alex and me. Naturally you can't get down to Anscombe while he's so young . . . so I came."

She was nervously dismayed by Castle Sinclair. "God, Julia, how can you *live* here? All these stairs and stone passages. It would need an army of servants to make it reasonably comfortable. To heat it . . ." She shook her head.

"We manage . . ."

"*We.* You mean you're one of them now?"

"No, but my son is. I have to remember that. He will never know his father. His father's heritage is all he will have to cling to, to give him some identity as he grows up."

"Father and Luisa were rather hoping—"

"Hoping that I'd come to Anscombe to live?" Julia finished for her. "Is that what the visit is for, Connie? They know you too well, darling sister. They know you couldn't tell a lie. Obviously they both mean the message to be that I should come back to Anscombe. As Luisa so kindly put it, Johnny and my baby could grow up together. All very suitable and nice, and a damn sight more comfortable than living here." Together they stood over Alasdair's cradle in the Red Tower Room. She would take him down soon to feed him in the housekeeper's room. "But don't you see, Connie, that that would be their life? Not mine. It's Luisa's house now. I would be a permanent guest, however welcome. It's not a large house. It has no place for another woman and her child. Even if it were bigger, do you think I want my child to grow up always slightly inferior to Luisa's? They might appear to be equals, but they wouldn't be."

"And here he will be king in his own castle, is that it?" Connie retorted with uncharacteristic acerbity.

"I think he has more chance of being an equal of the children of the farm workers here than he ever would be at Anscombe. The future laird of Sinclair he might be, but there's no one in this country who's prepared to doff a cap or bend a knee to anyone whom they don't think deserves it. So . . . what if it is cold in winter? What if he doesn't grow up with all the little luxuries he might have at Anscombe? He will grow up independent. I can't give him anything more than that. He could be in real danger of growing up to be Johnny's whipping boy—or else his manipulator, if Johnny turns out to be the weaker character. I can risk neither."

"But what will *you* do?"

"The best I can. Why is everyone so anxious that I make great decisions so soon? There's time. He's so young. . . ." She bent over the cradle and knew her tone conveyed the sense of yearning and loss that was forever with her. "And it's such a little time since Jamie went. I haven't gotten used to it . . . trying to plan for a future when there seems to be none. Life would be a great deal less complicated if there had been no child. But now that I have him, I can't imagine life without him.''

Connie touched her shoulder. ''Julia, I'm sorry. I've blundered unpardonably. They didn't really send me with any messages. It was my idea to come. I wanted so desperately to see you both. Now I've seen him—well, I know you can do nothing else. If he were mine—''

''You'll have children of your own.''

''Someday, I hope. When the war is over . . .''

''Ken still won't consider marriage until then?''

Connie shook her head. ''Never. He has to be totally responsible for his wife and children. Life is too uncertain, he says. He could be killed. I could be killed. Children shouldn't grow up without parents. He's eager—he wants marriage. But this terrible sense of responsibility gets in the way. I'd marry him tomorrow, if only he'd agree.''

''Has Ken ever thought he could fall under a bus—even when the war's over?''

''The chances of surviving to old age are greater in peace than in war. And you'll see—he'll have taken out very prudent insurance policies.''

''Connie, how can you stand it—this need to be so careful about everything? How can you and Ken be so *sure?*''

''Because I grew up being so unsure. Father's and Mother's lives didn't make for certainty in anything. I know I'm a hopeless coward, but I need someone like Ken. I need to be sure of a few things in life.''

''To live is to take chances.''

''I know—I *know!* But I keep telling myself it will work out. I will sink back into domestic tranquility and have my children, I will have a loving and devoted husband who wouldn't know how to be unfaithful if he tried. He will not neglect his children. And do you know something else, Julia? I really don't care if I never attend another play, or go to another concert in my life. I want to forget the drama and excitement just as much as I want to forget the racked nerves, the screaming matches. I don't want the heights and the depths. I want a long, wide, smooth valley that gets a lot of sun.''

''Connie—you're so beautiful. You could—''

''People keep telling me that until I'm sick of it. I've got the wrong spirit for the body and face I was given. I should look like the dull little mouse I am. I can't help that." She dismissed the matter. "Now can we wake the young laird, and may I carry him downstairs?"

"Just as soon as we've changed him. You'll have to get used to such things."

"Believe me, I am. Luisa lets me do anything with Johnny—under Brenda's eye, of course. Johnny's inclined to be fractious. And, of course, he's spoiled rotten, even at his age. Luisa can't help it. But when he's with me, he just seems all smiles, bubbling with good humor."

Julia gently lifted up the sleeping child and handed him to her sister. "I hope you'll be godmother to him and endow him with all the gifts a good fairy should have at her disposal. He couldn't have better than you, Connie."

For the brief days she was there, Connie slipped with perfect ease into life at Castle Sinclair. "What a goodhearted, sweet soul she is," Janet declared. "For all those good looks, she's so unspoiled. If I dare say it, Mrs. Sinclair, your sister has the face of an angel."

"And the nature of one, Janet. You're not the first one to find that out."

Lady Jean warmed to her. Julia detected something close to wistfulness in her mother-in-law. It was almost palpably plain what her thinking was: If Jamie had not married the girl his mother would have most liked, why could he not have chosen this girl, instead of her sister? Julia was amused and interested to see that on her morning rounds of the fowls and the stable yard, her daily conference with William Kerr, Lady Jean actively invited Connie's presence. "She's so interested in everything. One thinks of these smart London girls—"

"Connie was never exactly a 'smart' London girl. She knows the farm at home pretty well, too. And she's been serving the WAAF since before war was declared."

"Well, she has a good head on her shoulders." Lady Jean asked William Kerr if he would take Connie on his daily round of the farm. "I think she would be interested. It would be good for some of the people to get to know one of Mrs. Sinclair's family." There was no doubt Lady Jean had picked Connie as the most respectable, least remarkable, except for her looks, of all Julia's family they were ever likely to meet.

"Oh, I've had so many cups of tea, and scones loaded with butter . . ." Connie complained. "This must be real Highland hospitality. Half the time I couldn't understand more than half of what they were saying. But they were all so welcoming. I always imagined the Highlanders were a stiff lot with people they didn't know."

"I'm very jealous," Julia said. "You've met more of them than I have. And they obviously love you."

"Well . . . don't forget I'm not Mrs. Sinclair. They're not going to live with me forever. But what a heavenly place it is here, Julia. No wonder Jamie loved it so. . . . I begin to understand why you want to stay."

"*No!* I don't want to stay. I have to stay for Alasdair. Where else is there? Father's given up the flat in London—and, in any case, who would bring a baby to London at this time? The filth and inconveniences and short rations. I can't do that. This is, for the time being, all I have."

Connie smiled gently. "Now that I'm used to it—great gloomy castle and all—I can think of worse places."

Julia returned her smile. "I think you're about the only person who's not hell-bent on getting me out of here to keep up with my so-called career. Even Sir Niall—who I think is very fond of me. He's coming for dinner tonight. Just him—*en famille.* He doesn't expect a banquet in the dining hall, like the one Lady Jean put on when I first came. The war has changed too much, even up here. You'll love him. . . ."

"I do love him. I met him at your wedding, remember? Well, perhaps you don't. Who remembers much about their wedding day?"

"I thought I had every second of it locked in my mind."

"You do. Everything that matters."

While Connie was at Sinclair, a letter came from Alex. Julia read it swiftly and kept it out of Connie's sight. When the morning chores were done and when the baby had fallen asleep in his crib in the kitchen under Janet's eye, Julia said, "It's such a beautiful morning. Connie's leaving tomorrow, and we hardly seem to have talked—I'd like a little walk. . . ."

"Certainly, Mrs. Sinclair. The young man's fed and asleep. He'll be no trouble. You and Miss Seymour are owed some time to yourselves."

They walked across the drawbridge and the bridge, Rory, Angus, and Duuf eagerly following. On the other end, at the entrance to the forest, Connie turned back to look at the castle. "It really is out of a storybook, isn't it? All the romantic things one has ever thought that a real castle should have. It really only needs Rapunzel to let down her golden hair."

"And it has a history as bloodthirsty as any in the land," Julia answered. "Sometimes I almost hear the cries at night. But it has served its purpose. It has given shelter and protection to the clan in times of trouble—and there have been plenty of them. There must have been happy people here over the centuries. It's only the tales of blood and horror that are remembered."

They walked along the road, crowded by the forest on both sides. The first frosts had already touched the leaves of the oaks and beeches and turned them to colors of red and gold and soft brown. With each slight stirring of the wind, leaves softly drifted down, making no sound as they touched the forest floor. "It's as different from Kent as one can imagine," Connie said. She pointed to the ledges and ridges of rock that showed through the trees. "Tough and hard—and beautiful. You're right. Your son will have to grow up knowing his land—his country. It will be good for Johnny to come here sometimes. To learn it's not all sweet and green and pleasant. And there's not always enough hot water to go around."

They had reached the McBain cottage. "I've noticed it as we've driven past and wondered . . ." Connie said. "No one lives here. Yet it's near the castle and close enough to the main road."

"A lot of people don't fancy living in the middle of a forest. They'd rather have open spaces—a view. I suppose if Mr. Kerr could get as much help as he'd like, it would be occupied. As it is, he has trouble enough keeping the roof in order." Julia walked toward it and lifted the latch on the door. "They used it as a shelter when they were felling, or dragging out windfalls. The forest isn't as well managed as it should be—but then, what is, at Sinclair? Not enough money—not enough workers." She went in and felt for the little niche above the brick oven where matches were always kept. The dry kindling laid on the fireplace caught at once, and soon she was able to lay a larger log on the fire. "Jamie and I came here—I'll come back here tomorrow and see that there's kindling left, and dry wood. It's like a moun-

tain refuge. One always leaves it ready for the next person. But
what we could really use is a dram of malt whiskey.'' She
dragged over the pile of old rush mats and sat down. The dogs
squatted beside them, crowding the hearth. Then Julia took the
letter from her coat pocket and handed it to Connie. ''I wanted
us to be alone when you read it. Sit down. . . .''

Connie unfolded the closely written pages, and Julia leaned
close to her to read them again. *This comes to you by favor of
someone I know in the military who is flying to London tonight
and will mail it to you. There wasn't any point in sending a
cable, since the worst was all over so long ago, and I know how
you must feel about cables. I will write to Father, and the same
person will mail that letter also. The sad, terrible, to me almost
unbelievable fact is that Greg is dead. I heard today from the
Red Cross that his name is on a list they got from the Japanese.
Greg died in Changi. They don't say how or why, or even when.
I suppose it doesn't matter to them. He could have died of star-
vation, or beriberi, or malaria, or cholera, or any of the other
plagues that infest those hateful places. My poor, sad, cheated
Greg. He has been cheated of so many years of life he might
have lived, of the things he might have written. I hate to think
of him living and dying, being buried in one of their stinking
prisons. But, dear little sister, I have to tell you that that is about
all I feel, apart from a strange numbness. I had already lost the
Greg that used to be, and I feel almost certain he knew it. The
few letters I had, especially in this last year, could have been
written to a distant cousin. I tried so hard not to let him know
that I had fallen in love with another man. But I'm not very
good at lying, particularly in writing. I think most of all he must
have missed my talking and planning for the future, as most
other wives would have. I wasn't able to carry the deception that
far. His death makes my sense of guilt so much worse. I wish I
had been able to write the sort of letters that gave him the will
to live. Perhaps I took away his future. Men without hope sometimes do lie down and die. But Greg was always such a fighter.
I just pray that he didn't show such defiance that he was tortured. That would be the other side of him. When it's all over I
know I will have to find the truth—find someone who was close
to him there who will tell me what really happened. It will not
ease my guilt, but I have to know. It never occurred to me that
I could love a man, and then not love him because he wasn't at*

*my side. Am I really as shallow as that? Or has the world of
power and influence that Elliot inhabits seduced me? It's equally
bad to think I can be swayed by things like that. Can I say I
simply fell in love? Elliot is fourteen years older than I—as Greg
was older, and so much more mature. Have I always been seeking a father figure? As I grew up, our own father seemed barely
there. He seemed to flit into and out of our lives. As Mother did.
There was always something they were doing that was more important—or so it seemed to me. The most stable figure I knew
was Grandfather Guy—as different as any man could be from
Igor Maslov. Why am I writing all this? It doesn't ease my heart
or my guilt but simply lays a burden on you—you, dear Julia,
who so much loved the husband who died. I suppose Elliot and
I will be married soon. No one here in Washington will be surprised. It has become a matter of "when," not "if"—the only
"if" being how long Elliot's patience would stand a situation
that was not to the liking of either of us. The waiting is perhaps
proof of his love. I have to believe that. Life will change very
much for me. To be a wife again—instead of a mistress. I want
to go on working. Elliot doesn't discourage the thought. I love
what I do. I particularly like to think that I, in small ways, help
people who are Allies on both sides of the Atlantic understand
each other a little better. I may have been a poor wife to Greg—
he deserved better. But I have not been a bad journalist. In that,
at the very least, I have tried to measure up to his standards.*

Connie looked at Julia with stricken eyes. "I didn't imagine
. . . no one ever said anything. She never hinted in her letters—"

"Not to you, Connie. You have such a powerful aura of innocence, which I think even Alex hesitated to shatter. But she's
written very frankly to me about it. And I think Father suspected. Possibly he even knew for sure. Through Wolfie. It was
Wolfie who gave Alex her introduction to Elliot Forster. Anyone
who heard the Washington gossip, as Wolfie was bound to, must
have known about it. But it wasn't just an affair. He always
meant to marry her. Even if he had to wait until the war was
over to do it. I don't think this is a slight or selfish relationship."

"I hope she's happy," Connie said lamely. "I suppose it
means she's going to be pretty important in Washington—being
married to Elliot Forster. It frightens me a little. There's so
much fame and money around. We've experienced fame before,

with Mother and Father. But now with Luisa and Elliot Forster there's so much money—and he has all the power that goes with being a newspaper proprietor.''

Julia smiled wryly. ''I don't think at this stage Alex is likely to be corrupted by money. And as for Father—well, Luisa has liberated him from any pressure of money. For the first time in his life he's able to turn down a part if he doesn't think it's right for him, because he hasn't got to consider the money side of it. And Luisa encourages this. No—I don't think Alex will be corrupted by money.'' Julia glanced around the tiny room, the small windows that the filtered light of the forest shadowed. ''Money isn't always corrupting, Connie. It can be used well.''

''I don't suppose I'll ever know. Ken's unlikely ever to be earning a huge salary.'' She read through the letter again. ''I wish I'd known Greg a bit better. But he was a . . . a remote figure to me. Rather frighteningly intelligent. But in such a different way from Ken, who I know is brilliant but sort of keeps it to himself. Greg must have thought me very stupid, because I don't remember having much to say when he was around. It can't matter now, though. But what a rotten way to die—what a terrible place to die . . .'' Her hand stole over and linked into Julia's, both giving and seeking comfort.

They remained there, saying nothing more, until the flames had begun to die. Then Julia pulled the rush mats back, away from even a dying spark. The dogs were up and waiting to go. She pulled the door closed behind her, and together, in silence now, they walked through the enchanted forest to the fairy-tale castle.

Julia took Connie to the Inverness station very early the next morning. The light wind had strengthened and now held the chill of the winter to come. ''When will I tell them you'll be . . . be coming down?'' Connie asked. Julia realized she had nearly said ''home.''

''I don't know. When the baby's older. When there's some reason to come.''

The guard blew his whistle, and Connie scrambled into the coach. ''I wish you weren't so . . . so terribly far away.''

Julia realized there were tears in her eyes as she returned the wave of the figure who leaned from the coach window. She was terribly far away; she had voyaged, for love of Jamie, to a remote and nearly alien land. She didn't know how to live here, nor how to go back to her former world, now that love no longer sustained her.

II

THE BABY WAS CHRISTENED Alasdair Michael James; Sir Niall was a godfather, and Lady Jean's brother, the earl, had traveled, rather unwillingly, Julia guessed, from Ayrshire to stand as another godparent. He and his sister did not seem to be on very good terms. But he was there at the ceremony at the kirk in Langwell and at the small party given later at Sinclair. He stayed the night and left very early the next morning. Connie and Alex were named as godmothers, and Julia insisted that Janet should be a godmother as well. "She helped bring him into the world. She will help shape his values," Julia argued. It was Janet who held him during the ceremony. That caused surprise among the small number who gathered to witness the occasion. The young laird of Sinclair could have had others who were not servants as his godmother. Even Janet had been dismayed at Julia's insistence. "It's not done, Mrs. Sinclair. Lady Jean's only grandchild . . . and I'm but the cook and servant here."

"I am his mother," Julia said. "His only parent. I have explained my reasons to Lady Jean. She accepts them."

"Aye—and hard to swallow they'll be," Janet said grimly.

At the small christening party, Sir Niall offered the toast to the now-sleeping child. "At his mother's wish, he was born here. He will grow up knowing his people and his country. He will never be a stranger in this land."

Christening presents were offered. A silver clan badge from the earl; from Sir Niall a silver cup at least two hundred years old, bearing the Henderson clan badge and motto. "My boys and Jamie grew up together," he said. "I look upon him as if he were my own grandchild." There were humble gifts of knitted clothing that came from unexpected sources among the tenants of Sinclair and that touched Julia deeply. And from Luisa and Michael, along with a gift of shares in an American oil company that could only have come from Luisa's portfolio, there was a diamond ring that might have weighed, Julia guessed, about fifteen carats. A note from her father accompanied it. *I know it seems an extraordinary gift to give to a young baby, but Luisa has made up her mind, and it's impossible to change in this matter.* From Luisa, another note. *Please do not refuse, my dear. It was my first engagement ring—from André. The second engagement ring, from Henry, I have put aside for whomever Johnny should marry. I can sell neither of them—nor can I ever wear them again. But I would like them to stay in the family.* Julia knew that Luisa proudly wore a much less significant stone given to her by Michael before their marriage. Julia regarded the ring with some awe, and again wondered at the unexpected generosity of this woman she had once not been prepared to trust. *We wish,* Luisa added, *we could be with you for the great occasion, but travel is just too difficult.* It made Julia feel that she had moved to a realm beyond even her father's imagination. Was this the sentiment of the man who had played one of the greatest Macbeths of the modern English stage?

The strangest gift of all came from Elliot Forster. *I'm sure you're not aware of it, but my second name is Calder, my mother's maiden name, so through her, I suppose, I may claim descent from the Campbells of Cawdor. Having studied the map of Scotland many times and visited your region twice, I know you are not very far from Cawdor, and very probably the present Thane is among your family's acquaintances. We are honored that Alex is among the godparents. I will see that she takes her duties seriously. So that young Alasdair may have some interest in distant American connections, I am sending him a small number of shares in Forster Newspapers. In time they may have some value to him—or if I make a botch of steering this group, they may be worthless. So I don't know what kind of fairy I am sending to attend your son's christening. A fairy of good fortune, I hope. Call on me if there is ever anything I can do for you or your son. Alex and I will be married very soon. I wish you could be with us. Alex cares deeply about you, Julia. She describes your Jamie as the "beau ideal" of romantic love, and a hero. She grieves for the man who was lost to her, but she knows he was lost long before he died. It is now my right, my privilege, to take her as my wife.*

She read the letter several times, thinking what a strange man it was who had written this. It seemed to bear little stamp of the press baron, the man of influence and power who did not, at times, hesitate to use that power, even when it hurt. She knew

his reputation as a tough and sometimes ruthless boss who refused to hand over the running of his empire to other men. He
controlled each day's events, took responsibility for hard decisions, and did not shirk from the unpleasantness of firing those
he thought had not performed as they should. He was both liked
and loathed; but he was respected. All of that had little to do
with money, and it was not for money or power that he would
marry Alex.

Quietly Julia showed these two strange christening gifts to
Lady Jean. The value of the stock, neither of them knew; Julia
was only aware that Forster Newspapers was not a public company, and it was very closely held. There was no way to value
it. But the ring caused Lady Jean to tighten her lips. "Ridiculous—to give this to a child! There is no telling what it is worth,
but it could be a great deal."

"Luisa means well. She said she wanted it kept in the family."

"In the family . . ." Lady Jean's tone suggested that she
wanted no truck with those of foreign origin who could fling
gifts like this at infants and therefore buy themselves a place
within this particular family. She seemed to indicate that gifts
of this value were to be mistrusted. The stocks, both in the oil
company and in Forster Newspapers, were more acceptable,
more understandable.

The ring and the stocks were deposited with the bank in Inverness where the family had always done its business, and, for
Lady Jean, virtually forgotten. Sir Niall's christening cup was
locked up in the almost unused butler's pantry with the rest of
the Sinclair silver. The small spark of pleasure and excitement
the christening had lighted died away. A feeling near to panic
possessed Julia, the same as had engulfed her when she had
waved good-bye to Connie. Why had she come here in the first
place? And what would she do now?

III

THE WINTER had already closed in when news of Alex's marriage reached her. It came in a telephone call from her father.
"Alex was married today. She asked me to telephone you. She
thinks you must be rather sensitive to cables."

"May she be happy," Julia breathed. "You've known for some time about Elliot Forster, haven't you?"

"Yes, Pet. These things do get around. I can only wish her happiness. She's going to have a full life, keeping up with her writing and broadcasting as well as being a wife and hostess. She's going to have a pretty rough row to hoe. There's a certain stigma attached to the fact of becoming someone's mistress when one's husband is in a prison camp. And then, she's made such a success of her job. The knives will be out the moment she makes any slips—and Washington is a very gossipy town. She *is* a foreigner. . . ."

"As long as Elliot loves her, making slips won't matter. She knows the ropes pretty well now."

"She still will be seen as a woman who took another woman's husband—and deserted her own. Pretty hard stuff to live down. Unfortunate that it happened this way. People will tend to think that she was out for money and position. We know differently, but who else?"

"I wouldn't worry." She was remembering Elliot Forster's letter. There was a strength of devotion in it that would ride over any difficulties. He was not a man to admit they even existed.

For a few minutes over the crackling line she talked with Luisa. They exchanged notes about each baby's progress. "I wish you would . . ." Luisa bit off the rest of what she might have said, the renewal of the invitation to come to Anscombe to live. She satisfied herself by saying, instead, "Don't forget, when you want to come to London, the house is always available. Michael is longing to see his grandson. What is the weather doing that far north?"

"Snowing," Julia answered briefly.

That was the fact of their lives now. Snow had engulfed them early, and there had been no thaw. The harvest was long ago taken, and the cattle put in barns. The sheep foraged on the hills for as long as they could. They had been brought down to lower pastures and ate what was left by the cattle, or the hay spread for them. "I feel sorry for the poor beasts—having to bear their lambs each year in snow and cold," Janet said.

"They are bred for it," Lady Jean said, "and Nature sees that they don't lamb until spring is well on its way. Better pity the men who have to drag them out of the drifts."

William Kerr had plowed through the forests to the main road by tractor. Every day, Rachel and Colin walked the two miles to the road to meet the bus, and each time there was a fresh fall of snow, Kerr determinedly plowed the road again, making it possible, although difficult, to get a car through. Not that many journeys were made. A careful shopping list was made for Inverness once a month; beyond that, they hardly ventured out. No one came to call. Life seemed to stand still for the long months of short days and bitterly cold nights. Julia marveled that the mailman struggled through each day, unless the weather made it impossible. Those were days when even the Kerr children stayed home. "It's dangerous," Lady Jean said. "When a little snow becomes a blizzard, they could so easily wander off the road, get too cold. Every mother in the Highlands learns to be a teacher of sorts. Mrs. Kerr is very good. They keep up with their books. They have their tasks and their hobbies. The girl is already very good at needlework, and the boy has taken to wood carving. We learn to have our own resources. . . ." Julia felt rebuked because she had none beyond reading. Slowly, by observing, she was learning some of Janet's skills of cooking, and she admitted that she enjoyed the warmth of the big Aga stove, as difficult and temperamental as it was. "We will just hope," Janet said, "that it holds out until after the war. There's not a chance of a new one, and I doubt even a secondhand one now. Even if there was the money . . ."

For the sake of warmth and economy, Julia and Lady Jean had moved down to the little cluster of what had once been servants' rooms off the passage to the kitchen. They all shared the bathroom with Janet. Despite advertising, they had never been able to replace Morag, who had gone to a munitions factory in Clydeside. "Ah," Janet said with a sigh, "who would want to come here when there's work elsewhere—or the forces to join?" The three of them fought a losing battle to keep the large rooms in an acceptable state. It was easier to forget that the dust gathered in the dining room and Great Hall, that the library smelled of mold, that the upholstery in the drawing room was damp to the touch.

Julia had become aware of how long Lady Jean stayed closeted in the small office, crammed with old ledgers and piles of papers tied in untidy bundles, which was almost opposite the housekeeper's room but which had its own entrance from the stable yard. It contained the only telephone, apart from one in the library, which no one used. William Kerr reported to Lady Jean in the small office regularly. Julia was not invited to join those sessions. "Ah, she doesn't want you knowing too much. As if there is much to know," Janet said, sniffing. "The farming barely keeps things going. The Sinclairs lost too much of their good land. Way back at the time of Culloden was the worst—so the history goes. Backed the wrong side, as usual. But then an awful lot of Scots did. But the rest has been going these past hundred years, I'd say. A bit here, a bit there. Bad investment, bad management. Master Jamie's grandfather nearly brought the whole thing to ruin—living the high life in London, as well as his crazy investments. He had a woman or two on the side, so it's said. He didn't seem to notice what provided the money was slipping away. Better send Master Alasdair to some agricultural place than Oxford. We don't need more Latin around here—but a good eye for a bull or a ram. In the meantime, we get on with it—and wait until the war is over for things to pick up. By then, the whole country will be so in debt to pay for the war that Lady Jean will be hard put to it to borrow more." Janet banged the pan on the stove with unnecessary ferocity. "And the best men we had have been taken . . . when they're needed at home, 'tis a shocking waste. I wonder how we'll ever recover."

So while the drifting snow piled against the castle walls, and sometimes the loch couldn't be seen for the driving snow, Julia had plenty of time to reflect what a marriage to Kirsty Macpherson might have done for the Sinclair fortunes. Doubts grew within her as the cold, bitter weeks of winter slowly dragged past. If Jamie had had to die, how much better that his widow be Kirsty Macpherson of Darnaway, who had the money to raise Sinclair from its depressed state; who, after the war, would have applied it and her energy and skill to its revival. Once she voiced this thought aloud to Janet.

"Ah, put it out of your mind, Mrs. Sinclair. Kirsty Macpherson is not the piece of perfection Lady Jean seems to think her. A mite flighty, and an eye for the main chance. If they had married, and Master Jamie been killed, it's my opinion she would have walked away from the whole thing and felt she owed it nothing. There's nothing about her to tell me she would have given her heart to Sinclair. That's what it needs—heart, and a wee bit of money would be handy."

Christmas passed, with a modest celebration at which Sir Niall joined them. They entered what Julia realized was the true depth of winter. The only thing that lightened those months for her was the joy of her child, and the slow, gradual, but seemingly inevitable turn in the tide of war. The Allied raids on Germany were making their impact, the Russians were recovering the territory taken from them at the cost of millions of lives, Allied forces were painfully pushing their way up through Italy, and the world was stunned by the bombing and final destruction of the Benedictine monastery of Monte Cassino, which was the key to a vital pass. American pressure was felt at the farthest advance of the Japanese in the Pacific; island by island the Americans continued until hundreds of thousands of Japanese were surrounded and immobilized. Janet and Julia continued to study maps on the kitchen table. "I never thought I'd learn names like these. Why, they're turning them around, aren't they? It didn't seem possible—the way they raced through those islands—how long ago was that? I can't remember. . . ." The newspapers always came by the mailman, who gratefully drank the hot, sweet tea Janet made him and ate her scones.

"The RAF dropped three thousand bombs on Hamburg last night," he announced cheerfully one day in March. "That should keep the place warm for a bit." Julia envisaged the destruction; what she had seen in London would be little compared to this. Roosevelt's declaration of "unconditional surrender" meant the Germans would fight on, and so must the Allies until that day of surrender came. She looked at her rapidly growing child and wondered how long before that day came. Jamie had been dead for less than a year. If only he could have stayed at Hawkinge there would have been a chance, a good chance, that he might have survived to the final day.

There were other matters besides grief and loneliness brought about by Jamie's death. One day Lady Jean invited Julia into the little office. A small fire burned in the grate, and she added a little precious coal before she turned and poured tea for them both. "I haven't wanted to trouble you with these matters. You've had enough to bear. But finally the tax people have been in touch. They have been conferring with our accountants in Inverness. They have taken their time and are willing to be patient—which shows a degree of sensitivity one doesn't associate with tax people. But inevitably they have their way. You might say the mills of the taxman grind exceedingly slow. . . ."

"Tax . . ." Julia had barely had to think of it before. She had been aware of what had been deducted from her salary when she had been performing onstage; there were still discussions going on with D.D.'s accountants and the tax people over precisely how much she owed them of the monies that came in from her share of *Return at Dawn*, but D.D.'s accountants had been very cautious and had placed in a separate bank account what they considered would be ample to meet any demand. What other tax could threaten her? She watched Lady Jean's face closely as the other woman bent toward the fire, the dancing light of the flames revealing lines more deeply etched than Julia had ever noticed before.

"Well . . ." Lady Jean's shoulders seemed to contract with cold. How much she had lost, Julia thought—her husband, both sons, and still struggling to hold on to this piece of earth that seemed so precious to her.

"You must remember that Jamie remade his will very shortly after you were married. Until then, I was next of kin. Then you became that. So his estate, which was left to him by his father, and which I held in trust until he was twenty-one, became yours. And now, of course, they want death duties. It seems to me we have only just managed to pay the death duties after his father's death. If Jamie had lived to . . ." She reached for her cup and swallowed tea hastily. "If he had lived to a normal age, he would have had a chance to recoup a little. To gather up some capital again. Jamie was not a foolish or flighty young man. I *know*, given time, he would have made something better of the place. But he wasn't given time . . . and now the taxman is beginning to make his discreet inquiries. How much is the land worth? How much a year do we make from farming? Even, dear Lord, how much is the forest worth? Oak is worth money. Never mind that to fell the oaks would destroy a beautiful forest. That would break my heart. . . . There isn't a picture in the house that's worth anything artistically. Just ancestors in their plaids done by very indifferent artists. There was a good one—a Canaletto bought, or won in a gamble, by Jamie's grandfather. But that had to go when my husband died. It would have fetched a great deal more money now. We have so little good land left. We'll be reduced to hill farming. . . ."

"The ring . . . Alasdair's ring," Julia said immediately. "The oil shares. The Forster stock . . ."

"We can't sell what belongs to Alasdair." Julia thought it was the first time Lady Jean had ever used "we" to include her.

"If we don't, then anything that's worthwhile for him to inherit here will be lost. You can't support a cottage roof, never mind a castle, on nothing—which is all hill farming brings. Just enough to pay the wages of the men and keep their families. How much do they want—the tax people . . . ?"

Lady Jean's mouth twisted. "Oh, they haven't come to that yet. They have to make an evaluation of the farm, the stock, the condition of the castle, how much it's worth. As if anyone would buy it in these times! Oh, they have plenty of time. They're in no great hurry. We have no great fortune to skip off with."

"Well," Julia said, putting her cup back on the tray, "that decides one thing, at least. If they give you time . . . I can make my contribution. And I don't rule out selling that diamond, nor getting Elliot Forster to redeem his stock. It's not on the stock exchange, so it would be up to him to decide its value." She raised her hand to stop the protest she saw coming. "I have a little money coming from my share of the films. Something I hadn't really thought about. But I have two film scripts that have been sent to me. One D.D. recommends to me, and another from Rank Films. I don't care much for either of them. But they're there. I have work if I accept it. No guarantee of a fortune, but something . . ."

"Work . . . ?" Lady Jean seemed almost puzzled. "The picture people want you to act again?"

"It usually follows, if one has a success. They've left me alone—because of Jamie and Alasdair. But I have a little Oscar for *Return at Dawn*. People will forget it if I don't appear in something soon."

"I see. You would leave here. . . . What about my grandson?"

"It wouldn't be immediately. Film people always have difficulty getting money together. They can line up the cast, even have a good script, but getting the backers takes time and persuasion. Myself, I'd be inclined to go for the Rank Films offer. D.D. is thought of as a theatrical producer rather than a film man. The money from Rank would be there sooner, but the script isn't as good."

"So . . ." Again she said, "I see," and there was some bitterness in her tone. "You will leave the baby here? It wouldn't be possible for you to take care of him and go to , . . go to work every day."

"I think that might be better, if you'd take care of him."

"Take care of him! Of course we will. This is his home."

Alasdair's home, Julia thought, but not really mine. She would never belong wholly in this place.

Before the snows of the Highlands had begun to melt, Julia was back in London, living in Luisa's house. She had made her decision on the Rank Films offer because D.D. had not yet managed to put his production together. "Not to worry, darling," he said. "By the time you have finished the little Rank effort, I will have everything in hand, and you can just go from one to another."

Her father's naval film had won acclaim and was doing well in the States. "Now I want him back on the stage," D.D. said. "That's where his heart is. He refreshes himself by these long, exhausting stage jobs when he could be earning far more money and be seen by millions of people instead of mere thousands. Another producer is tempting him with something. And Luisa . . . she will allow him to accept nothing but the best."

"Good for her," Julia said promptly.

She went down to Anscombe, mostly to see Luisa and Johnny, since her father was often in London, conferring with his agent and D.D. She exclaimed over Johnny's growth. "He will be tall—like Father. And so good-looking." She tried to thrust aside her heartache over the absence of her own child, only a few months younger than this one. Johnny had reached the stage where he was pulling himself on any piece of furniture within reach and taking a few wobbling steps before falling on his backside. He usually laughed at this, more pleased with what he had accomplished than frightened by the fall. "He has so much of Michael in him," Luisa said. "He is not solemn—like my family. He laughs so much."

"He looks very much like my father," Julia said, "and as far as I can see, there's quite a resemblance to my father in Alasdair, although I think he will remain fair, like Jamie. Though I don't say anything about the resemblance at Sinclair, because they all declare him the spitting image of Jamie."

"It's a pity . . . well, I shouldn't say it again, but I must say it. I wish you would bring Alasdair here, Julia. He could grow up with Johnny, more matched in age than any brothers. Johnny is your father's son, and Alasdair your father's grandson. Does that make Johnny Alasdair's uncle?''

They both broke into laughter. ''Absurd, isn't it? I think I must leave Alasdair where he is for a while, Luisa. I never thought I could feel so much about her—but I think it would break Lady Jean's heart if I took him away. She's lost so much. And there are so many worries. Sometimes I see her looking at the baby when she thinks no one notices. She doesn't cuddle him the way most grandmothers would. She sits with him in her lap and talks to him—never baby talk. There's such hunger in her, as if she's starved for love and the chance to give it. But she doesn't show it, except in bits and pieces. She's holding back. It's as if she's afraid to love him too much, in case he's taken away, too.''

''You said 'so many worries.' What worries?''

''Little that money wouldn't solve. We have none, you see.'' Almost against her will, the whole story of the state of the farm, the impending death duties, tumbled out. ''Forgive me, Luisa, but I even told her we'd sell your beautiful ring before we sold any more land. That was terrible of me—but I meant it. It seems such a rotten shame that someone who died fighting for his country should have his little estate taxed so heavily. He died too young. If he had been able to *give* it away to his son years before he died, it would have been untaxed. We have lost a generation, Luisa. This poor little estate may never recover.''

''You must not sell the ring,'' Luisa answered. ''I will speak to my advisers. We will find a way to help you. You cannot be put in this position. Alasdair must not lose his inheritance. I understand these things—my family was not rich, but we loved our land. We would have done almost anything to keep it, poor as it was. It was a stroke of luck that I and my sisters made good marriages. I do understand. . . .''

Julia said tentatively, ''I'd borrow on the Forster shares, even the shares you gave Alasdair, before I'd let you get into this, Luisa. It isn't fair. It would take so long to repay you.''

''I *know* Elliot Forster,'' Luisa flared. ''He would be mortally insulted if you borrowed on those shares without going to him first. Then he would simply buy them back at some highly inflated price. Do you want to begin your relationship with Alex's husband on those terms?''

Julia sighed. "Well, you know far more about money than I suspect I ever will. There's no haste at the moment. As Lady Jean said, the mills of the taxman grind exceedingly slow." She saw the frown of puzzlement on Luisa's brow. "It simply means we have time. They haven't made any demands yet. All in good time. Their time."

She went to work on the Rank film, a script for which she had only slight regard. This time, on the strength of her Academy Award, she had the leading female role. And opposite her, on loan from the U.S. Army and MGM, was William Fredricks, a veteran of many "B" pictures from Hollywood but someone who would guarantee the film's circulation in the United States. She was cast as the young wife of a Canadian killed overseas, left struggling to run a small farm on partly cleared land, partly in native woods, on the edge of a lake near the U.S. border. A German-American, detailed by his masters to undertake an espionage mission, was trying to cross the border. The Mounties and the U.S. Immigration Service were already seeking him when he took over the farmhouse at gunpoint. It was a claustrophobic film and meant to be tense, as outsiders came and went and she was forced to hide the fugitive. It was filmed mostly at Elstree, because costs were low by comparison to the United States. But to Julia's disgust, the whole cast was transported north to the West of Scotland to do the outdoor shooting. "Why in God's name didn't someone tell me?" she stormed at the director. "We could have done it on my back doorstep—the lake, snow, and all." Whereas with *Return at Dawn* she had been frightened by the director and his almost overwhelming presence, with this one she felt impatience. He crowded her and Bill Fredricks, nearly destroying whatever rapport they were trying to achieve. She knew the American had hardened himself against the jokes flying around the set about Errol Flynn winning the war in Burma single-handedly. Her leading man was seen in the same light, since he had yet to see any action except on the back lot of a studio. She hated the director's interference in what was supposed to indicate the growing intimacy between her, a lonely, shaken young woman, and the nervous and increasingly doubtful older man who rated his chances of success in his mission very small once he had managed to cross the border. She was intended to grow to care about him, to worry what would happen to him. Out of increasing despair and loneliness, they became, briefly, lovers. The director had other ideas about how the role was shaped, so that it would seem she had been taken by force; he almost destroyed what she and Bill Fredricks were able to achieve together. At last the German was shot in the back as he finally made his bid to cross the border. She saw his hands go up in surrender on the long, snow-covered space between the farmhouse and the beckoning woods. But the shot that killed him was fired after that moment. They photographed her in close-up at that moment, and the tears on her cheeks were real.

"All right, wrap it," the director said.

And they did wrap it. At a hotel in Oban, the gateway to the Western Isles, they had the traditional "wrap" party. There was plenty of whiskey, and the talk and the laughter were loud, but there was no feeling that they had made a great film, or even a good film. The best of the cameramen, who had always been assigned to take the close-ups of Julia, said, "You Scots—you really know how to pour it on." Julia didn't remind him that she had only been married briefly to a Scot. "I hope I'll work with you again," he added, not yet quite drunk. "You've got a wonderful face to photograph."

Bill Fredricks, in one of the quieter moments of the party, gave her a handmade woolly black lamb with a rather absurd bonnet in the Royal Stuart tartan that he had found in one of the few Oban shops with anything to sell. "For your kid," he said. "It was all I could find." Then he produced a standard studio photograph of himself; he had bribed the only carpenter on the set to make a frame for it. It was signed, *To Julia—here's looking at you, kid! Bill Fredricks.* She thanked him and realized that she would cherish both gifts. "I'll be talking about you back in Hollywood," he added. "I'll even be boasting about playing opposite the great Michael Seymour's daughter and telling everyone she's on her way to following in her dad's footsteps. Pity that godawful director got in the way. We could have made a better picture—you and I." He kissed her gently on the lips, and they turned back to join the party.

The next morning she traveled by train with them all to Glasgow; there all the others were changing for a train to London, and she, across country to Edinburgh and on up to Inverness. Many hands waved to her as she stood on the platform watching the train pull out; she waved back with the woolly black lamb. She held it in her lap all the way back to Edinburgh, and even during the wait for the Inverness train. She nursed it during the drive back to Sinclair. William Kerr had come to meet her in the old station wagon. "My wife sends her regards, Mrs. Sinclair, and hopes everything went well. We've missed having you around the place. . . ." She realized he had had to express that emotion in his wife's name. He drove her around to the kitchen yard. "Janet will have something good and hot waiting. . . . Good night, Mrs. Sinclair."

Janet received her with a beaming face. "I've kept him out here. I knew you'd want to see him the first instant—but he's asleep."

She looked down at the sleeping face of her son, and the tears started in her eyes. She laid the woolly black lamb in the crib beside him. His baby's face had altered slightly since she had seen him. She had missed part of his growing; it would never come back.

She hungrily ate soup and stew, often casting glances at Alasdair's crib. "Ah, he's still there, Mrs. Sinclair," Janet said. "And haven't we all missed you . . ."

Lady Jean did not concur with this sentiment, but she had greeted Julia with a dram of malt whiskey, and insisted she take a Drambuie with her coffee. "It will help you sleep. You look exhausted."

Mostly for Janet's benefit, she related stories of what had happened on the set, most particularly the parts they had shot on location near Oban. "I told them they could have done it here—and we could have made some money from it."

As she talked, she kept looking into Lady Jean's face when the other woman wasn't aware of her gaze. Like her baby's face, something had happened to alter it since she had left. It wore lines of strain she had never seen before; perhaps she had never taken time to notice, she chided herself.

When she had finished eating, since she had no little presents to give them, she brought out Bill Fredricks' photo, knowing it would please Janet. Janet examined it eagerly. "I've always enjoyed his pictures, Mrs. Sinclair. Just imagine . . . you making a picture with him."

In her turn, Lady Jean took the framed photo in her hands and read the inscription.

"How extremely vulgar," she said.

IV

A LAGGARDLY SPRING had at last come to the Highlands. The lambs born in late March and April were gaining some independence from their mothers and eating the new green grass. The forest had burst from bud into leaf. Julia slept heavily in the new silence of the world about her. She had lost weight during the filming, and Janet thrust food upon her. She played with Alasdair and she pushed his baby carriage along the rutted road through the forest. They were often at the main road when Rachel and Colin Kerr got off the bus on their return from school in Langwell. For them she saved the wrapped candy that came in the unceasing flow of packages from Alex. They chatted easily now to her and Alasdair, having lost their shyness. Julia always gave a secret little nod and smile to the McBain cottage as they passed it. It was all growing into a blessedly familiar routine. By now she had traveled with William Kerr on his rounds of the farm, so the tenants all knew her. She always carried Alasdair with her on these journeys, and the women were always eager to have a look at him. In the farmhouses where there were children, and that was most of them, she shared the contents of Alex's boxes of candy. Alasdair now had a full head of fair hair, much the color of Jamie's, and his vivid blue eyes. "Ah," said one of the older women, taking care of her grandchild in a remote farm cottage on the far side of the loch, from which the castle truly looked as if it had sprung from a fairy tale, "I remember them so well." She examined the baby's features, which now truly were beginning to form a shape that resembled Jamie's. "Your husband was the younger—the fair one. A very bonny boy—a real Gael. Such a handsome young man. But the older—he was dark. Took more after Lady Jean. They tell me Lady Jean's ailing . . . ?"

Julia denied the fact, not wanting to believe it herself. "Oh, no—nothing to be worried about. She's just tired. As most people are these days. The winters at the castle are difficult. No fuel to heat it. Hot water is a luxury, and we have only Janet to help us. Mrs. Kerr has enough to do to mind her own children. But Lady Jean will be better as the summer goes on. And, of course, now that we can begin to believe there really will be an end to the war . . ."

"Aye, that's the truth. We live on hope. We may have our men back again. But I wonder if Lady Jean has the heart for the struggle any longer."

Julia found the words tantalizingly enigmatic. What did this woman, living so far from the castle, who must only rarely have caught a glimpse of Lady Jean—perhaps at Sunday attendance at the kirk in Langwell—know that she, Julia, did not? She allowed for the chain of gossip that must radiate about all that went on at the castle, but had she been so blinded by her weariness after the filming, by her absorption in her baby, that she had not noticed what she should have?

That evening she took particular notice of Lady Jean's appearance. It was true; she looked more worn and thinner than when Julia had left for the filming. She was tired of the burden she carried; the hope she had cherished of Jamie returning to take it from her had been cruelly destroyed. But she had carried on, and continued to do so, taking her share of the household tasks, going over the books with William Kerr as carefully as always, no doubt in growing fear of what the tax people would demand of their meager possessions and only grudgingly allowing Julia some knowledge of their financial affairs.

"We manage. We survive. If it weren't for the tax vultures hovering . . ." They sat together before the fire with a last cup of cocoa. Janet had long ago gone to bed. Alasdair lay sleeping in his crib. "As soon as the snows were gone they were all over the estate, examining buildings, fields, the stock. They went all through the wood, with experts, no doubt, who could estimate how much each oak would be worth to the timber merchant. I'm sure they counted the spring lambs. Naturally, they have been to examine the books—a number of times." She added with bitterness, "All on the taxpayers' money, of course. I suppose we will know their demands in time. They have plenty of time. . . ."

She rose to put the cups on a tray, and Julia thought she saw a spasm of pain cross Lady Jean's face. Or could it merely have been the flickering of the fire playing on the lines of that delicate

skin? Those lines seemed to grow deeper each week. "Is there
. . . are you not well, Lady Jean?"

"Well? Well enough. Tired, like all of us. One worries . . .
naturally one worries. But we'll find some way around this tax
business. They are infinitely patient, these people. But we have
to recognize that in the end they get their pound of flesh, no
matter what." She gave a slight laugh, which ended in a cough.
"What a pity they didn't call them all up. We would have had
them off our backs for the duration. But they're all old and gray—
I think they were born gray—they with their neat, shiny gray
suits. If I offer them even a cup of tea when they come, they look
at me as if I were trying to bribe them. But they do take it, and
Janet's scones. But I make the tea weak, and just scrape the
butter on the scones in case they report us to the Ministry of
Agriculture for holding back food. . . ." She bent over Alasdair's crib and looked at the sleeping child. "We'll have to fight
them as hard as we can, won't we, baby? We mustn't let them
take away all that's yours—your father didn't die for that!"

The day came early in June when Julia came into the kitchen
with Alasdair in her arms. Dawn had long ago reached them in
these northern latitudes, and she had listened to the cries of the
birds in the forest, and the ones that nested in the craggy battlements of the castle. Janet was there before her, and the radio
was on. She turned an excited face to Julia. "They've landed!
Our troops have landed! Normandy, I think they said!" She was
studying the worn, smoke-grimed map that had been tacked to
the kitchen wall since war had come. "That looks a longish
distance—not the shortest way across the Channel, but perhaps
the shortest way was where the Germans were expecting them.
No real news yet—just that they've landed."

They had been expecting it for some time. The concentration
of troops along the southern and eastern shores had turned all
that area of England into one huge armed camp. A camp that
no one could leave. Weeks ago her father had moved Luisa and
Johnny and Brenda Turnbull to London, which was now virtually
free of air raids. He was starring in *Arms and the Man*, and he
could no longer move readily back and forth to Anscombe. One
letter mailed in London had reached Julia from Luisa. *Poor
Harry Whitehand can hardly turn around but there isn't a tank
or a truck full of soldiers in the road. A great many Americans
. . . all looking lean and fit, and, oh, dear, Julia, so young . . .*

so young. When I think of what they face . . . This is exactly what I am not supposed to write, but everyone knows they are there. Hundreds of thousands of them. The joke goes around that if it were not for the barrage balloons England would sink beneath the weight of all the men and the weapons. God help them, everything will be needed. Stella and Cook decided to stay . . . I suppose they are safe enough. There's little chance now the Germans could possibly launch retaliation attacks. But they said they weren't going to abandon Anscombe to these young lads running all over the fields, pitching their tents wherever there's room. Truth to tell—I think they want to be part of it all. They take a delight in passing out tea and crackers. Thank heaven for Alex's packages and those my loyal friends still send. We can afford to be generous. Do you hear anything up there of this rumor that the invasion might be through Norway? Surely that would be the hardest way of all. Reports are coming from D.D. that the word is that you have done very well in this William Fredricks film. A pity it was not with a better actor, but at least he's well known. Please come when you can, and bring Alasdair. We are longing for a sight of him. Connie is so enraptured with him that I am quite jealous that he has stolen her heart from Johnny. She is very—what do you English say—moony?—about the two babies. It amazes me that Ken Warren hasn't long ago married her for fear someone else will snatch her away and give her the babies she wants. Her fidelity to him is quite touching— and quite incredible. They will probably marry the second the war is over—only the good Lord knows when that will be—and they will be one of the few couples who live happily ever after. But it stretches my poor imagination to see Ken Warren as the dashing prince. But he seems to be the rock Connie has found to which she can cling. I wonder if she truly knows how beautiful she is and what kind of marriage she might have made. Perhaps she does and is wiser than all of us in choosing the way she wants to set her life. I hear from a friend in Whitehall that Ken Warren is highly regarded in the job he is doing, whatever that is. No doubt he sits there costing out how much the bombs cost, and how much the planes, and how much we will owe when the war is over. But who will care?—as long as the war is finally over. We'll face the bill then. You write nothing, Julia, about how you are facing the tax bill up there. Have the sharks presented it yet? I wish you would come down so we could talk

*further about this matter. And I don't care if the formidable
Lady Jean thinks it is none of my business. All that concerns you
is my business. Your father is well and seems happy with his
work. How magnificent he is! Surely the world's greatest actor
. . . and equally surely the world's fondest and most foolish
father to his young son. I swear I see some of your father's
gestures in the way Johnny waves his arms when he and his
father are having a conversation. I mean, your father speaks
words and Johnny makes noises, but to them it is a most marvelous dialogue. I have even heard Michael reciting pieces of*
Richard III *to Johnny and he answering back. To me, it is all
sweet music. Come soon, Julia. . . . Love, Luisa.*

But through the days of heady delight in the knowledge of
the slow advance of the Allied troops through Normandy and
the equal despair in the realization that the slowness of that advance must mean heavy casualties, Julia remained at Sinclair.
Each day the women studied the map on the kitchen wall, not
quite sure that what the newspapers told them was true but wanting to believe it. Softly, alone except for Alasdair, in the walled
garden Julia sighed for Jamie. If he had to die, how much easier
it would have been to bear the news at this time, when they
knew that victory was a matter of time, not of chance. He had
died at the moment of the turn of the tide, but had he known
that? He should have gone with a song of triumph in his heart.
Perhaps he had felt only doubt. *Tread softly because you tread
on my dreams,* he had written her.

His dreams had been entwined with Sinclair, and now she
knew that soon she would be making the major decisions about
its future. There was no longer even the faintest chance of de-
nying Lady Jean's illness. One bright afternoon Julia had set off
much earlier than usual on the road through the forest, determined to make the four miles to Langwell, where the children
attended school and where Dr. MacGregor practiced. She tried
her best to stop the dogs from following her, but they refused,
thinking it was the usual afternoon walk. So they trudged, Julia
pushing the baby carriage, and the dogs increasingly heavy-
footed, until they reached the village. She had to wait until almost the end of the afternoon's appointments before Dr.
MacGregor could see her. The dogs and the baby carriage
crowded the small waiting room, but the other patients didn't
seem to mind. In their immemorial fashion the women clucked

over Alasdair, and the dogs lay quietly, grateful for the rest, at
her feet. Everyone knew who she was and addressed her by
name. Finally it was her turn, and as she was called, she started
to push the carriage forward, and the three dogs rose to follow
her. "Ah, Mrs. Sinclair, you've no need of that crowd in there,"
one woman said. "I'll keep an eye on the wee child, and as long
as he's here, the dogs will be content."

Dr. MacGregor removed his glasses and rubbed tired eyes.
"I've been wondering when you would come. I know it's not
for yourself. You're looking bonny, lass, though, I might add, a
mite thin—though I suppose that's fashionable for actresses. And
there's nothing wrong with the wee lad . . . ?"

"It's Lady Jean."

"Ah, yes . . . well, Lady Jean. Well, she'll not thank me for
breaking her confidence. We doctors are not supposed to. But
you have seen it for yourself, and I know that stubborn old body
does not take kindly to questioning. Even when I sent her to
Inverness for a specialist's examination, and a week in the hospital while you were away on that picture business, she made
me promise that you would not be told. Only Janet knew, and
she had to make the same promise. The Kerrs thought she had
gone to meet the family solicitors in Edinburgh—that she was
meeting her brother, the earl, there. Well, they did a wee ex-
ploratory operation—and there was no point in going further.
She made visits several times a week into Inverness for radium
treatment, but it was only a last, desperate chance. No one expected it to have worked. I'm amazed she managed to keep it
from you as long as this. Seeing the tax people in Inverness, she
always said—or the accountant. Oh, I expect the Kerrs had their
suspicions, but how were they to be sure? She always went alone
by bus, took her treatment, which is not easy, and managed to
get back to Sinclair by evening, no doubt feeling terribly sick
and tired. She would let only Kerr meet her at the bus. Of course,
the doctors kept me informed. There was nothing I could do but
respect her wish that it should not be widely known."

"Cancer . . ." The word had a dull and hollow sound. It was
not a question.

"Aye—and it won't be long before everyone knows, no matter
what Lady Jean wishes. It is in the stomach, and the pancreas,
and it has spread. Metastasized. She has painkillers prescribed,
but it'll not be long, I'm thinking, before you'll be calling me

to the castle for morphine shots. But she's stood up to it better and longer than I expected. Tough body, she is. Comes of a good, strong line. But with cancer . . ." He shrugged. "We doctors have done what we could, but our knowledge is pitifully inadequate. Hit or miss."

"If I persuaded her to go to London . . . ?"

He shook his head. "I managed to get the best cancer man in Edinburgh to look at the results. He even traveled up to see her when she was in Inverness. They don't know anything medically in London that they don't know in Edinburgh. Finest medical school in the world, in my opinion—and many others'. Accept it, lass. If she sees it through to the end of the year, it will be a miracle—though we all know cases of remission. But you must understand we've tried all we know—there's nothing more we can do except try to ease the pain."

Numbly Julia waited outside the school for the Kerr children to come rushing out with all the others. They were surprised to see her, but she invented an errand she had to do in the village, and they accepted it unquestioningly, with their usual politeness. "Are we to walk, then?" Rachel asked.

"No, it's too far for you to walk. I'll just see you onto the bus and take my own time going back with the dogs. It's such a lovely evening. . . . Tell Janet I'll not be long."

But when the bus came, the driver, who by now knew her and the baby carriage and the dogs well from the many days when she had waited where the forest road joined the main road, insisted that she ride with them. "Ah, 'tis a long way to be pushing the child." He left his seat and between them they lifted the big carriage into the bus, the three dogs scrambling in behind them. The other occupants made room, and no one complained. The remoteness of their situation and the war itself had bred a high degree of awareness that many times they depended on each other. A few shy smiles and greetings came to her. Perhaps, she thought, it pleased them to see that the laird's wife and someone they thought of as a "film star" would share the humble necessities of war. No one went hungry on the farms of the region, but gasoline was a precious commodity. A few hands waved to her as the carriage was unloaded again, and she started with the children and the dogs on the road through the forest.

The castle, in all its ancient, forbidding splendor, was bathed in the warm afternoon light. No wind stirred, and the loch mirrored the farthest of the sheer walls but not its decrepitude. Just at the edge of the forest they had startled a doe, which had fled, with its light, graceful leaps and a flick of a white tail. Far above, coming from the mountains, they saw the soaring glide of what might be a peregrine falcon, or even a golden eagle. It was a scene of magical beauty; and within the castle Julia knew that only pain and approaching death awaited.

Through the summer they charted the Allies' slow and bitter progress through occupied France. But in mid-June there appeared a weapon whose existence had only been rumored or whispered about before. It was something Hitler had believed all through the years of the war would be the final subjugation of his enemies, that would, in the end, make Britain sue for peace. The "V" weapon, quickly christened the "buzz bomb," appeared, and fell on London and any other place that the bombs' launching pad at the Pas de Calais enabled them to reach. There was an unearthly menace in their droning whine, and everyone heard it, held their breath while it passed over them, and then wondered what happened to those under it when its motor cut out and it fell. A pilotless weapon, carrying far more power of destruction than any single bomb they had known before. The area along the southeastern coast became swiftly known as "Bomb Alley." London was shaken as it had not been, even at the height of the Blitz. A brief note came from Luisa: *Michael has insisted that Stella and Cook leave Anscombe. The houses are being so shattered and blasted here, and, of course, since one does not know until that deadly silence falls that the bomb is coming down, there is no use to take shelter. Over my protest, Michael has arranged that we all—the women and Johnny, that is—go to a cottage in Wales that some friends are lending to us. How I hate to leave him in London alone, but now I have Johnny to consider. Michael has very skillfully played on my fear for the safety of the baby. Oh, such joy and relief at the news of the invasion of Europe at last, and now we must be banished by this new terror. Will it never end? It has been so long. . . .*

The V bomb created a homelessness not known even at the worst of the Blitz. Connie wrote: *The little house Ken's mother and father have been sharing with his sister ever since their house in Hampstead was bombed has been so badly shaken, they have had to move out. They are in "temporary accommoda-*

tions,'' and I'm sure it's as grim as it sounds. Wooden prefabs, at the very best. Ken thinks that his father's worry about his mother's health has made him slightly deranged. He always did consider that he married above himself, and he feels ashamed that she had to endure these years of living in and sharing a house that belongs to any other woman. On Sundays, when it is fine, he takes Ken's mother back to the bomb site in Hampstead and promises her that very soon she will have a rebuilt house in the place where she was born. However much money his father has been clever enough to make during these years, by sheer hard work, it's difficult to see how he'll ever be able to keep his promise. Even when peace comes, as it must soon, getting materials and labor to build houses is going to be difficult. . . .

There could have been, Julia thought, few Sundays that summer when it was fine enough to go for expeditions from South London to Hampstead. It was universally damp and wet, with leaden skies. As the Allies slowly advanced into France, Hitler's determination seemed not to flag. The V rockets were mounted on pilotless planes and released so that they traveled as far north as Yorkshire and as far west as Manchester. It seemed an almost unbelievable irony to Julia that the Allied forces could be within striking distance of victory and yet the British population suffered killing and maiming and homelessness as never before. There was, she sensed, no longer the spirit of "Britain can take it." It had been a long, cruel, and infinitely tiring war. Even the courage of the bravest souls wore thin in this last, seemingly interminable wait.

The person whose courage did not seem to falter was Lady Jean. Sensing what Julia knew, she admitted the illness. "Mind— there is to be no talk of it. I will not accept pity." She was more than the "tough body" Dr. MacGregor had described. She possessed, Julia thought, a stoic soul, which would wage its hopeless battle with death, until death could no longer be denied. She had given up attending church on Sundays so that the congregation would not see her deteriorating appearance and so inquire about her health. Daily she seemed more worn, and she grew desperately thin. But she carried on her daily routine, helping Janet in any way she could. Her only concession was that she stayed a little longer in bed in the mornings, but she refused Janet's offer of breakfast there. She would take a cup of tea and nod her head in thanks, and then later appear in the kitchen, where she took a piece of toast, ignoring Janet's entreaties to have a little bacon, an egg, perhaps some fish. She did not go early to bed, and Julia could not bring herself to leave her alone on the sofa before the fire in the housekeeper's room. Alasdair slept peacefully in the crib beside them, and they sometimes talked, or read, or just gazed into the fire, always remaining until the last news bulletins from the BBC had been broadcast.

"I'm glad," Lady Jean once said, "that Alasdair seems to have inherited his father's temperament. Jamie was always a stable, self-controlled child. I don't remember temper tantrums. I feared he might have taken more of the 'artistic' temperament—from your family. Volatile—highly strung." She seemed suddenly to realize that her words might have given offense. "Oh, of course, I didn't mean that I wished he would not be so highly gifted. But his job in life will be here. For that he must have the temperament of an ox pulling a yoke, capable of the long, slow haul. The one thing that disturbs me, angers me, is that I shall not be here to help him."

Julia bit back the retort she felt like making. A woman bearing pain and facing a death inevitably soon, with such calmness, was not one to be quarreled with. She simply gathered up her sleeping child and prepared to take him to bed. "I'm glad he has inherited the Sinclair temperament, too. He will need it."

Julia had that summer made her own personal sacrifice. D.D. had finally put together his package for the film he had planned for her. He had telephoned excitedly from London, shouting over the crackling line. "Darling, *The Border* has turned out much better than anyone expected. Or else that stupid director suddenly developed genius in the cutting room. It has been taken by all the usual circuits who always take Bill Fredricks' pictures, but it's going to get extra promotion—something he could use, and it certainly will help you. Now Worldwide say that they will come in on my production and will use Rod McCallum to play opposite the part I had marked for you." When she did not immediately reply, he shouted more loudly. "Did you hear, darling? *Rod McCallum!* Of course, the script is his usual thing of taking on all the Japs single-handedly—I *had* to agree to script changes for that—and winning the war. But he's become a star doing that. Yours is only a small role—the girl left behind. I suppose rather like *Return at Dawn,* but this time the hero has to live. Wounded—heroic—but alive. Rod McCallum can't die,

or the war effort might collapse. But you see, darling, you are
the *only* girl in the film—the one whose photo he carries, and
talks to, in flashbacks, when he's not leading heroic charges. I
don't have to tell you any more—you know the plot. But, naturally, you won't have to go to Hollywood. They are talking of
location shots in Hawaii. A long journey, darling, but not nearly
so dangerous as crossing the Atlantic these days. You might even
fly, if we could get you onto a military transport. And I think
for Worldwide and for Rod McCallum, the U.S. Air Force would
be prepared to do that. After all—he's won a few Pacific islands
for them. On film. The chance of a lifetime. It will *make* you!''

She had taken the call in the little office, and Lady Jean had
discreetly withdrawn to the kitchen. She could hear the murmur
of the two women's voices.

''I can't, D.D. It's wonderful of you to have put all this together for me. It's wonderful that they want me. But I can't leave
here.''

''*What!*'' Even on the crackling line, the tone of sheer incredulity was evident.

''I can't explain now. I'll write you.'' Julia was aware of the
local operator who, she didn't doubt, would be avidly listening
to this conversation. ''I *can't* explain it now, D.D. But you'll
understand when you get my letter.''

''Darling, I have wrung my heart out to get this role for you.
Not a little British film this time, but one with a role opposite
one of Hollywood's most popular actors. All right—he's not a
genius. Who is?—with the exception of your father. But he is
big *box office*. And you can ride all the way with him. All you
need is your name coupled with his on the credits. You are
made! Your qualities as an actress far outweigh his as an actor,
but what does that matter?—for the moment. You need the audience. Soon you will be able to pick and choose.''

''D.D., stop it! It's breaking my heart, but I can't. I'll explain
it all in my letter.'' She hung up, to stop the further explosion
she knew was coming.

He tried further persuasion by letter after he had received
hers. She had impressed upon him that he must not again telephone Sinclair. *So the old harridan is dying. Why must you
sacrifice this magnificent chance—which, I must stress, may
never come again—for an old, dying woman who has always
disliked you, if not hated you? Oh, I do have eyes in my head.*

I spoke with her briefly at your wedding reception. You were as welcome as her daughter-in-law as a nest of vipers. Not good enough for her son. You, the daughter of Michael Seymour and the divine Maslova! What madness is this? What can you do to help her? She will die no matter what you do, and you will have thrown away the chance of a lifetime. I am now reliably informed that Rod McCallum has seen both your pictures, even though The Border *has not yet been released, and he is personally anxious to have you in this role. To have the cooperation of such a star any girl would give her eyeteeth. But the option does not remain open forever. You must telephone, or telegraph me by return. Worldwide and Rod McCallum do not wait forever. There are dozens standing in line for this part.*

From her father by the same mail delivery came a short letter. *Darling Pet, what a terrible, or courageous decision to make. I understand your feelings—or at least I try to understand them—and wonder how someone of your age can have such maturity. The actor part of me is amazed that you can turn down this offer—we actors are a selfish lot, as your wonderful mother learned, I'm sure often with heartbreak. But we must all live by our decisions, and I love and respect you even more. . . . You face a grueling time . . . telephone us, write us if you need help. Always your loving Father.*

It isn't just Lady Jean, she wrote to D.D. *As you said, she will die, no matter what I do. But how can I leave her here to die alone? With only Janet and the Kerrs, for as much as she will permit them into her life? How can I bear to go to Hollywood and think of her and my baby here without me? How can I leave my baby alone after she dies? It is too much responsibility to place on Janet's shoulders. Shall I go away and not care? Don't you think that every strain that crystal-clear girl Rod McCallum is supposed to love won't show in my face, no matter how they light and photograph me?*

Her father wrote back, having read the letter to D.D. *It is just this feeling, which will show in your face forever, which will make you, someday, a great star.* From D.D. there was only an angry, bewildered silence.

So she settled down for the long vigil with Lady Jean and Janet, well aware that many others knew that Lady Jean was ill, but only in Sir Niall had she confided the precise details. Occasionally Lady Jean would take the bus into Inverness, and request only that she be met on her return at the junction with the forest road. She guarded her little vial of tablets, supplied by her doctor in Inverness, jealously, still, perhaps, believing them to be secret. That July saw the original launching pad of the V rockets overrun by Montgomery's troops at Caen, and then in August, Paris was liberated. But still the V rockets continued to come from bases in Holland, until in early September the first of the greater menace arrived. The almighty blast and explosion it made on impact in a London suburb was described on the BBC as the explosion of a "gas tank." Soon they came so regularly, four to six a day, that they were known, with bitter humor, as "flying gas mains." It wasn't until November that the Government admitted the existence of what everyone knew, the "V-2" rocket, the ultimate weapon that thundered on Britain even while the Allied troops struggled to reach the bases from which they were launched.

The snows arrived in the Highlands before the Allies crossed the German border. Lady Jean held stubbornly to life. Dr. MacGregor had told them that there could be such cases of remission, the reason for which none of the medical profession understood. "Though in my opinion it has much to do with the spirit of the person who struggles."

Once, while they waited for the last BBC bulletins of the day, Lady Jean confessed to Julia, "I couldn't bear to go before I know that what my son was part of, in this sacrifice, had been accomplished. I only pray that Alasdair will never have to know such a time."

One of Alex's letters referred to the arrival of winter in the Highlands. Alex wrote, *Elliot has given me a small present— one of the many presents he gives me, but this, I think, has most meaning for us both. It is a paperweight he found while he was browsing in an antiques shop one day. I never imagined he found time for such things, but he takes it as a break from his desk instead of going for lunch. I think it was made in Germany— possibly Bavaria—about a century ago. It is the smallest image of a baronial castle, standing with its tall towers, and its drawbridge, and its flags flying. When I shake it, and the snow flies, I can imagine your Highland fastness. I share your vigil. I envy your courage. If only I once had stood so fast, I feel that Greg might still be alive.*

They celebrated Christmas quietly, with only Sir Niall as a

guest. Toys had arrived from all the family for Alasdair, in a bewildering variety, but not understanding what the fuss was about, he clung to the toy he seemed to like best—the little black woolly lamb given by Bill Fredricks. By now its tartan hat had mostly been chewed off, and it had the look of something well loved and well worn. Janet laid a crisp white cloth for the dinner and polished some of the Sinclair silver. "Ah—why not?" she replied when Julia protested at the extra work it made for her. "Won't it be the last Christmas the poor woman will know on this earth? I've been saving all the ingredients your sister Miss Alex sent, and those from Lady Seymour. As you know, Mrs. Sinclair, Christmas is not our great celebration here. It's New Year's Eve—Hogmanay, we call it—we toast. But it will be a mite quiet this year, and I doubt Lady Jean will stay up to see the new year in."

But she did stay up, listening to clocks chime the hour. There was a mild sense of celebration on the radio stations. Early in December the Home Guard had been stood down. "And about time, too," Sir Niall said with a growl. "Bloody useless we would have been if there had been an invasion—falling over each other's broomsticks. Those of us who had guns probably would have blown each other's heads off in the confusion." There had been no fresh snow for days, so he had made his way over frozen, icy ruts in an increasingly battered vehicle to see in the new year with them, stopping at the Kerrs' cottage with a bottle of whiskey and what he called "sweeties" for the children. For them he brought whatever Inverness could offer, modest gifts of toiletries for which he must have expended precious coupons. For Alasdair there was a white lamb "for when he decides not to be a black sheep." To be shared with them all, particularly as the hour of midnight struck, was a bottle of twenty-five-year-old malt whiskey. "Well, we have an interest in the distillery, and I gave up a few shares to collar this lot for my cellar. This is a special year dawning, for surely this is the year of victory."

He never referred to Lady Jean's illness, or remarked on her appearance. He never asked how she felt. There was an unspoken agreement between the two friends not to speak of the impending event.

The snows were deep around them in February when they learned that Dresden had been consumed in one enormous firestorm. The full news of the bombing drifted through only during the next few days. "The price of victory, I suppose," Lady Jean said. "But I wonder if we needed to go to these lengths. . . ." And then, with a thickening of her weakening voice, she added, "But they would not have hesitated to do the same to us if it had been possible."

She lived to hear the news of the Allies taking Cologne, to hear of them encircling the Ruhr. She stayed later in bed these days, and retired there after lunch for several hours. Her eyes were now far sunken into her face, but she wore the almost ethereal air of one who has looked at the worst and was not afraid. Julia believed that she was seeing before her own eyes a role so magnificently acted that it dwarfed any stage acting she had ever witnessed. Lady Jean wrestled with a devil that was grim and real, and she knew which would win. But she continued the struggle.

In April the snows dwindled into what for the Highlands were showers. They heard of what the Americans found when they took the concentration camps of Belsen and Buchenwald. The Russians occupied Vienna. "God help whoever is there," Lady Jean murmured as she held her grandson on her lap. When the news came that Hitler had committed suicide in his bunker in Berlin, she just nodded weakly. "A cowardly end—the only one possible for him."

She had delayed as long as possible the moment when she was forced to take permanently to her bed and to summon Dr. MacGregor for the stronger drugs she now needed. But now she returned to the tower room she had once occupied. "It is only fitting," Janet said. "You cannot really expect her to spend her last days down here next to the kitchen." The April days had lengthened to the long northern twilights, and she kept the curtains drawn back from her western-facing windows for as long as light lasted in the sky. Sir Niall shared their vigil. He came every evening, bringing bottles of his precious old malt whiskey, waiting for Dr. MacGregor's second visit of the day, when the injection that might give Lady Jean a few hours of sleep was administered. The gaunt figure sat upright in bed, wearing a faded bed jacket and agreeing to take a single dram of whiskey, which Dr. MacGregor said could only do her good. During the day, when Julia or Janet sat with her, she liked to have Alasdair's crib brought into her room, and she watched him seated on a blanket, playing with his toys and chattering his unknown language. The last of the V bombs had fallen in Kent in March. There was now, over the whole country, a quiet air of expectancy. They almost held their breaths. Early in May came the news that Berlin had been occupied by the Russians.

"A big mistake," Sir Niall observed to Dr. MacGregor when they shared their nightly dram with Lady Jean. "We should have raced to get there at least at the same time. Stalin is going to demand a king's ransom just to let us get our noses in there. Doesn't look good for the future." They always carried on a normal conversation, as if Lady Jean could participate if she wished. But her strength now would not permit her to sit up, and she whispered only a few words. Alasdair no longer played in her room. "Let her have whatever rest she is able to get," Dr. MacGregor said. Julia was aware that the doses of morphine must have been gradually increased, for Lady Jean seemed to spend most of her days in semisleep. In the last weeks Julia had brought, over Lady Jean's protests, a nurse from Inverness. "Can't pay," she said hoarsely. "The taxes—"

"The taxes be damned!" Julia had replied. "I have money from *Return at Dawn,* and I'll soon be getting some extra from *The Border.* There's quite enough to pay for what will make you comfortable." She sought for something to comfort the dying woman. "Did I tell you Alasdair has just received quite a handsome dividend check from his Forster Newspaper shares, and the American oil company . . . ?"

The other woman's hand gripped hers with surprising strength. "Not to be spent. Even for taxes! His education . . . he must go to his father's school. To Oxford . . . If he is to labor here for the rest of his life, he must understand it's"—Julia had to bend close to her to hear the words she struggled to say—"must understand it is worth it."

Daily Sir Niall brought the spring flowers from his garden, and they helped to dispel the smell of illness and impending death in the room. They were placed in many vases and pots, so that wherever Lady Jean could look, she saw them. Julia was strongly reminded of the rosebush dug up and sent to Anscombe, at Jamie's insistence, for Ginette Maslova's garden. She remembered the rosebush from Sir Niall that she had carried back from her first visit here. According to her father's letters, they both thrived and flourished.

Sir Niall and Dr. MacGregor were both in Lady Jean's room

on this, Dr. MacGregor's last visit on his rounds for the day, sharing their slowly sipped whiskey, when Julia entered to give them the news. The nurse hovered in the doorway, understanding that Lady Jean loved these few minutes when the men talked together as if the dying woman were perfectly able to join in their talk. "It's just come on the news," Julia said, "Churchill and Truman have declared that tomorrow is officially Victory in Europe Day. I think I'll just have a dram with you to mark the occasion."

Lady Jean's head stirred and half turned, painfully, on the pillow. "I think I'll have a sip. . . ." The long rays of the western sun mercilessly revealed the ravages of her face. She allowed Julia to raise her momentarily to take a small sip of the fine malt. "So glad . . ." she murmured. "So glad . . ." Instinctively the two men drew close to the bed. "So glad I lived for it . . . lived to know Jamie died for . . . for the ultimate victory." Slowly Julia lowered Lady Jean's head to the pillow again.

"Put in another pillow please. I want to be be able to see . . . to see the last of the light." Propped up, she stared into the spectacular sunset over the loch.

"Well, now," Dr. MacGregor said, coming to feel his patient's wrist, then to put a blood pressure cuff around her skeletal arm, "if you'll all leave us, I'll just give Lady Jean her little medication and hope she will have some sleep tonight. All right, nurse . . . all right! No need to stay." He was holding up a syringe and preparing it with liquid. "Lady Jean prefers it comes from me—with no offense meant to your good self. I'll leave a wee vial if she should wake during the night."

She did not wake.

2

June 1947

Chapter Seven

Julia wandered along the rock-strewn shore of the loch, the dogs following her at a sedate pace; they appeared to have had enough excitement for one day. Perfect June weather had graced Alasdair's fourth birthday. He was now asleep, exhausted from the turmoil and pleasure of the first birthday party he had been really able to comprehend. They had invited every child of a suitable age on the estate to attend, and somehow most had managed to get there. She had held the celebration over for a day so that it took place on a Saturday, when the children were free of school and the mothers could look forward to an outing. They had come, many crowded into small cars, they had come by horse and pony, some had taken a shortcut by coming with unerring instinct through the woods, or along the shore of the loch.

The afternoon sun had poured into the long dining hall of the castle. The dark corners had been filled with flowers picked from the wilderness of the garden. At each child's place was a festive paper cracker and several bars of chocolate, all of this sent by Alex. The crackers had in turn produced paper party hats. There had been cakes and jelly and cream, again made by Janet mostly from packages from Alex. Julia had written a month before that she planned a little celebration for Alasdair's birthday. Alex had responded by sending several large packages, extravagantly, by air freight, containing the sort of things few of these children had ever seen. It would not be a party at which Alasdair received presents, but at which they were given away. There had been a grab bag that had produced small dolls; soft, cuddly animals, and toy automobiles made on American models that had fascinated and puzzled the children. Appropriate trades had been made—dolls for automobiles, books for stuffed animals. The man who had played the pipes at that long-ago dinner party Lady Jean had given on Julia's first visit to Sinclair came again with his children and played the familiar reels. Some of the boys wore kilts, held in the families for generations; some of the girls had pleated tartan skirts and sashes and white blouses. The mothers and some of the fathers who had attended drank tea and ate sandwiches and cakes, and they smiled their appreciation as Sir Niall provided and himself poured the whiskey that made the celebration complete.

Julia had sometimes wondered how many of his distillery shares Sir Niall had sold to stock his cellar before the war. His generosity with its contents seemed boundless. He brushed aside Julia's protestations, as he had kept Sinclair stocked with whiskey through the years. "What else do I have to do with it? Drink it all myself? What a waste—and I'd be in my grave now if I had." He had watched with delight the ill-coordinated dancing of the children. Some of the older ones, though, were imbued with a natural grace and skill. "The old traditions go on . . ." he had murmured happily. "I remember some of the mothers as young lasses. . . . Everyone seemed to be pretty before the war. And I must stop saying 'before the war.' Everything has changed, and we know it. No use in looking back. . . ." It was true that the war had left them not only tired and, as a nation, deeply in debt, but also the austerity demanded to pay off those debts bit more deeply than when the war had actually been raging. They were short of everything, and now even deprived of the spirit to fight. The battles and the war had been won; peace brought its own emptiness of spirit.

The guests had finally departed, leaving behind little gifts that Julia knew must be accepted or she would give offense—jars of jam, for Alasdair a pair of woolen gloves clearly made from some other garment that had been unraveled and reknitted, socks made in the same fashion, and a hand-carved wooden stag with great antlers. Alasdair, his face flushed and smeared with chocolate, had shaken the hands of all of them, children and parents, as they left. He wore the Sinclair kilt that his father and his uncle Callum had worn at his age. Julia had found, in the closet where these things were stored, shoes with gilt buckles that had fit him. "Not a baby anymore," Sir Niall had said. Already, at this age, Alasdair bore an astonishing resemblance to Jamie—the same vivid blue eyes, his full head of blond hair growing in just the same way. Even through the still-childish features, Julia thought she could see Jamie emerging. Sometimes he made a movement, a gesture that was heartstopping in its likeness to Jamie. There were many moments of heartbreak for Julia as she had watched Alasdair grow, the sense of loss and longing renewed over and over. She remembered Elliot Forster's strange letter when he had sent his christening present to Alasdair: *She describes your Jamie as the "beau ideal" of romantic love, and a hero.* Yes, he had been that, and much more to her, and his son, tall for his age, stood straight and proud by the castle door to shake hands with his guests. Julia's eyes misted at the sight. Would the image ever fade?—the memory grow dim and less painful? Her love for Alasdair, her pride in him, was the double-edged sword that seemed forever lodged in her heart, because in Alasdair Jamie could never be forgotten.

She bathed him, heard his prayers, and tucked him into bed, her arms lingering around him longer than usual. If only Jamie could have seen him today . . . if only . . . The words echoed in her mind endlessly.

Sir Niall had waited while she put Alasdair to bed, and they had a simple supper from the leftovers, washed down with a bottle of good claret that Sir Niall had brought, along with the generous supply of whiskey. Julia and Janet had both watched as he had coaxed his ancient and rusting car into life and had set off jerkily from the kitchen yard to the drawbridge and home. " 'Tis just as well there's not much traffic around," Janet remarked. "Sir Niall has put away a skinful this afternoon. But how he enjoyed himself. What a pity—there he is in that great house, without wife or child, and only that dour old soul Mrs. Cummings to take care of his wants. No wonder he dotes on the child. . . ."

After all the dishes and glasses had been cleared and washed, Julia put on the old, heavy cardigan that hung in the kitchen porch, and heavy shoes. She realized how incongruous they looked with the filmy dress that had come in one of the many packages from Alex. She never for a moment resented wearing the castoffs from her sister. She knew they were equally shared between herself and Connie. "Darlings," Alex had said on one of the rare occasions when all three sisters had been alone together, "you know what social life in Washington is. . . . I'm

Elliot Forster's wife. I have to have a new wardrobe every season, when the cherry blossoms bloom, and when the leaves fall. It's so lucky we're all much the same height and build. Though I confess I have trouble keeping my weight down these days. Perhaps an inheritance from Grandmother Maslova, whom I remember as being on the heavy side—how strange that none of us inherited the musical genes. We had two generations going for us—and what did that produce? An actress and a journalist . . ."

"And a housewife," Connie had said and laughed happily.

Julia was thinking of all this as she walked along the edge of the loch, the dogs at her side. Only now, just past Midsummer Eve in these far northern latitudes, was the sun beginning to cast long shadows from the forest across the loch. It had been a day of excitement and happiness for Alasdair, a day when more than at most times she had longed for Jamie to be present to watch his son. She touched the stiff paper of the letter that had arrived that morning and at which she had had barely time to glance. She had saved it for this time of quiet, when she could read and reflect on it. It was a portent that her world would begin to impinge once more, and she was not certain that she wanted it, nor could she afford to dismiss it out of hand.

She thought of that little time two years earlier when they had been together—she, Alex, and Connie. Connie had married Ken Warren as soon as she could wangle her demobilization after victory in Europe. He had not then been released from the RAF. Luisa had organized a beautiful wedding at Anscombe; Julia had come south with Alasdair, and Alex had crossed the Atlantic with Elliot to be there. Connie and Ken had been married at the village church, and Connie had paused by her mother's grave after the ceremony to lay her wedding wreath there. It had been the first time that Michael's son, Johnny, and his grandson, Alasdair, had encountered each other. The meeting, and their stay at Anscombe, had been attended with as many blows and tears as smiles, but Michael professed himself delighted with the relationship. "Exactly as two boys should be. They'll be the greatest of friends as they grow up, just you see." It had been the first time for the family to meet Alex's husband, Elliot Forster. He was a naturally impressive figure, with the long, lean body of an aristocrat, and good looks that conveyed intelligence and breeding. "I was fortunate enough," he said to Julia, "to have had a great-grandfather who didn't lie down and die when he lost most of his land after the Civil War, and bought, for next to nothing, the presses and the name of a bankrupt newspaper in Richmond. And he went on from there. I've managed to buy back a little of the land the family once owned in Virginia, but the present owner of the old homestead refuses to part with the house itself, even though at the end of the war it had only a few chimneys left standing, and has been rebuilt piecemeal ever since. . . ." He had said this as they walked the perimeter of the Ginette Maslova rose garden. "I'm as tough in business as they come, as probably Alex has told you. But like most Southerners, my soft side is heritage—even though my father sent me to Harvard to get my perspectives right on such things. Harvard didn't knock it out of me completely, I suppose because they had their own brand of sentimentality about places and names there—because it's New England." The wedding had been in July, just after Alasdair's second birthday. The rose garden was in full bloom, and trellises that had been built since Julia had last been there were heavy with roses. Elliot Forster had paused beside one of them and had easily reached for and plucked a blossom from the tallest stem. "So, you see, I'm a natural sucker for all things that are old, that hold together a heritage. I hope you will invite Alex and me to Sinclair."

For only a second Julia had hesitated. "Of course. But you must expect fairly primitive conditions. We're . . . we're still on a wartime basis. I have only Janet to help."

He had nodded to her from his height, even while he still held the rose. "Madam, I'm a pretty deft hand at the stove, and I don't mind carrying hot water. I haven't been unaware of how you live—Alex always has shared your letters with me. I'm not as soft as I may seem. It's only your beautiful, wonderful sister who keeps me from taking off for the Canadian wilderness to fish a mosquito-ridden lake for a couple of weeks in summer. I'd like to try again a Scottish trout or salmon river. Now I think we had better go back to the festivities, or Alex will grow jealous. I rather wish she would be jealous. You do understand that I am forever fighting the ghost of Greg Mathieson, whom I highly respected as a man and a journalist."

"Well, then," Julia said, "come to Sinclair. I have enough of my own ghosts to fight there. It's just possible you'll encounter one or two of them."

At the time of Connie's wedding, war was not over in the Pacific. "Ken won't be demobilized until all the bills are properly set out, if not paid," his father had said to Julia at the wedding. He was a tall, thin, austere man, as gray as his suit, which she knew must have done as his "best" for many years. Ken's mother had the remains of a delicate prettiness and the look of perpetual weariness. She wore a prewar dress of frilly fussiness, and her faded fair hair was arranged in elaborate curls. Her husband was tenderly solicitous of her, insisting that she did not stay in the garden too long, lest she get a chill. Connie and Ken would start their married life in a prefab in Croydon. That fact seemed not at all to diminish Connie's happy radiance. "But I'll see that they do better," Ken's father had said. "We have the land at Hampstead, and the remains of a house. It will be possible, I believe, to make part of it habitable. I will find the builders—somehow. Goodness knows, there are enough bricks lying there to make several houses. I must have Mrs. Warren comfortably housed soon. She has suffered quite enough from the deprivations of this war. . . ."

So the wedding party had gone on, and things had seemed almost normal. With the war in Europe so recently over there still was an air of optimism, a sense that soon life would be as many people fondly remembered it. D.D. had said, "Now we *must* find something for you, darling. What a mistake to have turned down that chance with Rod McCallum. The film was a considerable success." His tone was heavy with reproach. She shrugged it off. There were other things to worry about.

The greatest worry had been the death duties, which had duly been presented shortly before Julia and Alasdair had come to Anscombe. Luisa had pressed Julia on the matter, and she had finally given in and told her what was demanded. "There's nothing to do, I'm afraid, but to sell some more of the best land. It's self-defeating, really, as it produces by far the largest part of our income." As Lady Jean had grown weaker, she had been forced to allow Julia knowledge of the details of the farm income, knowing that soon she would need that knowledge.

Luisa had been horrified. "Oh, not the land! That is the last thing. In Spain, my family was not rich. We are an old family, but land was all we had. The hard, dry land of Andalusia—good for cattle and goats and vines, but many acres are required to produce riches. We never had riches. I and my sisters all married well, so there are no worries, but we were taught that the land was sacred. As soon as conditions permit, I will go over to Burgundy and see how quickly the vineyards there can be put back into full production. My first husband knew I would always *care* about his beloved vines. He trusted me greatly. And there is the acreage in Gloucestershire, which Henry left me. As soon as the RAF vacates the house, I will see about selling it, as I know Michael will never live happily anywhere else but here. But the land—the land I will keep. It is bred in me—like a peasant. So, Julia, I cannot think of letting you part with the land that must be kept for Alasdair. I will have my accountants look at what those unpleasant tax people have produced, and we will set out the formal terms of an interest-free loan. You will pay me back whatever the farm can afford each year. Believe me, my accountants have eagle eyes. They will know that *I* could take over the Sinclair estate, and they also know that I will not. But we must have a proper agreement. That will make it look right in their eyes.''

"You must take back the ring.''

Luisa shrugged. "If you wish I will put it in the London vault, but I will never wear it again. I gave it to Alasdair as a christening present. I do not take back gifts. . . .'' Her manner grew slightly cold, and she dismissed Julia's stammered thanks.

Julia herself was uncomfortable, unhappy with the arrangement, but she saw no other way to go but to accept. It put her totally in Luisa's hands. She did not begrudge or resent the contentment her father had found in his second marriage, the unexpected arrival of a young son. But Luisa's hand was as firmly on him and his life, as it would, from now on, be on Julia and Alasdair's. Luisa was jealous of Michael's time and attention; she guarded him and his career as if they were as sacred as the land she talked of. Julia noticed that even during her brief visit to Anscombe for Connie's wedding, she and her father were seldom alone. Luisa was constantly at his side. She was involved in every aspect of his life in a way that Ginette never had been. Ginette and Michael had been two busy professionals—during their times together they had hardly ever, as Julia remembered, discussed details of each other's career; they had left each other to make their own decisions. Now Luisa weighed with even greater care than the devoted D.D. which move would best serve Michael's future. "She is very shrewd, and she can drive a very tough bargain," D.D. had observed to Julia. "But it is never just the money—every role must *do* something for Michael. She is a very possessive woman and is used to having her own way. I would not care to cross her seriously. It would be the end of my long friendship with your dear father. He grows more and more dependent on her—her judgment, the way she caters to all his needs. And she makes sure no one else does that. I take care that I always speak to Luisa before I speak of any new project to Michael. Never forget she is Spanish. I think she would be capable of tearing to shreds anyone who damaged Michael or little Johnny." He sighed. "Well, darling, let's go and find another champagne. It is your sister's wedding day, let's not forget. But *why* . . . ? He groaned, and struck his forehead with a deliberately theatrical gesture. "Why did she have to go and marry that fellow? He'll stay in Whitehall, of course, once he's demobilized. A born Civil Servant. He'll work his way up, and no doubt one day be regarded as a Treasury mandarin. In due course he'll get his knighthood. And that lovely, radiant creature will be totally wasted on him. She was meant to *shine*. . . ."

"But they love each other, D.D."

"Love is brief, darling, when you are saddled with little children, and pinching pennies, as they will be doing for years as Ken Warren dutifully climbs the Whitehall ladder. Oh, he will be very careful, and in the end he'll look just like his father. Now, who could love *that?*"

"I think Mrs. Warren does. We're not all meant to be stars, D.D."

He took two glasses of champagne—Julia had ceased to wonder where Luisa got her supplies—from the tray carried by a passing waiter. "Well, *you* are meant to be a star. If only I could dig you out of that miserable wilderness . . ." He started toward the house. "Ah, I think the bride and her lugubrious groom are about to depart. Dare we be so extravagant as to throw rice? I hear they will honeymoon in Bath. No doubt Ken Warren thinks that the waters will do them good. He looks as if he could do with a tonic. . . ."

For Julia, as she saw off Connie and Ken, there were only memories of her time with Jamie in the McBain cottage, the time their marriage had truly begun, the nights at the suite at the Ritz, their wild tumbling in the damp heather on Dartmoor from which their child had come. She knew that once past Anscombe, Ken would stop and remove the ribbons from the borrowed car and they would proceed at a sober pace to Bath.

Alasdair seemed to be confused by the sudden congregation of the guests around the front door of Anscombe and the little car. "They've just been married, darling. They're going away."

"Away . . ." He repeated the word mechanically, not fully understanding; his tone had the sound of misgiving.

"But they're happy, darling. It's a very happy day." He wriggled from her arms as he saw Johnny begin to dash after the departing car. He joined in the chase, the two little boys running together, pumping small, still-uncertain legs to their utmost. And then they collided with each other and fell. At once they struggled to their feet and began raining baby blows on each other's head and shoulders. Julia and Luisa raced after them and separated them. Julia found that she was immensely relieved to see that Luisa was laughing. "Oh, dear—boys will be boys—as they tell me here in England. Come, little ones. Time for bed now. An exhausting day. And perhaps a little treat for you both when you are in bed . . . provided you are good and quiet."

Julia was frightened to realize how grateful she was that Luisa had taken no offense at the incident. She was still hearing D.D.'s words: "I think she would be capable of tearing to shreds anyone who damaged Michael or little Johnny." Julia was beginning to know fully the implications of Luisa's having lifted the immediate burdens of Sinclair from her. A part of hers and Alasdair's life now belonged to Luisa. She was not only in Luisa's debt literally, but Luisa also held the key to her father's affections. There was no way in which she could be bypassed. Julia now knew that if a misunderstanding arose between her and Luisa, it would be she, Julia, who would be cast off. Alex had the independence of her husband's high regard and his wealth—and she had more, she had his love, Julia was sure. And Connie, no matter how humbly she lived, would always have the protection of Ken Warren. A sense of her aloneness almost swamped Julia as she helped Brenda Turnbull bathe the two little boys. But Luisa seemed to know exactly the moment to appear so that she knelt beside the two as they chanted by rote. *And now I lay me down to sleep* . . . It was Luisa who gave the chocolate to them both before they were tucked in.

"For once we won't spoil the taste by having you brush your teeth again." She kissed Johnny. "Sweet dreams, little man.

Mother and Daddy love you." She turned to Alasdair in the next
bed. "And you, dear little cousin—nephew—whatever you are—
you and Johnny will be friends forever."

Alasdair hadn't understood her, but he recognized her tone of
voice. Julia could hardly credit the pang of jealous that swept
through her as Alasdair suddenly put up his arms and drew Luisa
down to him for a kiss. Perhaps it was only a kiss bought by a
chocolate, but it had been quite spontaneous. She foresaw a
lifetime of being grateful to Luisa, dependent on her goodwill.

They had traveled back to Sinclair by car with Alex and Elliot,
because Elliot had demanded that they see some of the countryside on the way. The journey had taken three days, Elliot driving
a Rolls that had been produced for him by his London bureau
office. He appeared to have plenty of gasoline coupons, and
reservations had been made at the right hotels along the way.
Alasdair had been entranced by all the novelty the past ten days
had brought into his life. He was ready to love all those who
produced it. "What an extremely obliging, intelligent child he
is," Elliot remarked. "He doesn't howl, and he doesn't get car-
sick. . . . I think you have a sturdy young Scot there, Julia."

Julia had made a frantic series of telephone calls to Sinclair
before leaving Anscombe. Janet was informed of who would be
coming and what must be done to prepare for them. "Oh, Janet,
we need a guide for Mr. Forster. He would like to do some
fishing. And we give them the Red Tower Room. Thank God
it's summer. At least they won't freeze. . . . Janet, I'm nervous.
It's silly, since she's my own sister. But I do want them to enjoy
themselves."

"Don't fret yourself, Mrs. Sinclair. Between us, Mr. Kerr
and I will see that all is arranged. Oh, and I have managed to
engage a wee lass from one of the farms. She's not trained, of
course, but very willing. She will be a help. The young ones
are beginning to realize that with the war over, there aren't the
jobs in the cities there used to be. But . . . but, Mrs. Sinclair,
can we afford her?"

Julia, secure in the knowledge of Luisa's loan but increasingly
aware of how dependent she had become, said firmly, "Yes,
Janet, we can afford her—now."

They approached Sinclair in the late afternoon, and the forest
trees were beginning to cast long shadows; then they broke

through into the full light of the sun. Elliot stopped the car and sat silently for some moments, gazing. Julia thought she heard him murmur: *"The splendor falls on castle walls . . . The long light shakes across the lakes . . ."* He raised his voice and turned to Julia. "I never thought I'd see such perfection."

"Close to, it leaves much to be desired."

He gestured to Alasdair. "Anyone born to this would have it in his heart forever." Then slowly he proceeded across the bridge and the drawbridge, and they entered the castle by its first court-yard. Janet opened the massive oak door at precisely the moment the car stopped.

Julia always remembered the time Alex and Elliot spent with them at Sinclair with pleasure, and when they were gone, a sense of loss. They had fitted in so perfectly and never appeared to notice what was lacking. The house had functioned more smoothly than Julia could have hoped. The addition of young Kate, who was raw and inarticulate but who rushed to do what-ever was asked of her, was a considerable help, leaving Janet to do what she did best, which was to cook. Sir Niall had stocked the meager cellar with some splendid wines, and the neighboring families were generous in issuing invitations. Alex and Elliot brought with them the glamour of an outside world, but a world of power and money that in no way smacked of *nouveaux riches*. There were many invitations for Elliot to fish trout and salmon rivers, which he did with a skill that earned the admiration of the guide Sir Niall had loaned to him. Sir Niall also loaned his fishing rods. "There're not many men I'd do that for." Kirsty Macpherson had returned to her father's home after a divorce from the Englishman she had married during the war; she brought with her her little daughter, Betsy, about a year younger than Alasdair. With her mother now dead and her sister married and living in California, Kirsty was mistress of Darnaway. She displayed her talent in this direction in a magnificent dinner party she gave for Alex and Elliot. At Darnaway there seemed no lack of servants, or any other comfort. Kirsty appeared to Julia more beautiful than before, ever more assured. "Why," Elliot asked as they drove back to Sinclair, "is that lovely creature so jealous of you, Julia?"

"Jealous?—I doubt it. She might harbor a slight resentment. She was the one Jamie might have married if he hadn't fallen into my grasping hands. It would have been better for Sinclair if he had married her. Now we each have a child, and neither has a husband.''

''Perhaps better for Sinclair,'' Alex said, ''but not for Jamie.''

On the last day of their visit, a golden July afternoon, Julia walked, holding Alasdair's hand, with Alex along the shore of the loch. The dogs ran ahead of them. Occasionally Alex picked up a stone and skipped it along the surface of the water, and the dogs bounded after it. Since they couldn't retrieve it, and had to return disappointed, she began to search for some small pieces of windfalls from the edge of the forest. Deliberately she did not throw them too far, so that one of the dogs could retrieve it and return it to her feet, eyes begging to have it thrown again. Alasdair shrieked with delight and tried to squirm from Julia's grasp to join them in the game. At last they reached the point at which Alasdair began to tire, and they perched on rocks to rest.

''It's been perfect,'' Alex said. ''I've never known Elliot so relaxed. He's such a complex character. I've known him to be absolutely ruthless and cold when people make mistakes. He's not squeamish about firing someone he thinks has acted with bad judgment—even when they've worked for him a long time. Sometimes I'm almost afraid of him—suppose I did something that caused him to feel that way about *me?* And yet—well, I think he would forgive me anything—except disloyalty. He has this strange attitude that once something is his, it must be his forever. That's how his first marriage broke up—his wife had an affair with someone else, and he absolutely could not forgive it. This was about the time we met. When we fell in love he knew how I felt about being disloyal to Greg. That's why he was prepared to wait until the end of the war, so that I could tell Greg to his face that our marriage was finished. He couldn't condone a divorce from a man in a prison camp. A very strange morality—and I was twisted in knots of guilt over it. Still am, in many ways.''

She rose, reached for the piece of wood Rory had laid at her feet, and flung it into the loch. The scramble of the three dogs caused the water to fly high, and it flashed like crystal in the sunlight. It was Duuf who brought it back to her feet. Seated on the rocks, they were showered with water as the dogs shook themselves.

Alex gestured to them to be quiet, and she sat down again.

"There is one way in which our marriage is a grave disappointment."

Julia turned to her, puzzled, concerned. "But he loves you. I *know* he loves you."

"Yes, he loves me. I don't doubt it. I play my role of the Washington wife very well. And he enjoys the fact that I still write and broadcast. Of course, being Elliot Forster's wife doesn't hurt me at all in that direction—but I get paid good money by hard-nosed men to do what I'm doing, and he seems proud of me. He rather despises idle women. . . ."

"Then what . . . ?"

"I can't give him a child. That's what the doctors tell me. I have been to them all—Washington, New York—all over."

"Alex—you're sure?"

"About as sure as anyone can be. God knows, it isn't for lack of trying. And no fault of Elliot's. He's had all the tests. And his first wife was pregnant once—and miscarried. No—I'm the one with the problem. Do you remember that time when I was about fifteen . . . no, of course you don't remember, you were too young, and you were all in New York, and I'd demanded to go back to Grandfather Guy at Anscombe. I had some trouble then—an infection of some sort. They didn't know much about it, and eventually it cleared up. I just remember a lot of pain and a fever, and Grandfather Guy bringing some doctor from London because he was so worried. Well, it was the Fallopian tubes. Some sort of blockage. They don't hold out much hope. I used to wonder why I didn't get pregnant by Greg—but at that time I was enjoying my marriage and the freedom of being without a child too much, and it didn't bother either of us. And now—well, I want desperately to give Elliot the child he desperately wants. It hurts, Julia. I feel so . . . so inadequate. I've always thought that all the fuss about barren women—you know, the biblical stuff—was a lot of nonsense. Who needed children? I never thought I'd care much, one way or the other. Now I'm suffering all the pain and self-reproach that's supposed to go with this condition. I'm not a whole woman. It's a devastating thing to try to come to terms with."

"Elliot . . . ?" Julia said his name softly.

"He accepts the situation in quite a wonderful way. I wouldn't realize how wonderful if we hadn't often talked of the children we would have once marriage was possible. I've offered him a divorce. He won't hear it mentioned. I told you—once something is his, he never wants to let go. The only consolation I have in this whole sorry business is that he seems to want me more than he wants a child. I'm not going to be cast off. But I have to face the prospect for the rest of my life of being less than other women—even when I *know* I'm better than a lot of them, except for this biological flaw. In bed—well . . . with both Greg and Elliot—and one other person, very briefly, whom I won't talk about—I have the most complete satisfaction. And I think I give it. I'm always hungry for sex, and Elliot knows it. We have everything we could want from our marriage except the children we had hoped for. Unless some miracle happens. So now I find myself struggling to be the perfect wife, because in this respect I will always be imperfect. I find that I bend over backward to anticipate anything he could wish—to do everything as *he* wishes it done. Perhaps not always what I want. I can never rebel—and something of the rebel has always been in my nature. Sometimes I find I have views different from his politically. I try to stifle them—not to write them, in case I upset him. And yet—I know very well he doesn't want a doormat as a wife. I think that was what first attracted him. I always said what I thought. We would have the most wonderful arguments. And now I find I sometimes bite my lip and say nothing. I don't want to turn into a 'say nothing' woman, and yet, in many ways, I find I am. It's a pervasive thing, Julia—the sense of being a failure. I always believed I would be successful, whatever I did. And now Nature plays this dirty trick on me.'' She rose, cutting off any comment Julia might have tried to make. ''Come on. We'd better be starting back. I hope Elliot and Sir Niall have had a good day's fishing.''

They walked back, each holding one of Alasdair's hands to steady him. Even the dogs seemed to have caught their mood; they walked quietly beside them, not begging for anything to be thrown. It occurred to Julia that the Alex she had known all her life would not have worried about being a little late for anyone's return, nor if they'd caught a fish.

The three dogs trotted docilely at Julia's side; they, too, Julia reflected, were two years older than when she and Alex had walked along the loch shore on the last afternoon of their visit. She perched on the rock where she and Alex had sat with Alasdair; her hand touched the letter in the pocket of her cardigan, but she did not immediately get it out to reread it. The two years since that day when she and Alex had sat on this rock had, on the surface, been busy ones, and yet there still remained at the core of her being the feeling of deadly emptiness that Jamie's death had left. It hurt now in a much more subtle way than it had in the beginning. She now had the sense of her life stretching on endlessly in the same pattern that these years since the end of the war had shaped. She looked back to the fairy-tale castle on its island and thought, Is this it? Is this how it will always be? Would she be the custodian of a trust held for Alasdair until he was old enough to take over, or at least old enough to help in carrying the trust? Was she fated to repeat the pattern Lady Jean had set, of living to take charge of an inheritance until it was time to hand it over—perhaps to see Alasdair marry someone of whom she approved as little as Lady Jean had approved of her?

The end of the war had made farming no easier than it had been before. They were still rationed for gasoline and food, and the Ministry of Agriculture still demanded that quotas be filled. They had managed to buy two new tractors and to undertake the drainage of some land that until now had been only marginal. The Forestry Commission had advised the planting of a whole desolate mountainside, which had barely supported hill sheep, to conifers. Julia and William Kerr had not liked the idea—the squared-out acres of young pines looked alien in that landscape—but they both recognized that it was a better use of the land and would in a relatively short time produce a cash crop of needed timber. They had spread the little available money as far as possible—sometimes having to decide on whether it would go to the necessary repair to the tenant farms, or the building of new hay sheds or cow byres. However they added it up, there was never enough money. The debt to Luisa weighed heavily on her, and she was scrupulous in trying, each year, to repay some part of the sum. Luisa always had been soothing. "You are not to worry. It is a good investment. . . ." Julia realized she had mortgaged her and Alasdair's future, and the future of the Sinclair estate, to Luisa instead of to a bank. "A generous woman," William Kerr had said when she had been obliged to inform him of the arrangement. "The bank would have charged a great deal of interest, if they had agreed on the loan at all. . . ." But he liked the state Sinclair was in no better than she.

In that time she had made one film, a rather trite costume piece that had gone largely unnoticed. It had played briefly in the United Kingdom, was booked by a minor circuit in the States, and had vanished. Since the contract D.D. had arranged for her had not provided much money as a down payment but had a handsome provision for a share of the gross, the failure of the film had meant she had come away little better off financially than she had been before. She used the money to put a new roof on the house the Kerrs occupied and to provide them with a new indoor bathroom. Until then they had used an outhouse and had bathed before the kitchen fire in a copper tub. With the very little she had left over, she mended the roof of the McBain cottage, connected it to the electricity supply, and so was able to bring water from the well indoors. Her action had puzzled William Kerr. "What for, Mrs. Sinclair? The place hasn't been used since the McBains left—since the old laird was killed. Who will live there?"

She could not tell him why she would not see it fall into ruin. "Who knows? We could certainly use some help for you. It's the cottage closest to the castle. You never know when some young couple might come along wanting a job, and there would be a place for them to live. . . ."

"And what, I wonder, would we pay them with? The money would have been better spent on a new roof for the stables. The haylofts above would make quite good accommodation for anyone. There's already electricity laid on, and water. Wouldn't take much to put a bathroom in there—since we're now all connected to the septic tank that reaches into the loch." They didn't mention the fact that the mare Catriona was now the only inhabitant of the stables. With the purchase of the tractors, the oxen had gone. Catriona now seldom pulled the trap. She spent her days happily cropping the sparse grass that surrounded the outer walls of the castle, sometimes crossing the bridge to graze what little grass grew on the edge of the road through the forest. She was not tethered. Little traffic ever used that rutted road, and she could always be trusted to return of her own accord to her stable as dusk came down and it was time for her oats and water. Julia herself often groomed her, with some help, or hindrance, from the youngest Kerr child, Dugald. "I wonder why we keep you,

you silly old thing?'' Julia murmured as she stroked the soft
gray muzzle. ''Eating your head off . . .'' But there was never
any suggestion of the knacker's yard for Catriona. ''I suppose
there have to be some luxuries left in life, and you are one of
them.'' The rest of the farm horses, who still supplemented the
work of the precious tractors, were housed at the tenant farms
on the other side of the forest. The very site of the castle, situ-
ated on its small island in the loch, protected by the forest,
which helped create its unique beauty, was also its curse. They
were effectively cut off from the land and the farms that produced their sparse income. Precious gasoline was used each day
by William Kerr to get to the fields and the work he had to
supervise. They had not even the space to graze a milk cow.
The hens and roosters continued to roam the kitchen yard,
roosted in one of the disused stables. The Kerrs worked the half
acre of the vegetable garden. Milk and the rest of the food were
brought from the tenant farms. Julia remembered the easy access
to the fields of Anscombe, their lushness and plenty, the mild
winters, with something like disbelief that she had taken it all
so much for granted. She wondered what the magazines and
newspapers that had once interviewed her would make of the
life of the woman who struggled to keep the walls of Castle
Sinclair above the waters of its lovely but unkindly loch.

The two years had seen the birth of Connie's first child, a
daughter, who was named Margaret Ginette—the first name being that of Ken Warren's mother. As had been predicted, on his
discharge Ken had been invited into the Treasury. He held a
junior post, but he was firmly set in the course that, if he persevered, probably would lead to the office of the Permanent Under Secretary. That would be many years away. As always, the
road he traveled in the Treasury was nonpolitical. It would not
matter which party was in power; the day-to-day running of the
Ministry was in the hands of the Civil Servants, who were there
ostensibly to do the bidding of the current Chancellor of the
Exchequer but who were, in fact, his advisers and in many cases
his mentors. To the public, the most powerful of these Civil
Servants were nameless and faceless, but power they did hold,
and Julia didn't doubt that one day Ken would have that power.
His father, Clarence Warren, had managed by some sleight of
hand, or by sheer bribes, to get part of the house in Hampstead
restored. It was a more modest building than the one his wife

had grown up in, but it possessed the inestimable virtue of its seven acres adjoining Hampstead Heath. Connie dutifully moved out of their prefab in Croydon, to live with her parents-in-law in Hampstead. *There's loads of room for us all,* she had written, *and it's so marvelously comfortable after the prefab. We even have central heating on the ground floor, and that will be extended as soon as we're allowed more fuel. The kitchen is weird and wonderful, made up of bits and pieces of scrap that Mr. Warren has managed to salvage. He must know every inch of London to have put it all together. We each have our own bathrooms, which are furnished with rusty baths and cracked sinks, but they work, and we keep out of each other's hair. And the space—well, after the prefab, it's wonderful. Almost the best thing is the privacy of the garden. Of course, it's a wilderness, with only the vegetable garden functioning. Ken and Mr. Warren work like dogs there every weekend when it isn't raining. Mrs. Warren goes out in a big hat left over from God-knows-when, and picks the peas and beans when they're ready. We grow parsley by the row. Ken's become very good at preserving the seeds of everything and hands them around Whitehall. Oh, it isn't heaven by most people's standards, but it is to us. We all have our meals together. I've become quite a decent cook. On Saturdays when it rains, Ken and Mr. Warren go off hunting for furniture. Each week we seem to get something that's needed—a wardrobe, a dresser—sometimes something pretty, perhaps a little antique side table, an old mirror whose frame is only a bit chipped. The curtains are the most wonderful mismatch you've ever seen—but they cover the windows. I don't really know how Mr. Warren has managed all this, what with building regulations and all that. He's been very patriotic and put a lot of money into War Bonds during the war—but he must have made some money on the side somewhere—and of course during the war there was nothing to spend it on. But at last he's got Mrs. Warren back where he thinks she belongs, and she has every comfort he can provide. Theirs is the only bedroom with central heating, but he insists that she is delicate and needs it. It's as if they were still both very young and still very much in love. Nothing and no one comes before her. They both adore Margaret Ginette, and I am made to feel very much the daughter they never had. I know it all sounds impossibly ordinary and domestic, but I am happy. . . .* The same letter announced that she was pregnant with her second child.

Julia sighed with something near envy as she thought of her sister. The quiet and peace Connie had craved, the dream of it she had clung to all during the war years, had come her way. Julia didn't doubt that Connie worked very hard in that nearly-large house Clarence Warren had rebuilt from the rubble of the old building; she would have turned her clear, methodical mind to making the best of the slender rations they were allowed—grateful for the things sent from Anscombe and from Alex to supplement them but capable of managing without them, and she would most likely have become more than "quite a decent cook." Julia wondered if she hadn't also become something of a servant to Mrs. Warren, but the woman had not appeared to be a tyrant or martinet. Perhaps they truly had formed a mother-daughter relationship. But her loyalty to Ken was fully, almost blindly committed; she would find nothing done for the little family group to be too much. She craved no excitement—she had had all that. Julia often thought that Elliot Forster, in his demand for loyalty, might have considered Connie the perfect wife—except that, for all her beauty, she totally lacked Alex's spark of vitality and wit. Another child—that Elliot Forster would have given much for, and the news must almost have broken Alex's heart. How they both, for different reasons, she and Alex, envied the sister who had wished for nothing but peace and the humdrum of life. She possessed her own wisdom that none of them had truly appreciated.

Luisa had been to visit Hampstead. *Ken and Mr. Warren have worked wonders when one remembers they started out with nothing but the ruins of the old house. One day it will be beautiful. Of course, they lack much, but who doesn't these days? They are touchingly grateful for the little things I send from Anscombe. Connie seems so happy . . . I don't think one ever need worry about her. I ask Mr. Warren for tips on where to go to get workmen, and bits and pieces we need for both the Wilton Crescent house and Anscombe. He is a dedicated sifter through rubbish, and Mrs. Warren has an eye for pretty little pieces they seem to pick up for nothing, but many of which are really quite good. What does it matter if the hand is missing off a Staffordshire figure? No one notices these days. Ken seems to have developed a passion for restoring furniture. I suspect someday he will be an excellent judge of antiques, find them in unlikely places, and pay the proverbial song for them. Unlike most economists, he seems to know the value of money in an everyday sense as well as being able to juggle billions around in his mind. Of course, the true value of their house is its position. Seven acres of wilderness, but it borders on Hampstead Heath. Ken has cut a path through to the old stone arched gate that opens onto the heath. It must cost a fortune in taxes to own such land in London, but one day it will bring more than a fortune. Mr. Warren also has his own unique gifts in understanding money.*

That, Julia thought, coming from Luisa, who understood money in her own way, was more than a compliment.

Luisa continued to guide and direct Michael's career, and he seemed more than happy to leave it in her hands, even when she disagreed with D.D. on what should be the next project, whether this or that offer should be accepted. Always Michael's career seemed to run into Laurence Olivier's, even though the two were good though not close friends. D.D. suggested filming *Hamlet*. "How can I?" Michael had replied. "Larry's is already the definitive version, and if I must wait until the public is beginning to forget how he played it, I'll be far too old for the role." There had been a time when D.D. proposed that Michael and Julia should film their first stage hit together, *King Lear*. Luisa had been very doubtful, but she had allowed D.D. to make his approaches to sources of funding, promising that if he raised a certain amount, if he could interest a major Hollywood studio in putting up half the budget, she would find a way of matching the amount. Michael, for once, had stepped in and forbidden her to participate. "It's madness, darling. *Lear* on the London stage is tricky enough. It's simply not for the one-and-sixpennies on a Saturday night, who want, now more than ever, a bit of glamour." But D.D. had persevered and had, at last, admitted defeat.

"No Hollywood studio will go for it. When one of their story editors reminds a studio head that it is Shakespeare and will star Michael Seymour and his daughter who won the Academy Award, they say, 'Who needs the story of a mad old man who gives away what he should be holding on to? Who will buy it in Des Moines?'—wherever that place is. But it seems to be their measuring stick of what makes money. Art they know nothing of, and don't want to know."

All this had been going on while Julia had been at Pinewood filming the slight, forgettable costume drama. Her father was then appearing as Chebutikin in Chekhov's *Three Sisters*. While Hollywood had turned down the very idea of *King Lear*, they had enthusiastically responded to the film Michael had made of *The Skin of Our Teeth*. It had a major critical and box-office success in the States; and Luisa, who had backed it from the beginning, purred with satisfaction. Michael was currently preparing for the role of Solness in *The Master Builder*. D.D. was planning a production of *Uncle Vanya* with Michael as Astrov when *The Master Builder* had run its course. D.D. also was trying to interest some Swedish filmmakers in starring Julia in Strindberg's *Miss Julie*, but without any apparent success. "You were made to play Miss Julie," he said with a sigh. "But I shall not throw out the idea. I will keep it for when I find the right people."

While Julia was filming at Pinewood she had lived in Luisa's London house, and Alasdair had lived at Anscombe with Luisa and Johnny. It coincided with the time when Michael was resting, but also preparing for a revival of *The School for Scandal*, so the family had remained at Anscombe during that whole period, and Julia had seen Alasdair only on Sundays, when she was free. "I keep Michael at Anscombe when he is not working," Luisa said. "So much better for him. Quiet days, a regular routine, the country air . . . just a few people on the weekends so that he doesn't get bored. Do you not think he looks splendid? I encourage him to work in the garden—and doesn't the Maslova garden flourish? He gets contributions of bushes from everywhere in the country. It has become famous. I have difficulty in keeping curious strangers out. Did you know that one rose-grower is proposing to call his very best hybrid 'Ginette Maslova'? Such a charming compliment, don't you think? But the grower hasn't achieved quite the shade of red he desires, so we must be patient." The garden had been extended to enclose part of an adjoining field, as she had said it would. Slowly walls were rising, made from the old bricks Michael had salvaged from the ruins of the oasthouse—and Luisa had put out the word all over Kent and Sussex that they would buy any usable old bricks that were available. In the aftermath of the bombing of the Battle of Britain, and the time of the V rockets, there seemed tons of old rosy brick to be had, if one was prepared to pay the prices Luisa could. It steadily piled up in the stable yard and adjacent areas until Julia realized that there was far more than the walls of any rose garden would need. There also began to appear pieces of ancient lead guttering and downspouts, some of them bearing crests of ancient families. "Oh," Luisa explained, "I have learned much from the admirable Mr. Warren. I have become a regular scavenger."

"But why . . . ?"

"My dear, as soon as it's possible, we shall remake the stables as guest suites. Anscombe is a delight, but it is . . . well, a trifle pokey. Big in the eyes of the people of the time when it was built, but when one has carved out space for bathrooms, and extra closets, and the day-and-night nursery for Johnny— which, of course, will become his own rooms when he is finished with Brenda and goes to school—well, there is little space left over. So I thought it would be comfortable to house guests in their own suites, with a bathroom and little kitchen, so they may make their English morning cup of tea themselves, without which no one seems able to manage. I try every way I can think of to make Michael's life smooth. He works hard enough when he is on the stage . . . why should he be bothered with domestic matters . . . ?" Julia remembered the sometimes chaotic life Michael had lived with Ginette Maslova, and on which he had seemed to thrive. But that now seemed many years ago, almost a lifetime. They had passed from war to peace; all of their lives had changed. Her father was no longer young; he appeared to need the cosseting Luisa gave him.

She sensed that Luisa was not altogether displeased when the whole idea of filming *Lear* had to be given up. It had been a wild scheme of D.D.'s, with only a small chance of success, but Julia wondered if Luisa had not slightly feared what replaying that part of daughter to father might have done. For once she would have been outside the relationship, not able to control it. She noticed how quickly Alasdair had slipped into Luisa's control, cherished as a companion for Johnny and as Michael's grandson. Already Luisa was talking about the time they would go to prep school together. "I promised," Julia said, "that Alasdair would go to the same schools Jamie and his brother went to."

Luisa waved a hand airily. "Oh, does that matter so much . . . I mean, particularly prep school? Afterward the public school . . .

well, perhaps that is different. But wouldn't they be such a help to each other when they first left home? Back each other up? They are such good friends, even though they're hardly more than babies."

"We'll see . . ." Julia answered vaguely, determined that it would not happen, but afraid, just at that time, to offend Luisa. This was what it was like, she thought, to be perpetually in someone's debt—for all Luisa's kindness, her generosity, it really was no better than owing money to the bank. True, it did not carry actual interest, but it was worse in that it was a family debt, and carried its own particular interest and penalties for default.

The shadow of the castle had begun to fall across the loch, reminding her that she soon must start back. The dogs had not yet been fed, but they still lay patiently at her feet; perhaps there had been enough scones and pieces of cake slipped to them during Alasdair's party to keep them content. She remembered Alasdair's pleasure in the whole event; she remembered that Sir Niall's eyes had been bright with what seemed like tears as he had watched the children go fumblingly through the sometimes intricate routines of the Highland dances. Kirsty Macpherson had brought her daughter, Betsy, over to join the party. Even her air of aloof superiority had mellowed as she watched the children. "Alasdair has all Jamie's grace. We used to have dancing lessons together when we were children. He was the only one I ever wanted to dance with . . . all the others seemed so clumsy by comparison. . . ." Remembering how Kirsty and Jamie had danced together at Lady Jean's party, the quick lightness of his movements, Julia was hit once again by the sense of hurt and loneliness, and that strange jealousy of all of Jamie's years she had missed.

She put her hand in the pocket of the sweater and felt the letter there. She wondered if she would reread it now, or let it wait until she had her cup of cocoa on the sofa in the housekeeper's room. It was from D.D. and quite long and considered, unlike his excited, impatient telephone calls, which always demanded an instant decision. As usual, he was wildly enthusiastic, but more cautious than she had ever known him. It had been at his request that she had allowed a man from Pinewood to spend a day at Sinclair almost a month ago, looking over the whole property, walking the loch shore, taking many photographs, eyeing the castle as if he saw it through the lens of a camera. He also had asked some very practical questions about electricity supply for lighting purposes indoors, had viewed the Great Hall and the dining hall as if he saw them in a film setting, wondering if the floors, where they were not flagstone, would bear the weight of cameras and dolly, if a generator could be hooked up to boost the power supply. He asked about which bedrooms and bathrooms might be available for various members of the cast of a projected film, which he carefully did not name. He went off, committed to nothing but saying he must check accommodations in Inverness, since it was obvious that many of the cast and all of the crew would have to stay there, and travel to Sinclair each day. He had checked out the kitchen and wondered aloud if Janet would be prepared to provide a simple meal at lunchtime and if she could cook dinner for the principals in the evening as well as give them breakfast. "Wouldn't it be easier," Julia had replied, "if everyone stayed in Inverness? Your stars aren't going to find it very comfortable here."

"You understand, Mrs. Sinclair, that this might not turn out to be the location our client is really seeking. I have merely come, with your permission, to look it over. It is one of a number on my list."

Julia then recalled her anger when they had all been sent on location to the Western Isles for *The Border,* and she had raged that the location shots could have been done on her own doorstep—realizing how much money she might have earned in those few weeks. Now here it was in writing from D.D. A very handsome rental for the use of the castle for filming purposes for at least six weeks, very possibly longer. They would, at their own expense, make arrangements to boost the power supply from the main road to the castle, and they would pay the fees of a surveyor of Mrs. Sinclair's own choice to survey the property before and after the filming and make good any damage done, although every care would be taken, the principals being aware of the antiquity of the castle and its historic value. They would send a catering staff to supplement Janet in the kitchen and order whatever provisions were necessary. It seemed, because they would be paying in much-needed dollars, that the Ministry was prepared to supplement their food rations, and they would be allowed to import costumes and scenery where necessary, though they would also require the help of local electricians and carpenters, paying them going union rates for London, which were well above the average for the Highland region. They had decided that the castle site was suitable, though filming indoors might prove somewhat difficult. The were especially anxious to use the long daylight hours for shooting that the latitude of Inverness provided in the summer; they also would run the shooting into the autumn, using the forest setting as well as the disused RAF station a few miles away, for which the Ministry of Defense had already given permission. They might need to return for some snow scenes immediately after the first fall—although these could be faked, if necessary, at Pinewood. But the star of the film very much preferred the real thing.

The star of the film was Rod McCallum.

She remembered the stormy fight with D.D. when she had turned down the chance to star with Rod McCallum, although the part had been tiny, in one of his most successful war films. The girl they had found to take the part she had turned down had gone from that beginning to better things and was now in demand in Hollywood. And she, Julia, sat here by the shore of the loch of Sinclair and was virtually forgotten.

Well, no part was being offered this time. It was doubtful that Rod McCallum knew, or any longer cared, that she was the Julia Seymour who had turned down his offer of glory—because Rod McCallum was the stereotypical actor who had become famous and had had huge box-office during the war, whose films automatically shed a reflected glory on whomever he agreed to have play opposite him. The choice had been very much his. She hadn't any doubt that some beautiful girl, destined for a very much inferior role, would appear with him.

At last, D.D.'s careful letter broke from its restraint. *Darling, you must seize this chance. There are other moldy old castles in Scotland, but McCallum has chosen this one. And Worldwide offers a more than generous price. If you and the surveyor are clever, you can invent a little damage they did not actually cause. It might help a little with the plumbing.* D.D. had heard enough from Connie and Alex about the state of such things at Sinclair that he never ventured to pay a visit. Nor had her father and Luisa, even when she had wistfully suggested they come north in the middle of the summer, when the region was at its kindest. There was always a reason why they could not come. Michael was in a play, Luisa had to go to Burgundy to see to her estate there. Behind it, Julia knew, was the reason that Luisa dreaded the discomfort of the castle they had heard described. She was kind—infinitely kind—but the kindness did not go as far as disturbing her creature comforts. Instead, they had urged her to visit Anscombe—even to go to France with Luisa. They had sent rail tickets for her and Alasdair. Last summer she had spent two weeks there at Anscombe, and she and Luisa had been amused and delighted over the growing relationship between the two boys when they knocked each other around in the rough and tumble of their play but seemed never to carry a hurt or a grudge into the next day. Julia wanted very much for Johnny to come to Sinclair by himself, if Luisa could not be induced to come. But Luisa had not yet reached the stage when she could trust Johnny totally to another's care. "When he is a little older . . . I know I try to protect him too much, but he is my treasure. . . ."

Think, D.D.'s letter continued, *just a few weeks of inconvenience, and I am sure it won't cause too much inconvenience, and none at all to your farm, since I have heard that your farming is all away from the castle. I think McCallum likes the position of the castle and the forest. It is some script he had written for himself—something to do with, I think, some American soldiers holed up in a castle, preparing themselves to make a raid into Germany as a guerrilla unit, to take out some scientist who is in a somewhat similar castle, who has signaled that he wants to be taken out. Carrying his scientific secrets with him, of course—realizing that the Nazis have lost the war. Of course, there will be a beautiful mistress of the castle where they train, and I suppose McCallum will play his usual tough role. Myself, I put out a little feeler about you playing that part yourself. It would seem so natural. But I got no response to that. Myself, I think it is a little late for this sort of film—or else it is ten years too early, when moviegoers would look back at it as history. But then, who knows? With Rod McCallum's name it should go well enough at the box office. And why should you care if it does well or not?—except that it could make your castle famous, and tourists will want to see it. You could start a souvenir stand. But whatever the outcome, darling, you will have the money for the rent in your pocket. Be assured I will have a watertight contract. They will pay for every single second they occupy your house,*

*for every nail they bang into your old walls. Do not let pride
stand in the way of this, darling. And who knows? If the star is
happy, he may go back to Hollywood talking about you—things
may come of it. I shall make sure Luisa entertains him on his
way through London, as she does so supremely well. Just one
thing, darling: They will want to start filming in August, so you
must be prepared by then. It does not mean you have to do
anything—but the advance unit will arrive before then. Already
there is a man ready to go to Inverness to make arrangements
about the extra electricity supply. It seems from the visit of the
man who came to see you that the local authorities are ready to
cooperate in every way. Not only because the Treasury assures
them the dollars are badly needed hard currency, but also because of the publicity for the region. You must be prepared for
little inconveniences, but the reward is handsome. I write all
this because I want to give you some time to think it over. Please,
I beg you, when I telephone, do not say "No." You will disappoint your old D.D., who loves you, so much.*

There was really no option but to accept. As D.D. had
shrewdly guessed, she could not allow pride, or pride for Alasdair's sake, to stand in the way of what would, in real terms,
amount to more than they made in a whole year from the farm.
She thought of the sum she would be able to repay Luisa. Pride
did not count against even that small degree of independence.
Already her mind was wandering over which of the many needed
improvements the money would make possible. And, after all,
what was so shameful about renting a facility for some weeks?—
in fact, the longer the better, the more money they would earn.
The contract would cover, D.D. had promised, extensions of
time, any extra household help needed, and all the requirements
of the cast who stayed at the castle. She could almost name her
own price on that. She began to hope that they would decide to
stay until the snow flew.

She rose, and slowly the dogs did also, stretching their fore
and back legs after their long wait. She scratched behind the
ears of each of them. "Prepare yourselves, my loves. We're
going to have lots of guests, and you'll probably be spoiled
rotten among all of them. There's only one thing you can't do:
You can't run in front of the camera when they're shooting. . . ."

As she walked back, a chill came to that evening air even on that June day. She was preparing what she would say to Janet. She already knew how she would answer D.D. when he telephoned.

Chapter Eight

I

THE INVERNESS PRESS was alerted well in advance of what would be taking place at Sinclair, and there was a small stir of excitement over the news—and it seemed to Julia that almost the whole of the region reacted the same way. She sensed that some of her neighbors did not approve of this invasion of foreigners, but most people seemed to think she had acted with canny good sense. "A body must make a living some way" was Janet's reaction, and it seemed basically to be that of most people. Janet seemed unperturbed by the thought of her kitchen being taken over. "Ah, what harm can they do? Except burn their fingers. And as for the evening meal, well, you know, Mrs. Sinclair, you may safely leave that with me. We will make the rooms as clean and comfortable as we can, for whoever stays here, and with Kate to help and a wee hand from the Kerrs, we'll manage just fine." A weekly salary had already been allocated in the budget for Janet and Kate and extra help to be brought daily from Inverness, a sum that caused Janet to open her eyes wide. "It must be millionaires they all are!"

"One has to be more than a millionaire to make a film, Janet. It's just too bad I won't be able to pay on that scale when they're all gone."

"Well, a wee nest egg I'll put aside. And how many millions do you think they will spend on this?"

Julia shrugged. "I don't know the film budget, Janet. But D.D. did indicate that Rod McCallum had personally invested some of his own money in this. It seems he commissioned the screenplay and then had to persuade Worldwide to back it. Well, they owe him one. He's made millions for them and, I wouldn't doubt, millions for himself. Perhaps they're only pampering him on this. It's a sort of weird story—if what D.D. says is right. Something about twelve men being specially trained for a secret drop into Germany to take out a rocket scientist who has managed to send the message that he wants to come over. Well, they train at a remote castle in Scotland—dress themselves as Germans, think German—except when they get drunk, which I think they do regularly every evening. The castle is commandeered by the Ministry of Defense for their training, and no one is allowed near any town, or even the village, to talk about what's going on at the castle, or who the strangers are. So they chose a castle on an island in a loch, with mountains in the background, and a forest—as near to the conditions they'll find after the drop into Germany. We'll be seeing them clambering up and down the walls on ropes—all carefully rigged, of course. I just hope to God none of the old battlements come tumbling down on anyone's head. But D.D. assures me they're insured for millions if Mr. Rod McCallum should get clumped on the head by a piece of Sinclair stone. Though I imagine they won't risk their star in any dangerous position. The stuntmen are there for that.''

''You mean,'' Janet said, disappointed, ''that they really don't do those things themselves? I mean . . . the likes of John Wayne and such . . . Errol Flynn . . . they don't do those things?''

''You only see their faces in close-up in what's *supposed* to be some feat of daring. Long distance it's almost always a stuntman.'' She hated to see the disillusionment in Janet's face, but characteristically the other woman perked up.

''Well, at least I'll be sharing a house with the famous Rod McCallum for some weeks . . . and a handy wee bit of money to go with it. And Sinclair Castle will be seen all over the world. Well, haven't they come to the right place? A grander spot they could never find.''

Sir Niall seemed just as excited, but in a more restrained way. ''I'm sure that your D.D. steered them this way. Now, Julia dear, you must consider coming to stay at Finavon with me while they are in residence. You have to give up all your habitable rooms to them—whoever 'they' are. And what will you do in the evening?—dine with them in the dining hall? I don't think the cozy old housekeeper's room would be quite their style. And

Alasdair . . . he'd be underfoot all day. They'll either spoil him or curse him. It could ruin the child. . . ."

Julia smiled. "You're so kind. But I've already thought about what I shall do. I'll go and live in the McBain cottage. We can quickly furnish it, and it's quite good enough for Alasdair and me. And I shall be near enough to give Janet a hand with the breakfast in the mornings and with dinner. I shall leave Alasdair with Mrs. Kerr during the day. She won't stand any nonsense from him. I'm beginning to think I'd better leave the dogs with her during the day as well. They can come to the cottage with us at night. The only creature likely to be unaffected by all this is Catriona. I just hope there might be some wild, improbable scene when an old white mare could be trotted out. If I could only persuade Rod McCallum to get on her back and be photographed. She would be Queen for the Day—and forever after. We could sell a million postcards of her. . . ."

Sir Niall became alarmed. "Aren't you getting rather deep into this?"

"I know the film world, Sir Niall. It will be here one day and packed up and gone the next. We will have to settle back into our old routines, and the excitement will be gone. What no one understands here yet is how incredibly boring filming is. Scenes shot over and over again. If you get even a few minutes of film a day that's usable, that's good. You just sit around and wait for the next call—whatever the director decides needs redoing—it can be dozens and dozens of takes."

"But this is why I'm saying you and Alasdair must come to Finavon. You can't be involved day after day in all this."

"I have to look after my property, Sir Niall. I have to see that no one goes too far—however well insured we are for that period. And I must be around to help Janet. I can't afford to retreat like the grand lady. I have to help. And I have to keep my eyes open. So it will be the McBain cottage. . . ."

He sighed. "I am grieved. I would have loved an excuse to have you both as my guests. But you have a down-to-earth wisdom that one must also respect. But I shall—no matter what objections you make—see that some sort of bathroom and flush toilet are installed at the cottage. I don't care what laws I break. One can always put it down to the cause of earning very much desired hard currency—such as good American dollars. By the way—will the public flock here in hundreds to watch?"

"I don't think so. I suspect part of the attraction of Sinclair was the fact that it is cut off. All they have to do is put a guard at the entrance to the forest road, and no one can come in, unless they walk through the forest itself. It's private land, after all."

He nodded. "Yes—I see. Will you provide me with a pass, so I can get past the guard? I want to be part of the fun, as everyone else does—even if you think it's boring. I'm going to sell you—at a ridiculously low price—some of my very best wines, so that Janet can sell them at an enormous price to those who take dinner at Sinclair. You should pocket a very tidy profit, my dear."

It seemed unbelievable to Julia, but Sir Niall managed to convert the small third room of the cottage into a rough bathroom within a few weeks. She suspected he must have commandeered every available man on his estate and some of his neighbors' workers. The septic tank was dug in a hurry, on land sloping away far from the well and down toward the stream. There was no heating in the bathroom, but a secondhand immersion heater was installed, which served the bathroom and the living-room kitchen sink. "You must have been prescient, my dear, in having the place connected to the electricity supply." She suspected he had got no planning permission for what he did, since she had signed no forms. There wouldn't have been time for such niceties. The small room was mostly serviced from odds and ends of plumbing material lying around Sir Niall's estate. He did as Ken Warren's father had done and combed the scrap dealers' yards of Inverness for the bathtub, sink, and toilet.

The evening the last stroke of white paint was put on it, Julia met him at the cottage to share a dram to christen it. By the time she arrived, he already had a fire going. There were carpets on the flagstones, and chairs and a table taken from the castle, two beds in the adjoining room, and faded cotton curtains at the small windows. He flushed the toilet several times just for the satisfaction of seeing it work. "There, my dear, rough and ready, but it should do until they are gone and you are back home again."

He had brought along his special old malt whiskey, and his housekeeper had put slices of smoked salmon on thin brown bread for him to bring. She raised her glass to him. "Thank you—but how can I thank you? Why do you do all these things for me? I could never have survived here without your help."

"Oh, nonsense! What else have I to do? You're a brave woman, Julia—as Jean was. You are both my friends. What are friends for? There's not much in my life now. Not much to plan for. You and young Alasdair keep a spark going. We have all lost so much, we cherish even more what comes our way." He went hastily to top up his glass, and she thought the action was to disguise a quaver in his voice. She thought of the two sons he had lost, the two who had gone off with Jamie to join the RAF and win the war, the two who had been killed only days apart in the Battle of Britain, a day before Jamie's Spitfire had demolished the oasthouse where her mother had played Mozart. Often she had been tempted to tell him that it had been Jamie's plane that had caused the carnage, but loyalty to Jamie and a sense of the added hurt it might have caused him had kept her silent.

"No one could ever have a truer friend," she said. They drank their whiskeys, mostly in silence, finished the smoked salmon, and set off in Sir Niall's old car to Sinclair to have what they assumed would be their last meal together in the housekeeper's room until the filming was over. Janet treated it like a feast. The first unit of the film crew would arrive in two days.

II

NO ONE EXCEPT JULIA had imagined the near-chaos the arrival of the unit would cause. Men prowled all through the castle as if they owned it—as they almost did, since the company was paying a princely rent for it. They walked the shores of the loch, combed the woods looking for location shots. Julia had trouble keeping them out of the McBain cottage. "Hey, why didn't we know about this? It's got great possibilities. Mind if we do some exterior shots here?"

"Exterior only," Julia said firmly.

"Jeez . . ." one of them said. "Real Grimm's fairy-tale stuff, isn't it. Would this have been the woodcutter's cottage?"

"Not exactly . . ."

"Who's the old guy who goes around in kilts? Directing the traffic, sort of?"

"Sir Niall Henderson. He's the family's greatest friend."

"And what do we call you? Are you Lady Sinclair?"

"I'm Mrs. Sinclair. There is no title in the family."

"Is that a fact? I thought people who had castles were always lords and ladies. But who's this Lady Jean we keep hearing about?"

"My late husband's mother. It was a courtesy title. She was the daughter of an earl."

"Very confusing . . ."

The stable yard was beginning to fill up with caravans that would serve as makeup and costume rooms. The Kerr children were entranced and just a little frightened by all the activity and the strange American accents. The dogs quickly found the ones who would be their friends, the softest touches for handouts of food. At one of the quieter moments, after Julia had watched cable being strung over the Great Hall and the dining room and had then gone to see how the Red Tower Room was being re-arranged, the chief cameraman stood beside her for some moments. "I hope it doesn't tear your guts out to see this happening. It sometimes upsets people a lot."

"I expected as much—if not more."

He smiled slightly. "I know you're Julia Seymour. Saw two of your films. You were really good. Bill Fredricks still goes around Hollywood raving about you. Rod McCallum saw the movies, too. In my opinion he would have done better to have hired you to play the role of the lady of the castle—instead of the dumb broad he's got. But maybe he's still sore at you for turning down some part you were offered opposite him. He's not used to that. . . ."

"There were reasons . . . personal reasons he wouldn't have known about."

"Yeah . . . we all have our reasons for saying no, I guess. Well, good night, Mrs. Sinclair. We'll be back bright and early in the morning. You'll be fed up with us by the time it's all over. . . ."

She lingered; she stood by one of the windows of the Red Tower Room that looked down into a courtyard. All the equipment had been stored safely under cover. The last of the hired station wagons and cars revved up and roared over the draw-bridge and the bridge to the forest road. She would have to re-mind the production manager that both those structures were crumbling and beg that a speed limit be imposed. Well, D.D.'s contract couldn't take care of everything. In the sudden silence she turned back to look at the room. It was here that Rod

McCallum would sleep, but it would also be used in interior shots, so the four-poster had been moved nearer to the great fireplace, the massive chests rearranged. The long evening light fell across the polished floor, already scarred with the marks of the furniture moving and many feet. She remembered all the nights she had slept here—though never with Jamie. She remembered her tears for him, the pain, the joy of her son's birth. She remembered the nights she had wakened to the fancied notion of a woman's soft weeping, the long sigh. "Oh, Ellen . . . Lady Ellen . . . have we disturbed you too much? Don't let them drive you away. Just wait for me, and don't show yourself to anyone. I'll be back with you soon. . . ."

She shook her head. Was she going crazy here in this isolation, talking to a ghost she wasn't even sure existed? She closed the door softly and went to inspect the other rooms that were available to the cast and director. They were grand in size—but rather dismal in appearance despite the heroic job of cleaning they had all pitched into. Nothing could disguise the frayed silk brocade of the curtains in the folds in which they had hung since the castle had been refurbished in Edwardian times. Only the stout lining held them together, as with the bedspreads. The Blue State Room, the Culloden Room, the Prince Charles Suite—grand titles and little else. There was the rather smaller room Lady Jean had used, with its humbler, faded rose chintz. The Rose Room, it was euphemistically called. Two bathrooms existed at this level of the castle, and they would have to be shared. There was another, small bathroom in the tower above the Culloden Room, but the two rooms up there were the ones Jamie and his brother, Callum, had occupied. Julia saw no reason why anyone should need to go up there, but nevertheless Janet had insisted on cleaning them thoroughly and making them brighter with rugs and quilted bedspreads and cushions borrowed from Sir Niall's housekeeper. "You never know, Mrs. Sinclair. There could be others who might prefer to stay here besides the number they told us to prepare for. All extra money, Mrs. Sinclair . . ."

"And more work . . ."

Julia had carefully locked away in a closet all the personal things the two brothers had left behind—their bats and tennis rackets, the school photos, the badges and caps. She now inspected the rooms with a sense of sadness. It was as if Jamie and Callum had been banished. Both rooms, being at the top of the tower, gave splendid views of the whole loch and the sweep to the mountains. The bathroom was small, the bathtub slightly rusted. It would need the full-time service of the man they had hired to help out, who would stay with the Kerrs, to tend all the fires that needed to be kept going and to stoke the boiler. They had striven to give the rooms little welcoming touches, bowls of potpourri, little woven rush baskets with good soap, and small bottles of cologne and after-shave. All these things had come from Alex, once she had known about the project. She had also sent huge packages of linens, sheets, and pillowcases and soft, thick towels, all embroidered with the single initial "S." Janet's larder was stocked with cans of whatever could be of use.

From room to room Julia went, glad now that she had decided to anticipate the money she would earn and had replaced the old boiler and the hot-water tanks—she had shamelessly exploited the excitement the whole project had created through the region to get the necessary permits for these luxuries. But her high-paying guests would have the hot water they expected, and afterward, at the castle, they would enjoy the benefits. D.D. had even produced a letter signed by Rod McCallum stating that he and the cast and crew would make more than ordinary demands on the facilities. So it had been possible to get the new boiler and tanks, and even a new Aga for the kitchen on the strength of that letter. It was useless, at this stage, to sigh over what the place lacked. She had done her best. The man from Pinewood had seen what was offered, and what was offered had been accepted. Doubtless most of these people were used to far tougher, more spare location places than this. She remembered how they had all made do with whatever was available in Oban when they had gone on location there. She paused for a moment, remembering Bill Fredricks—each year they had exchanged Christmas cards. She had once sent a photo of Alasdair with the black woolly lamb. Then mentally she shrugged off what was lacking. She would not apologize for it. They would make do—these Hollywood people. They would have to—or they would leave, and she still would get the full money contracted for. D.D. had seen to that.

She descended the circular tower stairs, the long staircase into the Great Hall, which was decked with flowers, although the set dresser would ruthlessly get rid of them, as the castle of the film story was to be bare and spartan. She had arranged them just to make a first, good impression. She was aware now just how much she counted on making in money above the contract price—by serving as hotel-keeper to the principals and the director; how much money to be made from food and wine. Once the sense of misplaced pride had been overcome, she determined that these next weeks, or months, would be made to pay handsomely. She moved through the dining hall, where the silver candelabra made a handsome display, and on out to the passage leading to the housekeeper's room and the kitchen. Then she turned back. She had meant to check the North Tower—the carpenters had been doing some last-minute work there. Until now there had been only some rough planks nailed at a height that would keep Alasdair from gaining entry. Inside was the perilous state of damp and decay that made the whole tower unsafe. It had never troubled her that they did not have the use of this tower. Who needed another tower in this turreted castle? Now she saw the whole entrance had been boarded up, almost obliterating the ancient, magnificently carved oak doors. They looked safe, and stout enough, but she knew that what lay behind them was almost a ruin. A rough fence had been placed around its outer walls so that the Kerr children—and anyone else—were aware of the danger of its crumbling stonework, which let in water with every storm, and the whole fabric decayed still further. She shook her head over those lovely oak doors covered up; it was better that way. She then looked into the library. It had always been a wonderfully handsome room, reached by a little curving passage from the dining hall. They had decided that this was the only place possible for the guests, the tenants, the stars—whatever they called themselves—to sit in their spare time. They had had fires going here for more than two weeks, in the two fireplaces. She touched the upholstery of the sofas and found it still slightly damp. Perhaps, if they had had enough whiskey and wine with their dinner, they wouldn't notice. The cellar was stocked with wine that even her father couldn't call mediocre. Sir Niall had refused her check, even the ridiculously small sum he said it had originally cost him. "Pay me when they pay up—and don't forget to deduct the amount *I* drink." Julia suspected she would have difficulty making him accept any payment at all. She touched some of the books as she made her round of the room and was dismayed to see that many of the leather bindings were spotted with mold. She didn't go up to the gallery—from this level it looked grand, but the state of the books did not bear inspection.

She went back along the passage and through the dining hall to the drawing room, and checked to see that it was locked. There had been no hope of refurbishing it, or making it look more attractive. It was impossible to heat it; they had to conserve their fuel for what was essential. They would have to learn—this invading party of Americans—what things were like in postwar Europe. Slowly she walked back to the kitchen. She had planned a pickup supper with Janet and Alasdair in the kitchen, and then she would go to spend their first night in the cottage.

But she found Sir Niall on one of the sofas in the housekeeper's room, reading a story to Alasdair, who was half asleep, worn out with the excitement of the many people who had thronged his house in these past days. Sir Niall looked up sheepishly. "I just couldn't stay away. I'm just as fascinated as any of the youngsters. I've brought a picnic basket and a bottle of wine. Shall we have it here, or at the cottage? I thought—maybe a little bit of housewarming . . ."

"The cottage," Julia said. "It will be Alasdair's first meal there. No one better to introduce him to the place than his best friend."

They went in Sir Niall's car. The old station wagon had been declared beyond repair, fit only for scrap. They had replaced it with another secondhand vehicle, which William Kerr had to use for the farm work. This had been another reason for Julia's refusing Sir Niall's offer of hospitality while the film was shot. She would have been dependent on William Kerr to carry her to and from Finavon each day—it would have wasted his time and used precious gasoline. She thought, as they drove along the forest road, that the money from the film might just stretch, after she had made a decent payment to Luisa, to a small car for herself. It was a thought that already gave her a wholly new sense of freedom.

Alasdair ate the supper of cold meat, Scotch eggs, bread, and cheese at the table in the cottage before a roaring fire. Sir Niall gave him a sip of the wonderful claret. Alasdair shivered with a kind of delicious excitement. "I like it here," he pronounced. But he was sleepy again as Julia washed him and put him into his pajamas in the bedroom they were to share. There was a fireplace back-to-back with the one in the living room; she had lighted a small fire there to give it cheer, but he didn't need it. He put his arms around her wearily as she kissed him goodnight. "I always wanted to live in the cottage in the wood," he said—he, who had been born in the castle.

There were another few days, of the various units gradually getting the lay of the land, of the assistant director laying out the preliminary shots, and then the director himself, John Gunn, arrived. Julia knew his fame, and greeted him with the hope that everything would work out all right. He grinned at her cheerfully. "Nothing ever does, Miss Seymour. *You* know that. It's part of the business to take it all as it comes. I caught a couple of your movies—very nice. You did very good work." He stood with his hands on his hips and gazed at the castle walls rearing above them. "As they say back home, 'Some place you've got here.' It's going to be hell to work in, but it'll look like a dream on film, or my name's not Gunn."

"Gunn's a Scottish name."

"Yeah. Great-grandfather went to Canada when they threw him off his croft—if that's what you call it—to make way for the sheep. Never been to Scotland before, myself. Nearest I got was Pinewood during the war. This is some introduction. . . . Say, you know what the Gunn family motto is? *Either Peace or War.* That about sums up a director's life. If we don't fight with people we don't get a good movie. Now, McCallum's all right. He takes direction well. Not the world's greatest natural actor, but shrewd as a cat about seeing the best pieces of what a director is aiming for—and he gets all the best shots himself. Naturally. He gets to be teacher's pet. Not that he doesn't have a few flaws. He can be just about under the table with booze at night, but he'll be on the set, all made up, lines learned, exactly at the time he's supposed to be there. I suppose you'd say he was a real pro. That's what's made him over the war years." He was silent for a moment and then shook his head. "I have more than a few doubts about this script. It's a bit confined for his sort of action— but audiences have had just about enough of really broad war heroics. This is a bit more subtle. I just wish he'd gotten a better actress to play the female role. She's a knockout to look at, but she can't act for little green apples. Well, he put a pile of his own dough into it and got Worldwide to do the rest. It's his baby. Worldwide just sent me along to do the best I could. I'll give it

all I've got.'' He raised his eyes again to the ancient walls above
them and turned to look over the loch. ''After all, it's a sort of
homecoming for me.''

''Welcome to Scotland, Mr. Gunn. You are home.''

He smiled at her, waved a hand in acknowledging salute and
thanks, and made his way to where the assistant director was
waiting for him.

Julia had made friends with the production manager, Mike
Pearson. He was a friendly, seemingly tireless young man. Two
days ago the scenery shop, set up in the stables, had made two
elaborately scrolled signs, one posted at each end of the bridge.
*Notice! This bridge is made of spun sugar. It may disappear and
dump you in the lake if you speed. Five miles per hour, max.*

Two ladies from Inverness appeared each day to help Janet
and Kate with the lunch; two more would come to make up the
bedrooms each day. A giant coffee urn stood in the kitchen, and
a load of freshly baked scones and buns came with the first
station wagon each day. Dozens of loaves of bread came for
sandwiches, and the meat and eggs to fill them. Julia knew that
some arrangement had been made with the Ministry, but it wasn't
her business to worry about that. The crew spread themselves
around the long kitchen table and spilled over into the housekeeper's room and even into the dining hall. Janet and her help-
ers cooked gigantic meals. Julia knew from other film sets how
important it was to keep the crew well fed. Patience could wear
very thin; a well-looked-after crew gave its efforts more whole-
heartedly. She was glad to see that whoever had organized the
provisioning—probably Mike Pearson—also had provided plenty
of cigarettes. There was no alcohol available on the set, but she
didn't doubt that the bars in the various hotels in Inverness that
housed the crew did a roaring trade in the evenings. She kept
the office locked, and only she and William Kerr held keys; they
had a hurried conference each morning. The life of the farm still
had to go on, though it all seemed remote from the activity here.
Sir Niall came almost every day, took up his position in the
housekeeper's room, and, as he put it, was ''just keeping an eye
on things. Silver's well and truly locked up, I hope. They seem
a very decent group to me . . . of course, I can't understand
half of what they're saying. But I did catch a nice description
yesterday. 'Who's the old guy dressed up in the costume who's
always hanging around?' Am I in the way, my dear?''

"If you weren't here, I'd go mad! Alasdair would either be spoiled silly, or he'd fall into the loch and drown, just showing off. I don't know how we're ever going to get the dogs back to normal. They're more excited than the children. . . . Mrs. Kerr can't wait for school to start again and get them all out of the way for the day. Dear God, I don't know what we'll do if they really do stay for the final shots in the snow. We'll all be out of our minds. . . ."

"Let *them* go out of their minds. You'll just get that much more rent."

"Canny old Scot, aren't you."

He chuckled. "It's bred in us, my dear."

Julia walked with Alasdair through the forest on the evening before Rod McCallum, Claire Avery, and two of the other principals were expected. These four would stay at the castle, along with John Gunn. She had just made a last inspection of the rooms. She was weary, and so was Alasdair. His feet dragged. They had all eaten in the kitchen—there was always such a mound of food left over from the lunch and afternoon coffee break. She thought longingly of a hot bath, and she blessed Sir Niall again for the bathroom and the immersion heater.

The long Scottish twilight was beginning to descend. It had only been such a short time—Alasdair's fourth birthday party, at the end of June—since all this had its beginning, but it seemed much longer; so much had had to be done in the time. Rod McCallum, having gotten his script and his backing, was unwilling to wait another year for the autumn fall of the leaves, or the falling of the first snow. It seemed he would not be satisfied with what the back lot could produce. He wanted the real thing and was paying for it, in time and good money. Julia hoped it all would go smoothly. She knew it was vital to stay on schedule and within the budget. The worst sin one could commit was to run over budget, and as some of this budget came from Rod McCallum, he would no doubt be an anxious taskmaster, even of such a brilliant director as John Gunn. She wondered how the combination of star and keeper of the purse would work out.

She and Alasdair rounded the bend in the forest road that revealed the cottage. Four cars were lined up before it, and a number of people were standing around. She grasped Alasdair's hand more tightly and hurried forward.

"Yes?" she called. "Can I help you?"

They all stared at her silently. No one seemed to want to speak. "Can I help you?" she repeated.

A man strolled around from the back of the cottage; he came toward her with an easy walk, glancing at her, then at the trees above, then back at the cottage.

"Who are you?" he said.

"And who are *you?*"

One of the men laughed. "There's something of a fan for you, Rod. The lady doesn't know you."

He held out his hand. "I'm Rod McCallum. And I know who you are. You're Julia Seymour, the girl who turned me down."

She accepted the outstretched hand. "My son, Alasdair," she said. "The dogs will get just as much underfoot as he. Rory, Duuf, and Angus."

"And where, Miss Seymour, are you walking to at this hour?" The famous face seemed slightly amused; the deeply set eyes, a strange dark gray seen so often on the screen, were beautiful in their way, but rather guarded, set under thick, straight, dark brows. His mouth, when he was not speaking, followed the same straight line. It was a perfectly balanced face. She judged there was no camera angle that would be a less than favorable one for him. He was as tall and as broad-shouldered as he appeared on film, but his movements were light and easy. She realized what a gift he was to a cameraman. How little makeup he would need, she thought, wearing either his Army helmet, or his broad-brimmed cowboy hat. He was, as they said in the theater and the films, "a natural." She was experienced enough to recognize those qualities the camera loved, a kind of charismatic presence that would make him stand out from most people around him, the depth and timbre of the voice, the unexpected quirk of the raised eyebrow.

"I'm known as Julia Sinclair around here. And Alasdair and I were going home to bed." She nodded toward the cottage. "We didn't expect you until tomorrow."

"Made better time than we thought from London—where your gracious stepmother entertained us handsomely. I know we were supposed to stop in Inverness tonight, but I just couldn't resist coming on here. I hope it doesn't inconvenience you."

She shrugged. "You have more or less owned the castle for the past ten days, Mr. McCallum." She took in the line of the four station wagons, two of which had held the passengers and two of which contained piles of luggage; there was a driver for each vehicle. She tried to make her smile welcoming, but her mind was racing over the logistics of feeding them all and settling them in for the night.

The familiar, rather charming frown she remembered from the screen came to Rod McCallum's brow. "Home? You live here?"

"For the time being. While you are in residence. The castle *looks* big enough, and Lord knows, it's a regular rabbit warren, as you might expect. But we're . . . we're rather short of amenities such as bathrooms. I thought I'd make some room for you."

Rod McCallum then introduced Claire Avery, whose face Julia recognized—a beautiful but rather vacuous face. As they shook hands, Julia had the distinct feeling that the young woman was rather nervous. The two men who were Rod McCallum's chief supporting cast greeted her in a much more relaxed fashion, with pleased smiles. "Martin Calder . . . and George Harvey. Mrs. Sinclair." Their manner suggested to Julia that they would not be very demanding or difficult guests.

After the introductions were over, a petulant cry came from the second car in line. "For God's sake, are we going to be here all night?"

A look of profound annoyance crossed McCallum's face. His voice assumed a rough tone. "Stacia, we've all had a bellyful of your bitching all day. Now get your ass out of there and come and say hello to Miss Seymour—Mrs. Sinclair."

Slowly the car door opened, and a young woman—no, Julia thought, a girl about to be a young woman—emerged. Even in the fading light Julia saw that she was beautiful in a perfectly natural way that had no artifice about it—not at all like the manicured beauty of Claire Avery. Her sulky movements had the grace of a cat, her downturned mouth was a sensual pout. "Mrs. Sinclair, this is Anastasia Rayner, my adopted daughter. Your hostess, Stacia." A reluctant hand was held out.

"Hi . . ."

"She was supposed to stay in London, but the friend she would have stayed with is . . . is ill, so she had to come with us."

"And when," Stacia said, "do we get to the castle?"

"It's a mile farther on," Julia said. "But I think I'd better come with you. There's only Janet and Kate there tonight. To-morrow we've got another two ladies coming from Inverness. But Janet will need some help. . . ." She recognized the girl— or she recognized the name, and a very startling likeness to a face made famous in a very few films, the inimitable Anne Ray-ner, for her brief life a pouting, infinitely enticing symbol of sex whose pictures had adorned the walls and lockers of every American service base around the world. She had been blond and beautiful in a memorable way, with full breasts and but-tocks, and improbable long legs, the face of an angel that looked as if, tempted enough, she might sup with the devil. A little more than a year ago she had taken a curve on the Pacific High-way to Santa Barbara too fast, and her body had burned in the wreck of the car. She had then been married for almost three years to Rod McCallum. The girl who stood there in the gath-ering dusk bore a startling resemblance to her famous mother, but a resemblance somewhat marred by an expression of fero-cious resentment and animosity.

"Well, do we have to stand here? What's so special about this little shack? I came to live in a castle."

"And so you shall, my dear, unless I leave you to walk the rest of the way, as your charming manners deserve. Now look how this little boy stands here and says nothing. Behaves him-self."

"Well, he's only a kid. Probably too dumb to say anything."

"You'll excuse her, I hope, Mrs. Sinclair. She's only a kid, too, and it's been a long day. . . . I really shouldn't have pressed on like this. Only I was wild to see the castle. We've invested a lot of hope as well as money in this mad dream of mine. . . ."

"I understand. Could you give Alasdair and me a lift back to the castle? I think he's falling asleep on his feet."

"Right!" Rod McCallum gave a signal, and everyone piled back into the cars. He himself took Alasdair in his arms and carried him. The child sat quite contentedly on his lap as they bumped their way back to the castle. They caught it at the magic moment of sunset in which Julia had first seen it, its silhouette dark and brooding, its crumbling imperfections hidden.

"Wow!" It was the first word Julia could remember Claire Avery saying.

* * *

There were hectic first hours after the arrival of the little group at Sinclair. Julia laid Alasdair on Janet's bed, covered him with a quilt, and left him to sleep. Then she rushed to the Kerrs' cottage to ask the favor of the man, Reevie, who was to do the fires, and stoke the boiler, to come at once, to see that hot water was available and the fires lighted in each room. Then, after they had had their first drink, she showed the new guests to their rooms. John Gunn already displayed his knowledge of the place by helping her sort out the baggage and directing the drivers to take it to the right rooms. John Gunn had already chosen the Rose Room as the most comfortable. He told the others that they would have to toss a coin for the three remaining rooms. Rod McCallum was plainly disturbed because the whole length of the gallery separated him from Claire Avery, who had been given the Blue State Room. She was impressed by the name of the room, if not the room itself. That left the Culloden Room and the Prince Charles Suite to Martin Calder and George Harvey. There was no place to take the sulking girl, Stacia Rayner, but up the narrow tower stairs to the top, which contained Callum's and Jamie's rooms. Julia made a swift decision and opened the door to Callum's room; she was not prepared to share Jamie's room with a stranger unless it was absolutely necessary. At first the girl looked pleased. She was surveying the world outside as the dusk settled. "You mean I'm to be up here all my myself?"

"Yes. I hope you'll be comfortable. We really weren't expecting anyone else to stay. . . ."

"Oh, this'll do. Where's the bathroom?" When she saw it, her nose wrinkled a trifle. "Well, at least I'll have it to myself— I suppose. Of course, Claire will be in Rod's room most of the time, so she can use *his* bathroom. Are the other bathrooms like this?"

"A little bigger—perhaps a trifle grander. This was where— where the children slept. It wasn't considered necessary to have a large bathroom for them. Reevie will be along soon to light your fire. He'll bring extra coal and wood. . . . Later Kate will bring hot-water bottles for the bed."

Kate had raced upstairs with a pile of sheets and towels over her arm. Together she and Julia made up the bed while Stacia stood and watched. She didn't volunteer to take the towels to the bathroom. One of the drivers struggled up the narrow stairs with three large suitcases belonging to the girl.

"Not much hanging space, is there?"

"No," Julia said shortly. "Now, if you'll excuse me . . ."

She left the girl brooding over the darkness gathering on the loch. She had said no word of thanks to either her or Kate, or to the man who had brought up the bags. Mentally Julia shrugged. Let this unexpected, unwanted guest settle in as best she could. But at the same time she blessed Janet for the shrewd guess that there could be someone extra needing a bed.

She went down to the Great Hall, where the men had returned for their second drink. John Gunn was doing the honors, saving Julia the task of pouring for them all. "Everything settled with Stacia?" Rod McCallum asked. "I just took a chance on there being a bed somewhere for her. Of course, I should have telephoned from Inverness . . . but I was really mad to get here before dark."

"Perfectly all right, Mr. McCallum," Julia said smoothly. "I'll learn how hotelkeepers cope with these little things. I think your stepdaughter will settle in all right. She has her own unique little eyrie right at the top of the tower. Shall I take another drink up to Miss Avery?"

He sprang to his feet. "No! You're not the waitress around here, are you?"

"There will be more help tomorrow."

"Well, let her come down when she's finished preening."

Julia raced back to the kitchen, frantically filling a bowl with more ice from the new refrigerator they had got, almost entirely for that purpose. None of the Scots ever took ice in their drinks. She deposited it hastily on a chest in the Great Hall and fled before anyone could say anything. Then she helped Kate lay the table in the dining hall for dinner, and after that, the table in the housekeeper's room for the drivers. The meal for everyone would be the soup Janet had already prepared, cold roast beef, baked potatoes, and a tossed salad that Julia made of everything she could lay her hands on in the pantry. They would serve the apple pies made for tomorrow, cheese and biscuits. Julia raced around preparing bowls of celery and radishes; she remembered the canned nuts Alex had sent, and dispatched Kate into the Great Hall with them. Perhaps that would keep their guests satisfied until the potatoes were done. She remembered to serve drinks to the drivers in the housekeeper's room. All but one of them would return to London tomorrow, leaving three cars behind for the use of the company. Reevie kept coming and going with scuttles of coal; he had no choice but to walk through the Great Hall, where their guests sat around the now roaring fire with their drinks. Julia knew he was outraged at being dragged away from the Kerrs' comfortable sitting room, but all they heard from him were a few rebellious mutters. "Boiler's coming on," he said. "If they don't run off all the water just now, they might all get baths tonight. Really don't know if the hot water'll get up to that top tower room. Never tested it for that far."

The drivers were served as quickly as possible, and they departed, leaving the first courtyard jammed with cars. Julia returned to the Great Hall, bearing a glass of canned orange juice that Alex had sent, for Stacia Rayner, who accepted it with a look of resignation. She would not yet know, Julia thought—if she ever troubled to learn—that fresh oranges were reserved for those with children's ration books. She offered the wine list to Rod McCallum and saw his brows raise slightly as he read it. "You run to some pretty fancy stuff here."

"Only for your benefit. It's not our everyday fare."

He made his choice without consulting the others, a fine red Burgundy. "As many bottles as it takes," he said. "And we all hope you'll eat with us. John here is getting fed up with dining in lonely state."

"It's kind of you—but I can't accept. I'm . . . well, I need to see to things. And I should be getting back to the cottage with Alasdair. I've already eaten."

"Oh, come on! You can't play the great-lady-servant role all the time, you know. In any case, I know the kid's dead asleep. I'll drive you back as soon as we've finished."

She was obliged to stay, and sit and pick at some food with them, barely tasting Sir Niall's very expensive wine. They were all tired, and the talk never touched the subject of the film. She wondered if they felt a little oppressed by the size of the dining hall, by the great height of the carved ceiling above them, lost now in shadow. At last Claire Avery rose. "Well, I've just about had it. I think I'll go up . . . I'm dying for a good soak in the tub. . . ."

Julia went to show her where the light switches were for the stairs, hoping that all of them wouldn't want baths, because the boiler wasn't yet up to its full capacity. Only the price they were paying for this rather primitive accommodation stopped her from suggesting that they all return to Inverness and let the hotels take care of them.

"Any ghosts here?" Stacia asked when Julia returned.

"A few, I suppose. Some people claim they have seen ghosts, but I've never encountered any," Julia lied. "Old places like this always have odd noises—I think it's mostly the hot-water system protesting about being put in a situation it was never designed to take."

"Then why do you stay here?" the girl demanded.

"Stacia—shut up! You don't ask questions like that," Rod McCallum said. "Or don't they teach you things like that at your fancy schools?"

"I'll answer it, though," Julia said calmly as she began stacking dishes to carry to the kitchen. "I stay because I really have no other place to go. And it's my son's home."

"You could always sell it," Stacia said coolly.

"I said it was my son's home. It's not for sale."

The table was cleared, and Janet left coffee before the dying fire in the Great Hall; Julia showed Rod the long dresser in the dining hall where she had laid in a great selection of drinks and liqueurs. "You must, please, after this, just help yourselves." Then she smiled. "It's all included in the cost, which even an American must realize is very steep. But then I can hardly keep count of every drink served. Of course, the wine is extra—I made very special arrangements to get it for you. I had to get Ministry of Food help to stock the bar. We're quite severely rationed, even here, where whiskey's made. It's a very special export that earns us precious dollars. Of course, we don't have a license to sell spirits—that's why it had to be an all-in price for room and board. You are—very special of course—paying guests here. It is still a private house, not a hotel."

He made a mock bow. "We'll try to remember it, ma'am, and behave accordingly. Look, I'll just pour a brandy for John and Marty and George and pack Stacia off to bed. I apologize for the kid, Mrs. Sinclair. She's not always this bad. But last year her mother—"

"Yes, I know, Mr. McCallum. I think you'll find we understand such things. When she begins to relax she may be happier. I wish there were some young people her own age about—"

He poured three measures of brandy, and his short laugh was

harsh. "Young people aren't Stacia's scene, Mrs. Sinclair. She's never been young in her life."

He carried the brandy out to John Gunn, Martin Calder, and George Harvey. "Toss another log on the fire and I'll join you as soon as I've driven Mrs. Sinclair back to the cottage. And you, Stacia, off to bed."

Reluctantly the girl dragged herself out of the big chair. "I don't suppose it'd occur to you that I might have liked a drink myself."

"No, it didn't. And it won't for a long time. Now move your ass."

"I'm not sure I can remember where my room is. Did those hot-water things get in?" she asked of Julia.

"I believe Kate took them up."

"I'll probably freeze."

"Then freeze, as long as your tongue freezes with you," Rod McCallum said. "And don't go poking your nose into what doesn't concern you. We're only renting—remember. Paying guests. *Guests.* Remember that."

Rod McCallum carried the sleeping Alasdair out to one of the cars and laid him on the backseat. Julia noticed that his actions were very gentle as he handled the child. While he struggled with the unfamiliar gears for a moment, she said, "You're a little hard on your stepdaughter, Mr. McCallum."

He got the first gear at last and moved slowly over the draw-bridge and the bridge, stopped to read, by the light of the head-lamps, Mike Pearson's notice, and laughed. "Some guy, Mike. I picked him especially. You've got to have stamina to be a production manager, but it's helpful, especially in a foreign country, if you have a sense of humor as well. The well-being of the whole crew so often depends on the production manager, as you well know. Mike costs a fortune, but I think he's worth it." They reached the forest road. "I appreciate what you did for us tonight, Mrs. Sinclair. Dropping out of the blue on you, as we did. And no, I haven't forgotten your question about Stacia. I wasn't ducking it. It's just unfortunate—the way she is. Naturally, the kid's still upset by her mother's death. But she was that way before her mother was killed. I'll let you in on a well-known secret, Mrs. Sinclair. Her mother was pretty drunk when she ran off the road. Only the studio didn't release that small detail. She was mad as hell at me over something—I can't remember what, now. We were yelling at each other, and she just dashed out into the night. Story of my life. Dames—sorry, ladies—are always dashing out into the night.''

''Stacia's father, though . . . ?''

His harsh, short laugh came back. ''Stacia's father is nowhere to be found. He deserted them when she was a baby, and before Anne—whose real name was Anastasia, too—became famous. I never had a kid. I've been married before, but kids really aren't my scene. But with Anne came Stacia. When she killed herself, I was left with Stacia. What could I do? Throw her out? She's been in two boarding schools in the past year, and *they've* thrown her out. What do I do with a fifteen-year-old who's a walking mantrap? She can't help it. That same quality made her mother famous. . . .''

Julia was aware that Rod McCallum was proceeding along the forest road at the same speed prescribed by Mike Pearson's sign. She doubted it was because he was a timid driver.

''You have your problems, Mr. McCallum.''

''Don't we all.'' It wasn't a question.

The headlights struck the whitewashed cottage. ''Why are you living here, Mrs. Sinclair? Surely that huge old heap has a spare room or two?''

''Not really. Just a few little rooms down near the kitchen. Scottish castles—fortress castles—go up and up, Mr. McCallum. And the farther up you go, the farther from a water supply. In any case, I thought I needed a place of my own—just a little privacy. Someplace Alasdair and I could stay away from all the fuss. He's so young. . . . He could get carried away with it all. Spoiled. He wouldn't be able to understand what was real and what was make-believe. So I decided to come here.''

''Perhaps you're wise. Though I didn't appreciate you waiting on us as if you were a servant.'' He was lifting Alasdair gently from the car and carrying him to the cottage.

''I have to remind you again, Mr. McCallum, that we are charging you very stiff prices for staying at the castle. I don't mind pitching in to make you comfortable. One is not a servant unless one has the mentality of a servant.''

''Spoken like Michael Seymour's daughter. *Touché,* ma'am.''

Inside the door she groped for the light switch. One small table lamp cast both light and shadows in the room, with its very basic furniture and its sink. ''So you've put in electricity . . .''

His question faded away. "In there . . . ?" He nodded to the door of the bedroom.

"Please."

She watched him lay Alasdair down very gently. With swift fingers he untied the shoes, took off the socks, eased the boy out of his sweater and pants and shirt. Alasdair woke momentarily.

"Mummie?" She took over the rest. "I'm here, Alasdair. Now your pajamas. We can skip doing your teeth tonight."

"Prayers . . . ?" he murmured.

"We'll say double in the morning."

She kissed him, then left the door a little ajar so the light from the sitting room partially lighted the bedroom. Rod McCallum had stayed all through this, and now he followed her.

"Mind if I sit down?"

She hesitated. "Well . . ."

"Yes, I know you're tired, and the last thing you want is a late-night guest jawing his head off. But there are a few things I'd like to tell you. By the way, it's confidential what I tell you. I wouldn't want the rest of the cast or the crew—I don't want the press knowing it. I suppose you're the one person I feel like talking to about it."

"Sit down, Mr. McCallum. I don't have brandy to offer you, but there is whiskey."

He nodded. "Thank you. Will you call me Rod?"

"Not when other people are about—not for a while."

"I understand. I'll try to remember." He accepted the whiskey from her when he saw she had poured one for herself. She sat down in the chair opposite him. "May I light the fire?" he said.

She tried not to sigh. Lighting the fire meant he intended to stay for more than a few minutes. She would have to make up the fire again in the morning. But there was something strangely vulnerable in his expression as he made the request, nothing at all that resembled the "tough guy" image of his films. She nodded, then waited while he applied a match to the paper, carefully fed the kindling in until it was well alight, and laid on one sawn length of wood.

"Yes—that's what I was hoping for."

"Hoping . . . ?"

"To see it alight again. You may have wondered why I had everyone stop here this afternoon."

"I certainly wondered when you mentioned the electricity . . ."

"You noticed. Of course you would. You're a smart as well as a very talented woman. You don't mind if I say you're beautiful also." He held up his hand. "No—I'm not trying to make a pass at you. I watched those two films of yours very carefully— I saw them several times. I even caught that awful costume piece you did. Waste of talent. Did you know that Bill Fredricks still goes around Hollywood raving about you? No, I didn't think so. He's just like a schoolkid with a crush on you. His talk is too innocent—and Bill is no innocent with women. He sort of put you on a pedestal. He was trying to help. Talking to directors and producers about you. Even talking to studio bosses. After all, you did get an Academy Award."

"Supporting actress," she reminded him.

He shrugged. "And how many get that? It was a pity you couldn't accept my offer of the film with me."

"There were circumstances . . ."

"Those circumstances have been explained to me. There was the old lady . . . dying. And the kid . . ." He nodded toward the bedroom. "I did, finally, understand. In the beginning I was sore that you turned it down."

"That wasn't what you wanted to say to me—at this time."

He took a small sip of his whiskey. "No—not that. Not that it wasn't important. It was. You would have made a great leading lady. But this . . ." He looked around the room with great care, taking in every detail. "I saw from walking around behind this afternoon you changed the old back room into what looks like a bathroom."

"So you *do* know this place."

"Julia . . . Mrs. Sinclair, I was *born* in this place. And my brother and sisters. I was the eldest, and I can't remember how many hundreds—perhaps thousands—of times I've lighted that fire."

She took a swift gulp of her whiskey and almost choked. "The McBain cottage," she said with a gasp. "You're a Mc-Bain!"

"Yes—McBain. My father was a gamekeeper for Lady Jean's husband. Your husband's father."

"Then why . . . why did you leave?"

"We didn't leave, Julia. We were thrown out. My father kept the reason to himself until one night he got drunk. . . . I was about ten when we left. This cottage—the castle—the forest, the village, Langwell, everything we passed through on the way here was my whole world until I was ten. Then it was finished and we went to Canada."

"Thrown out—it doesn't sound like Jamie's father."

"No—I suppose he wasn't as hard a man as that. But if you don't trust your gamekeeper, you can never go shooting with him. Trust is everything in that relationship."

"What happened? Why?"

He gestured vaguely toward the fire, looking into its heart as if trying to conjure up things as they had been. "How much does a kid of ten understand? All we had ever known was trouble—of one sort or another. My father had money problems—but then, who didn't? Adam Sinclair himself had money problems. We all knew that, even though he was laird of Castle Sinclair. Hell, it was just after the First World War. Everyone was on low wages, even the people employed by men far better off than Adam Sinclair. Adam Sinclair—as an officer, of course—and my father, and about a dozen of the estate workers all went marching off with the Argyll Highlanders to do their duty for King and country. And a fat lot of good it did them. My father and Adam Sinclair were two of the very few of that little group who survived that particular wave of patriotism. My father came back with a limp, and the little finger of his left hand gone to frostbite, and an abiding hatred for all the stupid brass who pushed them into a war that couldn't be won. A chip on his shoulder so big you could see it. And no great love of Adam Sinclair—because he belonged to the class who had made those crass blunders and wasted so many millions of lives. Naturally, he was desperate for money. He was trying to support his parents in an Edinburgh tenement. One of my uncles came back so badly gassed he was never able to do a day's work again. Another uncle didn't even bother to come back. Just slipped away as soon as he was demobilized, and he was never heard of again. They suspected he went to Australia, but who would know? Another uncle was killed. I was four years old when my father went off to war, and I had two younger sisters. I got a brother almost nine months to the day after he got back. He drank whatever spare money there was—I can remember him stumbling into this place when we were all asleep, and rousing the whole lot of us. He wasn't particular where the drink came from. People used to have their own illegal stills in those days—even as late as that. Rotgut, most of it. He used to go and drink in the village, then come home and beat us all up.''

He looked away from the fire, directly at Julia. ''I had been brought up being told he was a hero for going to the war, and he came back a brute, and I hated him.''

''Yes . . .''

''Yes . . . yes . . .'' His voice almost softly mimicked hers. ''Your husband was born just a little after my young brother. Those who survived were eager to breed. Jamie's brother, Callum, was born after his father left for war. Lady Jean would have been about twenty, I suppose. Those years when he was the only thing she had in her life made him some sort of a god in her eyes. In fairness, you'd have to say the chances of his father getting out of that war alive were pretty slim. People like her cherished the children they had—in case there weren't any more. But not my mother. Three kids in three years, before my father went off, and a private's pay to support them on. No wonder she didn't want any more. But she got them. And we had some bastard stepbrother somewhere in Inverness. My father got a girl pregnant, and her father demanded money. God, I can still hear the rows going on. We heard every word of them.'' He looked around the small room. ''Where is there privacy in a place like this? We heard the rows, and we saw the way he would push my mother on the bed and just treat her like an animal. Not pretty memories, Julia.''

''No. Ugly. Horrible. . . . But women put up with things like that because they had no other choice.''

''True.'' He held out his glass. ''I know I'm keeping you up. Do you want to throw me out? I'll go—peacefully.''

She refilled his glass. ''What you're saying is important to you. That you came back is important. It wasn't out of love for the place. You aren't here for sentimental reasons.''

''No—that I'm not. Just the desire to actually see the place again. To make sure what my memories were really like. Was it all a fantasy? Now that I'm here, it's much worse than I remembered. . . .''

''But you could have come at any time since the war. You

could have come and looked. You didn't need the excuse of a film to bring you here.''

"But I did. I didn't want to come as a tourist, coming to look at the old cottage where I was born. Now I'm the privileged tenant of Castle Sinclair. I think I wanted to grind my father's memory into the dust, but along with that, I don't mind paying to spit in the eye of your husband's father—even though neither of them is alive.''

"Strong feelings, Rod. I wonder, if your father was so wretched, so burdened with money and family problems, why he didn't just take off like his brother—and leave the whole mess behind? So many men would have.''

"Might have been better for us if he had. Though we would have lost the cottage . . . Well, who knows what was in his mind? All I know is that he was a bloody fool. Instead of going to Adam Sinclair for a loan—though I'm not sure he hadn't done that several times—well, he went and took a piece of the Sinclair family silver. I'm pretty sure it wasn't a thing they would normally have missed. One of those great silver dishes with lids they had at the top of the pantry shelves and wouldn't have used in ten years. Mind you, if there'd been a butler, it would have been spotted at once, or the pantry would never have been unlocked. But the Sinclairs couldn't afford a butler anymore. My father was asked to do all kinds of odd jobs that didn't strictly fall into the category of gamekeeper. He was family friend and retainer, trusted—always around the house. I suppose Adam Sinclair imagined they shared some sort of comradeship because they had come all through the war together. What my father was experiencing—poverty, drunkenness—all that was pretty common to his class. The way he treated his wife and family was a man's own business. He was McBain, the trusted one. Well, one day he just went over the top and took the silver. No one noticed it was gone. On his next trip to Edinburgh he took it to a jeweler—he didn't even have the sense to take it to a pawnbroker, which would at least have shown some intention of trying to redeem it in the future. No—he took it to a jeweler, who gave him whatever price he could beat him down to—I don't imagine my father knew anything about what silver was worth. But the jeweler recognized the Sinclair crest—he didn't have to be a great mind to do that. Except my father said *his* name was Sinclair. The jeweler looked up their records and found they had made the piece for the Sinclairs about a hundred years before. Jewelers do keep those sorts of records—well, it would have had their hallmark on it, wouldn't it? My father was too dumb to think of anything like that. So, naturally, the jeweler got in touch with Adam Sinclair, and, yes, they finally looked into the cobwebs on the top pantry shelf, and the great stupid thing was gone. God knows how my father got the thing out of the castle, or how he hid it from my mother, or what story he told the jeweler. But he did have the run of the place—trusted, as I said. Well, the trust was smashed then. And so was my father. He had to go. Adam Sinclair did what I suppose his class would call 'the decent thing.' He didn't tell the police. He paid back the jeweler whatever he had paid out. He didn't prefer charges. He just told my father he had to go. He even—and I think that was what my father resented most—paid our way, steerage, to Canada. 'The gentry looking down his long nose at me,' he said. 'Handing out charity. I've earned more than charity.'

"This all spilled out of him one night when he was drunk— and he was drunk whenever he could find the money for it. But it also happened to be the night my mother died, giving birth to her last child. The kid died, too. We were somewhere freezing in Canada—we were always moving on somewhere. The grieving widower lined us all up ready to go into any orphanage that would take us. Well, I was too old to go off meekly just where he sent me. I lit off on my own. Made it to Vancouver. Held a few jobs. Slept in basements. Did anything for money—stole when the opportunity presented itself. Eventually I got across the border into Washington State—illegally. Then I drifted east to Montana—worked a couple of years on a ranch there. A rough life. I learned to ride a horse, and I learned that where they needed fancy riders most was Hollywood. Hell—what did I have to lose? I discovered Los Angeles was my town. I never wanted to leave it."

"Your sisters and brother . . . ? Your father . . . ?"

He shrugged. "Don't know. I never called myself McBain again. I didn't make any inquiries. I didn't want to know. Eventually I got myself fixed up with papers—and said my name was Roderick McCallum. It's a wonder I didn't call myself Sinclair."

His face was contorted with the sort of pain he had never been able to project on the screen. Dumbly he held out his empty glass to her, and she filled it, her thoughts swinging wildly between fear and pity. But neither must show. She gave him the refilled glass.

"But *why* have you come back? Come back to these wretched memories?"

"God knows. I'm certainly not sure myself. Trying to lay my own ghosts. The thought of Castle Sinclair and this cottage had always obsessed me. I've never told another living soul about these things. Am I drunk?—or mad to be telling you? Both, I suppose. I've always just followed the line the studio publicity department made up for me. Poor Scottish immigrant boy—only child. Parents dead. Can't remember where he came from, or who he is. That's what I told them. They bought it—thought it made as good a story as any they could come up with. It saved a lot of questions. Exactly where in the Highlands did I come from? Were there any family left there? How was I to know? I was just one of the millions streaming through New York and Boston in my mother's arms. It got over a lot of awkward questions, and shut up the Immigration Department, who might or might not have had their own opinion about how I got where I was. In any case, I wasn't an 'undesirable.' I was earning my own way, and in time I fought the Battle of the Pacific so many times—graduated from horse opera—that I actually began to believe I had done all those heroic things. Of course I joined up right after Pearl Harbor—every red-blooded American was supposed to do that. But the studio made sure I was never in any danger—I just did basic training, and then there was a film waiting that was meant to show Americans that they weren't beaten by the Japs. I was back in Hollywood, and I never left it. Oh, a few weeks back at some soft job in some camp in the States—the studio wouldn't even risk my getting as far as Pearl Harbor in case the ship went down. Then I'd be back in Hollywood, loaned out to whatever studio had something ready for me. It was a great war. I never got farther than being a private because I never spent enough time with the Army to be anything else. Even the studio couldn't swing a first lieutenancy for me—not even a sergeant. Oh, God, I was having a good time. I was living my old man's war in my head and at the same time being the best-paid private the Army ever had. In my head I was *buying* the Sinclair family silver. I was building my own castle, all here in these woods where this cottage stood. I knew I'd come back someday. But I'd never tell a soul why."

"You've just told me."

"I must be mad. I am mad—and I suppose I'm drunk. But being drunk hasn't ever loosened my tongue about these things before. There was a sort of door closed that time I ran away from my father and my sisters and brother. That kid called Rod McBain no longer existed. There was no one in the world who could claim kinship. There never would be. I used to half expect some letter turning up at the studio from one of the family wondering if I wasn't their long-lost brother. I guess I looked different up there on the big screen. I would have bet anything I had my father never saw any of his children once he had handed them over to the orphanage. He wouldn't have worried a minute about the one who disappeared."

Julia said slowly, "You could have gone through this whole venture and not said a word. *I* wouldn't have guessed. Nor, I think, would anyone around here. Your face on the big screen must look rather different from the boy of ten who left here. People tend to see what they want to see. Why tell me? . . . Why tell me anything at all?"

"I don't know. I don't understand myself. Even stopping the cars on the way here was a mistake. I could have given myself away by that. Then I saw you and Alasdair . . . I nearly came undone when I realized that you were going to be *living* here instead of the castle, or taking yourself off to visit your father, or one of your sisters. I never expected to find Mrs. Sinclair showing my foolish little stepdaughter to her room and waiting on table. I didn't expect to find her living in *my* house. Things got terribly mixed up, and now I'm babbling away to you, pouring out things like a whiskey cask that's had the bung removed. That's what undid me. I shouldn't have come in here. But just watching you putting the kid to bed in the room I was born in— the sort of gentleness my mother was too tired to give any of us. Lighting the fire again. But this time without the thought that I'd get a box on the ears if it smoked. Having to carry the water for the kettle from the stream before the well was dug. It was all too much. I've trusted you too much, Julia Seymour. Are you going to betray me?"

"Why should I? Can you trust no one?"

He shook his head. "No. I've never completely trusted anyone once I realized that promises are made—and broken. I've had a lot of pals. I don't think I ever had a friend. Just someone to have a good time with. Someone to get drunk with. Never anyone to talk to. Oh, there is one—but he doesn't count in the real sense. I've had two wives, and I don't ever remember having talked to either one of them. It was either bed, or escorting them somewhere—proud that they were better-looking than any other dame in sight. Sorry. I'm getting maudlin. . . . I had fantasies of you when I saw your movies. Mrs. Sinclair . . . who was also Michael Seymour's daughter. The kind of theater royalty I could never aspire to. You became a sort of princess in the castle to me. That's why it was such a shock to find that you were living *here*. Princess—Sinclair Princesses—should always live in castles.''

"Was that why you wanted me for the film?"

He shook his head. "The studio doesn't let anyone live out fantasies—not on their money. No, I had a perfectly good reason for wanting you. Your acting, the way you photographed—and the Oscar, above all, were quite enough. You would have done very well out of it, Julia.'' He held up his hand to dismiss her protest. "Yes—I know. You couldn't leave here. Lady Jean—the kid. I haven't ever known that sort of woman before. Career would have come first, last—and always. I guess I began to think of you the way my father thought of Adam Sinclair. You are Michael Seymour's daughter. And I've never come within spitting distance of an Oscar. You could have been looking down your long theatrical nose at me."

"If you only knew how I would have welcomed the job—and the money. It was just too far to go—at that time.''

"I can imagine you needing the money. I had a few inquiries made. After all, the Sinclairs weren't well off back in the twenties. After I got over being sore at you, I understood some of it. It wasn't until I saw you this evening with the kid that I understood the rest.''

She took his empty glass from him and made no move to refill it. "Then we seem to have some things straightened out. I think we understand more about each other than we ever could have expected to. I'm glad you told me . . . what you did. I'm glad you trust me enough. No one will ever know. Not from me. And don't be surprised at any of the things I do at the castle—or make any sort of protest. I have placed a certain trust in you, too, Rod. I may be the mistress of the castle, but pride doesn't stop me turning my hand to whatever will make an honest penny.

I don't look for handouts. We've never been able to afford much in the line of pride—either the Sinclairs or the Seymours. Remember—both my father and mother worked for a living. Worked very hard at times.''

"Acting and playing the piano—it never seems very hard work to people who dig ditches. I'm street-smart, Julia, but there are an awful lot of things I don't know. Can't remember when I've ever admitted that to anyone—especially a woman—before.''

"Go back," she said, "and go to bed. You'll have forgotten half of this conversation in the morning. And don't worry about the rest. It stays with me—only with me. Always.''

He got to his feet slowly. He held out his hand. "Thanks. Thanks a lot. You're a great woman, Julia Seymour." She opened the door. "I think I'll just leave the car here—walk back. Remember how many times I've walked this road. Maybe it'll clear my head." He stood in the open doorway, taking deep breaths. "So you smell it?"

"Smell what?''

"The woodsmoke. That faintest bit of chill in the air that tells you fall is coming. I can remember smelling the seasons in this forest. In California you really don't smell anything. Except women's perfume. May I kiss you, Julia?''

"No.''

"Oh, for God's sake, I didn't mean it that way. For once in my life I want to leave this doorway with a kiss of gentleness on my lips, instead of a cuff around the ear, or a curse. Kiss me, Julia? Please?''

She raised herself on her toes to brush his lips softly, quickly. "Go back and sleep. There won't be any nightmares, Rod. No kicks or curses. Sleep deeply and dreamlessly. The ghosts are all being laid to rest.''

"I'll remember that.''

He had only dim starlight to guide him back. She watched the forest road swallow him up.

III

SOMETHING CAME TO LIFE in Julia in the weeks that followed— something she scarcely recognized, or could put a name to. She began to realize how much she had missed the company of people of something like her own age, how she had missed the repartee, the mock insults, sometimes genuine anger when something went wrong. The crew became faces and real names. She got to know their idiosyncrasies, their weaknesses and strengths. She heard laughter, often curses when a piece of equipment didn't work as it should, or John Gunn demanded yet another take on a scene they had already gone through a dozen times. She began to perceive the strengths and weaknesses of the script also and to know what a gamble Rod McCallum was taking. He had chanced a great deal for his brief tenancy of Castle Sinclair. She began to wonder at the compelling force of feeling in a man that could lead him halfway across the world to take a great risk with his future just for this chance, briefly, to possess Sinclair.

A friendship grew between them steadily, but what they had talked of that first night was never again referred to. Now she almost always stayed to have dinner with Rod and Stacia, Claire Avery, Martin, and George. She always helped cook and serve the meal and then sat down and ate with them. Alasdair slept comfortably on a sofa in the housekeeper's room. Now she brought pajamas and a bathrobe with her, and he hardly wakened on the journey home. Janet refused to let her help with clearing the table and washing up. "Well, aren't Kate and I well able to do it?—I've only been doing it all my life. Go back to the fire with them, Mrs. Sinclair. It does you good. You've been here long enough by yourself. A bit of young company . . ." It was the loneliness of the past years that Julia suddenly recognized. She listened to them swap tales of Hollywood, location stories. They drank a lot—but not too much. The irritations of the day seemed to fall away from them over the evening meal. She was pleased that Sir Niall so often stayed to eat with them. He, too, had had his years of loneliness. They seemed to welcome his company once they discovered the sense of humor and the genuine kindliness that lurked behind the formal exterior. Every Sunday the whole crew was bidden to lunch at Finavon— any who cared to come. His housekeeper laid on a buffet lunch. Where they got the food, Julia never asked. She suspected there was some collaboration between Janet and Sir Niall so that supplies that were meant for Castle Sinclair were redirected to Finavon. Surprisingly, most of the crew turned up. Inverness on a Sunday held no particular attractions. There was the continuing joke about one or another of them seeing the Loch Ness monster—"Old Nessie." Some of them went fishing, but when the rain pelted down, Finavon seemed a warm and friendly refuge. Many of Sir Niall's neighbors were invited for the Sunday buffet, and to Julia's surprise, many of them came. At first they came out of curiosity. Rod McCallum's name alone was enough to arouse that. Some were stiff and inclined to be condescending—they didn't return. Curiosity satisfied, they were content to leave with the impression that film people were as they had always imagined—loud and vulgar. But some seemed to realize their own insularity and welcomed the arrival of these unconventional, relaxed strangers, to whom the bounds of class seemed to mean nothing. The crew recognized only two things: that Rod McCallum was a star and that John Gunn was an Academy Award-winning director. That was their own class system. Any respect and deference they had went in that direction. Some of the crew didn't like Rod McCallum or John Gunn and stayed away from them as much as they could. But they all recognized each other as professionals. They were on this job, on this location, to exercise their skills. There was a budget and a schedule. Too many takes were expensive. Bad weather when they planned to shoot outdoors was expensive. Julia thought some of them might have been inclined to drag their heels to add a few more weeks' pay, but John Gunn and Mike Pearson between them kept a tight hold, and there was little chance for anyone deliberately to disrupt shooting. Rod McCallum proved to be as he had been described: a pro. He was present on the set, made up, his lines learned, whenever John Gunn was ready for him. Except for the Sunday break, he did not drink during the day.

"It's all very amusing, my dear," Sir Niáll said to Julia. "I find them all interesting. Types I'd never get to know in a million years if we weren't all stuck here together in the wilderness. It's very decent of them to pass the time of day—spend time—with an old fellow like me."

"You're very entertaining to them, Sir Niall. And I don't mean 'funny.' They'll remember you. Some of them will meet up on other films—other locations. They'll say, 'Remember that marvelous guy with the kilt and the cane who gave us those great lunches and great drinks?' Years from now, when one or another of them meet up, they'll talk about you. With affection."

"Bless you, my dear. How kind. But I know half of them are madly in love with you."

"I think rather more are madly in love with Kirsty Macpherson."

Kirsty was always present at the Sunday buffets, and by becoming familiar with those who guarded the entry to the forest road, she was free to drive to the shooting whenever she felt inclined. She always brought her daughter, Betsy, with her. Betsy and Alasdair played together on the fringe of the shooting, by now well trained not to get in the way of the men with the cameras and cables. They even took to acting what bits of the plot they could comprehend—a sort of variation where cowboys and Indians turned into commandos and guards.

The person who roused Julia's pity, although she couldn't bring herself to like her, was Stacia. She remained forever on the outside of the group. Any of the crew who tried to talk to her, with the exception of the continuity girl, Barbara, were quickly frozen out by a glance or sometimes a warning word from Rod McCallum. She had been driven into Inverness and pronounced it "boring." She had gazed at Loch Ness in the pouring rain and wondered aloud what all the fuss was about. The driver and all of the crew were strictly forbidden to take her into Inverness at night or to travel with her alone.

"What else can I do?" Rod McCallum had said to them all assembled around the fire when Stacia had gone to bed. By now she had been commanded by Rod to learn to fill her own hot-water bottles. "She's a walking mantrap, and at her age *someone's* got to be responsible for her. She can't help that she's her mother's daughter. I feel sorry for the kid sometimes, but I don't know any other way to keep her out of trouble." No, Julia thought, it wasn't Stacia's fault that she possessed a body of almost full-blown sexuality, the famous pouting lips of her mother that promised what someone of Stacia's age should hardly know about. She was aware of the feelings she roused in men; she seemed to handle them as a grown woman would—yet there was still a raw, gaping wound of vulnerability evident in her. It was this that roused Julia's sympathy. She knew the girl was desperately lonely, and perhaps still grieving over her mother's death. She tried to include her in conversations, but the girl wouldn't be drawn, usually answering in monosyllables. "It isn't much use trying," Rod McCallum said to Julia, "though it's

kind of you. She's pretty dumb—well, not dumb, but not edu-
cated. She never stayed at one school long enough to learn anything. I had her pick a whole lot of books in London to bring
up here, but I don't think she's cracked one of them. Film magazines, that's all that seems to interest her. And men. I don't
know how I'm going to keep her tied down until she's of age.
Once she's old enough for me to let go the reins, she'll fall into
one affair or marriage after another. But I won't be responsible
for her then. That person I had lined up in London to take care
of her—well, she spent one afternoon with her and decided she
was too much of a handful. Just the looks she gets when she
walks down the street. I was going to pay a basketful of money
to this lady—who came highly recommended and who has two
daughters around Stacia's age. But as badly as she needed the
money, she wouldn't take the responsibility. 'I don't want to
hand her back to you pregnant, Mr. McCallum,' she said.
Straight out, like that. She'd gotten everything planned—a round
of museums and galleries, theater, ballet, movies. Stacia was
going to have lessons with a sort of tutor in the mornings, and
then the afternoons were for all the rest. Well, the lady formed
the opinion that no man under eighty was safe with her. God,
all they did that one afternoon was to go to tea at the Ritz—just
the lady, Stacia, and the two daughters. It was enough. I had no
choice but to bring her here, even though I knew she'd be miserable. And I knew she'd be a disruptive influence. Look at what
happens when she goes to Sir Niall's on a Sunday. All the men's
eyes pop out, and the women would like to see her drop dead.''

So Stacia hung around the fringes of the set, sometimes getting more in the way than Alasdair or Betsy ever did. Everyone
knew that she knew better and that she did it deliberately. The
less tolerant would order her away rudely: ''Out of the way,
kid.'' She would plump herself down in what was meant to be
a gesture of contempt but always turned out to be an act of
provocation, in the chairs she knew were sacrosanct—Rod's
chair, John Gunn's chair, Claire Avery's chair, Barbara's chair—
and wait to be asked to vacate it. When the weather was fine
she could sometimes be seen taking solitary walks along the
edge of the loch. At first Rory and Duuf and Angus followed
her, hoping she would toss sticks for them, as most people did.
But she ignored them, and they gave up. Never at the tea or
coffee breaks did she offer them the scraps that it seemed to

delight the rest of the crew to do, and they gave up coming to her. Julia realized the loneliness in the girl and felt powerless to assuage it. She was still a hurt, bewildered child trapped in a woman's body, not knowing how to handle her physical or emotional situation.

But Julia had little time to watch much of the shooting and therefore little time to try to draw Stacia more into her confidence. Helping Janet and Kate and the two women who came daily from Inverness to cater for the crew was a day's work—as well as being there to serve breakfast and dinner. She partly welcomed the reprieve; there was always boredom in seeing shots taken and retaken—and this must have added to Stacia's boredom. But Julia was also experiencing the doubts some people felt about the script. At times the scenes shot within the castle seemed too claustrophobic for Rod McCallum's style. The bitter wrangling of the commando troop shut up within the confines of the castle to train for their desperate mission into Germany seemed to place too much strain on his abilities as an actor. The maneuverings among the small band of men for the favors of the mistress of the castle, played by Claire Avery, seemed contrived. But Julia did try to get away from the kitchen, always taking Alasdair by the hand and inviting Stacia to come with them, to watch some of the scenes as they, or their stand-ins, did their training sequences. They scaled the castle walls while Julia held her breath and hoped the walls themselves would not come tumbling down. They raced and crawled through the falling leaves of the October forest. The bitter quarrels they had around the long table in the dining hall as their mission was planned gave way, when the crew had packed up and gone back to Inverness, to the pleasant, amiable dinners, the brandy before the fire, either in the Great Hall or the library, which was also being included in some "atmosphere" shots that Rod McCallum had demanded once he had seen the great room. Julia thought the double use of the set a mistake. The castle should have been reserved as the setting of the film's conflicts. They should all have returned to Inverness every night, and come back to Sinclair to take up the roles they played, the animosity and strains geared up freshly every day. But a trace of the good-humored bonhomie of the night before always remained. This was entirely Rod McCallum's fault, Julia judged. His passion to be master at Sinclair, even for these short weeks, had overruled good sense.

He was more inclined to play the laird of the castle than the commander of the small, tight group preparing for their mission either of success or death.

When they went to the small, abandoned RAF airstrip to shoot the scenes of the practice landings and takeoffs, supposedly near the fictional castle in Germany, here Rod McCallum seemed more the actor screen audiences were accustomed to. His actions were natural, his voice of command rang true. It was his element, as when he moved through the forest to approach and take and hold the castle for the brief time needed to get their scientist out. That part of the film, Julia didn't doubt, would work, the suspense skillfully maintained by John Gunn. Rod McCallum at the table in the dining hall with his men, or in the Red Tower Room or the library with Claire Avery, was less convincing. John Gunn was using the projection room of a movie theater to view the daily rushes. If he was not happy with what he saw, he never said so, nor did he display any great enthusiasm. ''That's John's way,'' Rod McCallum said. ''He never says a word about what he's got. He saves all his likes and dislikes for the cutting room.''

What Rod McCallum's real relationship with Claire Avery was, Julia couldn't quite fathom. He usually treated her off-handedly and never seemed to listen to much she said. Julia noticed, as the weeks went by, that Claire said less and less. The vital spark of confidence needed for her role as mistress of the castle seemed to desert her. Julia watched one day a brief shot of her descending the stairs from the gloom above, and the men at the table, discussing refinements to their plans, suddenly freezing as they realized she had overheard them. ''Damn!'' she heard John Gunn mutter. ''She moves as if she hadn't ever come downstairs in her life. She's mistress of a castle. She makes it look more like a brothel. It'd have been far better, Rod, if we'd asked for Julia Seymour for this part.''

Julia faded back into the crowd and made her way to the kitchen, wishing she had not heard. There were many things she now regretted about agreeing to the whole arrangement—except for the money. What would it be like when, inevitably, they all left, when the big lights went out and the talk and the laughter and curses were stilled? The loneliness and the silence would descend with more weight than she had yet experienced. She and Janet and Kate would sit it out here through another winter, remembering the laughter and the fights, the daily turmoil. They would eagerly await visits from Sir Niall. That would be about all there would be to wait for. Alasdair would be bereft of all these fascinating and entertaining companions who petted and spoiled him. The stillness and austerity would return. Inexorably the trees of the forest became more bare, and the time of the snow came closer. They were approaching the shooting of the climactic scenes.

She had grown used to Rod McCallum driving her and Alasdair back to the cottage in the evenings after dinner. Even the nights when Sir Niall was there, Rod would come along when Sir Niall dropped her off at the cottage, saying he enjoyed the walk back. Many evenings he came in, lit the fire for her, and had a whiskey poured by the time she came back from laying Alasdair in his bed, having heard his prayers. Only very occasionally did he ever refer to what this cottage had once been to him. They talked of other things—about his slow, hard rise in Hollywood, the years in Westerns when he didn't even have a speaking part. He told me how he had gone to a voice coach to have the last of the Scottish burr rubbed away. "I needed to be an American. It cost more than I could afford, but I had to know when I did get my first few lines, they'd come out right. I went to an acting coach, Ernest Wilcox. I used to live in a dump to pay for that, but he taught me a lot more than acting. He told me how to dress, which fork to pick up when I was lucky enough to get to be invited to someone's party. He told me what newspapers and magazines to read. He told me which books I should know about—even if I didn't read them all. Very decent fellow— an Englishman. He's still around. I still see him. He still gives me reading lists. He knew I hardly spent a day in school after I was ten, but he'd gotten all the rough edges rubbed off by the time I was offered some speaking parts. Not that I was ever going to be a rival to Cary Grant—but, you know, he didn't want me treated like a dumb oaf. I've tried to pay him back. I'm always sending other actors to him. In a while I'll even send Stacia to him, since she's bound to end up in the movie business. He has a ballet school picked out for her when we get back. He helped her as much as anyone could after her mother was killed. Drove her around—talked to her. And I knew she was safe with him. He's a homosexual. He admires beauty in women, but he doesn't want it for himself. And he plays it straight with men he knows are straight. If I have any education at all—if I can even sit here and talk to Michael Seymour's daughter—it's because of what he taught me and what he made me learn. . . .''

She found these moments of humility in him endearing and touching. In turn she shared her memories of her time at RADA, of what it had been like to step onto the stage for the first time to play Cordelia to her own father's Lear. He questioned her closely about all her small experience of the stage, a medium he knew nothing about. Since Jamie had been part of this whole period, his name often came into her telling. He listened, even though she sensed he did not want to hear about Jamie. But he heard her out in a kind of respectful silence, as if he owed her the return favor of listening, as she had done for him. The parting kiss was now something he expected, and she began to understand that he would have come for that alone, even if there had not been the talk, the sense of shared experience, that assuaging of old hurts and hungers. But it was not the cool kiss she had first given him. Now their embrace held passion. She dreaded the eagerness of her own body meeting his. This, too, had been part of the loneliness—this yearning of a healthy young woman to be loved physically, to be held in a man's arms. No words of love were spoken between them in those first weeks. Just their embrace grew fiercer and stronger, and she knew that she lived all through the day for that moment at night. She didn't know if she was in love with Rod McCallum, but she needed him.

At last, drawing out of his arms, she brought herself to say, ''Claire—are you going back to Claire now?''

He gave a soft laugh. All their words in the cottage were soft because of the sleeping child in the next room. ''Jealous? I hoped you might be. No, I'm not going back to Claire. That part of our relationship is over. You must have seen that for yourself. All she wants now is to finish her scenes and get out of here, and I'm happy to oblige. I've had John reschedule some of the shooting so she can leave earlier. We're shooting out of sequence as it is—so it doesn't matter. But we have to be sure we've got all we need from her before she goes. But you can see as well as anyone she isn't working out in the part.''

''That may not be her fault. She was supposed to play a part she had in real life. Now it doesn't exist. She is acting something she wasn't prepared for.''

"Now, listen—I didn't promise her anything. Sure, we had a relationship. But we never talked about marriage. Never. After two marriages—especially marriage to someone like Anne Rayner—I wasn't going to rush into anything. Of course, the studio made sure that we were never seen to live together. She never even stayed a whole night in my house, or I in hers. This is the first time we've ever spent whole days or nights in each other's company. And, frankly, she bores me."

"And you've told her?"

"I didn't need to. She's not as dumb as she sometimes seems. She understands how things are. She knows that when you're around, she hardly exists. Perhaps that's why she seems to be disappearing from the film. She hasn't even the spirit to be jealous—or to fight. You notice how she slides away from you. She doesn't confront you, because she knows she can't match you. She knows, as a few other people have noticed, that I'm in love with you."

She drew away from him slowly. "Are you sure you're in love with me?—or are you in love with the mistress of Castle Sinclair?"

"Is there a difference?"

"Yes—and you know it. One is a position, the other is a woman."

"I'm in love with the most womanly woman I've ever known. Someone with tenderness and grace. Someone I thought would be beyond me all my life. Beside you, Julia, I'm rough and rude. When I'm with you I fall back into being the Rod McBain who grew up in this little place. The kid who only knew the cuffs and kicks. The gentler things of life have not come my way, Julia. I've scratched and clawed my way up, and Hollywood taught me nothing different. There was only one way: my way; the hard, rough way I learned from my father. The people who lived in the castle were creatures of another world. They thought differently—they *were* different. If I had known what was going to happen to me, I might have dropped this whole idea of filming at Sinclair. Or I would have asked you once more to play opposite me in a film. I think I wanted to make this high and mighty lady of Castle Sinclair regret profoundly that she'd ever turned me down—because she wasn't going to get another chance with me. I wanted to humble Julia Seymour—more than that, I wanted to humble the mistress of the castle. And what's happened? I've fallen in love with a woman who is neither of the persons I've had fixed in my mind. I've fallen in love with a woman called Julia. I don't remember ever saying that to any other woman in my life. Love was something for screenwriters. I knew it was something I was supposed to feel when I went to bed with someone. For the first time rough, tough Rod McBain is in love—with a woman he's never even been to bed with. When Claire leaves, will you move back to the castle? Can we be with each other just for a little while?''

"No." She said the word quietly. "No. I can't do that. Life will be hard enough when you go away. If we grew any closer, when you do go, it would be as if my lover had died again. I don't think I could stand that."

He turned and wrenched open the door, and for the first time she had known, he slammed it, with no thought for the sleeping child.

The remaining scenes with Claire Avery were quickly shot, as if Rod McCallum couldn't wait for her to go. Everyone on the set recognized the situation. Coolly Kirsty Macpherson sat on the wall of the bridge well away from the activity of the crew, smoked her cigarette, and observed to Julia, who found herself unaccountably alone with a woman who still had the power to make her feel unsure, nervous, as if she were still the young girl who had first come to Sinclair: "Well, you've done it again. You've taken a man I rather fancied. Not that I'd ever have married him, as I wanted to marry Jamie. Beside Jamie, Rod McCallum is scum. But I do fancy him. With the Avery woman out of the way, it should have been simple. But you got in the way. Is he good in bed?''

"I wouldn't know."

"Oh, come off it. Don't give me that frozen-faced virtue. What woman having the chance of Rod McCallum wouldn't take it? When he looks at you he has that lean and hungry look. What are you holding him off for? Surely not marriage. You wouldn't last six months together. Well—he'll soon be gone. You'd better make the most of it." She stubbed out her cigarette and turned to toss the butt into the loch. Her tone altered to a pitch of incredulity. "Oh, God—no! No!''

Julia turned to look where Kirsty pointed. At the loch's edge, about a mile away, they could see the fast-moving figure of a horse and rider. For another heart-stopping minute Julia watched. The figures became plain and recognizable. It was Stacia, mounted on Catriona—that unmistakable dappled gray, and the bright, flying hair of the rider, laying into the flanks of the old mare with a riding crop.

"God!" Kirsty shouted. "Stop!—you fool!" Stacia couldn't hear her, and Julia doubted she would have obeyed if she had. "Cat hasn't been ridden like that for more than ten years! The old thing will drop dead, if they don't kill each other before that."

Her shrill cries had interrupted the absolute silence demanded when a scene was being shot. The commandos of the cast were all in their military dress, going through yet another torturous training exercise. Now they all, cast and crew, spun in the direction of Kirsty and Julia at the end of the bridge. Every eye followed Kirsty's pointing arm. Even in this moment, John Gunn's professional instincts did not desert him. "Quickly!" he shouted to the two cameramen. "Shoot it! Shoot it! Get whatever you can of it." The cameras were turned hastily, and the wild flight along the loch shore was recorded in whatever fashion the cameramen could manage.

But Julia and Kirsty were already down off the bridge and running to meet the approaching rider. Very quickly Rod McCallum, Mike Pearson, Martin, and George had caught up with them. "Crazy kid!" Rod yelled. Now that they were down at the same level as the horse and rider, the situation seemed more dangerous than ever. At first Stacia had swerved Cat around boulders at a pace that would have taxed a show jumping horse. Now, as she recognized the figures running toward her, she began to set Cat to jump the lower rocks, which were strewn like obstacles along the loch edge. It was a terrain no horse should have been taken through at more than a careful walking pace. The two parties had almost reached each other when what had seemed inevitable happened. In a last gesture of defiance, Stacia put the mare to jump a long, low boulder, all the time beating her fiercely with the riding stick. The tired, terrified animal made a gesture to refuse until the crop came down again. With a scream of protest she backed off, almost threw Stacia, and made another try to clear the hurdle. Her forelegs clipped the rough, hard edge, and horse and rider plunged headlong into the dark earth.

By the time the runners reached them, Stacia was on her feet, but Cat was still on the ground, rolling and screaming in agony. They stood and gazed at the animal; the spasms of pain caused a shaking in every limb. She foamed at the mouth, and the places where Stacia's crop had fallen had brought red weals to the gray-white coat. Rod McCallum pronounced what most of them had already decided. "Leg's broken. She'll have to be put down."

"No!" Stacia screamed. "She'll be all right!"

"Shut your mouth, you bitch. You've killed the animal. Someone, for God's sake, get hold of William Kerr. He has to have a gun around. . . ." The set was full of guns, but they were all filled with blank ammunition.

Almost as he spoke, Julia recognized the figure of William Kerr running along the loch shore, scrambling over rocks, sometimes taking to the water because it gave easier passage. He carried a shotgun with him. It was just pure luck, Julia thought, that this afternoon he had chanced to be at the castle and not out at some distant farm.

He reached them at last, when Julia thought she could bear the sound of Cat's agonized screams no longer. The mare's struggles were less; Julia thought her heart might give out before the merciful gun ended the nightmare. William Kerr assessed the situation in seconds.

"She is gone," he said. "Nothing to be done." He loaded the gun, and risking being kicked by the thrashing hooves, he managed to place the barrel against the gray temple.

"No!" Stacia cried once again. By answer, Rod McCallum turned and struck her with his full strength across the mouth. Her cry of pain and shock and the mare's final death scream came at the same time. The gray-white limbs continued to tremble and flex for a few seconds longer and then were finally still.

The roar of the shotgun echoed around the loch and the hills, and the echoes died away. A terrible silence fell on everything and everyone.

Rod McCallum was the first to move. He moved with purpose toward his stepdaughter. Reading his expression, she stepped backward in fear, but his long arms easily reached her. One after another the blows rained on her. She retreated farther, and he followed her until they were both standing knee-deep in the water of the loch. She tried fighting back in the only way she could. Long nails raked deep scratches in his face, and then she put up her arms to try to defend her own face.

"Now you're killing, are you?—you stupid, dumb bitch. You killed that animal as surely as if you fired the gun yourself. Well—take that—and *that!*"

Mike Pearson was now struggling in the water with them both, trying to get between Rod and the girl. "For God's sake, man, stop it!"

He in turn got a blow that knocked him backward into the water. Stacia's screams now echoed round the loch as Catriona's had. Her lips were running with blood; she had lost her footing and fell into the water. With manic ferocity Rod dived after her and brought her up with both his hands closed around her throat.

"Jeez—we've got to stop this! He'll kill her!" George started wading into the icy water, and Martin more reluctantly followed. William Kerr laid down his gun by the dead mare and he, too, strode in. Stacia had fallen again under another blow, and now Rod dragged her up by her trailing, sodden hair. Mike Pearson interposed himself again, and again he took a blow that was meant for Stacia. Rod dropped Stacia as she began to sag into unconsciousness, and he started pounding George and Martin with the skill and ruthlessness and mean cunning that spoke of dozens of fights in which no rules but survival were followed. Among them, George and Martin and Mike were at last managing to take some sort of grip on Rod's arms, but he was still kicking, and it seemed that he might even be able to shake them off. Stacia, on her knees in the water, received one of the kicks, and she toppled sideways. She managed to bring herself upright again and began crawling toward the edge of the water.

Julia wasn't aware of whatever cries of protest she might herself had added. She found herself reacting without thought but that all this must be stopped. She picked up William Kerr's gun.

Through the din she heard Kirsty's sharp voice: "Julia—don't! For God's sake, don't!" It was perhaps, Julia thought, a good thing William Kerr hadn't reloaded the gun. As Rod struggled to throw off the four men now trying to restrain him, she waded into the water, judged the moment when it was right, and brought the butt of the gun down on the back of Rod's head. For a few seconds he remained upright, and then slowly his knees began to buckle.

"You'd better put him on dry ground, or he's likely to drown," she heard her voice say, this unknown voice sickened and made harsh by what she had witnessed.

Rod had not been knocked unconscious; within a minute he was shaking his head to clear it, on his knees on the ground, his feet still in the water. He had given up his struggles with the four men. "Okay—okay," he said. "It's over. I just wish I'd had time to kill the murdering little bitch."

"And lucky for you there wasn't a bullet in the gun, or I might have killed *you*," Julia said.

To her astonishment a slow smile broke over his features. "You know—I really think you might have. Come on. Let's get back, or we'll all freeze where we stand." But for a moment he stood over the dead mare. "Poor old girl. She'd earned a better end than this. And to think it was me who taught that silly bitch to ride. . . ."

Then he held out his hand to each of the four men who had struggled with him. "Thanks, guys. Sorry if I hurt any of you. I guess it got a bit wild. You may have saved me from a man-slaughter charge." He looked toward the figure of Stacia, who was running in a hobbling fashion back to the castle. "I really don't think I would have killed her. I suppose sanity might have come back before that. All I know is that I wanted to beat the living daylights out of her—to give her the thrashing she's had coming to her all her rotten little life. Well, will anyone shake my hand?—or am I condemned for getting blind mad at sense-less cruelty to an animal?"

Slowly each of the men took his hand. "Take back your gun, Mr. Kerr. Thank God you were here to put Cat out of her mis-ery. I think it was her screams that drove me mad . . . well, whatever, I did a pretty terrible thing, and yet it'll be some time before I get around to thinking Stacia didn't deserve it."

Kirsty had picked up the riding crop Stacia had dropped. "I once remember my father giving me a few belts with one of these the day I kept a horse at an all-out gallop far too long and nearly ruined her. I never tried it again. What amazes me is that Cat stood it for so long. She could have just stopped short, and Stacia would have gone straight over her head."

"Not Stacia. First I taught her to ride, and when she showed she enjoyed it—that kid never enjoyed very much—I sent her to one of the best stunt riders in the business. He taught her all kinds of tricks about how to keep her seat. Maybe too much."

They walked in their sodden clothes in Stacia's wake, the boots of the men squelching water. "I hope John has the good sense to be ready to take a few close-ups. I guess we look as if we've really been through the wars.''

As they climbed back onto the bridge, Rod greeted his director. ''Hi, John. I guess shooting's over for the day. But save the footage. It might splice in somewhere pretty well.''

Julia summoned Dr. MacGregor, who had already treated some of the crew for minor injuries and who was familiar with most of them, having attended some of Sir Niall's Sunday buffets. ''Well, lassie,'' he said to Stacia, who was in bed, with Janet applying cold compresses to her face, ''it seems you were a mite more than foolish. Let me see what the damage is? Poor old Cat. You were mad, you know, lassie. She was too old, and no one had ridden her like that for many years. And *no* one would ever have ridden her along the loch shore. It's a wonder you didn't break your own neck.'' He was looking closely at the cut on her left eyebrow. Blood had congealed there, and Janet had not dared disturb it. ''Or perhaps it's a wonder your stepfather didn't break your neck for you.''

''He tried to,'' Stacia spat out. ''He would have killed me if he could. He would have loved me to break my neck, and then he would have been rid of me—just the way he was glad to be rid of my mother. And as for the horse . . . well, we just went for a ride. God, I'm so *bored* here. He doesn't let me do anything at all. We just went down the forest road and through the woods a little. I could tell Cat was enjoying it. Then on the shore I gave her a little tap—just to see what she'd do. That set her off. She just went into nearly a gallop.''

''Cat was a bit of a Thoroughbred. Blood always tells. She didn't take kindly to being put between shafts when the time came. But she settled down to it—just as long as she was well treated. She was always a gentle soul, for all that her sire was fiery. Pity. You did know she's been out to grass for some time now . . . ?''

''How was I to know?'' was the reply. ''No one here talks to me. I just saddled her up while everyone was having lunch. She seemed to enjoy being ridden. It wasn't *all* my fault.''

''Well, maybe you'll leave old horses to their justly deserved rest in the future. I don't much care for the look of this eyebrow. We'll just clear this blood away. . . . Sorry, I know it hurts. . . . Janet, if you could just take the shade off the lamp, I'd see it better. Warm water, Janet, if you please." A fresh bowl was brought, to which Dr. MacGregor added some disinfectant. "Well, I think I'll just have to take a few wee stitches here— otherwise you could end up with a wee bit of a scar."

Stacia jerked away from him. "A scar!" she screamed. "A scar! He's scarred me, the bastard!"

"He's done nothing of the sort. Of course, from the looks of it you are lucky he didn't break your jawbone. You're going to have a very sore, puffy face for a wee while, young lady."

"You're not going to put any stitches in me. I won't have some country bumpkin messing me up. I'm going back to London. Get me a decent plastic surgeon—"

"By the time you get to London this may have started to heal with a separation on the hairline, where no hair will ever grow again. If this old country bumpkin draws it together so that it heals that way, there's a good chance it will never show. Maybe a wee spot of remedial work later, but you stand a much better chance of that being successful if I do this job first. However, that is your choice. . . . You're not going to bleed to death. I can just put a plaster on it, and you can go to London and hope for the best."

Stacia slumped back against the pillows. "Do it, then! I suppose I have to believe you know what you're doing."

"Ah, I've had a wee bit of experience. Surprising what old country bumpkins are called upon to do. What with drunks fighting, and nasty farm accidents, and children falling off things and into things . . ." He was swiftly threading suture through a needle with skillful, practiced hands. "Yes, quite surprising what things come our way . . . Now, this may hurt just a wee bit . . . but it'll be over in a second. . . . Try to keep very still."

Stacia clamped her lips closed, and her face assumed a look of perfect composure. She did not permit herself to wince as each of three small stitches was taken, but Julia saw her fingers grip the sheet very tightly; she was rigid, immobile.

"There—it's over. You're a brave wee lass, even if a foolish one."

"Brave!—nothing!" Stacia snapped at him. "Do you think I want my face ruined for life? I'm going to be a film star. A *great* star."

"Well, then, young lady, I suggest you don't do any more stupid things like putting a poor old mare up to tasks she's long past. I suggest you think before you take your fences in the future. Think of others as well as yourself. Now, Mrs. Sinclair, I'll just leave these wee pills with you for the pain and to help her sleep. She's going to be very stiff and sore all over for a few days, and not a pretty sight. But she'll survive, which is more than poor old Cat did." He returned his instruments to his bag. "Now I'd better go and see to the mayhem your stepfather wreaked on innocent bystanders in what I can only think of as a fit of righteous anger. It all could have been worse, I suppose. At least there is no *human* to certify and bury. You're not sending Cat to the knackers, are you, Mrs. Sinclair?"

Julia shook her head no.

"I thought not. Well, a grave for a horse is a formidable undertaking, but I'm sure you'll get help. I would like to see some little marker put up—something that reads a bit like *Beloved Catriona. Here lies the testimony to human folly.* Good night, young lady. I hope you sleep. I'll look in on you tomorrow."

Dr. MacGregor went downstairs to the six men, who were soberly sipping their whiskey before the fire. Rod had insisted that William Kerr return and have a drink with them as soon as he had changed his clothes. But Rod himself had gone back to keep a vigil by Cat's body until darkness fell, and John Gunn had come to persuade him back to the warmth. Dr. MacGregor accepted a whiskey and looked around the group assembled around the library fire. "Well, that was a wee bit of a fracas, wasn't it? I hope you washed those scratches with antiseptic, Mr. McCallum. Pity about poor old Cat. I can understand why you went a bit wild, man, but you could have been in a very serious state with the law if these good friends hadn't done something to stop you. And the young lady upstairs may yet take it into her head to prefer charges against you for assault and battery."

"Then I'll haul her into Juvenile Court—or whatever court you have in this country—on charges of extreme cruelty to an animal. I think she knows it. It's a standoff. I *am* her adoptive father."

"Well, I'm not the law," Dr. MacGregor said. "You're a bit of a wild man, Mr. McCallum."

"No wilder than my stepdaughter—or daughter, as she is in law. Have another dram with us, Dr. MacGregor."

"Well, as I see it's Niall Henderson's best, that I will. I'll just dispense a few pills around for aches and pains and be thankful that's all I have to do."

Sir Niall arrived, having been telephoned by Janet about what had happened. Along the way he had met Kirsty Macpherson driving home, and he knew all the details. He looked around the group; for once his face was not amiable. "Well, this is a sorry business. Julia, I've made arrangements about Cat. There isn't soil deep enough here on the island or anywhere I can think of along the forest road to bury her. So I've arranged for my men to take her away. Getting her along the loch shore is no easy matter—especially in darkness. They've taken a tractor and a five-barred gate. It all has to be done by flashlights and the tractor headlights. She can be buried on my land, if that suits you."

"Thank you," Julia murmured.

"Any expenses—" Rod McCallum cut in hastily.

Sir Niall waved his hand in dismissal. "It's nothing I wouldn't do for a friend or a neighbor." He slumped into a seat and absentmindedly took a whiskey from Julia's hand. "What I can't understand is what got into the girl's mind. It was an act of sheer, almost criminal folly."

"She was probably hopped up on something," Rod McCallum said in a low voice.

"Hopped up? I don't understand. . . ."

"Drugs, Sir Niall. They're in use in Hollywood. Uppers—downers—whatever way you feel that you want to change, there's a nice little pill for it. All quite discreet. What I'd like to know is where she's getting them. I myself searched her baggage before we left Los Angeles—over her strong objections, I may say. I found nothing. She could be getting something from one of the crew here. I haven't got eyes in the back of my head, as much as I try to watch her."

"Drugs . . . at her age." Dr. MacGregor didn't seem as surprised as he might. "We see very little of it here—we're not a very sophisticated world. I suppose you could justly say that alcohol is our drug. But occasionally one reads an article in one of the medical journals, the word is passed at medical conferences. One hears it is not uncommon in London among certain types. It hardly seems to mean more to them than a dram of

whiskey or a cigarette. Does Miss Rayner drink, Mr. Mc-
Callum?''

"Not when I'm around, she doesn't. Have you missed more
than the usual from the store, Julia?''

"So much drinking goes on here, I wouldn't notice an extra
bottle or two. *I* haven't got eyes in the back of my head, either.''
Her head and body ached, her heart ached over Catriona, and
over Alasdair's tears when he had heard the news. He had witnessed, though from a distance, most of that scene on the loch
shore. Julia had managed to bustle him back into the castle before he had been able to see Cat's body. But he had refused his
supper and had cried himself to sleep in Julia's arms. Nothing
so violent had ever touched his young life. There had been no
disguising the shot that had ended Cat's life. There seemed to
be no confusion in his young mind between the make-believe
battles he had seen rehearsed so many times at the castle and in
the forest, and the real and terrible thing that had happened that
afternoon.

"I think," Dr. MacGregor said, "in light of what I have
heard, it might be better if you withheld those pills I gave you
for Miss Rayner. If she must suffer a little pain, it is infinitely
preferable to the consequences of mixing pills with drugs I don't
know about. How do children get hold of such things . . . ?''

"Stacia is a child only in years, Dr. MacGregor. Show business is a strange world, and the Hollywood version is the strangest of the lot. The studios make damn sure the public doesn't
read about it in the fan magazines, but that subworld does exist—
for some people. Call it what you want—sleeping pills, pills to
calm the nerves, pills to wake you up, whatever pills. It's there—
available," he said quietly. "It's a fairly open secret in Hollywood that Stacia's mother was hopped up with a mixture of
drugs and alcohol when she died. And it happened after she and
I had had a blazing row that Stacia can't have helped hearing. If
I went wild when I saw what Stacia had done this afternoon, I
think it could be put down to more than a fit of temper. I'm
afraid of what that girl could do—either to herself or to someone
else. I heartily wish her off my hands.''

Julia didn't sit down with the assembled men. She went to the
kitchen to give Janet and Kate some help with preparing the
meal. But she let Janet serve it alone; she had no heart this
evening to stay with the company, and she felt her presence

would not be missed. She didn't know if Rod McCallum had forgiven her for that blow on the head; at the moment, she didn't care. Finally Sir Niall came into the housekeeper's room, having declined the offer of dinner. "Are you ready to go, my dear? I'll drop you off."

Alasdair wakened and went eagerly to Sir Niall's car. Janet had filled a basket with cold game pie, cheese, bread, and a bottle of Sir Niall's own wine. All three of them ate it before the fire at the cottage. Then she put Alasdair to bed. "Mummie, has Cat gone to heaven?"

"Yes, dear. Cat's in heaven. No more aches and pains. She's young again—skipping about."

"Has she met Daddy?"

The question caught at Julia like a sharp pain. "Yes, I think she's met Daddy. I expect they've had a wonderful meeting." What had she done, bringing these strangers into her house, to bring with them a stench of corruption, of hatred, of violence into a child's life, to make him doubt the simple, innocent things he had been taught? She stayed holding Alasdair when the tears came again, stayed until he had exhausted himself and finally slept.

She was dressing the next morning, preparing to go to the castle to help Janet and Kate with breakfast, when she heard a gentle tap on the door. Rod McCallum stood there, in his hand a bunch of greenery.

"I don't know whether they're weeds or flowers. I don't know about things like that. I've come to say I'm sorry." Green and brown bruises were showing on his face, as well as the scratches inflicted by Stacia. "I've come to say I'm sorry," he repeated. "To say I'm sorry for what Stacia did, but most of all I'm sorry for the way I behaved. Even though I knew she'd destroyed something that was precious to you, I should never have reacted in that mad way. It *was* mad. How do I say I'm not always like that?"

"And I hit you. It didn't occur to me then that I might have fractured your skull—or even killed you. I just wanted to stop it all. As I wanted to stop Cat screaming . . ." She sighed, taking the weird bouquet of herbs and wild vines and weeds that had almost choked the castle garden, and she opened the door wide. "Oh, hell," she said. "Let's try to put it behind us. Do you want some tea?"

"No—Janet has coffee on the stove at the castle. I just thought I'd walk there with you and Alasdair. Did it scare him terribly?"

"He's very sad. He's known Cat all his life. He thinks she's just met up again with his father—both, of course, in heaven."

"Poor kid—we wrecked a bit of heaven for him."

Two days later—Julia learned that through Sir Niall Rod McCallum had dispatched telegrams to every reputable horse dealer across the Highlands—Sir Niall's horse box came into the stable yard at Sinclair. Rod McCallum waited until the crew had packed and gone for the night before he brought Alasdair around to see the back opened. What emerged was a beautiful, almost pure-white pony, dappled with a little gray, wearing a red harness, with a proud lift to its fine head and a high Thoroughbred's step. Alasdair gazed at it in wonder, his thumb going back into his mouth in the babyish habit Julia thought he had long outgrown. Rod McCallum squatted beside him as William Kerr trotted the lovely little creature around the yard. Sir Niall looked on. "See, kid, it's sort of like this," McCallum said. "When someone goes to heaven, like Cat, they often send back themselves in some other form to the people they loved. This one's come back to you like Cat must have been when she was very young. She's not going to grow big, like Cat. She's only going to grow a little bit more, perhaps she'll get a bit whiter, like a proud princess—so you'll be able to ride her for years and years before you grow too big for her. She's not quite like having Cat back again—but she's a little Cat."

"Is her name Cat?"

"I expect so. If that's what you want to call her."

"When can I ride her? Cat was too big for me."

"I'll show you how to ride her. Nice and slowly—easily—gently. We'll take everything very easy. She's a real sweet pretty little creature, this Cat. Her mouth is tender, and we won't go sawing at it."

"I never saw a horse with a red harness and saddle before."

"Well . . . that's because she's special. Like something . . ." He bit back on the words that might have revealed that the harness came from a circus, something else that had had to be speedily arranged. "Well, we have only to put three white plumes on her harness and she's ready to carry a princess—or a young prince."

"A princess . . ." Alasdair repeated. "Princess Cat." Slowly but without fear, he went and ran his hand down the soft white muzzle of the pony. William Kerr slackened his hands on the bridle and stepped back, leaving the pony and child standing alone. Julia caught her breath, fearing that a wrong movement from Alasdair would startle the pony, that she might kick or shy away nervously. But the two stood side by side for some minutes, Alasdair continuing to stroke her muzzle, her neck, standing on tiptoes to touch her ears gently, all the time talking in such a low tone that none of them could distinguish the words. With very slow, quiet movements, Rod McCallum put some lumps of sugar into Alasdair's hand. The child took them as if they had appeared from nowhere. As the pony munched them and then put her head down to look for more, they heard Alasdair's words. "Princess Cat . . . oh, Cat, you've come back!" He put his head against the pony's, and they saw the silent tears start down his cheeks. "Cat, you've come back. Princess Cat."

He had to be carried away from the stable that evening. A cold October wind was blowing, and rain was starting to fall. He refused to leave until he had seen the pony unharnessed, fed, and watered in Cat's stall. He could hardly eat his supper for fatigue and excitement, and occasionally tears came again. He fell asleep in the housekeeper's room, and Julia went to join the rest at dinner. Stacia had not yet emerged from her room.

"Let her stay there," Rod said. "If I could, I'd lock the door and throw away the key. But she has to get to the bathroom, I suppose."

The sense of camaraderie had returned to the group at the castle. John Gunn had taken some close-ups of the battered faces of the actors. "Makeup never looks quite that real. . . ."

Sir Niall drove them back to the cottage. "He's doing his best—McCallum—I suppose. But I never did think that very expensive presents to children did much to mend broken hearts. Though the tale he spun about the pony just may take Alasdair's mind off Cat's tragedy. God knows—he paid a fortune for this one. I went and looked her over myself. Saw that she was fit, and looked right, with the right temperament. And I didn't want McCallum paying over the odds—though he didn't place any limit on price. Getting the harness was a real problem. They certainly stung him for that. Julia, I don't know what to make of this whole business. Myself, although I've enjoyed having them here, I'm beginning to feel that I won't be too sorry when they've all packed up and gone. I don't expect you'll feel quite that way. It's been good for you to have some young company about. Life is very lonely here, as you've found out. Perhaps it might be a good idea to tell that D.D. fellow that he should look out for something for you. . . .''

"It isn't as easy as that. He tries—I know he does. But very few scripts come my way these days. Most of the theatrical profession think I've vanished permanently into the Highlands. The film people have almost forgotten me. Perhaps just as well, for Alasdair's sake. He's far better growing up here than anywhere else, even with Johnny and under Luisa's eye—as he'd mostly do if I got regular stage work. You see what happens to young ones, like Stacia. . . .''

His mouth twisted in disgust. "I wish I were a good enough Christian to say I pity her. Good night, my dear.''

The next morning Alasdair kept urging her to a swifter pace as they walked the forest road to the castle, eager to see that, like some fairy gift, Princess Cat had not disappeared during the night. When they emerged from the cover of the trees, Julia saw that the far, high mountains had been capped with snow during the night. Very soon it would move down to the hills and the valleys. They would have perfect conditions for filming those last scenes in the forest; Castle Sinclair would be transformed into the fortress in Germany when it was seen through the filter of flying snow. Soon they would all be gone. In these last few days she had believed she would welcome that; now that it was almost upon her, the doubts began to creep in again. Perhaps she would, after all, press D.D. to find some work for her. But as she watched Alasdair race to Princess Cat's stall, she wondered if she could do it.

All the rest of the company were aware of what the snow heralded. They knew exactly what their camera positions would be in the forest, how they would shoot the castle once the snow fell in earnest. Julia saw the rolls of barbed wire come out as the crew prepared to form the impression of the German fortress-castle.

After they had served breakfast and eaten their own, Kate came down from Stacia's room bearing her breakfast tray. "Ah, she's only picking at her food. And she's asking, Mrs. Sinclair, if you could spare a few minutes to see her.'' So far Julia had only been present in Stacia's room during Dr. MacGregor's visits. Stacia's face was almost unrecognizable, with swelling and bruising, but that was gradually reducing. The cut on her eyebrow was healing well. In another three days the stitches would come out. Dr. MacGregor was quietly pleased with the results. "With the stitches out, there'll only be a red mark for a few weeks, and that will fade. A tiny hairline scar, maybe. It would probably give your face a most interesting appearance."

"There was nothing wrong with my face until he—"

"True beauty always has its imperfections, young lady. The perfectly symmetrical face is a rather dull object, in my opinion."

Julia went to Stacia's room with some reluctance. The girl had stayed there since the accident, and the fight, not because Rod McCallum had ordered her to but, Julia guessed, because she wouldn't allow herself to be seen by anyone until her face healed. Seeing her again, without Dr. MacGregor's shielding presence, Julia wondered again about those few minutes of madness they had all experienced by the loch, and she tried to thrust it all away.

Stacia was dressed, and standing by one of the tower windows that looked down into the stable yard. She turned at once as Julia entered. The room was tidier than Julia could remember seeing it since Stacia had occupied it; there were some books piled on the bedside table.

"Thank you for coming," she said. "I'd better get it out right away and say I'm sorry for what happened. I should never have taken Cat without asking. I should never have ridden her like that along the shore. I began it—I didn't think it would turn out the way it did. . . ."

Julia leaned back against the door. "Did Rod tell you to say this?"

The girl shook her head no. "I wouldn't have said it if he had. I haven't set eyes on him since it happened—except down there. . . ." She nodded toward the stable yard. "I guess I upset everyone pretty badly—especially Alasdair. I didn't think about any of that when I took Cat. I just wanted to be away from all of you—from the whole damn shooting match for a while. I went carefully as I could through the forest. Cat seemed to enjoy it. She was very careful where she put her feet, and I didn't hurry her—just let her go at her own pace. I swear I didn't abuse her.

The wet leaves were pretty slippery in places, so we took it real easy. When we got out on the shore she just seemed naturally to want to trot. I gave her a little tap, and she went into a canter by herself. I think she has been bored, too, and she was sort of remembering how things were when she was young. I guess we both wanted to kick up a bit. Well—you know the rest." The rest had also included the weals on Cat's gray coat from the riding crop. "I'm sorry," Stacia continued. "I saw Alasdair yesterday with the white pony. I've done a pretty dreadful thing to him as well as to Cat."

Julia went and sat down on a chair near the fire. "And I'm sorry you're so unhappy. With your whole life. Is there something you want to do that Rod doesn't let you—something that would make things better?"

Stacia shook her head. "It's never been right—either for me, or my mother. My father disappeared, you know. That's when I was a baby—before she was a star. I guess life was pretty tough for her. I can remember there were lots of different men when I was growing up. I didn't know one from the other. Some of them were pretty rough—with me as well as her. I got used to being kicked and cursed. Then she got her break, and after two movies where she had the lead role, she was a big star. The men still kept coming, but they were a better lot. I guess the studio kept a pretty good eye on her. Didn't want any scandals. She used to get drunk, and she'd cry a lot. She had a gorgeous house and a pool and all that . . . and she'd sit and cry. I guess she got taken for a lot. My mom wasn't the smartest girl on the block. She'd gotten a whole raft of lawyers and money people— money manager, accountant—and they took her to the cleaners. I suppose they stole most of the money. Bad luck, they called it. Investments that didn't go right. She was absolutely broke when she met Rod McCallum. The house was mortgaged. She owed money all over town . . . she was in hock for what she'd earn from the next movie.

"I have to hand it to him—he didn't seem to care that she didn't have a cent. He just took us out of that house and put us in his own. But it was *his* house. Not theirs—his. And we belonged to him. We did what he said. The house is great—all Spanish-Mexican style. And furnished with Spanish things—big leather chairs and long dark tables. He got one of his friends to put together a library for him. He actually read some of the books. Everything had to be spotless. No fingermarks—no foot-prints on the tile floors. I hardly dared walk on his Navajo rugs. He'd even check on my room, and if there was a mess, I'd get a few slaps to remind me that it wasn't my property. My mom just couldn't take it. I guess she was pretty sloppy—there were plenty of servants, but things always seemed to get into a mess, and that'd send Rod wild. They were always fighting—and mak-ing up. I guess they were pretty hot stuff in bed. Maybe that's what kept them together. About three years it was. He kept her on as tight a rein as if she'd been an unbroken horse. He closed all her charge accounts, fired all the money sharks, and generally put things back in order. But she was still working off her debts—he didn't pay them, he just stopped them from getting any worse, and finally she was in the clear. He set up a trust fund for *me*—and anything she earned went into it. She told me all this herself. She said, 'Listen to him, Stacia, he's got his head screwed on right. Don't get into the mess I did.' He picked all her clothes for her and got them cut-rate because she was going to wear them to some big do. But her underwear was cheap. I guess he liked her better with her clothes off than on. They drank quite a lot—but when they were alone at nights, they'd dance together. It was pretty—and kind of romantic.

"He was nice in ways—like the way he taught me to ride. He took trouble about things. Sending me for diction lessons and dancing lessons. He was always trying to improve me. I guess he thought Mom was past improving. As long as she showed up on the screen the way she did, so that the fans were crazy about her, he didn't care. Perhaps he was afraid of spoiling whatever it was she'd got. Then he picked schools for me to go to to learn to be a 'lady.' That's what he called it. He didn't approve of the pals I had at Beverly Hills High. A bunch of spoiled brats, he called them. They were my friends. Well, I got the heave from school—acting up, they said—and he sent me to boarding school way up past San Francisco, miles from nowhere. They were a bunch of snobs. I didn't wait to be kicked out. I just ran away. The police picked me up pretty quickly, and I ended up back at Rod's house, told not to leave my room, not even to use the pool. I wasn't to call any of my friends. My meals were sent up. I guess he was trying to think of what to do with me next. I wanted to do something real wild—do anything to hurt him. Lock him up—or something. I wanted to run—as far away from there as I could get. But I didn't have any money—and my mom didn't either. They were quarreling all the time about me—and just about everything else. And I'd sit upstairs and hear them hollering away at each other. Sometimes I'd go out on the stairs and listen. He thought she was seeing some other guy, but I don't see how she had the chance, because he had her watched all the time. We were kind of locked up in that place. I remember—before I ran away from school—that he gave swell parties, and everyone must have thought they were a great couple. That's what the fan magazines said. I just kept my mouth shut when any of the gossip columnists came around. He dressed me like a little girl—and blamed my mother because I looked too sexy even in that rotten school uniform.

"I was there the night of their last fight—they'd been screaming at each other for hours. Both of them were drunk. Even the help must have heard it—and they lived in a separate building. She screamed at him that she was leaving, and he just laughed. 'Don't forget to take that bastard kid of yours with you' was what he said. He didn't expect her to go. He kept a tight watch on all the car keys, but he didn't know she had duplicates for some of them. She just rushed out into the garden, and I suppose he thought she'd be wandering around there for a few hours until she got cold and tired—and sober. And then we heard the sound of the engine. It must have been three years since Mom had driven a car—he had her driven everywhere—easier to keep an eye on her that way. She didn't get to stop at stores and spend money, or shack up for an afternoon with some guy. I heard the car go. The wheels were spinning like mad. I was on the stairs, and I saw him go to the front door. She'd left it open. He stood there for a long time. Long after she'd gone. Then he just closed it very gently and went back to his drink. The police came in the morning and told him they'd found the burned-out wreck at the bottom of a canyon.

"If she'd remembered me—if she'd done what he said—if she'd taken that bastard kid of hers, I'd have been there in the wreck with her.

"So he was left stuck with me. And I'm stuck with him until I'm old enough to earn some money and get away."

"Why," Julia said, "did you decide to tell me all this? In a little while you'll be gone. You'll be free of *this* place, at least."

"Because I felt real sorry about Cat. Sometimes I feel real

wild inside and want to go running myself. Anywhere. It doesn't matter. Just to be free. Just to be free of men. And yet I like men. My mom warned me about that. She said a lot of them would like me too much, and perhaps I'd never find one who loved me. But I told you this because what I did with Cat was stupid. When I saw Rod running toward me, I just wanted to show him that I didn't care. I forgot Cat wasn't a jumper. I wanted to show him I'd slipped the reins.''

"Did he ever beat you before this?"

"Not like this. Just a sort of slap when I'd made a mess in the house, or my grades at school were rotten—which they were. He'd call me a lazy trollop. I had to look it up in the dictionary. I said to Mom I couldn't be a trollop because I'd never had a man. She said, 'Well, watch it, honey—or you'll turn out just like me.' Like I said, he could be real nice at times and take a lot of trouble explaining things. And then there were times when he was mad over something—or drunk, and I made myself scarce. I think he hit my mom once or twice, but she sort of expected it. Sometimes I think she wanted it. She once said she'd had it all her life. Why should things change?" There was silence between them for a few moments. "Well, I guess that's about it, Mrs. Sinclair. I wanted to say I was sorry. But I wouldn't have done it this way if *he'd* ordered me to. I suppose I would have said something, but I wouldn't have told you all these things. I watched the pony come yesterday—and, well, I guess I cried. I haven't cried since my mother died. I guess I felt so rotten about Cat. And I wanted someone to care enough about me to go to all the trouble Rod did to try to make it up to Alasdair. Kate told me she's called Princess Cat. I like that. . . ."

Julia stood up. "Thank you for what you said, Stacia. It explains a lot. I'm sorry I haven't had time to be with you more. I wish you could have enjoyed your time here."

The girl shrugged. "Not your fault for dragging me off to this place where there's nothing to do. I could have stayed in London, but *he* didn't trust me. I don't suppose he ever will. I'll just have to stick it out until I'm old enough to go. And I'll go the minute I can.''

The snows finally came; the takeoff and landing scenes were shot at the RAF airfield, the silent crawl through the forest so long rehearsed went smoothly, John Gunn got his shots of the castle-fortress in Germany ringed by barbed wire filmed through an almost whiteout of snow. The crew were cold and impatient, and the takes as few as possible. The German scientist was taken out and handed over to those who needed his work by the small band of commandos who had gone in. Rod McCallum was at his best in all these situations. The last shot was of him returning, alone, to the castle in Scotland. They had Julia stand in for Claire Avery as she was shot from behind at the open doorway of the castle as Rod McCallum walked across the bridge. No words were required to be said.

John Gunn finally said, "Cut. I guess that's it. Let's wrap it."

The wrap party was more cheerful than Julia thought possible, given the mood of the crew as the cold had closed in and their frayed tempers. It was becoming increasingly difficult to keep the castle warm, and the men huddled over the fires during their lunch break, saying little, laughing less. She sensed it wasn't quite so much the cold and discomfort that the snow had brought; the change in the mood had seemed to stem from the day of Cat's death. Like Alasdair they had all witnessed violent death and violent retribution, which owed nothing to the make-believe world of filming.

To Julia's relief, Rod McCallum had decided to have the wrap party at the Caledonian Hotel in Inverness. She doubted that Janet and Kate and the women who came to help could have stood the strain of yet another demand made on their stretched resources of energy and willingness. For once they would be part of the party and not the makers of it. They dressed in their best and drove with the Kerrs into Inverness, looking forward to an evening free of worry after a relaxed day. Rod McCallum had declared that Sir Niall was the guest of honor. He had sent to Edinburgh for a silver tray engraved with the name of the film, the cast, and the director, to be presented to Sir Niall. For each member of the crew there was a silver-plated badge, mounted on wood, of the Sinclair crest—with its upstanding cock. There was some ribald laughter about the clan motto: *Commit Thy Works to God.* Julia heard one of the crew say, "Only time in his life I'd bet that McCallum committed anything to God. But God had better be in the cutting room with Gunn to paste this lot into shape. He just might have committed his whole future to God, and maybe God just ain't going to be around.''

"Damn cheek!" Sir Niall muttered when he saw the badges being distributed among the crew. "He's no earthly right to the Sinclair crest."

Julia shrugged. "Does it matter?—they'll all take them back home, and put them on the mantel, and say to guests, 'Yes—that was the movie we shot at that crazy place in Scotland, Castle Sinclair.' I'll bet their wives like them. Rod has just about enough good and bad taste to know what would go down well back at home. He can't give them all Dunhill cigarette lighters . . . which is what is being presented to the cast and John Gunn and Mike Pearson—all with the Sinclair crest engraved on them." She thought that Rod McCallum must have cornered the entire stock of lighters from London. These would be by no means the first lighters given to these people, but they bore the snobbish name of Dunhill and were solid gold.

Rod McCallum had ordered Stacia to appear at the party—the first time she had been seen by any of the cast or crew since Cat's death and the ugly fight on the loch shore. She appeared almost a different creature. The swelling and bruises had disappeared; as Dr. MacGregor had predicted, there was only a slight red mark on her eyebrow, and the skin had knitted together perfectly. She had lost weight, and she moved with a dignity and decorum that were entirely new. Her golden hair, pulled back into a severe ponytail, revealed cheekbones, a chinline, and beauty of a kind her face had only promised before. The prominent, pouting lips were still there, an indelible reminder of her mother. Her movements, though quiet, were as sensuous as ever. She wore a simple green dress, whose very simplicity served only to accentuate the curves of her body. She wore one ring on her right hand—two amethysts setting off a small, dull diamond. "My mother's engagement ring," she explained to Julia. "I suppose my father gave it to her. That's what she told me. But I suppose it could have been any one of a dozen guys. She said it was the only thing she kept when Rod told her she had to sell her jewelry to pay off her debts. It's worth so little I suppose he didn't mind her keeping it. When they went to big parties—or gave them—jewelers always loaned her whatever she wanted, like the dresses the designers provided. They wanted the advertisement."

Kirsty Macpherson and a number of the regular guests at Sir Niall's Sunday buffets attended the party. "Things are going to be a little dull around here during the winter, aren't they," she said to Julia. "Oh, well, we'll just go on with our own dull routine. My father expects me to find another husband and have children. But with things as they are—austerity—not much chance to travel to visit other people—no house parties—how does one meet anyone to marry? We can hardly arrange it by mail, as they used to do. I've only got Betsy, and my father wants a grandson. I don't see what he can do about it. He can't manufacture a husband or a child for me. I'd light out for London if I could—but he holds the purse strings and doesn't approve. He thinks one disastrous marriage to an Englishman is enough. Una, my young sister, is so happy in her California heaven that she couldn't care less what happens at Darnaway. But you're in the same position, aren't you? You don't have any money to go with Sinclair. That situation doesn't exactly bring suitors flocking from all over the Highlands."

"I am not," Julia said with great deliberation, and then swallowed the remainder of the whiskey in her glass and put it down, "remotely interested in your matrimonial prospects—which are much greater than mine."

"Goody for you!" Kirsty retorted. "The nun of Sinclair is going to remain chaste and pure—and damn lonely, I'd say, in her Highland retreat. Well, good luck, Julia. I'll take—well, perhaps not the first—but the best man who comes along. And he doesn't have to be one hundred percent proof—because there just isn't any man like that."

The cars carrying those who had stayed at Sinclair during the weeks of shooting followed William Kerr's lead car through lightly falling snow. Alasdair had been left in Rachel Kerr's care for the evening; he was quite happy to be sleeping so close to his beloved Princess Cat. Rod had taken to getting up an hour earlier each day to give him riding lessons. They were the moments to live for in Alasdair's day. Julia and Rod were in the last car that moved away from the Caledonian. They reached the forest road, and then Rod turned off into the little clearing in front of the McBain cottage. "Can I come in for the last time, Julia? Light the fire, which is probably out by now—have one last dram with you here?"

"Of course you can come in. But why the 'last dram' bit? You and Stacia are staying on for a few days."

"Well . . . naturally I assumed you'd be moving back to the castle as soon as John and Marty and George moved out."

"Oh—I'm in no hurry. I think Janet and Kate should get a bit of a break. And Alasdair needs to settle down after the excitement of these weeks. So do the Kerr children. Mrs. Kerr says the schoolmistress has sent a note complaining that they are inattentive. No wonder . . . they've seen more of life in these few weeks than in all their collective lives. The trouble is that it isn't real life."

Rod was kneeling before the fire, slowly placing kindling on its dying embers, stooping farther to blow them into life. "What you need here, Julia, is a good set of bellows—and a good man to go with them."

She handed him a glass of Drambuie; she had stocked it since he had taken to driving her back and having a nightcap here.

"The bellows we could find. A good man is hard to come by."

"Would I do until someone better comes along?" He took a large swallow of the liqueur. "I've waited so long, Julia. I knew you wouldn't permit it while Alasdair was in the cottage—so close. That's not your style—though it was all we knew about people making love while we lived under this roof. It didn't sound like making love, as I later came to understand it. My father was usually drunk—my mother unwilling. I want so much to take you to bed—to make love to you in a way it has never been done under this roof. Oh—I forgot. This isn't the moment, but then back at the party wasn't the moment, either. Your wrap present. It's not a bribe. I've been having things sent from Edinburgh and London for weeks, choosing what I thought would please you most—the sort of thing you should wear." He pressed a small box into her hand.

She didn't open it. "I can't accept presents from you, Rod. You know that. And I can't make love to you here . . . now. In a few days you'll be gone. . . ." She was remembering the first time she had come to this cottage, when she and Jamie had tenderly undressed each other before this fire, had made love tenderly, knowing that in the midst of war, their loving might have to last a lifetime. And it had—Jamie's brief lifetime, and she left only with the remembrance of it. No man but Jamie would ever make love to her under this roof.

"Goddamn you!" He crashed the glass down on the hearth, and for a moment the fire sparked with the spirit that had splashed on it, the shards of glass reflected the light.

"Goddamn you!" he repeated. "I'm not good enough for you. You've been married to James Sinclair. You've been married to a genuine hero. A hero of the Battle of Britain. One of 'the few.' DSO. DFC and bar. While I stayed in Hollywood and played toy soldiers. Why on earth did I tell you I was born in this cottage? Why did I tell you that I fought to climb out of this background? Why did I trust these things to you? Only because I thought I could love you—in a way I've never loved a woman in my life, in or out of bed. Why did I trust you? I thought you were different. I told you things I've never told any other person—never mind a woman—in my life. And you won't give me one short hour in your bed. Nothing to make these weeks significant. It's all right to talk to me, to kiss me, to let me give presents to your son. You're too good for me—that's it, isn't it? Well, Mrs. Sinclair, I won't force myself upon you, nor impose any longer. Stacia and I will be gone in the morning."

"Rod—" He was gone, the door left wide open. She listened to the motor of the engine being gunned, the wheels momentarily spinning as they struggled free of the snow. Then the car was driven at reckless speed down the last mile of the frozen, rutted tracks of the forest road.

She ran to the door. "You don't understand. You didn't give me time to explain. . . ." All she saw was the red rear lights of the car disappearing around the bend. She ran back for her coat and scarf, dropping his wrap present into the pocket of her coat. Then she slammed the door behind her and set off, for the first time in her life, in pursuit of a man.

All the stored hunger of her empty years gave her strength to run the mile through the woods. Far away, she heard the rumble of the car as it crossed the bridge. She was panting, almost exhausted, as she let herself in by the kitchen door. She moved quietly past the rooms where Janet and Kate slept, turning on lights only when she had to. She went through the dining hall, guided by the few wall sconces left lighted in the Great Hall. She started up the stairs, feeling the wetness of her coat, her fear, feeling once more the vast emptiness of the place. Cameras and cables no longer blocked her way, there was not the faintest sign of a dropped chewing-gum wrapper on the wooden floors, nor the butt of a cigarette. Those real and make-believe people had departed; now the ancient, authentic ghosts would repossess their rightful place.

Her steps had grown slower as she had mounted the stairs. She was beginning to be unsure. The terrible hunger that had impelled her along the forest road seemed to lessen. When she finally knocked on the door to the Red Tower Room, the sound was so light she knew it would not be heard. She summoned the will and the energy to knock harder.

Rod opened the door. He had taken off his jacket and held a lighted cigarette in his hand. "You! I thought I heard a mouse knock."

"A mouse may be all I am. Can I come in?" He held the door wider, and as she entered, began to remove her wet coat.

"A mouse would have had better sense than to come running through the snow. You're frozen—look at your feet—shoes and stockings must suddenly have come off ration, because you won't be wearing this lot again." He drew her close to the fire he had relighted from the embers of the old, as he had done in the cottage. "What can I do for you, Mrs. Sinclair?"

"I should have explained—back there, at the cottage. You didn't give me much time."

"You didn't give me any time at all. Not the time of day—or night."

"I said—I should have tried to explain. The cottage means two different things to you and me, Rod."

He tossed the cigarette into the fire and thrust her back into one of the high-backed carved chairs, and gently removed her shoes and stockings. He pulled the chair closer to the fire and began to massage her feet. Restored to its usual order, the Red Tower Room welcomed her again. She saw the furniture back in its familiar place, the wide-canopied bed where it had always stood.

"You have lovely feet, Mrs. Sinclair. Much smoother than your hands are sometimes. Lovely hands that get rough through washing dishes, and lovely feet, which few people have ever seen, I'll bet. I didn't ask for a servant, Julia. The moment I saw you, there at the bend in the forest road, your hand in your son's hand, I wanted a lover. I've held off all these weeks. God, you don't know how hard it's been. . . ." Her shoes and stockings lay on the floor. His hands had begun to touch the intimate, almost secret places that no hands had touched in that way since Jamie. She gave a little sigh of pleasure. He was kneeling, but his head was level with hers. His hands ran from her thighs up the length of her body. "All I've had to feed off were those few kisses, knowing all along that you were listening for Alasdair to wake, were using any excuse your mind or body could invent to keep me off. Well—now you've come. And I know what you want, just as surely as I want it."

He raised her, undid the button at the neck of her dress, and with gentle hands found the zipper. Then he turned away, and she thought he had left her. But it was to turn off the only light that burned at the bedside. Now the firelight sprang across the floor in the way she remembered it. He slipped her dress down off her shoulders, and it fell on the floor. Then her slip and bra and panties. His hands went slowly down her breasts, to her waist, to her hips. Then he knelt again to kiss the curling hair between her legs. "The mound of Venus . . ." he said, his voice as gentle as a whisper. "You're more beautiful than even I had imagined . . . and I've imagined a great deal. I've lain here at night and imagined how it would be if you were here with me. But I never thought you'd come. I never thought you'd come running through the snow to me."

"I have come. . . ."

As he took off his own clothes his movements were hasty, almost clumsy. He scooped her up in his arms and carried her to the bed where she had lain so many nights alone, thinking of Jamie, the bed in which Jamie had been born and in which his son had been born.

"Now, my lady," he said as he pulled the blankets around their naked bodies, "my lady of the castle—my lady of the lake. My lady of all my desires. Are you mine now?"

"Of course I'm yours. Haven't I come running? Did you force me? I came. You're the first person I've loved since Jamie. But the thought of *you* has filled my nights, too. Only I was afraid. . . ."

"Afraid of what . . . ?" As they whispered together, their hands explored each other's bodies, gently, quietly, without hurry.

"Afraid of what it would be like when you had gone. The emptiness more empty. The well of silence never filled . . ."

"You know something, my sweet lady? You talk too much." Only when they were joined, and their bodies moving in what seemed to her a perfect rhythm she had never before experienced, did Julia know how absolute the emptiness had been. She had desperately missed her young husband. Her body had yearned for his. But she had never known what it was to be loved in quite this fashion. Her senses seemed to slip back to the time when she had been a young, untried woman, never knowing the totality of a male. She felt her body give itself completely to his, and a fury and energy and finally a sweet release that was quite new to her engulfed her. She lay under his body, sweating, kissing him, hands and arms clinging fiercely to him. "I didn't know . . . realize . . . part of me realized it, and I wouldn't understand. Didn't understand." They had fallen apart slightly but still clung together, breathing hard, sounds that were near sighs. "Oh, I *feel* you, Rod. Every part of my body shakes because of you. I know what it will be like when you're gone. Worse than I imagined. But worth it—to have known this. I—my husband—we were both so young. Pretty inexperienced, I suppose. There should have been time to find our way—to times like this. But we ran out of time. And I've never known . . . But you will go—and I will remember. Forever."

He stroked her wet hair back from her forehead. "You still talk too much, my sweet, beautiful lady. Can't anyone shut you up? One of the things I've loved most about you was your silences. Most women talk too much—talk away the intimacies, the little revelations. You have listened so beautifully to my outpourings. Kind and gentle. And like a hellcat in bed—which was not exactly what I expected. That is—if I ever got you into bed. There was no certainty in that. I knew you belonged to this world, and I didn't. You could have held me off forever with the icy aura of the lady of the castle." He kissed her again, lingeringly, knowing that he was once again arousing both of them. Then he deliberately fell away from her, back onto the pillow. "Why do you keep talking about the time when I go away? I don't want to go away from you—ever. Did you look at your little present? Was that what brought you running?"

"No, I didn't look at it. I just grabbed my coat and came running. It's there—I think I put it in the pocket before I came.

Perhaps I thought I was going to return it—but I would never have opened it without you being with me.''

He sprang out of bed and went to her wet coat draped over the back of a chair. He found the small box she had thrust into a pocket, and he brought it to her. He pulled the blankets around them both again, and only the firelight illuminated their actions.

She pulled off a pure silk ribbon, removed expensive wrapping paper she would have believed unavailable in these times—or perhaps Bond Street could produce anything for money. She fumbled for and then found the small catch of the fine leather box and opened it to reveal what lay in its dark velvet depths. The cuts of a large solitaire diamond refracted the moving light of the fire; it glowed in a thousand mysterious ways, something of almost heart-stopping beauty. It had a majesty about it she had never seen in a single stone.

''My God—how beautiful! How magical . . .'' She took her eyes from it and looked at him. ''I couldn't possibly take this. It's . . . well, it's beyond anything. . . . Rod, this must have cost a king's ransom.''

''Well . . . perhaps a princess's ransom. I'm not good with jewels. Never have understood why people go for them. I guess that's the rough side of me—the part that's always thinking of what a fraction of that would have done for us at one time. But— well, I guess I never thought about a jewel for a princess. A jewel on a hand I loved. Makes a difference.''

She kissed him gently. ''You know I can't take it. Dear man, it would break my heart even to look at it when you have gone.''

''You're in a hurry to get rid of me, aren't you. You haven't even looked at what's behind it.''

''Behind it?'' She turned the solitaire over in her fingers. ''Is there some inscription? I can't see.''

''No, little stupid. Where's the box?''

He was propped up on his elbow watching her as she searched among the blankets and sheets to find it. He didn't help her. Then when she did find it she saw the thin plain gold band slotted into a niche in the velvet behind where the diamond had sat.

She stared at it for a long time. ''Do you mean it?''

''Why would it be there if I didn't? The other hunk of glitter is just that—glitter. This is small—and for real. It means everything that I have to give you, Julia. But there's one thing you must do first.''

"Yes . . . ?''

"I have to see you take off your husband's wedding ring. Take it off with your own hands. I won't do it. You have to give away the past—stop living with ghosts. If I see you take off that other gold band and put this one on, I'll know you're mine. Don't forget your brave young husband—that would be a rotten thing to do. But open your heart and yourself to the future—a life with me. If you can't do it with a whole heart, then just keep the piece of glitter and I'll keep the gold band.''

Very slowly, with tears starting in her eyes, she took off the plain gold band she had worn since Jamie put it there. She didn't attempt to disguise the tears. "I've lived in the past so long, Rod. Now you show me the future.'' She held her bare finger toward him. "Now you put it on.''

It was slightly too big; it slipped around on her finger. "Well, we can't always guess right. Should have known the finger of a princess would be finer than any other woman's.'' Jamie's ring and the solitaire dropped somewhere into the bedclothes. "Hope I can remember the words . . . never said them to anyone else. Let's see . . . how does it go? With this ring I thee wed. With my body I thee worship. With all my worldly goods I thee endow. How about that? I remembered. You are going to marry me standing up in a church, aren't you, Princess? But that's a formality. If I have your consent, we're married now. Are we married?''

"I think we must be married, Rod. It feels like being married. I want nothing else.''

"You have me, Princess. With all my faults, my misdeeds. With all the truth that's in me. If you hadn't agreed I would have left a large chunk of my soul—funny, I didn't know I had a soul before—behind me here. The way ahead wouldn't have been easy. It won't be easy. It never is. But if you'll come with me, I'll be eternally grateful.''

She said softly, *"Whither thou goest I will go; and where thou lodgest I will lodge: thy people shall be my people, and thy God my God. Where thou diest, will I die, and there will I be buried.''*

He kissed her with a gentleness and a subtlety she had never imagined him capable of. To her astonishment there were tears on his cheeks as well as on hers.

"I never thought I'd be married to the sound of poetry."

"We've just both been married by the words of the Bible and the Book of Common Prayer."

He buried his face in her shoulder. She felt a convulsive heave through his body and wasn't sure whether it was the end of his tears or the beginning of his laughter. "Well, that does it." His tones were muffled in the bedclothes. "I guess we're married."

She woke once again, when the fire was just embers, to the familiar sound, this time mixed with the sound of Rod's heavy breathing beside her. She thought, once again, that she glimpsed that vague shape by the mantel, the shape that disappeared as soon as she tried to focus directly on it. The sobbing . . . gentle, soft, heartbreaking. The sobbing that this time did not so quickly trail off into the long sigh. She actually spoke to it . . . to the direction from which the sound came.

"Oh, Ellen . . . Lady Ellen . . . why do you weep so? It is joyful . . . good. Do you weep because you never knew this happiness . . . ? We love each other. We are married. . . ."

Beside her Rod stirred sleepily. "I thought I heard you talking to someone."

She turned and leaned over to kiss him. "No . . . just talking to myself. About happiness. About the strangeness of being married again. I never thought I would be married again. Rod, you're sure? This has to last . . . I couldn't bear—"

"Shall I show you how sure? Tell you? Let you feel it? This will last as long as I live."

Their bodies came together with sureness, tenderness, and more passion than Julia had ever known. And it would be a long time before she again heard the sound of Lady Ellen's tears.

Chapter Nine

I

THEY REMAINED at Sinclair for almost another week. Julia and Alasdair moved back into the castle, and Julia stayed each night with Rod in the Red Tower Room, not being secretive about it, though she knew Janet did not approve of this arrangement. Stacia had taken the news with a shrug of her shoulders. "So what's new? I knew all along he wanted you. You're a big step up in the world for him, Mrs. Sinclair."

"I love him, Stacia."

"That's fine. That's a plus, at any rate."

Julia telephoned the news to her father, Luisa, and to Connie. To Alex she sent a cable. The reaction from her father was somewhat puzzled. "Are you sure, my darling? I mean . . . it'll mean living in Hollywood with all the razzmatazz. Well, I shouldn't be a mealy-mouthed old man, begrudging you your chance of happiness. As long as you love him. I do confess I've wondered what the rest of your life would be like living up there in the wilderness. You're so young, Julia. There's so much ahead of you. I was afraid you'd end up like so many young war widows— a widow forever. It's just your choice of a husband that's startled me. But . . . so what? If he's your choice, then he must be good. He just struck me as one of your run-of-the-mill film stars, for all his fame. But then, that's judgment based on only one meeting—which isn't fair."

"He's been kind . . . and tender, Father. After Jamie . . . well, I suppose I became rather choosy. He's very different from Jamie. But I can't build my life on a ghost. Nor give Alasdair a father who isn't here."

"I understand, my darling. As long as he truly loves you . . . takes care of you. And makes you happy."

"I hope I make *him* happy, Father. He could use a bit of happiness. His life's been rather short on that."

Luisa purred over the news. "Darling, Julia, this is wonderful! We worried so much over you. So young to be alone. Now, you must leave all the arrangements to me. We'll have the reception here at Anscombe, it is really 'at home.' I think you had better be married at the registry office in Brighton, and just be here to greet the guests. How we will cope with the press, I'm not quite sure, but we'll work out something. Can you give me a few weeks? I'll do the invitations. If Rod wants friends over from Hollywood, it would just give them time to get here if he sent cables. Yes, I think it should be Anscombe. The press will be anxious to see that this marriage has your father's approval. Thank heaven they have finished the conversión of the stable block into guest rooms. Connie and Ken and the children will want to stay. And I'm sure Alex and Elliot will try to be here. Oh, I am so excited! You have a charming, handsome husband—and some money to go with it. I have heard he has been very careful with his money and hasn't flung it around, so you will be well looked after. His films must have made millions. . . . Do I hear a disapproving silence, Julia? Please don't think I'm entirely mercenary. I know you'd never marry for *money*. That's not you. But it is a relief to your father and myself that you won't spend your life rotting away in that moldering old castle. Your father will just have to accept that Rod is a film actor and not a stage actor. I'm a practical woman, Julia. You know that. I have to be glad that you're not marrying another penniless Scottish laird, or an actor with a bit part in a West End comedy that will close in a week. Leave everything to me. Come to London as soon as you can. Stay at Wilton Crescent. You'll need to buy some clothes—at least a wedding dress. Somehow we will find the coupons for a few more things. . . ."

Connie's reaction was simple. After Julia's telephone call she wrote: *I'm so happy for you, darling. We both hope you have a very happy life together.* Her second child had been a boy. *We're managing very nicely. Gradually Mr. Warren gets things in the house in better order. Before the baby was born, he managed to get another two rooms and a bathroom built*

*on. Don't ask how. Of course we share the same kitchen, but
as I'd be doing the cooking in any case, that's no problem.
Mrs. Warren eats like a bird, and Mr. Warren doesn't care
what he eats. I have a "daily" in the house, and now Ken
thinks there should be a nanny. But that would squeeze us up
again. In the meantime, Ken hacks away at the garden every
weekend. I wish there could be time when you're in London to
come and visit us—just for a quick meal. . . . And, of course,
we'll be at the wedding. . . .*

Julia began to wish that she and Rod had gone to the registry
office in Inverness and married quietly there. But Rod seemed
pleased with what was being arranged. "Yes, of course we'll go
and visit Connie. I want to meet all your family." A cable had
confirmed that Alex and Elliot would be at the wedding. "No,"
Rod had answered when Julia had suggested that he might like
some Hollywood friends with him. "John Gunn's in London,
working at Pinewood on the cutting. He'll be best man. I have
a few old buddies in London at the moment. No use expecting
people to drag all this way. We'll have a big wingding when we
get back to Hollywood. Everyone will be dying to meet
you. . . ."

"Well . . . we could skip all the London part of it. It's still
possible to get married here in Inverness."

He shook his head. "No—you should have your day with your
family and friends. Time enough for mine."

"What he means," Stacia said, "is that he wouldn't miss the
London publicity for the world. He wouldn't miss being photographed with your father. Those sorts of pictures get printed in
newspapers all over the world. And he'll have it all over again
when you get to Los Angeles."

"What a sweet little creature you are, Stacia. Don't you think
it would give Julia's family some pleasure to share our wedding
day? They're going to be *my* family now. I don't in the least
mind taking some time to meet them."

"Well, that's put me one more rung down the ladder, hasn't
it. I'm not related. I'm not your daughter—"

"You're my adopted daughter. Naturally, as long as you refuse to use my name, you'll appear to the world as my stepdaughter. I've tried to see that your life was as good as you'd
allow me to make it. A little cooperation on your part would
help."

"Oh, yeah . . . ? Well, am I going to be a bridesmaid or something?"

"Julia's sisters come before you. And in any case, Julia doesn't want a bridesmaid."

"Oh, please, can't we stop fighting?" Julia pleaded. "There are other things to think about."

She had broken the news to Alasdair, who seemed almost indifferent to the fact that she was going to marry Rod. The weeks Rod had been at Sinclair had made him into the only permanent male figure Alasdair had known besides Sir Niall and William Kerr. He hardly knew what having a stepfather meant. He had never known his own father. What he cared about was the separation from Princess Cat. Rod had soothed his agitation by telling him that he had arranged for Princess Cat to come down by train to London and be shipped to the stables at Anscombe, to be stabled in the new block Luisa had built for Johnny's pony, and the pony she had given Harry Whitehand's youngest child. "And what then?" Alasdair asked. "Do I have to leave her forever with Johnny's pony?"

Rod breathed hard. "No, I think I can arrange that Princess Cat comes all the way to Hollywood with us. We don't have any stables at my house there . . . but I have quite a few acres up near Santa Barbara, in the hills. The place has a little shack on it where I go when I want to get out of Hollywood. I keep some horses there, stabled with neighbors. Princess Cat wouldn't be lonely. But then, we'd have to bring her all the way back when we come here next summer."

"We're coming back—*here?*"

"Naturally we're coming back. It's your home. We'll come back every summer. I've got all kinds of plans. We're going to fix the place up. You know—patch up the walls that are falling down. Put in some more bathrooms and get in some workable central heating. Give Janet a new kitchen."

"You're going to change it all! I like it the way it is."

"Your son," Rod said later to Julia, "is being just as difficult in his own good-mannered way as Stacia is. He wants the world he has here to stay exactly as it is—and yet he's plainly excited about seeing the world outside. Can I give him both?"

"Just a little bit at a time." Julia said. "Don't keep promising him the moon. It's quite enough that Princess Cat is taken down to Anscombe, to be with Johnny's pony and the Whitehands'.

Gradually, if you explain to Alasdair what it would be like for Princess Cat on a sea voyage, and then that long train trip across to Los Angeles, I think he'll see that it's better to leave her there. And she'll be waiting for him when we come back next summer. Do you really mean we'll come back every year?''

"Every year, Princess. I'm going to fix this old place up in a way that no one will ever notice—except that we'll be warmer, and there'll be a bit more plumbing. And the bridge won't fall into the loch. Make the Kerrs a bit more comfortable. He's a valuable man, William Kerr.''

"The money . . . The farm just about pays its way now, and there's the loan from Luisa I have to keep paying off.''

"Why don't you let *me* worry about what gets spent on the castle. After all, I expect to spend a lot of time here . . . it's where I belong.''

Long afterward, Julia remembered her initial feeling of happiness at those words.

The wedding celebration went off in a fashion that only Luisa could have planned. Rod was disappointed that they could not be married in the Anscombe church; but his first divorce made that impossible. But Julia, dressed in the finest pale blue gown and hat that Luisa's influence and coupons could make possible in that short time, stopped at the church on the way back from the registry office ceremony to lay her bridal wreath at her mother's grave. The vicar was waiting for them. ''There is nothing I know of that prevents me from saying a word of blessing on your union—outside the church—since you have made it in honor and good faith. Though it may get me into trouble with my bishop later.''

So the press photographed Julia, with Rod at her side, laying her wedding wreath at Ginette Maslova's grave. She was photographed with him at the lych-gate of Anscombe church. The moment, which should have been totally joyous for her, was momentarily overcast for Julia as she looked at the beaming face of her son. He was so innocently happy because people had told him that he would now have a father. But the young face, so vividly resembling Jamie's, recalled that earlier marriage, Jamie at her side, having sworn vows of love and loyalty, love of which this happy child was the result. The sharp pain of loss returned. She did not believe that Jamie's spirit had meant to haunt or darken her second wedding day, but his spirit was there in the beloved form of his child.

But there was no time for any more such thoughts when they reached Anscombe. There were many photographs with all the family, the children and dogs, outside the house itself. The official photographer had difficulty getting order into that boisterous jumble of family and friends. Janet and Sir Niall had traveled to London—Janet to stay at the Belgravia house, Sir Niall at his London club. They, with Stella and Cook, were included in the family group. At the last moment Harry Whitehand brought along Taffy, Johnny's pony, and Princess Cat, and they, too, got into the family photographs. There was a lot of laughter at this, even from the press. Michael stood between the bride and groom and beamed. Only Stacia was reserved and withdrawn, and Julia had to coax her into the family group. But the press picked her out—Anne Rayner's daughter, bearing such a striking resemblance to her famous mother. The short December afternoon gave a rare burst of brilliant sunshine. D.D. kissed Julia before the flashing cameras. "Happy the bride the sun shines on. Ah, my dear, your career is almost out of my hands now."

"I don't think there'll be a career—except as Rod's wife."

He shook his head. "Wait until they get you in Hollywood. They will use you. At last you have come out of the wilderness."

Luisa had decided that the only way to deal with the press was to allow the most important of their members to join the reception. A huge, heated marquee had been joined to the side of the house, with the entrances from the French doors of the drawing room. It was blue, like Julia's dress, and had its own French doors, which looked into the winter drabness of the Ginette Maslova rose garden. But the warm, rosy brick wall, and the wrought-iron gates, standing open, gave a promise of summer delights to come. The tables were loaded with an array of food impressive in those days of rationing. When questioned about this by the sharp-eyed members of the press, Luisa waved a hand vaguely. "So much was sent by Julia's sister Alex—and then my friends in France have all made their contributions. The champagne comes from them. We have the white wine from my own vineyards. Everyone has helped. All our neighbors from around here have contributed ingredients for the cake . . . such good friends. One is fortunate to have them. Everyone is so happy for Julia."

Rod's ring was examined and exclaimed over. One woman journalist wanted to know the carat weight, which Julia refused to give. "It's such a rock," was the reply. "Film stars don't usually keep secrets of things like that. I expect you'll be living in Hollywood now, Mrs. McCallum."

"Well, naturally—that's Rod's home, and where he normally works. But we'll try to get to Scotland every summer."

"Oh—you're not giving up the place there—what's it called—Castle Sinclair?"

"Why should it be given up? It will belong to my son when he comes of age. The Sinclairs have lived there for centuries."

"Your husband doesn't mind?"

"Why should he? He loves the place."

"Now, really," Alex broke in, "isn't that enough questioning of a bride on her wedding day? Sinclair is an absolutely captivating place. There wouldn't be an earthly reason for giving it up."

The journalist instantly turned her attention to Alex. "Is it true, Mrs. Forster, that the President and the First Lady recently attended a small dinner party at your house?"

"One doesn't talk about the President's private social life."

Connie, seeing her sisters together, joined the group. Her daughter, Margaret Ginette, was clinging to her hand, her face smeared with icing from the cake. Even at that young age, she had her mother's features and coloring, the promise of beauty to come. "And what does it feel like, Mrs.—er, Mrs. Warren—to have two such famous sisters and a famous father—as well as being the daughter of Ginette Maslova? Are they sometimes a bit hard to take?"

"How impertinent!" Alex protested. She moved closer to Connie, as if to protect her. But Connie only laughed.

"I just wonder how I came to be so lucky. We *have* stuck together, even though we live so far apart. I remember when we were children there were all the usual rows and squabbles. Now that we're adults, there's just the comfort and pleasure of having such a wonderful family." She blushed a little. "A loving family." Connie was wearing an outfit of deep pink that Alex had brought over for her to wear at the wedding. She looked as beautiful as Julia had ever seen her.

The journalist was scribbling rapidly. "Well—that's nice. Just one big happy family. That should go down well with the fan magazines. I've been asked to file a story for Reuters. Of course, it'll be in a lot of American papers. I wonder if we could have just one exclusive photo of the three of you together? Mr. Forster might even want it for one of *his* papers.''

Rather reluctantly they grouped together and smiled. Margaret Ginette refused to release her mother's hand and so had to be included. Rod thrust Alasdair into the group, though he stayed out of it himself. Later they found that after the picture of Julia with Rod at her mother's grave and at the lych-gate, it was one of the most widely circulated pictures.

"The charmed circle," Julia heard someone behind her remark. "Beauty, fame—and money." She turned swiftly to try to identify the speaker, because the tone had been less than kind. But everyone seemed engrossed in conversation with someone else, and she never learned who had used the words. Then inwardly, she shrugged. It was her wedding day—a wonderful wedding day, a day that had come twice in a lifetime. An unexpected blessing. Why let a small voice of envy spoil it? She turned back, and of her own volition suggested another photo, this time with her husband and son. "And Stacia . . . Connie, do you think you could extract Stacia from that nest of photographers who are begging for just one more photo? We must have a family one of just us four.''

"I see you're determined to make it a real family, Mrs. McCallum."

"Absolutely. And please see that that gets in the story, too."

Julia spent her wedding night at Anscombe. "We really don't need to sneak away by ourselves." Alex and Elliot and D.D. were staying for the night. Alasdair was sharing Johnny's room. Stacia was staying in the main house, the rest in the guest wing, which Luisa had made into a place of charm and beauty, furnished with materials for curtains and bedspreads that Alex had sent over, and with antiques that the auction galleries and Bond Street shops were starting to show again. Finally even the most stubborn guests were starting to leave, Sir Niall being among the last of them. He held Julia lingeringly. "Ah, lass, it'll be a lonely winter up there without you. I've never been sure about this marriage, but seeing you so happy today, I must say I've been mistaken. Be happy, dear Julia. I'll miss you so much. Don't forget your old friend. . . .'' He blew his nose vigorously as he led Janet out to the car he had managed to borrow for the day.

So the family gathered around the dining table, with no one needing anything to eat, but picking at things the caterers had brought in from the marquee tables, drinking Luisa's château-bottled wine. Tomorrow, except for Luisa and Michael, they were all going to visit Connie and Ken. Luisa had seen that the Warren car, already packed with Ken's parents, Connie, and the two children, had its trunk stuffed with leftover food and her own wine. "Connie does so much—works so hard for them all."

"She seems to thrive on it," Rod remarked. "She's a bit of a knockout, isn't she, your Connie? What on earth does she see in that odd man—who's going to be just like his father in a few years?"

"That's Connie's secret," Alex said sharply. "She has her own kind of happiness. That's very plain. What she sees in Ken is entirely her own business."

Stacia had stayed silent during the meal. She had seemed to Julia just the faintest bit overawed by Sir Michael and Lady Seymour, by her surroundings, but puzzled by the informality of the occasion, the very lack of the show-business quality that would have been an essential ingredient if it had taken place in Hollywood.

"I think she's just beautiful," Stacia said suddenly about Connie. "And nice. And I think she's very lucky. She's about the luckiest person I've ever met."

"Why—what a perceptive young woman you are," Michael said and favored her with his most charming smile. As she returned the smile and warmth came to her face, Julia realized how seldom she had seen Stacia smile spontaneously. The whole character of her face altered.

"What a strange child," Luisa whispered later to Julia. "Is she always so . . . so remote? Almost sulky. But, poor child . . . such a terrible death of her mother. No doubt she misses her very much, although Rod is so good to her. And what an extraordinary remark to make about Connie."

"Connie is happy," Julia said. "I don't think Stacia's encountered many genuinely happy people in her life!"

It was the same the next day when they all drove up to Hampstead to visit Connie and her family. Only D.D. had declined the invitation. "All that domesticity is very well in its place. But it's not my place."

All through the visit Stacia followed Connie's every movement, offering to help in the kitchen, to wash dishes, asking if she might hold the baby. The Warren house was a strange mixture of what Clarence Warren had been able to salvage from the ruins of the house that had stood there, and what he managed to scrounge from all his scrap-dealer friends. Stacia didn't seem to notice how ill-matched were the curtains and carpets, the rust in the bathtubs, the lack of the luxuries she had taken for granted for much of her young life. She held Margaret Ginette's hand as they explored the seven acres that bordered Hampstead Heath. "Oh, you have your own private gate," she said, as if the gate led to some fairyland of almost lost memory. "That's special."

"Very special, Stacia," Elliot Forster said. He then addressed himself to Clarence Warren. "How wise of you to hang on to this acreage, Mr. Warren. In the future, when building starts up again, it will be worth a fortune."

Clarence Warren looked shocked. "Why, I'd never dream of disposing of it—although it costs a fortune in rates. It was Mrs. Warren's home." That seemed to end the matter for him. "She is so happy to be back here."

Julia wondered if she was the only one to catch the look of almost pitiful longing on Stacia's face. Then her expression seemed to close again, as if she once again felt excluded from this magic circle of people who actually knew happiness. She dropped Margaret Ginette's hand. "It's cold," she said, and turned back toward the house.

After four days in London they all traveled to New York on the *Île de France*. Rod was obviously happy at the gathering of the press at Southampton, by the fact that he was traveling in the company of Alex and Elliot Forster. Their suite was filled with flowers and champagne. They all went up on deck for the final photos. "What a long time it seems since I last crossed the Atlantic," Julia said. "Sometimes with Mother, sometimes with Father as well. Waving good-bye at one end to Grandfather Guy, and if we were lucky, and he wasn't too busy, waving to Grandfather Maslova at the other."

"I'll bet it was always first class," Rod joked.

"Not always. It depended on how funds were at that time.

We were always either broke, or the money was pouring in. It always got spent, however much or little of it there was. My parents were never very good at putting anything away for a rainy day.''

"Perhaps they never expected a rainy day," Stacia put in abruptly. "Like my mother." She wandered away from the group.

"She's going into one of her moody spells," Rod said. "We'll have to watch her. Not easy on board ship."

It was Alex who noticed the glimmer of tears on Alasdair's eyelashes, which he tried to rub away. She bent down to him. "It's all right, darling. Princess Cat is going to be quite happy. She wouldn't have been very comfortable on the ship or the train. You saw how quickly she made friends with Taffy and the Whitehands' pony. She'll have plenty of company and plenty of exercise. . . .''

"But she'll forget me. By the time I get back she'll love Johnny—not me.''

It had finally been Connie who had persuaded Alasdair to leave Princess Cat behind; she had said, if he would prefer it, they would bring Princess Cat to live with them at Hampstead. "Ken would put up a wooden stable for her very quickly. Of course, Margaret Ginette is a bit young to ride yet. But wouldn't she be happier with the two other ponies, and Johnny, and all the Whitehand children? Mr. Whitehand promised me he wouldn't let Johnny take her over. You'll be back so soon, Alasdair. Isn't it a tiny bit selfish to drag poor dear Cat so far, and then bring her back again? Rod has promised you can go riding at stables near him in Hollywood—up in the hills. Los Angeles would be awfully hot for dear Princess. . . .'' So in the end Princess Cat had stayed at Anscombe.

Connie had come to Southampton to see them all off. At the very last minute she had produced wrapped presents for them all. "Not to be opened till Christmas. Nothing like you send us, Alex—but sent with love. I can't tell you how Mrs. Warren has been knitting—even with her poor, arthritic hands. She *loved* the wedding. Said it was like old times again. That made Mr. Warren so pleased he would have given you all the earth if that had been possible.''

"Dear Connie . . .'' Elliot Forster bent to kiss her cheek. "If

I love Alex just one degree more than you, it's because I've known her longer. If I'd seen you first—"

Alex laughed. "Not a chance! She's been in love with Ken Warren since the day she met him. And if you think, Elliot Forster, I would have given you to my sister, however sweet . . ."

The last "shore" calls came, and Connie dashed down the gangplank. They waved to her as the tugs gently nudged the liner out into deeper water. They bunched together at the rails, the perfect picture for the cameras, except there was no sign of Stacia.

They were greeted in both New York and Washington in much the same way they left Southampton—with the flash of camera bulbs and the shrill questions of reporters. This was beginning to irritate Elliot, who enjoyed his privacy, but he put up with it for Julia's sake. Slowly Alasdair was getting used to all this, and he talked without guile or thought to any reporter who asked him a question. "What was it like when they were filming in your castle, kid?"

"Good fun," he answered, "until Cat got killed." Whenever that was mentioned, Stacia seemed to manage to fade out of the group. But Alasdair wanted to talk about Princess Cat, and the press wanted to ask about Claire Avery, and how did he feel about his mommy getting married, and how did he feel about coming to live in America? He had almost forgotten Claire Avery. He talked about "the cottage in the forest," and every word was taken down. In the garbled versions that appeared in the press it seemed that Rod McCallum had rarely been absent from the cottage in the forest.

"Out of the mouths of babes," Alex commented. "You know what the press is like, Rod. Or you should." Only Elliot Forster's own newspapers were respectful and reticent, usually just the last paragraph of their stories mentioning the fact that the new Mrs. McCallum, Julia Seymour, daughter of the famous actor and known to American audiences for her Oscar-winning performance in *Return at Dawn,* was the sister of journalist and broadcaster Alex Mathieson, wife of newspaper proprietor Elliot Forster. Even Stacia, who had tried to evade the cameras, was dragged in. Her likeness to her mother was too startling to be overlooked.

''Well,'' Elliot said as they settled down to drinks in the drawing room of the beautiful Forster house just off Dupont Circle, ''it's only what one might expect. Think of how many hundreds of thousands of ex-servicemen remember that face on their locker doors and pinned up in the mess. The poor kid has a legacy to live with. Not easy at her age . . .''

''I've done my best,'' Rod replied rather shortly. He had been at great pains to treat Alex and Elliot with the deference he thought their due; Julia knew that it was a deference that did not come easily to him. For years he had been famous in his own world, the world of the Hollywood factory system that had made him a star. He was less at ease with money that had been made in other ways, with power that was exercised in a different manner than that of the Hollywood tycoons. He appreciated the subdued splendor of Elliot Forster's house, the quiet sense of wealth, the smooth service of well-trained servants.

''I know you have,'' Elliot replied. ''And in very difficult circumstances. It can't be easy either keeping your head or your feet in your world, Rod.''

Rod relaxed and smiled, warming to Elliot's approval. ''If you only knew quite how humble the background I came from is, Elliot . . . the Scottish part of it I barely remember, but I can remember far too well roughing it in Hollywood until the breaks came, and then I had to learn which fork to pick up in a house like this. I can hardly believe that someone like Julia has agreed to marry me.'' He smiled at his wife. ''I call her Princess, you know.''

''I suggest,'' Alex said softly, ''that you don't let Stacia see too much of how you regard Julia. She is a very hurt and bewildered girl.''

Rod shrugged. ''What am I to do? Pretend I don't love the woman I'm madly in love with just to spare the feeling of a kid who wouldn't know decency or good manners if she ran headlong into them? Of course she's had a rough time—but I'm not responsible for all the years that turned her into what she is. I just happened to marry her mother—who was a woman half the men in the civilized world seemed to desire. I found that a little tough to deal with myself. I don't think I did very well—but Anne was finding all that a bit hard to handle herself, even when we married. For Stacia—well, first Anne, then the two of us did what we thought best. Anne wanted her to have an education.

So did I—since I hadn't had one myself.'' He gestured with his glass; the movement encompassed the quiet elegance of the room. "We didn't come from a background like this. We did the best we could for Stacia—I guess we were too dumb to know what was the best." He added, without malice in his tone, "I envy people like you. You were born knowing how things are done. I'm still learning—and learning a lot from Julia. I know she'll try to pass all the lovely qualities she has on to Stacia. Perhaps we'll be able to give her what she's never had. . . .''

Julia's eyes brimmed with tears. She didn't know if Rod was acting. If he was, it was possibly the best piece of acting he had managed in his life. She didn't doubt his declaration of love for her, but she knew that his intention had been to win Elliot's final and total approval of him. He seemed to have won it, even given Elliot's instinctive reserve about everyone and everything that had its origins in Hollywood.

"Please," Elliot said, "remember that Alex and I will do anything we can to help."

It appeared to Julia that Rod had passed that particular trial.

He gave Julia money to buy Christmas presents. They were all going to spend Christmas at Elliot's Virginia estate. "You'll know what to buy, my love. I know it won't be the Hollywood sort of thing. No glitz. But do try to find something special for Stacia—well, I suppose I want you to find something special for everyone, but things that don't look like Hollywood. There's no limit on price. . . . I'm just beginning to catch on that money shouldn't look like money. The best actors—like your father—have always underplayed things. Only the hams go over the top.''

They went to Elliot's house Westmount on Christmas Eve. It was even more subdued than the Washington house, but it glowed with the beauty of polished floors and good paintings. Rod asked Elliot to take him on a tour of the paintings, naming the artists. He particularly liked the Stubbs and Munnings canvases. "If I ever have more than a few bucks to spare, those are what I'd like," he said.

The presents Julia had bought in the Washington stores, which had excited her with their lack of austerity, seemed to please everyone. Stacia even dropped a light kiss on Julia's cheek for the red cashmere dress she had found, and prettily thanked Rod for the very simple gold bracelet Julia had chosen. They opened Connie's assortment of handknitted gloves and scarves, and

Luisa's more lavish gifts. Rod presented Julia privately with the sapphire ring he wanted her to wear on her right hand. "Rod! it's too much! After the diamond there shouldn't be any more jewelry. I don't want to be decked out—"

"Like a princess," he said. "I hope there'll be other things to wear in the future. . . ."

In the crisp, clear winter days, Stacia and Rod and Elliot rode together. Elliot had borrowed a pony from a neighbor for Alasdair to try out. Rod spent many hours with the child in the stable yard, teaching, training, encouraging his growing confidence. "They are both of them superb riders," Elliot said of Rod and Stacia as he hung back for a moment to watch them ride out. Alasdair had been left with a groom, to ride the pony on a leading rein.

"Well, it's been Rod's passport into big-time movies," Alex said. "And for Stacia—well, it's about the first time I've seen her quite at ease. Pity about the accident with Cat . . . it must have shaken her quite a lot. . . ." Then Elliot mounted his own horse and hurried to follow his guests. The sisters wandered back to the house, to have coffee before the fire in what would, in a past generation, have been described as a morning room. Alex poured, and passed a cup to Julia. "I wonder how long it is since you and I sat down like this. Not since the housekeeper's room at Sinclair. Oh, Julia, what a long passage it's been for both of us. And you're about to embark on an even further passage. . . . I wonder how you'll manage it. The strangeness . . . Hollywood. Don't forget it's possible to telephone me now without too much trouble. Remember it. I'm always available."

"Do you think it will be so strange—so difficult?"

"Difficult enough, from what I hear of Hollywood. And with Alasdair and Stacia to cope with. It isn't as if you and Rod were starting a fresh life. You both bring your baggage with you. . . ."

"We can't discard the past. Without Rod there would have been precious little for me in the future. A repeat of Lady Jean's life was about the best I could expect."

Alex lit a cigarette and gazed into the fire. "Now you have the possibility of more children. You're still so young, there's no reason why you and Rod shouldn't have your own family. That I envy you. . . ."

"I would like more children. But it will be a very mixed family."

"Don't worry about that. You'll manage. . . ." Alex drew deeply on her cigarette, then tossed it into the fire. "I wish I could be presented with that problem."

"Is there really no hope?"

For a moment Julia didn't think Alex would answer her. The stillness of the room was complete. "For a blissful two months I thought it would happen. I dared to think—yes, even the doctors confirmed it—that the miracle would happen. That this blocked tube had somehow straightened itself out. I *was* pregnant—so the tests said. They put me to bed, and I was quite prepared to stay there for the rest of the nine months. But it didn't last. A spontaneous abortion—that's what the doctors call a miscarriage. My one hope. I don't think it will ever come again. Elliot was marvelous about it. He kept on repeating that all that mattered was me. But I know he wants a child—children—quite as much as I do. Perhaps even more." She lit a fresh cigarette. "So strange, Julia. I've done so much better than I could ever have hoped at my job—at the no less demanding job of being Elliot's wife, and keeping up all the social side of things that *his* position demands. If anyone gets on Alex Forster's list for dinner parties in Washington, they know they've made it. I can juggle ambassadors, and even the President and the First Lady will occasionally consent to dine. We are always being asked to the White House. Elliot's newspapers are very influential. We have everything any reasonable person could want. But there is that vital ingredient missing in our marriage. Something so much desired and that we can't have. I feel so inadequate . . . incomplete. Elliot has told me if I mention divorce once again, he'll consider it on grounds of aggravation. I've suggested adoption. He can't quite bring himself to that. It may come someday. He really doesn't want an unknown child. Someone not of his blood . . . it's the part of the dream that didn't work out, Julia."

Mixed with her concern for Alex, her sympathy, Julia also experienced fear. If Alasdair were to die, there would be nothing of Jamie left. She shook away her absurd fear. But the memory of the day the news had come of Jamie's death returned. Nothing was sure—guaranteed. She thought of Alasdair riding the borrowed pony, enjoying himself. Not all her love could protect him forever, as it had not protected Jamie.

On the way back to Washington, Elliot drove them ten miles

farther south, to a place on a low hill that overlooked a large white house partly obscured by trees obviously planted many years ago. Even at the distance they could see that the house had all the beautiful characteristics of an antebellum mansion.

"There," Elliot said as they stood and looked down on the house and its serene surrounding acres. "That was what my great-grandfather lost in the Civil War. It's called Forster Hill—*still* called that even though the owner gave it another name, which didn't stick. Almost completely burned down. Someone from the North picked it, and the land, up for a song when my family were desperate for money. It's been rebuilt to the original plan—and it's one of the few things I can't buy, for love or money. The man who owns it doesn't agree with my politics—or rather the politics he reads about in my papers. I'm the last person he'd sell to. I hear he's short of cash, but he'll hang in there . . . somehow. He has three sons who are thriving lawyers, and they'll hold on to it, by whatever means." As he spoke, his arm was laid absently around Alasdair's shoulder. "So, young man, you take care of Sinclair. Don't let it go to anyone. Don't sell your birthright. . . ."

Alasdair didn't understand what the words meant, but he understood the tone. "Yes, sir . . . I mean, no. I won't sell Sinclair. But no one wants to buy it, my mother says."

"It's just a house," Stacia said. "The one you have is much better, Mr. Forster."

"No matter—this is what I *want.*"

Julia glanced swiftly at her sister, who was already moving back to the car. Alex's expression was tight and closed. There was something else in life that Elliot Forster was denied.

The journey to Los Angeles by train was slow, but infinitely exciting to Julia and Alasdair. The vastness of the land they saw was a constant source of wonderment. "When do we *get* there?" Alasdair kept asking. It was a matter of puzzlement to him that he could go to sleep in his berth, and wake up to find the train still heading west. He had thought the change at Chicago was the end of the journey. "Just wait, kid," Stacia said. "You'll get as bored with this journey as everyone else does. We could have gone by plane—that's how the smart people do it these days. But no—Rod had to show you America."

Rod had taken a quiet satisfaction in their amazement at the seeming endlessness of this land. He stared out of the window for hours as they passed through prairieland, mountains, desert. Julia felt sure he was reliving the years of his survival in such places, of his brutal struggle to pull himself out of them. He was pleased that she and Alasdair reacted as they did. "But just as well Princess Cat didn't come," Alasdair finally said. "It would have been a bit much for her—the ship, and then this. . . ." He was looking tired, Julia thought, and acted a little nervous. Too much, she thought, had happened to him in these past weeks for him to comprehend. He was only just beginning to understand how totally life had changed. She encouraged him with Rod's promise that they would all return to Sinclair in the summer and was aware of how much she herself counted on it. "Princess Cat will be waiting," she kept reassuring him. She was proud that he did not whine or complain, even when the train journey seemed to have become of interminable length. "He's a tough little kid," Rod said. "It makes a nice change from Stacia."

They were greeted in Los Angeles by the now-familiar horde of press and photographers. "Put on the best outfit you have," Rod had advised her. "This is like a photo call." Julia, who felt weary and grimy, did her best, but it was difficult to summon up the smiles of her wedding day. "You'll get used to it in time," Rod said. "But the whole of Hollywood will right now want to see the new Mrs. McCallum—and her family. Not that they haven't seen you years ago on film—but memories are short. I suppose they wonder who's brave enough to follow Anne Rayner."

"I don't consider being married to you an act of bravery. It's *our* life, Rod."

"You'll find out that in Hollywood you have to fight hard to have any sort of life of your own." The train had begun to slow at the approach to the station. "Brace yourself . . . and act like the princess you are."

Somehow the first ordeal was over—the posing, the questions asked—and they moved toward the limousines the studio had sent to meet them, Rod making small talk to the studio executive deputized to be there. His agent, Phil Westin, was there also. Julia found that more people remembered *Return at Dawn* and *The Border* than she had expected. Then, lounging against one of the limousines was a familiar figure, a face she greeted with delight. Bill Fredericks flung his arms around her. "Here's looking at you, kid," he said, repeating the words of the inscription on his photograph. The photographers recorded their embrace and kiss. Then he held her away from him. "Well, let me really get a look at you! Lovelier than ever. Damn—why did I have to shoot off my big mouth about you? I was planning to marry you myself—only my wife didn't really cotton to the idea."

"Come back to the house with us," Rod said. "I'm a mite nervous about carrying my bride over the threshold. My family's suddenly become much bigger."

"I know you," Alasdair said to Bill Fredericks as they drove away from the station. "You're the one in the photograph Mummie has. I've brought that black lamb Mummie said you sent me. I like him. Mummie made him a new bonnet—she says I chewed up the first one. And this one's made of the Sinclair tartan."

"Gee—that's right. I'd forgotten it was the wrong tartan. Sorry."

Julia was taking in her first glimpse of this fabled land where film stars were made and broken. The palm trees; the stretches of concrete; the bare, brown hills; the sense of seediness lurking only a block behind a glittering facade of shops and restaurants. It was just as all the photographs and all the stories of those who had come and gone had told her. She had to remind herself that this was real, not the playback of a film clip. She was seeing it for the first time and yet recognizing almost at once its unreality. A city created from orange groves to make movies because the sun always shone here.

In many ways Rod's house also had an air of unreality—except that it had its own kind of beauty. He had been too superstitious to give it a name, but the architect had called it simply "La Casa del Sol" because of the way Rod had demanded that it be positioned—so its angles gave it the utmost of the sun, although from the road below it did not appear too impressive. Julia was aware that across the high hedge was a mock English Tudor house, but this was a carefully put together mixture of Spanish and Mexican. She loved its long, cool, arched loggia; the warm, burnished tiles; the brilliant bougainvillea that wreathed its walls and made it a curved rather than an angular building. In the distance she could hear the sound of splashing water. Two Mex-

ican servants appeared, bowing slightly, smiling warmly. "Maria—José—this is *la Señora*. You must do everything exactly as
she wishes it."

It was as Stacia had described it. Earth-colored Indian rugs
on the tiled floor of the main hall, with its shining wooden stairs
and elaborate wrought-iron banister. A massive saddle studded
with silver was mounted on a block, and the walls were adorned
with masks from the ancient Mexican cultures. Brilliant blue and
white pots—Spanish, Julia guessed—stood around, filled with
masses of differently colored flowers, as if they had been picked
haphazardly but betraying a hand of great skill in their arrangement.

Rod looked at her anxiously. "Well . . . ?"

"It's beautiful. So much more beautiful than I expected."

The house had been built with an interior patio. Massively
carved wooden doors were flung open to the sun, and the vision
of a pool made brilliant by small Mexican tiles of blue and
green. Bougainvillea climbed the center walls of the two-storied
building, and around the pool were massed hundreds of multicolored glazed pots filled with flowers for which Julia as yet had
no names. It was a day in early January, and yet the place was
alive with sunlight and colors, the flickering of butterflies, the
sounds of bees working the blossoms. Arches behind the pool
led to a vista of a hillside covered in sprawling ground-hugging
plants and hibiscus. The scent of eucalyptus was in the air; she
recognized the tall, whitish bark among the gray-blue leaves.

"Oh, beautiful . . ." Julia said again.

Alasdair tugged at Rod's sleeve. "Will you teach me to
swim?"

"Can't you swim? Well, I suppose there aren't many days
you'd want to go swimming in the loch. Of course, I'll teach
you to swim. Stacia might help. She swims like a fish."

"I'm not here to give kids lessons. . . ." She had already
started to climb the stairs. "I suppose I'm still in the same room?
I mean, I don't have to sleep downstairs with Maria and José?"

"Little bitch," Rod said in words so low Julia scarcely caught
them. Then he put his arm around Julia. "I'm glad you like
it. . . . I thought it might seem a bit of a comedown from a
castle."

"Oh, rubbish . . . it's very beautiful, and you know it."

He led them into a living room that was rather what Julia had imagined, from Stacia's description of how life was lived in Rod McCallum's house. Here were the leather-covered sofas, the Indian rugs, the carved wooden chairs, the massive fireplace made of stone which looked as if it had come untouched from the earth. There was a high-beamed ceiling; simple off-white curtains, which Julia guessed were handwoven, hung from wooden poles and rings. Duplicates of the blue and white pots filled with flowers stood around, sconces from wrought iron lined the walls. Floor-to-ceiling windows with wooden shutters decorated with aged green copper studs opened both to the loggia and the pool. The room was filled with splashes of sunlight and the darkness of shadows.

"Some place, isn't it?" Bill Fredericks said. "You'll see plenty of places that are trying to look like Versailles in this town, but this is the real McCoy. It's been photographed by just about every magazine in America. Rod built it himself. . . ."

"With the help of a pretty good architect," Rod said. He was at a dark oak chest that held a drinks tray. "What'll it be, buddy?"

"Oh—rum and something." José was already in the room, his soft-soled shoes making scarcely a sound on the tiles, carrying a tray with a pitcher of lemon juice. "Maria thought for the niño . . . Mr. McCallum."

"Good idea. Fresh lemon juice, Alasdair?"

"He's never had that in his life before. I don't think he's even seen a lemon. Oranges are hard enough to get. . . ."

"You can put a squirt of that into the rum," Bill said. "Rita sends her love and hopes you'll come to dinner tomorrow night— if you're not too tired." He turned to Julia. "I married a gorgeous Mexican lady—which is why I wasn't free to court you that time in Scotland. But sometimes I hate Rod because Rita's always on about me not building her a house like this. I keep saying I will—when I can afford it." Then he raised his glass to her. "Well, here's *really* looking at you, kid."

Julia tasted the rum and lemon for the first time and thought it delicious. Alasdair smacked his lips over the lemon drink, into which Rod had spooned sugar. "Kid . . ." he repeated. "Everyone keeps calling me kid, and now you just called my mother kid. Who's who?"

"Little wiseacre, aren't you?" Bill answered. "Just for purposes of identification you'd better be kid from now on, and your mom is Julia. But don't forget, Rod, I saw her first. She was the best thing that happened on that film. She really warmed up that icy bit of Scotland they shipped us off to.''

Rod put down his glass and turned to Julia, his arms outstretched. ''Princess, in all the fuss, I forgot to welcome you in the traditional style.'' He took the glass from her hand and swept her up into his arms in a practiced stroke which spoke of his years of athletic training, on and off horses. She was carried out onto the loggia and then beyond the arches into the sunlight. He gave her a light toss in his arms, then he turned and reentered the room. ''Welcome to your new castle, Princess.''

He deposited her lightly on a sofa, and as he gave her back her glass they became aware of Stacia standing in the great stone arch that led into the room. ''Do you think, just for once, I could have a splash of rum in the lemon? I think I'm a bit older than the kid.'' She had already changed her dress for something of cotton that looked as if it had been woven of a thousand colors, something that reflected the colors of the flowers and the pool. Her legs were bare, and on her feet she wore rope-soled shoes. Her hair was brushed out straight and lay in a long golden fall over one shoulder. Bill gave a soft whistle. ''Gee, you sort of grew up while you were away, Stacia.'' She shrugged, and the pouting lips pursed provocatively. Julia was startled by the display of sheer sexuality in that small gesture. ''Most people do grow up, Bill. When they're allowed to.''

''All right—all right,'' Rod said. ''Yes, you may have a splash of rum in your lemon. And remember that, legally, you're not grown up yet. I have to look after you.''

''Yeah . . .'' She poured her lemon juice and added a large shot of rum. ''Like you looked after my mother. I saw you carry her just like that into this room the day you were married.''

''The reason I carried her in was because she couldn't walk. She was dead drunk. She slept off our wedding night on that sofa.''

Bill refused an invitation to dinner. Julia learned that Alasdair was not expected to eat with them until he could manage a knife and fork. He would eat in a simple but comfortable room off the kitchen with Maria and José. ''That's so he won't put messy fingers on anything,'' Stacia said. ''But don't worry. He'll learn Mexican Spanish. But I don't see how you're expected to teach

him good table manners from a distance. I had the rudiments
when I came here, and Rod soon saw that I learned the refinements—which is a load of—'' She pressed her lips closed over
the last word. "Rod is all for refinement and elegance. I guess
that's where he and Mom came unstuck. She was a great broad,
but she wasn't exactly what you'd call elegant."

"You're a beautiful young woman, Stacia," Rod said quietly,
"but you'd be a lot more agreeable to be with if you had a touch
more elegance in your manners. . . ."

Julia quickly learned, though, that at least part of what Stacia
had said of Rod was true. He was immensely proud of his house
and liked to say that it had been earned only by his own efforts
and that he didn't owe a cent on it. It was coolly immaculate, and
he intended it to stay that way. Two Mexican women came each
day to help Maria and José. It seemed to Julia that they spent a
great deal of their time wiping away the faint dust marks left on
the dark tiles by the shoes of anyone who walked in from the
garden. The pool was constantly being vacuumed by one of the
two Mexican gardeners. Any petal that fell was instantly picked
up; paths were raked, no weeds appeared. Julia began to realize
how the unavoidable untidiness of Castle Sinclair must have irked
Rod, especially when the rooms were festooned with the essential litter of cameras, cables, and lights. A kind of hush hung
over this Casa del Sol, sweetened by the sounds of the birds,
and the splash of the small artificial waterfall that trickled down
the hill into the pool and was recirculated to the top again. Julia
remarked on it as they made a complete tour of the house the
next day. She had been admiring Rod's collection of Wild West
drawings and sculpture in the living room. "Remingtons," he
said briefly. "Not quite like owning those Stubbses and Mun-
ningses of Elliot Forster's—but they belong there."

"It's a beautiful house, Rod—but unexpected. I mean—it's
very masculine. One knows it's *your* house." She waved a hand
in dismissal of the protest she could see coming. "Oh, I know
you'll say it's the architect—or the interior decorator. It's *you*—
but so tidy, so neat. It hardly goes with the Wild West image."

"I've left the Wild West behind, Julia. The Wild West was
Scotland, and the kick and the shove and the clawing to get
where I am. To own this house—and never to owe anyone in the
world a cent. I don't have to scrape or grovel anymore. And I
want things as they never were in the cottage in the forest. I

want order, and peace and quiet. I can't stand laziness or waste. I pay this Mexican lot a good rate for what they do—but if they get sloppy, or I see the *mañana* attitude creeping in, out they go. And they all know it. No sentimentality. I value Maria and José exactly for what they give me, and no more. I'm not a soft touch, Julia. That's what Stacia can't get into her head. She grew up in a mess. Her mother was always jumping from one money crisis to another. She was cheated left, right, and center because she never knew where the money was going, and she trusted everyone. Stacia thinks I'm tough about money. She doesn't know how close her mother came to being flat broke. I put on the reins. Neither of them liked it. Neither of them liked the fact that I tried to tidy up their messy lives. . . .''

"Yes, I see," Julia said, but the sense of unease was still with her. "Look, Rod—can we do something about Alasdair eating with Maria and José? I mean, they seem a perfectly nice couple, but he can't talk to them. He can't really be shut out forever. . . .''

He smiled at her. "Sweetheart—did what Stacia said last night get to you? Yes, I did say he'd have supper with Maria and José. Just the way he had breakfast this morning. Princess, we're still on our honeymoon. There's a perfectly nice, pleasant *small* dining room next to the kitchen. That's where I usually eat and where we'll eat in the future—except that the kid has to go to bed earlier, so you'll just have to sit with him. I was just showing off last night. I couldn't exactly tell Stacia to eat with the kid, but I wanted that first meal alone with you—in the dining room, looking as it should. We *are* a family, Julia, but sometimes I'm going to want to have you just to myself. Not surprising, is it?"

"I love you, Rod," she said.

"Keep it that way."

They went to dinner with Bill and Rita Fredericks, in a house not unlike Rod's but without its calm space and touches of splendor. On their arrival Bill had joked, "Bit of a comedown, eh? Let me introduce my wife, Rita—the reason I didn't dare to try to carry you off in Scotland."

"I am jealous," Rita said, but embracing Julia at the same time. "Of course I saw *The Border*. But you are more beautiful now." She was of the distinctly Latin type, handsome, with black hair, olive skin, and deep brown eyes that Julia was relieved to see appeared to be genuinely welcoming. Their dinner was of traditional Mexican food. "Bill said I must make it for you. But don't let either of them fool you about the sauce. It will burn your tongue off."

The talk was of the film business—who was making what picture, who was on suspension, who had had a contract renewed. Julia was to learn that that was what the conversation usually was. "I hear the Big Boss asked you both to dinner," Bill observed.

"Where did you hear that? I only got the invitation this morning."

"Word gets around—you know how quickly word gets around in this town. You're going to be looked over, Julia."

The Big Boss was Bill's name for Morris Meadows, the head of Worldwide Pictures. She had heard Rod's rather clipped acceptance of the invitation on the phone. Clearly he was not pleased, but just as clearly it was an invitation he could not refuse.

"I meant to keep Julia under wraps until we had our party, which is fixed for two weeks from tonight. I don't care if you both have a date. You're our first guests. . . ."

Julia looked at Rod in puzzlement. "We're having a party in two weeks? You didn't say anything. . . ."

"Don't worry your head, Princess. It's all arranged. I just called the caterers. A temporary secretary comes tomorrow to handle the details, and everything gets done. . . ."

"But I didn't know."

"You don't have to know. All you have to do is look beautiful. Tomorrow we'll go shopping for the dress. . . ."

She got back to find Alasdair still awake, and with traces of tears on his cheeks. "Stacia wouldn't come down from her room. I had supper with Maria and José. They're nice, Mummie—but I don't understand anything they say. Maria put me to bed, the way you said. She even heard my prayers. She knelt beside me. I missed you. . . . There are funny sounds outside."

"Just the cicadas, darling. Little insects that make a big noise." She stroked his forehead and kissed him. "You'll be all right now, darling."

"Are you going to be away every night?"

"No, of course not . . ." But she wondered if she was making a promise she could not keep. "And we'll make some other arrangements. You won't be having all your meals with Maria and José. You're still tired from the journey, Alasdair, and it's all strange, but we'll all settle in. Trust me, darling.'' She doubted if he understood all she said, but her tone seemed to satisfy him. But he still clung to her hand, and she stayed there seated beside him until finally he slept. She looked at his fair young face, lying on the pillow, even in sleep so like Jamie's, as she had watched as he, too, slept. She looked at Jamie's photo on the chest of drawers—the young, cocky, confident Jamie of his early days in the RAF Volunteer Reserve, when he had learned to fly for the fun of it. Then the later one Lady Jean had insisted he have taken, the one with the changed face of the veteran flier, the campaign ribbons, the DFC and bar, the downward wound across his cheek, the jagged hairline where the bullet had clipped. She gazed at the sleeping, now peaceful face of her son. She wondered if she had committed an act of utter selfishness in marrying Rod, in bringing Jamie's child to this alien place, which, for all its luxuries, was strange and bewildering to him. When she had gone to Sinclair for Alasdair's birth it had been because she had been determined that the child, which was all she had left of Jamie, would grow up to know and understand his inheritance. She remembered how during that visit she had made to Sinclair with Jamie he had spoken of his dreams for the future—humble enough dreams, simple dreams that envisaged only the slow improvement of Sinclair, dreams that did not gloss over a life of hard and patient work he had seen for the future. *Tread softly because you tread on my dreams.* She had agreed to be part of those only half-formed dreams. Had she betrayed them? For a moment she dropped to her knees, taking her gaze from her young lover's portrait, bending to kiss their son's fair, smooth cheek. "Oh, God," she murmured, "don't let me ever betray Jamie's dreams."

Finally she went to the large bedroom she and Rod occupied. It had two dressing rooms, and two bathrooms off it, but the severe Spanish influence had given way only marginally to traces of femininity. It was obvious that Anne Rayner had never been permitted to alter anything from what Rod had originally decreed. An enormous four-poster bed had a cover and canopy of handwoven wool that incorporated all the bright colors she imagined were the essence of Mexico, but the headboard was of dark carved oak, as were the posts. A large blue-figured antique carpet was laid on blue and white tiles. Two austere carved chests were the only furniture apart from wooden chairs almost as large as the ones in the dining room. A magnificent refectory table held flowers, books, and magazines in orderly piles, and wrought-iron candlesticks. The two long windows opened onto balconies that gave a view of the lighted pool below. She had been too tired and confused the night before to take in what now struck her forcibly—translated into this more exotic setting, and without the wooden floors and the fireplace, it was not so very unlike the Red Tower Room at Sinclair.

Rod was wearing a dressing gown and standing by one of the windows, smoking. He half turned as she entered. "You were a long time." She wondered if she detected a coldness in his tone.

"Alasdair was still awake. Stacia didn't have supper with them. He was a bit upset—he still isn't used to not being able to understand what Maria and José say between them. They're very kind but . . . well, I suppose we have to allow for him being a bit homesick—"

"*Homesick!* What the hell's he got to be homesick about? He's got everything he wants, hasn't he?"

"Rod . . . Rod! He's only four and a half. There've been big changes in his life in a few weeks. Nothing is familiar. . . . I think he's worn out with the novelty of it all. If there were someone like Janet . . ."

"Yes . . . Janet. I hope he's not been mollycoddled. But I guess we'll have to find someone who can be a sort of governess for him and Stacia until he goes to school. Someone to teach them both—if such a person exists. Damn, why are kids such a bloody pain in the neck?"

"Will you think that way about the children we'll have, Rod?"

He stubbed out his cigarette and came to her swiftly, enfolding her in his arms. "Princess, why do I always put things so badly? I love you . . . and he's a damn nice little kid. And I'll love him no different from the kids we'll have. What I meant was . . . well, I've never had a kid of my own—not that I know of. Until Stacia arrived, I didn't know what a lot of things they need . . . but you have to admit she's a special problem. The kid will do fine, you'll see. He'll settle down. We'll find some decent old dame to keep an eye on both of them. I'll ask the studio to help with that. We should have brought one of those fancy English nannies with us. The sort with the funny hats and the frumpy shoes. That would have knocked everyone's eyes out. Like having an English butler.''

"Somehow I don't think Stacia would have taken to an English nanny. You either send her back to Beverly Hills High, or get a live-in teacher for them both. She can't be left without some teaching. She's intelligent—and quick, when she's interested. . . .''

"Yes, Princess. But we'll think about that in the morning. At this moment all I desire is your presence in my bed.''

"Isn't it my bed, too?''

He lifted her face to kiss her lips. "It's our bed, you lovely fool. It's been waiting for you for so long. I didn't know who I was waiting for until I saw you. Forget Anne. She hardly knew she was here. I've been waiting for you for so long . . . so very long. I guess from the day I walked out of that cottage in the forest with my mother and father and all the kids. Perhaps someone told me about a princess who lived in a castle. This is *your* bed, your home, your castle.''

"Where thou lodgest, I will lodge. . . ."

He swept her up in his arms. "May I have the privilege of undressing you, lovely lady?''

Rod took Julia shopping for clothes—not just the dresses she would wear at the Meadowses' dinner party, and the party they would give, but also for everything else he deemed she needed. She protested that she was quite happy wearing some of the things Alex had sent to her.

"That was all well and good in that time, Julia. I know you were all on clothing rations, and you aren't exactly flush with money. But now you're my wife. I can't have you wearing *anyone's* castoffs, even if they are Mrs. Elliot Forster's.'' The faint edge of jealousy was in his tone, something he could never quite rid himself of when he spoke of those who had had the advantage over him of education or breeding. So she went with him, and bit her lip against commenting on things that she found outrageous in cost, and sometimes in style. "Princess, this is Hollywood. Tinsel Town. You're not dressing for a party in Inverness—or even in London. Yes, I agree—some things are a little over the top. You just keep to your quiet good taste in most of the things you wear—they're your style. But just once in a while you have to show that you're an actress and can carry off *anything*. Think of them as costumes—wear them as if you were onstage. Everything looks so great on you. . . .'' But she realized that when prices were discussed, there was a considerable discount because she was Rod McCallum's wife. He missed no chance to strike the hardest bargain. He bought her lingerie and dressing gowns that she thought far too grand, because they would be seen by no one but him. She kept remembering what Stacia had said about her own mother's clothes: ''But her underwear was cheap . . .''

A compromise had been reached about Stacia; Rod had agreed to allow her to attend Beverly Hills High once again. ''But so help me, if your grades aren't up to scratch, or if you start messing around with the boys, or coming home late, I'll yank you out of there so quickly it'll make your head spin, and you'll be back in that place near San Francisco. A car will take you to school and pick you up in the afternoon. You can bring your friends here as long as you don't make too much noise or mess up the place. But you've got to crack the books, you understand? You're a smart kid, Stacia, and you'd do very well if you'd just apply yourself.''

She was so pleased to be with her friends that she actually thanked him, and made promises that she would work hard. ''After all,'' she said as they ate in the pleasant, small room near the kitchen that was their normal dining room, ''I really don't want to seem to be a dummy. . . .''

''Attagirl,'' Rod said approvingly. ''I thought you'd see reason. Another year and a bit, and you'll graduate. You don't want to be bottom of the class, do you?''

The studio had found a pleasant young woman, Jenny, who had just graduated from Valley State College and had taken a secretarial course, who would act as a part-time secretary and Alasdair's companion-teacher. Rod was already in correspondence with Luisa about finding an English nanny willing to come to Hollywood. Julia was blessing Elliot's christening gift of shares in Forster Newspapers that could pay for this and whatever lay ahead. Rod was talking about a prep school in the East when it was time. Julia was silently determined that it would be an English school, even if she had to fall in with Luisa's plans for Johnny and Alasdair to go to school together. The complexities of her marriage to a man who lived so far from what she still thought of as ''home'' struck her more forcibly every day.

Again she began to wonder if it had been a monumental act of selfishness to marry Rod—to bring her child into this land. Had her hunger for him, her need, the prospect of long years of loneliness made her too hasty? These thoughts were dispelled by Rod's kisses. But he was shrewd enough to guess them. "Try not to worry, Princess. These things have a way of working themselves out. I promise every summer you'll go to Sinclair, whether I'm filming or not. Alasdair won't lose his roots. But try to remember that one day you will have to let him go. One day, however far off it seems, he will marry, and you'd be just a nuisance mother-in-law. But we'll have our family here. . . . Sure he'll be different from them, but they'll be *ours*. We won't be trying to live our lives for them, no more than you can live your life for him. I suppose people thought it a little odd that you married Jamie Sinclair instead of someone in the profession—or at least one of the boys who lived near Anscombe. You might have married a musician, or a London stage actor. Instead you married a Scottish laird, and then a Hollywood actor. Stranger things have happened . . . and worked. Just let's see that this works."

"Of course it will work. You're . . . you're very understanding, Rod."

"I love you, Princess. And I'm not as dumb as some people think. Now stop moping, and go and have a rest before the Big Boss's party this evening. Maybe he'll have looked at a few minutes of your pictures. Maybe he won't have bothered. But you're Rod McCallum's wife and Sir Michael Seymour's daughter. They're a pretty rough lot, these studio bosses—all came from nowhere. But they can generally recognize class when they meet it. And I rate you the classiest dame in Hollywood, and I'll kill anyone who says anything else."

She wore the pale lilac chiffon dress Rod had selected, and the necklace of gold, with a single pearl studded with diamonds, that had been her father's and Luisa's wedding gift. Rod's two rings gleamed on her hands. At Rod's insistence she had spent half the day at a beauty parlor having her hair arranged in an elaborate upswept style, her nails and even her toenails attended to. "You're very lovely," he said as they mounted the steps to Morris Meadows' door, which was already held open by a butler. "And now that you've stopped washing dishes, those rings have found their proper place." She wished, rather uncomfortably, that she didn't feel quite so much like a piece of property on display.

Morris Meadows bowed slightly as he took her hand. "Ah—the lovely bride. Congratulations, Rod. Mrs. Meadows and I have been looking at your films. Very nice—very well done, for low-budget jobs. And you have that little man, Oscar, on your mantel, which is more than Rod has. Not that we don't value him highly. Perhaps this next picture . . . who knows? Let me introduce you. . . ."

Mrs. Meadows' decorator had decreed that the house should be all white, with bare touches of gold. Julia found it excruciatingly boring, as was the dinner party for twelve. It seemed that nothing happened in the world except making movies. Box office was discussed, as bankers might privately, over port and cigars, have discussed the stock market. Well, it was much the same, Julia thought. She began to understand her father's misgivings about her coming to live here. Things might have been a little more fun in his time, in the thirties, when the industry was finding its way in the new world of "the talkies." Now it had become "The Factory," churning out movies and sometimes counterfeit stars. It had its gods and goddesses, some of whom were entirely manufactured by publicity, some of whom had the truly magical quality that came across on the screen. Some, like Rod, were in between, hung on, and prospered. Some, like Anne Rayner, the system had appeared to destroy.

"You were a great hit," Rod said as they drove home. Julia wondered how he could tell. After dinner they had watched the screening of a movie not yet released by the studio; it seemed the usual thing to do, as it was the usual thing to congratulate Morris Meadows on the film, which Julia had frankly thought bad. "He said he would be coming to our party."

Rod's austere house was transformed for his party—Julia thought of it as "his" party, since she seemed to have little or nothing to do except attend it. But at its basic level it was much like any other Hollywood party she later attended, the marquee, the flowers, the food. It was expensively and well done, and she kept thinking how Rod must have hated the thought of the hundreds of feet tracking over his floors, the thought that a cigarette butt might be stamped out on one of his rugs. But most of the "right" people invited turned out—whether from curiosity or desire, she didn't know. She found, in the midst of all the talk, the music, the elaborately orchestrated sense of gaiety, that she strongly missed her family. There was no one, apart from Bill and Rita Fredricks, she could count her friends. Rod kept reeling off names to her—some of them famous, some of them obviously important to him, and she smiled and talked and did what was expected of her. But she longed for a glimpse of her father, Alex, Connie, Luisa and Johnny, Sir Niall, Janet. She tried to shake off the feeling of being a stranger in a strange land. Hadn't she known what she was coming to?—hadn't this condition been part of what she had promised when she had married Rod? Hadn't she gone into a strange land to bear Jamie's child? A terrible sense of homesickness assailed her in the midst of the compliments, some of them genuine, that were offered to her. She thought of Alasdair, with the tears of homesickness on his face.

In one of those quiet moments that sometimes occur, Stacia appeared at her side. "It's all like this, you know. They're all smiling at each other, and most of them hating each other's guts. They're talking about grosses, and most of them are trying to sell something—a script, a new starlet. Why, I almost sold *myself* to an agent a few minutes ago, until he remembered I was still at school. He said he'd call me, and sign me up a few years from now." She was wearing a reasonably demure dress that Rod had picked out for her, in which she managed to look anything but demure. "I even wondered if Rod would let me be here, you know. Or if he'd say I had to stay upstairs and do my homework. Well, you're a success, at least."

"How can you tell?"

"I can tell. It'll be all over school tomorrow, but I don't need the other kids to tell me. They're such snobs here—they die for that English accent. Has Morris Meadows offered to sign you up yet?"

"No."

"I think he will. But Rod will strike a hard bargain. You won't be starting at a starlet's rate of pay."

Julia looked at the young, alluring face, which was nearly that of a woman. "You know an awful lot, don't you—for someone so young?"

Stacia shrugged. "Rod thinks I've never been young, and he might be right. But if you want to know anything about this town, ask me. I do know—as you call it—an awful lot." She half turned from Julia. "Now I'm going to find the best-looking, the most famous guy in this crowd and make him dance with me. People shouldn't forget Anne Rayner. God knows, they took enough from her. . . ."

A little later Julia saw her on the dance floor with a man of almost fifty, whose name and face were known all over the world. The way he looked at Stacia as they danced did little to disguise what his feelings were. Anne Rayner was being born again.

II

REPORTS FROM JOHN GUNN, still working in the cutting room at Pinewood, were that *Drop into Danger* was turning out better than he had hoped. "John was always cautious," Rod said. "It sounds pretty good to me. It had better be good—I've got a lot of my own money riding on it, and it's my break for some independence. I'm coming to the end of my contract. I don't want to be tied up for another five years—no matter what the money. Two at the most. Let them come back offering more at the end of that. Someday—oh, God, wouldn't I love it—I want to produce my own films. Tell them all to go to hell. Only it takes a mountain of money and your own studio to do it. Getting our own location at Sinclair and renting Pinewood was the only way I could swing *Drop into Danger.* I don't know when I'll get another chance like that."

"Wasn't it mostly that you wanted to come back to Sinclair?"

"Partly. I always wanted to go back. But not as a tourist. I wanted a script that would work there . . . and enough money to buy a big share of the action." They were in the library, a room of which he was more proud than any other in the house, in which old and battered leather-bound volumes resembled no other library she had yet seen in Hollywood. He had explained it briefly when he had first shown her the house. "Well, my old friend Ernie Wilcox, who taught me most of what I know, went on the hunt for real books. He didn't go just for the matching bindings. You remember him at the party, don't you, Princess? The old guy with the cropped hair—looking around for any suitable young man. We'll have him over to dinner—should have done it sooner. . . ." He reread the letter from John Gunn and looked at the rest of the mail. A very large package with an

Edinburgh postmark was the last thing he touched. Julia sensed he had been holding it off, saving it. He went to the fine old refectory table, and spread out the folded papers. He was silent for a few minutes, studying them. "Want to look at this, Julia?"

She stood beside him and gazed down at what she recognized as elevations of Castle Sinclair and appropriate ground plans. Suggested alterations were outlined in red. Silently Rod handed her the letter that accompanied the drawings. It was from a well-known firm of Edinburgh architects. They discussed proposed alterations, the additions of bathrooms, the complete reworking of the ancient central heating system; they also stressed the difficulties they were encountering in making precise measurements because of the age of the building, and the different dates at which various parts had been added, with no plans of that period to work from. They spoke of the difficulties of masking pipes needed for the bathrooms, and the central heating, the obstructions they would meet in walls that were built from stone, not brick and plaster. *It is mutually understood that the facade of the castle must not be altered—an opinion with which we entirely concur. We will merely make safe that which is crumbling and adhere to the essential quality and historical value of the building, which is unique. The problems of the interior renovations and added amenities will have to be solved as they occur. We regret it is quite impossible to give you a cost estimate of what is involved, owing to the nature and antiquity of the castle. But we await your opinion of our suggestions of interior alterations.*

"What have you done?" she said. "This is outrageous, Rod. You're proposing to put a fortune into a building that's falling down. Why?"

He shrugged. "Well, I thought you knew. We're going to spend summers there. Might as well be comfortable. It won't cost quite a fortune, Princess. I told them to go easy. Just get the place tidied and cleaned up a little. Stop the pieces from falling off the battlements . . . no big deal . . ."

"It sounds like a fortune in my kind of money," she said. "The cost is open-ended. You don't know what you're getting into. These old places . . . Rod, most of those walls are more than four feet thick. Getting pipes and electrical wire through there—"

"Why don't you let the architects worry about that, Princess?

That's what they're paid for. At any rate, what's the objection? Just makes the place better.''

''Rod—you're proposing to spend a great deal of money—call it that, or a small fortune—on a property that isn't yours. When Alasdair comes of age, it will be his. Jamie left his estate to me. The castle and farm belonged to him. His mother had a life interest until he came of age. But in the will he made after we were married, he left it to me, even after he knew we were going to have a baby. But when he is twenty-one, I shall make the whole thing over to Alasdair. I don't believe in a mother holding the purse strings—particularly when he decides to marry. Lady Jean had nowhere else to go—no money to go anywhere. And why should she have? She held the place together for so many years, waiting for Jamie to grow up. But I don't intend to be another Lady Jean.''

''Right, Princess. Because you're married to me. Look, it's a long time before the kid will be twenty-one. We have a lot of summers. Wouldn't you enjoy a mite of comfort until then? Maybe he'll be nice and invite us back after he becomes the young laird. There are a lot of years to enjoy it. I'd look forward to it. Remember, they gave Eisenhower the use of a part of Culzean Castle for life. Maybe Alasdair will grant us the favor . . .''

It was her castle, and her consent was needed for any work to go ahead. She felt herself inexorably drawn into a web of Rod's wishes, his will. How could she refuse without angering him, perhaps endangering their whole married life? Instinct warned her not to let it go forward. She knew her own weakness when she said, ''Well . . . if that's what you want. If the cost isn't too outrageous . . .'' She wondered what she was giving away.

But whatever she was granting only by word was matched by what he gave to her. He called his lawyers to a conference. After a week she was presented with papers that gave her half of La Casa del Sol and half of the ranch in the Santa Ines Mountains, which she hadn't even seen yet. She watched as Rod signed, and had witnessed, the new will he had made, making her his sole beneficiary. ''Stacia's taken care of with the trust,'' he said. ''I just want to be sure that if I get rammed on the freeway, you'll be okay, Princess.'' And she had, with some misgivings, allowed him to adopt Alasdair. ''He needs to know I want him as

a *real* son. It should be done before we have a kid of our own,
so he knows he came first.'' Put in those terms, she found it
impossible to refuse him. He had taken care of Stacia with some
harshness but real concern. But she wondered if she hadn't sac-
rificed too much of Alasdair's independence. But independence
of what? she had to ask herself in fairness. Rod had asked for
nothing in return. He was willing to pour money into Sinclair,
which he knew would never be his. Among the papers she
signed, in that flurry of signing, was a power of attorney she
gave to Rod. He explained that it was necessary for him to have
it to make dealing with the studio possible, to procure the best
possible contracts for her. ''Phil Westin's all right . . . in his
way,'' he said, ''but don't forget he has a lot of other clients to
peddle to the studios. I won't have you sold off in a job lot with
six others. You're special, Princess—and I can't let you start out
here as a starlet. I want to be able to dictate the terms of any
agreement you sign. You're far too soft, you know. You weren't
brought up in the hard school. Stage actors have always played
for peanuts. That isn't going to happen to you—not anymore.
Listen, Princess—I know this game backward. I know more than
Phil Westin. I know the value of money—the power it gives. I've
had better salaries than many people here in Hollywood would
believe—but I keep my mouth shut about them, and so does
Worldwide. They're afraid other people would start asking for
the same. I've even had a percentage of the gross in the last
three pictures. And they were *big* box office. But I live in the
same nice, tidy, but, by Hollywood standards, fairly modest
house. And say nothing. I don't rouse anyone's envy. That
wouldn't do. The only thing Hollywood envies me at this moment is *you*. They just don't understand how a rough cowboy
could capture a princess. I'll work my ass off to see that you get
good pictures and the best terms going. . . .''

He knew this world, and she knew nothing. She signed the
power of attorney.

III

THE DAYS FLOWED evenly on. Julia was growing accustomed to
the rhythm of her new life, not resisting it, trying not to let
backward thoughts of England and Scotland distract her from

the life she was building with Rod. She enrolled Alasdair at a kindergarten for four hours a day. The rest of the time he spent with her and Jenny, a bright-eyed, attractive young woman who loved the glamour of the job she had just landed. But sometimes Alasdair was near tears when he returned from the kindergarten; his accent was called "funny." " 'You talk funny,' they keep on saying."

"Listen, kid, you just punch 'em in the eye. I'll show you how," Rod said. And he did. Alasdair returned one day with torn clothes, a badly bruised cheek, and a complaining letter from the principal. "I gave him worse," Alasdair said. Rod loudly applauded him. Julia said nothing. If Rod was going to be the father Alasdair had never had, she would not interfere with the rites of passage into masculinity.

Stacia was quiet and, as she had promised, not only improved her grades but also her manners. Sometimes in the afternoons she brought some of her friends home to swim, to eat cookies and drink lemonade in the small dining room. "You know," Rod said, "I think she might have come to her senses. Of course, it's your influence, Princess. She might be beginning to see some virtue in quietness and dignity." Julia had more the sense that Stacia was biding her time, having realized that any revolt against Rod's edicts would result in banishment to a harsher regime. She ate her evening meal with them and even began to contribute to the conversation. When they had guests to dinner, Rod included her in the company, provided that she had finished her homework. She carried drinks and cups of coffee, and the pouting mouth often seemed to smile. But Julia still saw no happiness behind the smile, no pleasure. Stacia seldom laughed.

Rod was reading scripts, but so far no new picture had been assigned to him. He was busy with forward publicity for *Drop into Danger,* and there were many interviews they had to give together—the new Mrs. Rod McCallum, the actress Julia Seymour. Sometimes the studio decreed that Stacia must be photographed with them. "Damn . . ." he said privately. "They won't let Anne Rayner's ghost lie down. You're following a hard act, Princess."

John Gunn returned with what he had finally decided was the finished print of *Drop into Danger.* They viewed it nervously and decided it had come off. Morris Meadows was as enthusiastic as his nature would allow. "It ain't great. But it ain't bad, either." He began to prod his writers to come up with a script for Rod. "Don't let him get cold," he warned. "No point in being yesterday's star."

"Damn him!" Rod said. "You'd think I was eighty-eight instead of thirty-eight. But I'll have to be a little choosy about scripts in the future. What I need is a writer like Dashiell Hammett—I need to create a character like Humphrey Bogart . . . or should I go on trying to outdo John Wayne at the box office?" While he waited for the right script, the studio continued to pay his very handsome salary.

On a few weekends they went up to his ranch house in the Santa Ines Mountains. The house was tiny, but Rod's nature seemed to expand with space around him. He owned over seven hundred acres there—mostly bare, and to Julia's eyes, barren ground. But his love for it was evident. "I won it at poker," he said, "when I was a bit player without a line to speak. I came up here and felt like a king—owning land. One day, when I'm finished with Hollywood, I'll put cattle on here—really work it." He kept horses stabled with neighbors, and true to his promise to Alasdair, there was a pony for him. "Not quite as pretty as Princess Cat, but she's a very nifty little lady." Alasdair was enchanted. Rod had been sending him for riding lessons at the same school Stacia attended—he had become used to the Western saddle and showed a natural aptitude. "He'll do fine," Rod said. The child basked in his approval. Julia and Alasdair both reveled in the warm sunshine of the February days, the clear, cool nights. She felt no longing for the snows piled against Sinclair's walls. At the ranch house they mostly ate reheated food cooked by Maria and brought with them. The old kitchen stove was falling apart, and Rod objected to Julia spending time cooking. Stacia helped with the washing up and seemed less restless there than Julia had ever known her. She even brought books to read. They sat before the fire at night, oil lamps lighting the dark. After Stacia had gone to bed, Rod poured brandies for them both. "It seems to be working, Princess. Anne could never stand the place. Too far from the bright lights."

But the bright lights had to be part of their world. They had to attend the obligatory parties, whether the hosts were friends or not. Julia came to realize that it was part of the studio system. Rod could virtually be ordered to be present wherever the studio thought he should be. It was part of the contract, and for his thousands-of-dollars-a-week salary, he had to comply with its demands. On a day late in March he came home from a meeting with his agent, Phil Westin, with a thin, rather worried smile on his face.

"Well, it's coming—as I thought it would. Meadows wants you and me together in a movie. Don't ask me what the movie is. They haven't written it yet. But he thinks you're much too good publicity to miss—and, of course, there's that little Oscar. You'll get a good contract—I'll see to that."

The studio insisted that both Rod and Julia go on a publicity tour to coincide with the release of *Drop into Danger*. "Too bad," Rod said, "but we've got to do it. It's a real pain. Even if you've got a smash hit, it's a pain. If it's a flop, or a medium success, it's a whole lot worse. But you have to keep on smiling no matter what happens."

For Julia it was total bewilderment—a succession of trains and planes, press conferences, and individual interviews. As it opened in each major city they had to attend a premiere—each time a different dress for her, her hair immaculate, a flashing smile. And each time the film seemed worse to her. It had received mixed notices—some praised Rod's effort to break out of the mold into which he had been set. He was, as Julia suspected, weakest in the moments when he had to play off his men, one against the other, but he rose to a sometimes stunning best when action was demanded. He became again the studio idol he had been during his wartime pictures. Claire Avery was clearly miscast. John Gunn had retained the footage of Stacia riding Cat along the loch shore—at that distance she was a figure of grace with blond hair streaming in the wind, her face indistinguishable; she could have been Clair Avery. John did not include the fall scene. It was one of the most atmospheric pieces of footage in the film, one that had the impact of reality that only a one-shot piece ever attains. Rod had insisted that Stacia's name appear among the credits; she came right at the end of the cast of characters and was simply credited as *Girl on the Horse*. The shot had absolutely no bearing on the plot but established the wild beauty of the loch, with the forest behind, as no planned shot did. Stacia had received an honorarium payment and was highly pleased. But she had the good grace not to say anything to Alasdair about it. To have earned money from the death of Cat would have been an outrage to him, even at his age. Julia wondered how long it would be until his memory of that day would fade enough so that he would be able to see that last ride again. She would keep him from seeing *Drop into Danger* for as long as possible. The single thing that pleased Julia most was the credit *Filmed entirely on location at Castle Sinclair, Scotland.*

The box-office figures were respectable but not sensational by the time they returned to Los Angeles. *Variety* was speculating on where Rod McCallum would go from there, as well as being laudatory for his courage in filming without the help of the studio backlot.

"I'll tell you where he's going," Rod said. "He's taking his bride back to Scotland. It's time we inspected what those architects are doing. The studio says they'll have a script ready for us by September—at the latest. So let's have that summer I promised. . . ."

They stopped briefly in Washington to see Alex and Elliot. *Drop into Danger* was politely commented on. Julia knew that both Alex and Elliot were stretched to find words for it. "Pity you didn't have the female role, Julia. It really needed someone who understood castles to play it," Elliot remarked.

"Elliot," Rod said, mustering patience, "she turned me down once when a part in one of my pictures was offered to her. How was I to know the great Michael Seymour's daughter wouldn't turn me down again? I didn't even know she'd *be* at Sinclair. Yes—it was a great chance missed . . . I kick myself every time I think of it." No one even slightly hinted at the fact that Claire Avery had been his mistress at the time.

They went on to London and again the waiting press. Rod was impatient because he knew he was expected to stay at Anscombe for at least two nights. Michael and Luisa welcomed them warmly; Alasdair and Johnny waited only minutes before Alasdair volunteered to show Johnny how Rod had taught him to punch. Luisa managed to stave off the demonstration, and the two boys ran immediately to the stable to visit Princess Cat. The pony had already been booked on the train to go north with them.

"You know Cat won't like it," Michael said. "She's used to company—Taffy and the Whitehands' pony. She's a slightly temperamental little beast. She's spoiled, of course. She's so much more striking than the others."

"Well, I promised the kid . . ." Rod said. Julia sensed he was slightly on the defensive in the presence of her father, as so many film actors were around those who had mastered both the stage and the screen. Both Michael and Luisa had graceful excuses as to why they had not yet seen *Drop into Danger.* "You know how it is . . ." Luisa gestured vaguely. "With Michael working all week, there's only Sunday and part of Monday to relax. The play has had an unexpectedly long run. . . ."

Julia knew that her father had scored yet another acting triumph, in *Arms and the Man,* and negotiations were under way to mount a Broadway production, though Actors Equity was protesting about importing the English cast in full. It was the sort of thing Rod might have hungered for but that never would be his. He was earning far more money than her father ever had, but he would never know the heady excitement of carrying a live audience with him through the evening.

That Sunday Connie and Ken came down to visit, with their two children. Clive was now walking and had the air of one who knows exactly what he is about. He was very tall for his age, taking after his father, but both children had been touched by Connie's grace and beauty. Since it was June, the rose garden had to be inspected in minute detail. Michael took them to almost every bush, naming it and explaining its virtues and defects. "Beautiful, this one—but no scent. A big bloomer here, but it fades quickly. They all have such oddly feminine personalities. . . . The Ginette Maslova rose is almost ready to spring on the world. The grower tells me it probably will be ready for the next Chelsea Flower Show."

"We hardly have a peaceful Sunday during the summer," Luisa complained. "Some rose fancier or other wants to see Michael and the garden—give him advice, give him his latest product. Of course, the commercial ones want the publicity if Michael decides to grow it—but there are some rather sweet ones who write so politely and just ask for the privilege of seeing the garden. They're the ones whom Michael usually invites to stay on for tea, and then it's drinks, and then it's a pickup supper, as Michael always calls it—as if Cook and Stella weren't supposed to have the day off. So I always have pâté and a ragout of some sort waiting for Sunday supper—infinitely stretchable."

Michael touched her cheek fondly. "Luisa's an angel. There's one rose grower who's waiting to produce a particularly strong

gold, which is very hardy, and it's going to be called 'Luisa.'
The Ginette Maslova is a brilliant red.''

''When someone has produced the perfect white, persuade
them to call it 'Princess,' will you?'' Rod said. ''No trace of
color in it at all. Perfect and pure.''

Michael glanced at him with a puzzled frown. ''My dear boy,
you're asking for a rose grower's dream.''

''Well, let them dream away. . . .'' Suddenly he caught up
Clive and hoisted him onto his shoulders. ''Hold on tight. . . .
Here we go—'Charge of the Light Brigade.' '' He went gallop-
ing off along the center path of the outer rose garden.

''Is he always like that?'' Ken inquired. ''I mean—so impul-
sive. I must remind him Clive was India, not the Crimea.''

''It won't make a difference, dear,'' Connie said. ''Neither
one of them will care.''

''I don't suppose they will. Clive will learn one day. . . . I
must say, there were some terrible inaccuracies in that film of
his, Julia. All fantasy, of course. Could never have been done.''

''Cinema audiences buy fantasy, Ken,'' Julia answered. ''If
you make it convincing enough. Father's been trading on fantasy
all his life.''

Ken shrugged. ''I expect he has.''

Julia took her drink to the kitchen to sit with Stella and Cook,
while Connie and Luisa set the table and started to make salad,
and prepared to toast bread for the pâté. They pressed Julia with
questions about Hollywood—was it really so glamorous? She
had brought pictures of the house—was it really so beautiful, so
very different? Was it possible to swim in the middle of winter
in the pool? Stacia sat in the kitchen with them, saying little.
Alasdair and Johnny were being bathed by Brenda Turnbull and
Jenny, whom Rod had decreed must come with them for the
summer. ''I want some time with you by myself,'' he had said.
''The kid can't take all of it.'' Clive was already sleeping in
pajamas, ready to be carried to the rather rundown car Ken
Warren drove, when the time came to leave. Margaret was upstairs with the two boys, pretending to help but putting off her
own bedtime. ''They're both so like Ken,'' Julia said to Stella
at one of the times when Connie was absent from the kitchen.
''They seem to take life very seriously. The wild Maslov strain
seems to have run out.'' She was looking carefully at her old
nanny, noting the deep lines in her face, the stoop of her shoul-

ders. ''They were rather wild times, weren't they?—Mother and Father living such a hectic life, and you trying to keep us all in order?''

''Sometimes I wish they were back—those times. It gets too quiet here during the week when Sir Michael and Lady Seymour are in London. You'll be sending Alasdair back here to school, won't you? He can't really grow up in Hollywood.''

''We'll have to see,'' Julia replied cautiously.

Stacia made one of her rare utterances; Julia had almost forgotten she was there. ''He *shouldn't* grow up in Hollywood.''

Sir Niall and Janet were waiting when they arrived in Inverness, and there was a horse box for Princess Cat. Sir Niall seemed more stooped than Julia remembered, his tall figure shrunken. ''How I've missed you,'' he said simply, his words seeming to embrace them all. Janet knelt by Alasdair.

''How you have grown! Oh, it is grand that you are back here for your fifth birthday.'' She put her arms around Julia, the first time she had done so. ''Oh, it's been a long, lonely winter without you, Mrs. Sinclair. . . .'' Then her face flushed. ''I beg your pardon, Mrs. McCallum. Mr. McCallum, we've all seen the picture . . . everyone here loves it. It's grand the way the castle came out.''

''I think the castle was the star of the picture . . . still, might sell a few postcards,'' Rod quipped. They moved toward the waiting press, who in deference to Sir Niall had uncharacteristically hung back. They had also been interviewed when they had changed trains at Edinburgh. The questions were more or less the same, but now they had closer relevance. How long would they be staying at Sinclair? Was Mr. McCallum pleased with *Drop into Danger?* Any more plans for pictures filmed in the Highlands? And, last, because they had local knowledge of it, did the extensive alterations at Castle Sinclair mean that they intended to spend a considerable length of time there in the future?

One last reporter pursued them to the waiting cars. ''We wonder, Mr. McCallum, if we could have an interview at some later date for *The Enquirer.* About your Scottish background. Your memories of Scotland. There's nothing on file of where exactly in Scotland it was you were born.''

Rod smiled and shrugged. ''You know as much as I do. My

parents died before I could really ask them. Grew up in an orphan home. They didn't ask questions there. Just took me in. I wasn't the only Scottish emigrant who lost his roots. I don't intend to advertise in newspapers for my family—I have one now.'' He waved a flippant good-bye. There would never be an acknowledgement from Rod of the cottage in the forest.

All the Kerr family were lined up in the courtyard to welcome them. Even Mrs. Kerr's usually solemn face wore an unaccustomed smile. ''I couldn't believe you'd be back so soon. The place is a fair mess, but no doubt Mr. McCallum will be able to make sense of what the building people are doing. . . .'' The three dogs, Rory, Duuf, and Angus, greeted them joyously, but less boisterously than before—the black muzzles of the collies had turned almost white.

They looked up at the scaffolding that wreathed two towers of the castle. ''And not before time,'' William Kerr said. ''Very dangerous they were getting. I have to thank you, Mr. McCallum, for the additions to our quarters. It's a little palace we have now. . . .''

Julia had not been aware, from the plans she had seen, that Rod had provided for improvements to the Kerr house. He was generous in unexpected ways. And yet she was uneasily aware that every gesture of this sort made him appear to be more the master of Sinclair, as he was the accepted authority in his Beverly Hills home, the only person the servants looked to for orders. Instinctively, her arm went around Alasdair as they entered the castle by the great double doors.

In the Great Hall the scaffolding went above the height of the stairs and gallery, to the roof itself. ''They found some dry rot in the beams, Mr. McCallum. The architects have had to scour the country for master carpenters to make the repairs. And of course there're the water lines and the electric wiring. A lot of it was in a dangerous state. We've held off tackling the kitchen and the bathrooms on the ground floor—otherwise there'd have been no way to give you anything to eat, except what was carried from our own kitchen. . . .'' He went on with his explanations as they walked on to the dining hall.

Here Julia gazed with dismay at the scaffolding that also reached to the ceiling. Some of it was swathed in canvas. ''To try to keep the dust off you,'' William Kerr said. ''But we really thought you'd be more comfortable using the housekeeper's room to eat in and the library to sit in—as they haven't gotten around to that yet. You mustn't worry, Mrs. McCallum. We've had all the pictures stored safely, and Sir Niall has had the silver removed to the bank vault. . . .''

"Looks like a bloody mess, doesn't it," Sir Niall said. "Yet, when I heard it was to be started, I knew it would have to go this way, or not at all. These old places . . . one never knows where the end is. I have enough trouble and expense holding my own place together, and it's quite a few hundred years younger than Sinclair. The architect will be here tomorrow to take you through the finer points of it all. But I've climbed up on some of that scaffolding myself, and I'd say what you're doing has come just in time. You don't see the rot until you get up there with a strong electric light. Well, it's your money, McCallum, and good luck to you. You're a braver man than I am.''

Kate and the Kerrs had carried the baggage to their various rooms. Julia and Rod would have the Red Tower Room—Rod had given strict instructions that the magnificent Victorian paneling of the bathroom was to be left intact, as well as the original porcelain fittings with their *fleur-de-lis* pattern. All he wanted was heat and plenty of hot water. Stacia was to have the Culloden Room. Alasdair would have a room next to Janet on the ground floor. All of this Rod had arranged beforehand. It was Jenny who did not know where she was to go. "Oh, Miss," Janet said, "Kate will be sleeping with the Kerrs for the time you are here, so you'll have her room. You'll share the bathroom with Master Alasdair and me, if that suits you.''

"Why, sure . . ." It was the first time Jenny had spoken since they had driven over the bridge and under the portcullis. Usually she was not at a loss for words, but the sight of Sinclair had baffled her. Suddenly it came in a rush. "Well, I've seen *Drop into Danger* about six times, but I didn't expect—well, I didn't expect it to be so *real*. It's sort of . . . bigger, and yet smaller than I expected. Those close-up scenes, Mr. McCallum . . . I can see how difficult they must have been. Imagine, this whole place was a *studio set!*" They had reached the room Jenny would occupy: Kate's room. Julia's mouth dropped a little as she saw it. A carpet of velvety green had been laid over the room's original flagstones. The walls had been replastered and painted a lighter green; there was a sink surrounded by a chintz skirt, there were pretty chintz curtains, a matched bedspread, and a chintz-covered armchair. A tiny antique dressing table stood before the narrow window, from which, through the break between the stable block and the Kerrs' house, it was possible to see a little of the loch. "Oh—isn't it quaint!" Jenny exclaimed. The transformation of Kate's room amazed Julia. She had known nothing of these plans.

"The bathroom's a bit primitive, Jenny, but we've added an electric heater at a safe distance from water—so you wouldn't freeze, or get electrocuted. This part of the house, I can assure you, is always warmer than those grander apartments upstairs. . . ."

"Oh, Mr. McCallum . . . I couldn't complain. Just the thrill of staying in a *real* castle. Wait till I write home. . . ."

Julia was beginning to think that Rod was using even Jenny in his subtle game of publicizing what was happening to Castle Sinclair. The next shock was the housekeeper's room. She had been expecting its familiar comfortable shabbiness, but it also had been transformed. It was a violent and uncomfortable mixture of the Sinclair and McCallum tartans. The carpet and curtains had been woven to the predominantly red pattern of the Sinclair tartan. Even the seats of the dining chairs had been recovered. The walls, like Kate's room, had been freshly replastered and painted. A bright fire was burning in the fireplace. Elaborate crystal decanters, which Julia remembered had always been in cupboards in the dining room, stood filled with whiskey and gin and were on a silver tray on a small and beautiful gateleg table new to that room and as far as Julia could remember, new to the castle. So much had been done without consulting her.

Rod looked at her expectantly. "Better, Princess? A little more comfortable? Next year we'll be living in state in the big rooms. . . ."

Sir Niall stayed for dinner, but only when he was pressed. He seemed to have become a little more hesitant in his manner toward Julia—acknowledging that Rod's was the more proprietorial interest. He filled them in on the news of the district. "Napier died," he said. "Couldn't seem to take much interest in life after he lost his son. The daughter sold off the estate . . . she's married, and living in London; no time for taking care of the place. I think they wanted the money—she married an artist. Prime land. Sold very reasonably. I was very tempted, but I thought I had enough on my hands. Oh—I should have written you. Allan Macpherson died, and Kirsty Macpherson married again. She married a Macdonald—a Macdonald of Clanranald. He has a whiskey distillery over on the Western Isles, but Kirsty wouldn't move there. Can hardly blame her. Her sister, Una— did you ever meet her?—well, she settled for her part in the estate in cash. She's still in California. MacGregor was laid up for part of the winter. Bronchitis . . . ah, none of us getting any younger. How was it at Anscombe? How's the rose garden doing . . . ?'' Jenny had taken Alasdair to have his bath and put him to bed in the room next to hers, which had not yet had its renovation. Julia slipped in to say good-night and kissed his sleepy face. ''Tomorrow you and Princess Cat will have a great time together.''

''Are we back for good now, Mummie?''

''Not for good, Alasdair. But we'll be coming back very often. . . .''

They sat over a Drambuie at the fire, the fatigue of the journey slipping away. ''Nice to be back,'' Stacia said finally. She had been given wine with the meal, and Rod, without asking, had poured her a crème de menthe. ''I hope people are forgetting about the accident with Cat. It *was* an accident.''

''Ah,'' Sir Niall said, ''don't fuss yourself, lass. Accidents happen. You might have been killed yourself—''

''Well, Rod would have killed me if the others hadn't gotten together to stop him—''

Sir Niall rose. ''Well, I'll be bidding you good night, my friends. I've taken enough of your time. Shall I expect you to dinner tomorrow night?—or have you had enough of my company? Kirsty is planning a big 'welcome back' for Sunday night— she said she'd telephone you. Of course, mine is just a simple meal. . . .''

''We'll be there,'' Rod said quickly. ''Thank you.'' The dogs barely stirred from their places by the fire when Sir Niall left. Julia had to force them outside for their night's walk.

Later, when she lay in Rod's arms in the Red Tower Room, with the smell of dust that no amount of canvas could keep out, she said faintly, ''That was McCallum tartan in the house-keeper's room. But your name was—is—McBain.''

She felt his body tense against hers. ''I once told you something in confidence. I trusted you. McCallum is my official name. That's how it's going to stay. Do you think all this bloody clan system had any justice in it? They all took the name of the chieftain who led them into battle—and they were ordered into battle, whether they liked it or not, just because they farmed a little piece of the laird's land. They couldn't read or write. Might as well belong to whatever clan they told you you belonged to—or who your laird was. McCallum—McBain. Maybe McCallum was my mother's name. Who cares? It's really a whole load of nonsense.''

"But you cling to it—all that tartan downstairs.''

He yawned. "Why not? It's amusing, isn't it? No one said I couldn't do it.'' It had long ago struck her that Jamie's brother's name had been Callum. Had Rod appropriated that also?

The summer passed with days of golden splendor and days of slashing rain. The work on the castle continued all around them, the air hideous with the sound of hammering and drilling, and dust all-pervasive. Kirsty Macpherson's husband, Douglas Macdonald, offered them the loan of horses, and in good weather they rode in the forest, or took picnics in favored places. Rod had acquired an old U.S. Army jeep, which took them into places where they might otherwise not have ventured. They spent two weeks at Gleneagles, leaving Alasdair to stay with Sir Niall so he did not have to be parted from Princess Cat. The neighbors who had known the Sinclair family for generations issued invitations to dinner and didn't expect a return of hospitality since it was known that Castle Sinclair was barely habitable. Rod countered by hosting a grand dinner party, with dancing afterward, in the Caledonian Hotel in Inverness. The hotel became private for that evening only, all the rooms being reserved for those who felt like staying the night. Julia could sense the opinion that Rod McCallum was splashing money around like a fool, but she noticed that very few invitations were not accepted—nor was the offer of a room for the night. A lavish buffet breakfast was served the next morning, and those who wished it had champagne. "Well—have to hand it to him. The fellow has a sense of style.''

"Theatrical'' was the reply Julia overheard. "But I must admit I've never known the old Caledonian to look so festive. They say he had the flowers sent up from London. . . .''

Rod's love of order had been outraged by the state of the

walled garden at Sinclair, and two gardeners went on the payroll to put it back in order. "I can't afford them, Rod," Julia said. "Who asked you to? I hired them. They've nothing to do with the farm." Week by week they saw the old paths cleared, the tangle of briars and old roses removed from the rotting trellises, the herbaceous borders dug ready for replanting in the autumn. A landscape gardener was called in to advise on the new planting, the only condition being that he keep to the style and character of the old garden. "Wise to renew the plants," he said to Rod and Julia. "There've been so many improvements in horticulture since this was planted. New varieties that will stand this climate. When this is done, I'd like to dig out all the old daffodils around the edge of the island and replace them. They've been left far too long without lifting and dividing, and they're in poor condition. If that were done, and with the—I must say wonderfully discreet—repairs you're making, this island and castle could become one of the sights of Scotland in the spring." He was calculating how many thousands of bulbs would need to be planted.

"Do it," Rod said. "Send me pictures next spring."

"Next spring will be only the beginning—they'll multiply like weeds."

After that, and many meetings with the architect, Julia had once more tried to protest about the money Rod was spending. "Quit it, Julia," he said sharply. "I never commit to anything I don't know I'm easily able to afford. I'm not the sort of guy who doesn't know where the money's coming from, or where it goes. I know I've got a bit of a reputation for being a tightwad, but that's only because I insist on seeing every bill, checking it out. With big things and small things. Do you think I let Maria and José feed twenty cousins on my grocery bill? No way. When the big money started coming in, I was very cautious. I didn't just turn it over to some accountant and say, 'Take care of it for me.' Some of it went into the stock market; a tiny percentage went into risk ventures, some of which have paid off handsomely. I bought little pieces of real estate on the fringes of Los Angeles through little companies, so no one knew Rod Mc-Callum was buying. I've got plots of land just outside the Palm Springs city boundaries—they're going to be worth a fortune someday. When I wasn't working, I had a hobby of driving around that whole area—the San Fernando Valley, out into the desert—seeing what I could find cheap. These are all 'futures.' A lot of money went into good, sound investments and they throw off a pretty healthy income, apart from my studio salary. Don't mistake me—I'm not pretending to be a financial wizard. I listened to the money men, paid them for their advice. Sometimes I took it, sometimes I didn't. Sort of played it fifty-fifty. Perhaps being a little too cautious. But the millions I made stayed *my* millions. I don't believe in fairy tales. You could say I'm very Scottish in my attitude toward money.''

"Then why are you throwing it into Sinclair? It can never be yours. There aren't any dividends to be paid out of these old stones.''

"I'm aware of it. It's something that amuses me. All through the war, when I was into one picture after another, I didn't spend much money. I built my house—carefully. My first wife left the scene years ago; she had no claims on me. Anne Rayner came only at the end of it. I didn't have very extravagant tastes. I just worked and made money. For a few years I don't think there was an actor in Hollywood making more money than I was. I didn't go in for yachts or fancy cars. I didn't go for fancy women. Anne Rayner came into my life because she wanted to—not because I bought her. You're the only woman I've ever given jewelry to. Perhaps the only one I've thought worth it. . . .''

She kissed him. "You're very sweet at times, Rod. You seem so tough—and yet there's a soft place.''

"Well, maybe you touched the soft place. Don't worry about the castle, Princess. Maybe it's become my hobby . . . like your father's rose garden.''

"My father's rose garden costs nothing by comparison with this. And he's married to a very rich lady.''

"And so am I. I'm married to a very beautiful lady who makes all the work, and the small pictures, and the clawing my way up worthwhile. So perhaps I'm trying to present her with a fairy castle . . . perhaps, in some ways, I want to live up to those millions I put away. I'll soon be forty, Julia. What am I waiting for?''

As if to prove it, he had a Rolls-Royce delivered from London. Stacia was ecstatic, Julia rather dismayed. "Rod—it's not like you at all. What will you do with it—here?''

"Oh, just drive around. It was supposed to be ready when we got to London—but I'm told handmade cars take time. We'll ride back to London in it. It'll stay there until we're ready to use it next summer.''

"I think you've gone mad.''

He shook his head. ''No . . . What's that I remember from the Bible?—about there being a time for everything? Maybe this is the time for me to stop saving everything I can and loosen up a bit. I fought so hard for everything—now I suddenly realize that the money's not there to be counted every day. Some of it is to be spent.''

During the summer Rod had paid for his acting coach, Ernest Wilcox, to come over for a week. The small, rather tired little man, who made a brave effort with his clothes and movements to appear much younger, was entranced by Sinclair. ''How wonderful, Rod, that you've got this. It's so much your image. When it's finished you must let me alert the decorating magazines in the States. They'll all want to photograph it.'' He borrowed overalls and lithely climbed the scaffolding to inspect the work. ''They're doing a first-rate job. After this, it will stand another couple of hundred years.'' He had long conferences with the architect and the landscape gardener. Most of all he savored the library, its shabbiness intact, its bound leather volumes in need of repair. ''There are some very fine first editions tucked away there,'' he observed. Julia kept a fire going in the library all day, since, apart from the housekeeper's room, it was the only place where they could sit. The drawing room had not yet been touched, and there was a perpetual smell of dampness in it. About the housekeeper's room Wilcox said nothing, except to remark to Rod that it was ''very cozy.'' Later he added, with a wink, to Julia when they were alone, ''He went a bit mad with the tartans, didn't he? But on the whole, he's doing a great job. I'm proud of Rod. He was all rough edges when he came to me for voice coaching. But he wanted to learn—well, everything. I gave him all I could. And he's stayed a friend ever since—not ashamed to acknowledge old Ernest Wilcox.''

Stacia had greeted Wilcox's arrival with pleasure. ''Poor child. It was very bad for her after her mother died. I seemed to be the only one she would talk to—and that was not very much. We just went driving around a lot. . . .''

Stacia asked if they could have the jeep, and together they went off picnicking to the places that apparently she liked best. She took him to visit Sir Niall and Kirsty Macpherson.

"Shouldn't have done it without telephoning first," Wilcox protested, "but they were exceedingly civil."

He left after a week. "Mustn't overstay my welcome. Thank you, dear Rod. I will enjoy my week in London. . . ." He bowed and kissed Julia's hand. "What a lovely lady of the castle you make. So much more your place than Beverly Hills. But then, we all go where life sends us, don't we?" To Stacia he said, "I'll be expecting you for lessons as soon as you come back. Remember your breathing exercises. And I expect those plays to be thoroughly read by the time you get back."

"A week in London?" Stacia questioned when he was gone. "Are you paying for a week in London for him—as well as the fare here?"

Rod shrugged. "Why not? He didn't ask for a fancy hotel. No doubt he'll be looking up some old chums, as he calls them. He was born in London, remember."

"I never asked," Stacia said. "Am I really going to have lessons with him when I get back?"

"Since you're bound and determined to get into the movies, you might as well start to acquire some techniques now. He won't steer you wrong. And how about going back to your ballet lessons? Not that you're ever going to be a ballet dancer. But it might teach you to hold your head up. That sideways glance under the lashes is wonderfully sexy in close-up, Stacia, but you have to be taught how to move."

"You do so much for her, Rod," Julia said later. "But I wonder why you make it all seem like a punishment."

"If she's anxious enough, she'll grab at it. And I think she's got enough brains to see what'll help her. Anne was just letting her run wild. Well—I sort of figure that among school and Wilcox and ballet lessons, she'll be so worn out she won't have any energy to go fooling around with guys. Give her a little pride in herself—who knows? She might turn out all right."

She kissed him. "You're a strange, dear, unfathomable man. So afraid to show that you may love someone. I think, for all your fights, that you do care about Stacia. . . ."

He drew her into his arms. "I love you, Princess. I'm just getting used to the feeling. Maybe that makes me a little more generous with Stacia and guys like old Wilcox. I've given him presents before—clothes, a watch he can flash around. But nothing in the annals of Hollywood will ever come up to the visit to a Scottish castle—the way he'll tell it. By the time the story goes around Hollywood, it'll turn out to have been like an invitation to stay with the Royal Family at Balmoral.''

They left Sinclair in late August, but early frosts had already touched the forest trees, dappling them with a light color. Alasdair complained that they wouldn't be traveling by train with Princess Cat but driving the Rolls. ''What are we supposed to do, kid—shove her in the trunk? As it is, half our luggage is going by train. Princess Cat will be in London long before we will. We have to have an overnight break somewhere—York, isn't it, Julia? For Stacia and the kid to look at the Walls and the York Minster. We have two nights in Lady Seymour's house in London, and Princess Cat will be all nicely settled back in her stall with all her friends.'' His voice hardened a little, as it always did when he was challenged. ''Or maybe you want to ride in the freight car with her? Suit yourself. I'm sure Janet will make sandwiches for you. . . . Okay, don't look like that. I was only kidding. . . .''

''But I wasn't kidding,'' he said later to Julia. ''It would do him good to bunk down on the straw with Cat, with a tag around his neck to tell the guard where he was headed. I don't want him to get the notion that the world is made of money and that it's to be spent for his benefit. It's taken me long enough to rattle that idea out of Stacia's head.''

They stayed two nights at Luisa's house in Wilton Crescent and then went down to Anscombe. The run of *Arms and the Man* finished, but it was settled that Michael, and possibly more of the cast, would go to New York to open it in October. ''The unions are being very sticky,'' Michael said. ''They'll take me—but not the whole company. Do you think you could come to New York for the opening?''

''We'll be filming,'' Rod answered swiftly. ''We're due to start in September. And there are a few location shots—or so they tell me. I haven't even seen the script yet. It's supposed to be something dreamed up just for Julia and me. And she's been put on a two-year contract for the biggest salary any newcomer to Hollywood has ever been given. I wouldn't agree to any of these dirt-cheap deals they make for the Johnny-come-latelys. Most people have forgotten that Oscar Julia has—but I don't let our agent or the studio bosses forget it. They're getting quality, and they'd better not forget it.''

"I must say, Julia, you have a determined man to fight for you.''

"My privilege,'' Rod said. Alasdair bade a tearful good-bye to Princess Cat, being pleased, though, that he had been able to demonstrate his riding skills to Johnny, who was friend as well as rival. They went back to London, where Luisa gave a farewell party at Wilton Crescent to which some members of the press were discreetly invited, which pleased Rod. D.D. was there. He had a slightly worried frown when he found a few minutes to talk to Julia. "I do hope this script is *good,* darling. It's so terribly important, since it's such a long time since you made a film. I didn't have much of an opinion of *Drop into Danger,* and I wonder if Rod is really a good judge of a script. Of course, the studio is exploiting your marriage—and the publicity. They'd be mad if they didn't. But I worry. . . . If I could just have seen it before it went into production . . .''

"Don't worry, D.D. Rod only wants what is best for me.''

"I don't doubt it for a second. But I wonder . . . well, never mind. I am glad you are back in films. I wish I could look after you as I once did. But marriage is good for you . . . even though it takes you so far away.''

Connie and Ken attended, Connie radiant and proud as she told Julia of Ken's recent promotion at the Treasury. "He's small fry yet, but he's made the grade younger than is usual. The extra money is useful, too. . . .'' She laughed. "Of course, we'll never be rich. Civil Servants don't get rich.'' She was wearing a dress Alex had sent. "Thank God for Alex's generosity. I get such fancy things from her I'm able to put all our clothing coupons into the essentials. But she is a dear . . . there are always things for the children, and socks and so on for Ken. And the food packages still come . . . and are needed.'' She looked at the loaded buffet table. "I don't know how Luisa manages all these wonderful spreads. . . . And she always has a package ready for me when we leave. Sometimes I think Ken would like to refuse. His pride is a little bit hurt, as if she's implying he can't provide for us. But then she always says something like, 'The chocolates are for your mother, and I thought your father might enjoy the wine . . . it's from my vineyard,' and he feels he has to accept. We're building on two more rooms. Mr. Warren has said Ken must have his own study. I swear before he's finished Mr. Warren will have that place the size of the house that was bombed. I don't think he scruples to deal on the black market for the materials—his 'contacts,' as he calls them. Of course, all the effort is for Mrs. Warren. He wants everything she had when she was young. And she just sits there and says, 'Yes, dear. Thank you, dear.' ''

"Don't you sometimes wish you had your own house?''

Connie looked faintly shocked. "But Ken—the family—are all they have in the world. Mrs. Warren worships the children. At any rate, what Mr. Warren would do is build another house on the grounds. It's far more economical if we all stay together. We manage so much better with food and heating. . . . I don't mind. Really, Julia, it's far easier to run one house than two. Mrs. Warren never interferes with what decisions I make. She just says, 'Yes, dear,' the way she does to Mr. Warren.''

"I hope,'' Julia said, "you won't find in a few years that you are giving your whole life to two elderly people—'' She stopped when she saw the closed, almost angry look come to Connie's usually serene face.

"We'll face that when we come to it. Until Rod came along you were willing to bury yourself in that wretched castle until Alasdair was old enough to take it over. Now, if ever I saw *waste*, that was it. Even if Rod does make it the most comfortable castle in the kingdom, you're still saddled with a monster. I wouldn't swap my little piece of domesticity for all your grandeur. I know Ken and I seem so *ordinary* by comparison to all this.'' She waved her hand to indicate the beautifully furnished rooms, the smartly dressed guests, the good food, the famous faces. "Do you know what I think? . . . I think we're a jolly sight happier than most people here. At least we know who we are and where we're going.''

For the first time she could remember, Julia saw her sister turn from her in what was almost a gesture of anger. She stood quietly for a moment, surveying the scene, trying to see it through Connie's eyes. Was the noise just a little frenetic? The talk was mostly, she knew, about business—either show business, or the business of getting ahead in the world, the world in which there was no time for mere social pleasantries. Every minute of it counted. No time to waste. Some of them, she thought, even the famous ones, might even be wondering if next month's rent check would bounce. That fear would never enter Connie's life, and she knew it. There was such rocklike security in Connie's world that Julia experienced a moment of fierce envy. She glanced down at the rings on her fingers, the expensive Hollywood dress she wore; Connie did not even remotely desire such things. She had no fears. She would not worry when the first lines appeared around her eyes, when the gray appeared in her hair. She would always be beautiful, and she would always be loved by Ken. Julia realized it was an experience she herself would never know.

Alex came to New York to meet them. "Elliot couldn't get away. He wishes you'd come down to Virginia for a few days."

"We're starting a film," Rod said. "You know that."

Alex shrugged. "Well . . . okay. So I'd better do an interview and have it ready to file when the picture's released. What's it about? What's it called?"

"We don't know," Julia answered. "Better save the interview until it's finished and we do know what it's about. Special starring vehicle for me, courtesy of Worldwide. For the first time I play a lead role. Of course, they're betting on Rod to carry the film. . . ."

A flicker of doubt crossed Alex's face. "Well, good luck. Tell you what—we'll make a deal. You give me the first exclusive interview when it's made, and I'll see it's carried all through the Forster newspapers. Elliot would go for that, although it's rank nepotism. But it would make great copy—especially as I could say I was your sister. . . ."

Rod was smiling at last. "It's a deal. You'll come to Hollywood."

"Naturally . . . I was wondering when you were going to ask us. It would suit very well if the film happened to get finished around January. It would be bliss to get a few weeks in the sun at that time of year. I'm going to have a fine time covering Father's opening on Broadway. I understand Luisa's going to give one of her celebrated bashes for the opening. Aren't I lucky to be related to such famous people?" She smiled and winked at them. Then she added, "How's Connie?"

"Radiant," Julia said. "Very grateful for all you send to the family, Alex. But I suspect she would manage very well even if it weren't forthcoming."

"Dull," Rod said. "Ordinary. No ambition. I haven't the faintest notion what Ken does in life. Real Civil Service. If the wallpaper were gray, he'd vanish into it."

"People like Ken," Alex said, "usually end up with a knight-hood and a good pension."

"Big deal—if that's what he wants."

For the first time, during the tea they were having in the McCallum suite in the hotel—except to thank Alex politely for the silk scarf she had brought her—Stacia spoke. "She'll be better off than any of you—just wait and see."

Rod turned to her, almost in anger. "Better off? That guy will never have any real money."

"She'll be happier," Stacia said, then lapsed again into silence.

Chapter Ten

I

THEY FLEW BACK to Los Angeles—more and more people were now using the quicker means of transportation. "Thank God," Stacia said, "we don't have to go through the train journey again. I always felt like a bag of bones rattling together."

Alex, who had come to see them off, said coolly, "You don't look in the least like a bag of bones to me. I wish I could pretend that every man in this airport isn't staring at you. I think some of the ones on your flight are praying they get the seat beside you. . . ."

"They didn't," Rod said. "She is next to Alasdair."

For all her welcoming the plane instead of the train, Stacia looked rather strained as they took off; beside her, Alasdair was bubbling with excitement at his first flight. By the end of it, with the refueling stops, he was exhausted. Jenny carried him up to bed as soon as they arrived at the Beverly Hills house.

Neatly bound copies of the film script were waiting. "Better take a day off before reading it. It will seem better then," Rod said. "By the way, did you notice your paychecks in the mail?"

"I don't remember ever signing a contract."

"I signed it for you. Don't you remember you gave me your power of attorney?"

"I did?" She remembered well enough. It had seemed an innocuous enough document at the time, although she had pondered it. But not to have signed it would have been to slight and anger Rod. She had put very real power in his hands. But they had proved very capable, very generous hands. "Yes—that's right." She looked at the paychecks. "And these are wonderful!'' She smiled, but the unease persisted. Why be uneasy?—hadn't he given her far more, a half share in all his holdings? And she now realized how much he valued them because of the hard work they represented. He had taken on the responsibility of her child. It had been a gesture that most women would have been happy to accept. She thought of Connie's willing acquiescence to Ken's wishes. But what would Alex have done? Somehow she thought that Alex would have waited and thought a great deal before she signed papers, and she would never have signed what she hadn't properly read. What, in those first heady days of kisses and lovemaking and the sweet scent of flowers in this house, had she signed away?

When she read the script, Julia was doubtful that they should make the film at all. Rod brushed her worries aside. ''Oh, hell, Julia, all movie scripts read like horse—Well, they're lousy on the first reading. Look, the studio's had four of its highest-paid writers working on it.''

''I think that's the trouble. They may be highly paid, but it reads as if it's been put together by a committee. And it's too much like *Drop into Danger.*'' It was the story of an American airman who had escaped from a prisoner-of-war camp, passed along the French underground network, and then been stopped short at a point when the next ''safe house'' had been discovered, and those who resisted the German rulers had either been sent to concentration camps or executed. Julia, who played the role of a young French widow who ran the farm where the American sheltered, did not know the stage beyond the one to which she was expected to deliver him. For the sake of security, each unit knew as little of the total network as possible, or torture could bring down the whole system. Week after week she hid the airman, wondering when the Germans might come and search the house thoroughly, discover the airman, send him back to the prison camp, and send her to a concentration camp. She had two German officers billeted on her, and she cooked for and looked after their needs while feeding and caring for the American, who lived and slept in the specially excavated part of the cellar hidden behind a row of wine butts. Inevitably they would fall in love. There were some good scenes where Julia was to take him out into the fields on the darkest nights so he could get some fresh air and exercise. ''I don't even get to see the stars,'' he would say. Finally the broken link in the network was reestablished, and he left her for a safe house on the way to the Spanish border, not knowing that she was pregnant. He made a promise to return to her when the war was over, but he was recaptured when the next safe house proved to be known to the Germans, and an ambush set. The last two shots were of Julia being pushed aboard a cattle car on the way to a concentration camp, and Rod being placed in solitary confinement in the prison camp from which he had escaped.

Again, Julia thought, the script had the claustrophobic feeling of *Drop into Danger,* the scenes that Rod couldn't handle with the ease of a born actor. He would be at his best in the early stages of the film, the life at the Fighter Command station in England, the rendezvous with the bombers as they head toward Germany, the dogfight when he is shot down, the escape scenes. She hoped he had learned enough to be able to handle the scenes when they whispered to each other in the cellar, in near-darkness, with the German officers overhead; and the dark, rain-sodden nights when she had smuggled him out of the farmhouse and they walked the fields so he could have exercise, fearing German patrols or informers each step of the way. It could be that she would have to carry many of those scenes herself, and she guessed the writers had counted on that.

"It'll work," Rod said. "A few changes here and there. We've got a good director. Hank Humphries is one of the best. A real easy guy to get along with—ready to listen if you don't feel something is right."

"I should speak French sometimes," Julia complained. "All this talking with broken accents in English is mad. I *do* speak French—after all, my mother grew up in France."

This annoyed Rod. "Oh, hell, Julia—we've been playing French and Germans and Italians and Japanese with broken accents since the movies started. Who'd understand you if you spoke French? This isn't a little art-house movie. It's meant for mass circulation. It's meant for every movie house in the World-wide network. We're doing the location shots in Canada—over toward the East Coast—the French part."

"Well, we should get some good broken French accents there," she said tartly.

She learned how movies were made in Hollywood—mostly on the huge sound stages where, it seemed, everything could be

faked. They had all the facilities that Rod had lacked at Castle
Sinclair: The dogfight scene, in which he was shot down, was
taken from old film clips of the real thing; the prisoner-of-war
camp had been used, with some changes, in a dozen other movies, and it was on the back lot. She wondered why they bothered
to go all the way to eastern Canada for the outdoor scenes, except that the trees and hedges and fences looked different from
California. "Wouldn't it be simpler to go to France?" she asked.

"Union problems, Julia," Hank Humphries answered her.
"We'd have to pay an arm and a leg to get our own crews over
there, and even then every one of them would be doubled by
one of their own guys. We'd be paying for two teams . . . as
well as taking a lot more time on the travel bit. Time is money,
Julia. You know that. If I run overtime, I run over budget. The
Big Bosses don't look kindly on running over budget unless they
know they've got a real big box-office movie on their hands.
They're not quite sure of this one. . . . But, I'll tell you, Julia—
you're one of the best actresses I've ever directed. I guess it's in
the blood. You might even manage Best Actress for this—but I
wonder how Rod would take that. He's not likely to get the Best
Actor Award. We hear rumors he's going to be cast in one of
the big Bible epics. The Bible's big business now."

"What's he going to be—the Christian or the lion?"

He touched her shoulder lightly. "Hey . . . hey . . . what's
the matter? You're not happy with the movie?"

"No, I'm not happy. I'm not happy being told which film I'll
play in—no matter what I think. I used to be able to pick my
films."

His expression grew cold. "Well, Julia, this is Hollywood.
One day you may be a big star, but you'll still be a contract
player. You'll go into whatever movies the Boss say's you'll go
into—or you'll go on suspension. Suspension means no work—
and no pay. Think about it."

The location shots were filmed in North Carolina because
Canada was under its winter blanket of snow—no one had been
sure when the film would finally be shot. "I wonder why they
didn't just bring some nice French trees and hedges here, along
with a Normandy farmhouse, and we wouldn't have had to
move," Julia said to Rod.

"Princess, take it easy. This is how films are made. Your
father could have told you. . . . What we did at Sinclair was

both an extravagance and an economy. I just bet everything on our being able to do it all on that location. On the snow coming in time. And it paid off. It *did* look better than if we'd done it on the back lot. But you just don't find the perfect location every time. You know, the studio did send a second unit to France for some of the background shots. We just didn't have to stand there and act in front of all their houses and trees, that's all." He bent to kiss her. "Be patient. This is the rough and tumble. Don't tell me your mother didn't put up with lousy concert halls, untuned pianos, and conductors she didn't respect. Your father's done the same. You work *with* the grain, Princess, not against it. And you'll come out of this like a bright penny."

They were finished filming in January, as was planned. Hank Humphries declared himself satisfied with the takes and set to work in the cutting room. There were some gestures of approval from Morris Meadows. "I hear you came out real good, Julia," he said paternalistically.

Alex came for her promised visit, and to Julia's surprise, brought Elliot with her. "I just forced him to take a break. Things can run themselves for a few weeks without him. We might even go on to Honolulu. . . ." She smiled as she said this. She toured and admired the house, and Rod glowed with pleasure. Elliot made a careful study of Rod's Remingtons and congratulated him on a fine collection. Alasdair was delighted to see them. Julia realized that in all his recent traveling, Alex and Elliot represented being halfway "home." But any mention of "home" other than Beverly Hills obviously irritated Rod.

Alex was less than pleased by the party Rod had planned for the second night of their visit. "We really wanted a rest . . . Washington is nothing but parties—going to them and giving them."

"Well, this won't take more than a few hours of your time," Rod said stiffly, "and it would give Julia and me a lot of pleasure to introduce our friends. . . ." There weren't really many friends, Julia thought, just the people it was important to know in the movie capital. She could see how much it pleased Rod to be able to associate himself with the power of the Forster newspapers. He had a very special guest whom not even Hollywood could command, and he intended to display him.

But Julia noticed that before eleven o'clock Elliot was nowhere to be seen among the crowd. She drew Alex to the far side of the loggia, away from the music and the bar. "Alex, is something wrong with Elliot? He's seemed a bit—well, quiet since he arrived."

Alex looked around her, made sure no one was within hearing distance, and took the time to light a cigarette before she replied. "We *hope* there's nothing seriously wrong with Elliot. The fact is, a month ago he had a mild heart attack. At home—during the night. Of course, I got him to the hospital immediately. We managed to keep it out of the newspapers. To anyone who knew he was in the hospital we said it was a scheduled hernia operation and that he'd be taking things easy for a few weeks. Forster Newspapers is a very tightly held company—it never went public, so we didn't have to worry about stockholders panicking and dumping shares. But it certainly scared the hell out of me! Even in those worst times, when I thought Elliot and I could never get married, I didn't realize how much I needed him. I seem to be busy enough with other things, but he's become my total life. I could drop everything and live just for him. In those first hours I was willing to make any bargain with the Almighty that was offered. I thought it was bad enough that I couldn't have children—but if I lost Elliot . . ." She went to the nearest flowerpot and carefully ground out her cigarette in the damp soil. "He's been told he's to take it easy. Avoid stress. I could have died laughing if I hadn't been so near to tears. Avoid stress. Stress is a newspaperman's lifeblood. I ought to know. I married two of them. Even though he's proprietor and not editor of any of his papers, he lives on every breaking news story. He's never off the telephone to the editors. I think he drives half of them crazy, and he's lost one or two good ones because he can't keep his hands out of what rightly is their business. But that's Elliot, and he'll never change—or I don't believe he can change." She stared out at the gardens to which the twisting paths, lighted at intervals, gave an air of mystery and enchantment. Julia noted her clenched fists. "I don't know how to make him change. I can't lose him, Julia. I can't. But I feel so helpless. . . . 'One day at a time,' I tell myself. Alter little things here and there." She turned back to the light, and Julia saw that her lips trembled. "He must have been feeling tired, or he wouldn't have left the party. One part of me wants to run up to see if he's all right, and yet I know he'll be furious if he knows I've left the party.

People would notice. Don't say anything to him, Julia. Don't tell Rod. Just don't say anything. And let's try to keep the pace as easy as we can without making it seem obvious. . . .''

"Would he agree to something that's less than simple—even primitive? There's Rod's little ranch place up in the mountains. There isn't even a telephone. We depend on our neighbors—the Russells—for just about everything. But he could ride. . . .''

Alex seemed to clutch at the idea. "Yes—that's what we'll do. That's what he needs. Peace, quiet, sun . . .''

They had two weeks there. With some reluctance, Julia left Alasdair alone with Jenny; Stacia had to stay in school. Rod was uneasy about the arrangement, and he remained at the ranch only a few days. He pleaded the need to consult with Hank Humphries, and to sound out Morris Meadows about the next picture. "Truth is,'' he said to Julia, "I'm nervous about leaving those two kids alone in the house. How do we know Stacia won't start giving wild parties? Jenny's too young to handle Stacia—I *knew* we should have gotten one of those English nannies.''

"There isn't a nanny alive who could handle Stacia,'' Julia answered. She glossed over the reasons for staying on at the ranch. "Alex is worn out. She's been told to rest.''

"She could rest just as well by the pool at the house. . . . Oh, well, if this is what she wants, let it go. I never thought a man like Elliot Forster could go for a place like this—I mean, he's what people think of as an aristocrat in America. I never thought this rundown little place would be his style.''

"It obviously is. People like Elliot do enjoy simple things.''

He relaxed and smiled. "Well, as long as you can manage . . . I must say, you and Alex are better at cooking than I thought. That old stove . . .''

"You didn't see the stove we once managed on at Sinclair. Even at Anscombe, it wasn't exactly luxury.''

"Well, then watch out for the rattlesnakes. The Russells will help you any way they can. . . .''

Elliot spent a lot of his time just sitting on the porch staring at the outlines of the distant mountains; he read from the pile of books he had brought with him. Every day the three of them rode the horses Rod had stabled at the Russell ranch. Every day they picked up the newspapers from the box at the entrance to the ranch, two miles away. They went down into Santa Barbara for groceries. Alex refused to let Elliot get in touch with friends he had in the town. By now he must have been aware that Julia knew Alex was protecting him, but he never made any reference to it. The days were warm and sunny, the nights crisp and sharp, the stars burning in the clear skies; the silence was broken only by the occasional howl of a coyote. They stayed longer than the planned two weeks. Julia telephoned from the Russells for news of the household in Beverly Hills. "Stay," Rod urged. "Just as long as you're all enjoying yourselves there."

Alex confided to Julia, "I don't know whether to be pleased or frightened. It's almost unthinkable for Elliot to go for this length of time without telephoning around to his editors, or firing off telegrams to them. . . ."

They returned to Beverly Hills, and Rod was annoyed when Julia refused all invitations to entertain her sister and Elliot. "People will just think you think they're not good enough for the great Elliot Forster."

"Let them think what they want. Alex has been ordered to rest."

"From where I sit, it looks more like Elliot who needs the rest. But I did hear him giving hell to someone in Washington this morning—something about some story one of his papers ran. I didn't mean to listen—but brother, when that man gets mad, he doesn't really need a telephone. He'd just have to put his head out the window and shout in the direction of Washington."

Alex and Elliot left a week later, to make the slow journey back East by train. "He'll be off the train at every stop, telephoning someone or shooting off wires to them," Rod said as they drove back to the house. "Well, that's that. They've been here almost a month, and all that happened was one lousy party."

"It wasn't lousy, and one party was quite enough. They don't need parties."

"Guess you're right, Princess. When I was trying to make it, getting invited to a good party was what I lived for. Showed I'd made the grade. I suppose it never occurred to me that there are people who think parties and dinners are just another chore."

"In their world, it is. A quiet evening is a luxury."

"Well, if that's so, we sure heaped them with luxuries. . . ."

II

JULIA LATER REMEMBERED those weeks at the ranch as the last peaceful ones of her life. Rod had not entirely been making excuses when he had said he had to confer with Morris Meadows about the film, which was called *The Betrayal*. Some of the studio executives protested that the French widow becoming pregnant by the American airman, even their being lovers, would not be acceptable to the Hays office, which ruled on all matters of morality in the films that Hollywood turned out. Part of it would have to be reshot. Rod put up vehement protests, even at one time refusing to return to the film or to allow Julia to do so. Julia had her own feelings of resentment and misgiving—she felt that the consummated love between the young widow and the airman was the strength of the story line. In wartime, she said to Rod, people had not waited to be sure that all would turn out well—they had taken love and happiness where they could find it and did not count the consequences.

"Of course they didn't!" Rod shouted. "They never have—war or no war. Do you realize that in this town they can't shoot a film in which a husband, fully clothed in pajamas, sits on his wife's bed without keeping one foot on the floor? It's all a load of phony claptrap, but Hollywood must be seen to be holier than thou . . . don't offend the Legion of Decency. Don't bring a twitter to the little old ladies of Dubuque."

"Those scenes in the cellar don't make sense unless we make love."

"Well—they're saying we have to reshoot them, or the film won't be released."

"Well, why did they pass the script in the first place?"

"Perhaps no one read the same script."

So they did reshoot the offending scenes, and the weaknesses of Rod's acting when he was in an intimate scene seemed doubled to Julia because his barely concealed resentment came strongly to the surface and communicated itself to her. They were more like antagonists than potential lovers. Hank Humphries realized it as he watched the daily rushes. Other scenes had to be rewritten and reshot, so that it began to seem that the young widow truly did resent the presence of the airman, resented the danger in which he placed her, resented almost ev-erything about him. What had been intended as a love story became a protracted battle; more writers were called in, more scenes were written and shot. In the end, the young widow's refusal to betray those around her, the next in the line of escape, those who had sent the American airman to her house of refuge, the torture she endured seemed to be done in the name of patri-otism only—and nothing for love. The scenes of her being pushed onto the cattle car on the way to a concentration camp, of the American being thrust into solitary confinement were only the consequences of war. The film faded out with no hope that the two would ever meet again or would have any desire to do so. It was a downbeat ending that only a great script and great actors might have made acceptable to audiences of the time. It did not go down well with the executives of Worldwide Pictures.

"It's turned into a dog" was Morris Meadows' comment. Julia privately agreed with him. The mixture of the scenes when she and the airman were involved in a passionate love affair, and those when she resented his presence, his overlong stay in the farmhouse, were ludicrously ill-matched. To save it, the whole film would have had to be rewritten and reshot, and Worldwide would not accept that idea. They had no intention of throwing good money after bad, as Morris Meadows put it. "We'll release it with some glossy advertising and hope McCallum's name will pull it through." The word, although Hank Humphries tried to keep it from Julia, was that Morris Meadows' opinion was that she was the cause of the film's failure. "Too damn stiff and British. We should have put Anne Rayner's kid into the part. That would have made great publicity. Should have thought of it. . . ."

Through the grapevine at Beverly Hills High, this opinion, embroidered, added to, elaborated, came to Stacia. Her mood turned from one of trying to please Rod to one of smoldering resentment. She had been cheated of a lead role that might have made her career in Hollywood. And it had been Julia who had denied her that role. Julia could almost sympathize with the girl if she had not been so sick at heart herself. In the rewritten version, the smoldering mood, which came naturally to Stacia, would have been excellently conveyed. Stacia was not a young woman of tenderness but repressed sexuality. She might well have perfectly conveyed the emotions of the young widow by simply acting herself. The role she might have played to perfection became, in her mind, one that had been stolen from her. She made little attempt to hide her feelings.

"So how long will it be, Your Majesty," she said to Rod one night over dinner, "before I'm allowed off the string? I know you can do anything you want until I'm twenty-one. Are you going to keep me tied down until then, or am I going to be given a chance?"

"Shut up, you ungrateful little bitch! You'll get your chance when the time comes. Don't start biting the hand that feeds you. Oh, sure, you could play the part of a tart or a trollop very well. Just like your mother."

"You didn't mind marrying my mother—no matter what you thought of her. Tart or trollop . . . she was famous. It was good publicity for you *then!* And you enjoyed every minute of boozing with her, and getting high together, and acting like wild animals. If it hadn't been my mother who went into the ravine that night, it would have been you. You were smashing her up . . . and she just ran. Remember—I was here."

His answer was to stand up and strike her across the face. "Go to your room, you little slut. You're made of lies. You live on lies. Don't mention your mother to me again. Anne Rayner is dead."

Holding her mouth and cheek, Stacia pushed back her chair with such violence that it crashed to the floor. "Anne Rayner will not be dead as long as I'm alive."

At the doorway she turned and looked at him again. "Well, you married your Ice Princess. You married the Castle. You married the Seymours and the Forster newspapers. You made lots of money, but until you got *her*"—Stacia's wild gesture toward Julia held more than menace—"you didn't think you had any *quality.* Never mind that being married to my mother made you one of the most envied men in the world. She was dirt to you—my mother. A tramp. I heard you call her that a hundred times. Oh, but you made money out of *her,* too, didn't you. Fabulous publicity. All the poor little slobs who went to see your lousy movies just to see who had been lucky enough to marry Anne Rayner. And then you killed her. You killed her with the drink and the dope. And you got the Ice Princess. . . ."

* * *

Julia knew that when Rod hit Stacia he had been drunk. During the reshooting necessary on *The Betrayal* he had often drunk too much at night, and always, miraculously, seemed to have recovered fully by the next morning, ready for their early drive to the studio, his lines, such as they were, studied and learned as the studio chauffeur drove them. But now, with the film over and the reaction of the studio so cool, the empty days seemed to bring Rod no occupation except to sit by the pool, slowly, endlessly sipping at a drink that José was called on to refresh whenever Rod desired it. A vacancy of mind seemed to fall on him; he seemed very far away, totally uninterested in what went on around him. He hardly seemed to notice Julia or Stacia, and Alasdair's presence seemed to annoy him. He barely seemed aware of Julia in his bed. She had been hurt by Stacia's dubbing her "the Ice Princess," but now it was Rod who seemed to do the rebuffing. She would have come gladly to him if he had seemed to want her. When they did make love, it was a hurried affair, with little tenderness involved, something Rod wanted over and done with, almost passionless. Every morning he slept late, coming downstairs only to swim a few lazy laps before calling José for his prelunch drinks. He read the mail that arrived, passed some over to Jenny to answer, phoned Phil Westin, and in the afternoons seemed to slip into a somnolence Julia had never witnessed before. Only if they were dining out or having guests to dinner did he show any interest in what was going on around him. On those days he hardly drank at all and was the usual charming, attractive man Hollywood· had always known.

"Watch it," Stacia said once to Julia. "He's hitting it again."

"Yes . . . he's drinking too much. But he'll come out of it."

Stacia gave her a look of near-contempt, as if despising her ignorance. "Drinking? That wouldn't affect him much. He's got two hollow legs. He was always much better able to handle it than my mother. It's drugs. . . . You mean you haven't noticed? Jeez—how dumb can you be? He's in a daze most of the time—until he's got to go out to dinner, or there are people coming. Notice how he perks up? My mom could never take it quite that way."

Julia didn't want to believe her. But the pattern that Stacia, wiser and more knowledgeable in the ways of this strange culture, pointed to was discernible. Julia began to fear what she saw.

"Where do they come from . . . the drugs?"

Stacia shrugged. "They're around. They've always been around. Just as long as nothing gets into the press, the studios don't care. Present a good face to the public—they can't control *everything* anyone does in their own time. Have you noticed how often Ernie Wilcox is visiting these days? Ernie has contacts. . . ."

Julia was startled. The pleasant little man, who so loved books, who loved to talk to her about her father's background in Shakespearean theater, who had taught Rod most of what he knew, made him wish to know more—could such evil exist beside such intelligence? She had reason to doubt what Stacia implied, but she was acutely aware that Ernest Wilcox had been the only person Rod had particularly invited to visit Castle Sinclair. There was so much she didn't know, but things she would have to find out.

Rod's mood hit a low point when he read the script of the next film Worldwide proposed for him. "Damn!—it's nothing but another stinking horse opera. Not a quality one—just the sort of thing I used to do before the war. Except this time I get most of the lines!"

Julia read it and experienced the same misgivings. "Well, if they could get John Ford to direct it—"

"No such luck. If John Ford would direct it, John Wayne would star in it." Rod demanded rewrites, and the studio fell in with his wishes. But the script did not improve as it went the rounds of the salaried writers. In the end, it hardly seemed to make sense to Julia; she could only hope that the photography and the location shots would compensate for the deficiencies. It was, in fact, the sort of movie in which Rod showed to best advantage, where the power of his presence, his superb horsemanship, his startling good looks could carry almost banal scenes. But his mind was fixed on the fact that he was back making a Western, and although he was the star, it felt to him that he was being pushed back to the humble parts he had once played. He demanded more rewrites—or a totally different script.

"Who do you think you've turned into—Cary Grant?" was the brutal remark of Morris Meadows that Rod reported to Julia. But they agreed to more rewrites.

In April *The Betrayal* was released to almost universally bad notices. They were no worse than Julia had expected, but still they hurt. It was to have been the picture that would have established her in a leading role, but the mismatching of the new takes with the old, the patching together of the plot made the film at times pointless and without meaning, with the two stars hardly seeming to know from one scene to the next what relationship they had to each other.

Alex telephoned from Washington. "I'm sorry, Julia, but the syndicated review that's going out in the Forster newspapers isn't good. Elliot will fight to the death with an editor if he doesn't agree with his political line, but he never interferes with a critic. He can order all kinds of articles about you and Rod, if that would be any help, but he's never muzzled any of his critics. I'm sorry, Julia. . . . I can, if you want, ask him just not to have any review of it appear—"

"Don't!" Julia answered sharply. "We have to take what comes. The film's pretty awful. We both know that. But if it were ignored by the critics, it would be worse."

Rod was enraged by the reviews, enraged with the studio, enraged with life. It was the kind of anger that burned beneath the surface of his silent moodiness. He barely spoke to anyone in the household. Julia noticed that Alasdair kept out of his way and that Stacia did not bring home any of her friends from school. A pall of rage and bitterness hung over the house. No one telephoned to invite them to dinner or a party. "Well—that's the way of this town. If it had been a hit, there wouldn't have been enough nights in the week to take in all the parties we'd be invited to. Rotten, stinking hypocrites. I wonder why I ever thought any of them were important. . . ."

The only one who seemed to be there almost constantly was Ernest Wilcox. "Don't think anything of it, old chum," he said. "You've come a long way, and the old green-eyed monster never dies. By the time the next one comes out, they'll be back licking your boots."

"Don't bet on it," Rod said sourly. But he seemed to welcome the little man's appearance in the evening when his coaching classes were over. He sipped Scotch with Rod beside the pool as the shadows lengthened and the lights in the garden were turned on. Julia knew that without much pressing he would stay for dinner with them, and dinner must be served in the formal dining room, with gleaming crystal and lighted candles. Rod seemed to need this proof of his success, his possessions. He liked Julia to dress up in the evenings, to wear her jewelry. But in bed he left her alone, falling almost at once into a deep sleep, as if she had played her role for the evening and was of no further use to him. She wondered what mixture of drugs could make him so frenetic and then so somnolent. She no longer doubted what Stacia had said about him taking drugs. She had begun to recognize the signs: the sudden elevation of mood, then the plunge into deep depression.

"Rod . . ." she ventured once, "you don't look well. Maybe you should see a doctor."

"What do you mean, I don't look well? I'm fine. And Dr. Sam sees me at least every two weeks, and what he gives me makes me feel just fine. . . ."

"You're seeing Dr. Fields? Why? What's wrong?"

"Nothing. I just drop in for a talk. He takes my blood pressure. He's got half of Hollywood beating on his door. He knows all the dirt. He knows exactly what it's like to be in my position. He's seen it all before. Smart old bird. Does me good to talk to him . . . we don't say much. Just sort of pass the time of day. But he never forgets to send his bills. His time of day is pretty expensive. . . ."

"Can't you talk to me?"

"Isn't the same thing. You don't know the things he knows. In this town, lady, you're a babe in the woods. You don't know the half of it, and you need me to keep you from knowing even that much. You really weren't made for Hollywood, Julia. You know that?"

"You'd like me to go. Is that what you're saying, Rod?"

"Who said anything about going? When it's time for you to go, I'll *tell* you. What do you want now? To have Hollywood laughing its head off because Rod McCallum can't keep his high-and-mighty English wife in order? If I could get Anne Rayner, I could get anyone—and don't forget it."

"But you didn't keep her, did you?"

That was the first time he struck her. She slipped on the polished tile floor and her head struck one of the legs of the heavy Spanish-style wooden chairs. He didn't move to assist her when she struggled to rise. Her face stung with the pain of the blow; she could taste blood on her tongue. Slowly she pulled herself to her feet, and moved to a sofa and lowered herself carefully onto it.

"I hope you didn't mean that. I hope it's just because you're drunk and—what do you call it?—'hopped up' to your eyes. What drug is it, Rod? Heroin? Whatever it is, it's stronger than marijuana—''

"So you've noticed, have you? Well, you should try it sometime. Might make you relax. Might make you thaw a little. Stacia wasn't so far out when she called you the Ice Princess."

"You want me to start taking drugs so I'll end up like Anne Rayner? Rod, I'm not going to have my baby born a drug addict."

"Baby? What baby? *Whose* baby?"

"Whose baby would you think it is? It can only be your baby."

"Baby! Since when? I've hardly touched you—''

"And well I know it. Just enough to make me pregnant. Since February. Of course, I wouldn't expect you to notice. You don't notice anything these days. Well, maybe there won't be a baby. Maybe you knocked me hard enough. I'll let you know if there's a miscarriage."

"The hell you will. You should have told me long ago."

"What difference would it make? Don't you want your baby?"

"I don't know," he said slowly. "I really don't know. Perhaps you should get rid of it. This isn't the time—''

"I'll get rid of you before I get rid of my baby."

"So it's *your* baby now. I had nothing to do with it."

"As far as you were conscious of it, you really didn't have much to do with it. Just an accident. And not an accident of love. It could have been anyone . . . so, yes, the baby is *mine.*''

He advanced rapidly, and this time the back of his hand caught her across the jaw. She held her arm up to defend herself, only to receive another blow on the other side of the face.

"If the baby is mine, then it's *mine.* But I don't want you to have it. I'm not ready for a kid just now. Things are a big enough mess. You ruined my last picture. Now you're going to tie me down with some kid I don't want. Well, you won't. I'll see that you don't. . . .''

She watched his stiff, upright walk, the controlled walk of someone who is drunk. She watched him go and said nothing. Reaching up, she turned off the lamp on the table beside her and sat in the darkness, alone, for a long time. Occasionally she felt her jaw where he had hit her, felt the pain, felt the dried blood on her lips. She remained there in a kind of daze, hardly able to believe what had happened to her, what she had allowed to

happen to her life. She remembered the days back at Castle
Sinclair when there had been little to worry about but the struggle to survive. How simple it all seemed now, uncomplicated.
Loneliness she had known, an aching longing for Jamie that had
never gone to rest. What she had not known was the fear that
now possessed her, the dread uncertainty, the desperate need to
find some escape. She needed sanctuary for herself, for Alasdair, for her unborn child. For the first time she began to perceive how Anne Rayner might have felt that night she had fled
this house and gone to her death. Should that fact alone not have
warned her? Had she been so blind with passion, and the fear
of loneliness for the rest of her life that she had not calculated
that Rod himself must have had some part in that death? Whatever Anne Rayner had done of her own volition, Rod had not
tried to prevent her doing. There was, of course, the fact, as
Stacia herself had said, that no one had expected her to take a
car, to go careening through the canyons of the city. But no one
had gone to try to comfort the woman they believed had intended
only to wander through the garden. And no one had started in
pursuit when they heard the car roar off into the night. Why did
the thought of Anne Rayner so possess her, when her own problems were so many? She had a much surer escape route. She
could go to Alex. Alex would take her in, would counsel her,
Elliot would see that her interests were protected. He would
advise her on American law. She could go to Anscombe until
her baby was born; Luisa would be delighted to have Alasdair
as a companion to Johnny, and her father would be compassionate toward her difficulties. There was also Connie, who would
give her love, even shelter, if she needed it.

But her mind and body were trapped in the circle Rod had
woven around her. The power of attorney she had signed with
such lack of thought and prudence. Why had she done that? Rod
hadn't seemed to press it at the time. Did women usually do
such things upon marriage? Only fools, she thought. And only
a woman made stupid with a spurious love, worried about the
future of her son, would have allowed Rod McCallum to adopt
him. That had seemed natural enough at the time, an act of
generosity on Rod's part, to make Alasdair feel wanted, a part
of their small family. But what of the coming child? This was
Rod's own child. She would never consent to its being destroyed,
as he seemed to demand. But even now she doubted that he had

meant that demand. When he had sobered up, she thought that he would be pleased at the thought of being a real father, not the stepfather to two children of different mothers. But she knew with terrible coldness that went oddly with the burning pain of her face that she did not want to bring up this child with Rod. She did not want either of her children, born and unborn, to grow up with him as a father. And yet he had a legal claim on both of them, if he chose to exercise it. Perhaps, after all, he had meant he did not want the child. Then she would be able to bargain with him for the freedom of herself and both the children. She would go back to Scotland without him. He could get a Nevada divorce, and she and her two children would be gone from his life. Yes, in the morning she would talk to him—before he had time to become drunk. She would talk reasonably, clearly—even sweetly, if that was necessary. She would make him see that it had all been a mistake and that their lives did not belong together. She would ask nothing from him. No money for the coming child, no alimony, no settlement. She would ask for freedom. And later admit to her family the mistake it all had been. Tomorrow they would sort it out.

But she did not go near the room they shared, where she knew Rod would lie in a drunken, drug-heavy sleep. She went instead to the suite that Alex and Elliot had used, one that it was Rod's pride to keep always in readiness, as if guests dropped in to stay the night every other night. Here were flowers, sheets on the beds, towels in the bathroom. From its windows she gazed down on the still-lighted pool, lights that were kept on all night. Across the atrium formed by the pool was the room where Rod slept, a room that had been meant to be hers equally, but in which she somehow, even after all this time, felt still a guest. She thought of its immaculate order, the flowers, the books, magazines of his own choosing. Not so much as a slipper of hers had ever been allowed to disturb its severe serenity. Even her nightgowns had been laid out by Maria in the dressing room. He would not miss her, she thought. For a time his pride would be wounded that another marriage had failed. But he would declare to Hollywood, as he had to her, that she had never truly belonged here. And it would be the truth. She never had.

She let the shower run on her body for a long time, feeling the warmth of the water relieve her aching face. She ran her hands over her still almost-flat stomach. No pains there. Her fall seemed to have brought no ill effects. She thought of the baby living there, growing. A son or a daughter, it would need a special kind of loving. Different from the love she had for Alasdair, for she would have no romantic tale of a hero who had died for his country, a distinguished and decorated hero, to give this child. She would have instead the story of a marriage made in haste to a fictional hero, the star of a make-believe world. She tried to think of ways she could make Rod sound kind and good and loving. When the time came, she would find them. Back in the purity and sparseness of Sinclair the stories would come.

She dried herself off, then looked into the mirror to see that her face was already hugely swollen. She dashed it many times with cold water to try to minimize the swelling. Tomorrow she would meet the curious gaze of the staff as well as Alasdair's outright questions. She knew the contemptuous, knowing looks she would receive from Stacia. But tomorrow she had to persuade Rod to let her and her children go. That was all that mattered.

She took some aspirin from the stocked bathroom cabinet and slid her naked, tired, aching body between cool sheets. Once again she stroked her hands across her belly, as if to reassure the child who lay there. "It will be all right," she whispered in the darkness.

"Señora! Señora!" Julia had not bothered to draw the curtains the night before, and bright sunlight flooded into the room, making it difficult to open her eyes fully. She had been wakeful until almost dawn and then had slept an exhausted sleep. It was Maria's urgent hand on her shoulder that fully shook sleep away. A torrent of Spanish swept over her, not any of it understood.

"Maria—speak English! Slowly."

The woman took a deep breath, her pudgy face screwed up in anxiety. "Señor McCallum. I take his coffee—he always wants strong, black coffee at this time if he does not come down to breakfast. I cannot wake him! I shake . . . shake him. He will not wake up. I call José. José cannot wake him—no way. I am looking for you. Cannot find you. Then I find you here. . . . Come quickly!"

Heedless of the fact that she was naked, Julia raced to the bathroom to get one of the bathrobes that hung there. Together with Maria she ran to the other side of the house, where Rod's louvered shutters were still closed against the late-morning light. José bent over the huge bed, alternately shaking Rod's limp body and bending over to listen for a heartbeat.

Maria hurried to open the shutters. Light reflected off the surface of the pool bounced across the ceiling and fell on Rod's still face and his inert figure.

"His heart beats, Señora," José said. "But I cannot wake him."

"Turn his head on the side," Julia said. She opened Rod's slack lips and drew his tongue forward so he would not choke on it. Her own efforts to rouse him failed, as José's had done. She reached for the phone at the side of the bed, then paused, suddenly afraid to dial for emergency help. "José, quickly. Go and get Dr. Fields' number. Bring the special telephone book from the library."

While he was gone, she had Maria help her turn Rod's body over. It was unresisting, but a dead weight. She turned his head once more on its side, throwing the pillows aside, climbed on the bed at Rod's head, and knelt over him. She arranged his arms, with elbows bent, just above his shoulder blades. She was frantically trying to remember what she had learned in the first-aid course she had taken at the beginning of the war. Her hands went to a butterfly position just below his shoulder blades, and she straightened her arms to exert the deepest pressure she could. Beside her, Maria looked on in wonder and uttered what Julia didn't doubt were little prayers in Spanish. Then Julia began to raise Rod's bent arms at the elbow, working them up and down until she began to feel the resistance of the muscles. Then she went back to repeat the cycle, her own breathing coming hard as she labored to return him to consciousness.

José came at last, carrying the leather-covered book that contained all Rod's personal phone numbers. She had to stop her labor on Rod to help him find the right name. His English seemed to have deserted him. "Dial it," she said, pointing to the number. He did it quickly.

Julia heard the secretary's voice answer, and she snatched the phone from José's shaking hand. The secretary protested that Dr. Fields was with a patient and could not be disturbed. "He *must* be disturbed," Julia shouted, "or I'll hold you responsible for the consequences if Rod McCallum dies!" She was put through to Dr. Fields immediately. He listened without comment to her brief report. "Keep pumping," he said. "Make sure the air passages are clear. I'll come at once. Don't telephone anyone else. We'll arrange the ambulance."

The time it took him to arrive seemed an eternity; afterward she realized he had been surprisingly fast. She continued to work over Rod's limp body, barely pausing to feel that a pulse still flickered. She issued orders as she worked. "José—make sure the gates are opened."

His eyes widened. "It is almost noon, Señora. Naturally they are open."

"Maria, bring bowls, basins." She didn't know exactly what pumping a stomach entailed, but although he had not said so, she imagined that that was what Dr. Fields would do. She was dripping with sweat, aching all over, careless that her bathrobe was slipping from her shoulders. She heard, as they all did, the sound of a car in the driveway. José was waiting by the door downstairs. Dr. Fields swept into the room. "Okay, I'll take over." He took one quick look at Julia as he stripped off his coat and rolled up his sleeves. "Seems you've had a bad night. How much did he take?"

Wearily Julia slid off the bed. "I haven't any idea. He was drunk. I suppose he just took too much—of whatever he takes."

They heard the sound of another vehicle, doors being slammed, feet running on the stairs. "Well, they got here in extra-quick time. But we'll have to do the job here. He might not last until we get him to the clinic." He felt Rod's pulse and put a blood-pressure cuff around his arm, watching the meter as it rose and fell. Two white-coated men entered the room. "Okay, Doc?—need some help?"

"It's an OD—the usual" was the laconic reply.

Julia wrapped the bathrobe more tightly around her and walked barefooted into Rod's bathroom. She didn't realize, until she entered the room, that in her bewilderment and fatigue she had turned in the wrong direction. This matched her own bathroom in every respect except that hers held an assortment of jars of cosmetics, bottles of perfume, and the light-framed mirror that she had always suspected Anne Rayner had demanded. This bathroom, she had only ever made a cursory inspection of before; Maria and José knew that their jobs depended on its being immaculate at all times. She splashed cold water over her face, then turned on the shower and permitted herself two minutes under it before reaching for one of the towels and wrapping it around her wet hair, with another towel to dry herself hurriedly. She took the fresh bathrobe that belonged to Rod to wrap herself in, dropping the sweat-soaked one to the floor. In the last moment before she left the room her tired senses focused on the hypodermic syringe and bowl that Rod had used to mix whatever powder he had injected himself with. Traces of the powder remained. She stood for some moments staring at them. With a morbid fascination she picked up the syringe. It was empty. She wondered if she would ever know if Rod had deliberately meant this as an overdose, or had been too drunk to understand how much he was taking.

She went back into the bedroom carrying the empty syringe and the bowl. The contents of Rod's stomach, the nauseous mess of what he had eaten and drunk the night before, and, she hoped, the poison he had injected, were in basins and bowls. The white-coated men worked efficiently, Dr. Fields watching them. Julia touched him lightly. "This is what he took—whatever it is." She showed him the remains of the white powder and the empty syringe.

"Drop it in my bag," he said noncommittally. "He'll be okay. But he's going to feel pretty rotten after this, so I'll take him to the clinic for a few days."

"Rod won't like that."

"He'll have to like it. You'd need three nurses here to take care of him. It's safer in the clinic. They get paid handsomely to be discreet."

He stepped a distance away from the bed and the two men. His tone was low as he spoke. "The clinic's nice, small, discreet. Owned by me and a few of my buddies. We see that the press doesn't get in, and only what we say as medics is ever published." He nodded brusquely toward Rod's body on the bed. "You don't think this is an unusual occurrence, do you? We dry out drunks and get them back on their feet. We have the best plastic surgeon in Hollywood so when the lifts and tucks have to be done the patients can recover in nice surroundings— and, above all, in privacy. Guess Rod overdid it this time. It happens. These people are under more pressure than anyone outside the industry realizes. I knew the last picture—the one you were in—the next one they wanted him to make—were bugging the hell out of him. Glad we made it on time. You did a nice job, Julia—in the circumstances. Pity you didn't get to him earlier.''

"I was asleep—in another room. Rod's been so late getting up these last weeks that Maria didn't even try to wake him— well, I suppose it must have been eleven.''

He drew her closer to the window. With amazingly gentle fingers he tilted her face toward the light. "Gave you a little going-over, didn't he? Any special reason?''

"He was drunk. He often is these days. And I'd just told him we are going to have a baby.''

He let out a soft whistle. "You okay? I mean—no pains? There hasn't been any blood, has there?''

"Not that I've had time to notice.''

"You'd better throw on some clothes and come along with me when we go to the clinic. I'll have one of our guys look you over. Was it just your face . . . ?''

"I fell when he first hit me.'' She put a hand gingerly to her throbbing head. "I think I've got a bit of a bump here.''

"It's a wonder you're in one piece. He's a hell of a big guy. . . . Yes, better come along with me. I think we might have you stay a few days in the clinic, too. You don't want to lose the baby, do you? Or do you?''

"No!'' She realized that she had shouted the word, and one of the attendants looked up curiously. "No,'' she repeated quietly. "But last night Rod seemed to want me to get rid of it.'' She looked at the figure on the bed. "If I had any sense, Alasdair and I would be on the first plane out of here, and out of his life before he has time to know what's happened.''

"If you want to keep the baby, you'll have a couple of days in bed. You're not fit to travel. The rest will sort itself out in its own good time. How far on are you?''

"Almost three months.''

He looked at her steadily. "There's time to do something about it, if that's what you want.''

"I don't want anything done.''

"Okay . . . okay. I'll tell Rod myself when he's able to take it in. I think you might find he's changed his mind. I'll tell him you saved his life. I'll tell him the kid's the best thing that could have happened.''

"The heroin—or whatever he's on—can't you get him off that? *That* would be the best thing that could happen.''

He shrugged. "Julia, I try. But people get hooked, and it's the devil's own job to get them off it. Sometimes he manages on a very low dose, but I think he'd come apart altogether without it. We don't have the means to cure. We just try to help them handle it."

She felt an infinite sadness sweep through her. "Do you supply him?"

He sighed. "Julia, I told you I have to help him. If I can't get him off it, I have to help him manage on as little as possible. He'd need to be in treatment for a very long time to come right off it. And then you can't tell that he wouldn't be back on it again the first time something he couldn't handle came up. Dependence. That's what it is. So, yes—I supply him. And try to help him." He touched her arm. "Don't think he's the only one. You'd be surprised if you knew some of the names that show up in my office. Now, be a good girl and go and get dressed. Sling a few things in a bag for a couple of nights in the clinic. We have to look after you, too."

"Alasdair . . . ? I can't leave him. I don't need to be in the hospital."

"Do as I say, Julia. Alasdair will be told that Mommy had a fall on the stairs and bumped her head. You'll be home in a few days. We don't let kids into the clinic. It upsets the patients. And they can't keep their little mouths shut. Go along now, Julia, like a good girl. Believe me, if you want to keep this baby, you need rest. You're only in the first trimester. Excellent time for a miscarriage."

"That's what Rod would like," she said bitterly. "Perhaps that's what he meant to happen."

He shook his head. "I know Rod better than that. He was so hopped up he didn't know what he was doing. He's been pretty down lately . . . one thing and another."

"Yes. I suppose the news of the baby, and my wrecking the film—his whole career, he seems to think—was just too much for him. That's the way he thinks."

"That's the way he thought last night. He'll be different the next time you talk to him."

It was as Dr. Fields had said. She lay in bed in a shaded room for two days. The gynecologist who examined her advised as much rest as possible. "You've had a little shaking up. Working over Rod like that—that probably was much harder on you than the fall. Just feed yourself up—you and the baby. When the bruises have gone, you can go and see your own doctor. But my guess is that you're all right. Strong girl, really.'' He patted her hand. ''Rod McCallum is crazy if he lets you go. I don't think he's *that* mad. He's been a hell-raiser in his day, but basically he's decent. His wife used to be my patient—''

She shrank back into the pillows. ''Anne Rayner? What was wrong with her?''

He looked surprised. ''Why do women ever need a gynecologist? Anne had her problems, like a lot of other women. Sometimes she just needed someone to talk to. I took care of Stacia for a while after Anne was killed. The kid was badly shaken. Not surprisingly. Rod was good to her, though. Did whatever he could to help. Of course, being Anne Rayner's daughter is no passport to a serene life. Emotionally, Anne and Rod are—were—like two volcanoes ready to blow their tops. Anne had irregular periods, too much bleeding, which used to leave her wrung out, cramps, headaches. The lot. And nerves strung like tight wire. Stacia still comes to see me sometimes. Nothing I can do for her except tell her she'll grow out of it. Maybe.''

''She never told me she sees you.''

''She wouldn't. The girl's jealous of you. Frightened. Rod encourages her to see me because he knows she trusts me. She is able to say things to me she can't to anyone else. You're very threatening to her, Julia. The very idea of any stepmother is. But you—you're something else again. Different. Foreign. She would have liked Rod never to remarry. You know how young girls get fixations on people. If she could, she would have married him herself. Just to keep him. When you came along, it nearly broke her. I really don't think, Julia, with your background, you can imagine what Stacia's life has been like. Never knew her father. Anne lived with a number of guys, not all of whom treated her very well—or Stacia. There was no order or security in her life until Rod came along and started to clean up the mess. He might not have been the ideal guy for Anne, but he really wanted to get her life straightened out. And he nearly succeeded. But she was kind of deadly in her own way. I don't think Rod would be in the state he is with the dope if Anne hadn't wanted a companion when she was on it. I don't blame him for the accident. It was something waiting to happen.''

"Stacia blames him."

"So she says. It would have happened. Anne was one of the most beautiful women I have ever laid eyes on—dressed or undressed. And a gynecologist sees a lot of undressed women. But she was very vulnerable. If you believe in predestination, she was destined for doom. She expected nothing good from life— just to be used by one man or another. Or the studio. Stacia seems to expect nothing better from life. If you can help her . . ." Then he touched her hand in parting. "But get well yourself, first. Think about yourself and the baby first. . . . Everything else will fall into place . . . in time."

When he had gone, Julia thought of his last words as platitudes. If she were well enough she would have taken Alasdair and fled. She did not want to be part of the doom that seemed predestined.

Rod came to her room the next day. He said nothing when he entered, but stooped and kissed her tenderly on the lips.

"What use is it to say I'm sorry? You must know I am. I was half crazy after I'd hit you. I'm only just beginning to remember that part of it. And some of the things I said to you. About the baby. Of course I want the baby. My own. Somehow I never thought of it that way. Just another thing to worry about. But a baby isn't a thing. The doc told me you were going to be all right, Princess. No thanks to me." He touched her face where the bruises were still obvious, but the swelling had gone. "I must have been out of my mind. I *was* out of my mind. I can stay off the stuff—I know I can if you'll stay with me."

Afterward she couldn't remember what she replied. Perhaps she said nothing. She was afraid of the power he seemed able to exert over her; she was afraid of her own weakness. She wished he had not come, had not asked forgiveness. Alone, she would have had the strength to gather herself up and go. But listening to his words, hearing his tone, she was aware once again of the feeling she had known when he had asked her to marry him. Another chance, he had begged. She thought of the unborn child and knew that it deserved another chance.

"Doc said you'd better rest a few more days," he said cheerfully when he realized that she was not going to resist his pleading. "But I'd better get back home. I have to tell Alasdair he's not to worry. You'll be home soon. And Stacia . . ." He shrugged. "Sorry, Princess, but we're going to have to have Stacia with us for a spell yet. Can't just abandon her. Can't just let her drift down the road her mother took. Princess, I love you." At the door he turned back. "I'll never let you go. You know that."

He had smiled as he said it, but to Julia it sounded like a threat.

She returned to the house three days later. Alasdair clung to her fiercely. "I thought you'd never come back."

"But I promised you she'd come back," Rod said patiently.

"I did come back, darling. I'll never leave you—not forever." She was anguished at the sight of his face. If it was possible to say that a child had aged in such a short time, then Alasdair had aged. Gone was that enchanting smile that was Jamie's very own. There seemed to be a darkness under his eyes that no child should have. What had she done to Jamie's child? What had happened to the promises she had made to her young husband, most of them never spoken but all of them solemnly vowed in her heart? She had made promises; she now had to find a way to keep them. In a kind of a daze she saw Alasdair's features meld into Jamie's beloved ones, and back again, a child's face again, and he was beginning to smile the smile that was Jamie's own.

She was determinedly cheerful as they all ate dinner in the small dining room. As carefully as she had covered the remains of the bruises on her face, she knew that no one was deceived. She asked Jenny what she and Alasdair had been doing; asked Stacia what was going on at school. Maria and José carefully avoided looking fully at her as they served dinner. To outward appearances they were a normal family, with Rod keeping up the stream of conversation, but Julia felt her gaze return again and again to Alasdair, trying to reassure herself that he did indeed believe the promise that she would never leave him. Rod drank only a little wine, and she saw him bite back his impatience as he noticed that Alasdair only pushed his food around on his plate. Stacia remained stubbornly resistant to his attempts to engage her in conversation, as if she would have no part in this charade of a happy family that had not just come through a time of trauma. Her sensual, beautiful, but still vulnerable face reminded Julia ever more strongly of her mother. But she had

an air of world-weariness, a sad wisdom that Julia doubted Anne
Rayner had ever possessed.

In the days that followed, Rod was tenderly solicitous of Julia's well-being. He insisted that she rest every afternoon. "You
have to take care of yourself. . . ."

She reminded him that this was her second child and that she
was not an invalid. "But Princess, it's *my* first child. I want you
both well. I need you. . . ."

She felt his almost desperate need to reassure her. He often
sat quietly by her side, reading, and he did not drink. She
watched him patiently coach Alasdair in developing a smoother
overarm swimming style. "That's it, kid. You're going to be
world champion. . . ." He did not mind how long Julia stayed
with Alasdair at night reading to him, talking about Princess Cat
and Sinclair, until the child drifted into sleep. Before her eyes
the haunted shadows on Alasdair's face lifted and Jamie's open,
trusting smile returned.

Rod went several times to the studio, and when he returned
he was disinclined to tell her what he had done there, whom
he'd seen. "Oh, it's those damn writers," he said dismissively.
"I just can't seem to get a decent script out of them. This horse
opera thing—it just seems to get worse. I've complained to Morris about it, and all he does is give me something a little worse
to read as an alternative. It's all those damn musicals they're
making. They can't seem to think of anything else. Trouble is,
I can't seem to turn myself either into Fred Astaire or John
Wayne."

He thumbed through the scripts in the library, chain-smoking.
"It's all garbage," he exclaimed. "If they want to kill me stone
dead at the box office, almost any one of these scripts would do
it. But Morris keeps insisting the first one they offered me is the
right one, and the one they're going to shoot. I keep telling him
no!"

"How long can you keep on telling him that?"

"As long as it takes them to come up with something that's
decent. Something I feel has real meat in it. They've always been
a rotten outfit to work for—every studio is, I guess. But still—I
did tell him about the baby. He came over all smarmy. Said it
was good to see me settling down to being a family man. He
was gracious enough to say you'd be kept on the studio payroll.
At a reduced price, naturally—as you can't work. Big of him. I

told him I was perfectly able to take care of my own family. My wife didn't need to work.''

"But your wife does need to work—because that's what she's been trained to do.''

He gestured to placate her. "You think I don't know it? The itch is always there, isn't it? Well, Princess, once the baby's born we'll go on a big hunt for something really special for you. Perhaps we can commission something from one of your writer pals in England. You don't just have to take the garbage they offer to you here.''

She laughed weakly. "Well, it won't be a musical. I've got a rotten voice, and I'll never be a threat to Ginger Rogers.''

"Just be yourself—that's enough.''

Two days later, Morris Meadows' office called and asked Rod to come in "at your convenience.'' He returned in a cold rage. "So that's it. If I don't take the horse opera garbage, I'm suspended. Me! *Suspended.* I've made millions for these guys, and they think they can kick me around because the last film was a flop! Who hasn't had flops? No salary until I decide to make whatever script I'm told to make. Well, I told Meadows where he could shove his script. I told him I'd find myself a decent script, and Worldwide would damn well make it. The bastard actually had my contract on the desk, and started to read the fine print in it. I told him where to put the fine print, too. That stupid agent Phil Westin let me sign it when it seemed a good thing—and he's been making money out of me ever since. It's a tough one to get out of, Princess. Making *Drop into Danger* independently was a one-shot deal. I persuaded them that they owed me that one. But I'm not going to let them push me around like this. I can hold out. I've got plenty of money. . . . I can hold out forever, if that's the way it's going to be. . . .''

"But you'll want to work. No one retires at your age, Rod.''

"Don't they? Well, when you've been working at some damn job or other since you were old enough to walk, perhaps the thought of not working at all doesn't seem so bad. But I'll beat these guys. They'll come up with a decent script. . . .''

Phil Westin arrived and spent the next hours arguing with him. Time for the evening meal arrived, and they were still closeted in the library, and from the sound of their voices, Julia knew they were not in the mood for a family meal. She sent in sandwiches and fruit and noticed that José was summoned to refill the ice bucket and supply a fresh bottle of Scotch and one of gin. The tones of the voices from the library grew louder and angrier. Julia helped Jenny put Alasdair to bed. "Why are they shouting, Mummie?"

"A little argument about a film your—your father doesn't want to make. He's right."

"Does that mean we're going to be poor? Stacia told me when a studio sus-suspends someone, they don't get any money."

Julia was appalled that he had so quickly learned the values of Hollywood, where suspension might mean poverty and therefore disgrace. "We'll never be poor, Alasdair. We have Sinclair. Don't ever forget Sinclair. We weren't well off there, but we were rich in ways people here don't understand. You had everything you wanted, didn't you?"

"Yes—and I had Princess Cat. Do you think she's sometimes lonely for me? I miss her. . . . I think Johnny's going to make her love him more than me. I miss a lot of things, Mummie. The forest—the Kerrs. It's nice here . . . the swimming pool . . . the riding and tennis lessons Rod gives me. But well . . . it isn't the same." He put his arms around her. "I'm glad you've come back. I was afraid you wouldn't. Rod was good to me—read me stories at night. Took me to the drugstore for sodas. But I thought he was trying to hide from me that you weren't going to come back. . . ."

"I'll always come back. I promise."

Rod went back to Dr. Fields' clinic for two days on an invented story that he had developed ulcers and wasn't fit to begin a new film. "We'll play for time," he told Julia. "Hope that something better turns up." But the studio demanded that their own doctors examine him, and on Dr. Fields' refusal to grant that permission, Rod was formally suspended from the payroll. He returned home at once. "All right, I'm supposed to be sick. I'll take sick leave. We'll all go to Scotland. I'm going to spend the summer recuperating. . . ."

They packed up and left, but Jenny, perhaps uneasy at what she had witnessed and overheard, decided it was time she had a different job. "Alasdair's quite old enough to do without her," Julia said.

"You're sure, Princess? We could pretty easily find someone

else. I don't want you tiring yourself out looking after him. He's a pretty lively kid.''

She shook her head. "All we need is someone local at Sinclair to see that he doesn't fall into the loch. Since the war, there are enough young girls looking for a job—particularly if it's just for the summer.''

"Perhaps, after all, we'll get one of those fancy English nannies. You'll certainly need one after the baby's born.''

"The best ones, I hear, come from around Edinburgh. At least they're Scottish. The purest English—and all that rubbish. I think if we got one of *those* we might be rather afraid of her.''

He grinned. "Whatever you say, Princess.''

Alex came to New York to see them. Julia was alone at the hotel when she arrived; she showed Julia a clipping from *Variety*. "I wondered if you'd seen this.''

Julia took it from her and read the headline for a front-page story: *Rod McCallum for Scottish Lair.* The story followed: *Rod McCallum, suspended from Worldwide, has retreated to his castle in Scotland, according to him, to nurse a stomach ulcer. But according to Worldwide, to think over his suspension until he agrees to make the filmscript currently offered to him. The castle, a hideout in the far North, has been associated with his family for hundreds of years. It was the locale for his film Drop into Danger. It is a castle located in the middle of a lake. As one studio executive remarked, "a great tent to crawl into to sulk." His British-born wife, Julia Seymour, with whom he made the box-office disaster The Betrayal, accompanies him. All is cozy domesticity between the McCallums as they await the birth of a child.* The item ran on, peppered with misinformation and supposed quotes from Worldwide.

"Julia, you didn't *sell* Sinclair to him?''

"Of course not! That's all rubbish. Sinclair is for Alasdair. You know how these stories get twisted around. Rod's spent a lot of money on Sinclair, but I couldn't stop him from doing that. It was something he wanted to do. It was to be our place to go in the summer. God knows, it needed the work, as you and Elliot know. Rod knows it was left to me and that I'll turn it over to Alasdair when he's twenty-one.''

"Then what's this about it being associated with his family?''

Julia flushed. "Oh, nothing. It's just something that papers invent. They think just because his name is Scottish that he has some ancestral ties with Sinclair. Look, not even Elliot's papers get it straight all the time. He doesn't even know where in Scotland he was born. Parents dead—brother and sisters in an orphanage that is since burned down, with all the records. He doesn't even know where his brother and sisters are.''

"And not looking very hard for them.''

"Nor they for him.''

"Sorry. Really none of my business. I was under the impression he was an only child. It just gave me a nasty sensation when they made out that it was *his* castle. Of course, newspapers go on elaborating on the same misapprehensions.'' She laughed and made a gesture of apology. "Even Elliot's.'' Then she added, "Is it true about the ulcer?''

"No. That was a cover while he tried to play for time.'' She was aware of how many lies she was telling Alex—lies of omission. She could not bring herself, now, to tell her of the awful night when Rod had struck her, the night he had nearly killed himself with an overdose. Least of all could she tell the canny Alex of having given Rod her power of attorney in those heady days when their marriage had been new and the prospects nothing but bright and happy. She realized she had never mentioned the fact that Rod had adopted Alasdair. It now seemed such a betrayal of Jamie—and yet to have refused it at that time, when it had been Rod's gesture to try to form a united family, to make Alasdair seem wanted, would have implied a lack of trust. She had had one chance to leave it all behind, but these factors—and a stubbornly held sense of hope and trust—had kept her with Rod.

"Is it true about the baby?''

"Yes.'' It was her reason for clinging to the hope that their lives together could be salvaged.

Alex drew on her cigarette and took a sip of her martini. "I can't help saying it, Julia. I'm fiercely envious. And you do have the special glow some women achieve with pregnancy. When's it due?''

"November. It's one of the reasons Rod wanted to go back to Scotland. He didn't want me bothered by the press in Hollywood—and he wanted me out of the summer heat. He's carrying on like an oversolicitous father already. Trying to feed me up—making me put my feet up all the time.''

"And so he should. A baby is a precious thing.''

"It's his first—or that's what he says. I don't have to paint a picture for you of what sort of life Rod's had. Perhaps there are children he doesn't know about. But no one's ever come forward to claim he's the father of their child."

"Didn't he want a child by Anne Rayner?—having a child with the world's pinup goddess would surely have been something he wanted?"

"After Stacia was born, Anne Rayner had two abortions. It seems the last one was bungled. She couldn't have children after that. I don't think she cared."

Alex gave a faint shudder. "Women throw away what other women so much desire. She wasn't very intelligent, Anne Rayner."

"She'd had a hard life." Julia wondered why she was defending this woman she had never known. But she knew she was also defending Rod, although he had been the father of neither of those children.

"And Stacia—how does that sulky little bundle of sex take this news? Another rival for her—as well as Alasdair."

"You've noticed, have you?"

"Who couldn't? If Rod hadn't married you, it wouldn't have been long before she had him in bed with her. I think she tolerates Rod's tight control of her because she just wants him to know she's there. You'll have to watch her, Julia, and as soon as it's possible, get her out of your house."

"How can I? She's underage. Rod doesn't trust her to handle herself yet. No one wants a teenage pregnancy—an illegitimate birth."

Alex shrugged. "I wish you were free of her. I can't help thinking she won't wait until twenty-one to get married, and then she's off everyone's hands. Where are they?—Rod and Stacia and Alasdair?"

"The plan was to go to Saks to shop for cashmere sweaters and tweed skirts and all the things that Stacia hates. Nothing sexy. But since Scotland is exporting everything it can produce, we're not going to be able to pick them up in Inverness." Julia could hear her voice become almost pleading. "Rod does his best, Alex. He tries to act like a father—even if it's sometimes clumsy and overdone. He still hasn't gotten past the stage of thinking that spending money on someone is a measure of love. Well—it's understandable. For him, money came the hard way.

He's been very careful with it. He's made some very good investments, and he's richer than a lot of people imagine. But to him, money is money. Not like us, Alex. Remember how it used to be when we were growing up? Some times were flush—when Father and Mother seemed to be earning heaps. And then the lean periods. But they never worried, did they. They believed in their talent. I seem to remember it was a bit of a joke for us when we had to economize. I don't think Rod has ever considered being short of money—or having to dodge a bill collector—as being some sort of game, the way Mother and Father did. So when he spends money, he means it as some sort of gesture of love. I hate to think what he's poured into Sinclair, but he doesn't seem to mind. Perhaps it tickles his fancy to have *Variety* making up some nice fantasy about him returning to an ancestral home. After all, Hollywood makes up the backgrounds of most of its stars, as well as giving them new names. . . .'' Then Julia changed the subject to Elliot's health; Alex just shrugged.

"He appears to be fine. The doctors say it was just a minor incident. Basically Elliot's healthy—and will stay that way if we could only get him to stop trying to run every one of his newspapers and radio stations himself. . . . He gets on the editors' nerves, I know. But it's like trying to stop Mercury flying around.'' She smiled. "He's full of energy and life. I won't worry so much anymore. He's in Baltimore now, where there might be another paper for sale; otherwise he'd be here. And as for me—I'm busier than ever. I've even got a once-a-week radio interview spot with one of Elliot's rivals—so that means they really want me. It isn't the boss buying a slot for his wife.''

Julia sighed. "Sometimes I envy *you*. You're doing something you love and are very good at. Me—I'm grabbing at straws now. I hate being blamed for the flop of *The Betrayal*. It was a thoroughly messed-up script—and reviewers find it easier to blame me than Rod. I'm the outsider. Sometimes being Sir Michael Seymour's daughter is a distinct liability. American film fans seem to prefer the homegrown product.'' Then she laughed ruefully. "But Rod's not complaining. And if it goes on like this I'll soon be old enough to play batty character roles.''

Alex laughed, too. "They'll have to make you up very heavily.''

"Well, I won't even be thinking about anything until at least six months after the baby's born. . . . Perhaps some dream of a script will turn up.''

Alex talked of Michael's triumph in the limited run of *Arms and the Man* in New York. The unions had finally prevailed, and he had not been allowed to bring the company to New York. But his performance had won rave reviews, and he had gone home happy and satisfied, to prepare for a run in *Richard III*. Alex and Elliot had attended the opening night in late October. True to his conviction, Elliot had not tried to influence the theater critic for the Forster newspapers, but the review had been laudatory. Alex had done a magazine interview with her father and recorded a radio interview. "Luisa was beside herself with pride. Strange how I used to think she would be a bad influence on him. But I was younger then—and thought I knew it all." This talk of their father was broken off when Rod, Alasdair, and Stacia returned. It was a situation Alex seemed to understand instinctively. Julia could remember how Rod had read the review of the play in *Variety* in silence and without comment. He would always find it difficult to conceal the envy he had of those who won critical acclaim for their acting.

Alex was at the ship the next day to see them off. Rod toasted her in champagne, of which he took only a few sips himself. "Thanks for coming, Alex. I've got swell in-laws. Why don't you try persuading Elliot to come over to Sinclair this summer? It'll just be family—and I promise you it'll be a damn sight more comfortable than it was before. Everything inside is just about finished and refurbished. Not at all like the primitive little ranch in the mountains. This is a *real* star's home.''

From the quick exchange of glances between Julia and Alex, both realized that they each wondered which star he was referring to and whose castle it was.

They arrived in London to a welcome from Michael and Luisa and a rather rowdy reunion between Alasdair and Johnny. Johnny had had a tutor rather than a governess during the past year. He had had his sixth birthday and was lording it over Alasdair because he would not reach that exalted age until the end of June. Michael, looking younger than Julia had thought possible, had scored a huge artistic success in *Richard III,* which had now been playing for three months. Rod refused to allow them to stay at Luisa's Wilton Crescent house, so they stayed expensively at the Savoy, in two suites. Rod gave interviews to carefully selected journalists, making light of the failure of *The Betrayal* and of his suspension. "Well, ulcers are ulcers. I've been told to rest. And my wife's going to have a baby. We thought the peace and quiet of the Highlands would do us both good. . . . It's nice to have it to go back to. . . ."

"You've often said you didn't know where in Scotland you were born, Mr. McCallum," one skeptical journalist said.

Rod shrugged off the question. "Oh, I just faintly remember being told about the Highlands. *Where* exactly I couldn't say."

They went to see Michael on the last night of *Richard III*. Though it was still playing to nearly full houses, D.D. had decreed that it was time it came off, in the flood tide of its success. All through the performance, Julia could sense Rod's unease. It grew as Michael was recalled for many curtain calls. He gathered the cast around him many times, but the heady applause was for him. It continued for fifteen minutes. Rod stood on his feet and kept up a seemingly hearty applause because he knew it was expected of him. Many eyes turned to him during this time, to note his reaction.

They went backstage to congratulate Michael and then to wait while he removed his makeup, and changed to have a late supper with them at the Savoy. Stacia was with them, wearing a red dress of the simplest cut, high-necked, with the thin gold chain Rod had given her the past Christmas. Her long golden hair was brushed back from her face and tied with a red bow. But even in this most innocent appearance, she still caused heads to turn at the intermissions and as they entered the Grill at the Savoy, even though she trailed behind two men whose faces were famous, one of them much loved by London theatergoers. "My dear," Luisa whispered to Julia during supper, "the men cannot keep their eyes off her. Of course, she so much resembles her mother, but her own quality . . . like some firecracker waiting to go off. How old is she?"

"Not quite seventeen," Julia said unhappily, aware of the reaction Stacia caused and beginning to wonder how much longer Rod could exert control over her, whatever her age.

Afterward, in their suite, Rod poured himself a large whiskey. He had drunk far more that evening, before the performance, during the intermissions, and at supper than he had since the night he had beaten her.

"Damn it, Julia. I suppose your father's a nice guy, but I just can't stand him. He looks down on me—don't tell me he doesn't! In his eyes I'm still a bit player who can just about get out the line 'Reach for the sky, mister.' And he's playing this great Shakespearean role that I can't even understand. I don't get it— the whole of London going mad over a hunchback cripple dragging himself all around the stage declaiming. Well, they might love it here in London, but it wouldn't go down in the sticks in the States."

"I don't think that's my father's object. But he did give a superb performance."

Rod shrugged. "And I'm still a hack in your eyes. . . . Well, what does it matter?" He poured himself another drink.

"It doesn't matter. You both do different jobs. You both do them very well."

"But you'd still rather watch your father play a cripple than Rod McCallum storming a Japanese-held island. I watched your face during the performance. You were mesmerized. . . ."

"I haven't seen my father onstage for quite some time. Is it so strange that I was interested?"

"Interested! You were worshiping him."

"Rod, this is pointless."

He shrugged. "Like comparing the best wine in the house to cheap stuff. Go to bed, Julia. I'll just sit for a while and contemplate my ulcer."

"Please, Rod . . ."

"Go to bed!"

It was hours before he crashed down, only half undressed, onto the other bed. She knew he was terribly drunk. Any fragile structure of confidence he had managed to rebuild in the past weeks seemed to have disintegrated since their arrival in London.

The next day he nursed a hangover, something Julia had not ever known to happen to him before. Johnny and Alasdair went riding in Hyde Park on Princess Cat, and Johnny's own pony, Taffy, which had been shipped up with Princess Cat to stables near the park just to keep her company. Princess Cat would travel north by train when they left London. Julia knew that Luisa was overseeing the two boys for the day, so she took Stacia shopping. They went to Harrods and Harvey Nichols and Liberty's, but Stacia was contemptuous of what she saw on display.

"Jeez, isn't this country ever going to get over the war? There's nothing to *buy*. The people look so shabby. . . ." The only things she showed any interest in were the displays of English bone china. She admired the richness of the Royal Worcester Imari pattern. "That's really something." When told it was for export only and that there would be a two-year wait to fill an order, she simply shrugged and ordered a complete dinner service for twelve.

Julia gasped in protest. "Rod will never allow that! It's so terribly expensive. What can you possibly want it for?"

"You don't think I'm ever going to have my own house, have my own people to dinner? I'm not asking *him* to pay for it. By the time it comes, I'll have a contract, and I'll have made a couple of pictures. I'll pay for it myself." And then she went to the Crystal Department and ordered a dozen handcut red and white wineglasses, and a set of tall, green-stemmed glasses for Rhine wine, called hock in Britain, although Julia doubted that she had ever tasted hock or even knew what it was. When it came to placing a deposit, Julia wrote a check. "I don't think you'd better tell Rod about this—not just yet. Wait until the film contract comes up."

"You don't think I'll get one, do you."

"I haven't the least doubt that you will," Julia said tartly. She didn't credit this sudden burst of nest-building instinct in Stacia, but she recognized some yearning in the girl to achieve adult status. Ordering a highly decorated, highly formal dinner service and crystal for a house she did not yet possess, and a way of life she would never live easily with, was just a flare of independence, like a little girl inexpertly applying her mother's lipstick and wearing her high heels.

"I'll be able to pay for it," Stacia protested. "There's the trust my mother left—that's what pays for all the things you think Rod gives me. It pays for my clothes, all the extras at school, the lessons with Ernie Wilcox. He doesn't spend a red cent of his own money on me—but he controls it until I'm twenty-one. I can't wait to be twenty-one and get out from under. Of course, if I got married, he wouldn't be running my life anymore, would he?"

"Have you got anyone in mind?"

Stacia looked her fully in the face. "Don't you think I could pick up a guy any day of the week? And not a nobody, either.

I'm just a little choosy, that's all. I don't have to take whoever throws himself at my feet.''

"I'm glad to hear it. Well, now that you've made your big purchase for the future, I think we'd better be going. We're having tea with Luisa, remember? And Connie and Ken are coming to dinner tonight.''

"I'd rather we were going to dinner with *them*—at their house. I like that place—all the crazy mix-up of things. I know it drives Rod wild.''

"Well, just remember that Connie and Ken might just like an evening out for a change. They've got two little children and not much money. It'll be a long time before Connie's able to afford a dinner service of Royal Worcester.''

"But everyone says Ken's such a smart guy. Why doesn't he make money?''

"He's in the Civil Service. In the Treasury. One day he'll have very senior rank. He'll make a good salary, but they'll never be rich.''

"If he's so smart, why doesn't he go into some Wall Street broker's firm? *They* make millions. . . .''

"Not Ken's style.''

"Oh . . . style. Well, I guess that's what all you people think I'll never have. Style. Well, I just bought my first piece of it this afternoon. One day I'll pour tea from a silver pot—and it won't belong to Rod McCallum.''

They arrived at Luisa's house, and because the boys were back from riding, tea was served in the dining room, under the watchful eyes of the tutor and a young woman who was neither governess nor nanny but simply there to help Luisa cope with the energies of a young boy. During tea Stacia said little, except to remark that she hadn't seen any cakes such as these for sale in any of the shops. She sat silently as Luisa insisted that the boys eat their share of bread and butter before being allowed any cake. "I thought butter was rationed . . .'' Stacia remarked.

"It is . . . but . . .'' Luisa shrugged. "From the country we manage. You will see that Janet is not short of it at Sinclair.''

Stacia's eyes had examined everything in that exquisitely furnished room. In particular she eyed the two tall cabinets whose upper shelves displayed a service of elegant, very finely wrought porcelain, bordered in a pale green and gold and decorated with flowers. She pointed to it. "I didn't see anything like that to-day."

Luisa smiled. "You would have to hunt the antiques shops for even a piece of it. It is Sèvres—French—almost two hundred years old. The set belonged to the family of my first husband. We put it away for safety during the war."

"Could I . . . ?"

Luisa was obviously anxious to please her awkward guest. "You would like to look at it more closely . . . ?" She took a key from the drawer of one of the cabinets. As soon as the glass doors were opened, instead of reaching for one of the smaller pieces on the bottom shelf, Stacia raised herself on tiptoes and took down the centerpiece of the whole collection, a magnificent soup tureen with lid. Luisa gave a little gasp as Stacia rested it on the small ledge between the top and bottom halves of the cabinet. "I bought some china today—can I see the mark underneath? They told me all the good ones have a mark." Before Luisa could intervene, Stacia had lifted the lid with one hand and turned over the tureen with the other. "Oh, I see . . . yes, it must be very old. Nothing you could order today . . ." Watching her, Julia thought she deliberately released her hold on the tureen. It smashed on the parquet floor. Stacia held the lid and looked at Luisa like an appalled child. "Oh . . . I'm sorry. I'm not usually so clumsy. I expect it was very valuable. Of course I'll pay . . ."

Luisa stepped over the fragments on the floor. "I see you still are a child. You cannot pay for two hundred years. Think nothing of it. An unfortunate accident."

Stacia had put the lid in the place where the tureen had stood. Luisa had already engaged Alasdair and Johnny in conversation about their ride in the park, as if nothing had happened, but Julia saw that her face was tight with the effort of controlling her anger. Stacia went back to her place at the table. For some minutes she stared at her teacup without raising it, as if in contrition and dismay. Then when she did lift her eyes, Julia was looking at her directly. For more than a few seconds Stacia's lips quivered, not as if she were trying to control tears, but to hold back laughter.

Chapter Eleven

I

THEY HAD BEEN DRIVEN around London by a chauffeur in the Rolls that Rod had bought the year before, something Julia had almost forgotten. But once they were ready to head north, the chauffeur was let go, and Rod took over the car, his features tight from the effort of staying on the left side of the road. His mood was not gentle. Julia guessed that he still had not recovered from the storm of applause that had been accorded to her father as he took his many curtain calls. He was unkindly abrupt when Alasdair wondered aloud if Princess Cat would be well cared for on the train journey. "Listen, kid, if you were so worried, you could have gone with her and slept in the straw. So shut up. She'll be perfectly all right. People are *paid* to take good care of valuable animals." Julia knew he was right. Sir Niall had promised to meet the train with a horse box, and Princess Cat would be happily bedded down at Sinclair long before they reached there.

It was an uneasy journey. Julia had decided, as a gesture to Stacia, that she should read the map and sit in the passenger seat beside Rod. They got hopelessly lost several times, especially as they got farther north and left the big cities of the Midlands behind. On the second day Rod insisted that Julia take over reading the map; he got unreasonably annoyed when she asked several times for him to pull over so she could check her reading. As the roads grew narrower, and the distances between the villages and towns greater, Julia noticed that many of the prewar signposts, which had been removed to bewilder a possible invading enemy, had still not been replaced. In these wilder, lonelier places north of the border, presumably one was expected to know where one was. But she fared hardly better than Stacia. "Why are women so goddamn stupid about maps . . . ?"

"Well, I suppose you know the map of the Pacific pretty well," Stacia remarked. "Seeing that you won back all the islands. . . ."

"Do you want to get out and walk, young woman?" After that Stacia remained silent, and with relief Julia knew they were firmly on the road to Inverness. She knew by heart the turn they would take to Sinclair before they reached the city itself. They came to it and eventually drove through the familiar village of Langwell. Alasdair began to drum his heels against the seat with excitement. "Watch it, kid. That's real leather—real expensive."

"I thought expensive things were supposed to take wear," Stacia said. "In this country it's posh to have your leather—and your clothes and houses—looking a little tacky. Shows you've had money for more than a few years. I suppose the castle's been all smartened up and shiny, like Cinderella at the ball. And all those snooty friends of Julia's are going to die laughing. . . ."

They had made the turn into the forest road. Rod slammed on the brakes. "Out, Stacia! Get out! We'll see you when you make the castle. Enjoy your walk."

"Rod!" Julia protested. "That isn't fair. It's two miles, and she's tired. . . ." But he had already slammed the door after Stacia had slid out of the seat, and he drove off quickly.

"Do her good. She needs to stretch her legs—and maybe she'll be in a sweeter mood when she gets to the castle." Julia did not reply, and Alasdair cowered in the backseat, apparently afraid that the same thing would happen to him, and his reunion with Princess Cat be that much more delayed. They traveled on in uncomfortable silence. They passed the McBain cottage, which Rod favored with only the briefest glance. But when they came to where the forest opened out to the shores of the loch, he slowed the car to a crawl, savoring all he saw. The castle stood in the golden splendor of the May evening, sunlight falling on the ancient gray stone in the way Julia had held as a picture in her heart ever since they had left. She could feel Alasdair's breath on her neck as he perched on the edge of the seat to get his first look. It was he who spoke first. "It really doesn't look changed at all. But it's . . . well, sort of . . . tidier." The work on the battlements had been skillfully done, so that the occasional gaps were still there, but the formerly crumbling stonework was now made safe. Rod eased the Rolls over the bridge and the draw-bridge, but Julia felt that caution was no longer necessary. The reinforcing of the arches had been done quite unobtrusively. The rusted portcullis was still in its frozen position; nothing would be done to render it workable again—even Rod had agreed that to attempt it would mean its complete replacement, and create the look of newness the architects had been at pains to avoid. No doubt watching for them, and hearing the car on the bridge, Janet stood ready by the great double doors of the inner court-yard, which were flung wide in welcome. With her were William Kerr and his wife and three children. A girl of about eighteen tried to hide herself behind Mrs. Kerr.

William Kerr sprang to open the door on Julia's side, while Janet went to Rod. "Welcome back to Sinclair, Mr. and Mrs. McCallum," she said with simple warmth. "Ah, but it has seemed a long time since you left us." Julia felt a new, sharp stab of sadness when only Rory joined the group in the court-yard. He wagged his tail as Julia and Alasdair knelt to embrace him, but he hardly seemed to hear their voices; his eyes had the haze of old age. During the winter Duuf and Angus had died, a few months apart. Rory looked bewildered at all this sudden fuss, and he turned and went back into the castle, to the fire, his hind legs dragging.

Rod beamed upon Janet and everyone else with all the attrac-tiveness of his sudden mood of good humor. "Great to be back. How are you all? Mr. Kerr? Mrs. Kerr? How the children have grown. Rachel will be finishing school soon, I suppose. . . ." All graciousness and charm. "And who's this nice little thing, trying to hide back there?"

"Well, now, Mr. McCallum, this is my sister's eldest, Ros-mairi. Kate's still with me, but Rosmairi's come to lend a hand—and perhaps look after Master Alasdair between times. 'Tis only for the summer. In September she'll go to a secretarial school in Inverness," she added proudly. A pretty young girl with red-dish hair half-bobbed a curtsy. Julia could read what was going on in her mind; she was torn between the respect her parents' generation had given to the landed gentry, however hard up they may have seemed, and the living presence of a film star of Rod McCallum's stature and fame.

William Kerr could hardly contain himself. "Oh, Mr. Mc-Callum, it's a wonderful thing you've done for Sinclair. It is all sound of wind and limb again and will last another five hundred years." All his former reserve about an American film star taking charge at Sinclair had vanished. Any man who was willing to spend good money, and a great deal of it, to restore a building that was not his earned William Kerr's respect and a slight sense of wonder. "Never in my lifetime have I seen it like this. But I'm sorry, Mr. McCallum, we have been reading in the newspapers that you have not been well, and here I have not had the manners to inquire about your health."

"My health is going to be perfect once I've had a few days' rest here," Rod said. "And no doubt you've also read that Mrs. McCallum is going to have a baby."

"That indeed we have, sir. But one doesn't know what to believe of the newspapers these days. I hope you are well, Mrs. McCallum. And here's Master Alasdair—so grown since last year—and come to have his sixth birthday with us. How well I remember—and Janet more so—the day he was born, there, in the Red Tower Room—as a Sinclair should be. . . ."

This observation did not seem to interest Rod very much. He was marching eagerly toward the open doors. The small entrance hall, where the stairs led down to the guardroom, was virtually unchanged, except that the central heating had been extended to here, and one of the Sinclair battle colors that had hung, heavy with dust, its silk tattered, from the Great Hall balcony had been skillfully repaired and cleaned, and hung against the stone wall. The Great Hall, with the scaffolding removed, was bigger than Julia remembered. It looked virtually untouched, except that she knew that now it must be in good repair. Concealed lights, turned on for the occasion, lighted the portraits of the Sinclair ancestors. "I resisted having them cleaned," Rod said to Julia. "They might have looked too new."

"Perhaps just as well. The art's of very dubious quality. One wouldn't really want to see them. But the rest—well, it's beautiful." Obviously Rod had also resisted the temptation to have the Sinclair tartan in carpets and curtains. But the predominant red of the tartan was in the plain velvet curtains and the velvet pile carpet, which did not entirely cover the polished wood floor. "We'll still be able to have dancing in here," Julia murmured.

Rod put his arm around her shoulders, the first gesture of

affection he had shown all day. "Like it, Princess? Yes, we'll have great times here." The doors were open to the dining hall, which also had remained similarly restrained, except that silver sconces shone on the walls, and two silver and crystal chandeliers hung over the long table. A warm glow was cast over the old paneling of the walls, giving the room a charm and grace Julia had thought it could never possibly possess. Here also were plain green carpet and curtains. Apparently Rod had seen the mistake of the multiple tartans of the housekeeper's room. He led her along to the library—it remained virtually unaltered, except that there were many more lights than before. The books remained, but the sofas and deep chairs were covered in a green chintz pattern whose color exactly matched the subdued mossy green that was predominant in the McCallum tartan. Plain curtains of what Julia judged to be handwoven wool echoed the green. Flowers were massed in copper pots; two beautiful gate-leg oak tables, new to Julia's eyes, held the current newspaper and magazines. Books with glistening new jackets stood beside them. "I thought this would be our sitting room. . . . The drawing room's been done, but this has a much better aspect—and I like the books." How had he done so much, she wondered, from such a distance? She would have staked a bet that he had overseen almost every detail, examined swatches, approved drawings from an interior decorator as well as the architect's plans of major alterations. One totally new thing struck her, but even here the work had been executed in old glass and looked as if it might have been in place for many years. In the center of the three tall windows a piece of stained glass had been fixed. Rod drew her close to it. "I didn't think you'd mind—since you're married to a McCallum. I don't suppose you recognize it. The clan badge. A castle argent and masoned sable. The motto *In ardua petit.*" He translated: *"He has attempted difficult things.* My one conceit, Princess."

She raised her lips to his. "Rod, darling—you have attempted difficult things and achieved and earned every one of them. It's perfectly right here. This will be our family room. . . ."

"In time we'll have the books re-covered—and the really old and important ones restored. The decorator has been in touch with the people who bind the King's books. There are some here that made Ernie Wilcox's eyes pop." His hand was actually loving as he caressed the worn leather of the books, touched the old wooden shelving. His eyes anxiously scanned the walls for any sign of all the new electrical wiring that had been put in, and apparently he could see none. The great second tier of books in the gallery was still in mysterious shadow, but Rod flicked light switches that had never been there before, and it sprang into radiant life. "They did a good job. Apart from the carpet and curtains and so on, you'd almost think no one had touched the place." But then he nodded to the stained glass. "Except for the rank outsider." Julia's heart warmed to him. He seemed to have such a hunger for all that was fine and old—the house in Beverly Hills reflected that. He was obsessed with detail to a degree that was almost hurtful. Whatever his hunger for the honors the acting world had not bestowed on him, as it had showered them on her father, he had contrived to sublimate in this passion for serene and quiet perfection. What had been patiently contrived here was a world away from the vulgar conception that a Hollywood decorator might have thrust on them. She felt he had fully earned the clan badge in stained glass in the window— except that McCallum was not his name.

"You have created a wonder," she said. And was afraid to say more—to remind him that he did not own this house.

Together they looked at the bedrooms. Here things had also been left understated—plain colors, but done in rich damask in the state rooms, in pretty chintzes in the lesser rooms. Bathrooms had been squeezed into what to Julia had seemed unimaginably small spaces. Had this really been the housekeeper's linen closet? And this one had been a moldering closet whose doors had always stuck and in which nothing could be left because of the dampness. Perhaps just to show that it worked, Janet had turned on the central heating. A gentle warmth pervaded each room—except for the Culloden Room, where, for some reason, the engineers had failed to produce more than a background heat. Rod pursed his lips over this: "It's the end of one leg of a run, but still no reason why full heat shouldn't get here. We tucked a massive heating and hot-water system into the bottom of one of the towers. Just let's hope the whole place doesn't crack apart from the heat."

They had returned to the Red Tower Room—unchanged except that the curtains and bedspread had been as skillfully repaired as the Sinclair battle flag in the entrance hall. But here again flowers were massed; an old table stood under the windows with the now-expected books and magazines. There was even a huge bowl of what Julia suspected was ancient Imari filled with a potpourri of rose leaves. She ran her hand through them, and the scent of last summer came to her. "It's inspired, Rod. You are a real artist."

She realized nothing she could have said would have pleased him more. She drew him to the window. "Look—he did what he said. That landscape gardener." She pointed to the thousands of faded daffodil blooms surrounding the island on which the castle stood. "We missed it by a few weeks. But as they multiply, it will be, as he said, one of the great sights of Scotland every spring. Maybe we'll be here next spring to see them."

His arm went around her again. "I hope next spring we'll both be very busy filming. But we'll see. I'm glad I've managed to please you, Princess."

She looked at him, and then around the room once more. "You said so little about it. I thought you were looking at plans of the electrical wiring, and the plumbing—I didn't imagine all the curtains and carpets were being done. And so carefully. Everything that was best has been preserved, and where it had to be replaced, it's been done so well." She stroked the old polished surface of the table. "Such lovely things. I didn't think they could be collected in only a year. . . ."

"When I say 'hurry,' I mean it. Everyone got paid handsome premiums for being in a hurry. Though I do have to say by comparison with Beverly Hills prices, what they charged here seemed like peanuts."

"But this is a great work of restoration. Far more difficult than building from scratch—and much more expensive. You should get a medal—or something of the sort—for preserving a part of Scotland's heritage."

"People will see it, Princess—and know. That's all the recognition I need."

Once again she looked, and took in more details of the room in which her son had been born. At the very last her gaze stopped at the mantel above which the carved crest of the Sinclairs was dominant. Since the hangings and bedspread had only been repaired but not replaced, with the few pieces of plain but beautiful oak furniture added the room hardly looked different, except that it no longer really needed the fire that burned in the grate as a welcoming gesture. "Ellen," she whispered. "Lady Ellen . . . ?'' She did not think that pale shadow had been disturbed by what had taken place.

"What did you say?" Rod demanded, as if jealous of any thought she did not share with him. He stood at the entrance of the dressing room, which now held floor-to-ceiling mahogany hanging cabinets. They very nearly matched the wood of the bathroom, which he had already checked to make sure that no one had marred its Victorian perfection.

"Nothing . . . just that it's better than I could possibly have hoped.''

Once again his arm came around her. "I'm glad that you don't think the only thing I know about is horses."

"You have wisdom bred in the bone," she said softly.

"Well, let's hope our son inherits it." She did not reply, unwilling to destroy his pleasure by reminding him that whatever he had done at Sinclair, it still would belong, not to his child, but to Alasdair.

Downstairs tea was served in the housekeeper's room. Here the Sinclair tartan had been removed; the carpet was the same mossy green that matched the McCallum tartan. Stacia was seated at the table, piling butter on Janet's freshly baked scones. "Enjoy your walk?" Rod said. "Thought a bit of fresh air might do you good.''

"Ruined a pair of shoes, but otherwise it was fine," Stacia replied with a shrug. "Whoever you got to do the work did a great job. At least we're warm—and this room doesn't look like a great big mistake.''

Rod laughed, now restored to high good humor. "Pour me a cup of tea, will you, Stacia, like a good girl? I hope you're not going to be too bored here this summer. I had them send over all the textbooks you're going to need at school next year. Don't forget you're going to *have* to graduate next year. You're already a year behind. I'm sure you won't want anyone to think Anne Rayner's daughter is a dummy.''

"I'll graduate, don't worry. And people already know I'm not a dummy. Will I get to make a movie when I'm finished school?''

"Depends. Depends on whether something's offered to you.''

A deliciously provoking smile spread across her face. "Then I have no worries." She carefully poured tea for them both, politely offered milk and sugar. "Have some of this Dundee cake, Alasdair. It's very good. . . ."

William Kerr came to have tea with them formally, as the right of a trusted retainer. He addressed most of his talk to Rod, lovingly detailing aspects and little dramas of each piece of alteration and repair. "The things they found—you'd hardly believe. Nooks and crannies that had been bricked up years ago—a whole new section of the cellars. Had a few near-misses—taking down what looked like partition walls and finding they were bearing walls. The new wiring—"

"Any skeletons found in the closets?" Stacia inquired hopefully.

William Kerr looked as if he wished she hadn't asked. "In fact, in the uncovered part of the cellar they found human remains. The pathologist in Inverness said they were the bones of a young woman. They were given Christian burial. We did not know what to put on the marker stone, so we just put 'Sinclair.' I didn't write that, Mr. McCallum. I thought it might upset Mrs. McCallum. For all we know, they were not a Sinclair's. Probably not, or they would have had a normal burial."

"Where is Lady Ellen buried?"

He frowned. "I don't recall a Lady Ellen in the family history, Mrs. McCallum. Of course, I'm not an expert. . . . Perhaps you'd better ask the minister. There are so many Sinclair graves and mausoleums in the kirkyard. He would have all the records—as far back as they go."

Suddenly Julia wished she had not mentioned it. The pleasure of seeing Sinclair restored was dampened. They might have driven away Ellen's presence from the Red Tower Room. Could it have been her bones they discovered? She thought of Jamie. It had been her choice, at the end of the war, not to have Jamie's body brought home to be reburied with his ancestors. But at that time she had felt it was better that he lie with his fallen comrades in the dry earth that had claimed him. Perhaps it had been a mistake. She had denied Alasdair the sight of his father's place in the kirkyard. Perhaps someday they would go together to see where he had been killed and where he was buried.

She shook off the thought and said she wanted to visit the kitchen again. She and Rod had glanced in there quickly, but she wanted to see it in more detail. "Oh, it's very grand we are here now," Janet said. Her gesture displayed the modern fittings, the stainless steel double sink and counters, the large refrigerator. She opened the doors to a hanging room for meat. "Everything a body could imagine is here. And a lot of it sent from America. I cannot believe the sums Mr. Kerr had to authorize to be paid out in duty for what has been sent. The refrigerator. No one has seen the like. And all the hot water anyone could want. The tank is enormous—"

"Like the gas works," Kate put in. She had greeted Julia shyly but warmly. Rosmairi was having her tea at the long, Formica-topped table, and she had sprung to her feet at Julia's entrance. Mostly, Rosmairi gazed down at the newly tiled floor.

"I hope Alasdair won't be too much of a bother to you, Rosmairi. But he'll be spending most of his time with the Kerrs as soon as school is over. . . ."

"Rosmairi is having the room Miss Jenny had last year, with your permission, Mrs. McCallum. So, like Kate, she'll be handy to help . . . unless, of course, you'd like her to board with the Kerrs."

"No—naturally you'd like her near you. I hope you'll be happy with us this summer, Rosmairi." The girl nodded shyly.

Kate, more bold because she knew Julia, stroked the gray-flecked Formica. "Beautiful it all is, Mrs. McCallum. Just to think I'll never have to scrub that old table again . . ." Julia had been rather fond of the old wooden kitchen table—but she recalled the times when she had scrubbed it herself and had been less fond of it. She looked at the two gleaming white electric stoves, the stainless steel . . . the old days were gone from Sinclair, and here in the kitchen, they had no regrets. But Julia was pleased to see they had kept the Aga; that, she thought, would have been at Janet's insistence. There were some dishes that only reached perfection from its slow cooking.

Janet then took Julia on a tour of the little cluster of rooms that opened off the passage to the kitchen. The old bathroom had new fittings and was tiled, and the radiator gave off a gentle warmth. Janet showed her own room with pride. "I've never been so comfortable in my life. So grand I am, with the carpet and everything new." Her small treasures stood around—family photographs, a Bible by her bedside, an ancient silver-backed brush and mirror proudly displayed on a pretty little chest of drawers; built-in closets went from floor to ceiling. "Mr.

McCallum said I was to have the choosing of the wallpaper and the curtains and the rest myself.''

"And a very nice choice, too, Janet," Julia said. "I'm glad you're comfortable at last. It's been a long wait. . . ."

Janet shrugged that aside. "Sinclair has been home to me. I didn't really notice what it lacked." She led Julia on an inspection of the rest of the rooms. "Rosmairi will have the room Miss Jenny had last year, and they've fixed up this one for Kate . . . just as pretty as anything she's ever imagined. And this one—well, we put in an extra bed, as it's the largest. This will be for Master Alasdair, so he can be near Rosmairi." Julia couldn't even remember this room. "It was a sort of catchall place, Mrs. McCallum. Do you not remember? We put anything we didn't have a real place for in here. Full of old odds and ends and spiders. The decorator found some pretty pieces here, and now they're scattered all over the castle—that is, after they'd been to the restorer's. And all the rooms are heated, with electric heaters ready for when the weather doesn't need the central heating to be on. But such a comfort in the evenings . . ." This whole cluster of rooms, which had once seemed to Julia a little like a cellblock, grouped around the ancient bathroom, was cheerful and bright, with sinks and built-in closets, and the gay splash of color created by the plain carpets and pretty chintzes. Only the unevenness under the carpets betrayed the old flagstones. Even the office had been tidied up but not refurbished, except for a fitted carpet under the old, worn Turkish one. But its lovely mahogany fittings had been repolished. The stacks of old papers had been arranged into leather-bound file boxes, the mahogany keyboard had been refinished and its brass keyhooks shone, all the keys in their place, neatly labeled. "The decorator had a special person to come to do this. William Kerr was not for having any family papers disturbed or destroyed." The desk where Lady Jean and later Julia had daily discussed the farm business with William Kerr had had its old leather top repaired; it shone. Now swept clear of its piles of papers, it revealed a severe neatness. "It's a great wonder Mr. McCallum found time to direct so much to be done from that far away."

Then she showed Julia what she privately considered the greatest wonder of all. Just at the entrance to the corridor from the dining hall to the kitchen, two old closets, which Julia could never remember seeing opened, had been turned into half bathrooms—for ladies and gentlemen, as the beautiful ceramic signs, bearing the Sinclair badge, proclaimed. "Who could imagine," Janet said, "that they could ever make something like these from what were only storage cupboards? Big enough, mind you—we used to walk into these. But they were just for odd bits and pieces of dishes no one ever used, bits left over from broken sets of china. It's all stored out in the stables now—and good riddance!" The two rooms were small but magnificently furnished. Julia noted the gold fittings on the toilets and sinks, arched swans' heads for faucets, fluted ceramic pedestals for the sinks. Julia wondered why Rod had not brought her here to display these things himself, and then realized he had been clever enough to leave Janet's realm to her, to be exclaimed over, admired, praised.

"It is a convenience we have always lacked at Sinclair," Janet said. "Sometimes I have been ashamed to show people into the old bathroom down the passage, or take them all the way upstairs. . . . Oh, a beautiful thing Mr. McCallum has done with the castle," she pronounced, as if setting the final seal on it. Julia could see that all doubts, all reservations about the American, although Scottish-born, had gone. Memories of the chaos and the demands of the days when they had made their film here were fading. Rod McCallum had given them comfort in an ancient, lovely, but difficult house. He had spent good money on it. He was now totally accepted. "Will you stay until the baby is born, Mrs. McCallum? It would be grand to have it born in the castle."

Julia murmured something noncommittal and retreated back to the housekeeper's room. Even they were beginning to think that Rod's child had an equal place with Alasdair here.

In the beginning it all seemed to Julia so normal, almost serene. She and Rod inspected the refurbished walled garden before dinner that evening. It was neat, its herbaceous border impeccably dug over and replanted; even in this far northern climate all the buds of early summer were there. The rose trellises had been rebuilt of hardened wood, and already the climbing roses, with their interwoven clematis, were grasping to cover them. "In a few years it will be a wonder," Julia said.

They went through the new wrought-iron gates to the walled vegetable garden that Rod had paid to have rototilled and replanted but that the Kerrs took care of themselves. The produce would be shared between the Kerrs and whoever was at the castle. "Myself, I don't think it's worth the money and the effort," Rod said. "Except that, being on an island, it's just possible to keep the rabbits out. But at any rate, it's a bit of a bonus to the Kerrs—and I guess the kids work pretty hard at it. Working on a vegetable garden is hell. The birds and the rabbits and the snails and God knows what take half of it. . . ."

"Have you worked on a vegetable garden, Rod?"

"Princess, it's easier to ask me what I haven't worked on. The way up is . . . well, interesting, when you start from the very bottom. But I was always an opportunist—and a good liar. When I got my first job—the time when my father was going to march us into the orphan home—I told them I was almost fifteen, when I'd just turned twelve. I was a big boy—even then. People would believe anything—as long as they paid almost nothing for wages."

"What was the job? Where?"

"A little family hotel on the outskirts of Vancouver. I carried the bags, cleaned the shoes and the brass, split the wood, and did any damn thing they could think of to keep me busy. I slept in the basement—at least it was warm. The furnace was there."

"How did you get the money to get to Vancouver?"

"I stole my father's money, Princess. I figured if he was going to dump us all in an orphanage, I had the right to fight my way out of that situation. With whatever money he had. It was mine, too, I thought. So I got as far away from him as I could—and after that, my name was McCallum. And as for vegetable gardens—once I'd managed to sneak over into the States, I worked a summer near Portland—I worked vegetable gardens when it was so hot I could water the ground with my own sweat. Those were the twenties, Princess—and I wasn't a Wall Street broker. There were lots of poor people in America. Then it was on to Montana, where I was so cold I was glad enough of having been brought up in the Highlands, or I don't think I could have stood it." Then he tugged at her arm impatiently. "Oh, let's forget it. We'll go back and have a drink in the library before we get dressed. Guess who's coming to dinner?"

"On our first night?"

"Who else but our old friend Sir Niall? You don't think I'd

be so discourteous as not to thank him for picking up Princess Cat. At any rate—we owe him.''

Julia bathed in the now warm and cheerful bathroom, prepared for dinner, and wore one of the three gowns Rod had produced for her. ''That little shopping expedition to Saks with Stacia and Alasdair . . . well, I didn't leave you out.'' They were all of fine cashmere, plain, green, blue, and red, fashioned in a flowing style that she could wear right through her pregnancy. She wore his two great rings and saw the pleasure glow in his eyes.

But she was surprised at the fierceness of his grip on her arm as they went forward to greet Sir Niall. ''It's been worth it, Princess—every bit of it. I've come home.''

Sir Niall wore his dress kilt and velvet jacket for the occasion. Julia did not have time to ponder Rod's strange words before she was enveloped in Sir Niall's arms. ''Welcome home. It's impossible to say how I've missed you. . . .'' He warmly shook Rod's hand and then in turn took Alasdair's hand before succumbing to the temptation to embrace the boy. ''Home for your sixth birthday. We'll make a grand thing of it.'' Then he turned to Stacia, who had hung back with an expression on her face that said she expected to be left out of this special greeting. He spoke to her, smiling broadly. ''My dear—is it possible that you're lovelier than before?'' He bowed formally, and to Stacia's evident delight raised her hand and kissed it.

Alasdair was permitted to stay up; they ate in the dining hall by the soft gleam of the chandeliers and lighted candles. After Rod had poured the wine, Sir Niall raised his glass to him. ''What a very splendid thing you have accomplished here.''

Rod nodded and permitted himself the briefest smile. Julia thought she read beyond his slightly masked expression. He must also have been remembering the child from the McBain cottage, the terrible struggle of the boy who was already a man to carve a future for himself in America, the handsome man whose face the camera loved who had clawed his way up the Hollywood ladder. He was now experiencing a triumph that achievement of money and fame had so far never given him. But he also believed Sinclair was his—it belonged to him and his child.

When Alasdair had gone to bed, they spent a last companionable half hour with Sir Niall over a Drambuie in front of the library fire. Then they went to the front courtyard to say good-night. Just as Sir Niall was about to get into his car, he turned to Julia. "My dear, I'm sorry about Duuf and Angus. William Kerr asked me to come over each time the vet came. They were very old and very tired. Duuf lasted only a few weeks longer than his brother. And there's old Rory . . . deaf as a doorpost and just able to drag himself from one fire to another. He hasn't much time, my dear. I remember them all when they were young. Jamie's beloved companions . . ." He slammed the car door swiftly and set off into the night with uncharacteristic speed. Rod's expression told Julia that Jamie's name was not now welcome at Sinclair.

II

AT ONCE there began a round of social activity that Julia had never experienced at Sinclair. All the people who had been invited to Rod's well-remembered party in the Caledonian in Inverness the year before were invited now to Sinclair, to see, to admire, to praise what he had accomplished. The restraint he had exercised in the restoration was not spoken of openly, but Julia knew it was noticed. Only once did someone speak frankly about it, and that was Kirsty Macpherson. She drew on a cigarette and looked at Julia with a half smile. "Well—frankly, I didn't credit your cowboy with such good taste. And he's even nicely modest about it . . . but we all know around here that he's supervised every detail. Can't keep these things secret in a little community like this. . . . He's annoyed and bothered the architects and decorators no end." She nodded, with a flicker of approval. "Good for him. And we hear you're having a baby. . . ."

"Yes."

Kirsty shrugged. "Well, good luck. I suppose I should have another child. Douglas would love a child. A boy. But the thought of pregnancy makes me sick, without actually going through it. Besides—it hasn't happened, even though I've done nothing to prevent it. . . ." Her expression changed abruptly as Rod approached them. She smiled her pleasure at his invitation to tour the newly planted garden. Julia watched them go with a faint sense of misgiving. It was not easy to be married to a man who seemed able to charm almost any woman he fastened his attention on. Lady Lowell eased her arthritic body onto the sofa beside Julia and accepted a second cup of coffee from the smartly uniformed Kate.

"Watch him, my dear. I've known his kind before. Can't understand what he's doing in this backwater of the Highlands. Isn't as if he has any connections around here—according to the newspapers. But Americans are terribly sentimental about what they consider their homeland. Watch Kirsty . . . she'd have him in two seconds if she could. Oh, my dear . . ." Her thin hand touched Julia's momentarily. "What a rude, arrogant, unthinking old bore I've grown into. You're pregnant . . . I have no right to say such things. As long as he's devoted to you—and an ideal of Scotland—there's nothing much wrong with the man. . . . I really must arrange a dinner for you both. And that girl, Stacia—what an extraordinary-looking creature she is! You really will be an oddly mixed-up family when the baby arrives. Still . . . perhaps it's better that way. One doesn't get bored. . . ."

There was little chance to be bored in the weeks that followed. Although Rod presented a facade of calm good humor to the outside world, Julia knew that he was seething from the lack of response by Worldwide to his departure from Hollywood after his suspension. No official word reached him from the studio. "I feel as if I've sunk into the loch," he said bitterly to Julia one morning as he scanned the morning's mail. "Here's the usual soothing note from Phil Westin—he's working on it, he says. Well, he'd better begin working pretty hard, or I'll find myself another agent." He looked across at her. "That would mean another agent for you, too, Princess."

"Do you think I'll ever make another film?"

"Of course you will! You're talented and beautiful. We'll find you something good. . . ." He flung down the letters. "Oh, hell, let's not bother with the whole damn thing. They'll come to their senses in time. Perhaps something better than I've ever had will turn up. Nothing like a little show of independence to make them realize that Hollywood isn't the only place in the world. I could hang out here forever without another goddamn cent of their salary. Aren't many movie stars who can say that."

But Julia was aware that he was often on the difficult and unreliable transatlantic telephone line, trying, within the eight hours of time zones that separated them, to talk to Phil Westin.

Rod cursed the fact that every call had to go through the Inverness exchange. "I really can't say a thing, even when I do manage to catch Phil. They're all listening. I'd hate like hell to let anyone know I care a damn about what happens. But I can't have Phil asleep on the job. . . ."

They were invited to lunches and dinners, and Stacia always was asked with them; they always drove grandly in the Rolls. When Rod discovered that William Kerr had been obliged to abandon the old station wagon to the scrap heap and had replaced it with something hardly better, he had insisted that Kerr must have the jeep he had bought the year before. He even had the papers made out in Kerr's name so that ownership was not disputed. On the occasions where they were invited out, Rod seemed to Julia unnaturally bright, exuding charm and bonhomie even beyond his normal measure. And then he would return to Sinclair and a darkness seemed to descend on him. He drank in the way he had in Hollywood, when things had not gone well for him. Not vast quantities at a time, but steadily. He seldom walked in the forest. He was not interested in accompanying Alasdair and Princess Cat. He forbade Julia from going into the forest herself. "What—do you think I want you falling and losing the baby? You could be out there for hours without anyone knowing where you were."

"Well, come with me. At least walk to the cottage with me. It would do you good."

"Don't want to see the damn place again as long as I live. It annoys me every time I pass it. It should be torn down. It's no good to anyone."

She knew it was the last shred of his past he wanted to destroy. "You can't do that. It isn't yours to tear down. It may be needed someday—when we can afford more help for the farm. It costs money to build cottages, Rod. It would do as a makeshift place if one of the young farm workers wanted to get married. . . ."

His face flushed with anger. "Don't you tell me what things cost. Have you any idea of the fortune I've spent on this place? No!—you didn't want to know. All those months in Beverly Hills you knew what I was doing here. I don't remember you asking to see a plan, or asking about what anything cost."

"You never *let* me ask! It was all your business—your concern. I was to keep out of it. I didn't think you were spending less than a fortune, but every time I tried to talk about it, you shut me up. Were you afraid to be reminded that you were spending money on something you didn't own?''

''Alasdair's a kid . . . plenty can happen before he takes over. He might be grateful to be rid of the whole thing.''

''But Alasdair doesn't own it, even when he comes of age. He will own it when I *give* it to him.''

A slow, teasing smile came to Rod's lips. ''Then we really needn't discuss it now. Do you remember that I have your power of attorney?''

''You'd never exercise it that way!''

''Try me. I'll do anything I damn well think fit. Alasdair isn't laird of the castle yet.''

''You do anything to take this place away from me—or Alasdair—and I'll—''

''Do what?'' He rose from the sofa in the library and went to the drinks tray to refill his glass. ''Difficult thing, Princess. After all, I put your name on the Beverly Hills house and the ranch. Gesture of a loving, trusting husband. And in turn you trusted me to look after your affairs and to adopt Alasdair. Gave the kid a father, didn't I? Gave him inheritance rights . . .'' He raised his glass to her. ''Let's drop the matter. Tell you what I think we'll do. We'll give the kid a slap-up birthday party. Have all the estate kids here in the afternoon and have a banquet in the evening for the adults. Think I'll get on the telephone to your father and say it's time he paid us a visit. Maybe Connie and Ken could come. Yes . . . that's what we'll do. Make it a birthday party no one will forget . . . Not much time to arrange it, but it can be done. Oh, did I tell you Ernie Wilcox is arriving in a few days? And the birthday party could just about coincide with Margot Parker's visit . . . nice little touch for her to write about. I've given her a first shot on the place—the story. But that's only two weeks before the Condé Nast people are here— with cameras. I had Phil Westin offer the story and pictures to Forster Newspapers, but for some reason they weren't very hot on the idea, even though Margot Parker's their Hollywood correspondent. So Margot's going to do it for one of the top fan magazines. Can it be that that brother-in-law of yours is cold-shouldering us? Or is it Alex? Have I taken too much of you from her, Julia? You're not her little sister anymore. You're my wife. And you're going to have my child. . . . A child is something I suspect Alex would very much like, and high and mighty Elliot even more. What's wrong with them? Aren't they up to it anymore?''

Julia felt choked with rage and impotence. ''You've done all this—made all these arrangements—without even consulting me? You know Margot Parker's pure poison. And you've invited her *here!*''

''Margot Parker's just about the most powerful woman in Hollywood. I don't have to tell you that. After all, she's syndicated in Forster Newspapers. And fan magazines. They *believe* what she writes. Even the studio bosses believe half of it. She's a very smart woman. And a very dangerous enemy. Better make her a friend. As soon as I knew the place here had turned out well, I cabled her to come on over. I even threw in expenses, so she's a free agent, and she'll have an ocean voyage on us. She should be as sweet as sugar when she arrives.''

''I don't believe it! You can't have done all this without telling me.''

He shrugged. ''Why not? Got to make the most of what publicity we can get. God, wouldn't I love to see Morris Meadows' face when he reads it. If he thinks I'm hiding in some little cabin in the Highlands, waiting to be called back to his horse opera . . . well, he'll think again.''

Julia got to her feet. ''I'll never allow my father to become involved in this cheap little publicity stunt. I'll warn him. *He* doesn't need Margot Parker—''

She winced as Rod grasped her wrist. ''I think you'll fall in with whatever I arrange, Princess. It would be plain stupid not to. After all, you don't want to ruin the kid's birthday, do you? You don't want to make everybody unhappy. . . . I'll tell him, you know. I'll tell him Mummie doesn't want him to have a good time. I'll tell him Mummie doesn't want Johnny to come and see him. Perhaps . . . maybe Princess Cat just might be so homesick for her pals at Anscombe that she has to be sent back there.''

''You devil! I think you'd do it.''

''Yes, I would, dear Princess. Don't think any of the niceties of your precious little world cut any ice with Rod McCallum.''

''I'll . . . I'll leave you—divorce you. I won't let you take over like this.''

The strange, otherworldly smile that she now knew came from

drugs deepened on his face. "You'll have a tough battle, Princess. Haven't I laid the world at your feet? There are no grounds you could possibly prove as a reason for divorce. There hasn't been any other woman—"

"You assaulted me—beat me—"

"Did you lodge a complaint with the police at the time? Did you leave my house? Did you leave me?"

"There are those who can testify . . . Maria and José . . . Dr. Fields . . ."

He laughed openly. "Do you think you'd get any of those people to open their mouths? It's the Hollywood code. Maria and José would never get another job. No one would enter Sam Fields' clinic again if they thought anything that went on there might be reported. You're sweet, Princess—and very unworldly."

"I'll leave you."

"Do—if you want to. And I'll fight you in every court in the land, and in the United States, if I have to, for custody of our child—and Alasdair. I'll use that power of attorney to take away every single thing you think you possess. I can fight you for our child—and my adopted son. I can even take this castle away from you—Alasdair's inheritance, as you keep reminding me. Oh, it would be a very ugly and messy affair. After all, how would it look? I'm the star, and I tried to make you a star. I have the money—and what did you have? A crumbling castle, and a hand-to-mouth existence. And I've been generous, Princess. Just look how I've treated Anne Rayner's child—what has she lacked? She's had indulgence, sympathy, care. I've never let her run wild. . . ."

"You take drugs . . . that doesn't make you a fit father for anyone."

He shrugged. "I occasionally indulge. But I can come off drugs anytime I please. No one is going to prove that against me. If you get a legal order for a test, I can show up clean as a whistle. Oh, it'll be one great fight—one you'll wish you never started.

"So just calm down, Julia, and leave things take their course. It was all right in the beginning, wasn't it? You didn't mind anything I did then. You were happy to be married—and married very well—and out of this dump. You didn't want to grow old here, did you, Julia? Grow old—alone. Watching the snow pile up every winter and wonder if you'd make it through another farming season. Everything mortgaged up to the hilt. Oh, I know the whole story. William Kerr opened the books to me when he realized how much money I was spending on the place—and how much I could be persuaded to give to the farm in time. He's worked with women too long. They have their place—but it's not running things. That was to be next, once the castle was put in order. The farm was to be looked at thoroughly. Improved. New machinery. Any good land that came onto the market I would buy. But anything that was done would be in my name—I would agree to it and sign for it. He knows I have your power of attorney, and it seems perfectly right and proper to him. Women were not meant to run business affairs. . . . To him, like any good Scot, money is money, and I've put my money where my mouth is. That counts. It always does.

"Think again, Princess. It can all be so nice and easy. We'll give the kid a swell birthday party—and all the people we've invited to come will come. Including Margot Parker. And anyone else I feel damn well pleased to invite. This is *my* home. We'll put this little upset of yours down to the fact that you're pregnant, and pregnant women do strange things. Like throwing away a perfectly good husband when there isn't another waiting in the wings. You'll never have it so good again—you and the kid. Don't forget what you're going to be doing to him. And *our* son. Don't forget, Julia. Go away and think about it."

She began to move toward the door. "I detest you! I'm not strong enough now to fight you, but after the baby is born I'll—"

"After the baby is born you'll be a happy and satisfied mother. You'll see that everything I do for you is for the best. You'll understand then. . . ."

"I'll get away from you, Rod. No matter how it's done, I'll get rid of you—and I'll have *both* my children."

He threw back his head and laughed, a wild, manic laugh. "You'll have to kill me to do that."

She jerked the door open as she turned to shout her last words at him. "I *could* kill you. I could kill you for freedom—for the right to do what is best for my children. Yes, even kill you!"

When she faced the passageway Stacia was there, and behind her, Kate, bearing a tea tray. And at the entrance to the little passage were Alasdair and Rosmairi, who had washed him and combed his hair in preparation for the tea ritual that they shared every day in the library. The young girl and the child stared at her with wide eyes, and Julia saw that Alasdair's lips trembled. She had no idea how much of the talk in the library they had all overheard.

"Kill him, would you?" Stacia said. She smiled the enigmatic child-woman smile. "That's what my mother used to say. But in the end *she* was the one who wound up dead."

"Dead!" Alasdair's cry was nearer to a scream. "Mummie, you can't get deaded. You can't!"

Rod had moved to the door and put his hand gently on Julia's shoulder. "That's right, sonny. Your Mummie can't get deaded. She's just a bit upset because she's not quite well. As soon as your little brother is born she'll be just fine again. I promise."

Julia jerked herself away from his touch. She brushed Stacia aside and ran along the passage. She took Alasdair's hand and half dragged him through the Great Hall and dining hall. Rosmairi followed. "Oh, ma'am . . ."

They reached the housekeeper's room. Janet had heard the commotion of their running steps. She stood at the kitchen door and then came to the housekeeper's room. "Go to your tea in the kitchen, Rosmairi. 'Tis none of your business . . ."

By now Alasdair had begun to cry. Julia sat down and took him in her lap, struggling to control her own tears but unable to subdue the trembling of her whole body. Alasdair called beseechingly to Janet, "Stacia said Mummie was going to get deaded. You won't let that happen, will you, Janet?"

"Why, never! What a foolish thought. Why ever would your mother get—well, why ever would she die?"

"I don't know. But Stacia said her mother got deaded. And Mummie will, too."

"That girl's tongue—like a snake . . ." Janet went and took Alasdair from Julia's arms and into her own. "Why, child, I've cared for you from the moment of your birth. I'd never tell you a lie. Your mother will not die. I don't care what anyone says. It is all foolish nonsense. She will not die. You must not be troubled by such thoughts." She had her handkerchief out, wiping his tears, making him blow his nose. "Well, well—that's better. Your mother will be very well indeed once the little one is born. It does upset ladies sometimes, Alasdair. Something you'll understand when you're a little older. When the baby comes—"

"I don't want the baby!" Alasdair screamed. "I don't want a baby brother. Why can't it be the way it was—before *he* came? I think I'll kill him—my mother said she'd kill him, but I'll do it before she does. Yes, I'll kill him, and then it will all be the way it was before."

Janet laid her finger across his mouth gently. "We'll have no more talk like that, Master Alasdair. There will be no killing—or dying—in this house. It will be sorted out. Peace, child—peace. Go and sit with your mother. Take care of her. I'll bring your tea in here. . . ."

"Bring a cup for yourself, Janet." Julia felt an urgent need for the woman's presence, the sense of comfort and protection it conveyed.

Janet returned with the tray, but besides the tea and scones it contained, there was also a whiskey glass, which seemed to Julia to contain a double measure. "A wee dram, Mrs. McCallum. 'Twill settle your nerves. Now, Master Alasdair, you have your tea, and let us hear no more talk of dying. No one is going to die. Here you are, almost six years old, and no more sense than when you were two. Would Janet let anything happen to you—or your lovely mother? Never! We all have many years to live yet. Of course, for the old folk—well, that's a natural thing."

"My uncle was only young when he drowned out there in the loch. My father got deaded in the war. My grandfather was deaded out here in the forest. People get *deaded*. Before they're old."

"Who told you this, child?"

"Rod told me. Stacia told me. Just the way she told me about her mother."

Janet caught the child and held him to her. "It will not happen again." Across his head she said softly to Julia, "The tongues of snakes. What have we here, Mistress? A nest of vipers?"

Julia said nothing, but wondered if she could last out the months of her pregnancy before she began the actions that would end this dangerous misalliance.

The next weeks passed before Julia's gaze as if some surrealist movie track rolled, with her a trapped and unbelieving viewer. Rod hired a temporary secretary, Miss Grant, who came daily from Inverness; they virtually took over the library, and one or the other of them was constantly on the telephone. Julia, Alasdair, and Stacia used the housekeeper's room, or sat in the drawing room, which, as Rod had pointed out, was splendidly refurbished, but somehow it lacked warmth or charm or individuality. Perhaps Rod's interest had run out at this point. Through Rod, everything was organized. Alasdair's sixth birthday party was elevated to something that far exceeded what had seemed a rather elaborate affair two years ago, the day she had received the letter with the offer to hire Castle Sinclair as a movie set. Only two years? Julia's weary mind tried to throw away thoughts of the past. She had never mentioned again the row that had taken place in the library—the threats offered and exchanged. It all must wait until she was better able to cope with what she knew must be done.

This time the birthday favors and ingredients for the party and the banquet that would follow were mostly ordered by cable from New York and sent by air freight. They were much more elaborate than those Alex had sent for Alasdair's fourth birthday. But apart from the toys, every child, and that included anyone under sixteen on the estate, would have a woolen sweater and cap. "If they don't fit, they can swap them around," Rod said. He treated Julia's passive attitude as entirely normal, something he had expected once he pointed out all the difficulties in her path. The list for the evening banquet included all the best-known families of the area. If they seemed a little reluctant to accept the invitation, both telephoned and written in Miss Grant's copperplate scroll, the added inducement was that Rod had persuaded Julia's father and Luisa to bring Johnny to Alasdair's party. "You owe the kid," Julia heard him say one evening on the telephone to Michael. "His birthday celebrations . . ." Alasdair's birthday fell in the middle of the week, but Rod switched its celebration to the weekend, so that more could attend, and the farm workers and tenants could have their own Saturday afternoon party, with lavish food and drink laid on in the housekeeper's room. The Caledonian Hotel had agreed to hire out its two chefs for the occasion, and waiters and waitresses, and would lend extra china and glasses. "It will be," Miss Grant said primly, "the first time the Caledonian has not operated on a Saturday night since Mr. McCallum hired it for his private party last year." She seemed pleased to be associated with the event. Life was still hard and austere in Britain, many things still rationed. An event that promised to bring back memories of the good times before the war was welcomed. Rod had had slaughtered several cattle and sheep, which were already in the hanging room, along with six sides of ham that had arrived from London. Sir Niall contributed two sides of venison. Janet's pantry filled up with sugar, flour, containers of butter, and bowls of eggs. Julia was consumed with guilt. She could remember passing butcher shops in London that had displayed the value of the meat any one customer could buy that week—it had been down to sixpence. It would have taken the ration books of three people to buy a single lamb chop. When she protested, Rod just laughed. "Princess, don't be so damn moralistic. Everyone knows it goes on. It's called the black market, if you don't already know. This isn't the war, remember. Ships aren't being sunk, and people losing their lives to bring in food. Those who can pay, get. Those who can't—stand in line to buy their sixpence worth. It's always been that way. In war and peace. I ought to know better than most."

By telephone calls and a fulsome, handwritten letter, which Miss Grant had helped him compose, Rod persuaded Connie to bring her two children for the event; he enclosed first-class rail tickets. By booking and paying for a sleeper ticket he made it possible for Ken to travel overnight to Edinburgh on the Friday evening and take the early train to Inverness the next morning. A rather flustered Connie telephoned Julia. "Do you really want us?—I mean, the two children and Ken and me—we'll take up an awful lot of room and eat an awful lot of food."

"Food is our least worry," Julia said rather wearily. "This is practically Aladdin's cave. Have you got anything to wear for this absurd banquet, or do you want to borrow something of mine?"

"Alex has just sent the most wonderful dress. I doubt it's been worn six times. Now that Ken and I have to attend official functions, she sends more than ever. . . . Mrs. Warren is knitting socks for Alasdair—and some little things for the baby. . . ."

Julia thought of the precious coupons expended and of how Rod would provide for his child, and she bit back her objections. What was done in love and with the sacrifice of scarce resources had far more value than anything bought with money.

Money seemed far from Rod's thoughts in those few hectic

weeks. He planned without regard for expense. "Princess," he said, "I'm having the time of my life. This beats any Hollywood party I've ever given—or I've ever been to. A man in his own castle! What can beat that?"

Julia did not say then, nor would she before the celebrations were over, that it was not his castle. She began to ponder what she could do to extricate herself from the legal muddle her trusting heart had landed her in, in the early days of her marriage. She looked at the great jewels on her fingers, thought of her name being placed on the deeds of the Beverly Hills house, and the ranch, of the gifts Rod had lavished on her and Alasdair, of the money that had been poured into making the castle the dream of comfort and beauty it was now. Surely all these things had revealed a man of almost reckless generosity, which was difficult to believe in someone who came from his hard background and upbringing. But since the night he had beaten her and almost killed himself, the dark doubts about him would not disappear. She told herself she must wait—wait until the baby was born. She felt the swelling of her belly and told herself that no other great traumas must impede its healthy passage into the world. She looked at Alasdair's fair young face, becoming with every year so much more like Jamie's, and thought she owed this coming child no less than he had had. So she tried to banish the thoughts of trouble, the nearly deadly anger she had experienced, and concentrate on the superficial pleasure of what Rod was arranging. Ernest Wilcox had arrived and clearly was enjoying every moment of his stay.

"Rod's been great to me—always. He doesn't forget old friends, even though he's made it big." He entered into every detail of the planning with delight. He helped Miss Grant on the details and spent a long time discussing the flowers with the florist in Edinburgh. He sighed with pleasure over the Sinclair family silver, the Meissen dinner service that came down from the top shelf of the butler's pantry. "I can't count the years since it's last been used," Janet said. Ernest helped her wash and dry each piece with reverent care. That afternoon, as he escorted Julia on her walk through the forest road, he said, "I can't tell you how proud I am of Rod. The Beverly Hills house is very fine in its way—but this is the real thing. He consulted me a few times about details, but mostly it was all his own choice. He's a very bright man—oh, I know—no formal education. But he soaks up things like a sponge. Pity he doesn't have *quite* what it takes to be a great actor—unlike your father. I can't wait to meet your father, Julia.''

They were almost at the McBain cottage when he said those words. She clamped her mouth on what she might have told him of the precise details of Rod's beginnings. She was beginning to wonder if Rod himself regretted what he had told her that first night they had sat by the fire there. He had trusted her with a story that he might now deny and that he never referred to. But had that been to win her sympathy, or the shattering of his nerve at the encounter with the tiny rooms in which he had been brought up?

Rod and Ernest made several trips to Edinburgh in the Rolls. ''Just getting a few bits and pieces, Princess. Ernie's talking to the florist. . . .''

At Rod's insistence, Ernest had stayed in New York for three days, his bill paid, at the Waldorf-Astoria, to do some shopping. He had produced gowns for Julia and Stacia that he unfolded with loving pride. ''I do hope you like them. I had to consider your condition, Julia . . . something flowing, but still magnificent.'' It was a gown of gold cloth, hand-embroidered in gold thread, that stood away from her body stiffly, with a high mandarin collar. ''You look like an empress,'' Ernest said. There was a gown of ivory silk chiffon with a band of red sequins around its neckline for Stacia. When a seamstress in Inverness had taken a few tucks in it and fitted the bodice more exactly, it revealed her woman's body to a startling degree. Julia could remember one of Anne Rayner's films in which she had worn a similar dress. The likeness between mother and daughter became even more evident. Stacia twirled before them all with radiant delight. The alterations now showed off her neck and the deep cleavage between her full breasts, and her skin glowed with a sheen greater than the silk chiffon.

''Great!'' Ernest said.

''A little—well, grown up, isn't it?'' Rod said.

''But I *am* grown up,'' Stacia hurled back at him. ''You're the only one who doesn't see it. But you will pretty soon. . . .''

Alasdair had been fitted for his first dress kilt, velvet jacket, frilled shirt, and buckled shoes. Rod had objected that it was the Sinclair tartan that had been chosen. ''He's my adopted son. It should be McCallum.''

Sir Niall, who had taken Alasdair to his own tailor, demurred. "It wouldn't do, Rod. Whatever legal changes have been made, to people around here, he'll always be a Sinclair. Don't shock them too much."

Rod shrugged. "Well, it's done now. There isn't time to argue."

He and Ernest were busy with the allocation of the rooms. "Do you mind, Princess, if we give up the Red Tower Room to Margot Parker for just those few days? It'll sound sensational in her column. You and I can use the Blue State Room. Now that it's got its own bathroom, it's quite comfortable. And of course your father and Luisa must have the Prince Charles Suite. That little sitting room makes it really nice." Ernest already occupied what had been Lady Jean's room, still called the Rose Room, though its faded chintz had been refurbished, the worn carpet replaced by something of a true rose color. He had protested about taking up such space. "Oh, just tuck me away in some little closet," he had said, but no one believed him. The Rose Room had once shared a bathroom with the Blue State Room, but now it had been connected to a bathroom fashioned from what had once been the old linen cupboard.

Rod had been more than a little annoyed when a stiff "regrets" letter had come from Alasdair's godfather, Lady Jean's brother, the earl. "We're not good enough for him, I suppose. He might become tainted with Hollywood. . . . Just as well, because we really don't have anywhere suitable to put him and his lady wife—unless you and I, Julia, took the little rooms above the Red Tower Room." There had not been time to renovate these, although the plumbing and electricity lines had been run up there. Not everything could be accomplished in the short time Rod had allowed; he accepted the situation unwillingly.

Connie and Ken and the two children would be occupying the two tower rooms that had been Callum's and Jamie's. Here, too, the bathroom had been refurbished with new fittings and central heating. The bedrooms were both done in shades of blue and green—no chintz or tartan. Stacia grumbled mildly about having to give up what she considered her own tower eyrie. "But . . . as long as it's for them. It's nice that they're going to be here." She had been allocated the Culloden Room, grand enough but with its heating still not working. A number of electric heaters had been placed around, but the water still ran lukewarm in its bathroom and radiators. "You'll just have to put up with it for a few days, Stacia. When you want a hot tub, you'll have to ask Julia, so you can use our bathroom. It won't be for long. . . . Perhaps just as well Alex and Elliot weren't able to get here. The Culloden Room would have done beautifully for them . . . if it were functioning." The Culloden Room, with its unique paneling, probably would be the most magnificent in the castle. It infuriated Rod that the heating engineers were still defeated in their efforts to get enough hot water to the radiators to heat it. Rod had railed at them ceaselessly about whatever fault caused this, and therefore the delay in fully redecorating the room. They had shrugged, and the architect had pored over the plans of the plumbing lines and shrugged also. "You have to remember, Mr. McCallum, this is a building which goes more upward than outward, and when it was built, the only water came from a well in the kitchen courtyard. We just must increase the size of the pumps. . . ."

"Then increase, for God's sake! And make the water get up there—good and hot! I could have used that room this summer . . . we have important guests."

The architect lost the patience he had clung on to precariously in the eighteen months Rod had been his client and Castle Sinclair had been his nightmare. "Man, will you ever realize that we have achieved miracles here—*miracles?* Believe me, there's no architect in Scotland who's envied me my job. I have combed the land for the finest joiners and stonemasons. I have set almost impossible tasks for the plumbers and heating engineers. Man, do you not realize what you're dealing with here? This isn't any Hollywood fake! This is the real thing—"

"Okay, okay . . . keep your shirt on," Rod said. "Sure, you've done a great job. I'm just a little impatient. I apologize. I mean that. And just to show I mean it, will you now sit down and have a wee dram with me, and we'll discuss all the terrific things you have been able to achieve here? And they are achievements. I hope you and your lady wife will grace us with your presence at the dinner we're giving on the night of my stepson's birthday." The actor that he was, Rod quickly fell into the Highland lilt and speech pattern, but was clever enough not to overdo and make himself ridiculous—or worse, seem to mock his hearer. "It's a pity we haven't a room to offer you—but as you said, space here goes upward."

The architect shrugged and accepted the whiskey, carefully not committing himself to accepting the invitation. "Someday, if you're brave enough and feeling very rich, we might attempt to redo the North Tower. A mighty task. As you saw, we've rendered the outside walls safe and weathertight, and redone the roof, but the inside is a ruin . . . quite unsafe. It's the least favorably sited of the towers. Any sane man would just keep the doors to it locked and forget about it. But, as you've noticed, we've taken away that ugly barricade. Those doors on the North Tower are as magnificent as anything in the castle. We've truly tried and tested the lovely hardware and lock. They're sound and in good working order. I turned over the key to Mr. Kerr. Now, if you *really* want additional accommodations, there's much easier and less expensive work that could be done to the buildings in the stable block."

"We'll see . . ." Rod murmured. Julia listened, and silently prayed that his ambitions for the restoration of the castle, and his willingness to spend money on it, had run their course. She and Alasdair were already too deeply in his debt; she vowed that there would be no more gatherings like this. Surely once the columnists and the magazines had had their field day, once he had reveled in the triumph of what had been done, the fact that every magazine would picture and credit him as being its owner, his ambitions would be satisfied.

Then he said, "Oh, Princess, I forgot to tell you. A cable from Bill Fredricks this morning. He and Rita are arriving in Southampton tomorrow. They'll be able to make it up here in time. The pity is they'll have to stay at the Caledonian." He glanced at the architect. "Not enough room here. Pity . . . They should have had the Culloden Room, and we could have put Stacia—oh, hell, maybe we'll just have to do something about the North Tower."

"I tell you, man, leave the North Tower alone! It's only one room piled on top of another, and I doubt there's a boiler in the world big enough to heat it properly. We're still living in hard times. You'll have used up more than your coal ration before the summer's out. And after that . . . well, make sure that every pipe to every room that's not actually in use is drained, or you'll have burst pipes and water ruining all your finery."

"We'll keep heat in the place," Rod said, his lips tightening with annoyance. "I won't let it go back to dampness and mold."

The architect sipped his twelve-year-old Scotch and permitted himself a little smile. "I didn't hear that last statement, Mr. McCallum. Where a man gets his supplies of coal from is none of my business. But be sure you have an able-bodied man here morning and evening to stoke the boiler. That monster eats coal— and it's no job for a woman."

Julia had begun to think that the castle itself might become an engulfing monster.

"We'll convert to oil as soon as this miserable government is able to get its act together and provide us with what every other European country is now able to get. Even the Germans, who lost the war—"

"This country is broke, Mr. McCallum," the architect said. "I haven't any idea when we'll ever pay off our debts from the war."

Rod gestured impatiently. "Well, I have plenty of good, sound dollars. They buy a lot over here."

"Fortunate man," the architect said, and finished his drink in one gulp.

They began to arrive. First there were Bill and Rita Fredricks, then Connie and the two children, Margaret and Clive. Rod went to the station at Inverness in the Rolls to greet each arrival, and almost before they had time to draw a breath, they had to take a tour of the castle. It obviously irked Rod that there was no room for the Fredrickses at the castle. He had recently bought another jeep, and it was for Bill's use while he was there. "And mind you, stay on the left-hand side of the road. . . . We expect you here every day for lunch and dinner—unless you want to take a picnic somewhere. There's some good fishing around. Sir Niall is very generous about inviting people to fish his river. . . ."

Connie was stunned and awestruck by what she saw. "I can hardly believe it. I was here during the war, you know." She spoke to Rod. "It was . . . well, not at all like this. Everyone was living in as few rooms as possible, trying to keep warm."

"You don't have to tell me, Connie. We filmed here when it was just like that—only we paid a bit more to keep fires going in what rooms were habitable. I hope you'll be comfortable this time around. . . ."

Connie laughed aloud. "Rod, do you remember what *our*

house is like? We're still growing—a little bit here, a little bit there. Somehow, even the money Mr. Warren was able to make during the war doesn't seem to get us what we want. Things just aren't available. And he's afraid now of stepping outside the law. He's terrified of doing anything that might harm Ken's career.''

"Ken's career? How's he doing?''

Connie sighed. "Climbing the ladder. The Civil Service is not notable for swift advancement. But he has a very responsible job. He works terribly hard. . . . Some people say he should have gone into politics. He would have made Chancellor of the Exchequer someday.'' Her face brightened into a smile. "I'm so very glad he didn't go into politics. He couldn't sell himself to the crowd. Chancellors come and go, but Permanent Under Secretaries last forever.''

"Is that what he'll be?'' Bill Fredricks asked. "It sounds important—I mean, the *permanent* part of it. Is it forever?''

"In the upper ranks of the Civil Service—yes, it's forever, unless you do something outrageous or dishonest.''

"Well—hell, how do they switch politics every time a new party gets in?''

"They don't. Their own personal politics don't have anything to do with the job. The new Secretary—or Chancellor—comes in, and in the beginning they have to teach him his job. Discretion is everything. A Secretary or Chancellor may never know which party his Permanent Under Secretary votes for.''

"Can you imagine,'' Ernest said, "the White House being staffed half by Democrats and half by Republicans? There'd be blood in the corridors.''

"Will you let me come and visit you when we get back to London?'' Stacia said. Surprisingly, she had taken Margaret and Clive to sit on each side of her on a sofa and was helping them to put jam on their bread and butter and to cut their cakes.

Connie looked a little surprised. "Why—of course. If you'd like to. There's nothing very entertaining . . .''

"Have you still got that little door into the park—no, I mean the heath?''

"Yes, naturally. Mr. Warren would never part with any of the land—it would upset Mrs. Warren.''

"He will,'' Rod said. "In time. When the taxes go sky-high, for that situation, and he realizes he could make a fortune by selling off for building sites.''

"He'll never sell—while Mrs. Warren is alive."

Rita Fredricks said gently, "You don't mind—this living with your husband's parents? You don't want a place of your own?"

A kind of radiance bathed Connie's face, making her, Julia thought, even more lovely. She had, as she matured, developed the sort of features that in old age would reflect not only a bygone beauty but also an unbreachable security and serenity. Not for the first time, Julia envied her. "Why—goodness, no! I'm so fortunate. They're such dear people, my parents-in-law. They love the children so much. We share the house so comfortably." There was just the faintest shade of reproach in her tone. "You know—we're much more comfortable than most people. Sharing a household means we can plan our rations better, and then Alex keeps sending such loads of canned food. We're quite spoiled."

Bill Fredricks leaned back in his chair, having, at Rod's urging, exchanged his teacup for a glass of Scotch. "I think I've heard everything now. I much look forward to meeting this husband of yours. He really must be something special—having landed a gorgeous woman like you who also is a contented housewife—and produced these two beautiful—and, may I add, perfectly behaved—children."

Connie blushed. "We're nothing special."

"That's what makes you *very* special," Stacia said. Her voice was soft and husky, and Julia realized it was the voice of a woman, not a girl. And it could have been her mother uttering one of the lines in a movie that had made her seem more than merely sexy, but also a very fragile, nearly helpless human being. There was an element in Stacia that craved, as perhaps her mother might have craved, the element of simplicity and security that Connie's life held.

The big moment for Rod was when he went to Inverness to meet the connection to the night sleeper from London that brought Sir Michael and Lady Seymour and their son, Johnny. The newspapers had been alerted and were present at the station. Alasdair had been near tears because he was not allowed to accompany Rod on the early-morning journey to meet the train. "Johnny's my best friend!"

"Then if you're a nice little boy, you'll just have to remember that your folks have luggage with them, and we wouldn't want them to be uncomfortable, would we? And you're going to be—

have yourself, aren't you? No leading Johnny astray . . . no doing anything you know you shouldn't . . ."

"Johnny and I will be all right," Alasdair said sulkily. "But I think you're mean. I wouldn't take up much room. . . ."

He spent the time while he waited for his grandfather, Luisa, and Johnny grooming Princess Cat, with the help of Colin Kerr. They harnessed and saddled her, and before anyone could stop him, Alasdair was riding over the bridge. He rode through the forest road and was waiting there when the Rolls turned off the main road. He accompanied them through the two miles of forest. Rod obligingly slowed down to allow for the pony's pace. Alasdair kept shouting at them. "See, Johnny—isn't it like I said? All wild. Grandfather, don't you think I ride better than Johnny? I've had special lessons. . . ." He bent low and looked carefully into the car. "Mama Luisa, you look beautiful. Most people look terrible when they come off a night on the train."

"God bless the child," Luisa murmured. "How does he learn these nice things to say? I suppose he's quite sophisticated for his age. Hollywood and Washington . . . and all the travel he's done."

Alasdair held out his arm to signal that he would precede them across the bridge, so Rod stopped the Rolls altogether and they had their fill of the picture of the castle. "Photographs don't tell it all," Michael said softly. "It's magnificent. Julia has written us all about it, of course—but somehow I didn't quite expect so much. She's told us in great detail everything that's been done. . . . I know the sort of decay it was in before, though we never saw it. She always considered it would be too uncomfortable for Luisa and Johnny. . . ."

"I hope you'll be *very* comfortable and happy this first visit. The first of many, I hope."

"Thank you, Rod."

They got out of the car to Julia's welcoming arms. There was the ritual of greeting Janet again. They had not met since Julia's wedding. They went through the introduction to Ernest Wilcox, the Kerrs, all the children lined up—to Kate and to Rosmairi. Connie and the children embraced them. As always, Stacia hung back until Luisa put out her arms. "How good to see you." In the warmth of her tone, the incident of the Sèvres china was dismissed; Julia silently blessed Luisa's generosity. Alasdair was already leading Johnny off to the stable block. "Here," said

Alasdair, "I've brought you some carrots to feed her. So she'll remember you . . ."

"She remembers me. Don't you worry. She knows me better than she knows you, don't you, Cat?" He fed the pony the carrots and stroked her muzzle. "How are you, girl? Are they looking after you here? Miss your stablemates? Here, Alasdair, don't be a pig. Get down and let me get up on her." Effortlessly the two changed places, and Johnny trotted around to the first courtyard where the welcoming ceremonies were still going on. He was wearing smart gray pants and navy blazer. His mother's mouth stiffened at the sight of him. "Oh, you two! Are you going to be naughty together all the time?"

"Not *all* the time, Mama. It's just so nice to see Cat again."

"Well, get down, and come in and change before you get yourself quite filthy."

"Come inside to some proper Scottish hospitality," Rod said. He had, with some reluctance, agreed to having this meal in the housekeeper's room. "We can't be on ceremony all the time, Rod," Julia had objected. "You know how simply everyone lives at Anscombe. . . ."

Rod agreed that the bags be left in the hall and that they would go immediately to a midmorning breakfast. "I'm starving," Michael said.

"And I'm dying for coffee," Luisa confessed. Janet was now used to the demand for coffee and had it ready. Almost every week cans of it arrived from Alex. The sideboard was laden with great silver dishes above spirit lamps. Michael helped himself lavishly to liver, bacon, smoked haddock, and ham, with a fried egg on the side. Luisa eyed his plate with horror. "Michael! It's almost lunchtime." She helped herself to one griddle cake. Julia looked and marveled at her slim, lithe figure, the nearly lineless face, although Luisa must now be close to fifty. "Julia, how do you resist all this? But, of course, you must now eat for the baby."

"Not too much," Janet said sternly while pouring coffee. "Dr. MacGregor says she is not to gain too much weight."

Luisa smiled wryly as she apologized to Janet for not being able to sample all the fare. "I did have a biscuit with tea on the train. . . . Johnny, come here at once and have your breakfast. Have you washed your hands . . . ?"

"Nothing wrong with them. . . . Just fed Cat some carrots. . . . Oh, all right. . . .'' He followed Alasdair to the bathroom next to the bedroom they would share.

Luisa sighed with pleasure over her coffee. "Ah, worth waiting for. What a happy welcome." She looked around the room. "And what a pleasant room—I expect you spend a great deal of time here. I wish we had such a room at Anscombe—a sitting and dining room, and close to the kitchen."

Michael was stuffing himself with everything on his plate. He spoke with his mouth still half full. "Marvelous food, Janet. Yes, I wish we had a room like this at Anscombe. Gets a little cramped at times." Rod almost allowed himself to smile at this artlessly given evidence of the superiority of Sinclair over Anscombe. "But you should see what Luisa has accomplished at the château. Really beautiful little place. Not so little, really. She's got the vineyards going splendidly again. If you can manage by the end of the summer to come over for the harvest—it's a great time. Best of all is when we get invited to visit the other châteaux and taste *their* wines. Great rivalry . . . Oh, forgot . . . sorry. You'll probably be back in Hollywood working then. And D.D. says we're taking *Richard III* to Broadway in October for a limited run. The *full* company is coming this time. And Julia . . . well, the baby will be due. You can hardly come this year, but I hope we may expect you next year. . . .''

He turned to Ernest Wilcox, who was seated beside him and hanging on every word but looking just the faintest shade disappointed, as if he hadn't expected a godlike figure such as Sir Michael Seymour to talk of the ordinary things of life, or to eat the quantities a hungry truck driver might have consumed. "Do you come each summer, Mr. Wilcox? You must come over to the château with Julia and Rod. You were born in London, I understand, and Rod tells us he's endlessly indebted to you. . . .'' The effortless charm was poured on, even though he didn't stop eating. Julia considered her father's face. He looked very well, and despite his eating, it was evident that he did a lot of gymnastic work to keep up with his Shakespearean roles. They said in London that he still was the best in a swordfight. She envied the contentment this second marriage had brought to him, remembering those despairing months after her mother's death when it seemed he would never stop drinking—never return to the stage. She blessed, again, D.D.'s inspired thought of bringing them together in *Lear;* how long ago the days of *Lear* now seemed. The days of her first love for Jamie, the innocence of their romance while the city was bombed around them, and daily, nightly, he had flown in the face of death.

Her father was not all absorbed in his food. "Why, Julia . . . you're crying. . . ."

"Not really. Just a bit misty-eyed. Just the pleasure of seeing you all here. My family . . . they do say pregnant women get a bit emotional—"

"And more than a bit tense," Rod interrupted. "This is my first pregnancy to go through. It's hard to guess Julia's mood from one minute to the next. She doesn't at all approve of this wingding we're throwing for Alasdair at the weekend. But I thought—what the hell! Why not? He'll have a great time with all the kids on Saturday afternoon. And he and Johnny can surely stay up to greet the guests in the evening. What better house-warming . . . eh? Everyone for miles around is coming. Mostly to meet you, Sir Michael."

"Rubbish, man. If I know the Scots, they're not at all impressed with personalities. They're coming to have a good time, and from what I've sampled already, they'll have it."

Rod, Julia thought, was looking well himself. He had drunk almost no spirits in the past week; his eyes and manner did not betray that almost frenetic quality they had when he was taking drugs. Perhaps it was true, as he claimed—that he could leave any drug alone when it was necessary, or as he desired. Seeing his welcome to her family, she once again began to doubt her judgment of the dark moments—the moments when he threatened her future, and the future of Alasdair and their child. She was certain that he experienced his own dark moments of doubt. She thought of his determined outward attitude of cheerfulness in the face of his suspension from Worldwide, his pleasure in what had been accomplished at the castle. It was his party, more than Alasdair's, she well understood. She vowed, silently, that she would do or say nothing to spoil it. Their differences could all wait to be resolved.

The few days before the weekend continued to unroll before Julia's eyes in a kind of ordered chaos. Several more of Janet's young relations appeared to help in the house—they were boarded with the Kerrs, but Julia couldn't imagine how they all fitted in. Everyone seemed determined to keep any housekeeping problems from her. "Do sit down, Mrs. McCallum," Janet would order her, "and don't be fretting about anything." She gave a half smile. "And if it's something I or Mr. Kerr can't cope with, then you can be sure Mr. Wilcox will take care of it. I never knew such a man for fussing over details—mind you, I don't object to him doing the flowers for all the rooms, or giving a hand with the dishes."

Miss Grant hovered among various tasks, asking several times if perhaps Sir Michael might not want to dictate some letters—she was always at his service. Unhappily for her, Sir Michael was determinedly on vacation. He borrowed Rod's Rolls and took Luisa and Connie and the children to see the countryside and Inverness. He walked with them in the forest. He continued to sample Janet's cooking with great enjoyment.

Kirsty Macpherson had sent over a pony for Johnny to ride, and a horse for Stacia. The girl had taken very seriously her responsibility to watch over the two boys on their daily rides, still trying to expunge the memory of the tragedy of Cat's death. "They'll be quite safe with Stacia," Rod reassured Luisa. "She's a wonderful horsewoman, and she won't let them get up to any tricks." Luisa smiled nervously, perhaps remembering the fate of the Sèvres tureen.

Julia and Luisa walked often in the garden together. "I hope all is well, my dear," Luisa said. "Rod is taking his suspension from the studio very well. He seems very cheerful—very happy with what he had done with his castle—"

"It's *not* his castle," Julia said, as gently as possible. "I can't either make him understand that, or get him to stop pouring money into what can never be his. Eventually it must belong to Alasdair. It is his birthright."

"And what of your little baby—still unborn?"

"Rod's baby will have every advantage a baby could have. But he—or she—Rod is positive it must be a son—will never be a Sinclair. *That* this baby cannot have."

"Yes—true. I know Michael cares for me deeply. But I cannot ever be Ginette Maslova."

Julia turned quickly and caught her by the shoulders. "But you must know how happy you have made him! When you married, I doubted that." Her hands gently dropped away, and they continued walking. "You have so much money—and somehow I didn't think the love he needed went with that. That was a stupid mistake. You have given him everything—love, cosseting—everything he needed. Space and peace to work at what he wanted, rather than take whatever was offered. He and my mother didn't ever have peaceful lives. Oh, yes, I'm certain they loved each other very much. But it was love and war. In this marriage you are the giver."

"Perhaps. For me, it is a good marriage. Calm—peaceful. And my precious child. Michael gave me Johnny. I do not feel at all like the woman you describe—the woman of wealth and of looking after affairs. Sometimes I think I resemble dear Connie, who only needs her Ken and her children. *She* is a very rich woman indeed."

"Yes . . . you are both fortunate in your marriages."

"We are not disturbed by ambition, Connie and I," Luisa ruminated. "We both have everything we need. You and Alex— you are both talented and troubled by talent. There is little peace for those so afflicted. It is always there—gnawing. You could say we are a privileged lot of people—we, and our charmed circle of success and fame. But you who have the talent must pay the price. I have seen Michael at times so exhausted, so unhappy with his performance. And Alex is worried—"

"Worried?" Julia turned to her in alarm. "What is wrong?"

"Elliot's health. He will not slow down. He will not give up any of the things he feels he must do. He will not delegate. She says at times he is very close to exhaustion, and he will not admit it. To the rest of the world, he appears as he has always done. Only Alex—as I with Michael—see the other side. It is difficult for Alex to make commands that he take things easier— he has always run his own life. She does not say so in so many words—not in her letters. But occasionally we talk on the telephone. I sense her worry. She wanted to come to England this summer—and to come back here. But Elliot says he is too busy. She would not leave him behind."

"No—she wouldn't."

They had reached the place where her father and one of the gardeners had decided that some of the sharply pruned roses he had brought with him should be planted. Michael wore baggy old trousers and an equally battered hat. Ernest Wilcox hovered but offered no advice. Michael greeted their arrival. "Well, I know it's mad to be planting at this time of year. I should have packed them up and sent them in the spring. But you are so far behind in weather here—I thought they had a chance. If they don't do, I'll send some more in the autumn. I just couldn't resist having a bit of the Ginette Maslova rose garden here—I can't forget that Lady Jean sent me one of the first roses I grew—an absolute beauty. And one of the cuttings of that is going back in here. . . ."

Luisa smiled at him encouragingly. How could Ginette Maslova ever be thrust into the background when Michael fostered a cult, and made a shrine of her in his own garden?

Stacia appeared from the arch of an arbor where she had been watching. She was still wearing riding pants and a sweater, having just seen the boys back safely to the stables and being drawn by the sounds of voices in the garden. "I wish," she said in a low voice, "that one day someone would love me enough to make a rose garden for me. . . ."

Luisa buttoned her cardigan and held her arms with her hands. "It's chilly, dearest. I think I'll go in. . . ." Julia accompanied her back to the house.

The next day, Saturday, was the day of the official celebration, though Julia felt it had already been going on for a week. Margot Parker arrived, in a vicious mood because she had had little sleep on the train, had not appreciated having to change at Edinburgh, and was furious that the photographer she had brought with her could not be accommodated at the castle and had had to be left behind at the Caledonian. "I thought it was a castle," she said by way of greeting to Julia, "where you had loads of space. I've seen Windsor Castle—"

"Well, as you now see, there are castles and castles. This is just one of the ordinary sort," Julia answered with a calm smile. She didn't care what Margot Parker thought; she was almost beyond caring what was happening during the next few days. They were Rod's arrangements, Rod's doing, his responsibility. As long as Luisa and her father were comfortable, Connie and the children happy, as long as Alasdair and Johnny got along in their strangely loving, quarrelsome relationship, she didn't worry about anything. Ken Warren had traveled up by the same train as Margot Parker, but the two had not made contact until Rod had introduced them at the Inverness station.

"Who's that gawky guy who came along with us? I don't remember . . ." Margot Parker asked as Julia accompanied her to the Red Tower Room. "You had room for *him*. Will you be picking up the photographer for the kid's party this afternoon, as well as for the dinner? I want lots of pictures—"

"Of course. Bill Fredricks and Rita and staying there. We didn't have room for them, either. But he'll drive the photographer—and there are taxis. The man you met at the station is my sister's husband. Works in Whitehall . . ."

"That's something like Congress, isn't it?"

"Not exactly. He's not elected. He works in the Treasury— and sometimes they send him, with the Chancellor, to brief the Prime Minister. . . ."

Margot's bad temper was beginning to fade. She had taken in the Great Hall on their ascent of the stairs and was now examining the view of the loch from one of the windows of the Red Tower Room. "Must ask him about the Prime Minister. . . ."

"He won't answer. You'll get some gloriously vague reply. They never talk, you know."

Margot nodded. "Should have been in the Diplomatic Service. Except he's not good-looking enough." Julia showed her through the dressing room to the bathroom. "Say—I've got to have photographs of this!" She pulled the ceramic chain over the mahogany-seated toilet decorated with the *fleur-de-lis,* then ran the water in the sink. "It actually works!" Julia slid back the panels to show her the bath. "My God—everyone in Hollywood will switch to mahogany-paneled bathrooms with enclosed baths. Did you say it's Victorian . . . just fancy . . . ?"

When she was ready, Julia brought her downstairs to the library, where everyone was assembled for morning coffee; the long table usually spread with books and magazines was given over to every possible temptation of scones and griddle cakes, jam, honey, and marmalade. There were Scottish toasts spread with game pâté. Michael and Luisa were there, Michael bowing gracefully over Margot Parker's hand, Luisa stunning in a Chanel suit. Alasdair and Johnny had been brought in from the stable yard and still wore some of its grime. They munched griddle cakes, quite unknowing and uncaring of the importance of the new arrival. "Don't eat too much, boys," Julia cautioned them. "There's lunch and the party this afternoon." They looked cheerful and happily careless in their riding pants and stocking feet—muddy riding boots had to be left on the kitchen porch. Bill and Rita Fredricks arrived, with the photographer in tow, who did not seem at all put out about having to stay at the Caledonian. Ernest Wilcox, who had known Margot Parker for years, was self-effacing. Finally Julia got to Connie and Ken and the two grave-faced but beautiful children. "You've met Ken. This is my sister, Constance, my niece, Margaret Ginette, and my nephew, Clive."

Margot Parker spent a long time looking at Connie and her two children. "God, where do you get it from, you people? Of course I've met your sister, Alex Forster—her husband's sort of my boss—and she's stunning. But you . . ." She inclined her head toward Connie. "You're the best of the lot. Ever made any pictures—or been on the stage?"

Connie drew closer to Ken. "I'm a housewife. I take care of my husband and the family."

"Damn waste," Margot said. She turned as Janet offered her coffee. "This actually smells like the real stuff—and you know how to make it. I haven't had a decent cup of coffee since I got off the ship." She nibbled at a buttered griddle cake, talked for a few moments to the Fredrickses—they didn't rank high on Margot Parker's order of importance in Hollywood. But she did listen for a few minutes as Ernest Wilcox pointed out some of the treasures of the library.

"We'll have to have them cataloged someday," Rod said as he roamed the room with her and even enticed her up to the gallery. "Some of them are really good—rare. So Ernie says. No one seems to have taken much of an inventory of what's in the castle."

"Any ghosts? A castle ought to have ghosts. . . . How old is it, anyway?"

"Parts, they say, date from 1200, or thereabouts. But they've built and torn down . . . hard to say. As for ghosts . . . some people claim to have encountered some. I haven't . . . but I'm not a Sinclair. Alasdair's the last Sinclair." He pointed out to her the crest and the clan motto inset in the big window. He translated the motto with some pride.

"Well . . . yes, I guess you have attempted difficult things . . . and they've, on the whole, worked out pretty well. Good for you, Rod." Her mood was mellowing rapidly. "You must show it all to me . . . I'll need to know what the photographer should shoot."

"We'd better do it now. . . . Luisa, do you mind if we put

our heads into your suite? Margot would appreciate it." Luisa nodded yes. "We'll go out into the garden before it starts to pour—as it frequently does in the Highlands. Might as well take you through the kitchen area. The courtyard there has the old well that supplied the whole castle with water; if they had enough grain and cattle inside the walls, they could withstand any sort of siege. . . ."

Julia thought he must have taken her on a thoroughly exhaustive tour of the whole castle and the island. They returned just in time for lunch, with Margot looking windswept but quite good-humored. "It's really something special. . . . I hope it doesn't rain this afternoon—we'll want some exterior pictures. If we could get Sir Michael with his grandson . . ." Drinks and lunch were being served as a buffet in the housekeeper's room. The team of waiters and waitresses had arrived from the Caledonian and were setting up long trestle tables for the afternoon children's party, with places set for sixty. Connie and Ken had spent their time blowing up balloons; Ernest had finished the task he had begun two days earlier of wrapping in fancy paper and ribbon all the presents for the children. There was the constant sound of hurrying feet in the passage outside. Sir Niall had arrived and was introduced to Margot Parker, who seemed to think that the tone of the party had improved. She drank several large whiskeys and piled her plate with food—some of the dishes new to her, and all to be tried. Smoked salmon, cold game pie, and Scotch eggs took her fancy. Sir Niall sat with her on a sofa all through lunch, explained the food, went to refill her plate with what she liked best, and saw that her wineglass was never empty. At the end she was smiling at everyone in the room. "What time do the kids come . . . ?"

"Three o'clock. And they'll all be here sharp," Rod said. "They don't get a chance of a party very often up here. Some of them will be wetting their pants with excitement. But don't expect too much from them, Margot. They're far too shy of strangers—no matter how charming. Especially a stranger who brings along a photographer."

She was downstairs again before three o'clock, her dress changed, her hair tidied. Rod looked at her anxiously, to gauge her mood. She beamed, taking in the lavishly spread tables, the groups of balloons that brightened every dark corner of the dining hall. Ernest had festooned all the stags' heads with ribbons and tied bows on each of the huge antlers. Johnny was smartly dressed in a gray flannel suit that seemed almost to match the one his father wore—probably made, Julia thought, by the same Savile Row tailor, with clothing coupons that Luisa ''just happened to pick up.'' Alasdair was looking as shy and self-conscious as any of his prospective guests. He was wearing the Sinclair kilt, with plain shirt and tie; a tweed jacket cut to the shorter style of the Highland dress; a sporran; long, thick socks; and stout, laced shoes. Sir Niall stood by him protectively as Margot took it all in and emitted an uncharacteristic giggle. ''Why, he *does* look like the little lord, doesn't he? What's under the kilt?—I've always wanted to know.'' She advanced on Alasdair, but Sir Niall hastily dragged Alasdair back from her. ''You'll have a wee dram, Miss Parker?''

''Don't mind if I do. Say, doesn't it all look cute . . .'' Sir Niall hastily pressed a drink into her hand as the first arrivals came through the Great Hall. Julia had given specific instructions that all guests were to come through the front doors of the castle. There would be no entry by way of the kitchen courtyard. They came with reticence on the part of the parents, shyness with the children. But the sight of balloons, the bows tied wickedly on the stags' antlers, set the children into fits of nervous laughter. Every light in the renovated hall was lighted, and a fire blazed, even though it was June; the long tables were spread with white linen and bowls of sherry-laced trifle, jellies, tarts, little iced cakes, and dainty sandwiches. Most of the ingredients had been sent by Alex, or ordered by cable by Rod. Julia remembered the party of two years ago, when Alasdair had barely been able to understand what was going on. It had seemed lavish at the time—but the dining hall must have appeared rather gloomy by comparison to what now met the children's delighted eyes. ''Quickly,'' Margot shouted at the photographer, ''get them! Get them as they're saying 'Happy birthday' to little what's-his-name . . . !'' The children blinked in the glare of the flashbulbs, momentarily put off. But they greeted Alasdair with warm familiarity. Many of them wore kilts, as he did, perhaps preserved for generations, so that each son had inherited his father's or uncle's or his brother's; a number of the girls wore plaid skirts and white, frilly blouses. Kirsty Macpherson had brought her daughter, Betsy. She clapped her hands at the sight of the bedecked hall. "About time someone showed some humor around here."

Gravely Alasdair, remembering more names than Julia had thought possible, introduced the children to Johnny. "This is my uncle, Johnny Seymour. It's not his fault he isn't Scots."

As the children inspected the "uncle," they went off into more laughter, even the older ones, who wanted to seem aloof from all this childish game. As they relaxed, Ernest wound up the gramophone and played Scottish airs, most of which the guests knew by heart. Janet was at the door leading to the house-keeper's room, beckoning to the parents. "Now you just go on in there, and there's your own party. The wee ones will be all right here. There is tea, and good whiskey, if that's what you fancy. . . ." In the short time since the buffet lunch, the house-keeper's room had been restocked, the long table and side-board decked with silver dishes of sliced ham, beef, and chicken, and the same sherry trifle and iced cakes that dressed the chil-dren's table. Kate was in charge of pouring tea; the sideboard held a formidable array of bottles of whiskey, of many brands.

"You sure *do* things," Margot Parker had said when she had gone to explore. The photographer followed her everywhere, photographing the children at their party, opening their presents, the gaiety that came once their shyness had fallen away. The adults crowded back into the dining hall to see Alasdair blow out the candles on his cake. Many of the children had never tasted icing such as it had. Janet had declared that this work would be hers alone, and she was proud of the result, while telling everyone where the ingredients had come from. That over, they danced a few reels to the music Ernest played, then fol-lowed Alasdair and Johnny to the stable yard, where Princess Cat had been decked out in her red circus harness and three white feathers, and took turns to ride her and the pony Kirsty had loaned to Johnny. But Cat was the favorite. William Kerr kept a sharp eye on all this, making sure that none of the older and heavier children was mounted. Stacia helped support the smallest of them with her hands and encouraged the ones who were timid. Princess Cat took it all with surprising good humor, as if she regarded herself, properly, as the star of the afternoon. It came to an end as the rain began to fall. An exhausted Alasdair stood with Rod and Julia to shake hands with each of the de-parting guests, adults as well as children. "Come again next year,'' he kept saying. Margot Parker got her wanted shot of him with his grandfather, Sir Michael Seymour, as they fed Princess Cat her deserved treats of apples and lumps of sugar. This, Julia thought, would be for the fan magazines—and whomever else Margot could sell it to.

In the dining hall, the trestle tables were being removed, and the two long stretcher tables were being clothed in fresh linen for the dinner that night. The balloons had been distributed to the children, Ernest was removing the bows and ribbons from the stags' heads, the Sinclair silver was being laid out. ''Are the two kids going to stay up for this . . . ?'' Margot Parker wanted to know.

''Just to say hello to the guests . . . the two of them will have had a couple of hours' sleep.'' Rosmairi had already shepherded them off to their room. The Fredrickses were driving back to Inverness to bathe and change. ''Be sure you don't lose that photographer in the bar. I told him to wear a tuxedo. . . .'' Margot Parker ordered. She went up to the Red Tower Room to rest before dinner.

''How do you stand her?'' Michael said quickly when she was gone and they had assembled for drinks in the drawing room. Kirsty Macpherson and Sir Niall had lingered; Kirsty's daughter was half asleep in her mother's lap. Kirsty laughed over Margot Parker and the photographer, which annoyed Rod.

''You don't 'stand' her—you're damn grateful if she shows up. Thank God it didn't rain when I was showing her around outside. If her hairdo had been ruined, the story would have gone sour.''

''But is it necessary, dear boy?'' Michael asked.

''You're darn tootin' it's necessary. That's how one stays alive in Hollywood.'' He turned to his brother-in-law. ''I'm grateful to you, Ken. I could see she was pumping you with questions about the bigwigs in Whitehall, and you were very patient.''

''Being patient is part of my job. She's more intelligent than she seems—if she put her mind to the right things.''

''She earns a fortune writing the rubbish she does.''

Luisa put a hand on her husband's. ''I'm so glad Michael doesn't have to bother with such things.'' It was said with just the faintest trace of smugness. Just for once, Julia thought, Luisa was publicly saying what she must often have privately savored— that her money protected Michael from the vulgarity of having to sell himself. For all the enjoyment of the guests—adults and children—Julia recognized it all as a giant public-relations effort on Rod's part, using Alasdair's birthday as a pretext. She was seated, as Rod had insisted, lengthwise on one of the sofas, cushions at her back, sipping tea. Together, she supposed, they must have presented the picture of domestic tranquillity. She forced ugly memories from her consciousness.

From the end of the room, where she perched on the wide window ledge, Stacia spoke. "No one had better be anything but real sweet to her. She was telling me Morris Meadows thought he had a script that might be just right for me. I don't want her dropping a few words of spite in his ear."

All afternoon Stacia had, Julia acknowledged, acted as if her sole ambition in life was to see that their guests were happy and well attended to. She had dished out helpings of trifle at the children's party, had carried more platters of food from the kitchen to the housekeeper's room, had even poured whiskey into proffered glasses. She had looked her most innocent and most seductive in the plain green dress she had almost outgrown. She had known that the men's eyes had followed her every movement; she had deliberately charmed with a sweet demureness, a willingness to please that even the sharp eyes of the women could not fault. The terrible incident of Cat's death two years ago was about to pass into local legend as the act of a brave but foolhardy young girl who had since learned better.

"No movies till you've finished school," Rod said. "Do you think I'd let myself be labeled as a child-exploiter?"

"Plenty of kids go to school at the studio. It's the law."

"Yes—and they come out idiots. There'll be plenty of movies for you when I say you're ready."

"I suppose that'll be never," Stacia replied. "One day I'll get out from under you, you know."

Kirsty Macpherson rose hastily. "Time I got this one," indicating her sleeping daughter, "off to her proper bed. It was a great party, Julia . . . Rod. I'll just have time to dash home, get her settled into bed, and don the glad rags for tonight. And my precious husband, who wouldn't deign to attend a children's party, will be here in full colors."

"I'd better do the same," Sir Niall said. "Nicely done, Rod," he said, as if trying to cover Stacia's words. "The children really enjoyed it. Enough of them have seen your films to be quite enchanted at the sight of you—er—in the flesh. I'm sure you didn't disappoint them. It was a magnificent spread. I always know when the farmers and tenants are enjoying themselves. They liked the castle filled with good food and drink, and music, and the sounds of the children laughing. . . . Good show!''

Connie returned as they were leaving. Ken at once poured her a drink. She had had nothing but tea all during the afternoon. "Do you think I should? I mean . . . this evening . . . it'll be pretty heavy going, won't it . . . toasts and all, from what I hear of Highland gatherings?''

Kirsty stopped by her and smiled warmly. "Don't worry. There's your Ken to take care of you. Children in bed now?''

"And asleep,'' Connie said, taking the well-watered drink from Ken. "Janet's going to sit with them for most of the evening, in case they wake and take it into their heads to go wandering around. She's more than done her day's work and is just as thankful not to be mixed up with the tribe from the Caledonian. She can't be expected to take orders in her own kitchen . . . so just as well to stay away.''

Surprisingly, Kirsty leaned over and kissed Connie lightly on the cheek. "You know—you're the nicest and the sanest of them all. And don't ask me to explain.'' She turned to everyone in the room. "See you later. Gorgeous afternoon for the children, Julia. But after this I'll be pestered to come up with something to match Princess Cat. . . . *That* won't be easy.'' She looked at Sir Niall. "Perhaps I'll set this old devil onto the task.''

Julia still thought she was seeing film scenes slowly rolling before her eyes; the evening had a quality of unreality about it, beginning with her stiff gold brocade gown. She was dressed and ready when Janet slipped into the room. "Here, Mrs. McCallum, you must wear this as a birthday treat for your son. It belonged to Lady Jean.'' Suddenly she was fixing a silk sash of the Sinclair dress tartan around Julia's left shoulder, one end crossing her back and the other her breast, knotting both ends gracefully on the right hip. Then she pinned it in place on the shoulder with a Sinclair clan badge. "There—you do your son honor, Mrs. McCallum. Better go down now. I hear the cars coming over the bridge.''

With some misgivings, Julia descended the stairs. Rod stood in the arched doorway between the Great Hall and the entrance hall. He looked up as she reached the end of the staircase. "Jesus . . . you look wonderful." Then his expression sharpened. "But that's the Sinclair tartan—not the McCallum."

"I would have worn neither," she said simply, "since I wasn't born in Scotland. But Janet came at the last moment and said it was to honor Jamie—no, to honor Alasdair. . . ."

His face relaxed a trifle. "Well, Princess, if I'd known I would have had the clan badge made in gold, to match your dress, and studded with diamonds and rubies for the cock's feather's."

"I really don't think that's done. But you look splendid yourself, Rod." She understood now the trips to Edinburgh with Ernest. Rod was magnificently dressed in the full dress of the McCallum clan—dress kilt, green velvet jacket adorned with silver buttons, silver-buckled shoes, a sporran of baby seal, the clan badge. He had totally taken over the identity of the name he had chosen to call himself. She wondered if he ever thought about the night he had told her his name was McBain.

"Mummie—look! Look at me!" Alasdair cried, perhaps jealous of the attention Rod was receiving. Sir Niall presented the boy proudly. Alasdair was dressed in the Sinclair tartan, a velvet jacket, finely woven socks in the Sinclair pattern, a shirt with a lace jabot, and an even softer sporran than Rod's, the Sinclair tartan over his shoulder, held by the clan badge, and thin-soled, silver-buckled shoes. She realized that Sir Niall had given all his attention to having Alasdair perfectly turned out for each of this day's occasions. She kissed first Alasdair and then Sir Niall. "Only you could have done it. Thank you."

"Say, we just have to have a photo of you three there, all dressed up." Margot Parker's voice behind them. Rod quickly bunched them together, although Julia could hear that guests had arrived in the entrance hall, and they should have been ready to greet them. Disregarding the guests, Margot insisted on pictures of Sir Michael and Julia and his grandson; then the whole group, including Johnny and Luisa, whose gown outglowed and outglittered all of them. With the photographs over, Julia turned with some embarrassment to greet her guests, the families who had made them welcome at their tables, had accepted Rod, had long ago accepted her. Kirsty Macpherson arrived in a dress of wonderful stiff white silk, wearing her Macpherson silk tartan sash. Her husband, Douglas, was handsome and almost as dashing as Rod in his own Macdonald kilt. Just about all the guests had arrived, and been greeted, when Stacia appeared at the top of the stairs. Even the new lighting did not entirely obliterate the shadows. She came down slowly, trailing a hand on the banister. She was wearing the dress Ernest had brought—its chiffon folds outlining her body, the single band of red sequins highlighting her woman's breasts. Up in the shadows she was the embodiment of Anne Rayner; as she moved down she became something more her own—even though the resemblance was still startling. Julia heard a few murmurs among the guests. Anne Rayner's face and body were still fresh memories from the wartime years, but this girl had an added dimension—she was more knowledgeable, more worldly-wise, and yet retained that air of vulnerability that had made her mother a woman men had wanted to protect as well as possess.

"Get a picture—quickly!" Margot Parker ordered. "Here comes our next big movie star!"

Julia was never afterward quite sure how the evening went. Everything seemed perfectly arranged and moved smoothly. Alasdair and Johnny, who was dressed in neat navy blue, stayed while drinks circulated among the guests, and then Rosmairi came to see them to bed. Miss Grant, in a tartan skirt and white blouse, fluttered around, checking the seating arrangements. The guests, charming, informal, climbed to the gallery to see the restoration better and even ventured as far as the housekeeper's room and put their heads into the kitchen. Almost all of them had known the castle in earlier times, when the decay had been very evident. They seemed genuinely pleased to see it returned to its former pride. She guessed, though, that there was some low-voiced comment among them of Rod's clan dress, and the stained-glass window in the library. But the general opinion seemed to be that he had earned whatever rights he now claimed.

Dinner was announced, and after two courses, the haggis was piped in by three pipers. Words of appreciation were voiced. Alasdair, though absent, was toasted on his birthday, and Rod and Julia were toasted. Afterward Julia led the women out to the drawing room, where coffee was being served. But the men joined them soon, and the pipers started up the first of the reels in the Great Hall, where the floor had been cleared of the carpet for dancing. Waiters circulated with trays of liqueurs and seventeen-year-old Scotch. Julia sat in one of the high-backed chairs and watched the dancers spin and turn, the kilts and sashes rising in the air. Memories came back to her of the only other time she had seen people dance here—the dinner party bravely mounted by Lady Jean in some of the darkest hours of the war, scratched together with whatever little help and food she could muster. Once again the scene took on some of the polished perfection of a movie set—clean, precise, smooth, and strangely lacking in reality. She imagined that if she went around the stone walls she would see the wooden structure that held up the painted set.

Eventually the guests left, with many invitations issued for them to visit during their stay. Being suspended from the studio didn't seem to mean much to these Highland gentry; they had no idea of how long Rod would remain, or if the summons to return to work in Hollywood would arrive tomorrow. Rod saw them all, like a good host, to the door. There were good-natured calls to each other as cars backed and filled to get out of the confined front courtyard. Others, more knowledgeable, had left their cars in the stable yard; still others had driven to the kitchen yard and had entered through the back door.

"My dear," Luisa said, "are you terribly tired? Such very energetic people. It quite wore me out just watching those dances. . . ."

Rod had returned to the little group who had deserted the Great Hall and gone to the library, flushed with pleasure and a kind of manic excitement. "Great evening, wasn't it? Nice to be able to do it in our own house, and not having to hire a hotel. I've been invited to more fishing and shooting than I could fit into another lifetime. . . . Maybe we'll stay, Princess, until the snow flies—the way we had to for *Drop into Danger*. At least this time we'll be warm."

He and Stacia had energetically joined in the often intricate pattern of the reels—their sure actors' instincts telling them where and when to move, their occasional mistakes readily forgiven. With her ballet training Stacia had easily been the most graceful woman on the floor, a fact that Julia thought she instantly knew and exploited. Julia realized that invitations had been issued to Stacia alone, by some of the young sons of the families who had attended, but they would not have been for fishing and shooting, but dinners in Inverness, picnics on the wild lower slopes of the far mountains. She had been invited to at least two weekend parties. Julia wondered if Rod would permit those invitations to be accepted. Stacia also had Rod's look of flushed success. She sat demurely on the window seat, but her whole manner proclaimed that this had not only been the celebration of Alasdair's birthday but also her emergence into full womanhood.

"Nothing will hold her now," Ernest Wilcox said to Julia. "Rod's going to have to let the reins slip, or she'll get the bit between her teeth and bolt."

Julia had no reply. She felt heavy and weary. She kissed her father and Luisa and then went to Connie, sitting as close to Ken as she could. Julia knew that the evening, however smoothly it had gone, had seemed rather wild and strange to Connie. She, too, could remember how it had been here in wartime, the old, uncomfortable days that somehow, in both their memories, Julia guessed, had seemed warmer and more intimate. "Thank you both for coming," she said to them. She didn't know why she thanked them more than any of the others. She went then to the room where Alasdair and Johnny lay sleeping. She let the light from the passage fall on their faces; she listened to their smooth, even breathing. The photographs of Jamie were in place on the chest of drawers, the young Jamie, laughing at the thought of combat, and the scarred war veteran. She looked from Jamie's face to Alasdair's. Everything in his being had seemed to relax and become more natural since his return to Sinclair, as if the time in California had been exile. He belonged here, as Jamie had. She pressed her hand against the swelling mound of the child she carried, resting under her heart. With every part of her being she wanted this child born at Sinclair, as Alasdair had been, she wanted them to remain here, to grow up as Jamie had grown up, knowing the fierceness of its winters as well as the splendor of its summers. From the photographs Jamie's face smiled at her, encouraged her, challenged her to find a way to do it.

Chapter Twelve

I

THE WORLD seemed to break apart in small pieces, a little at a time, after that. Julia found it impossible to get to sleep—the day had overtired her; the sense of excitement, undercharged, in some of those who had been there during the day or evening, with a sense of envy, malice, a shade of resentment, disturbed her and would not let her rest. Beside her Rod snored in the deep sleep that his day of drinking had induced, to which he had added some pills, of what sort she didn't know. She had merely shaken her head when he had offered some to her. "Come on, Princess—you look all in. Do you good to get a long sleep."

"I'm pregnant, Rod. I can't take medication the doctor doesn't prescribe."

He shrugged impatiently. "Okay. Have it your own way. Life could be a lot easier for you, Julia, if you'd just relax a little. What the hell harm can a few pills do?"

"I don't know. That's what I'm afraid of."

She was awake when the early dawn in this far northern latitude had begun to lighten the sky; she could see it through a gap where curtains had not been fully closed. She hugged her baby in her arms, the soft, growing mound in her body, and whispered softly, "Sleep, dear little one—sleep." Then she heard the lonely sound of the telephone ringing, faintly, far below. She glanced at the clock beside her. Just after four.

The one thing the architect had not been able to wangle, nor bribe sufficient people for, was the telephone extensions Rod had demanded. There were two telephones in the castle, one in the little estate office, one in the library, and a further extension in

William Kerr's house. With the telephone systems almost destroyed in all the great cities during the war, getting a battery of telephones installed in a remote Scottish castle would have stretched to the breaking point the black-market system under which the architect had been forced to maneuver to get the restoration done. "I cannot put my name to official papers, man, and maybe end up in jail. . . ." he had said. So the telephone rang and rang and finally was silent.

Then she heard the gentle knock on the door. Janet, bundled into a heavy bathrobe Rod had given her, cautiously peered around the door. "Mrs. McCallum?" she said softly. "Are you awake, Mrs. McCallum?"

Julia jerked upright. Beside her, Rod did not stir. Julia swiftly slipped on a robe. When she went to the door, Janet whispered, "It's Mrs. Forster—on the line from Washington."

"Alex . . . ?" Julia started running down the stairs.

"Mrs. McCallum . . . not so quickly. You can fall. . . ."

Why was Alex calling at this hour? Even if she had been trying to reach them all day to wish Alasdair a happy birthday party, she was aware of the time difference. Julia raced into the office and snatched up the receiver, praying that the transatlantic operator had not become impatient and cut them off.

"Alex . . . ?"

"Julia." There were many seconds of silence. "I thought Father might come to the phone. I told Janet to get whoever was nearest. Connie's with you, isn't she?"

"Yes—we're all here."

Again a very long pause. Julia listened with growing anxiety to the static on the line through which no words passed. "Alex—what's wrong?"

Alex's voice, always so strong and sure, seemed feeble, diminished. "Elliot. Elliot died this evening. Eight o'clock—or near it—our time. We had just begun dinner . . . he just slumped in his chair. He was dead by the time the ambulance reached here. Julia . . . he had seemed so well . . . he hadn't been overdoing things. Not by his standards. I was beginning to hope it was all past us. But no . . . he had to be taken from me. My beloved husband. I've never loved or respected a man so much—even after being married to Greg. I don't know what I'll do. . . . I feel so helpless. Me, Alex . . . helpless."

Despair and agony dragged at Julia's heart. "Oh, dearest . . .

oh, love. This is terrible. And I have nothing to say for your comfort.''

"To hear your voice is good, Julia. Do you think you could get Father and Connie . . . if I can hold the line long enough? Suddenly I need the voices of home. Do you understand?''

A Scottish voice interrupted. "We will hold the line as long as you wish, madam." And on the other end an American voice responded.

"Sure will. Just you hang in there. . . .''

Janet had already gone to wake their father and Connie. They arrived, exchanged shocked words with Alex, words of love, sympathy, distress for her distress. But both of them groped for words, just as Julia had. "God, I wish we could be with you,'' Michael said.

"Later, Father. Later I shall need you very much. I need you now, but you can't be here in time to help me through the . . . the funeral . . . and all the rest.''

"Child . . . dear child . . .'' Softly Michael began to weep. "Luisa and I will come over as soon as possible.''

"Thank you. I'd like that. It's not just Elliot's going . . . I won't get over that in a few weeks. It's what I have to do in the future. Nothing that anyone else can take on for me. When Elliot had the first attack, he remade his will. I didn't want the conditions, but I was afraid of upsetting him if I opposed him. So I let him do as he wanted . . . I thought later I would make him change his mind. But there wasn't enough time. We ran out of time . . . Elliot and I just ran out of time.''

"What is it that troubles you so much about his will?'' Michael looked up at the faces of his two daughters gathered around him as he listened, wishing that they also could hear the words as Alex spoke them.

"I have been left his entire estate—apart from bequests to charities. There were very few shares ever issued in the company—only to those who had served him well and whom he trusted deeply. But he still retained more than eighty percent of the shares. And the stricture is that I may not sell or delegate their voting rights unless the company is in desperate financial straits. That means—Father, that means *I* must make all the decisions about the papers and the radio stations and *Insight*. Elliot trusted me to carry out his policies. But I have to try to do the job he did. I have to hire and fire editors. I have to watch over it all—day after day. I suddenly realize I have power over public opinion that very few women have ever had to exercise. . . . Father, I'm so desperately afraid. I'm so lonely. He's only been gone—dead—a few hours—and already I find myself turning to him for advice . . . listening for his voice. I can't quite bring myself to ask the question I have to ask from now on: What would Elliot have done?''

''For a time things will run themselves, Alex. You don't have to take up the reins immediately.''

''But that's what he *expected* of me. That's what the will says. I know. . . . He discussed every clause of it with me before it was signed. I don't need any lawyer to read it to me. There are no surprises. Except the awful fact that he's dead. He isn't *here* anymore. He was my whole life, Father. We used to discuss every day what his feelings were about editorials. I shared his misery when he felt he had to fire someone. But rules were rules, and while he cherished independence of thought—originality—they could go only so far from his line. He was great at recognizing good work—and rewarding it. It's well known that Forster editors earn a lot more than most—but they had to put up with Elliot Forster as the price. He has given me an impossible task— one I never thought I'd have to carry out. I can't sell it or delegate it—or give it away. I have to *try* to be Elliot, and I know I can't ever be that. . . .''

''He trusted you greatly, Alex, or he never would have done it. He *knew* you could do it. A very grave responsibility to carry, child. But think what an inspiration you will be to other women. This is no fairy-tale job that came your way because you are good-looking, or can act or sing or dance. Your whole life has been a preparation for this. Elliot knew you were ready, or he never would have given you this hard load to carry. You can do it, Alex. He knew that. But you don't have to begin doing it tonight.''

''I do. I have to see the proof of the obituary that all our newspapers will carry. He wanted it straight and simple—warts and all. What I can't control, of course, is what the other papers will say about him. Father, I miss him so desperately. I couldn't . . . really, I still don't believe that he is gone. I have no husband . . . no children. Nothing but a lot of newspapers and radio stations. And a lot of money.''

''Alex, be thankful for the task he has set you. It would have been a lot worse if he had left you money but no purpose in life. He has left you what he regarded as a sacred trust. You can never be an idle or bored woman. You always have his trust to carry out . . . a heavy burden, Alex, but something to which to anchor your life. A formidable task, my darling child. But what is life without work? I knew that sort of hell for those months after your mother was killed. I saw no purpose . . . without Julia and D.D. perhaps I never would have pulled out of it. You cannot refuse your burden—hard as it is. . . .''

They talked for some time longer, and then the connection faded. ''Try to get her back,'' Connie urged.

Michael shook his head. ''I've said all I can for the moment. I think perhaps she wanted to stop, too. There's only so much one can stand at one time. I hope to God she's got some good friends around her to help her through these next days. Intimate friends . . .''

Julia sighed. ''I doubt it. She and Elliot were so totally wrapped up in each other and in their jobs. They had a hectic social life, because it was part of their job. But I really wonder if there's anyone's shoulder to cry on at this moment. Of course, half of Washington will attend the funeral, unless she announces that it's private, but I wonder if there's anyone to take her arm whom she completely trusts. . . .''

Janet had made tea while Alex had talked on the telephone; she put her head around the office door several times and gathered the essence of Alex's news. ''Poor wee thing,'' she said. ''It's very hard to lose a best friend—as Mr. Forster was to her. Very hard to lose two husbands—and she so young still. I've started a fire in the housekeeper's room, if you care to sit there. And I've been upstairs to wake Lady Seymour and tell her the sad news. I couldn't wake Mr. McCallum. He's there snoring his head off. I didn't think you'd want Mr. Wilcox with you just yet . . . and we'll leave the wee boys sleep until their usual time. Troubles come soon enough. . . .''

Ken had come down with Connie. He was already working on the possibility of at least Michael being able to fly to Washington before the funeral, which Alex thought would be on Monday. None of them had yet flown the Atlantic. It was still a novel thing to do. The scheduled flights were few and tended to be erratic. And Michael must first get back to London. ''I did suggest getting there by plane, but she said not to. She could not hold back on the burial on the faint chance that I could make it to Washington in time. Best, I suppose. It would only keep her on tenterhooks. Better to have it over and done with. Luisa and I will get there as soon as we can—there are many weeks before I open on Broadway, and even then Luisa could stay on with her, if that's what she wants. What an awesome responsibility to bequeath her. He must have trusted her judgment implicitly. Far better that she has work to do than not—but this is a monumental job.''

"She will do it," Ken said quietly. "Don't ask me how I know. I suppose one just develops an instinct for people who can do a difficult job. One can tell it with a new Minister within a few weeks. Some of them really never grasp the fundamentals. In a sense, Elliot has been grooming Alex, since the days they first met, to take over.'' Julia realized that Ken was well aware that the relationship had started long before Greg's death. "Though I wouldn't think either of them expected she would have to take this up for quite some time. Even if there had been children, she would have had to hold the fort for them until they were grown up. And perhaps . . . well, Alex has a true newspaperman's instinct. He couldn't have had a better heir. . . .''

Luisa had started crying, quickly holding on to Michael's arm as they sat together on the sofa. "Poor girl . . . to lose two husbands . . . I lost two husbands, but fate was kind to me and gave me Michael. I suppose it's always possible that Alex could be fortunate enough to marry again—to the right man.''

It was Connie who spoke. "I don't think—even at this moment, when it's all so strange and hard to take—I don't think in the future Alex will *ever* find that man. I think she would see it as a betrayal of the trust Elliot placed in her. She might think it would distract her from the task he has set her. It's really as if she's married to him—and the newspapers—forever. I think she will make an enormous success of it—but I suspect she may be deeply unhappy." She moved closer to Ken as she spoke, her hand automatically going to his.

Silently, Julia nodded.

The rest of the household learned the news at breakfast. Margot Parker showed a frantic interest. "Do you think I could interview her? I mean—it's the biggest newspaper chain in the States—

and they do carry my column. I could tell her everything about what it's like here. . . . Perhaps that would comfort her.''

"Lay off it, Margot," Rod said. His eyes were red-rimmed, his manner listless. Julia realized how little he was in control of himself by the way he spoke to Margot. No star in Hollywood ever spoke to Margot in that tone. "Alex is a very aloof lady. I'd bet my bottom dollar *nobody* will ever interview her about Elliot—or perhaps about anything else. She's withdrawn into the inner sanctum, hasn't she? In the future *she* will give the orders about who will be interviewed, and sometimes she'll do the interview herself. Maybe, like the President, or the Secretary of State—or the King of England, if anyone ever gets to interview him. Alex is one smart lady—and she doesn't spill her guts to—''

Margot stiffened. "All right! So she's Mrs. Elliot Forster, and she now controls Forster Newspapers. She just became, more or less, my boss." The implications were beginning to sink in. "Well, I only suggested it as a sort of . . . well, a gesture of sympathy, since I'll have been so recently with you all. It needn't be an interview. I could, perhaps—just go and see her.''

Rod shook his head. "Margot—you know the whole world will be trying to get to see her. To get one word out of her mouth. If I know Alex, they'll get nothing. She belongs to a very closed little group: this family. They only ever really talk to one another. The rest of us are left outside.''

Margot flushed, and lifted her coffee cup to her lips to hide her expression—a mixture of fury and fear, Julia thought. Suddenly, in Margot Parker's expression, Julia read the true magnitude of the power Alex now wielded.

It was a distracted and grief-stricken day. The telephone rang constantly as the news was carried on the radio bulletins and as people rang to commiserate. A little after midday they managed to get a call through to Alex; she was awake and said she had had some hours of sleep. "The doctor gave me some pills.'' Her voice sounded weary, and a touch of resignation had crept in. "It hasn't properly sunk in yet—and yet I'm being asked already for decisions. I approved the obituary—I wonder what woman has ever had to approve her husband's obituary? They had it ready and up-to-date, of course. What hurt me most was that they only had to put in the date of his death. Of course, they're carrying it as a news story—all the other papers are, too. Someone like Elliot doesn't die without it being news. It's terrible to see pictures of me and him—and everything in the past tense. I know part of me died with him. What I can't get used to is the rest of me being expected to function as if he were still alive. The funeral will be on Tuesday morning. I've chosen the place where his parents and grandparents are buried in Virginia—that brings him back close to the old property he so much wanted to buy back. We haven't announced the time or place—and hope that people will stay away. There are a few friends to come with me—that's all. No, Father, it's useless to try to get here in time. I will look forward to having you and Luisa with me when you can manage it. . . ." She talked again with her sisters and spoke a few words to Luisa, then abruptly hung up.

"She sounded as if she would weep—but she won't let herself," Luisa said sadly. "As if she must begin her job from the second he died. It is not right—there should be time for grieving. . . ."

They were a silent and gloomy group over lunch, of which no one ate much. Bill and Rita Fredricks drove out to offer sympathy. They were eagerly pressed by Rod to stay for lunch. Julia thought they accepted rather reluctantly. "Don't leave me alone, pal," Rod had said, as if he were the bereaved. Julia remembered his remark to Margot Parker. "They only ever really talk to one another. The rest of us are left outside."

The two boys had stayed outside all morning; without enthusiasm Stacia had taken them on a ride, but only as far as the main road and back. She was evidently anxious to stay with the group in the house, though all she had said when she had been told the news was "That's real tough. . . ." Alasdair and Johnny had eaten scones and drunk milk in Mrs. Kerr's kitchen; they seemed to prefer the company of the Kerr children to that of the adults in the castle. They only vaguely understood the grief that had engulfed the family. Death was not yet a personal thing to them, and Aunt Alex and Uncle Elliot were only dimly perceived identities. Of the newspaper empire and the responsibilities Alex now carried, they had no notion at all. All they knew was that the castle that yesterday had laughter and fun and decorations and dancing was now plunged into gloom. They instinctively kept their voices low. This being Sunday, it was Rosmairi's day off—a day to attend a church service, and visit her family in Inverness. She had suggested to Julia that this time she should remain.

Julia refused. "There's really no point in it. Mrs. Kerr has offered to let them stay with her family all day, if that's what they want. They can keep each other company. Janet has Kate to help her. . . ." So Rosmairi had gone to take the only bus that went into Inverness on a Sunday.

Bill Fredricks had brought Margot Parker's photographer back to the castle with him. She and the photographer had gone quietly from room to room, taking photographs of the interior but not disturbing the group in the housekeeper's room. The photographer had returned to Inverness by taxi.

After lunch Sir Niall arrived to pay his formal visit of condolence. "Elliot Forster was a fine man. I much enjoyed the time we spent together—especially the fishing. One has to like a man a great deal to enjoy fishing with him. . . . Poor Alex, I imagine she will take it hard and try never to let anyone know it."

Rod pressed him to come into the library, where a fire burned and where he had been dispensing drinks lavishly to anyone he could persuade to take them. He had been drinking ever since he had come downstairs—late, and showing the excesses of the drinking the day before. Julia could see that he was annoyed by the fact that he had not been wakened early—as soon as the news had come. "What was the point?" she said wearily. "I thought I'd let you sleep it off before you were hit with this."

Margot Parker was uncomfortable and retired to her room after lunch to rest and do her packing. She would be taking an evening train to Edinburgh, to transfer to the sleeper to London. Ken would also be on that train—he had to be back in Whitehall the next morning. Julia could see he did not relish the thought of having some hours of Margot Parker's and the photographer's company, but he would do his polite best. At the moment he sat at the far end of the library, reading from the childish books his children handed to him; Julia could see he did it readily and with love. It was the piece of attention he gave undividedly to them before Connie took them upstairs for their afternoon nap. They had declined to join Alasdair and Johnny at the Kerrs'; their sense of the gravity around them led them to hold on to their parents' company.

The day had become overcast, and after lunch the rain had

started, long, slanting lashes stirred by the wind blowing off the loch. Margot Parker had shivered as she had started to go upstairs. "I don't think I'd like winter here. I expect there's a lot of snow."

"A lot," Julia said firmly. If they stayed the winter, as they might do if Rod's suspension was not lifted, she did not want there to be any suggestion of Margot Parker coming to photograph and record a Scottish Christmas or New Year. She put on her raincoat and went across the stable yard to take Alasdair and Johnny back to the castle. "Ah, let them be, Mrs. McCallum," Mrs. Kerr said. "They're no trouble . . . they're happy enough playing with Dugald—there are all the toys and books I've saved from the older ones. I imagine you'd rather spend the day quietly, and children do need amusing. Are you sure Mrs. Warren's little ones don't want to come over?"

"She's already taken them upstairs for their nap. She'll stay up there with them. The place is too big to leave children on their own. . . . Alasdair, have you seen properly to Princess Cat, and Mrs. Macdonald's pony?"

"They've done that, Mrs. McCallum. They've been properly rubbed down, and they mucked out this morning—or helped to. Rachel supervised it, and Mr. Kerr put his head in to see all was well."

Julia thanked her and went back to the gloom of the library. She wished the boys had come with her. She could have made an excuse to stay in the housekeeper's room with them. The telephone kept ringing, and always Rod picked it up; Julia could see his barely suppressed irritation when it was one of their guests of the night before, expressing their sympathy. Rod had to hand the call over to her father, or to her, and there were brief words at the end of the conversation, thanking them for the hospitality the night before. This should have been Rod's great day for receiving praise for what he had accomplished at Sinclair. It had turned wretchedly sour on him. Michael and Luisa received so many personal calls from their London friends that Michael could not leave the library to have the rest Luisa urged on him. She had been reassured that Johnny was quite happy with Alasdair at the Kerrs' house. Stacia and Ernest Wilcox had remained very quiet, barely speaking. Stacia had retreated to her room after lunch, and Julia guessed Ernest would have liked also to do that but had not dared, because Rod demanded his presence, the sense of reinforcement his company gave him against Julia's family.

Finally Bill Fredricks rose. "We'd better be heading back, pal—that is, unless you'd like me to wait and take Margot to the train. And—er—Mr. Warren."

Rod shrugged off the suggestion. "Couldn't put Margot in the jeep. She'd have her teeth shaken out—and in this rain . . . ? No, I'll take her. Sure you won't stay for tea?"

"Thanks, Rod. Rita and I are plumb tuckered out after last night—and what with the news this morning. Real bad luck. And on your great day, too." He slapped Rod on the shoulder, then went around the room shaking everyone's hand. "Sure nice to meet you, Sir Michael. Sorry it had to end up this way. Rod, Rita and I will be taking off tomorrow for London. We've decided to take the day train down from Edinburgh. Take in some of the scenery . . . So I guess it's good-bye, pal, until you're back in Hollywood."

"You *can't* go, Bill—once Margot's gone, and . . ." He just prevented himself from uttering any of the others' names. "Well, there'll be plenty of room here. I was looking forward to having you stay here with us. Don't go, Bill. . . ." It was as close as Rod would ever come to a plea.

"We'd love to stay, Rod. But I promised Rita at least a few days in London before we started back. Mighty long way back to Hollywood. I'm due . . . well, I've got a picture starting soon, and I'd better not be late on the set."

Julia knew how Bill hated saying those words. They could only signify to Rod that Bill Fredricks was wanted back in Hollywood by his studio, and Rod had not yet received the summons. Steady work, in Bill's quiet fashion, had been the cornerstone of his career. He had never been a great star, but someone always wanted him for a movie. So he was going back to work, while Rod McCallum was still shunned.

Rod and Julia went with them to the front courtyard, where the jeep was parked. Rita kissed Julia swiftly. "We'll see you in Hollywood—soon. I'm so sorry about your sister. . . ."

They arranged to leave the jeep at the Caledonian. Julia watched them run through the slanting rain, a sense of depression settling more deeply on her. Bill was such a safe outlet for Rod's feelings, a stabilizer; it would have helped them both if he and Rita had stayed on after what she realized would be a

general exodus very soon. Tomorrow her father, Luisa, and
Johnny would leave; the day after that, Connie and the children.
She thought of Alex in her loneliness and near-despair. The
emptiness would fall on the castle, as it had in Alex's life. They
waved to the occupants of the jeep, then watched it disappear
over the bridge and onto the forest road through a curtain of
rain.

"Pity they couldn't have stayed longer . . . there'll be plenty
of room after tomorrow," Julia said.

"It's because the damn place has turned into a morgue. Who'd
want to stay? He didn't say anything about a picture. But then
people like Bill always have a picture coming up. They can fit
him into any little slot they like. It's not like being a star. . . ."

"No . . . not at all like being a star." They closed the doors
and went back into the Great Hall. Someone—Kate, Julia supposed—had lighted a fire there. There was the general sense that
they all needed comfort. At that moment they heard the clatter
of Margot's heels on the stairs.

"Well—well, I'm all packed and ready. Whenever you are."

"Right after tea," Rod said. "I'll be taking you to the station,
and Ken will take you to dinner at the hotel at the station in
Edinburgh before you get on the sleeper. It's called the Caledonian. They don't seem to be able to think of any other names.
But it's quite good—as these places go." He put his hand on her
arm. "Don't look like that, Margot. Ken's a very decent guy.
One of the real English. If you think he's a bit of a stuffed shirt—
well, you just should meet his father. The salt of the earth—and
all the rest of it. Kept Britain going during the war. He lost his
brother in the war."

"Oh, rotten luck . . ." Margot's face relaxed, betraying a
very rarely seen warmer side of her personality. "Well, Julia,
Rod . . . it would have been a great visit if it hadn't ended like
this. I enjoyed yesterday. I guess the newspaper world is going
to be standing on its ear until they see what sort of job Alex—I
mean, your sister—is going to make of running the show. Big
job. Pity I couldn't take your condolences to her personally . . ."
The edge of her voice became harder.

"Perhaps later," Julia said hastily. "She can barely speak to
us just now. In a few weeks—I'll suggest it. . . ."

"Yes, do that," Rod said quickly. "The sisters are all very
close, Margot."

"So people tell me. Until I met Connie I couldn't understand how really close they are. Now, if *she* wanted to go into pictures . . . You know, Julia, I could do a long feature article on your family—Sir Michael and the three of you for a national magazine. It would make a great—"

Her words were choked off as they suddenly heard a deep rumble, as if some giant animal stirred in the depths of the castle. Then came the crashing sound of masonry and tearing wood. Next came the screams of a child—or more than one child. For a second they stood transfixed, wondering where the sounds came from. Then Alasdair came running from the entrance hall. His clothes and hair were coated in dust, and tears were already beginning to make tracks on his face.

"Oh, Mummie—quickly! Come quickly! Johnny's hurt!" He grabbed her hand and was leading her at a run through the entrance hall, along the narrow passage that led to the always locked doors of the North Tower, which now stood open. "We just went up the first flight of stairs . . ." he shrieked through tears. "Just stone steps, like the other ones . . . and then we opened a door . . . it was all cobwebs inside. But there was an old chest. We just wanted to see what was in it. Johnny got there first. And then—well, I felt the floor going, and I moved back. Johnny fell. . . ."

They had reached the North Tower. The smell of the recently disturbed dust of centuries was choking. "I tried to pull him out, but more stuff started to fall."

Rod carefully opened the door to the ground-floor room. Narrow stone stairs twisted around the tower; the stone core that helped support the stairs seemed to quiver, as if in an aftershock. On the ground-floor room they saw the chaos of fallen beams and floorboards, the rising dust almost impenetrable, like a dense smoke screen. Within the rubble they could hear the sound of Johnny's sobbing cry.

With one swift movement of his arm Rod barred the entrance to them all. "Don't move—any of you! Don't set foot in here. Don't breathe until I say you can. Do you understand? Just shut up—and for God's sake, stand still! You, too, you little bastard!" This was directed at Alasdair. He dropped his jacket on the floor. "Johnny, stay still! I'm coming!"

Julia grabbed Alasdair's arm, and Margot instinctively withdrew, trying to stifle her coughing. Julia watched as Rod carefully picked his way through the fallen beams, lifting with the greatest delicacy those that blocked his path, not hurrying, making sure the way was safe except for the danger of more falling debris. Julia looked up at the ruined floor above and realized she could see through to the story above. The outer stone walls and the twisting stairs of the tower stood firm, as the architect had told them he had rendered them, but the inner, wooden structure of the building still seemed to quiver with the shock waves of the fall of its timbers. The rooms were mercifully small, but every step Rod took threatened to dislodge more from above. Ancient paneling had toppled and obstructed his way. Julia looked down at Alasdair, whose tears had stopped flowing, as if he, too, held his breath in suspense, and wondered how he had survived the attempt to reach Johnny. Her heart lurched violently, and the baby in her womb seemed to turn and kick.

Rod had found Johnny and lifted him in his arms, the movement making the child scream in pain. ''Just stay with it, buddy,'' Julia heard Rod say. ''We'll be out of here in no time.''

With infinite care he was picking his way through the path he had cleared through the debris. Julia held her breath as she saw him straddle the large beam he had been unable to lift. The two figures emerged fully, at last, through the dust. ''Close the door—and get out of here.''

The great carved double doors had come out of alignment with the force of the air implosion behind them. Julia tried to close them securely, but as she struggled with them, more pieces of the floors above began falling, and it seemed to set off a chain reaction. From far above they heard the sound of the screaming tear of rotten wood giving way. They all started to run.

Rod had laid Johnny on a sofa in the library. He put surprisingly skillful, gentle hands on the boy, running them over his whole body. Luisa knelt beside the sofa, holding one of Johnny's hands, and wept. ''Oh, my darling—''

''Knock it off, Luisa!'' Rod ordered. ''Does it hurt here, kid? And here? Got a bad bump on the head, didn't you? Did you fall on your head, can you remember? Well—it doesn't make any difference now.'' Janet had entered, carrying a bowl of warm water, well salted, and a towel. With great caution Rod sponged the cut on Johnny's head where the blood still oozed. ''Don't want to disturb it too much—just get the dirt out.'' When he had finished doing that, he turned to the assembled, shocked group. "For God's sake, do I have to do everything? Hasn't someone called an ambulance yet? The kid's got a broken leg, at the very least. Perhaps a dislocated shoulder. God knows what to his head. Someone has to snap the shoulder back into place. He can't be moved until there's a proper splint on his leg. I don't know whether it's a simple or a compound fracture. Don't want to make things worse."

"I telephoned the ambulance," Sir Niall said. "Of course, they have to come from Inverness—wanted to know which doctor had ordered it, and I just said, 'an emergency.' They'll be here as quickly as possible. . . ."

"Well, we can be thankful someone here still has some wits about them." Rod rose from his knees. "Well, kid, it's a rough deal, but you're all right. You're not going to die."

Johnny was sobbing gently. "My head feels as if I'm going to die. Will I ever be able to walk again?"

Rod hooted. "Walk? You'll be an Olympic runner! You're a little kid, and your bones knit easily. Listen, pal, you should have seen some of the guys I've seen after they've had a riding fall—stunt guys, and guys riding in rodeos. You've only got a little scratch by comparison." He moved to the side table where the drinks stood. "Can't give you any of this, pal—the doctor wouldn't like it. But we used to give a real stiff shot to the guys who hurt themselves. Pretty rough and ready it was—but when they come to take you to the hospital, they'll be as gentle as angels, I promise." He poured a large measure of neat whiskey and swallowed half of it. He looked around the assembled group. "Well, can't someone get rugs and cover him properly? Build up the fire. Don't give him any tea, or anything to eat, in case they need an anesthetic to set the leg."

Luisa wailed. "It's as bad as that?"

"How the hell do I know? I'm not a doctor. He's probably got a concussion, but I don't suppose his neck's broken. At any rate, he's not dead." Janet had come with blankets. Ernest was kneeling before the fire, piling on logs too rapidly and causing a lot of smoke. "Lay off it, Ernie. You're killing the damn thing." He finished his whiskey with another impatient swallow and went to undo some of what Ernest had done. "Give it some air, man. Jesus, I swear I have to do everything around here." He used the bellows on the fire. "Looks a little better. Push the sofa nearer—and go easy! Oh, for God's sake . . . !'' His words heralded Connie's entry, with Margaret and Clive, both fully dressed and with their coats on, as if ready for evacuation. "What is this? A convention?''

"Well—I heard the noise. As if half the house were coming down,'' she said defensively. "What was I supposed to do?—stay up there and cower?''

William Kerr had entered without knocking. "It's the North Tower, isn't it? I had a good look around. Nothing's fallen on the outside—but they did make it all good and sound. Inside—did it just cave in?''

Rod was back at the whiskey decanter. He gestured around the room. "Anyone want some?'' He thrust a glass into William Kerr's unwilling hand. "Damn thing didn't give in of itself. Stupid kids got in there. I thought the doors were locked.''

"They always have been,'' William Kerr said. "As long as I've known, the doors to the North Tower have always been locked.''

"And the key?''

"Hanging in the office, where all the other keys are.''

"Well, so that smart-ass kid can just put up his sneaky little hand and get it anytime he likes.'' He gestured toward Alasdair, who had climbed into a large armchair with his mother and lay quietly sobbing in her arms. "Look at me, you little bastard. You took the key, didn't you? You didn't just find the doors unlocked?'' He put out his hand and wrenched Alasdair's head around so that the child cried out in pain.

"Mr. McCallum! . . . sir!'' William Kerr intervened. "I suppose it was partly my fault. Master Alasdair said they would go back home to tea, and I just watched them cross the stable yard and go in through the office door. I didn't imagine—''

"*Master* Alasdair is six years old. *He knows* the rules. *Everyone* in this house knows it's expressly forbidden to go into the North Tower. We only took the boards off the doors because we *thought* everyone had the sense to stay away. Why the hell didn't the bloody architect board up the inside doors while he was on the job? Then even little wiseacre kids couldn't half kill themselves . . . or someone else.''

"The paneling, Mr. McCallum, is old and valuable. He didn't like to touch it without consulting you. There was barely time to make the outer walls and the staircase safe. No one ever imagined—''

''I pay people like him to have an imagination! I pay people like you to keep keys safely.''

William Kerr stiffened and put his untouched glass firmly on the table. ''The key was on the highest rack—and clearly labeled.''

Rod once more viciously wrenched Alasdair's head around. ''Look at me, you little snot! You climbed up there and got the key. You could read what it said, couldn't you? You knew exactly where you were taking Johnny. A bit of adventure? Well, I'll give you adventure. You'll wish you'd never heard of the North Tower.'' With a swift and heavy hand he smacked Alasdair's ear, and the child howled. Julia thrust him back farther into the chair.

Immediately Sir Niall was beside him, deflecting the next blow. ''Here—don't you raise a hand to that child. He's in enough trouble. Can't you see he's in shock, man? What sort of person are you?''

''Shock?'' Rod turned away and laughed contemptuously. ''And what about Johnny? Johnny could have been dead. And come to think of it, so could I.''

''At this moment, I wish you were,'' Julia said quietly. ''Save one child and beat another . . . makes you feel good to take it out on someone. You're suffering from shock yourself, Rod McCallum—hero of a hundred heroic victories—on the screen. Tell me, did you ever *hear* a shot fired in anger, much less do it yourself? Of course Alasdair was wrong. He knows he was. He doesn't like to see Johnny—''

''Well, he damn well sees him, doesn't he?—and no, madam, I didn't hear a shot fired in anger, except when I was growing up. Not like your hero husband, who only shot other men out of the sky but never saw the whites of their eyes. That's part of the trouble with those glamorous fly-boys—they never got dirty during the war. They either lived or they died. But they never got dirty—''

''Enough!'' Sir Niall said, his tone furious. ''I lost two sons in the Battle of Britain, in which Jamie distinguished himself. I suppose it's a clean death to be burned alive in a cockpit, as one of my sons was. The other one was just blown to smithereens. Don't you tell me—''

"Oh, for pity's sake," Margot Parker wailed. "Someone get me out of here. The kid's got a broken leg, and he and Rod and Alasdair might all have been killed. And now we have to refight the war. I've had enough. Is there anyone to get me to the station? I don't care how long I wait for the damn train. I just don't want to hear any more of this."

Rod snapped to attention. "I'll take you, Margot. I'm still your host."

"I wouldn't let you drive me five yards. You're drunk as a coot—stoned to the eyes with God knows what!"

"I'll take you, Miss Parker," Sir Niall said quietly. "I gather you've packed. I'll just go and bring your bags down. I think it would be as well if we all left Johnny to be as quiet as possible until the ambulance arrives. . . ." He left the room quickly, and Margot followed.

"Connie," Ken said, "will you get packed, please? I'll take care of the children. We'll all go on the train tonight. You and the children can have my sleeper—if there isn't another one available, it doesn't matter. It won't be the first time I've slept sitting up. . . ."

"What is this—evacuation time?" Rod demanded. "You're just going to leave us? After what's happened to Johnny—and to Alex?"

"We can't help Alex—and we can't help Johnny by staying," Ken said quietly. "In my opinion, the sooner everyone in this house quiets down, the easier it will be for Johnny and Luisa— and Sir Michael. I think you can rely on Sir Niall to steer you through the hospital business." He squatted down beside Johnny. "We're not leaving because we don't care, Johnny. We're just going to help things calm down. You've had a nasty shock. . . ." Very gently his fingers touched the scalp wound, where the blood had started to congeal. "That looks a lot more frightening than it is. You'll be healed up and well again in no time. Aunt Connie and the children and I are going only because having the house quiet will be less strain on your mother and on Aunt Julia. Just you lie as still as you can until they come for you. You do understand, Johnny . . . don't you? Aunt Connie was due to leave the day after tomorrow, in any case. It's just as well if they come with me tonight. We're all a bit upset—Aunt Alex's news upset everyone. You're a very brave boy, Johnny."

Johnny started to nod his head in understanding but then

stopped, grimacing with sudden pain. "Yes . . . we know that. Alasdair and I know that. I suppose that's why we went to the North Tower. You were all moping in here. We shouldn't have gone . . . but I said if there were any ghosts in the castle, that's where they'd be . . ." He started to cry again, and Luisa tried to hold her arms under his shoulders, but the movement seemed to give him pain. He cried out. Alasdair flinched as if he had been hit.

Ken rose to his feet. "It's really better if we go. You don't need this crowd around at this time." He went to Julia. "Thank you for making everything so wonderful—until this morning's terrible news—and now this." With an uncharacteristic gesture, he softly touched her cheek. "Try to take care of yourself. You don't look as well as you might. Get some rest. Telephone Alex whenever you can. She needs whatever support she can get, poor woman." He bade a formal good-bye to Ernest Wilcox. As Ken shook Michael's hand, his other hand went up to touch his father-in-law's shoulder. "It's a terrible thing that's happened to the whole family. It sounds ridiculous to say 'if there's anything I can do . . .' What can I possibly do for people like you?"

Michael held his hand firmly. "You take care of my daughter and my grandchildren splendidly, Ken. No man could wish for a better son-in-law. Stay in touch. Johnny might be coming on little visits to Hampstead while his leg is healing . . . if it is a fracture. Any nice warm day he could be out in the garden . . ." His mind was clearly running into the future. "I think I should go to Alex. She needs some family with her. . . ."

Julia felt like crying out that she needed some family with her also, and she knew the terrible selfishness of the feeling. She watched as Ken bent and kissed Luisa's cheek. "Try not to worry. As Rod said—he's young. Children get over these things very quickly." He gave a final squeeze to Johnny's hand and went to Alasdair. "It's a fine thing to be adventurous, Alasdair, but try not to get into danger—for your mother's sake."

Suddenly Alasdair gave a sudden surge out of Julia's comforting arms and leaped up to hug his uncle. "I wish you weren't going—but I suppose you have to." Julia realized that Alasdair had the same frightening sense of being left alone as she did. Alone—but she had people all around her. She knew that she was frightened of being left alone with Rod.

Ken's handshake to Rod was formal. "Damn good thing you were there. It could have been much worse. . . ."

Rod had turned back to refill his glass. "Yeah—I know. That damn little sniveler there could have gotten half-killed as well as Johnny. Would have taught him a lesson. Trouble is, the kid's spoiled rotten. Thinks he can do what he likes. He's only got to run to Mummie, and Mummie will fix everything. Well, that wasn't the way I was brought up—and things are going to be different from now on. He'll learn—believe me, he'll learn!"

Julia heard the sounds of their departure in Sir Niall's car— William Kerr had volunteered to take the jeep to accommodate the luggage. Connie came in for a hurried farewell, kissing everyone, anxious to be gone. "Kiss me, too," Stacia said. "Kiss me for good luck. You're the luckiest one of us all."

Connie looked startled but didn't comment. She put her arms around Stacia and kissed her on the cheek, holding her close, and lingering for a moment to stroke her hair. "Good luck, Stacia. Come to see us in London."

"Yes—I'd like that. If it works out . . . Thanks . . ."

Ernest Wilcox had slipped away. There was an unhappy silence in the room while they waited for the ambulance, punctuated only occasionally by a little, half-stifled whimper from Johnny. Luisa perched on the side of the sofa, holding his hand. From time to time Julia saw her hand reach to his forehead, as if to soothe him, and then withdraw, as if she feared starting the scalp wound bleeding again. Rod refilled his glass. Michael paced the room and went several times to the entrance hall, as if his going to look could hasten the arrival of the ambulance. Then he went upstairs and got together coats, and went to Johnny's room to get pajamas and some toilet things, presuming he would be kept in the hospital. Finally Rod laid aside his glass.

"I'll go and get out the car."

"We'll ride in the ambulance with Johnny," Michael said stiffly.

"Well, you'll need some way to get back here."

"I'm sure there's a taxi . . ."

"I'll follow the ambulance," Rod said loudly. "Don't you trust me?"

Michael didn't reply.

The ambulance came. The two men arrived with their stretcher. They made a quick examination of Johnny and decided to put a splint on his leg. "The rest can wait until the doctors get a look at him, sir. Hang on, young man!" They rolled him carefully onto the canvas and inserted the rods. Michael slipped a coat on Luisa's shoulders. Julia and Alasdair went to the courtyard to watch them go. Rod followed the ambulance in the Rolls, his driving as steady as if he had drunk nothing all day. The little procession disappeared into the driving rain.

Julia closed the door, and Alasdair buried his head in the folds of her dress, against the mound of her swelling stomach, as if he wished he could be back in her womb with the new baby. He wept quietly for a moment while she held him. Then he raised his face to her. "I know it was wrong. But Johnny was bored with being at the Kerrs. But it was pouring with rain . . . you said I had to keep him entertained. . . ."

"You're making excuses, Alasdair. You knew it was wrong . . . you should have come into the library. You could have played Chinese checkers . . . or anything. We would have found some way to keep Johnny entertained. . . ." Then watching the tears stream down his face, she knelt down, rather clumsily, to hug him. "I know you didn't intend anything terrible to happen. I suppose we just didn't explain to you how dangerous the North Tower is. I don't think any of us really understood, or we would have left it boarded up—or gutted it completely."

"Are *you* going to beat me, too?"

"No! Good God, no! You've had your punishment—you saw how Johnny was hurt, and I know you didn't want him to be hurt. I know you'll never do anything as dangerous and silly as that again in your life." She hugged him more fiercely. "Oh, my love. I could have lost you. You both might have been killed. You understand that, Alasdair. You both might have been killed."

"I understand. I got so frightened by everything falling down. Rod saved him. I deserve to be beaten. . . ."

Julia didn't know how to answer. Janet took the matter out of her hands. She had been hovering in the entrance hall, also watching the ambulance and the Rolls leave. "Well, there, Master Alasdair—it's all over now. They'll look after Johnny very well, and in a little while he'll be mended. And you'll both have learned the lesson of your lives. Enough of this crying now. I'll give you a wash—and you'll have some tea. Rosmairi should be back soon. The bus is almost due. Ah, what a pity she went this morning. If she'd been here, it would never have happened. She'd have been with them. . . ."

"I don't know, Janet. A lot of things have happened this weekend that seemed out of kilter to me. Half the time I didn't know if things were real or I was dreaming them. . . ."

"I understand, Mrs. McCallum. I think I understand. I've always known the difference between the pictures I go to see, and the real thing. Some things in the past few days haven't been quite real. And I'll not be sorry," she added with swift grimness, "when Mr. Wilcox has left—for all he's so polite and helpful. But it's a shame your father's stay was ruined in this way—on top of this morning's terrible news from Miss Alex." She was leading Alasdair rapidly through the Great Hall and the dining hall, to the little bathroom they all shared. "It's that, I think, got the little boys into mischief. It's been such a sad day, and children don't know how to handle the sadness of adults. They're not used to people dying. . . . Now, Mrs. McCallum, you go into the housekeeper's room and put your feet up. You've had enough for this day. Kate," she called. "Kate, would you please bring Mrs. McCallum some tea? And a scone, and a few wee things. And poach an egg for Master Alasdair. He needs something in his stomach, or he'll not sleep at all this night. Maybe a wee bit of aspirin we should give him, with some warm milk, Mrs. McCallum. The child had a bad shock. He's no coward, I'll say that for him—attempting to go in there after Johnny." But her parting shot as she waved him into the bathroom was, "But it's no use being brave after you've been foolish and naughty. . . ."

Julia stretched out thankfully on the sofa and took the tea that Kate brought her. Sensing that calm had descended on the house, Ernest reappeared. He drank tea with her while they watched Alasdair eat his poached egg and toast. Janet had bathed him, and he was wearing pajamas and a bathrobe. Rosmairi returned, her coat and shoes sodden, and kept an appalled silence when she learned what had happened. Janet told her to change and have some tea. Then she would sit with Alasdair until he fell asleep. Besides the egg and the warm milk, Janet put a few small iced cakes before him. "Naughty boys don't deserve cakes, but we can't let you starve." Alasdair looked up at her with loving gratitude. "Thank you very much, Janet," he said in a small voice. Despite her controlled fear and shock, Janet couldn't help giving his damp hair an affectionate pat.

When Rosmairi had taken Alasdair off to bed, Julia waved Ernest toward the drinks tray on the sideboard. "It must be well past drinks time, Ernest. Of course, in this house, drinks time is all the time—for Rod." She tried to refuse the small brandy he brought her. "I don't drink very much—because I'm pregnant. They say it's bad for the baby."

"Princess . . ." For the first time he used Rod's name for her. "It's been an absolutely terrible day for you. Between the news from Alex and what's happened now, I think having a good night's sleep would help the baby more than you tossing and turning all night. I have a few pills . . . you wouldn't know a thing until the morning. It will all look different then. . . ."

"Ernest, you know I don't take pills . . . or any of that stuff. I don't take whatever Rod takes . . . and I wish you'd stop supplying him with whatever you do bring him. It turns him into a devil sometimes—"

"Listen, Julia, I only do what Rod asks me to do. And whoever said I supplied him with anything? Rod's life is his own business. There are any number of sources in Hollywood who'll give him whatever he wants. You've got to try to understand Rod, Julia. He began from nothing. Look where he's ended! Who's to quarrel with that sort of success? As for what he drinks, and what he might take on the side—well, he functions, doesn't he? Has he ever not been up to a situation? Has he ever come on the set late, or not knowing his lines, or what he's supposed to do? Did he charge in there like a bull this afternoon to pull Johnny out? No, he went as if he were walking on eggs—and so they both came out alive, without the whole place coming down on their heads. Don't carp at the way Rod lives. He's doing all right. This business is full of pressures. He copes with them pretty well. This suspension from the studio—is he moping about it? No, he just thumbs his nose at them and gives a wonderful party . . ."

The door had opened soundlessly. "Glad someone has a good word for me, Ernie. You're probably the only one . . ." Rod looked directly at Julia. "Well, the kid has a broken leg—a compound fracture; a dislocated shoulder, which they snapped back into place; and a concussion. The head wound's pretty superficial, but they took some stitches. And Luisa and your father wouldn't agree to leave their darling in Inverness alone. They refused to come back here with me. *Refused!* And bloody Sir Niall showed up at the hospital, of course, and then got busy on the telephone arranging for a private ambulance to come from Edinburgh in the morning to take Johnny back to London—it'll take them a couple of days to make the trip, but the kid will have a private nurse with him, and his mother. Sir Niall has loaned your father his car to follow the ambulance all the way! Neither of them would hear of coming back here. I said Johnny could just as well convalesce here. He's got a room here on the ground floor . . . as soon as he's over the concussion he could hobble around here with a lot more space than in London—or Anscombe. But no—Luisa wouldn't have any of it. Wants the leg X-rayed again when he gets to London to make sure it was properly set—and a skull X ray, to see he isn't going to turn into a dummy. Doesn't trust anyone here—least of all Rod McCallum. Who saved her kid in the first place? Nothing I offer is good enough for little Johnny—and she doesn't want him under my roof again. She dropped all her nice manners, and became the real Spanish aristocrat who knows a peasant when she runs up against one! I'm like dirt under her feet. Your father said nothing. Only I knew he agreed with every word she said. They're staying at the Caledonian . . . even the hospital got fed up with Luisa's hysteria and said she couldn't spend the night with little Johnny—even if Sir Niall is pals with the matron. We can send on their luggage at our convenience . . . they can manage as they are until tomorrow, when they can buy some things. I even offered to bring their bloody luggage, but of course they wouldn't hear of it. No, thank you. So politely . . . and wishing I would get out of their way and out of their lives . . .''

He had poured a stiff whiskey and was taking it in large gulps. ''It's not as bad as it seems, old chum,'' Ernest said. ''She's overwrought. Only child . . . and all that—''

''And how would *you* know? How many kids have you brought up . . . ?''

Stacia had appeared. She walked around the table, absent-mindedly buttered a scone, and started to eat it. ''It's been a great day, hasn't it?'' she remarked, as if she were talking about the weather. ''Everyone just loves everyone else. Where have they all gone—your distinguished guests, Rod? Margot Parker will have a field day with it all. How you took the news about

Elliot—and has anyone even thought about Alex in the past couple of hours? How the roof fell in on Alasdair and Johnny, and hero Rod goes marching in and snatches the precious child from the jaws of death. Oh, that would have made a great shot if only the photographer had been around. Pity she had to see you beating Alasdair around the ears. That rather spoiled the fatherly image.''

"Shut up, you little slut, or you'll get beaten around the ears yourself. And where is the little brat?''

"If you mean Alasdair, I hope he's asleep now,'' Julia said. "That is, if your roaring hasn't wakened him—''

"*Wake* him! By God, I'll do more than wake him. . . . He's only had the beginning. . . .'' He strode toward the door, and Julia pushed herself quickly off the sofa.

"Rod!—don't do anything to him. He's had enough. He's had quite enough.''

"He has, has he? Well, there's more to come.'' He strode along the passage to the room the boys had shared, Julia following him. When he flung the door open, Rosmairi was sitting by the sleeping child. "And where were you?'' Rod shouted, and the girl shrank back in fright. "You were hired to keep an eye on them.''

"I told her she could go, Rod. Sunday is her day—''

"Bloody Sunday! Her job is here when she's needed.'' Rosmairi stood up, and retreated before him, as if his wild, thrashing hands were intended for her. Ernest and Stacia had followed Julia and crowded the doorway. Alasdair had wakened with the shouting, and now he cowered back against the pillows. "Oh, stop this crap, you little coward. You know what you did—don't you?'' He almost lifted the child from the bed by his earlobe, and Alasdair screamed in pain. "You've ruined the best party I ever gave. You've driven your grandfather and Luisa out of the house. They'll never come back. No fault of yours that Johnny isn't dead. That would have made the perfect day, wouldn't it? Just about all we needed. Now listen, you little sneak—I adopted you, and you're *my* son. Any kid of mine sticks to the rules, or regrets it, as Stacia knows. Well, you take that—and *that* . . .'' With each word he hit Alasdair across the face. Rosmairi screamed, and Julia flung herself toward them, tried to interpose herself between them. Rod shoved her roughly aside, and she fell across the bed. He continued to beat Alasdair, and when

Julia regained her balance, she saw that blood ran both from his nose and his mouth, where a lip had been split. Even Ernest was galvanized into action. "Here—steady on! You want to kill the kid? You could be had up for assault. . . . Rod, for God's sake—think if Julia took you to court."

"Julia is my wife—and Alasdair is my son. Who's to say a father can't beat some sense into a sniveling little coward who disobeys orders?" He turned, and Julia thought he was about to hit Ernest also. "Police don't interfere in family matters. A father has the right to discipline his son—especially when he's nearly killed someone through disobedience." Julia had now taken the chance to pull Alasdair down again onto the bed, and she lay across him.

"You'll have to beat me first before you get to him again!" she shouted.

Rod backed away. "I won't—you're carrying my child. But don't think this is the end of it. Punishment is punishment. I swear this kid will never forget this day as long as he lives. I intend to see that he never forgets it." His voice grew almost unnaturally calm. "I really want to beat the living daylights out of him—but he'd get over that in time. This is something he'll never get over." He walked back to the door. Ernest gave way before him, and Stacia vanished behind the doorpost. "Tomorrow Princess Cat will be put down. Do you hear that, you little brat? Do you understand what 'put down' means? It means that the vet comes and gives her an injection, and she dies. She dies—did you hear? Like the way you drown a kitten you don't want. It isn't your fault Johnny isn't dead, but it will be your fault that Princess Cat is dead. *That's* the punishment you'll never forget."

"You can't!" Julia shrieked. "I'll stop it! I'll never let you do it!"

"I can do what I like with my own property. Just try stopping me. I bought Princess Cat. She belongs to me."

"The vet would never do it. Never agree to it."

"There's always a gun, isn't there? And I'd make this brat stand and watch it. I swear he'll never disobey an order from me again. Think about it, kid. Just think about it the rest of the night—and have a good sleep."

Alasdair pulled himself free of his mother and ran toward Rod. "Don't!—*please* don't. I'll never do anything again I shouldn't. I promise. On my honor. *Please* don't kill Princess Cat. *She* didn't do anything. I did!''

"Then I should kill you—but I'm damned if I'm going to hang for a cowardly little weasel. You've heard of a whipping boy, haven't you? Or maybe you haven't. They were the kids who got whipped instead of the little prince. Well, Princess Cat is going to be your whipping boy. The thing you love most is going to die. So you'll never forget, will you?''

Alasdair had fallen on his knees. He tugged frantically at Rod's trouser leg. *"Please* don't do it! Please! Beat me all you like, but please leave Princess Cat alone.''

Rod lifted the leg that Alasdair held, and kicked him neatly under the chin, so that the slender young body was half raised from the ground and crashed back against a chest of drawers. Rosmairi screamed again and knelt beside him. He was only half conscious. Julia didn't go immediately to her son. She heaved herself off the bed and went to Rod's side. "If you do that—if you lay a finger on Princess Cat and ruin my son's whole life—I swear I'll *kill* you. I'll find a way. I'll kill you, Rod!''

He laughed in her face. "See you in the morning, Princess. I'll telephone the vet then and set the moment of execution. The brat has to be taught one way or the other. Let's get it over with. He's soon going to have a brother, and I don't want *my* child learning any of his sneaky ways. . . .''

II

Julia held her weeping son until his tears had exhausted him. Janet had come and bathed his face. There was a cut across his eyebrow. "Just like Miss Stacia got when Cat was killed . . . though at that time, I thought she deserved it. But this—this is a crime! Shall I telephone Dr. MacGregor? He should see this. Spanking a child is one thing . . . but this comes close to murder.''

Julia shook her head. "Stay as quiet as possible, Janet. Say nothing. Have Kate serve them a meal in the housekeeper's room—if anyone cares to eat it. Let them drink all they want— he and Ernest.''

"And what about the child here? You can't let the child see what he proposes to do. I'm ashamed of Rosmairi. She's fallen into a heap of nerves, crying her eyes out. Says she'll be leaving in the morning. Says she'll be the next one to feel the back of his hand. And you, Mrs. McCallum . . . you can't stay.'' Julia held her son, to whom they had given more warm milk and aspirin. She looked at his battered face, and hatred such as she had never experienced filled her. Finally he began to doze in her arms, but his body seemed to have violent spasms of trembling, which sleep did not overcome—as if he dreamed terrible dreams. ''All right, my love,'' she whispered to him, although she knew he did not hear her. ''It will not happen.''

Janet brought her tea and more aspirin and insisted that she eat some ham and cheese sandwiches. ''Try to eat, Mrs. McCallum. You must—for the baby. And if you're to be strong enough to stand up to him. I've had a word with Mr. Kerr. . . . He says no gun of his will be used on Princess Cat. I telephoned Sir Niall's house, but he has not yet returned from Inverness—I expect he may be having dinner with Sir Michael and Lady Seymour. I left a message that we would telephone first thing in the morning. I didn't want him telephoning here, in case Mr. McCallum took the call. There are a number of things Sir Niall could do. Speak to the vet . . . he could call in the RSPCA. Between us, we'll stop it. But I doubt any of us will have jobs here by tomorrow night.''

''For the moment, *I* own Sinclair. . . . No one is fired unless I say so.''

''May it be so, Mrs. McCallum. At the moment he's in there pushing food around on his plate and drinking enough to knock two men off their feet—and telling Mr. Wilcox he has the power to do what he likes around here.''

''I'll see that he doesn't use it. Somehow . . .''

When Alasdair was soundly asleep, she lay on the bed Johnny had used. She heard Rod and Ernest go by in the passage—on their way to the library. She heard no sound of Stacia's voice; she wondered if the girl had immediately reclaimed the rooms at the top of the tower that Connie and Ken had vacated. She thought of Alex and wanted to telephone her—and yet did not dare, lest the whole routine of the operator calling back when a line became free make Rod once again aware of her presence. She guessed that at this moment he did not care where she was. Soon, after he had had several brandies, there would be some of Ernest's pills, and he would be asleep. Let him sleep, she thought . . . let him sleep forever.

But she lay without sleep until the first streak of the false dawn touched the darkness. In the other bed Alasdair breathed heavily and sometimes eased his body into another position. Twice during the long night she heard him give a soft whimper, as if his tired, restless mind, his sore body, relived the horror of the day past, rehearsed the worse horror of the day to come. She had had Janet bring a candle, whose soft light showed her son's face; she went to him several times during the night when he had given his little cries, looking at him with love and anguish. On the chest of drawers the eyes in the two photos of Jamie seemed to follow her. They were both Alasdair's face, grown older, the face of her dear, sweet, innocent love that had been reproduced in their child. She knew that whatever happened, she must return Alasdair to the innocence his father had known. She had made vows, promises, that extended beyond Jamie's life, to Alasdair, even to the unborn child, who was not Jamie's but who must learn his values, live as he had done. She could do no less by this child than she knew she must do for Alasdair. The candle burned steadily, and through the night she looked many times at the face of the young man who had been her true, her real and everlasting love.

Alasdair still slept deeply when she eased herself out of the room. It was just light enough to see across the Great Hall and up the stairs. Even with the renovation, the timbers creaked slightly under her weight. The light was growing rapidly, and the birds had begun their twittering calls. She approached the Red Tower Room, wondering if Kate had remade the bed since Margot Parker had left and if Rod was sleeping there. The stout oak door permitted no sound to come to her. So she went on to the bathroom. The shelf above the basin, with Rod's toilet things scattered around, told her that he had taken up occupation again. She moved cautiously through the dressing room and listened at the door. The deep snores reassured her. She knew she could move almost at will, and he would not wake. She found the keys to the Rolls among the things Rod had emptied from pockets onto one of the chests, the detritus of a man's life, the notes and coins, the Dunhill cigarette lighter, the thin gold pocket knife, the most expensive brand of wristwatch in the world, the gold cuff links. The symbols of all Rod had striven for were there. She needed only the keys to the Rolls.

She went back through the dressing room, because she remembered that the door into the passage was stiff and sometimes creaked. She paused to take a heavy coat from one of the closets they had not emptied for Margot Parker's use. Then on to the bathroom. This time she paused to look at the things strewn around. On the mahogany table, made especially for this room and that held a selection of bottles of eau de cologne and shaving lotion, she saw what she had known would be there. There was a spew of pills of various colors, and there was a hypodermic syringe. The syringe was empty, but an almost full packet of white powder lay beside it. She thought of the morning she had had to try to shake Rod back into life in Beverly Hills. This time she would make no such attempt. But his strong body had survived so many assaults on it. She didn't doubt it would do so once again. When he finally woke, he would take more, as he had done many times, and he would come back into the world determined to kill Princess Cat and to break Alasdair's heart. She looked at the syringe and the multicolored collection of pills with distaste and left as quietly as she had come.

She went then to the Prince Charles Suite and hastily packed what toiletries and cosmetics she thought Luisa and her father would need. Downstairs she woke Alasdair gently and dressed him. "No time for a wash or teeth . . ." she said. "Be very quiet. We're going."

Still half-drugged with sleep, his face now quite hideously swollen, and dark bruises beginning to appear, he followed her to the stable yard. William Kerr was waiting there, with Princess Cat, who wore a bridle and leading rein, as she had asked Janet to have him do last night. "Mrs. McCallum—will you be all right? I should come with you." He drew in his breath at the sight of Alasdair's face. "It is well you are out of here."

"But I'll be back, Mr. Kerr . . . I'll be back very soon."

He protested that he should take them in the jeep, but Julia refused. "I cannot have you involved, Mr. Kerr. What I'm doing, I do on my own. Any blame is mine."

They eased open the doors of the stable that housed the Rolls-Royce. The motor purred quietly as she turned the ignition key. She put Alasdair in the passenger seat. "Now, it's your job to keep Cat on the leading rein. We can only go as fast as she can trot.''

"Where are we going?''

"To Finavon—to Sir Niall. Princess Cat will be quite safe there.''

"Well, can't I ride her? We could keep up.''

"Alasdair, don't argue. We have quite a way to go. You can't expect Princess Cat to carry your weight and keep up a trot all the way. Now just try to keep her head level with the car—your arms are going to ache, but you want her away from here, don't you? Thank you, Mr. Kerr.''

"Good luck, Mrs. McCallum.''

Alasdair knelt on the seat and leaned out, taking the pony's leading rein from William Kerr. Princess Cat started off briskly, holding her head high and eagerly sniffing the sharp morning air. Julia drove the Rolls in low gear from the stable courtyard, wincing a little at the sound it and the pony's hooves made on the wooden drawbridge. She wondered if Alasdair could manage the task she had set him. But he had already seen the difficulty, and he used the little riding crop to keep the pony at a safe distance from the car. "That's right, Alasdair. Try to keep her away. She mustn't brush against the car, or she'll get hurt. What a pity we don't have our own horse box . . . but we'll just have to manage. Keep talking to her . . . I think as long as she hears your voice, she'll feel all right. . . .''

The five miles to Finavon seemed an infinity of distance. Julia wondered if even the engine of the Rolls would stand being driven at this crawling pace for so long without overheating. Because of the early hour they encountered no other vehicle in all the long miles. Alasdair kept up a steady stream of words to the pony, words of encouragement, of praise, speaking her name very often. The pony seemed at times uneasy at this new method of travel. She tended to draw too close to the car. Alasdair was on his knees, leaning out of the open window, gently nudging the pony with the crop. "Cat . . . dear Cat, you've got to keep the distance. We'll soon be there, girl . . . oats and water for you. Carrots and apples. . . . Mummie, wouldn't it be better if I rode her?''

"No, I don't think so. In any case, you'd have to ride her barebacked, and she's not used to that. Just keep her going quietly and steadily . . . it's not far now.'' She prayed a silent prayer that the engine would not stall. If it did, she thought, they would abandon the car and walk the rest of the way.

But they made it into the stable yard of Finavon. Julia knocked at the door of the gamekeeper's cottage. He and his wife were already up and dressed. Julia explained briefly that she needed the pony watered and fed and that he should go and rouse Sir Niall. In barely five minutes Sir Niall had come to the kitchen door. "Julia!—for God's sake, come in. Alasdair, leave Cat with Mr. Lindsay." He was wearing pajamas and a bathrobe, and his hair was still rumpled from his night's sleep. "Good God! What's happened to you, child?" His housekeeper had come down, also in her bathrobe. "Mrs. Cummings, would you be so kind—"

He didn't have to finish. "I'll make tea immediately, Sir Niall. And a wee bite to eat. Good morning, Mrs. McCallum . . . and Master Alasdair . . ." In no way did she betray surprise at their appearance, or the state of Alasdair's face. Julia didn't doubt that word of yesterday's happenings at Sinclair had spread. Sir Niall probably had told her himself. She murmured softly to Julia, "I am very sorry to hear about your brother-in-law's death, Mrs. McCallum. A very fine man. I know Sir Niall held him in high esteem." Julia nodded her thanks.

In the dining room Sir Niall was trying to coax a fire into being. Julia told him as much as she dared to say in front of Alasdair. She didn't want the memories of the day and night before stirred too vividly. Alasdair had started to shiver, perhaps a reaction from the fatigue of leaning out of the car so long, perhaps from the realization that he and Princess Cat had escaped from Sinclair.

"Alasdair—why don't you go into the kitchen?" Sir Niall said. "It's warmer there. And Mrs. Cummings will have some plates and things for you to carry. A sharp morning like this makes a boy hungry. . . . And don't worry a thing about Princess Cat. She'll be on her way back to Anscombe in no time at all."

With him gone, Julia told him in more detail what had happened. "I haven't any doubt he would have done it—even if it had to be with a gun. I came to you because I knew you could get someone—even the police—to stop it. Rod's dead drunk, and drugged to the eyes. he won't stir before noon. . . ."

"Why on earth didn't you telephone me? I would have met you with the horse box."

"Afraid. I was afraid Rod would hear me telephoning—you

know there's only the phone in the office, and the extension in the library. I couldn't take the chance that anyone would know."

He shook his head despairingly. "Julia, how long must we be friends before you realize I'd do anything on earth for you? If you'd telephoned at three o'clock, I would have met you at the crack of dawn. At any rate, you're safely here, and so is the pony. Within the hour I'll have her in the box, and Lindsay on the road south. I have the horse box, and I even have something of Rod's that should pull it without difficulty. Yesterday, after I'd dropped everyone off at the station and soothed the Parker woman down as best I could, I went to the hospital. I hung back until after the ambulance from Edinburgh had been arranged and Rod had taken himself off—in a very ugly mood, I must say. I suggested to your father that he take my car to drive south with the ambulance. There would have been too many of them in it for comfort. He suggested hiring a car, and I told him it was a very unlikely event—hiring a car in Inverness to go to London— especially on a Sunday. I told him I'd just stop at the Caledonian and pick up Rod's jeep, which Bill Fredricks had left. I didn't say so—but I knew that returning the jeep to Sinclair today would give me an excellent excuse to see you and Alasdair. From Rod's mood—well, I didn't like the sound of things. . . ."

He made another attempt to coax the fire into more vigorous life. "I'd better think of someone to go with Lindsay. I doubt if he's ever been south of the Border before, and he'll need someone to map-read for him and steer him around London to Anscombe." He rose from his crouching position at the fire, bellows still in his hands. "I know! I'll get Kirsty Macpherson to go with him. She could even take Betsy if it suited. She'd just love to snatch something out of Rod McCallum's clutches. Lindsay's a good man, but he'll be bewildered over hotels, and where to get stabling for the night, handling money . . . and so on. I think Kirsty would love to do it."

Julia felt her humiliation and hurt grow deeper as she realized that she must be in the debt of someone who had once been a rival for Jamie's love—who once expressed, quite openly, that Rod McCallum could have made a good lover. But Kirsty Macpherson would never have made the mistake of marrying him. "Couldn't you go yourself . . . ?" Julia said tentatively. "I know it's a lot to ask—"

"I could, but something tells me I'm needed here more urgently. I have to be on hand to deal with . . . with . . . well, whatever arises." They didn't discuss the details of what might arise. Mrs. Cummings entered bearing a laden tray, and Alasdair carried a plate of buttered scones to complement the hot toast and coddled eggs. The sight of his battered face shocked Julia once again.

"Eat, Alasdair," Sir Niall said with unusual force. "You need food. Cat is having hers out in the stable."

"You won't let anything . . . anything . . . happen to her? I mean . . . you wouldn't let her be killed?"

Sir Niall put out his hand. "Shake, young man. On my word, Cat will be safe. And so will you and your mother . . . Now eat." He himself swallowed half a cup of hot tea and munched one piece of toast. "Now I must get on the phone to Kirsty . . . and get dressed. . . . You must stay here quietly and eat. Look after your mother. Make her eat something . . ."

An hour later, Kirsty Macpherson was there. Although, through marriage, she had changed her name twice, everyone in the district still thought of her as a Macpherson. Her face was alive and radiant. "Douglas thought I was mad to agree to do it . . . but he's getting used to my being mad. And Betsy can't wait to be on the road. I just threw some things into a bag for us both. I promised her a gorgeous stay at Anscombe, and then we'll have a couple of days in London on the way back. Oh, I'm so glad you're not lying down under Rod McCallum. That showpiece he put on on Saturday was just too much. And now this . . ."—she jerked her head in the direction of Alasdair— "Too much, altogether. I'd do anything to get Cat away from that swine. . . ." She pressed her lips closed on whatever else she wanted to say. She took a cup of tea and urged Betsy to eat some toast. "We can't stop for breakfast. We have to be well on our way before His Lordship at Sinclair realizes we're gone."

"Can't I come?" Alasdair asked.

"No, love. Your mother has much better plans for you. Don't worry. You'll meet Princess Cat at the end of it all. Betsy, get your coat on. . . ."

Lindsay already had the horse box hitched to Rod's jeep. It had already been fitted with a hitch by its previous owner. Princess Cat was loaded aboard. While Alasdair went to kiss the pony's soft muzzle, Kirsty said, with a wry laugh, "I do hope Rod doesn't take it into his head to report a stolen vehicle. . . .

I'd feel pretty silly behind bars. . . .'' She slung the single bag she had brought into the back of the jeep. ''I do hope the roof doesn't leak. Well . . . see you later. Betsy, you squeeze here on the front seat with me, and we'll tell Mr. Lindsay where he's to drive. That's exciting, isn't it?'' She was sorting through the pile of road maps Sir Niall had produced. ''Now, Lindsay, are you ready for this rescue mission? I'll spell you at the wheel every couple of hours. Lord, how lovely to be stealing something from Rod McCallum.'' She waved gaily to them. ''Good luck, everyone . . .''

It was still early when the porter at the Caledonian showed her to her father's and Luisa's room. ''It's Julia, Father.''

He opened the door almost immediately, clad in underwear with a towel draped on his shoulders. Luisa was sitting up in bed wearing only her elegant, lace-trimmed slip. The porter, who had had a long look at Alasdair's face, ventured, ''If I may suggest, Mrs. McCallum . . . I'll bring tea and toast up here . . . and maybe the young man would like a bite of breakfast. The dining room isn't open yet . . . but I'm sure Chef wouldn't mind doing a few eggs and such . . . with the staff, if that's all right.''

She thanked him, knowing that she needed time to talk to Michael and Luisa without Alasdair's presence. ''It's most kind of you.''

''A pleasure, Mrs. McCallum. Come along, Master Alasdair . . . I'm thinking you've never eaten in a hotel kitchen before.'' Julia let him go, knowing it was useless to try to hide the state of his face from everyone. The word would go around, whatever she did. Perhaps they would think it was the result of the same accident that had put Johnny in the hospital.

When he had gone, Michael said, ''In God's name, what's happened? Why didn't you telephone us? We waited till late last night . . .'' Luisa had draped a blanket around her shoulders.

''Tell us,'' she demanded.

As briefly as she could, Julia did. They listened in silence, their faces grim. ''Monstrous . . .'' Luisa said. ''The man is mad!''

They were interrupted by the porter bringing tea and toast. ''The oatmeal was ready—and Master Alasdair is eating heart-

ily.'' The porter's seamed face creased further, into a smile.
''And he's ventured that he'd like a fried egg. . . .''

Luisa shivered in the chill of the room. It being June, the
central heating had long ago been turned off. ''Of course he
must come with us,'' she said, sipping the tea gratefully. ''But
you must come also . . . you cannot go back there. . . . That
man—what will he do to you when he discovers what you have
done?'' For a moment her pursed lips turned upward in a smile.
''I should give much, though, to know how he behaves when he
hears that not only has Princess Cat gone, but his Rolls-Royce
and jeep also. Good for this Kirsty girl. I remember her—
very handsome—dressed in white? That was she? Ah, a good,
strong-looking face. She must stay as long as she wishes at Anscombe—and in London, too.''

''I have to go back—just to settle a few things. I'm not worried. Rod never stops reminding me that I'm carrying *his* child.
He certainly won't want to risk anything happening—''

''I don't like it,'' Michael said. ''It sounds like a very trou-
blesome mess you're in, Julia. I wonder why you ever gave him
power of attorney . . . why you let him adopt Alasdair—''

''Father . . . can't you understand? We were just married.
He was pouring gifts on me—including a half share in the house
and ranch. He was negotiating with his agent and the studio
on my behalf. He had adopted Stacia and has looked after her
affairs extremely well. I didn't think it foolish then to give Alasdair a legal father. I never expected . . . never imagined . . .''
Her voice began to waver. Michael hurried to take her in his
arms.

''Dearest, don't cry. You've only done what, with a normal
man, would have been a normal thing. We'll put it right. It's
possible to revoke a power of attorney. And somehow we'll see
that Alasdair's adoption doesn't take away your rights as his natural mother. We just won't worry about that until we've talked
with legal people in London. . . .'' Luisa was nodding. She had
given a cry of delight when she saw the bag of toiletries and
cosmetics Julia had brought.

''How thoughtful. Now I will go and have a bath and warm
up. The ambulance from Edinburgh cannot be here until eleven
o'clock. I think Alasdair should ride with Johnny in it. They
would keep each other amused. I don't know if we must spend

two nights on the road—I don't want Johnny shaken up by the ambulance hurrying too much. The concussion—one must be careful. . . ."

Julia went to the hospital and saw Johnny, Alasdair, and Luisa loaded into the ambulance, along with the nurse who had come to take care of Johnny. Johnny had greeted Alasdair with a yell of delight. "Well, you must have fallen on your head, too!" Julia had not coached Alasdair in what he was to say about the state of his face. She could not begin to teach him to lie. A tired young doctor in Emergency had looked at the congealed blood on the cut on his eyebrow. He cleaned it away and put in two stitches. "Should have been done yesterday. Chances are he'll have a scar. . . ." He seemed to take it for granted that the injury had been acquired at the time Johnny's had.

Julia sat in the Rolls for some time after the ambulance, followed by the car Sir Niall had loaned her father, had left. Michael's last words as he had kissed her had been, "Don't stay, Julia. Whatever you say . . . the man is mad. And mad in a cruel, vicious way. No one in his right mind could have devised a punishment so cruel for Alasdair. It's unnatural—even allowing for the drink and drugs. I don't like you going back at all. You may say he won't harm you because of the baby . . . but I'm not certain. I feel I should go with you . . . have it out with him."

"No . . . no. Luisa's more shaken than you think. You must be with her. And you'll be able to telephone Alex more easily from London. The funeral will be tomorrow. And none of us with her."

"We telephoned last night. She sounds . . . well, she's being Alex. Sounding tough. But so alone . . . We'll not tell her what's happened to Alasdair, and about Princess Cat. It can all wait until she's had more time to adjust. When I think of what I was like for months after your mother was killed . . . If it hadn't been for you, Julia . . . well, I think I would have just quietly drunk myself to death. It all takes a lot more time to adjust than one can ever imagine. Even to this day . . . no, I mustn't say it. It seems so disloyal to Luisa, who has been so wonderful in every way. Alex will not recover quickly from Elliot's death . . . if ever. It would be a very extraordinary man who could ever take his place. She gave him the love of a mature woman, and I believe it was wholehearted. I think . . . yes, perhaps that would be the thing. You and Alasdair could go to her as soon as you get away from Sinclair. Don't stay, Julia. I beg you. Have it out with him, if you must. But don't stay another night. I'll telephone from wherever we are this evening. . . ." He had embraced and kissed her again, and there had been tears in his eyes.

She wept her own tears quietly, tears of relief now that Alasdair and Princess Cat were safe, tears of fatigue, tears of fear at what she knew she must face. She caressed the child in her belly. "Oh—little one—preserve us both." She found herself praying. "God, preserve us both." Then she turned on the ignition, and the Rolls moved smoothly out into the leisurely Inverness traffic. She set her face toward Sinclair and what would await her there.

As she drove into the outer courtyard she found Ernest with his bags packed, waiting for the taxi he had telephoned for to come from Inverness. Stacia stood beside him, her expression at once both petulant and fearful. "You shouldn't go, Ernie," she said. "You know you're about the only one who can handle him when he's like this . . ."

"I've outstayed my welcome, I do believe," he answered. "All things must come to an end. I'll be seeing you again soon, Stacia—keep up with the reading list I've given you. Try to do your ballet exercises every day. And try to be a good girl."

"A good girl!" she retorted. "Where did that ever get me?"

With evident relief, Ernest saw the taxi start across the bridge. "Well, dear ones—this is it until you're back in Los Angeles." He took Julia's hand and kissed her briefly on the cheek. "Quite an exodus, isn't it?" He smiled blandly. "Well, you need a quiet time. *The tumult and the shouting dies; The Captains and the Kings depart* . . . eh?" Carefully he did not ask about Alasdair, nor whom she had been to visit in the Rolls. He preferred not to know, she realized.

She returned his kiss with some distaste. He was removing himself from the scene of more trouble he expected would erupt. "Have a good journey," she said mechanically. Limply she returned his wave as the taxi drew away.

Stacia jumped into the Rolls when Julia started it up again to take it back to the stable yard. "Where's Alasdair? Where's Princess Cat?"

"Mind your own business. You'll be safer that way."

* * *

Julia picked at the lunch Janet presented in the housekeeper's room; her stomach kept revolting against the food, and yet she tried to eat. Stacia sat beside her in silence, eating hardly more than she did. "I think I'll go for a walk," she said at the end of the meal. "It feels like a morgue around here. . . ." Julia realized she also was apprehensive of Rod's reappearance. When she had gone, Julia had Janet come into the housekeeper's room and bring a cup of tea with her. Julia told her then what had happened that morning; she had been careful not to tell either Janet or William Kerr exactly what her plans were. If Rod had come downstairs before her return, both of them would have been able to answer truthfully that they did not know where she and Alasdair and Princess Cat had gone. "You have done well, Mrs. McCallum—except that I do not think you should have come back here. I guessed you might have gone to Sir Niall . . . and, yes, Kirsty Macpherson would have thrown herself into an adventure like that. And fortunate it is that Mr. Lindsay has her with him. It was wise to take Master Alasdair to his grandfather. If Mr. McCallum should inform the police . . . well, a grandfather has rights also. Rosmairi was packing to go this morning, but I told her she must stay. She might be needed. . . ."

She paused and sipped her tea. "It's so very quiet now, isn't it, Mrs. McCallum? But not the quiet of the two winters you were away in America. When I lived with the thought of your return. Now . . . well, we must see . . ."

After Janet had gone, Julia went to the library and placed a call to Alex. At first the operator announced an hour's wait for a line. Then she called back to say the Washington number was busy. "Shall I keep the call in, madam?"

"Yes—please do, until Mrs. Forster is available."

Kate had come to light a fire in the library. Julia huddled over it. Janet told her that Rod still had not wakened. "I've put my head into the room several times, with a hot cup of coffee, but he was just there snoring. Well—best to let him sleep it off. . . . Time enough . . ." she had added, sharply, once again. "I wish you'd *go*, Mrs. McCallum. I don't think it's wise to stay."

"I won't stay, Janet, once I have settled what must be settled."

At last he came. She could hear his footsteps on the stairs. Then they receded as he went through the Great Hall and dining hall. Distantly she heard doors being banged. She did not go to seek him. He would come when it suited him. He would make his discoveries about Alasdair and Princess Cat, and then he would come.

Half an hour later, he did come. His face was tight with fury; it was also puffy, and his eyes red-rimmed. Before he spoke a word to her, he went to the tray and poured himself a neat whiskey which filled half the glass. Then he turned to her. "I suppose you think you've been very clever? You've taken them both away. Of course Kerr and Janet pretend they knew nothing of it—"

"They didn't. That's the truth!"

"A half-truth, if truth at all. You're just trying to shield them. As if I believed a word of it. You cunning, scheming little bitch. I would have done it, you know. I would have had the animal put down—and before that little brat's eyes."

"I knew that. I didn't doubt it for a minute. That's why they're not here."

"Where did you send the pony? To Finavon, I suppose. Well, I can always get her back from there. That fellow has no right to hold what is *my* property. Alasdair here or not, I'll have her put down. The final birthday present to the brat. Oh, don't think I don't know what's happened. The Caledonian was full of information when I called—and so was the hospital when I called to inquire about Master Johnny. Oh, he'd gone off in fine shape in the ambulance, with Master Alasdair to keep him company. Just a little surprised that I didn't know. So now we'll go and get the pony—you and I, Julia. So the news that she no longer exists will be the next message you give to your precious son."

She sighed, and wished her head didn't throb so much. "You're too late, Rod. You have to get up much earlier if you want to keep on top of everything that's happening. Princess Cat is very well on the road south. She's in Sir Niall's horse box, being driven in *your* jeep by Lindsay, and he has the charming companionship and guidance of Kirsty Macpherson and Betsy. They'll have made many miles by now—"

He slammed the now empty glass down and headed for the telephone. "That's theft! I'll report it to the police, and they'll have it stopped before it's even across the Border—"

"Oh, don't be such a fool, Rod. You'll make yourself the laughingstock of the whole British and American press. People like Kirsty Macpherson don't *steal* vehicles. She's not frightened or intimidated by police or press. She'll just state *why* she's taking Princess Cat south, and then your name will be mud, and the press will have a field day. Oh, I know here at Sinclair, you would have invented some story as to why Cat had to be put down, and you might have been believed. By some people. But you'll have touched a sensitive spot with the British public. Oh, they can turn the other way when people beat children, but cruelty to animals really gets their backs up. If you're wise, Rod, you'll just leave it alone. Kirsty will be the first to laugh when they come to arrest her for stealing a pony and a jeep. She'd even laugh at a night in the cells. But she'd have every newspaper in the country on her side by tomorrow. As well as the RSPCA. Offers would come pouring in to adopt Princess Cat. You'd be seen as the despicable—''

The telephone rang. Rod lunged forward and picked it up. ''Yes?'' he shouted. He listened for a moment. ''Yes, she's here.'' Reluctantly he yielded the phone to Julia. ''They have Alex on the line. . . .''

''Aren't you,'' Julia said mockingly, ''going to stay and say something to Alex? You haven't spoken to her since Elliot died. . . .''

''That stuck-up bitch! What the hell would I have to say to her? So her precious Elliot's gone. Who cares? Let her get on with it. . . .''

The room echoed with the sound of the door being banged as he left. ''What was that . . . ?'' Alex's voice on the line.

''The wind,'' Julia said. ''The door slammed.''

''I thought I heard Rod's voice.''

''You did . . . he didn't feel up to speaking to you, Alex. He's not good at that sort of thing. He thinks he's barging into a family matter. He was always slightly . . . well, a little bit in awe of you and Elliot.'' She cut off the subject. ''Alex, I have nothing in particular to say . . . I just wanted to hear your voice. To say, as Father's already said, how we wish we were with you right now.''

''Julia—I know he'll be here as soon as he can. The thought keeps me going. Tomorrow—the funeral—is a ritual that must be gone through. Elliot has left me—forever. I just have to carry on. . . . God knows what my life will be like without him—or how I'll measure up to what he expected of me. But I have to try. Julia . . . ?''

"Yes . . . ?"

"Father sounded very upset when he telephoned last night Not just about Elliot. He told me about the accident to Johnny. Is Alasdair all right? It seems Rod made a hero of himself.''

"That sort of thing comes naturally to Rod. He's rehearsed it a lot of times. But, yes—he did get Johnny out of a nasty situation. Just about all the beams in the tower came crashing down after he'd gotten him out. But he seems all right. I saw them off in the ambulance this morning. Alasdair has gone with Johnny. He'll help make the weeks while the cast's on a bit more bearable. I think they both—Alasdair and Johnny—got a terrible fright. But Johnny's taken the brunt of the physical damage. Luisa won't be coming over to you. She couldn't leave Johnny just now.''

"Julia . . .'' Now Alex's tone was soft, almost pleading. "Julia, do you think you might come over with Father? I can't ask Connie to leave the kids. But I just need . . . well, I need my family around me. I'll get through tomorrow all right . . . it's the days and the weeks after that I dread. Already I can hardly stand the nights. People have been kind. They've flocked around me. Distant cousins of Elliot's are staying with me now. Kind people—but I can't wait for them to go. I just need you— Father—Connie. Did you ever think you'd hear your tough sister Alex say such a thing?''

"We'll be there,'' Julia promised hurriedly, not knowing if she was making a false promise. She had no idea what the next days would bring, whether she would be advised that it would be unwise to leave Alasdair—she could be seen to be leaving both husband and child. And she was beginning to fear taking Alasdair within the jurisdiction of United States law. But she dared say none of this at this time to Alex.

"Bring Rod,'' Alex said. "He won't be parted from you for so long when you're pregnant. . . .''

"We'll see,'' Julia said cautiously. "I think he might just prefer to stick it out here until the studio relents and calls him back to work on a decent script. And then there's Stacia . . .''

"Oh, yes . . . Stacia.'' Alex's voice grew more distant. "Well, work out what you can. You're all welcome . . . God knows, the house is empty enough. . . .'' They talked for a few minutes longer—or rather Alex talked and Julia listened. It was talk of Elliot, rambling talk. Memories of the days during the war before they could be married. She even spoke of Greg. "It's as if my whole life were unwinding before me, Julia, like a film. I wonder what I did to deserve this. Was it because I fell in love with Elliot and planned to tell Greg as soon as he was liberated and able to bear the news? It was a rotten thing to do . . . but how can you help it if you fall in and out of love . . . ?"

"No one can help that," Julia said, thinking of her own reckless love of two men. "It happens, Alex. You're human, like the rest of us."

"I need some of your human touch right now, Julia. I need Father. I need Connie's dear, sweet touch—but she's never begun to understand me. . . ." Julia realized Alex was weeping, and then came the faint click as the receiver was replaced.

Julia herself wept quietly, not letting her emotions take too great a hold on her. She could not present a face of weakness to Rod. She wished she had allowed her father to stay with her; she wished Luisa had not been in such a vulnerable position at the moment. But the thought of Princess Cat being driven south by a defiant Kirsty cheered her, and the thought of Alasdair under the eyes of her father was even more comfort. And she herself would soon be with them.

Rod came back in. "Well, have you cried all your tears with Alex?" He immediately poured himself an even larger drink than the first one. Or perhaps he had had another from the decanter in the housekeeper's room while she had talked to Alex. Perhaps he had even listened on the telephone extension to their conversation. "Well, if you've got some tears left, now's the time for them. I've fired Kerr and Janet—the whole tribe of hangers-on. I'll make a clean sweep of this place. See if it can't be more efficiently managed. I don't like these old retainers who think they're better than I am—and they've got some proprietary right here. They're only servants. I can hire other people—"

"They're not yours to fire, Rod, *I* still own Sinclair . . . the farm pays their wages."

"Oh—is that so? Very soon I'll show you who owns Sinclair. You'll come with me now, my lady. I'll teach you what it's like to dispose of other people's property. . . . You'll see now!"

For a time she resisted his hands tugging at hers. Then he bent and lifted her bodily. It was useless to resist. He dragged her at a stumbling run through the house and out into the stable courtyard. Janet had come rushing to the kitchen door when she heard them. "Mrs. McCallum . . . ?" William Kerr stood in the doorway of his own cottage, his face wearing the stricken look of a man who has just had his past pulled from beneath him, his future totally unknown, uncertain. The Rolls stood ready, and Rod bundled Julia into it. "Where are we going . . . ?"

"Not far— not far at all."

He set off at a pace that rattled the wooden drawbridge and set the wildfowl, swimming and peacefully feeding on the shores of the island and the loch, into protesting flight.

They rattled along the forest road at high speed. At first Julia thought they were headed for Finavon but they went only as far as the McBain cottage. "Get out!" Rod ordered. She obeyed him only to the extent that she stood in the rutted road beside the car. When she saw the five-gallon can of gasoline he had taken from the tractor shed and put in the trunk of the Rolls, she uttered only one word of protest: "No . . . !"

Then she clamped her mouth shut on any other thing she wanted to cry out. Physically, she was powerless to stop what she knew he intended to do. He thrust the always unlocked door of the cottage open and strode inside. She opened the door of the Rolls and sank back on the car seat, not wanting to watch what she knew must happen, but compelled, just the same. He was only brief minutes in the cottage. She heard the sounds as furniture was dragged into the center of the first room. he spared the last of the gasoline for the doorframe. Then he went back into the room, and she gave a little despairing moan as she realized that now he was striking the match. The pile of old, dry furniture went up like a torch. He backed out carefully. She had thought for a moment he might himself be engulfed by the flames, but he had seen these things done too often by stuntmen on film sets to move recklessly, or place himself in danger. The wild flames began to light the small window, to light the shadowy corners of the small room. She saw the stone chimney breast illuminated. Soon the roof beams were on fire. The flames reached hungrily into the second little room, consuming the few things she and Alasdair had left behind when they had, at Rod's bidding, at her own desire, left the cottage and returned to the castle.

"There," Rod said, tossing the can into the middle of what was now an inferno. "That's the end of that! You loved that little place, didn't you?—you and the kid, for whatever reason you didn't care to tell me about. Well, it doesn't exist anymore. The McBains have left forever . . . wiped out."

She thought of the afternoon when she and Jamie had sheltered from the rain there, and built a fire, and became lovers—and had loved each other even beyond his death. She thought of the first night she had brought Alasdair to stay there with her, his arms around her as she had kissed him good night. . . . *I have always wanted to live in the cottage.* . . . This and the images of her own love affair with Rod came and went, glowing through the flames, brightening, darkening, dying. She felt the tears on her cheeks. A great part of her life went with the conflagration.

"Makes a good show, doesn't it?" Rod shouted above the crackle and roar. "Should have thought of a scene for the film so we could use it. . . . But you wouldn't have allowed it . . . and it hurts more this way, doesn't it? Doesn't it, Julia?" He tugged at her arm as he spoke.

He couldn't possibly know, but perhaps he guessed that this was an intimate and deeply felt part of her past, as it was of his own, for quite different reasons. He couldn't know that this was where she had given her virginity and love to Jamie. But he had certainly observed that she and Alasdair had been living lovingly and closely in this humble place—the place he loathed and despised as the scene of his loveless and battered childhood. The slates began to crack and slide down into the inferno as the roof beams burned through. "Nothing like old dried wood to make a good fire. Best fire I've ever attended. We should have had *this* as the finale to the party. 'Come to a cottage-burning.' Would have looked great on an invitation. Farewell to the past . . . good-bye to all that . . . and so on. People would have loved it."

All the time she had said nothing; now she put her head down in her hands and tried to block out the vision. Then Rod's hands, smelling of the gasoline, were on her hair, dragging her head upward again. "Look, you bitch, look! This is the sacrificial pyre. Princess Cat was to have been the sacrificial slaughter. But this breaks your heart, doesn't it?'' She screamed as the pull on her hair became too much to bear. At that moment what remained of the roof crashed in. It was the fall of the last of her good memories, her joys, her hopes, her loves. From now on, everything seemed as black as this charred ruin soon would be.

William Kerr and Janet had arrived in the jeep to witness the final act of the immolation. They stood silent, awed, perhaps even a little frightened at the ferocity of the anger of a man thwarted and filled with rage. They said nothing, just stood back and watched as the last of the cottage was consumed. The old stone walls and chimney breast stood naked to the sky. Around them, the leaves of the trees of the forest had shriveled where the heat had been most fierce.

Finally they came to where Julia slumped in the Rolls, her head propped against the soft leather where Rod had put it, forcing her to watch the spectacle.

"Are you all right, Mrs. McCallum?" Janet ventured. Julia nodded yes.

"We had no idea until we saw the smoke . . . thought it might be an accident. But I see it was no accident," William Kerr said. "No use to call the fire brigade. There's nought to save here."

"That's right," Rod answered him, "nothing left. There never was anything worth saving. Now you two get out of here and mind your own business. This is entirely the business of my wife and myself. Remember . . . you're both fired. You have only a month to get out. . . ."

"We'll be thinking about that," William Kerr answered. "It is Mrs. McCallum who has the final word in the matter."

"Mrs. McCallum does *not* have the final word!" Rod shouted at them. "So mind your own business." They left reluctantly, with many backward glances from Janet. The fire was beginning to die, though flames still sprang from the pile of charred wood. "A great ending, wasn't it?" Rod demanded of her. "I think my father wanted to do that the day he was forced out of here— something to make the Sinclairs think—to remember us by."

"Well . . ." She waved her hand. "You have your memorial now. And a dead one it is, too. Worthy of you."

The reply angered him freshly. "Shut up, you bitch. I've made my mark on Sinclair. And I've more to do."

He turned the Rolls swiftly, nearly putting it in a ditch. He raced along the road back to the castle, Julia had seen it count-less times from this point, but never had she viewed it with such hopelessness and despair.

Julia crept up to the Blue State Room, which was still made up, to lie down and to release the flood of tears she had barely permitted Rod to see before. So much had happened with such swiftness, and now the desolation of her situation swept over her. She tried to think logically, but the frantic events of the past few days swirled unceasingly in her mind, bringing only chaos. She was beginning to perceive the full threat to herself, to her child, from Rod's behavior. She had thought that with all the guests gone, with Alasdair and Princess Cat safe, Rod might return to some sanity. But this evening's senseless burning of the house of his birth made her realize that he was once again in the mood of dangerous savagery that struck him when the black dog of depression seemed to fall on him. She counted the things that had happened: Rod's witnessing of her father's triumph, as he himself had come away angrily defiant of suspension from the studio; the birthday party he had planned for Alasdair so that all their neighbors, but more important, the studio and all of Hol-lywood would know that other things occupied his mind and life; the news of Elliot's death, which had not allowed him time to savor his sense of triumph after the two parties; the near-disaster that the adventurousness of two little boys had almost brought on them; his unforgivable display of viciousness toward Alas-dair; the mad cruelty of his determination to kill Princess Cat; his final act of burning the place of his birth, as if by doing so he could wipe out all the slurs and hardships life had heaped upon him. She realized she could no longer cope with this mon-strous burden of deadly memories Rod carried with him. She must, by some means or other, fight her way free.

Exhausted, she slept for a time, then woke and prepared her-self for the talk she knew she must have with him—possibly the last, final, desperate plea before the real battle began. She bathed, carefully made up her face, and sprayed on perfume liberally. She chose the red cashmere dress he had bought for her in New York, and she put on both of the great gemstones he had placed on her fingers. She didn't know if she was making a great mistake; perhaps it would have been better to have dragged back her hair unbecomingly, to have left off his jewels, to have worn a white blouse and a skirt of the Sinclair tartan. Would battle have been better than this last attempt at persuasion? Could his mad anger have cooled in a few hours? She cautiously opened the door of the Red Tower Room on her way downstairs. The rumpled bed told her that Rod had also slept, or tried to sleep. She stood there for a few moments, listening to the silence of the great house about her, to the particular silence of this room. "Ellen . . . Lady Ellen . . . ?" she whispered; she did not hear that low, sobbing cry. Even this sad, kindly ghost of a woman long dead, who had also known great unhappiness here in this house, seemed to have deserted her.

When she reached the library, Rod was talking on the telephone, in his hand a large glassful of whiskey, which he sipped as he talked. ". . . Of course, Sir Michael. She's sleeping now. Needs the rest. Glad to hear Johnny and Alasdair are okay. Yes, I'll give her your message. . . . She'll probably call you back when she comes downstairs. . . ." And looking straight at her, he hung up and broke the connection.

He smiled at her, the beguiling, heartbreaking actor's smile. "Have a drink, Princess. Do you good. Everything's all right with those two little monsters. They've had plenty of time to think over their stupidity of disobeying perfectly natural orders for everyone's safety. Of course, it was my fault for not having the place boarded up—or the architect's fault. Johnny's head doesn't ache so much—so I guess he isn't going to die. Alasdair is licking his wounds and is glad they're not much worse. They all see sense in time."

She accepted the drink from him because she didn't want to upset him by a refusal. He lighted a cigarette and settled back into a chair, wearing the calm look of a man who has no worries, whose horizon is unclouded. She recognized the unnatural calm that came from a recent intake of some drug. "They've found some hotel in Newcastle—the number's there if you want to call back."

"Later," she said. She knew he didn't want her to call at all, didn't want her to talk to her father or Alasdair. For the moment, she would humor him. She sat and very slowly sipped the large drink he had prepared. He went again to refill his own glass.

Kate appeared. "Excuse me, Mrs. McCallum. Janet asked would she serve dinner in the dining hall, or the housekeeper's room—since there's only you and Mr. McCallum and Miss Stacia . . . ?"

Rod answered her. "The housekeeper's room will be fine, Kate. Keep it simple."

"Yes, sir."

He closed the book on forestry he had been skimming. "One of your pals—Forbes, I think it was—told me there's a nice little piece of property probably coming onto the market. Belonged to some old guy who's died, and his daughter's married someone in the South. Doesn't want to work it. So it'll be for sale. He said he'd like to buy it himself but is a bit short of funds right now. It adjoins some of our land—over on the other side of the loch. But it's good arable . . . the whole place was set to barley last year and gave a very good crop. Might be worth looking into. . . ."

"Yes," she said mechanically. "If you think so . . ." When, she wondered, when, if ever, would he realize that there was no "our" land in Scotland? What was jointly held was all of his giving, and it was all in California. Whatever was in Scotland must be held for Alasdair. But she could not make any objection to his buying a farm of his own. In the calm that had fallen on him, she dared not now raise his anger. He smiled at her benignly, and it was almost impossible to believe that this was the same creature who had, just a few hours ago, reduced to ruin a place that she and Alasdair had loved.

"Dinner is served, Mr. McCallum," Kate announced. Rod refilled his glass before escorting her formally through the Great Hall and the dining room, back to the housekeeper's room. Stacia was waiting for them there. "Hi" was Rod's greeting. "Haven't seen you all day. Have you been cracking the books?"

"Yes—a little. Walked a couple of miles around the loch. To that flat place where they're able to farm and keep cattle. A lady called me in and gave me tea and scones. Her kids had been to the party on Saturday. They were full of it . . . Jeez . . . I didn't know a sweater and a pair of socks and a few old party favors made such a difference."

"You haven't lived, Stacia," Rod said, but his tone was friendly. "You know—rationing, and not having much money make a big difference. Those kids would think that getting into Inverness was a real big thing." He waved his glass at her, and he put it down as he carefully pulled out a chair for Julia. "Listen, Stacia, why don't I pour you a wee dram, as they're so fond of saying up here. I suppose it's time . . . you're getting to be a big girl now. Just ease in gradually . . .''

"About time you recognized I'm getting to be a big girl," Stacia answered, but she was careful to smile as she spoke. "A couple of people gave me a few sips the other night. They were all so high they didn't care what they were doing—or how old I was. Just as well we weren't in California, or I might have been dragged off into the bushes by some of your horny old friends. At any rate, I'm not for dragging, I'll have to be led . . . when I feel like it."

"That's my girl," Rod said. "See . . . all the things your wicked old stepfather has been warning you about are real. You're going to do big things in time, Stacia. Just be prudent, my love. Cautious. You'll be twice the star your mother was."

"Never!" Stacia replied firmly, raising the glass Rod had filled for her. "People *loved* my mother. From a million miles off, up there on the screen, they loved her. I'm not as dumb as she was, and I won't let myself be used the way she was. But I don't think people will love me. If I'm good enough—which I will be—I'll be a star. But I won't be Anne Rayner's daughter. There will only ever be one Anne Rayner."

"Okay . . . okay." Rod rang the bell on the table impatiently. Almost immediately Kate appeared with a soup tureen. He watched her carefully serve them all. Julia realized that the exchange with Stacia, the mention of her mother's as yet undiminished fame, had brought anger back into him. "It's beef afterward, isn't it, Kate?"

"Yes, sir—with—"

"I don't want the whole goddamn menu. I just wanted to be sure I hadn't opened this priceless claret for a bit of tasteless fish." He gestured to the opened bottle on the sideboard. "What do you think, Princess? Château Lafite. Damn little of it around these days. Even our dear Luisa would open her worldly eyes at that."

"You work wonders, Rod," Julia said demurely. "Dare I ask where it came from?"

"Yes—that and a whole lot more. I've started laying down a proper cellar here. No more handouts from Sir Niall. And where did it come from? It came from money, my pet. Only money buys you the things other people can't get or have. Money buys contacts. Money buys everything. Money—''

"I guess you have enough money," Stacia said, "but your soup's getting cold."

"You'll have a hard job making someone love *you*, Stacia," Rod replied. "Even when you're up there a million miles away on the big screen." But he still smiled at her, and he ate the delicious vegetable soup with evident enjoyment. Jane and Kate came and served the sliced prime beef, tender in the way people seldom found it, because of its period in the hanging room Rod had installed, and in an amount almost unknown on anyone's table in those postwar years. Janet's face held a grim but resolute look, as if she didn't believe the money they had all received that afternoon. It seemed impossible that she would end her long years at Sinclair in a month's time. Julia guessed that Janet expected that Rod would change his mind about that when the next violent swing in his mood occurred. Rod poured the wine, sipped it, and then filled all their glasses. "Kate—go and bring another bottle, won't you please? It has to breathe a while. . . .''

They were served an excellent glazed apricot tart. Where on earth had anyone gotten apricots? Perhaps Luisa had brought them? But who knew what Rod hadn't arranged to have shipped from Fortum's or Harrods? Would the next thing they saw be that impossible prewar memory—a pineapple? "It feels like California," Stacia said. "Janet's a real good cook when she gets the right stuff, isn't she?" She edged her glass toward Rod. "Could I have more wine, please? It tastes real smooth. . . .''

He smiled at her, the film-star smile. "So it should, my dear. But I'm glad you like it. You'll find it hard to take rotgut after wines like this one. Always go for quality, Stacia. If you can't afford it, go without."

"My—I'm learning a few things tonight, aren't I? Well, this is the best teaching time. Nice and quiet, without all that mob around. I'll tell you—I was scared stiff the whole time Margot Parker was in the house. Those terrible things she wrote about my mom—I don't know how she could look me in the face . . . or you, either, Rod."

"Well, she will. And she'd better be sweet. Suddenly Julia's sister is just about her boss. How does that strike you, Stacia?"

"Funny as hell. I'll bet she's never worked for a woman before. No woman ever gave Margot Parker orders. Of course, she could always move to another syndicate. But that would put her on a lower rung than Crista Cowley, and she'd hate that.''

Rod raised his glass to Stacia. ''You know, when you're not pouting or sulking or being rude, you can be an interesting gal to talk to. Pity old Ernie decided to take off. I suppose the tower business scared the hell out of him.''

''I think *we* scared the hell out of him,'' Julia said. ''Deaths and near-deaths—and Margot Parker—don't make for a very happy stay.'' Suddenly her eyes brimmed with tears. She thought of Alasdair in some unknown hotel in Newcastle, of Kirsty making her way south towing Princess Cat, whose life was to have ended this day. She thought that in a few hours Alex's husband was to be buried, and none of her family stood beside her.

''Hey—Princess. No tears now. Everything's all right.'' He rushed to refill her glass, at the same time his own. He had already progressed to the second bottle. ''Everything's just fine. As soon as the baby's born, you'll understand that. A few changes here and there . . . I haven't done too badly so far, have I?''

She sipped the wine, which she didn't want, and nodded, as if in agreement. This couldn't be the same man who had burned down part of Alasdair's heritage and her sacred memories just a few hours ago.

Before coffee arrived, Rod and Stacia had drunk two more glasses of wine. When Kate poured the coffee, Rod said, ''Bring the Drambuie, Kate. It's time Stacia was introduced to the real wine of the country. . . .''

''Oh, I had more than several sips on Saturday night.'' She nodded in pleasure as she sniffed the liqueur. Over the coffee and the Drambuie, which it seemed to Julia, who was drinking neither, to take an interminable time, they exchanged gossip about Hollywood—news Ernest had relayed, things Margot Parker had said, the contents of the precious copy of *Variety* Margot had brought that had been read, and now was discussed page by page. For the first time they seemed to Julia to be forming an alliance—perhaps against her, perhaps against this alien world Rod so much wished to dominate but that he was, perhaps, just realizing would give him, no matter what lavish hospitality he dispensed, no more than the courteous nod they would give to any outsider. No matter what he did, no matter what name he claimed, whatever tartan he wore, he would never completely belong. As for Stacia, she only wanted to be back in Hollywood, free of all this dreary landscape and customs she didn't understand. She didn't care if Sinclair and Scotland rejected her. She was waiting for the applause of the whole world.

Julia felt the ache of exhaustion in her limbs. Her eyelids were heavy from her sleepless night, the hours of scheming and planning. She knew that Rod would expect her back in the Red Tower Room that night. She knew that she could never again share a bed with him.

"Rod . . . I'd really like to have a talk with you. I'd rather it be alone." She looked pointedly at Stacia.

"Ah, hell—let her stay. She's suddenly grown up. Can't keep her out of everything." He reached for the bottle of Drambuie, noted with annoyance that Julia had drunk none of hers, and refilled Stacia's glass and his own. "Spill it out, Princess. It's all in the family."

She took a deep breath. It would have to be said. She had promised that she would stay no longer than she had to. She now bore the responsibility of reversing all that Rod had done that day, of ensuring that Janet and the Kerr family were safe in their positions, that Sinclair continued to function as it had done before the day Rod McCallum had arrived with his film crew and his old hatreds from the past and taken over.

"Well . . ." She found it almost impossible to speak. She was afraid. She was glad that Sir Niall had stayed at Finavon— that he was near at hand. Surely nothing too bad could happen. "Rod, I think it's time we discussed the power of attorney I gave to you. Yes—I know I gave it. But I think it's time I took it back. I'm not incompetent. I don't really think I realized what I was doing. . . ." His features seemed so suffused with rage that she faltered.

But his tone was quiet enough. "Yes, my dear . . . do go on. I can't wait to hear all of it. So you think you're not incompetent. Fair enough. Not incompetent—just stupid. Like most women. And hopelessly sentimental. What have I done? Just poured a fortune into your precious ancestral castle. Given you things you could never have hoped to have—unless you had married one of the always unavailable Dukes of Scotland. So I'm not an aristocrat? So what? I don't recall it made any difference when we were married. With that marriage I gave you a great deal. I'm pretty good at managing business affairs—and you know it. Look

at Stacia here. She's got money from her mother in trust funds
that the shyster lawyers would have taken from her given half a
chance. When she comes of age, she'll have her own money—
thanks to me. I never took a penny of Anne Rayner's money. I
think that's well known. If not—go back and look in the attorney's files in Hollywood. Have I asked *you* for any money?''

''No, Rod . . .'' She pressed her hands against her temples,
trying to gather her argument and yet not make it sound like an
argument. ''It's just about Sinclair. You know I can't let it pass
out of my hands . . . it will be Alasdair's when he comes of age.
It must be. I can't allow you to fire Janet and William Kerr. I
can't allow you to take over everything. . . .''

His tone was still low. ''Ah, but you allowed me to throw
money at this heap. You didn't say no to what I gave you in
California—things that I loved.''

Her spirit quickened. ''Did you ever love what you destroyed
this afternoon? The cottage—''

''To hell with the cottage. That's where it belonged—in hell.
Would you expect me to love a place where I . . .'' With a swift
movement, he picked up the bell and rang it violently. Kate
appeared instantly. ''Bring another bottle of this. . . .'' He indicated the Drambuie. He sat in silence for the time it took Kate
to get the cellar keys from Janet and return with the bottle. Janet
had come to open the bottle; the trembling hands of the young
girl were not up to the task. Janet filled Rod's glass and then
hesitated before Stacia's.

''Go ahead—fill it up. It seems Stacia might be my only friend
around here.'' He raised his glass to Stacia, ignoring Julia.
''Here's looking at you. You and I might make sweet music
together sometime. Wouldn't it be something if Rod McCallum
made a film with Anne Rayner's daughter? Her first film . . .
think of it.''

''Yes . . . I'm thinking of it.'' She smiled.

''Well, we'll think a lot more about it. It'd make a lot better
box office than that stinker my dear wife and I made together.
We could do things with it . . . go places. It would be a terrific
box-office combination. The world has been waiting to see Anne
Rayner up there on the screen again.''

''Anne Rayner with a difference . . .'' To Julia, Stacia's words
began to sound slurred. Janet had stayed stubbornly at the side-

board, decanting a bottle of whiskey into cut crystal. Kate hovered by the doorway.

"Rod," Julia said faintly, "this wasn't what I wanted to talk about. I wanted to talk about—"

He waved his hand. "Oh, hell, out with it! Not in front of the servants, eh? Well, they might as well know it. They might as well know exactly what position you are in. Not yours any longer to grant favors, my dear. To keep people *I* don't want in employment. Tomorrow I will *buy* Sinclair. I'll use the power of attorney signed with your fair hand to buy this castle and all the land that goes with it."

"You can't! I'll stop it. I know I can!"

"Can you? I have a copy of the document you signed at La Casa del Sol. The original is safely locked in my attorney's safe. It should be good enough even for Scottish law. I will offer a more than fair price—a handsome price. No one will ever be able to say that I cheated you. I will use your power of attorney to sell your precious son's estate to myself. See what you make of *that,* madam."

"Well, you're being ridiculous! This isn't the Middle Ages. You can't force a woman to do what she doesn't want to do. I can revoke that power of attorney. I'll do it tomorrow."

He shrugged and uttered a contemptuous little sound. "Do what you like. Revoke it. Go ahead. I'll sue you for all the money I've spent on this place . . . acting, of course, under your power of attorney. Acting on your instructions . . . Oh, it'll drag on and on . . . as I fight you for this castle and the custody of our child. You haven't a penny now, Julia—except what the farm throws off. And that's peanuts. I can make out a pretty damning picture of how you beguiled me into spending all this money— and then decided you didn't want me. It won't look good that I've given you half of my California property. I have given you rights you have never given me. I'll fight you to the highest court in this land, by which time you'll have been forced to sell the castle and land to pay the legal expenses. . . . It's a no-win situation, Julia . . . so why don't you see sense? You'll lose it, one way or another. You might as well give it up at a handsome price, without a fight, as lose it by being so deeply in debt you have no other choice. You won't find so many eager buyers for this place. Too damned expensive and inconvenient to run—and the farm's no inducement to anyone."

"My family—"

"Your family . . . your *bloody* family. You think they'd do anything for you, don't you? Well, I know very well that none of them has ever seen the sense in your keeping this damned pile of stone just because your precious husband and son were born here. Luisa's helped you in the past . . . but there's a limit to that. You haven't even paid off *that* debt. Try Alex. You might find that that cool, calculating mind would say it wasn't worth the struggle."

Julia sat for some minutes in silence. Despite the warmth of the room, she could feel herself shake with cold. Janet stood transfixed by the sideboard, and Kate remained by the door. She felt the protectiveness of their presence; they may have stayed for that reason, or simply because they wanted to learn the full extent of Rod's plans. He had virtually ordered them to stay. It was as if he wanted them to hear, to know the power of the forces he would bring to bear against her.

She took a gulp of the Drambuie, although she already felt a pain in her head. "I would have to sign a deed of sale. You can't force me to do that."

"You don't have to sign anything. I have your power of attorney to do it for you. But you will sign—sooner or later. You will when the money runs out. When the lawyers' bills start piling up and you know you can't hang on anymore. You'll sell for pennies on the pound, just to get out of it all. Kind of a waste, don't you think?"

She straightened and tried to ease her body into a more comfortable position. The backache which had plagued this pregnancy was back, but worse; almost shooting pains racked her. "Why . . . ?" she said. "Why do you want it so much? What does it matter to you? Your life isn't here—it's back there—in Hollywood. Why can't *you* let it go? I could try to pay you back . . . slowly. I think Alex would help." In a last burst of desperation she said, "I suppose I could even use the money from your gifts of the California property to pay you back."

He looked at her intently, then deliberately turned his head and looked at Stacia, at Janet, at Kate. "I wish Kerr were here. Then he could hear it, too, and know that I mean to win. I'll have this castle, and I'll have my son, if I have to blacken your name in any way I damn well see fit. There are a whole lot of guys in Hollywood I could buy to say you had swift, sweet little affairs with them.''

''Never!'' The word came from Janet. ''Who would believe such lies? Of a lady like Mrs. Sinclair—''

Rod thumped his fist on the table and shoved back his chair. He walked around the table to where Janet stood. She held her ground well, but in the face of his ferocity, she seemed to will herself not to retreat before him.

''Until I divorce her, her name is Mrs. McCallum. After that she can call herself any damn thing she wants.'' He took the whiskey decanter from her hand and poured himself a large glass. Julia felt a shudder run through her as she realized what that would do to him after the drinks he had been taking all day, the bottles of wine, the Drambuie. ''And even that name's a fake. The real name is McBain.''

''McBain . . . ?'' Janet's whisper was incredulous. ''McBain! Then the cottage . . . ?''

''Yes—the cottage. I burned my rotten childhood. I burned the memory of that stuck-up son of a bitch who fired my father and generously gave him the money to get to Canada, to get us all out of his sight. They fought together, in the First World War, those two men. My father said he had saved Sinclair's life once . . . and the thanks he got was a pittance of a wage and no more. He must have been desperate to have pinched the Sinclair silver—but he was always a bloody fool. But even a bloody fool deserves more than being kicked out like a dog. So, yes— I burned the cottage. Tomorrow, I'll have those walls down. Not a stone upon a stone . . . isn't that in the Bible? 'Vengeance is Mine, sayeth the Lord.' Oh, they were good at preaching vengeance when I was dragged to church every Sunday. Well, I think my father had his own vengeance. We were due to go the day after Adam Sinclair disappeared—and go we did, as ordered. And it took them days to find his body, and it looked like a bad and stupid shooting accident. The sort that happens when a man slips with a loaded and unbroken gun. My father read about it in a Glasgow paper the evening we sailed. His body in the bottom of a ravine, lost in the leaves and bracken. I can remember my father laughed his head off and got right royally drunk. He wanted to talk, but my mother shut him up. Later he did talk— sometime later when I could better understand—so drunk he could hardly get the words out. Adam Sinclair. How he hated him. Wished him dead. Was glad when the other son drowned in the loch. If he could have engineered *that* death, I wouldn't put it past him—but he wasn't clever enough for that. Or too clever to take the chance. The night my mother died he got drunk, and he told me. He told me about following Adam Sinclair into the forest that day. He didn't have a gun with him. All the guns belonged to Sinclair. He said he went to have a final talk with Sinclair . . . to tell him it was a mistake to send us all away. To ask for another chance . . . even if he had to choke on the words. He didn't want to leave Scotland. He was afraid of what he would find on the other side of the Atlantic—and he was right. Adam Sinclair refused him, and told him to be grateful he wasn't prosecuting—was even paying his way out. Some stupid crap about that being his payoff for saving his life. My father said he hit Sinclair. Whether the gun went off, or my father fired it, I'll never be sure. My father was a liar. It made a good story. He'd killed the man who'd driven him out of Scotland. That's what he said.''

"I don't believe it!" Julia breathed. "It couldn't be so . . .''

Holding both the decanter and his glass, Rod came back to his seat. For the first time Julia detected a lurch in his walk. He topped up his glass. "I'm not sure I believe it either. . . . And none of you here in this room believe it. . . . You can repeat it, any of you, but who would believe it, and what could you do about it? Adam Sinclair is dead. I suppose my father is dead. The dead don't talk. It's all hearsay . . . the drunken ramblings of a man who had stolen a piece of silver and who might have made up the whole story of his revenge to make himself into a hero in the eyes of his son. We'd been through the Canadian wilderness by then—and men who used guns were heroes.'' He took a large gulp of his whiskey. "Oh, but the thirst for vengeance was there—whether that story is true or not. He believed Sinclair owed him. And so he did.''

"Did you intend to come back—all those years ago—when you were only a child?'' It was Stacia who asked the question. Her eyes burned with eagerness for the answer.

He laughed at her. "Kids don't have ambitions like that. I scraped by, and in my mind I let the Sinclairs go to hell. But when the money started rolling in—when I knew I was going to be more than a bit player—I began to think of Sinclair. I was old enough to remember it. Remember how I used to come to the kitchen door to get instructions for odd jobs—and a few coppers to pay for them, and if Cook was feeling generous, a bite of bread to eat and something to take home to my mother. My service to the laird of Sinclair was taken for granted—unpaid, if he was feeling stingy that day. All the family were in his service—and we lived in that damned little shack in the woods, and I would take off my boots to walk to school—yes, that same goddamn school—and put them back on—to save the soles and the family pride. Some pride! Oh, yes, I began to think of Sinclair then. I thought how I'd love to turn the lot of them out of the place and have it for myself. I had a fancy to live in the castle. To own the castle. At the end of the war I began to make inquiries. There was only the widow of the younger son, and a kid. Lady Jean was dead. But I wasn't rushing my fences. I waited until I had good and sufficient reason to come here—until I had a film script that suited the location. I thought maybe I'd hate the sight of the place once I saw it again, and that would be good-bye.''

"Did you . . . could you have married me just to get the castle?'' Julia said. She didn't want to say such a thing before all the people present, but she sensed that Rod would never again talk as he was talking now. By tomorrow they might never talk again.

He shrugged. "A bit of both, I suppose. You're a beautiful woman, Julia—and I needed a permanent woman in my life. You had the possibilities of being a star. And you just happened to own Castle Sinclair. An irresistible combination—''

"You lousy snob!'' Stacia suddenly shouted. "You were married to the biggest star in the world, and you threw her away.''

"The biggest star in the world threw herself away,'' Rod replied with quick sharpness. "Anne Rayner was dead. What was I supposed to do—live with her memory for the rest of my life? At least the woman I married wasn't a tramp. It might have worked out—given half a chance. But she never fitted into Hollywood, and I never fitted in with her fancy family. So now it's blown wide apart. I suppose . . . I suppose, in the end, the old fairy tales are true. Only the prince finally marries the princess in the tower. But this time the stableboy will keep the tower, and the princess can go . . . can go to hell. But not with my child.''

"You'll have none of it,'' Julia said. She rose to her feet

shakily. "You'll have neither castle nor child. I'll see to that. I may well go to hell. But I'll meet you there, Rod McBain. I'll meet you in hell."

The pain in her back was worse; she could hardly hold herself upright as she left the room. Dumb and awestruck, Kate moved aside to let her pass. Tentatively she raised a hand, as if to help Julia, and then let it drop, as if the whole situation were beyond help—gone beyond control.

Julia waited a long time, dressed and sleepless in the Blue State Room. She lay on the bed, a blanket drawn around her. She was frightened and terribly alone. It was raining, a light but steady rain that trickled in the gutters and downspouts. Downstairs, faintly, she heard the telephone ring. It could be her father, perhaps calling with the hope of speaking to her. She longed for his voice, for news of Alasdair, and yet she could not make herself go down to ask. She could not place a call to her father or Alex. She could talk to no one except the child in her womb. "I won't let it happen, little one . . . I won't." Part of her fear was for the child itself. Her panties had been slightly spotted with blood, and the ache in her back was steady. But when Janet knocked and came in with a cup of cocoa, Julia said nothing of her fear. If Janet brought Dr. MacGregor, that might bring Rod also. She wanted Rod to stay in the library and drink himself almost to oblivion, before he went slowly to the Red Tower Room to sleep it off. She drank the cocoa in silence, only nodding to Janet's inquiry. "Are you all right, Mrs. Sinclair? Won't you let me help you undress . . . ?" But she, like Kate, seemed numbed by what she had heard; she did not insist. She simply laid more logs on the fire. It seemed she knew enough words had been said for this one day, enough deeds done, enough threats made. Again Julia shook her head when Janet suggested that she might sleep in the adjoining room. She took the empty cocoa cup from Julia and softly wished her good-night. "I hope you may get some sleep, Mrs. Sinclair."

Julia waited through the hours. She heard footsteps on the staircase, light footsteps that passed her door, not pausing, but going on to where the winding stone staircase led to the tower rooms. Much later she heard other footsteps, heavy, slow. They would be Rod's. She held her breath in fear lest they turn in the direction of her room, but they faded. He had gone to the Red Tower Room.

She waited another two hours. The pain in her back had eased somewhat. She slipped off the cashmere dress she had worn and put on a woolen skirt and sweater. She carried her shoes as she tiptoed along the gallery and entered the bathroom of the Red Tower Room. She almost dropped the shoes when she saw the state of the bathroom. Rod must have been foraging in his store of barbiturates—they lay in a pretty, evil, multicolored display all over the bathroom floor. She saw the white powder—the deadly white powder sprinkled on the mahogany sink and also on the floor. Rod must have been very drunk to have been so careless with his precious supply—though undoubtedly he knew where to get more.

In the dressing room she took her warmest coat from the closet and searched for her gloves and handbag. She dared not turn on a light but used what came from the bathroom. When she had assembled these, she eased open the door to the bedroom. If he had done what he usually did, the contents of Rod's pockets would lie on one of the chests. She groped her way in the faint light that spread from the bathroom, barely enough to lighten the darkness, not enough to waken the sleeping man. But his manly possessions, of which he was so proud, the Dunhill lighter and cigarette case, the diary bound with a thin gold strip, the keys to the Rolls with their gold chain and tag, were not on the chest. His clothes—those expensive clothes of which he usually was so careful—lay where he had discarded them. She dropped on her hands and knees to begin a search of the floor of that large room for the keys to the Rolls. She had no idea how long it was before she found them. It had seemed an hour, and the pain in her back had returned with ferocity, but now it was accompanied by shooting pains in her stomach. She wanted to cry out in pain, but she willed herself not to do it. She cursed her own stupidity in attempting this venture at all. How much easier to have had William Kerr drive her to Sir Niall's house, but she had not wanted to involve him. She wanted to make this break freely and cleanly, with no one's help. Her reluctance to bring someone else in had also been mingled with a bitter anger, the anger of Rod's acknowledgment that there had been little love, but a great deal of calculation in his marriage to her, anger at the beating he had given Alasdair, resentment at Rod's threats, as if she were something he could shake off like an annoying pest. She had been belittled and ridiculed. She had remembered Kirsty's joyous acceptance of the jeep, shrugging off the possible consequences. Julia wanted Rod to have to get a court order, in the full eyes of the law, to repossess his Rolls-Royce. She wanted some of the humiliation she had suffered to sting him.

Then, with the keys in her hand, she rose to her feet. A stabbing pain in the abdomen nearly sent her back on the floor again. She steadied herself against the mantel. No fire had been lighted there that night—perhaps a signal of Janet's anger also. Then something about the room struck her as strange. There was no sound in it—no sound at all, except for the light trickle in the gutters and downspouts. There was no sound of Rod's breathing, certainly not the heavy breathing, even the snoring that usually accompanied one of his wild indulgences in drink and drugs. Was he not in the bed, after all? Where was he? She groped her way to the bed, and her hands lightly explored the shape of his body under the blankets—blankets that were partly thrown aside. She slid her fingers down his arm to his wrist. There she thought she felt a flutter of a pulse, but faintly. Or was it her own fear and pain that were growing worse, that made her unable to judge? She put her ear down to his mouth, trying to hear breathing. There seemed to be none, but the mighty pounding of her own heart could have blotted out all sound. Easing herself back from him, she managed to find the switch to the bedside light; she pulled it on, without fear now that he could do anything to hurt her, or stop her from leaving.

"Rod?" She shook him, and his slack shoulder seemed lifeless in her hand. Then she saw on the beside table the hypodermic syringe. She picked it up and held it to the light. It was empty. Despite his drunkenness, the spilling of the heroin powder, he had managed to make enough of a solution to inject himself. How large a solution? The answer seemed to lie in the bare fluttering of the pulse, the breath so slight she could not hear it. Rod was dying.

She turned to the door, still with the syringe in her hand. Then the pain struck with all its massive force, hurtling through her back and abdomen. All the strength seemed to flow from her body. She fell to her knees, and then facedown on the floor. The glass of the syringe crushed in her hand. She felt the rush of blood both from her hand and from her womb. "Help me!" she whispered. And then louder, and the loudest she could raise her voice: "Help me!"

The only answer came back from the sobbing, sighing spirit who had been her companion so many times in this room—the companion who had died in childbirth. "Lady Ellen . . . help me . . . for God's sake, help me!"

She felt the intense coldness of shock against the warm rush of blood before the blackness came.

She struggled to consciousness a number of times during the hours that followed. She got to her knees and made some progress toward the door before she collapsed again. She called for help, knowing it was almost useless. There was only Stacia, in the tower room at the other side of the gallery, and a whole floor above. How could she hear her cries? Impossible to believe, or even hope that Janet or Kate, far removed, next to the kitchen, could ever hear what little sound she croaked. Better to save her strength for the baby she thought she was miscarrying, to hope that Rod might survive until Janet came in the morning. Once, in a brief time of consciousness, she managed to get as far as the door and started hammering on it. The sounds were loud in her ears, but she knew that her movements were feeble, more like a cat scratching than the thunderous noise it would need on that heavy oak to wake Stacia, to bring anyone to their aid. Once again she heard the sobbing sigh; she raised her head and saw, far more clearly than she had ever seen it before, the gray, slender shape of an outstretched hand that seemed to beckon her onward, onward to peace and rest. She slipped once again into the darkness as the single light burned by the bedside. She believed that now they would all die here together, Rod, their baby, and she.

Janet's hands on her. "For pity's sake, Mrs. Sinclair . . . ! Will you not speak? What in God's name has happened here . . . ?"

She managed only one word: "Ellen . . ."

Janet ripped one of the blankets from the bed to cover her. "I'll be back in moments, Mrs. Sinclair. I must telephone for the ambulance." She was aware briefly that now light flooded the room from the windows. Morning had come, and she was still alive. She was also dimly aware of the journey to the hospital, of many hands upon her, of voices both familiar and strange to her. Then the darkness was real and deep as the anesthetic took hold. She awakened later to know that the baby had been incompletely aborted there in the Red Tower Room, and they had had to remove the pitiful remains from her womb. She suffered the strange and cold sensation of blood transfusions. She could not count the hours—or was it days?—when she slipped into and out of consciousness in the hospital bed in Inverness. Always, when she woke, either night or day, Janet or Sir Niall was seated at her bedside; sometimes she thought she sensed the presence of another person quietly seated, someone she did not know. The world seemed an icy wilderness of white, the sheets, the dressings, the starched white aprons of the nurses, the white coats of the doctors. She shivered in the grip of fever, even with the blankets and the frequently changed hot-water bottles.

Then one morning—she knew it was morning because the light had the particular and unmistakable quality of the dawn—she woke and was no longer cold, shivering. Gradually her eyes focused on aspects of the room—the pale green walls, a single picture. Then she turned her head to see that Sir Niall sat in the chair beside the bed, his head bowed in sleep. But again she sensed the second presence on the other side of the room. She turned her head and looked directly at the face of a man who did not sleep as Sir Niall did, a man who was a stranger to her and who did not wear the white coat of a doctor.

"You are better this morning, Mrs. McCallum," the stranger said.

His voice roused Sir Niall, who rose to his feet and gently approached her. His hand had already gone to the bell to ring for a nurse, but he was also feeling her forehead. "You'll be all right now, my dear. It was a bad time . . . you've had a severe infection. We thought we might lose you. . . ."

"I lost the baby, didn't I?"

"I am so sorry, my dear. Yes. That is so."

"Rod?"

He bowed his head. "Rod is dead. Not your fault. We all know you tried to save him."

"Alasdair?"

"He is well. He is with Luisa and Johnny. Your father has been to visit. But you . . . well, you weren't well enough to recognize him."

"But Rod—"

He silenced her by placing a finger over her lips. "There is no need for you to say anything about Rod, Julia. The gentleman over there"—he nodded toward the stranger—"is from the office of the Procurator Fiscal. One or another of them has been here since you were brought in. You are to say nothing about the circumstances of Rod's death. All that will come later—when you feel stronger. I say this on the advice of the solicitor we have engaged to represent you. . . ."

"Solicitor . . ." The word sank in, the implication of the man seated there. Had they thought, in these days, however many there had been, of her fever and near-delirium, that she might speak some words that would implicate her in Rod's death? Now that she was conscious and warned by Sir Niall, would they send him away? "How long have I been here?"

"More than two weeks . . . They had to . . . well, perhaps the doctor would be better at explaining. . . ."

She experienced a cold sinking of her spirits again. There had been a second operation. She remembered the glaring lights of the theater before the anesthetic had been administered. They had taken away more than the remains of her poor, pitiful child. She shivered.

By then the Sister and an attendant nurse were beside the bed. "I will ask you gentlemen to leave us now," the Sister said briskly. "We must attend to the patient. . . ." The nurse had applied a blood pressure cuff, and a thermometer was thrust into her mouth. "It was a near thing, Mrs. McCallum," the Sister said as she read the thermometer. "For a wee while we thought you might not pull through. Infections as severe as yours are difficult to fight. But you are strong, and we've believed you'd make it. Very devoted friends, you have . . . and your father is here. . . . Flowers . . . so many flowers we have filled all the wards. Now we'll just change the dressings and bathe you and you'll feel more comfortable. The doctor will be along shortly. . . ." Competent but impersonal words, words that related to the state of her body, not her mind. All the words she cared to say. Later, because it was so early, a young doctor came to check on her condition but evaded any questions. Later in the morning, the senior surgeon visited her. He had a bland cheerfulness about him. He came alone, without his bands of interns. "I'm so sorry, my dear. The infection was so severe we had to perform a second operation. It will not be possible for you to have another child.'' He patted her hand. ''But I know you have been blessed with a bonny young son, and you will bring him up to make a fine laird of Sinclair.'' She stared at him dumbly; her function as a woman seemed to have been fulfilled in the birth of a single child.

Dr. MacGregor came later. ''Ah, my dear—a sad business. But better than losing your life. It was those hours you spent lying on the floor, without help. I can't fault them here. They did what they thought best to save you. Sleep as much as you can—and eat. You lost a great deal of blood. You need building up. . . .''

Her father came, bearing roses. ''Luisa had them sent up— from your mother's garden.'' With feeble fingers, Julia touched the soft blooms. They had wilted somewhat on the journey, and petals fell. She touched them tentatively. *''Now sleeps the crimson petal, now the white,''* she quoted softly. And then she looked up to see tears in her father's eyes. Her father sank to his knees beside the bed, clasping her hand, and for a moment burying his head in the white quilt. ''A great loss, my darling, but nothing matters . . . as long as you live.'' Before he left he produced the little gray rabbit that had been her mother's good-luck mascot. ''I found it in your room at Sinclair. . . .''

She noticed that after that morning when she became fully conscious and lucid, the officer of the Procurator Fiscal was no longer present. The Procurator Fiscal, she leaned by questioning Sir Niall, was a legal officer who performed the function of public prosecutor and coroner. It was an office and a title that were unique to Scotland. As she grew stronger, she asked more questions. There had been a postmortem on Rod, as she had expected, and he had died of a massive overdose of barbiturates and heroin, which had combined in his body with alcohol. ''Will there be an inquest?'' she asked Sir Niall.

''We don't have inquests in Scotland, my dear. The Fiscal just makes his own inquiries. Nothing to worry about . . .''

She was walking, feeling weaker than she had imagined she could ever feel. ''I would like to see Alasdair. . . .''

''Not yet,'' her father said. ''He'd only be distressed by the sight of you in the hospital. And they don't let young children in to visit.''

She advanced to being able to walk up and down the corridor. She ate as they all urged her to do; they brought her magazines and books, but she noticed there were no newspapers. "What's been happening in the world since I blacked out of it . . . ?" Why did she feel no sorrow about Rod? She experienced only the sorrow that it had all gone so hideously wrong, that she had let the loneliness of the solitary years since she had come to live at Sinclair blind her into the belief that she loved him. But she remembered his better moments, his generosity, his care for her, and refused to believe that had all been a sham, a way of lulling her into thinking that her future was secure with him, that it had all been one gigantic and long-thoughtout plan to take possession of Sinclair, the object of his love and his hate. Surely there once had been real love between them?—it couldn't all have been totally false. And yet doubts echoed in her heart.

Her strength returned. She was able to make telephone calls to Alasdair at Anscombe. He seemed cheerful: Princess Cat was happily settled back in her stall beside Johnny's Taffy. There were plans for him to go to school with Johnny in September. When would she come down to be with them?

"A little later, Alasdair. When I'm stronger."

"I'm sorry about the baby, Mother." She guessed it was something Luisa had coached him to say. Then came the halting words. "I'm sorry about Rod dying. I didn't cause it, did I? I know we weren't supposed to go into the North Tower—and he saved Johnny. . . ."

"That had nothing to do with it, Alasdair. It would have happened, no matter what. I'll be with you soon. . . ."

"As soon as they let you out of the hospital?"

She hesitated. Don't promise him what you're not sure of, her senses warned her. "I'll have to rest a bit longer before I can make the journey."

"But they got an ambulance for Johnny—and *he* was all right."

By now she knew that two of Alasdair's ribs had been broken in the attack Rod had made on him. She thought of his courage in leaning from the Rolls and leading Princess Cat along without any complaint of pain—though it must have been near agony. He had traveled most of the way in the ambulance with Johnny on a stretcher. "I'll come as soon as I can. Do everything Luisa tells you—"

"Why does Grandfather stay up there with you . . . ?"

She cut the connection, unable to parry any more of his questioning. She walked back, weak and drained, to her bed, grateful, for the first time, of its sanctuary.

That evening her father, Sir Niall, and the solicitor they had engaged all seemed to drift into her room at the same time, something that was not normally allowed. She looked at them apprehensively. The young registrar also arrived, and the Sister, her starched veil seeming to add an air of bristling formality to the occasion. Her father took hold of her hand. "Say nothing, my darling. Say nothing at all."

When they were all assembled, a man she had never seen before entered the now crowded room. "Detective Inspector Logan, Mrs. McCallum," he announced. "I am here at the order of the Procurator Fiscal to charge you with the willful murder of your husband, Roderick McCallum. You have the right to keep silent. You will, at a later date—when your doctors permit it—be brought before the Sheriff at the Castle and charged in chambers. Have you anything to say?"

She shook her head. Logan's eyes swept around the assembled company, as if reminding them that although she was in a hospital bed, Julia McCallum was now a prisoner. As he left she saw that a uniformed policeman had taken up his station in the corridor beside her room. She sank down farther into the pillows as if trying to avoid, to drive out the words that had been said. The Sister was swiftly wrapping a blood pressure cuff around her arm; the doctor looked at the reading and nodded. "We'll leave you alone then—but I ask you, none of you, to stay too long. Mrs. McCallum needs rest. And I'm sorry to say that after this, visits will be restricted." He gestured toward the corridor. "That gentleman out there has his orders. All of you must, from now on, make application to visit Mrs. McCallum."

When the two medical people had departed, Julia looked around the others in bewilderment. "What has happened? No one—no one from the—the Procurator Fiscal's office has been to ask me a single question. How can they charge me with such a thing when they haven't even questioned me about what happened that night?"

The solicitor, Andrew Frazer, answered. "In Scotland, Mrs. McCallum, the Fiscal always conducts his own inquiry. The suspect is not questioned. They have extensively questioned those who had any part in the matter—about the night your husband died, and the weeks leading up to it. He believes he has a strong enough case to charge you with murder.''

She closed her eyes. "I don't believe it," she whispered. "I didn't kill Rod. He killed himself. Can't they see the evidence that was there . . . ?''

"They saw what they saw, Mrs. McCallum. It is their contention that you administered a dose of heroin large enough to kill your husband, given that he had taken other drugs and had been drinking heavily all that day. The syringe in your hand. Your fingerprints along with his. You had the motive, the opportunity. . . . I ask you to try not to worry, Mrs. McCallum. It is the duty of the Fiscal to conduct these inquiries. I have no doubt at all that when this matter is all over, you will be entirely cleared of the charge . . . it is a difficult case to prove.''

"Or disprove," Julia said slowly. "If it hadn't been for the miscarriage I suppose they think I could have done it—have even taken my fingerprints off the syringe and put Rod's back on it.'' Her mind was racing wildly, seeing all the possibilities she had managed to thrust away before this. She turned her head on the pillow. "Oh, God, I didn't do it. *I didn't do it!*''

"That we will prove to everyone's satisfaction, Mrs. McCallum. I shall leave you now with your father and Sir Niall. When I was informed this was to happen, I engaged the services of two of our leading King's Counsels to represent you. You will have the best defense in the land.''

"When?'' she whispered. "Do I have to wait . . . wait for a Circuit Judge, or something like that?''

"We are a little more civilized than that in Scotland, Mrs. McCallum. The trial must be concluded within one hundred and ten days of your committal. If necessary they *send* a Lord Justice to hear the case. You will not be kept languishing eternally until they get around to trial.''

Committal . . . trial . . . The words rang in her ears, blotting out whatever her father and Sir Niall said later. She felt their comforting hands, heard the reassuring tones of their voices. But her mind could only grope in stunned shock with the words that had been uttered. Committal . . . trial . . . murder . . .

Within a week—reluctantly, she thought—the doctors had agreed that she could be released from the hospital. "It's better to let you go, Mrs. McCallum," the surgeon said. "You will be as well treated as the facilities allow. No question of being forced to do anything beyond your strength. We really cannot find any more excuses for keeping you here. I've written out instructions for medication and diet . . . that is, if their kitchens can stretch to it.''

The skirt of the neat gray suit Janet had brought swiveled loosely on Julia's waist. She looked in the mirror at features that seemed to her changed beyond the mere look of illness. She had lived a nightmare and now must face worse. She had asked Janet to bring the wedding band that Jamie had given her.

The first of a series of shocks came when the policeman outside the doors, finally summoned by the solicitor, came and locked handcuffs around her wrists. She looked in bewilderment at Frazer. ''I'm sorry, Mrs. McCallum. It's the custom.''

She did not look at anyone as she left the hospital. The handcuffs seemed to have chained her tongue as well as her wrists. She could utter no word of thanks to the doctors, the nurses who had cared for her, the Sister. She was afraid of what she would see in their eyes now that her needs were no longer strictly medical—scorn, pity, indifference, the shrug of the shoulders that might indicate that she deserved whatever the law had in store for her. She was driven, seated between two police constables, the short distance to the hill on which was built Inverness Castle, a Victorian building that housed the courts, and the offices of the Sheriff. In a car following were Andrew Frazer, her father, and Sir Niall. She tried to close her eyes against the small crowd that had gathered to see her enter the office of the Sheriff. Then she realized there were cameras poised. Something inwardly prompted her to raise her head high, to straighten her back as she emerged from the car. The hideous handcuffs were only a thing of the moment. She was Julia Seymour. She was the daughter of Ginette Maslova and Michael Seymour. She had been the wife of James Sinclair. She would not disgrace them.

Andrew Frazer went with her to the Sheriff's chambers. Three men sat there. She had been prepared for this by Andrew Frazer. The Clerk waiting to take a written note of the proceedings, the Sheriff at his desk; on the other side, the Procurator Fiscal. She was formally charged, once again, with the willful murder of her husband. Andrew Frazer answered the charge for her, in the manner of Scottish law. ''No plea. No declaration.''

She was taken to Porterfield Prison, a grim, high-walled

building incongruously placed amid rows of small, respectable-looking houses, only a short distance from the Castle. There she handed over all her clothes to the wardress and put on prison clothes—drab garments that seemed to hang on her and that scratched her skin. It hurt her most of all that among the possessions she was forced to hand over was her mother's gray rabbit, which she had had in her handbag. The wardress was not unkind, just businesslike; she, no doubt, had witnessed many scenes like this, but perhaps none that she knew would be followed by the degree of worldwide interest that this particular prisoner would generate.

"The doctor will be along to examine you soon, Mrs. McCallum. You are ordered rest, and additions to your diet. He will, no doubt, confirm that."

She was in a cell by herself. Primitive, harsh. The wardress brought an extra blanket. "The nights are growing chilly. . . ." It seemed to indicate the length of time she would be there. She paced the small space restlessly when she was alone, trying to accustom herself to the feeling of the prison clothes, to the confinement, to the strange sounds around her, the rattle of key rings, the slamming of heavy doors. Finally she went to peer at what she could see from the high, barred window. There was sky—at least there was sky to see. Then she realized that she had slowly climbed so high on the way to this cell that she could see more—not the neat little rows of houses in the shadow of the prison walls, but the green, impeccably mown hill on which was perched Inverness Castle. She could make out the dome of the great central court where Andrew Frazer had told her she would be tried. One hundred and ten days—the utmost the law allowed from the time of committal to the end of the trial.

The end. It was 1949, and the penalty, on conviction of murder, was hanging.

Chapter Thirteen

A FIRST, EARLY, light snow had fallen on the green hill on the day Julia made her last journey to her trial from Porterfield Prison to Inverness Castle. She thought of it as she sat with the woman police officer in a small room across the corridor from the circular, high-domed, galleried courtroom in which the trial had taken place. Had there been, she wondered, snow at Sinclair yet? She might never see snow at Sinclair again. Outside the locked door of the room were, she knew, two male police officers. Here in Inverness, a prisoner was not confined in the room below the courtroom, nor had she sat in a prisoner's dock. Instead she had been led, for each session of the trial, which had lasted a bare week, in handcuffs, across the hallway to the courtroom. There she had sat on a wooden bench directly facing the Bench and the Lord Justice Clerk, Lord Sutherland. When she was in place, the handcuffs had been removed, put on each side of her, sharing her bench but with cushions provided for them, sat a police officer, both wearing white kid gloves and holding truncheons. Behind her sat her two counsels and their clerks. Robert Innes was the name of the senior King's Counsel—held to be, Andrew Frazer had told her, and the opinion was backed by Sir Niall, the best advocate in Scotland. The Procurator Fiscal, as agent of the Crown, had also summoned its own highly regarded advocates, headed by the King's Counsel, Charles Shaw, whom many might have regarded as an even match for Robert Innes, to act as its Advocate Depute. Julia found all these differences between Scottish and English law puzzling as well as intimidating. She felt small and helpless sitting there between the kid-gloved policemen. The kid gloves had been the only source of humor she had found in that grim week—that, and the thought that the truncheons were there to club her down if she evinced any sign of unseemly behavior—or, she supposed, to attempt the impossible, to escape. She had worn the same gray suit throughout the trial, with a clean white blouse each day, and Jamie's gold wedding band. Anyone who had expected some of the glamour of Hollywood here, some of the flamboyance or histrionics of an acting career, had been disappointed. She wondered what sort of spectacle she had presented to the world's press, seated there in the much larger space than was normally allocated in this court. She knew she had lost more weight. She could appear too thinly gaunt, with her hair swept into a French knot at the back of her head. They allowed her to apply some makeup in the prison before attending the court each day, and she used the skills she had learned in the theater to make the best of herself. A wardress had been present during this ritual. A mirror could become a means of suicide or of violence in the hands of a prisoner. She wondered if she had made a mistake about her clothes—perhaps overplaying the role of the meek and gullible woman who had been led so hideously astray by her husband's tactics. Perhaps a touch of drama would have served her better.

But nothing could upstage the drama of the court itself. When they were all assembled, she—without handcuffs, guarded by the policemen—the jury, the fifteen members of it—again another variation from English law—the Macer would appear, a man wearing a black suit with white shirt and bearing a mace on his shoulder. This was the signal for the court to rise and for the policemen beside her to hold their truncheons stiffly upright. Then the Lord Justice Clerk would appear, majestic in crimson robes and white ermine. The Lord Justice Clerk would then bow to the jury and to the assembled representatives of the bar. The mace would be hung on the wall behind him. The proceedings of her trial would continue.

Covertly, Julia often glanced sideways at the jury, trying to study their individual faces. Her counsel had used his five powers of challenge to try to rid the jury of any he thought might be prejudiced against her—they had all been professional people, and for once she had doubted his wisdom. They might have been more likely to understand the scene created by drink and drugs, jealousy and mangled pride that had pervaded those weeks and days leading up to Rod's death. But the empaneled jury sat there, four women and eleven men, listening to the evidence presented for and against her. She had been able to read nothing from their faces.

This morning the Lord Justice Clerk had presented the end of his summary, which had lasted for an hour. Nothing in it could she deny as being anything but strictly fair. It did not lean toward her in pity, or against her with any tinge of malice. He had instructed the jury to retire to consider their verdict.

And so now they waited. "It will not be long," the policewoman had told her. "The jury is locked up until they reach a verdict. That means they don't get taken to a hotel or anywhere else overnight. There they stay until they've decided. So verdicts usually come quickly."

In her case it did not come so quickly. She paced the little room while the policewoman watched her every movement, as if she might suddenly spring for the door and make a futile bid for freedom. She found herself unable to eat any of the sandwiches that were sent in; the hand that held the teacup trembled as she relived every moment of the past week, the things said and implied. She relived the weeks leading up to the trial, the fear, the hope, the long hours of despair when even her family had been unable to sustain her.

Alex had come. "I won't pretend otherwise," she said. "I'm telling you now so it won't be too big a shock. Just about half the world's press is sending a representative. The cameras will be there as you go into court from the jail every morning. The press will watch every little nuance—not only yours, but of everyone who goes on the stand to testify. And what they can't see, they'll invent. They're building it up as the trial of the century. Of course it isn't—it's just the trial of the moment, the one they can milk the most from. That's why I've decided that *I'll* do the reporting for Forster Newspapers. And I'll prove that I can do it evenhandedly—as Elliot—and, yes, Greg—would have wanted. Everyone will be waiting to see me bend toward your side, to fudge and play down whatever case the prosecution presents. And why am I doing it when I'm your sister and everyone will expect me to present only your side of the case? Well, I'll tell you: I had to fire Margot Parker from the Forster syndicate. She was adamant that she, and only she, was fit to report the trial—she knew both Rod and you, she'd stayed at Sinclair, she knew Hollywood. Only she could do it justice. *Justice!* I can still see that bitch's tongue hanging out. It'll probably cost the Forster chain a slice of readership, because undoubtedly she's the most widely read Hollywood columnist. But I knew how she would report it, and I wasn't going to have that muck in our newspapers. Of course, she immediately moved over to another chain—the Stephens Group. But they haven't got anything like our circulation. But then she's got those wretched fan magazines she writes for. So we can expect some acid in that quarter, but at least she has nothing like the daily circulation Forster gave her. My board of directors is furious with me for firing her, but they do know why. Oh, Crista Cowley for News Incorporated is here—Margot Parker's deadly enemy. Between them, they'll squeeze every agonizing drop of blood from it all. I didn't want you to get a shock when you saw them in court.''

Since Elliot's death, Alex's face had changed, as Julia knew her own had. What had been high cheekbones had sharpened as the hollows in her cheeks had deepened. Her eyes had a wary, almost defensive expression, as if she expected attacks from every quarter and was determined to stand against them. ''But I'm managing all right,'' she said in answer to Julia's questions. ''It's damned rough. I miss him so desperately. But when I heard what had happened to you, my troubles suddenly were in perspective. Sure—I'll miss him forever. As you'll miss your Jamie—so unlike Elliot. That sweet, dear, beautiful, innocent young hero. I know, of course, Julia—''

''Know what?''

''I know that it was his plane that plowed into the oasthouse when Mother was killed. I suspected there was something more than a chance meeting that brought you two together. He had to come to spill it all out to Father, didn't he? And you stopped him.''

''How did you find out?''

''I'm a reporter. It's my job to dig around and get the facts. Stella always suspected it, but she never was sure. Only his CO, whom I managed to trace, would admit it to me. Only he and your solicitor, Andrew Frazer, know about it. I had to tell Frazer in case the other side had gotten hold of it. Though I don't see how they could have used it except to prove that you were a saint to be able to forgive him—''

''But it wasn't his fault.''

Alex leaned across the table in the prison interview room.

They were not permitted to touch each other. "Don't you think I *know* that? I just didn't want the rest of the world to know what the connection was. But if they do—what use can they make of it except to prove how much in love you two were?" She had managed to smile at Julia. "You must promise me that when it's over I will have exclusive rights to the book."

"The book—what book?"

"Of your life, of course. Every publisher in the world will want it—every newspaper would give its eyeteeth to serialize it. I want to write it—right from the beginning. Our mad, wonderful growing up. Our grandparents, Mother, Father. What is most magical about your life, Julia, is that your love of Jamie transcended the knowledge that he had unwittingly killed Mother. It is a beautiful love story, which wipes out the sordidness of what Rod McCallum dragged you into. I've already staked my claim. I've told the press that I—and only I—will be writing your full story. They'll write what they feel like writing for their papers. I've just appealed to them to write the truth." Then she added the word "Alasdair . . ." She'd bitten off what she might have said, and Julia had known at once that even Alex harbored doubts of her acquittal. She had begun to think that if Julia should hang, Alasdair must come to her. He would be the child she had never had. Yes, she had allowed that thought to creep into her mind. "Alasdair," Alex had repeated, knowing her slip, "and you must come for a long visit to Washington when it is all over, and we'll do the book exactly as you want it done." She made a gesture toward her sister that almost allowed their hands to touch. "You must not worry. The press—and the jury—can't fail to see you as you are: dear, foolish, trusting innocent Julia. They *must* see it. . . ."

"They"—the jury she dreaded, those men and women now deliberating not just her future, but her very life in a room somewhere in this building. There could have been very few of them, although they were drawn from everywhere in the surrounding countryside, who did not know of Castle Sinclair, or of the Englishwoman who had married the young laird, produced his son, and then had married the famous film star who had come to Sinclair. Always, she would be regarded as an outsider—someone who had come to usurp a place and position that should by right have gone to some girl of Scottish birth and tradition. Even those who followed in her wake—her famous father married to a woman of immense wealth, her sister who had inherited not just wealth but power also, the other shadowy sister married to someone in Whitehall—local gossip placed Ken Warren much farther up the ladder of power in the Civil Service than he was—all were in their way alien. And wasn't she, Julia McCallum, half Russian, after all? And everyone knew what being Russian meant—traitors when they had made their pact with Hitler, traitors when at the end of the war they had turned against the Allies who had come to their aid; they had taken half of Europe, and it was their stated aim that one day they would have not only Europe but also the whole world in their grasp. To be Ginette Maslova's daughter was no great help to her, Julia guessed, in their eyes. The glittering and the famous would arrive to witness the trial of this stranger in their midst. They would discover the might of Scottish justice.

The family had come as often as they were allowed to visit her in Porterfield. Sir Niall and Janet she expected, but her father had abandoned his plan to open in *Richard III* on Broadway in October. He had taken up residence permanently in Castle Sinclair, making an unlikely companion to Stacia, who also stayed on there. He came faithfully, whenever he was permitted. Julia had agreed with his decision that Luisa, Alasdair, and Johnny should remain at Anscombe until it was all over. "We will try to make it seem as normal as possible for Alasdair, my darling. We think Anscombe is better. We are able to keep the press out of there by hiring a few people, and we make sure no newspapers that show any pictures of you or Rod—or even Anne Rayner—get anywhere near the boys. They're very happy in each other's company—but they're no dummies. They know they're being a bit restricted. All we've told them is that you've been very ill but are recovering and will come to Anscombe as soon as it's possible. I've engaged a tutor—who knows his real job is not just to go through the routine of lessons but also to make sure Alasdair and Johnny hear nothing about what's going on. Luisa invented some marvelous tale about why they weren't, after all, going to school in September. It's a bit of a battle—watching for the press behind every hedgerow—making sure neither of the boys goes to the kitchen when the news is on, just in case your name might be mentioned. We have made Johnny more of an invalid than is necessary. His leg is fine, but we don't let either of them do more than ride around the stable yard—and I even agreed to let them ride up the paths of the rose garden—can't worry about what havoc they make of it. Luisa is with them every second they are outside the house. . . .'' Every day he telephoned Anscombe, and each time he came to visit her, he would give little details of Alasdair. "He misses you— of course. Keeps asking about you. We keep making excuses about why you don't telephone. We have to keep reminding him about the baby. It's easier for him to understand why you have to stay here until you're well enough to make the journey.''

In the midst of the worry and deprivation Julia experienced, the loss of the baby was the sharpest hurt. She thought of the being she had nurtured and cherished, the one thing that had made her stay with Rod—it had been his child also. She had held perhaps foolish hopes that the birth of the child would have changed him. Naïve hopes. It seemed, as she reflected on the less than two years of their marriage in the long nights she spent alone, in the sleepless hours of the night, that she had been remarkably naïve during the whole time—hoping, trusting, believing in things that would never happen. The same naïveté had placed her where she was now. Who but she would have stayed on at Sinclair to try to argue out her case with Rod, even to plead with him to see that whatever he had done for it, Sinclair would, must belong to Alasdair? Instead she had witnessed the horror of his burning down the McBain cottage, had seen him turn from her to Stacia—punishing her through his promises to the girl of the things they would do together. The seduction of the girl had taken place under her own eyes, and, as an added humiliation, under the eyes of Janet and Kate. No one in her right mind, she had often bitterly thought, would have gone back to Sinclair when an alternative was offered. She just could have driven away with her father. She could have stayed with Sir Niall while they consulted solicitors about revoking the power of attorney. The very fact of her return to Sinclair might have taken on the aspect of an evil purpose. No one sane would have gone near Rod's room on the night when he was to die, just for the petty reason of taking away from him, for a time, one of his prizes, his Rolls-Royce. Everyone knew that she could have had William Kerr drive her anywhere she wanted to go. A telephone call in the small hours of the morning, when she knew Rod would be unconscious from drink, if not from drugs, would have brought Sir Niall. All this had been hammered into the minds of the jury by the prosecution. But she had gone, fatefully, stupidly, to his room. She had picked up the syringe, like an ingenuous child. And then the massive contractions, the latest of which she had herself admitted had been coming more frequently, had reached a savage peak, and she had collapsed, holding the syringe in her hand—the syringe, which even though broken into pieces, had held her fingerprints as well as Rod's. The scars of the little shards of glass that had penetrated her flesh were there, to last for the length of her life—long or short.

The office of the Procurator Fiscal had presented its case. Culpable homicide. The Advocate Depute had charged that she had gone that night to Rod's room, admittedly under the duress of the threats that he would take Sinclair from her and from Alasdair, and take away her unborn child. Knowing his habits and what she had seen him take of drink that night, she had been certain that he would be asleep and virtually unconscious—helpless—and she had prepared and administered a fatal dose of heroin. How she had intended to eradicate the traces of her act they had not dwelled on unduly, except to point out that once the syringe had been wiped clean it would have been possible to reimpose her husband's fingerprints on it in many positions, one overlapping the other, until it would have been impossible for even the most extensive forensic examination to say how many times and in what positions he had held it. Why would she allow her fingerprints to appear on the syringe?—except that she had not counted on her collapse, her inability to clear up the traces of her act. Even her gloves, laid out neatly in the dressing room, pointed to her intention. What woman in her distressed state would have thought about gloves? They had been there, the Advocate Depute alleged, to use while she placed Rod McCallum's fingerprints on the syringe.

In turn, her advocate, Robert Innes, had pointed out that a syringe with no fingerprints at all on it would have been an absurdity that even a women in Julia's overwrought state, the pain she was feeling, the fear of a miscarriage, would surely have thought of. Could a woman in such a state have been capable of acting so coolly, so methodically? He had called up the evidence of the post-mortem—that the arm of Rod McCallum had been riddled with puncture marks, several made a short time before his death. He could, in his drunkenness, have prepared a solution many times stronger than he normally took, and being unable in his befuddled state readily to find a vein, have made several attempts to inject himself. Along with the quantity of barbiturates and alcohol found in his body, it would have needed no action from Julia to cause his death. His death had been caused by his inability to resist the drug he had come to crave. True, Julia McCallum had, like an artless child, picked up the syringe to examine it. The hammer blow of the miscarriage had hit, and she had been unable to call for the help that might have saved her husband's life and her child's.

She had known that it would have been useless to plead with her husband—if he were capable of listening. She had gone to the Red Tower Room, as she had before, to take the keys of the Rolls-Royce. Undoubtedly an unwise action, but nonetheless an innocent one.

The prosecution had stressed that she would have had no need to clear up the deadly mess in the bathroom. It didn't matter how many of her fingerprints appeared there. She had used the bathroom, along with her husband, until the visit of Margot Parker. It was entirely likely that every inch of those mahogany surfaces had not been wiped clean of her fingerprints. The evidence of the spilled barbiturates, the dust of heroin would be there for all the world to know how her husband had abused them. As he abused alcohol. The Advocate Depute had made a strong claim that only a woman bent on destroying a man who clearly meant to destroy her would have remained at Sinclair after the burning of the McBain cottage. A normal woman would have fled in fear and in helplessness. She had plenty of neighbors who would have aided her; she would have had the support and assistance of William Kerr and Janet. And she had one man whose friendship she could never have doubted, a man who had demonstrated his concern and care many times: Sir Niall Henderson. A man not unknowledgeable in the ways of the law and able to bring assistance swiftly—even though that morning he had sanctioned, even arranged, the expedition of Mrs. Kirsty Macdonald in what was technically a stolen vehicle, with a valuable pony, known to be the property of Rod McCallum. Why had not Julia McCallum turned to him, instead of making her way to her husband's bedroom, with the obviously trivial excuse of taking the keys of his car? Only a very grave reason would have brought her to the Red Tower Room that night. The reason could have been no other than to finish the work of self-destruction her husband had begun. She had gone with the purpose of murder—a murder that would appear to be the result of his own excesses.

"And with his death her problems would have vanished. She would not only have been secure in her possession of Sinclair, and her child's inheritance, but also in possession of Rod McCallum's child, his property in California, and whatever else of his assets he had, in his will made shortly after their marriage, bequeathed to her—which was his total estate. The fact that she had given him power of attorney to act for her was a small thing compared to what he had given, and had been prepared to give, to her. He had already adopted her son and given him the same care and privileges he had given his adoptive daughter, Stacia Rayner.''

He went on to cite the fact that Rod McCallum had set up trust funds during the lifetime of Anne Rayner of which Stacia Rayner was the beneficiary. Until the advent of Rod McCallum, the financial affairs of Anne Rayner had been in chaos; she had been near bankruptcy. He had touched none of her money but protected it from her wild extravagances and her bad advisers, had seen that her child's interests were protected. Had he not done the same for Julia McCallum's son? Julia McCallum, in her turn, had made no will that gave her husband Castle Sinclair and its lands in the event of her death. Those, her only assets, would go to her child, Alasdair. The death of Rod McCallum had not been an accident, brought on by his own hand. It had been willful murder. If her plan had succeeded—if she had not collapsed and been unable to help herself—she would have been a rich widow, a woman freed of a husband who threatened her whole way of life, who had threatened to take from her her most cherished possessions—her son and the unborn child.

She recalled, as she paced that small room under the eye of the policewoman, how skillfully the Advocate Depute had played upon the feelings of the jury, acknowledging that she had been a woman under extreme duress, in a most terrible position. Her husband's former generosity, his gifts, his care for her and her son might well have turned to vengeful threats. It was not denied that he had beaten Alasdair in a horrific fashion in his fury when the boy's disobedience had almost led to the death of Alasdair and the young half brother of Julia McCallum. "But no threat, no pressure, no mistreatment in our society justifies the taking of human life. This woman, in desperation, set out to take her husband's life and succeeded. That cannot be condoned. Such an act cannot be unpunished.''

Vainly, her solicitor, Andrew Frazer, had sent to California to obtain depositions from the servants, Maria and José, from Dr. Fields, that once before Julia had been instrumental in saving her husband's life when he had been comatose from a drug and alcohol overdose. That she had summoned a doctor and help as soon as she had seen his condition, that she herself had then been in a shattered state, brutally beaten by her husband. If she had not let him die then, why now? But depositions bearing out her claims had not been forthcoming. Rod McCallum had been a patient in the clinic for a few days for treatment for gastroenteritis, Dr. Fields declared. The postmortem had revealed no trace of the ulcer Rod McCallum had claimed as his reason for turning down the scripts the studio had sent him and retiring to Sinclair. Julia McCallum had been in the same clinic because she was in the early stages of pregnancy, and there was some fear of a miscarriage. Maria and José would add only their sworn testimony to confirm the doctor's. Bitterly Julia remembered that that was exactly what Rod had predicted. Maria and José would never again have worked in Hollywood if they had betrayed to any others their employer's business. The clinic existed only to care for those people who did not want their medical or emotional problems known and written about and who were willing to pay for, above all, discretion. In questioning Stacia, before Julia had been charged, the Procurator Fiscal had learned that some such event might have taken place, and had employed Los Angeles attorneys to ask the same questions of the same people, and they had received the same answers. Julia's pitiful hope that her onetime act of saving Rod's life would speak for her now was destroyed.

Even in her most hopeful moments, and they had been few, she had known that her stated reason for going to the Red Tower Room must have seemed pitifully weak compared to the strength of the argument of what she had stood to gain by committing the act of which she was charged. How often in the long nights in her prison cell had she cursed the impulse to leave Sinclair secretly, in the dead of night. If she had stayed where she was, at least the baby might have lived. When Rod's death was discovered, there would have been nothing to indicate that she had

ever set eyes on him since she left the housekeeper's room after
the confrontation that had told her that she was going to lose
everything.

Over and over, as she sat in that room across from the great
circular courtroom, as she had paced it during the painfully slow
hours of waiting while the jury deliberated its verdict, she had
seen, in her mind, the faces of her family and the other people
who loved her. They had gathered, her family, to lend her what
support there was. Her father was endlessly photographed en-
tering or leaving the Castle on the hill, his hand protectively
under Luisa's arm. Luisa had come to Sinclair for the duration
of the trial, having tried to secure Anscombe as a kind of fortress
against the world and the press, having told the staff, under pain
of dismissal without references, that no single newspaper, either
accidentally or deliberately, was to reach Alasdair's eyes, that he
should hear no radio reports of the progress of the trial. She had
charged the tutor and Harry Whitehand with this and come north
to be with her husband as he sat in court each day, to signal her
concern to Julia. Julia wondered why she had ever doubted that
this woman could be less than good for Michael and the whole
family. Perhaps her great wealth had been a factor in the reservations Michael's daughters had held about her—the thought that
she was buying attention for herself through her famous husband. But she had done more than money would compel. She
had cared in an almost fanatical fashion for Alasdair. In the one
visit she had been permitted to make to Julia, they had sat separated by the table and were not allowed to touch each other's
hands. "They will see, my dear, that you could not have done
such a thing. Why you are even here, undergoing this ordeal, is
beyond my understanding." Then she let slip, in her final words,
her misgivings about the outcome of the trial. "I swear to you—I
give my sacred honor—that Alasdair shall have my care forever.
He shall grow up as Johnny's brother. . . ." Then her eyes had
misted, and she had risen swiftly, unable to give Julia the embrace she obviously had wanted to give. "But, of course, you
will be there to take care of him yourself. I give you my love,
Julia. I love you as I love your father. You were always his
favorite child—apart from Johnny. He is exceptional. . . ." Julia
had seen her handkerchief go to her eyes as she left. At the door,
which the wardress had already opened, she turned back mo-

mentarily. "They will see that you could not have done it. It is
not your nature. . . ."

They, the jury. It was the "they" Julia feared. As usual, they
were drawn from all walks of life. She was more acutely aware
than she had ever been that she was still an outsider to these
people, no matter how fiercely she had loved her husband Jamie
and tried to fight for her son's future position here in Scotland.
When the press had learned that Rod McCallum had actually
been born on the Sinclair estate as Rod McBain, a swell of
sympathy had grown for him. Newspaper sources in the States
had tried to delve and find his true background, and had, as
usual, come up with half-truths—those that Rod had uttered himself for press releases, and those pitiful little facts they were able
to place on the record as true. Some people, after these facts
were disclosed, came forward, claiming that they were the
brother and sisters of Rod McBain, but none could ever claim
that they had seen or known of him since he was twelve years
old, and they had been younger. The old tale of McBain's dismissal from Sinclair had been retold, with embellishments. There
were plenty in the neighborhood who remembered that. But neither Janet nor Kate had ever repeated the story they had heard
that last night from Rod's lips—the fantasy, or true story, of his
father having murdered Adam Sinclair. Because no one had asked
them. But when questioned by the Procurator Fiscal, and then
later by the Advocate Depute in court, Stacia had spoken freely.
She recounted all that had been said at that last dinner and thus
had forced Janet and Kate to be reexamined. They had admitted
they had heard a certain tale, but declared emphatically that Rod
McCallum himself had said he did not know if it was the truth,
or the fantasy of a drunken man, his father, who might have
wished to kill Adam Sinclair but had not actually performed the
deed.

As they were questioned, each of the three women on the
witness stand, they all had to admit they had heard those words.
Janet and Kate, knowing themselves to be bound by solemn oath
to speak the truth, had been unable to say otherwise. Only Stacia
had spoken willingly. Julia wondered how freely, how willingly,
she had talked to the Procurator Fiscal. She had responded
readily to an unexpected question from the Advocate Depute:
"In your recollection, what words did Julia McCallum last speak
to her husband in your presence?"

Stacia had appeared on the witness stand, to the delight of the world's press, dressed in the plain and simple clothes of a child—a white blouse and navy skirt. But even those clothes could not disguise what the press longed for and photographed lavishly once she was outside the court—the reincarnation of Anne Rayner, the same look of sensuality, the expression of a vulnerable child who has blundered into something she didn't fully understand. But she was a slightly more sophisticated version of her mother, a girl both protected, and abused by her adoptive father, a man who had made her life, as she told it, a kind of misery but whom the world could clearly see had used harsh measures to prevent happening to her what had happened to her mother, a man who had never touched a penny of the money her mother's estate continued to engender.

When asked, from the knowledge she had given to the office of the Procurator Fiscal, what had been the last words she had heard Julia McCallum say to her husband, Stacia had made a brief but dramatic hesitation, as if she knew exactly how to squeeze the situation of every ounce of attention it would draw to her. She had made the hesitation seem that she, like Janet and Kate, was recalling her oath of truth. Julia guessed, in fact, that she had waited and longed for this moment.

"She said, 'I'll meet you in hell.' "

The statement had caused an uproar in court, which the Lord Justice Clerk had had to silence with the threat that the court would be cleared. Stacia stepped down from the witness stand with the slightly smug air of someone who knows that her words would be repeated in newspapers in countries far and near, wherever her mother's and Rod McCallum's films had ever appeared.

Janet and Kate had been recalled to the stand to corroborate the truth of what Stacia had said. Julia had seen plain anguish on each face as they had been forced to agree that they also had heard those words. Rosmairi had broken down and sobbed when she had been forced to recount Rod McCallum's beating of Alasdair, his threat to kill Princess Cat. Stacia had little to do but confirm what Rosmairi had said. But it was Stacia, under questioning from the Advocate Depute, to whom she obviously had told the story before, who had recounted the events in the library the afternoon when she, Rosmairi, Alasdair, and Kate, carrying the tea things on a tray, had overheard and partly witnessed the scene between Julia and Rod. "Will you repeat what you heard?"

"Well . . . I can't be absolutely sure of the exact words. It's a while ago. It was a row. We all heard it. She said something like, 'No matter how it's done, I'll get rid of you—and I'll have both my children.' Then Rod laughed and he said, 'You'll have to kill me to do that.' Then she said. 'I *could* kill you. I could kill you for freedom, for the right to do what is best for my children.' I think she said after that, 'Yes, even kill you.' "

Rosmairi and Kate had been forced to agree that, yes, to the best of their recollection, words like that had been exchanged. Neither could look at Julia as they left the witness stand. Rosmairi openly wept, as if a betrayal had been forced on her.

The Advocate Depute had seized this change to repeat to the jury the words he had used in his opening charge against Julia, words well known in Scottish law: "And she did previously evince malice and ill will toward him."

Julia's advocate had brushed aside the exchange. "I do not say that such words were not exchanged, though Miss Rayner's testimony seems to be somewhat prejudiced, as well as unnecessary. Who among us has not been party to or witnessed a domestic quarrel in which wild and extravagant claims or threats have not been made? But are they always acted upon? Of course not. If we took seriously all the threats uttered during a domestic quarrel, this court would never be out of session. Because Julia McCallum uttered those words, or words like them, does not mean she carried out that threat. She was a woman under severe pressure, threatened and mistreated by her husband, carrying the burden of her child. She was threatened by her husband, and she uttered certain words in rebuttal. What sort of woman would she be if she had just allowed her husband to carry on as he was doing, made no protest, not declared she would fight him for what was, after all, her own property—particularly the right to her own children? It is natural for any woman to defend those rights. But it does not follow that she killed for them."

Round and round in Julia's head the phrases swirled during the days of the trial, and those terrible hours waiting for the verdict. For some reason, in those days when she had been in the courtroom and had been seeing the faces of those who loved her and those who might have felt less than love for her, the face that haunted her most was that of Connie. That sweet, beautiful, guileless face had mirrored the effect of every word that was said; her eyes had glazed sometimes in horror at what she heard, words damning to Julia. Julia had experienced a strange sort of pride that Ken had taken leave from his job to be here in Inverness with all the family to help sustain them in this ordeal. He had not distanced himself in any fashion. He had not been the cautious creature they all had imagined him to be. He knew his wife's anguish and had not let her come alone to face the drama and torment of the trial. He had come with Connie to visit Julia in prison just before the trial commenced. But he had been unable to prevent himself from uttering what evidently had been discussed with Connie beforehand: "You must not worry about Alasdair. He will always have a home with us, grow up as a brother to Margaret Ginette and Clive." Then he realized he had said what should not have been spoken then. His voice had been calm and deliberate. "But I know it will not come to that. They will believe you."

But did they believe her? Not instantly. That was now clear as the hours passed. They were still arguing. Alex had pointed out, before the trial, that on the whole, Inverness might be enjoying its small moment in the limelight. For the duration of the trial it had become, for many people, the focus of the world. Famous names, famous people were involved. The charmed circle that had seemed untouchable—those glittering with wealth and talent—had been dragged into a dark and sordid tragedy. They, her family, her friends had gathered around Julia as if to protect her with their presence. She thought of D.D.'s jowly face, looking haggard and worried. Her father was too accomplished an actor to let such emotions show on his features, but sometimes he had bent to comfort Luisa. Connie had sat, her hand clutching her husband's, drawing strength from his calm. Alex had scrupulously taken shorthand notes, her head bent over her pad. No one could tell from her expression what her thoughts were. Each evening she had telephoned her report to Washington, written with what everyone must see was scrupulous fairness. Only once, when she had ended her report of the beginning of the Lord Justice Clerk's summary to the jury, which had begun the afternoon before and not finished until this morning, had Alex permitted herself to stray from the role of the objective reporter, the observer.

It must seem from all the evidence given and heard that it is

impossible to prove that Julia McCallum did or did not murder,
or seek to murder, her husband. She is the only person who
knows that beyond a doubt. While a doubt exists, she must, in
law and in conscience, be acquitted. If truth and the law are to
be served, this must be the only verdict.

Julia thought again of the words of each witness as they had
been said in court, had seen the faces, the loving, troubled faces,
the faces of the merely curious. She had seen the faces of her
tenants in the court, she had seen faces she vaguely remembered
from the Fleet Street press from the days when Alex had been
married to Greg, familiar faces from the Hollywood press. Some
had seemed to extend hope to her, to wish for her acquittal;
some had registered a sort of open contempt that told her exactly
what her position had always been in this society—that of an
outsider.

Stacia's face had retained its little-girl look of wonder, as if
none of this could possibly be associated with her, the look of
vulnerable innocence that had made her mother so loved and yet
pitied. Stacia had seemed, by her expression, to appeal for the
understanding—indeed, the protection—of the world. None of
this was her doing, she seemed to say. But hers had been the
most damning evidence in reporting those two fateful confron-
tations with Rod. While Janet, Kate, and Rosmairi would never
have lied under oath, neither would they have gratuitously reported what they had seen or heard unless the questions had been
asked of them. Only Stacia could have given that information to
the Procurator Fiscal while the case against Julia was being built.
She had been able to stare at Julia from the witness stand with
an air of bewildered helplessness. How can I not tell them? she
seemed to say. After all, it had happened, and she had promised
to tell the truth. She had not even had to place her hand on the
Bible when she had taken the oath; here in Scotland it was
deemed that the sworn promise of a witness to tell the truth was
sufficient. She had committed no perjury, Julia conceded. She
had simply told more than was necessary. And the helplessly
innocent face of this girl-woman, who would, after this trial,
receive almost countless film offers, had conveyed to Julia and
to the waiting cameras outside the court that she had been the
unwilling witness to the sordid lives of Rod and Julia McCallum
and that nothing she could do or say would change that.

When questioned herself on the stand, Julia had regularly,

almost monotonously, repeated the events leading up to Rod's death—the events as only she could have known them. She did not deny the testimony offered of conversations overheard, events witnessed. Nor did she falter under the most ruthless questioning of the Advocate Depute. There had been no dissembling of the truth.

At a knock on the door, Julia spun around. The policewoman had opened it, and a few words were exchanged with one of the two policemen guarding the door. The policewoman turned back. "Right," she said to Julia. "The jury is coming in." For a second Julia staggered and was forced to sit down. "Come . . . my dear . . ." Was it an expression of pity? "Here's your jacket. You will need to stand, you know, when the Lord Justice Clerk appears. . . ."

Handcuffs were replaced for the brief passage back to the wooden seat facing the Bench; she was escorted, as always, by the two white-gloved policemen, truncheons sheathed. There was a moment to glance back to see the faces of her family. Even her father showed his emotion then. They were twisted in various degrees of anxiety, hope, and doubt—her father; Luisa; Connie and Ken; and Alex, whose face for the first time showed the strain of these past days. The handcuffs were removed. The jury began to file back into their places, deliberately, with no haste, as if they, too, relished the drama of this moment, the moment when Julia's fate would be pronounced. She grew fearful when none of them looked at her directly, none of the fifteen. She was aware of the tradition, the belief, that held that jurors did not look at the face of the prisoner on whom they were about to pronounce a verdict of guilt.

They all rose when first the Macer and then the Lord Justice Clerk reappeared, in the full might and majesty of his ermine and crimson robes. He bowed, as always, to the jury and the bar. He sat, and the court was totally silent. Julia felt herself hardly able to breathe. She noticed then what she had not seen before, and she was unable to suppress a shiver of sheer horror. Along with the Macer and Judge, another figure, never before present on the Bench, had come to take his place there. He was a minister of the Church of Scotland, in his black clothes and distinctive white collar. She could guess what his duty would be if the jury found against her.

The Clerk of the Court addressed the jury. "Who speaks for you?"

The foreman, elected by the jury, stood. "I do."

"Do you fifteen swear by Almighty God, as you shall answer to God at the great day of Judgment, that you will truth say, and no truth conceal, insofar as you are to pass upon this Assize?"

"We do."

"Have you reached a verdict?"

"We have."

"What is your verdict? Is the verdict unanimous or by a majority?"

The foreman hesitated for what seemed the length of her whole lifetime to Julia. Her stomach seemed to turn over; her bowels grew weak. She had not realized how fearful she had become. Then the foreman turned with an apologetic gesture to the Lord Justice Clerk. "My Lord, I do not know how to record this verdict. This is the first time—"

The Lord Justice Clerk made a gesture of impatience and annoyance. This was not according to the custom of the Court.

"What is your problem? If there has been a question of interpretation of the evidence presented, or a point of law on which you wished further instruction, you should so have informed the Clerk of the Court, and I would have given it."

"It is a matter of numbers, my Lord. The verdict is not unanimous. You see . . ." He looked at the paper he held, clearly intimidated by the Lord Justice Clerk's tone. "Among the jury we have a verdict of . . ." Another long pause.

"Five—Guilty."

"Four—Not Guilty."

Four and five were nine, Julia counted silently. No one in the court stirred, there was not a rustle of paper, a cough, a movement of uneasy feet.

"Six—Not Proven."

The Clerk of the Court glared at the foreman. Such numbers were not meant to be recited in or out of court. They were meant to be held as a secret of the jury room.

"The verdict, then, is 'Not Proven,' " he intoned, trying to suppress his wrath.

Not Proven. A verdict unique to Scottish law. She had not been judged "Guilty." She had not been judged "Not Guilty." The charge had been voted, but only by a plurality, "Not

Proven.'' She would not leave this court as an innocent woman or a guilty one. She would leave as a woman against whom the charge of murder had been "Not Proven."

Julia did not know from the tumult that broke out whether the verdict was popular or not. Her life had been spared by this strange quirk of Scottish law. The Lord Justice Clerk brought the courtroom to silence again.

The Clerk of the Court intoned, "I will now record the verdict." He dipped the nib of his pen into the inkwell and wrote in a large, splendidly bound volume. After he had written he read aloud, "The jury by a plurality find the charge 'Not Proven.' "

The Lord Justice Clerk then addressed Julia.

"Julia Svetlana Seymour—or Sinclair—or McCallum," using all the names she had ever borne, as was the custom, "in respect of the verdict of the jury you are discharged from the bar." He added words strange to her. "You have tholed your Assize." Later she learned that they indicated that she had suffered her punishment. She knew she would go on to suffer it for the rest of her life.

The Lord Justice Clerk then bowed to the jury and to the bar, and the slow procession of Macer, Judge, and minister of the Church of Scotland left the Bench.

She was free to go. She felt the hands, the arms, the kisses of her family. She remembered to utter words of thanks to her two King's Counsels before she passed in dazed bewilderment up the aisle of the courtroom. She hated the press of people around her, which seemed to impede her progress to liberty.

Outside she raised her face to the sky, trying to hold at bay the shouted questions, the flash of cameras, wished for just a few seconds that she would be allowed to savor this moment of freedom—freedom from guards, from handcuffs, freedom from her terrible fear. She did not know how the newspapers, whose cameramen jostled for position around her, would regard this strange verdict—if, in their own columns, they would brand her guilty, or support her innocence. She had received the verdict "Not Proven." Some on the jury had believed her guilty, some had not. And some had declared the charge "Not Proven."

She felt her father urge her into a car, driven by Sir Niall. She sat between him and Luisa, wordless, while Connie's and Alex's faces appeared briefly at the window to smile, to blow her kisses, until they were thrust aside by the cameramen fighting for just one more picture.

"We have a bag packed for you in the trunk, with our own luggage. We'll be clear of this in a very short time. By tomorrow we'll be in London. The day after, you'll see Alasdair."

"No!" she said sharply. "Alasdair must come to me here. I must go back to Sinclair."

"My darling," her father protested, "we were sure you would want to leave all this behind you."

"No!—no, I must go back to Sinclair. I can't run away from their verdict. I must live with it. It is Alasdair's home. . . ." She knew what sort of prison she was condemning herself to. She was the most notorious woman in Scotland. Many people would not believe in her innocence. That she must endure. She would have to endure it through her whole life—she would have to live with it here, among these Highlanders to whom she would always be an outsider. To leave might imply guilt. The only way she could help Alasdair to face the horror of this charge, the trial and its verdict, was to bring him up among his own people, bring him up to know and understand his inheritance. Her son would not be a stranger in his own land.

The car rolled slowly down the hill on which the Castle stood, still impeded by the following photographers. It was the very last moment of the sunset, and for an instant the white snow of the beginning of winter was shaded to a pinkish tinge. And then the dusk descended.

The dusk had become darkness by the time they left the outskirts of Inverness. Her father's hand had gripped hers tightly all the time. He spoke only once. "You're sure, my darling—absolutely sure? It would be so much easier for you—for Alasdair—to leave all this behind. . . ."

"Father, you have to try to understand. My salvation—and Alasdair's—lie here. I am not guilty, and I must be ready to look into the eyes of any who say I am. Alasdair will not grow up thinking he has to dodge and hide. He will grow up proudly—his father's son. The son of a hero. Never mind what people may think his mother is. In time I mean to prove to them what I truly am. That can't be done by running away. You do see . . . ?"

"I see . . . in a sense. But you carry honor and pride to an undreamed-of height. Courage . . . you are Jamie's match in courage."

In the darkness Luisa's hand came softly to take hers. "My family would be proud of a daughter such as you."

The rest of the way they drove in silence. Sir Niall made no comment on what he had heard pass among them. He was too wise to intervene, but somehow Julia could sense that he totally understood and approved the hard but necessary course she had set.

They could see the glow in the sky as they turned into the forest road. Sir Niall speeded up a little, perhaps through anxiety. When they came at last to where the forest opened to the loch and the bridge began, he stopped the car.

Never, ever, had Julia seen it quite like this, the remembered scene of many years, the years of her young love for Jamie, her maturing years as the mother of Alasdair, the brief, dark years of Rod McCallum. She wondered who could have done it. Janet, the Kerrs, Kate, and Rosmairi had all been in court to hear the verdict. One of them had telephoned to the castle. Only Rachel Kerr was there, with her two brothers. It could only have been she who had raced through the whole building, so that lights shone from every window, over every arch to each courtyard, as far up as the rooms that Jamie and Callum had occupied in the highest tower. Even the floodlights Rod had installed had been turned on, so that the old walls were bathed in mellow beauty.

Julia gasped, and for the first time in many months felt tears on her cheeks. It was a shining beacon of hope, beckoning her into a future that would be brighter than the past. It signaled to her plainly that those who knew her well had expected her to make this decision, had known that it was right that she should return here. The light in the darkness, the place where she could live out her past and have her future.

Slowly Sir Niall drove across the causeway and the bridge.

A slight figure stood outlined against the open double doors to the entry hall, with its great Sinclair battle flag hanging in honor and pride. Rachel did not rush to open the car doors, as Janet or William Kerr might have. Tentatively, with great subtlety, she slowly raised her hands and then her arms as Julia approached.

"Welcome back, Mrs. Sinclair."